AN·ECHO·OF·THE·ASHES

BOOK II

SHADOW

· OF THE ·

NIGHTINGALE

Printed in Australia
Cover and internal design by Shawline Publishing Group Pty Ltd
Images in this book are copyright approved for Shawline Publishing Group Pty Ltd
Illustrations within this book are copyright approved for Shawline Publishing Group Pty Ltd

First printing: November 2023

Shawline Publishing Group Pty Ltd
www.shawlinepublishing.com.au

Paperback ISBN 978-1-9231-0114-2
eBook ISBN 978-1-9231-0118-0

Distributed by Shawline Distribution and Lightning Source Global

 A catalogue record for this
work is available from the
National Library of Australia

AN·ECHO·OF·THE·ASHES
BOOK II

SHADOW
· OF THE ·
NIGHTINGALE

· ANTHONY KEARLE ·

Also by Anthony Kearle

Blood of the Eagle

To my dearest Nila,
A moon by name, but more radiant than the brightest sun.
Yours always

Acknowledgements:
To the map maker, Charles Thompson,
who turned sketches into magic.
Your work is unparalleled.

.

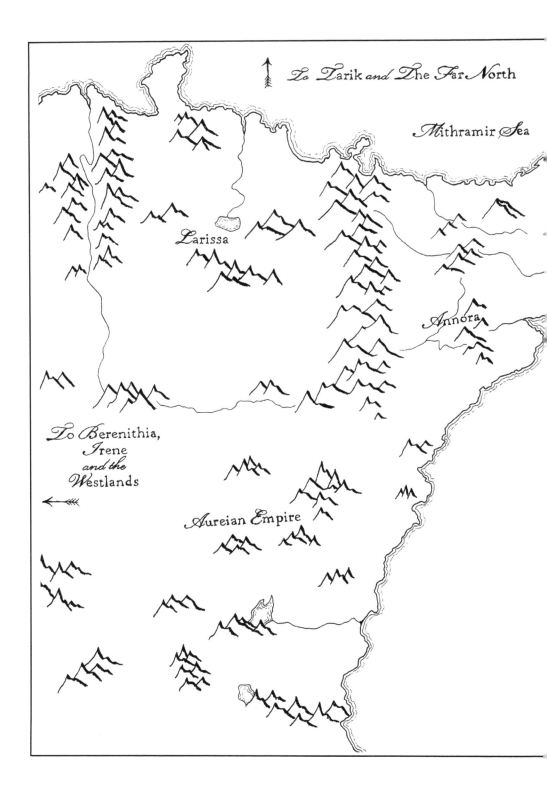

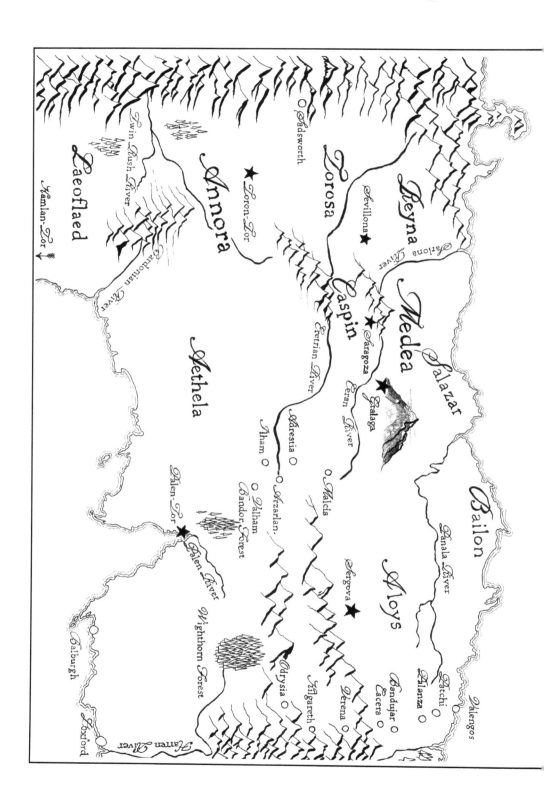

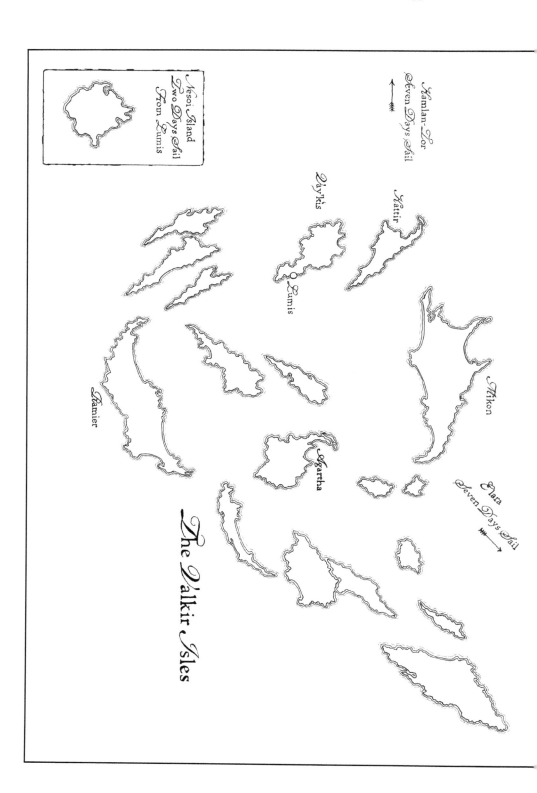

The Dalkir Isles

Nesoi Island
Two Days Sail
From Lumis

Kamlan-Lor
Seven Days Sail

Day'kis

Xattir

Lumis

Tikon

Lamier

Agartha

Tiara
Seven Days Sail

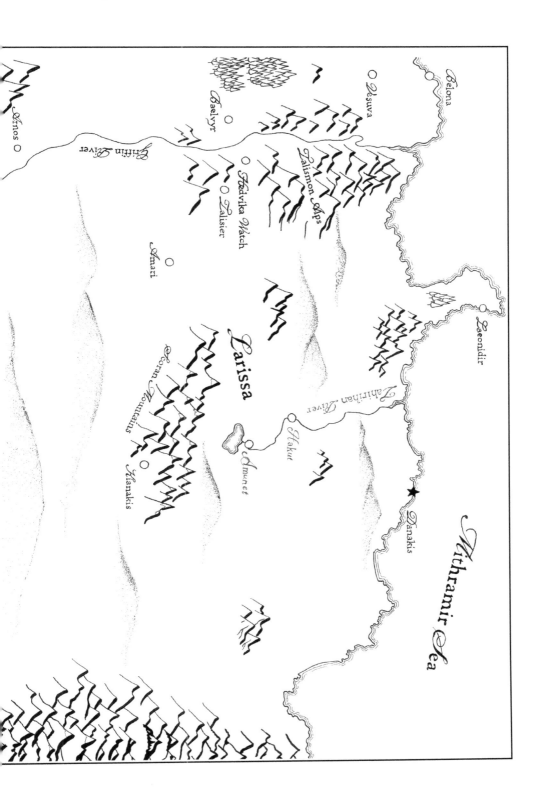

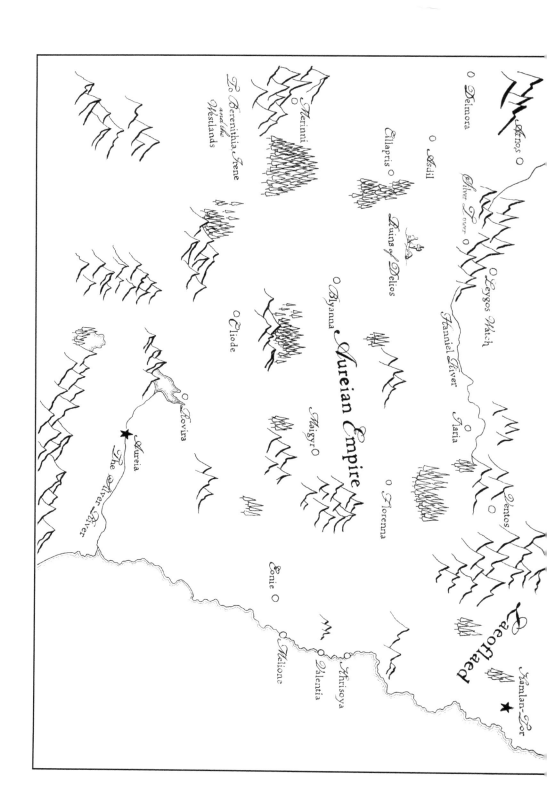

ONE

Island of Ephilion, Gulf of Lamrei

Ephilion, once the crowning glory of the Gulf of Lamrei, lay ruined. A haze of smoke arose from its ashes, while the bodies of the dead lay abandoned. Those that hung in steel cages were left to rot in the sun, a great feast for the crows. The ships once moored at harbour now rested at the bottom of the bay.

"Elara came," Luana Marquez murmured, as she led a dozen of her crew through the ruined harbour town. Her hand tightly clasped her broad-bladed sidesword. The sight of this once-beloved safe haven chilled her to the bone.

Like the rest of her crew, the captain of the Emeralis wore a sash of green tightly around her waist, beneath her wide belt. A dagger with an emerald imbued in its pommel sat atop her right hip, while a jade-coloured bandana kept her curling brown tresses at bay. Beads ran through her hair, and a trio of necklaces hung from her throat. Her fingers were covered in rings of emerald and jade. The Jade Queen, some called her, and for good reason. It was said that though she wore green, she had a tongue of pure silver. It was said that she led without mercy. It was said that that was why she'd become captain in the first place.

"That marks four settlements in as many weeks," murmured Luana's first mate. The simple loose-fitting garb that he wore, along with his foreign sword and eaglelike eyes, marked him as Tariki.

"Aye, Calvillo," Luana replied.

Her crew was quiet as they trudged toward the centre of Ephilion, for they all knew what its destruction meant. The conquest of the Gulf was now inescapably under way. Many were about to die. Many who had called Lamrei home.

Calvillo's ears pricked as a sound no greater than a whisper reached them. "Voices," he hissed.

He flicked his sword into both hands. Luana took up her dagger and nodded to her crew. Swords were readied, while two of their number nocked arrows into powerful bows. Luana set her jaw before she rounded the corner into Ephilion's town square.

Her eyes widened as she saw what lay ahead. Two dozen pirates stood in the square, the vanguard of not one but two crews. One man knelt beside the body of a boy who would have been no more than twelve. A pair of crucified men rose before the pirates. Luana knew them both, and the sight sent a shiver down her spine.

"Marquez," one of the pirates called, as he noticed her crew.

The mere act revealed how serious this had become. They may have respected each other, but every crew was rival to the next.

"Laven," Luana returned in greeting.

Garrett Laven was more of a schemer than a true-blooded pirate. A man who many sought for his wisdom. His ship, the Aglaeca, had plagued these waters for nearly ten years.

Luana sheathed her blade and made her way over. All was quiet as the boy whispered something to the second captain, Cillian Teague of the Oridassey was crouched above him. A fierce man, Aureian to the bone. One of the six. One of the old guard.

The boy's words faded with his breath. His grip on Teague's hand loosened, and his arm fell limp to the ground. Teague reached out and gently shut his lifeless eyes.

"Rest easy now, lad," Teague said, his voice quiet. "Drift deeper and deeper. The sirens are calling your name."

Luana did not allow the tears that threatened to flow. Not just for the boy, but for all the lives taken needlessly. For a haven from the cruel outside world, sundered before their very eyes.

"What happened here?" she asked.

Teague rose to his feet. His hand wrapped around the hilt of his sword so tightly that Luana could see the white of his bones. Now there was a true pirate in every sense of the word.

"When we arrived, they were long gone. The boy said that they came like ghosts in the night." Teague gestured up to the crucified men. "Aulous and Fabian resisted. They made the Elarans pay for every step they took with blood, yet in the end, they fell like all the others. None were left alive... blood, bones, and cinders. That is what's become of us."

Garrett Laven's lips curled back as he snarled, "Elara will bleed for this."

"And how do you plan on doing that, exactly?" Calvillo of Tarik asked him. "Look around you. Ephilion is no more. The fourth of our harbours, in little more than a month, to be left as ash and scorched earth. Landonsport has joined these invaders and now willingly supplies them. Aulous and Fabian are dead. The old guard are dead."

"Not all," said Teague.

"No, not all," Calvillo continued. "All the same, the days of fortunes pouring down upon us are over."

Fury etched itself upon Luana's heart. Its venom sprang from her lips. "And that is why we must fight back," she growled. "They are burning our seas from shore to shore. Each day brings them closer to finding those places that remain as our safe havens."

Captain Teague looked from pirate to pirate. He brushed the hilt of his sword as he stepped away from the boy's body. "When we of the old guard founded Lamrei twenty-five years ago, we did so with a single purpose," he started. "To create a place of freedom for all who sought it, free from the rule of tyrants and fools. Thousands joined as our kingdom of the sea grew."

He nodded to Luana, Laven and Calvillo in turn.

"Escaped slaves, banished men." Teague's gaze shifted to the dead boy. "And those just in search of a better life. All came together to make this place what it is… what it *was*. I can still hear the principle that started this all burning in my mind. Freedom. We are all just stories in the end. Let us make it a good one."

Teague's gaze shifted a final time. It moved to the crucified corpses of their former leaders.

"We have all stood idle too long. Do you agree, Laven?" Teague asked.

"Aye, I do," Laven nodded thoughtfully. "Yet the future is not a gentle river to carry us. It is the ocean in which we drown if we are not prepared."

Luana Marquez took a deep breath as her fellow captains spoke. A short life, but a good one. That was their code. Here in that place where all were equal.

"And so, prepared we must be," she said. "The old guard did it wrong. They tried to fight Elara alone, without the aid of their brothers, and they paid the price."

"What do you suggest?" Captain Laven asked with a frown. "We are pirates. Working alone on the seas is the only way… it is who we are."

"Then we must change," Luana replied with a deadly certainty, before she strode into the centre of the ruined square. "Friends, they come for us now. Circling like vultures. Waiting… watching for any sign of weakness," she cried as her eyes moved from face to face. "They think us defeated, broken. We who were once feared. I say that we remind them that they were right to be afraid. I say we remind them that we are more than just the dogs that they would brand us as. We are lions, and lions hunt in packs."

Eyes glowed as her words began to fade. Teague nodded. He slowly made his way to Garrett Laven. He looked Laven in the eye and held out a hand. They had spent so long working alone; it had been necessary to survive on the open water. Ending such a life was a hard thing for them.

Captain Laven gave a small nod, and they joined hands.

"And you, Marquez?" Teague asked. Again, he held out a hand. He watched her. He dared her. He stepped closer.

"We are lions, then," she told him.

They clasped hands. An alliance had begun.

Darkness covered the sea. It engulfed the waters that stretched from horizon to horizon in its ebony maw. The moon and its silver light were hidden beyond the clouds as they often were in the heart of autumn. Only the lamps of the Red Fortune broke the dark veil. The only sound was that of the vessel cutting through the gentle waves. The Fortune was an Elaran treasure galleon bound for the harbour city of Landonsport, a prospering town held within the clutches of the Gulf of Lamrei. Vanor Pasian, captain of the Red Fortune, sighed as he ran his gaze over the maps stretched out on the table before him. In his thirty-five years he had spent near twenty aboard ships. Fifteen of which had been with the Elaran navy. He had fought in dozens of skirmishes, against pirates, vagabonds, and even the Valkir, yet never had he been dragged into a conflict such as this. War had been declared on the filth that called Lamrei home. The scourge of the Sacasian. The ones who stole, burned, and murdered in cold blood. The orders had been simple. Kill or capture the pirates and burn their harbours. Imprisoning those who believed that they fought for freedom was poetic justice. The thought gave Pasian something of a smile.

Yet now Landonsport, one of the four great cities that had all but helped the pirates in creating their havens across the seas, had turned coat and thrown themselves upon the League's mercy. Magister Imrohir of Elara had accepted the surrender, but the surrender came with condition. The League would now use the port as a base, and the city would give over command of their fleet.

Pasian believed this folly for the people of Landonsport were no better than the rats. Now he was sailing a cargo of near unimaginable value to them. Food, supplies, weapons, and – most importantly – gold. Why have a turncoat ally when you could have a good friend?

"STARBOARD!" came a roar from the Fortune's deck.

Pasian's head snapped up as the cry was echoed once more.

"STARBOARD!"

The warning bell began to sound. Something large slammed into the side of the ship.

They were under attack.

Illis heard the screams from above as the Red Fortune was boarded. Fear ran down the boy's spine, as he heard the clash of steel and the cries of the dying. He had seen fights and brawls in his fifteen years, yet never anything like this. He was nothing more than a cabin boy and had never wielded a sword; let along swung one. He hid in the crews' quarters beneath the main deck. Here, at least, he would not be in the way.

Something heavy thudded into the boards overhead. It was followed by a snarl, and the unmistakable sound of steel being driven into flesh. The Elaran boy reached into his shirt and wrapped a hand around his amulet.

"Azaria protect me," he murmured, and shut his eyes as a great roar assaulted his ears. His blood turned to ice. Trembles rocked his thin body, as the men above began to chant.

THUD!

The door to the main deck was flung open. Illis snatched up his knife as a pair of boots began to descend into the bowels of the Red Fortune. He ducked around one of the side posts as the boots left the wooden stairs and reached the hard flooring of the crews' quarters. The sound of heavy breathing reached his ears as the wood creaked underfoot.

"Anything?" a savage voice called, no more than three paces from Illis' hiding spot.

"I'm not sure," another replied.

The boy could barely keep his frightful gasping breaths at bay as the footsteps drew closer. His trembling fingers tightened around the hilt of the dagger.

"I think I smell a rat," the first voice growled, and its menacing edge cut deep into Illis' terrified heart.

The boy turned his head as the blood left his face. Staring at him across the quarters was a man. His hair wild, and his face a mask of blood. His right hand was covered by the curling guard of a sidesword, while his eyes were gateways to hell. Illis stumbled back with a whimper as the pirate came toward him. Fear. It was all he felt. The dagger fell from his grasp and rang as it hit the wooden planks beneath. Illis' gaze was drawn to the pirate's bloody sword. A second pirate joined the first with a sneer and brought his vicious bearded axe into a two handed grip.

"You a coward?" he growled in disdain.

Illis' heart near stopped. The pirates could see the fear in his eyes. From birth he had been told about the bloodthirsty raiders of Lamrei. He knew how they treated their victims and prisoners.

"Please..." he stammered, as he backed into the side of the ship, "I'm just the cabin boy."

The man with the sword snorted. His hand shot out and grabbed Illis' arm. The boy screamed as the pirates dragged him toward the wooden stairs.

The deck of the Red Fortune was slick with the cold, salty water of the Sacasian, mingled with the thicker crimson coloured tide of blood. Splashes came from the sea as bodies were thrown overboard. The pirates were clad in their loose shirts, coats, and blouson pants. Under the moonless night, they appeared as devils.

Now that he was above deck, Illis realised how they had been taken by surprise. No lights had been kindled aboard the pirate vessel and so it had made its approach unknown. The dark sails had helped with the illusion. The boy's eyes widened as he was shoved toward the main mast. There, covered in his own blood, was Captain Pasian. Beside the captain knelt eight of the other crewmen. Their hands bound tightly.

Another man crouched before Vanor Pasian. A midnight-blue coat was pulled tightly around his strong form. A white shirt sat beneath the embellished coat, while a pair of belts were wrapped around him. The first ran from shoulder to hip, while the second was bound around his waist.

The pirate murmured something to Captain Pasian before he turned to face the boy and his captors. Everything about the man was evil and chilled Illis to the bones. A trio of scars ran down the left side of his head while his dark hair hung loosely down to his shoulders and disappeared into his beard. A slight frown furrowed his brow. His eyes burned deep into Illis' soul.

"Found him skulking below deck," one of Illis' captors told the man.

The scarred man raised his bloodied sword and placed it upon Illis' shoulder.

"Do you know who I am boy?" the menacing voice growled coldly.

Illis's eyes dropped to the deck, for he could not bear to look at that evil face any longer. There his gaze fell upon the gore below, and gods, did it frighten him.

"Cillian Teague of the Oridassey," the pirate captain told him, as he wiped his sword on Illis' shirt. He twitched his wrist and placed the cold edge of his blade upon the side of the boy's neck. "Time once was, if we took a ship, its crew would be offered the choice to join our brotherhood," Teague continued. "But those days are long gone. Do you know why?"

Illis' lip trembled, yet he clamped his jaw tightly shut. For such was his fear.

Teague leaned closer and cast his hot, stinking breath on the boy's face. "Sacira, Famier, Androna, and Ephilion, all washed away like the tides. Bodies left to rot in the sun as carrion for crows. Men, women, children... all dead. And for what? For what?"

"You are a traitor and a butcher, Teague," spat Vanor Pasian, as he glared up at the pirate captain. "No more than that. Here you stand under the moonless sky, attacking in the dark like a coward."

"Yet here I stand," Teague replied, "aboard *your* ship, with *your* men kneeling at my feet."

"The Crown will make you bleed for this."

"They have tried many times over."

Teague locked his gaze with Illis'. The boy could not look away from that consuming glare, that bottomless pit of burning rage, even as Teague spoke.

"Kill the crew."

The men of the Red Fortune cried out as rough hands seized their bodies. Pasian closed his eyes and bowed his head. He had failed his men. One by one, the pirates sank their blades into the throats of their prisoners and watered the deck with their blood. Illis began to sob as their lifeless bodies collapsed before his eyes.

His comrades. His friends.

Was he next to fall?

All he felt was the biting wind, and the numbing fear that chilled him to the bone. Tears spilled freely down his cheeks, as Teague turned those evil eyes back on him.

"Did you know that Pasian was my brother once?" Teague murmured. "No matter."

He lowered his blade and glanced to one of his brethren. "Prepare a longboat. We do *not* kill children."

Teague stepped away. He met Captain Pasian's eyes, and the man gave him a nod and a slight smile. Like the rest of the crew, Pasian had always been good to him. It was all he could do to stop the sobs from wracking his body.

"Is it wise, sparing the boy?" one of the pirates whispered to Teague, as the two drew close. "They do not know we are this far west."

Illis' heart skipped a beat. He had good ears and could just barely make out their words.

"And that is how it shall remain," Teague replied. "Trust me, brother – they will not be ready when we attack Landonsport from the north."

The captain of the Oridassey turned and gazed around the deck. "We have won a great victory here and it shall not be the last. Lock the Fortune's captain in the brig, and then we sail with our new prize."

TWO

"Kneel."

Sir Corvo's voice echoed through the silent chamber and pierced its quiet like a blade through water.

Kyler knelt before the newly minted acting grand master. He did not wear the travel-stained clothes of the boy he once was, nor was he clad in the garb of an initiate. The time for those garments was past. Now a midnight-blue surcoat, emblazoned with the white sun, covered his chest. A shirt of mail sat atop the sapphire gambeson he wore beneath while a brilliant blue cloak was draped over his shoulders. Steel bracers, pauldrons, and greaves were strapped over his limbs, and his amulet of the Twins hung free from his neck.

All eyes went to Sir Corvo as he wrapped a powerful hand around the hilt of his longsword and drew it in a single motion. Kyler clasped his medallion and stared at the cold stone floor. He felt not the chill that came from the floor, nor the gazes of all present. Not that of his mentor Sir Alarik Sindra, or the keen gaze of Sir William Peyene, the man who had been deemed worthy to take upon the mantle of warden. Nor did Kyler feel the kind eyes of Lysandra of the maija. He felt only a warm shiver run down his spine.

"Those who are soldiers of our citadel are soldiers of the gods," Corvo began. "Will you stand with us?"

"I will."

"We stand as Durandail's sword. A mighty instrument to bring justice to his people and strike down their enemies." Corvo kept his eyes forward as he spoke and did not spare the kneeling boy a glance. "We stand as Azaria's shield. To serve all in need and protect those who cannot protect themselves. Will you take up arms for your faith?"

Kyler's words were strong and loud as he spoke, for this was what he was made for. He knew it in his heart, in his very soul.

"Honour, valour, justice, truth, compassion, allegiance. These are the tenets that guide my blade, and in the gods' name, I shall bear it."

The orange glow of the flamelit torches glinted upon Corvo's sword as he raised it. First, he touched it to Kyler's right shoulder. "By the will of the Father of all Fathers." The steel came down on the boy's left shoulder. "And by that of the Silver Lady, I knight thee, Sir Kyler Landrey. Arise now as one of Durandail's chosen. Arise a Knight of Kil'kara."

"Knight of Kil'kara," the watchers chorused.

Kyler rose to his feet as pride blossomed in his chest.

Someday, I'll be a knight. Words he had spoken. Words he had lived by. Words branded upon his soul came to life. He took Sir Corvo's proffered arm, and the two men clasped wrists.

"Wear this title with honour, brother," the acting grand master said with a nod.

"Until my last day," Kyler swore.

Vows spoken and oaths sworn, those who had gathered finally parted. Boots rang on the stones beneath as Kyler strode through the corridors of Kilgareth.

"Pisspot."

Sir Alarik's parade ground voice echoed down the passageway. Kyler nearly rolled his eyes as he turned to face the battlemaster. Despite his new rank, some things would never die.

"I need a word," the veteran knight continued, as he beckoned the younger man. Something in his eyes seemed different. He was tired yet there was a flicker of an ember in his copper gaze. Kyler nodded. Whatever was on the battlemaster's mind was of great importance.

Kyler nodded. "What is it?"

"It's about Elena," he replied. "Follow me."

All elation fled Kyler's body. Instead, he felt a numbness slowly take hold.

"There are some who do not deem it wise to tell you about this," Alarik told Kyler, as he ushered him into his office and closed the thick wooden door behind them. "Yet I have lived long enough to know that a secret kept too long can be the thing that kills a man," he paused a moment, and a flicker of pity crossed his weary face. "And I know how much she means to you."

Kyler could not find words enough to reply. They had returned from Durandail's Vault little over a week before, and as of yet, he had heard *nothing* of the woman he loved – save that she had not come back with them.

He glanced around the small office as Alarik walked past him. The shortsword of an Aureian soldier hung above the knight's mantelpiece, while the purple and silver griffin banner of Aureia itself was draped across a wall. There was little decoration save those two relics from Alarik's past. It was a soldier's room, through and through.

A leather-bound book sat atop the wooden table in the centre of the chamber. It was flung open to reveal the contents of its old pages.

"When we returned," Alarik strode over to the great tome and turned it toward Kyler, "we returned with questions, many of which were of paramount importance. About the Spear that we recovered... and about Elena."

"What are you saying?"

Kyler frowned as he glanced at the open pages of the book. Two words written in dark ink, etched into the top of the parchment, made the blood drain from his face.

"The ruskalan?" he asked, bewilderment turning to shock. "Even if they did once exist, the ruskalan are gone. They're *gone*. Duran Cormac, the Inquisition, saw to that."

"Or so we thought."

"No... no... this cannot be..." Kyler gestured to the illuminated image of a ruskalan painted upon the page. "Look at them. Teeth like daggers, eyes of crimson, pointed ears. Elena was not..."

"Her blood ran *black*," Alarik growled, as his glare burned into Kyler's gaze. "When you fell, you were struck with a mortal wound. You should be dead."

Kyler's hand drifted to his chest. Beneath his armour, there was nothing. Not even a scar. Yet when he closed his eyes, he could still feel the steel bodkin tip of the bolt ripping through muscle and flesh.

Alarik planted his gloved hands on the table. "Listen to me. Corvo, the men, they're *all* saying it. No one, no man, no healer could've saved you. Yet here you stand, as though you had never been hit," Alarik said, and his gaze flickered back to the book. "They say that ruskalan blood has remarkable healing qualities. That it can bring a man back from the very threshold of the afterlife."

"No, you're wrong," Kyler said. 'She's human, like you and I."

He refused to believe it. It could *not* be true.

"I am sorry, truly," Alarik told him. He meant every word. Kyler could see it in his eyes. "Yet there is no mistake. Elena knelt at your side, knife in hand, its steel covered in her black blood. Her eyes burned like fire, and her teeth grew sharp. That is all we know. However she did it, Elena secreted herself amongst our ranks for nearly two years. Never betraying who she was... *what* she was. I went to Lysandra first, for I too did not believe.

You see, Kyler, after the Inquisition and the war, Duran Cormac destroyed every book, every scroll, every last word about the ruskalan beyond these walls. For such was their evil. Even in his time, few believed, yet now... now the ruskalan cease to exist to the outside world and long ago drifted into myth and fairy tale. Every word written lies in this manuscript." Alarik gestured to the book, "And none of it speaks of a ruskalan appearing human."

Kyler bit his lip, and dread filled him as he remembered. He felt as though he had been shot again.

"In Adrestia," he said, "before, even... Elena often spoke of how her mother was sickly. How it was an unknown illness, and that was the reason why she never left her home. At the time, I thought nothing of it, yet now this begs me to question it. Her mother stands as any human, of that I have no doubt, for my father once laid eyes upon her. Though so did she... so did Elena."

"Perhaps she is a halfcaste? A mix of our blood and theirs," Alarik replied, with half a shrug. "We may never know. Whatever her demons, whatever she is, Elena fled upon discovery and vanished as the ruskalan once did. Perhaps they are not as dead as we supposed."

Kyler felt numb. Had it all been a lie? Had *Elena* been a lie? For him, nothing had been truer. The battlemaster paused. His brow twitched into a frown as he looked at Kyler. Kyler knew what he could see. The dark rings beginning to appear around his eyes. The exhaustion.

"You've not been sleeping," Alarik stated.

Kyler said nothing. The truth was written on his face.

"You loved her, didn't you?" Alarik asked.

Kyler nodded as he swallowed his reply. He loved her. He loved Elena. He always had. Now the Elena he knew was gone. Perhaps she had never been real. It tore at him.

With a grimace, Kyler pushed these thoughts back.

"What comes next?" he asked.

The battlemaster let out a deep breath.

"These are dark times, and we will need to stand together to bring back the light. Until such a time as a new grand master is chosen, Corvo will lead in his stead. He will need us, Landrey. All of us. By now, the birds will have reached Rovira, and now the decision rests upon the shoulders of the cardinal and his inquisitors. Though, in my heart, I know what will happen next." He shook his head, expression grim. "We are on the warpath now. There is no stopping it. Not with the Spear in our possession. It will only be a matter of time before we are called to arms once more. And then war will follow. A thing known, is it not, that the gods do not want those heathen Salvaari to blight our land any longer."

"And so we shall finish what Duran started," Kyler said, as he at last understood.

The barbarian tribesmen had plagued their Medean brothers' borders for too long, raiding town after town. Killing and burning without care. The thought angered him to the core.

"Just so," Alarik replied. "If the call comes, we *must* be ready to fight and die."

"*Areut talc cuun'etc,*" Kyler murmured in ancient Aureian.

"Blood or immortality," the battlemaster agreed. "That is our fate as Durandail's chosen. We will rip those rats out of hiding, and if the gods will it, see an end to whatever demons still lurk in the shadows."

"General, Sir." The chainmail-clad soldier dipped his head in respect. "A rider from the south is here. He brings word from Rovira."

Ilaros Arran, commander of the renowned northern legions, glanced up from the many letters scattered around his desk. Letters from Ilaria, Ventos, Maigyr, and even the mother city of the empire, Aureia. His cold blue eyes washed over the soldier who had entered his tent. The soldier was one who served in his private guard. Kaelyn, his name was. A deep purple gambeson protected him beneath his garb of mail, while an equally violet cloak hung from his shoulders. Across his back, a great oval shield bearing the griffin of Aureia was slung, while a shortsword of steel hung from his hip. He looked like any other Aureian soldier, save the fact that his helm was crested.

Ilaros' lips twitched. Tidings from Rovira were a rare thing these days. "Indeed," came his reply, as he nodded to Kaelyn.

It was the only word he need say, for the guard knew him well. The general straightened his tunic as Kaelyn left to fetch the rider. He ran a hand over his beardless chin and folded his arms. His fingers brushed against the sun and moon medallion that he wore at his neck. Within a moment, Kaelyn returned, at his back a man dressed in a travel-stained cloak followed. The messenger kept his hair neatly cropped and his face cleanshaven, like any soldier of the empire. He was young. No more than in his mid-twenties. An embellished cuirass of steel bearing the symbol of the Twins covered his chest. He pulled off his white crested helm and bowed to his superior officer.

"General Ilaros," he greeted the man.

Ilaros gestured toward the golden jug of wine that stood on his desk. "You've had a long ride, friend. Would you care for refreshment?"

"Apologies, sir," the messenger shook his head as he replied, "I must reach Florenna by nightfall."

Ilaros glanced at him thoughtfully. A long ride indeed. "My man tells me that you bring word from Rovira."

"I am Farris Quinnal of His Holiness Cardinal Aleksander's guard," the rider told Ilaros, as he reached into his satchel and withdrew an unopened roll of parchment. "I bring tidings from the highest office in our faith."

Ilaros took the proffered letter with a slight frown. The sun-and-moon seal was unbroken, yet he could tell that Farris knew exactly what the contents of this letter were. He split the wax and unrolled the parchment, and from there his eyes grew wide. Ilaros read the words again, and again in disbelief.

He met Farris' eyes as he spoke, though his words were directed to his guard's ears. "Kaelyn, send for the captains. We're going to war."

"General?" Kaelyn's brow furrowed.

Ilaros handed him the parchment, and Farris broke the silence as he read. "His Holiness will wish to know how soon you depart."

Ilaros let out a deep breath and fingered the hilt of his sword. "I have ten thousand swords at my command. Two legions in all, scattered from Valentia to Ilaria."

He turned, shifting his eaglelike gaze to the great standards by the entrance of his tent. Lengths of wood like any spear, yet atop them were carved griffins, forged in bronze, coated with silver. Each legion had one such standard, the symbol of Aureia itself. The griffin stood as more than just bronze and wood. It *was* Aureia.

"It will take a week to call my legions and have them ready to march. Here, at the northmost garrison of our great empire, we stand sentinel, and now Cardinal Aleksander has sent forth his call. I shall send orders. The fifth legion will rally here, and we shall meet the seventh in Valentia. Tell His Holiness that we will reach Aethela in little over a month. It is a hard march through the mountains of southern Laeoflaed. From there we track northeast through Torosa. But make no mistake… our blades will have tasted pagan blood long before the other legions arrive. Of that you have my word."

Farris, seemingly satisfied, nodded.

"Then I will make my leave," he said.

"Light of the Twins go with you, brother," Ilaros tapped a hand to his chest as he replied. The messenger returned the gesture.

"And with you, General."

He left, vanishing from the tent as swiftly he had come.

"So, Durandail's Spear has been found, and for the gods we march," Ilaros whispered, as he clasped his amulet.

Now it would begin.

The great temple of Kilgareth was full, yet it was silent. Over a thousand men and women – knights, maija, and initiates – all watched on without a word as the caskets were carried down the aisle in the centre of the hall.

Kyler felt nothing but cold as he watched the coffins of his comrades move past him, held atop the shoulders of those who had known them for far longer. Neph, the once marathon runner from Larissa. Emir, from faraway Berenithia. The maija, Quinn, whom he had met long before he had arrived at Kilgareth. Sir Matias Valenquez, the great warden who had once saved his life. Torin Aureilian, the young knight from Rovira he had met in that filthy tavern in Malcia. They had been his companions, his friends. Now their light had been extinguished.

Kyler glanced to his side and placed a comforting hand on his companion's shoulder. Gaius Aureilian, father of Torin. The veteran of Aureia's legions kept his face near devoid of emotion, yet even Kyler could see a great sadness behind his eyes.

All those men, those great knights, had suffered the same fate. Cruelly taken from this life by the one they called Wa'rith – the shadow. Kyler could remember the shadow well. The hood and garb. The way he moved and fought. A demon made flesh. Kyler's hand balled into a fist as his anger stirred. One day, he would avenge his fallen friends and take that monster's head.

Five caskets belonged to Wa'rith's victims. The sixth, the one at the front of the procession, belonged to Amaris Delodrysia.

The fallen grand master of this fortress. He had passed in his sleep, that was what Alarik had told Kyler. He had died but two days after they had left Kilgareth to chase the riddle of the Spear. Once a great bear of a man, his veins running with his faith, now his eyes were cold and unseeing.

One by one, the coffins were laid out atop the dais. All bore a silver sun and moon upon their lid. Lady Lysandra, arc'maija of the citadel, stood before them. The robes she wore were of the purest white. It was her duty as head of her sect to lead the eulogy for their fallen brethren.

"Azaria once said each life has a season," Lysandra began, her strong voice carrying to the very ends of the temple, "and in this, we must remember that there cannot be darkness without there first being light. And it is in this light that we flourish."

She paused as her words echoed through the temple. Her eyes stared out at the crowd. For a moment, they found Kyler's, and he could not look away. He was frozen. It was as if she stared into his heart, seeing the pain, the anguish, the sorrow, the rage. So many dead. Elena gone. Only when Lysandra looked away could Kyler move again.

"Today we mourn the passing of our fellow knights and maija," she continued. "Men who gave their lives for our Order, for our faith. They were brothers and sons, lovers and friends. They gave their last so that we may embrace a future that was once only spoken of in hushed whispers. Each person here in this temple can attest to the fact that, though they gave their lives, they left this world in a far greater place than they found it. And now they rest in paradise."

Lysandra swept her gaze over the coffins as she spoke, "Amaris I knew better than most. He treated all as an equal, regardless of rank or standing. Brothers and sisters, all of us in this temple, were his children, and he loved all of us with the deepest part of his soul. He was the blood of Cormac. He was a great warrior and mentor, though above all else he was a great man and a dear friend. As he once told me, *Every man has a purpose to which he sets his life; let yours be the doing of good deeds.* An ideal worth striving toward."

Briefly, she closed her eyes. "He was my friend and brother, as were all taken before their time. Do not dwell on this moment of sadness, nor let darkness fill your heart. Instead rejoice, knowing that they bask in the light of paradise. And so, we send our brothers forth to their final rest. They go with the gods."

Lysandra wrapped her fingers around her medallion. "May their souls find the rest they well deserve in heaven. Cuun'etca hěy'læn."

Immortality in paradise. A thing well deserved.

THREE

The Sacred Grove, Forest of Salvaar

Galadayne pushed down hard upon the mercenary knight's wound. Blood was already soaking through the strip of cloth, and the man's breathing was growing shallower by the second.

The Medean gasped. His eyes flickered open.

"Easy now," Galadayne told him.

The knight winced as he tried to move. Pain burned through his legs and chest. The back of his head was covered in sticky blood from when he had fallen. He glanced down and for the first time saw the red bandage pressed tight to his neck. His face paled and panic began to set in. Galadayne saw the Medean's eyes widen as they took in the deep wound. "Don't look down. Look at me," Galadayne said as he placed a hand behind the man's head and forced his gaze up. "Look at me!"

"What happened?" the man gasped, as he fought for air.

Galadayne snorted. "Seems like your brothers left you to die."

He looked down at the man and for the first time he felt some kind of pity for the one abandoned by his companions. Horror washed across the Medean's face as Galadayne spoke the words.

"Now," Galadayne continued, "you are not long left for this world, my friend. The only question that remains is how you wish to leave it."

"My sword," the fallen knight stammered through gritted teeth, as he reached for the hilt of his blade. It lay barely two feet from his outstretched fingers.

"Tell me where they took the girl," Galadayne said.

"Give me my sword!"

"Tell me where they took the girl," Galadayne repeated, as he glared down at the knight. "*Where?*"

"You waste your time," the knight hissed. "I am already dead."

"Aye," Galadayne told him. "The only thing that can change is how you greet the gods. I could ease your passing and send you on your way painlessly with sword in hand. Or these next few hours could be your longest."

Galadayne drew his dagger as he spoke and placed its pommel upon the fallen man's armoured chest. If he pressed down even a little…

"Please tell me that I do not need explain further," he murmured.

The Medean spoke.

Bellec charged back into the clearing with purpose. Rage masked his face. The Medean knights, those slavers, had taken Kitara, his daughter. Now he would get answers. He would search for her for a week, a month, a year. However long it took.

He slid from his saddle and jogged toward Galadayne, with the Aedei moonseer, Aeryn, hot on his tail.

"Has he spoken yet?" Bellec called out.

Galadayne glanced up from the Medean. The mercenary released his grip on the fallen knight's bloody wrist and wiped his knife clean with his cloak.

"Vesuva, along the Mithran coast," Galadayne told him. "It is there that they will meet the flesh mongers and trade the souls that they so condemned."

"Aureia," Bellec cursed.

"Aureia," Galadayne agreed.

Aeryn slowly made her way over to the two men. She held Kitara's fallen sword. Blood still covered its bare blade.

"How far?" she asked.

"Nigh on three thousand miles," Bellec pursed his lips and met her silver eyes. "If the wind is fair, a little under two weeks by ship. On horseback? Perhaps two months."

"Then why do we wait?" Aeryn replied, before starting back toward her horse. "Each moment we delay grants them more time. Come, we must find a ship."

"We cannot just–" Bellec began.

"We cannot abandon her!" Aeryn snapped back.

Bellec started towards the Aedei scout and shot her a venomous glare.

"Listen to me!" he growled. "We would have to charter a ship from Medea, and that would not work. Do you know why? No captain... *no captain*... will take one of your kind aboard. Few enough would be willing to sail that far west past Larissa. Not to mention that as soon as we land, word of our arrival will spread. Two dozen sellswords with Annoran and Medean blood arriving mere days behind knights who fled those same people. We would get to Aureia, but as soon as we land our quarry would know of our presence. The mercenaries I can fight, but *not* an Aureian army. Finding a ship and a man to captain her is a lost cause. Do you understand?"

Aeryn grimaced. She could see the pain on Bellec's face, clear as glass. He was right. "Then what do you suggest?" she asked.

Bellec's brow twitched, and he turned to face Galadayne. The beginnings of a plan had started to take root.

"Gather the men and make them ready. We leave by daybreak."

"We have travelled a long road, you and I," Prince Lukas Raynor told his companion. "There are no words."

"Then do not speak them, my friend," Sakkar replied.

They were alone, sharing a last cup of ale before they departed this land. The Annoran knights were preparing to ride come morning. Lukas would be travelling at their head with his sister, and he knew full well that there would be a storm awaiting him in his homeland. He had disobeyed his father... his king. He had forced Dorian's hand in sending Sir Garrik and countless others this far north. Yet the worst was that Kassandra, his little sister, was being forced to wed that arrogant sod, Emilian Aloys. There would be wars to come, at least in the council chambers of Palen-Tor. He could only pray that they did not spill further afield because of his actions.

"No," Lukas continued, "there are some things that need to be said. Over two years ago, you swore me an oath that you would stay by my side until such a day comes that you might save my life in return."

"I gave my word," the Larissan told him as he let his gaze drift to the flames. "And I plan to keep it."

"How many times have we fought together, Sakkar? Side by side, shoulder to shoulder? You have followed me since the first without qualm or question, often foreseeing the blades of rivals that I have been blind to. In so doing, you have repaid your debt a thousand times over, brother..."

Lukas trailed off as he spoke, for every word was true. Without the Larissan, he never would have made it this far. He knew himself too well for that. He knew what he really was.

"Beasts die, friends and family die, and, in turn, I shall die. In battle, of that I am certain. Yet there is one thing that never dies." Lukas lifted his cup. "Reputation. Reputation that we leave behind... legacy, even. And my story is only just being written."

He could feel the truth of it in his very bones. It coursed through his veins like blood. As his brother Dayne had forged his own path, so too would Lukas.

"But I will not choose such a fate for you," he said. "Your oath is fulfilled. You can go home."

"You would free me of my vow?" Sakkar murmured with wide eyes.

"No. You freed yourself in Miera, in Salvaar. Times beyond count. We are here... *Annora* is here... in this land, because of what I did." The prince bit his lip as he spoke. "When I return home, everything will have changed... for better or worse, I cannot say. And that demands a response. In what form it will come, I do not know, yet that is a burden that I must bear."

Sakkar dipped his head slowly. "You grow more a prince every day."

"If it is fated," Lukas replied.

He had been deep in thought for days. He could remember the words of the Salvaari priestess, Maevin.

Turn away from the rule of man. Only then will you be free to do as you will. Only then can you accomplish greatness.

Lukas stared into the flames. "It is no secret that I have never desired my crown, nor the titles that come with it. Though if it must be so, I shall earn it."

"Whatever the next day brings," Sakkar said.

The prince of Annora held out his hand. "Then, tomorrow, at last we part ways."

Sakkar took it. "Tomorrow. Though do not think this will be the last time we share drink, Annoran."

A smile tugged at Lukas' lips as he saw the grin etched upon his friend's face. He knew that what he'd done meant everything to Sakkar. The Larissan would be able to go home to his family at last. An honour he well deserved.

The sound of galloping hooves hit Lukas' ears long before the rider emerged from the trees. The prince's hand hovered over his sword, and then he recognised the rider. Lukas knew not how he felt about the mercenary, nor could he name the emotions that arose within him when he saw *that* face. Not yet, at least.

"Bellec," Sakkar called out in greeting.

The mercenary's face threatened an ever-growing storm as he dropped from his saddle.

"I need your help," Bellec said.

Gentle waves brushed against the prow of the Lioness as it carved its path west through the Mithramir Sea. A day had come and gone since Kitara's capture at the hands of the Medean mercenary knights, and still not a word had been shared between captor and prisoner.

Kitara opened her eyes as she leaned back against the steel bars of her stinking cell and let her gaze run over her wounded thigh. She had long since bound it with a rag ripped from her shirt, yet the dry blood that had seeped through her trousers served as a sticky reminder of her failure.

She placed a gentle hand over the wound as she looked to the heavens – or, rather, the dark wooden planks above. Though deprived of cloak and brigandine, she barely felt the cold against her skin. The dampness and chill that froze men to the bone were both things well known to her.

The cells that lined the brig were filled with condemned prisoners much like her. All were Salvaari. Most were Káli. Few enough were warriors. A grunt came from the cell opposite as its captive shook the steel barred door in an attempt to force it open. The door, and its lock, easily held.

Kitara grimaced at the sound before speaking. "You can keep doing that all day, and the door is never going to move."

The Salvaari warrior slapped his hands angrily upon the bars and glared toward her. "So, what are you doing?"

"Trying to think," she replied, the slight taste of sarcasm beginning to play upon her lips. "You should not waste your strength."

"Well forgive me if I do not resign myself to this fate," the man growled back. "I have something to live for!"

"Urlaigh, enough," another voice cut in. A strong voice, one that commanded obedience.

The warrior, Urlaigh, painted in the black of the Káli, spared a final glare for Kitara before he glanced at the speaker and replied.

"Aye."

Kitara returned Urlaigh's stare as the big man lumber away from his cell door. Her eyes then went to the man who had commanded him to stop. Morlag of the Káli, brother to Chief Vaylin. Like his sister, Morlag's hair was dark, his eyes evergreen. His form was lean and strong. Beads adorned his beard. Like the rest of his tribe, Morlag's clothes were dark and the arm ring at his wrist was shaped like a viper. A simple cord adorned with a curved snake fang hung at his throat. A young girl, no more than ten or twelve summers, was curled up asleep in the crook of his arm.

"Morlag," Kitara called as she looked to him, "how is she?"

The chief's brother glanced down at the girl's sleeping form.

"Strong."

A door above grated as it was pulled open, and a streak of light flooded the brig. Footsteps.

Kitara set her jaw. She shifted her keen gaze to the two men who came down the thin aisle between the cells. They both held gnarled canes and vicious expressions. Almost as if they hoped that one of the prisoners would try to grab them through the cages.

"What do you want?" snarled Urlaigh, as the two men approached.

"Mind your tone, pagan," snapped one of the Medeans.

Urlaigh grinned savagely through the bars.

"Oh, *pagan* is it?" the warrior sneered.

Many of the Káli began to rise to their feet, their rage-filled eyes stabbing deep into the souls of their captors. If one of these cells was open but a little…

"You had best be praying that these doors hold," Urlaigh finished.

"Oh, they will hold," returned the Medean with a smirk, "and while you are busy howling like a dog, remember that you live only because we allow you to."

Urlaigh's grin widened.

The second man pulled a key from his belt and nodded toward Kitara. "We're here for her," he said.

Kitara frowned.

What could they possibly want with me?

"No," Morlag told them, as he rose to his feet and rested his strong hands upon the bars of his cage. "You will not take her, nor any other."

The man wrapped a hand around the hilt of his sword and drew it ever so slightly. "And you will not move an inch," he replied.

Kitara could hear a dark note in his voice. He would use the sword if he were tested, of that she was certain.

"It's alright, Morlag," Kitara told the chief's brother as she pushed herself to her feet. Her wounded leg protested, but she bit down on the pain and showed nothing. She would not give them the satisfaction. Whatever these men wanted, Kitara would not let any of the Salvaari get harmed in her name.

The Medeans opened the door to her cell and tightly bound her hands, before roughly shoving her up the stairs. The light was nearly blinding. Kitara had been in the darkness below for so long. The crewmen had led her halfway across the deck before her eyes had adjusted.

Dark blurs took colour and shape. Sailors crewed the deck and scurried across the ship like ants, each tasked with one job or another. Silver-clad knights patrolled the deck: the same men who had captured her in Salvaar. There were others, as well. Rough men with dangerous glints in their eyes. Mercantile soldiers, by the looks of them.

The Lioness was triple-masted, like many of the ships Kitara had seen. Each glimpse of white canvas sail and wooden decking brought back memories. Memories that she had repressed.

Now was not the time to dwell on the past. The Lioness was a middle-sized galleon, by the looks, and capable of carrying a crew of over one hundred souls. Whether this ship had such a crew, Kitara could not be sure. Perhaps fifty men were aboard, or perhaps two times that. Either way, there were more than enough to deal with the twenty-eight Salvaari prisoners below. Yet it wasn't the white-shirted sailors nor the clean blue sea that drew her gaze. It was the man clad in steel armour before her on the quarter deck. She knew nothing about him, yet she recognised his armour and those copper eyes.

"You're the one who killed my friend, Hektor," the knight said, as he met her emerald gaze.

"You're the one who left him to die," Kitara replied. She kept her face emotionless.

"Tell me," he replied as he clasped his hands behind his back, "should I have tied one with a broken collarbone and open neck to the back of my horse before beginning a hard ride? I think not. He would have died a far worse death. We had no time, for your people were nearly upon us. Should I have taken his life? Perhaps. I tried. I wanted to end his suffering. And yet I could not kill my friend."

This man, this Hektor, was one who Kitara could remember clear as day. His helm and armour had prevented her from killing him outright, so she had cut open his legs and sliced her blade down hard where his shoulder joined his neck.

"A shattered collarbone is a bad death," Kitara told him. "Yet I will not apologise. He tried to spill my blood, so I spilled his in return."

Kitara could see a hint of sadness behind his gaze. It was the look of a man who blamed himself for his friend's death.

"The curse of every warrior," the knight nodded slowly. "I am Rowan of Patchi, beholden to the lands of Bailon. What do they call you?"

"Do not flatter yourself. That is no business of yours." She raised her bound hands. "Though you bear the title of knight, though you try to speak to me as an equal, I stand as nothing but your prisoner."

She did not lower her gaze as Rowan stepped toward her. His hand wrapped around the hilt of his dagger. Kitara smirked as he drew the blade. The light of the sun danced across its steel length.

"You think that little blade scares me?" she told him, as her gazed flicked to the knife. "I do not fear death."

The blade sliced through the ropes that bound her.

"I have no doubt," Sir Rowan said, as he watched surprise drain the colour from her face.

He sheathed the dagger and turned his back. Rowan's gaze lingered upon the distant land to the south. The coast of Medea. The plains before were broken by the river which melted into the forest of Salvaar.

"I grew up in a small village not far from Salvaar, half a day's ride from those very trees. I was a boy, no more than ten, when your people crossed the border. I saw my parents slaughtered as my home burned around me. As your people took everything. I thought it would all end there, the day that my world fell. And yet life went on as if nothing had happened. Of course, things changed yet nevertheless many things remained as they had been."

Rowan turned back to her and once more clasped his hands behind his back. He did not want pity. Anyone could see that. The purpose of the story had been to give her understanding.

"You do not give me your name, and I do understand that names have power. Yet where I come from, it is considered rude not to introduce yourself, even to an enemy."

"Kitara," she told him, after a moment. "My name is Kitara."

"Well then, Kitara," Sir Rowan said thoughtfully, "I have a proposal for you."

She frowned. "And what is that, exactly?"

"Your people cause quite the commotion, and I would rather this voyage pass without unnecessary bloodshed."

Kitara crossed her arms and tilted her head ever so slightly. "You wish to make a bargain? I am not their leader."

"Indeed," Rowan said. "Yet tell me, what would happen if I sent for that man Morlag? What would happen if my men were forced to drag him from his cell?"

"The Salvaari would turn quickly," Kitara replied.

"And if, in turn, I was forced to harm his people in exchange for a word, I do not believe he would be so inclined to bargain with me."

"You want me to speak to Morlag. Convince him to keep his people quiet."

"Yes," Rowan replied. "As I said, I would rather not resort to violence."

She could see that he meant it. There was no lie in his eyes, and yet what if he merely wanted to keep as many of them alive and unharmed as possible, so to receive more coin once they were sold? Kitara wasn't sure, and yet there could be much to gain. She had seen how slaves and prisoners could be treated. Not so long ago, she had been caged and treated as a beast. Kitara could remember the cold, the lashing wind, and the beatings. Her body had been battered and broken, day after day. Even so, she had not given in back then. She would not give up today.

"And so, you wish to buy my tongue," Kitara told him as her resentment stirred. "I will *not* be your pawn. I will not betray my people."

"I urge you to choose your words with care."

Kitara stared deep into his eyes and let her anger flow. "You take us prisoner, lock us in cages, and now you come before me, your hand extended? I will not be a puppet to you, nor any man. Not while I draw breath."

Rowan returned the glare and took a step toward her. A new coldness came into his eyes. "Do not test me, Salvaari. I have shown mercy to an enemy. It would not be so difficult to put you on your knees and slide my blade across your face. Though it would appear that I would not be the first to do so."

Kitara's blood froze. Here she stood, a prisoner aboard a ship, destined to a life of slavery. Not for the first time. She could still feel Barboza's knife carving through her skin. She could still taste her own blood as it flowed that night.

The beatings.

The cages.

The betrayals.

All of it came back.

A shiver ran through her body. Kitara could barely make out what the knight was saying. His face seemed to warp into that of the pirate captain. The thick beard and golden ringed ears. Her breathing grew more ragged by the breath, and a bead of sweat ran down her pale face. She could feel Barboza's stinking hot breath upon her skin.

His eyes. His savage eyes.

He smothered her. She was drowning in her own blood. Kitara could barely see Rowan's lips move as he spoke, let alone hear the words that came from them. The only sound was the beating of her heart. She was scared. So full of rage. Kitara's hands grew white for her fists were clenched ever tight.

She lashed out.

She was unable to control it. The blow connected and slammed into the knight's chin. Rough hands gripped her as she tried to continue her assault. She screamed and struggled to escape, but she was held too tightly. Rowan returned in kind. His backhanded strike caught her across her face. Kitara's lip split and the iron taste of blood filled her mouth. She offered no resistance as she was taken below and hurled back into her cage. Shivers wracked her body, as she pulled her knees to her chest and curled into a ball. Kitara could not stop the tears.

"Why did you summon me?"

Cailean let his keen gaze run over the dark-clad man who knelt before the great tree. The druid's pale, weathered hand rested upon the tree's ancient roots. Long robes and a wide hood covered the druid's form and hid his scars from the outside world.

"The spirits call to me by day and darkest night. Their pain and anger keep me from my sleep," the musical voice replied, although its bearer did not turn to acknowledge Cailean. "Lycan the Great Hunter has called his pack and even now sets his gaze upon these very trees."

At last, the druid rose to his feet and faced Cailean. The spirit caller's eyes seemed to stare into the Aedei's soul, reaching in to devour anything they could find. Cailean suppressed a shiver as the dark man spoke.

"Do you recall, Cailean son of Raywold, what I once told your brother, here in this very grove?"

The druid slowly raised an arm and swept it around the sacred grove. It was lit by the silver rays of the full moon, while the orange flames of half-a-dozen torches flickered and cast great shadows.

"I did warn him. I warned you all. No matter how the crows feast, not *one* blade is to be drawn at Sylvaine, or no one will be able to save you. Cyneric ignored my words and, in so doing, angered the spirits."

Cailean bared his teeth in anger. "Kendrick was—"

"Under the burning gaze of Sylvaine herself," the druid cut him off with little more than a waved hand. "Your brother attempted to claim his life. He went against the will of the spirits. Of Sylvaine. And they who are as old as time itself do not forget. Nor do they forgive."

"He was poisoned by a traitor's blade," Cailean growled, remembering the look upon his brother's face as the life fled his body. That was something he would never forget.

"In payment for his desecration. However, his blood was not spilled by a traitor's sword, for was it not Henghis who took his life?" The druid's dark gaze flashed in the firelight as he spoke, "The very man who swore a sacred Raigath. An oath accepted by Tanris himself. Such vows cannot be so lightly broken."

Cailean closed his eyes. He could see it still: Henghis' sword driven deep into his brother's chest, Cyneric's lifeblood pooling upon the Stones of Tanris. First it had been Malakai who had fallen to the blades of the Catuvantuli, and then Cyneric had followed.

"What I feel now tears at the soul."

"For now, Cailean of the Aedei, the spirits have granted you their favour. A thing of which they could take away just as easily," the druid continued, never once turning his empty stare from the face of Raywold's son. "So, heed me now. Do *not* go against them. Let them guide you to the right path. For as one battle ends, another so begins."

Cailean let out a deep breath, as at last he looked back to the spirit caller. He felt a very real shiver run through his body. He knew of what the druid spoke, of what the spirits willed. Medea had once again come to the east and shed Salvaari blood under Salvaari skies. The spirits were angered to a fury.

The druid looked up into the heavens, as if his dark gaze could pierce the Veil and traverse into the other plain.

"The nights grow cold," he said, "and the wolf grows hungry."

A great pyre rose before the gathered host as the first rays of the morning sun seeped through the trees. There was a light mist and a cool breeze, unnoticed by those who had come to bear witness. Four torches perched high on wooden poles surrounded the structure, where hundreds of Salvaari had gathered. Their furs and pelts kept the chill breeze at bay even as it pulled at their grease-streaked hair. Men and women from all twelve tribes had come, and now as the sun rose through the clearing, the sorrow etched upon their faces could be seen clear as glass.

Lukas watched on as Cailean stood alone before the pyre. He wished to go to his friend, not to say anything, but to show that he was not alone. It was not his place. Instead, he stood in silence, just as the rest of them did.

One of the Salvaari broke from the crowd with a torch burning bright in her hand. Flaming red hair and the garb of the mountain tribe revealed her to be Etain of the Icari. Lukas had never spoken a word to her, yet he knew that her bond with Cailean was great.

She reached Cailean's side, and he turned to face her. Nothing was said, but something unspoken passed between them. It said more than a thousand words. Cailean took the torch, as Etain turned and stepped back to allow him a moment alone to grieve.

Silent tears streaked down cheeks. Pale faces watched on, as Cailean reached forth and lowered the burning flames of the torch to the base of the pyre. The flax oil caught alight and sent the fire coursing through the kindling and thin branches. Cailean stepped back and cast the torch to the ground as the great structure was engulfed in flame. Wood burned as the fire rose. Flames slowly caught onto the linen wrapped body of Cyneric; once the chief of the Aedei.

"May Cyneric's soul pass through the Veil and find sanctuary beyond the gates of the spirit plane," Etain said in the tongue of her people. She turned to face the crowd as her voice grew. "The chief is dead. Hail Chief Cailean!"

"Hail!"

The roar of the Salvaari echoed from this plane to the next.

Cailean closed his eyes.

Would the spirits smile kindly upon him? Was he strong enough to lead his people?

FOUR

Isle of Agartha, the Valkir Isles

The golden rays of the dawn sun crept through the shutters and assaulted Astrid's closed eyes. The jarl sighed and rubbed her pounding head.

Maybe she had drunk a little too much last night. Maybe.

Astrid bit back a groan and ran a hand through her wild black hair before she pushed herself up onto her elbows. The icy chill, so common to these Isles, barely cooled her warm skin, yet she felt it upon her cheek all the same. Astrid frowned as she looked around the room. The walls were all but bare and near unrecognisable to her eye. Then she remembered.

She glanced to her side, and let her gaze come to rest upon the man who lay next to her. An arm and half of his muscled chest hung out from the bedcovers. His copper hair was long and untamed, although his beard was short. She could remember it tickling her shoulder in the night and her chin before that.

Kol. Yes, that was his name. Kol Svanhild. A warrior from Jarl Ulfric's crew. One who had been all too eager to share the bed of the raven-haired captain who had toppled Magnus from his throne.

Astrid pushed her sheets aside and swivelled around to sit on the edge of the bed. The cold welcomed her like an old friend as her bare feet touched the floor. The jarl took up her carved raven's head necklace and placed it over her head. The cool wooden carving fell to her throat. She gazed at the amulet for a moment as she remembered everything. Her mother and father. Raol and Hélla. Everyone who she had lost.

Astrid pushed the memories aside and flicked her hair back. It fell over the black raven tattoo that sat upon the naked skin of her shoulder. A jagged scar crossed the top of her right arm where Erik's axe had once tasted her blood. Around the wound were burn marks from seared flesh from when she had sealed the injury with fire.

Astrid pulled on her blue and white dress, tied the small belt around her waist, and wrapped her fur-trimmed cloak about her. She gave Kol a final glance before walking out of his bare-walled house and into Agartha.

Even though autumn had long since pulled the Isles into its icy grip, the streets of Agartha were filled with a great throng of people. Fishing ships still had to be sent out, trading vessels still needed to bring back the goods required to survive winter, and some of the brave men still prepared for a final raid before the snows came down.

Though she carried no weapon, not even the humblest of daggers, Astrid could not keep her eyes wary. While many of the people saw her as some kind of liberator who had toppled a tyrant, there were those who still held Magnus to heart. Others yet held her accountable for burning their ships during her flight from the city. Erik insisted that she still carry the axe that he had once given her, and yet she could not do it. Not now, when she had no clear enemy. She was no warrior and would no longer pretend to be one.

No – now, Astrid had but one path to pursue. A dream, even. One worthy of even the greatest of navigators or sailors.

The passage south.

The thought gripped her mind as she hurried through the streets, often exchanging greetings with the people she knew. She ignored the few lingering dark looks, for they had long since ceased to cause her concern. After all, if someone had wanted her dead, she would have died a long time ago.

The warm flames of half-a-dozen braziers and cooking fires greeted her as she at last made entry into her family's longhall. Erik Farrin glanced up from the fire as she strode toward him.

"I sent someone to find you," he stated.

"Oh?"

Erik met her eyes for a moment. "The city is without a leader, and the people are undecided. There are some who still blame you for their misfortune."

"Well, here I am," Astrid replied, as she cast off her cloak. Her lips curled ever so slightly. "And as you can see, I am fine."

He watched her as she approached his seat by the flames. "You, more than most, must be on your guard. In moments such as these, cities can change hands as easily as silver."

"And we must keep our eyes ever watchful." Astrid nodded and crossed her arms. "Another of father's lessons. I remember them all, and I remember them well, Erik."

He frowned. "And I trust then that you had a... *pleasant* evening."

Astrid rolled her eyes to the heavens and gritted her teeth. She loved her brother, and she loved him dearly. They were two sides of the same coin. Yet he still had so much to learn. "Don't give me that."

"The people are beginning to notice."

She raised her eyebrows as she replied, "Notice what, exactly? That I am human, just as they are?"

"They are saying—"

"That I am a whore, no doubt," the jarl cut in. She snorted and turned away. "Let them talk. I care not."

"Well, you should."

"Indeed," she said. "However, as the wisest person I know once said, a good man should think with his head, but always, *always* listen to his heart."

"Who said that?" the bloodsworn asked.

Astrid turned and gave Erik a smile.

"Brother, you forget – *I* am the wisest person that I know."

Irritation flickered across his face. He did not understand. Not yet, at least.

"And so," she continued, "I tell you now, this world, as dreary as it is, as bleak as it is, holds many pleasures. Why should you not embrace them all, and take whatever joy you can from a moment, however fleeting it may be? So, let them talk."

At last, Erik sighed and placed his hands upon his hips.

"When Father died, I knew everything would change. When you laid your plans and Sven fell, I could feel it evermore. I knew that the path we went down, however dark it may be, would finally emerge into the light. And yet when victory was so close, when it was within our grasp, my heart was ripped from my chest. Yet still, I believed."

Astrid could see the pain in her brother's face as the trials of days past flashed through his mind. She knew that it was this final loss that wounded him so terribly. The loss of the last of their crew to fall to the tyrant's blade.

"I am sorry," Astrid told him, letting the sincerity she felt flow from her lips. "I know that Hélla was your future... I loved her as a sister."

"I know," he said quietly. "I know. She was the sun and will *never* rise again." Astrid bit her lip and placed a sorrowful hand on Erik's shoulder. He clasped her arm.

"I am afraid," Astrid's words were quiet, barely more than a whisper, "and do you want to know the truth? Despite the horror that has come to us, to our family, to Mother, Father, Raol, Hélla, all those who were ripped from this life..." A chill seeped through her veins, though not from the cold. "I do not feel a thing. Not pain, nor sadness, nor grief. And that terrifies me. For the first time in my life, I do not have an answer. I feel as helpless as a child."

"We will get through this, however long it takes," Erik told her. "Together."

"Your will, my strength."

The sun had risen ever higher when the siblings were joined by their crew in in the longhall. Laughter, song and the warmth of fire filled the hall. The great doors burst open, and in strode Torben, a great bear of a man. A grin spread across his face as he peered through the hall filled with his fellow crewmates. His eyes locked upon the siblings.

Cheers flooded the room as those within caught sight of their returned friend. Over a week he had been gone, yet now once more he stood before them.

Meaty hands were clapped upon his back and a drink swiftly poured, as he made his way to the centre of the hall. All eyes followed him, and joyous faces lit up at the sight.

"Torben, you old boar!" Erik grinned and embraced his friend and mentor. Torben let loose a bellow of a laugh and returned the hug.

"It is good to have you back, old man." Astrid couldn't stop the smile from spreading across her lips as she in turn embraced the man she saw as a second father.

"Been gone a week and you have all grown soft on me!" Torben roared.

The crew jeered in reply.

"You survived Lumis, then?" Astrid asked.

"Well enough," he said with a shrug. "Those men of Vay'kis… too lofty for my taste."

The scâldir laughed as he spoke, and they hungrily lapped up every word. They had all missed him. Astrid smacked her cup into his and together, they took a long draught.

"And Earl Arndyr?" Astrid asked.

Of all the people she had met, it was Earl Arndyr Scaeva she had bonded most with. They were as kindred spirits. Both had a love of the sea and discovery alike.

Torben nodded slowly as he replied, "Pretty as ever, but says he will join with us."

The roar that followed was deafening. Astrid clapped her brother on the back and exchanged a grin with him. From his pouch, Torben procured a sealed letter and handed it to her.

"He gave me no message for your ears, yet said that everything you need know is in this."

Astrid took the letter and opened it with a small smile playing across her lips. She scanned the document. Her gaze lingered on every last word.

"Little use that," Torben muttered, gesturing to the letter, "reading."

"Coming from a simple man, I am not surprised," Astrid shot back.

Like many of the Valkir – most, in fact – Torben saw no point in learning to read or write. Few of her people did, though that fact had long since stopped grieving her. Astrid saw it as an advantage, especially for one not fond of the sword or axe. Knowledge was power, and the ability to read unlocked it. Many things could be learned through book or scroll. Things long forgotten to most.

Astrid fingered the letter as her mind was filled. Arndyr wished her well and looked forward to the next time they met, and then he spoke of the plans that they had set in motion. The jarl passed her cup to Erik and, using a chair as a step, leapt up onto the vast table. All eyes went to the raven-haired captain as she held a hand up for silence.

"My friends, written here in this letter is everything. Our plans – our *legacy* – has been put in motion. Thanks to our brothers in Lumis, the gateway south, past the shores of Aureia, has been opened!"

The Valkir cheered as the words left her mouth. Feet were stomped, and a great chorus of sound echoed through the hall.

Astrid began to stride up and down the length of the table as she spoke, "In one moon, Arndyr Scaeva will grace these shores, and will bring his ships with him. In one year our journey will be a song that has become legend!"

Astrid let them roar for a moment as she spread her arms wide. This was it. The one thing that had plagued her mind for weeks now.

"This dream, to charter the unknown waters beyond the empire, may be seen as folly... yet I give you my solemn word that those who dare navigate those cursed seas will return not as men or sailors, but as heroes! Are you with me?"

The crew of the Wind Rider bellowed their approval.

Astrid climbed down from her perch and embraced her friends.

This was it. The one thing that she lived for. Sailing. Navigation.

Nenrir, the great archer of the crew, clapped her on the shoulder, while his ever-present brother, Laerke Redleaf, gave her one of his wide grins. Despite everything he had suffered at the hands of Magnus, Redleaf still believed in her fully. Just as he had done when she had asked him to stay behind and act as a prisoner, while she had made for Vay'kis.

"Well said," he told her, "Tyrantsbane."

Tyrantsbane. The Raven Jarl. Names and titles given to her when she had struck Magnus from this life. Titles that she did not want nor desire, yet it was impossible to stop the whispers from taking true form. There were worse names, she supposed.

Astrid glanced up as her helmsman, Fargrim, made his approach.

"Did you speak to Lodinn?" she asked him. "What did he say?"

"I did," the helmsman told her, "and he said yes."

"And the ship?"

Fargrim could not hide the grin from latching onto his lips.

"She is ready."

Elation took hold as the jarl left the hall and made for the harbour. A breeze whipped through Astrid's hair as the vessel cut through the water. Three massive masts soared into the sky. More sails covered its massive length to grant her speed, while the new hold allowed for more resources and a far longer voyage.

"Two notches port!" Astrid called out to Fargrim, as she held onto the railing of the quarter deck.

"Jarl!" the helmsman cried, and he pulled on the new wheel.

Wind rolled through canvas. The ship changed course. The sails billowed as they took on the force. The ship flew out of the bay and carved a path through the waves. Astrid couldn't stop the joyous laugh as it left her lips. The wind in her face, through her hair, and on her cheek, made her feel *alive*. Truly alive, for the first time in months.

Astrid ran across the quarter deck and leapt up onto the side railing. She had long since abandoned her dress for a tunic and trousers. She caught the taut rigging with her right hand, as she leaned out over the waves.

Thank the Sea-Father for the trader Lodinn. It had taken a vast sum, a king's ransom even, to get the man to part with his ship. The vessel was one of the best in the Isles, that much was certain. Eventually the trader had agreed to the sale. The Wind Rider could only hold enough food and water for a large crew for a few months, perhaps more if they rationed it. But this ship, this majesty of the sea, could store enough for them to survive near to a year before they even *thought* about rations.

Astrid didn't know what lay beyond the southmost tip of Aureia, but by the Sea-Father, she would be prepared. This ship could see her dream through. It could change everything for her people.

Lodinn was waiting for them when at last they returned to the harbour. The gangplank was lowered, and Astrid strode down as soon at the wood touched the pier. The old merchant watched her closely.

"It went well, then?"

"Lodinn…" Astrid held out her arm. Lodinn took it eagerly. "I have no words. She's beautiful."

"I know," the trader gave her a smile as he spoke. "Should do you well enough down south."

The jarl met his kind eyes and let hers show nothing but the gratitude that she now felt.

"I cannot thank you enough."

Lodinn snorted. "You paid for her. She's yours now. I will hear no more about it."

Astrid nodded as her crew began to disembark. She let her eyes wash over the ship once more, and took in every beam and sail, every last chip or fade in the wood. The vessel had character, and as her father had once said, *Never trust a man without scars.*

To Astrid, ships were like any person. Treat them well, and they in turn will look after you. Harm them at your peril. This path that she was about to set them on was unlike any other. She had no knowing of how it would end. Many had tried to conquer the passage south, yet in the centuries of trying none had yet returned. Astrid planned to be the first. If she succeeded in this undertaking, if *they* succeeded, her crew would be immortalised as heroes. Just like Iren Brightblade and Freydis Bluksvier had once been.

It wasn't the fame that concerned Astrid, nor the legacy that would come with it, that kept her awake at night. It was the dream of discovering new places and cities. In discovering what exactly happened to all those crews who vanished like ghosts. She had never been a glory seeker, she had never wanted it, but this voyage was the thing of legend. Reputation would come with it, no matter what happened from this moment on.

"A ship needs a name," Lodinn said, after a moment. "One that binds her to her jarl."

Astrid wrapped a hand around her necklace. The Raven Jarl, some called her. Intelligent birds were ravens, deceptive and full of tricks. Just as she was. It was time she embraced that.

"Ravenheart," she said.

FIVE

The Sacred Grove, Forest of Salvaar

The great red and silver host gathered as dawn's rays crept over the horizon. Swords, spears and shields were made ready, as the Annoran guard came together under the light of the sun. They were ready and each man was filled with the same excitement. They had ridden here to make safe their beloved prince, and he had been made safe. Now they could return to Annora and to their homes and families. Landon Montbard and Sir Edward rode at the head of the column with the eagle standard-bearer at their side. They had only to wait for the word of their commander and then they would begin the long journey home.

With the guard rode a second force five hundred strong. Eirian of the Káli, Vaylin's general, who had once fought by their side, and his warriors, were to accompany the Annorans as far as Oryn.

"All the men are assembled, my prince," called Sir Garrik Skarlit, the master at arms and captain of the royal guard of Palen-Tor.

Lukas gave a single nod. "Prepare them to ride," he said. "We can reach Oryn in a matter of days. From there, we turn west to Sergova."

"Lord." Garrik bowed and pulled on his red-crested helm.

While he swung himself up into the saddle and rode toward his men, Lukas turned to his companions. Bellec, Galadayne, the moonseer Aeryn, Cailean and Sakkar were gathered around him.

He would be parting ways with many of them. Perhaps some he would never see again.

"My father's blood would boil knowing that we fought side by side, no matter the truth," Lukas told Bellec, as he held out his arm. "Though for what it is worth, I wish you good fortune."

"Likewise," the mercenary leader replied, as he clasped the prince's arm.

"May the spirits ride with you," Cailean told them, as he tapped a fist to his heart. "Return swiftly, moonseer. We may yet have need of you."

"Yes, Chief," Aeryn replied.

"Bring her home," Lukas said. His strong voice was filled with the want to go with them. Kitara had saved his life, and not being able to return the favour hurt him. It was not his task, though. He had to get Kassie home safe and put an end to this foolishness with Aloys.

"We will," Aeryn vowed.

Lukas could see the fierce intent in her silver gaze. She was a hunter, yet Lukas could see something else in her face. Something that went beyond friends. Aeryn felt something for Kitara; that much was clear.

Bellec gave the company a final nod before he clapped Galadayne on the shoulder and strode toward his horse. There, the mercenaries had gathered, twenty in all. Each hardened to the bone from decades of fighting. With a tracker as skilled as Aeryn at their side, Lukas had no doubt they would find Kitara.

"Farewell big man," Sakkar's voice broke the silence as he held out his hand to Cailean.

"And you, Larissan," the Aedei said, and he swatted the hand aside and pulled his friend into a bear hug. "Take care of yourself, uh? And that bird of yours."

"Always," Sakkar told him as he stepped back.

Lukas met his friend's eyes, and in them were a thousand words.

They had travelled so far together. Had shed blood and sweat together. Had sang and danced and become the closest of brothers. Now, at last, they would part ways. They embraced as kin, as family. Their foreheads came together.

"I thank you for everything, brother," Lukas told Sakkar. "If not for you, I would not be the man I am today. Everything that I learnt about the values of nobility and honour… I learnt from you."

Sakkar clasped Lukas' shoulders with his powerful hands. "You and I will always be blood, from this day until our last."

"I wish I could go with you, truly," Lukas told him.

"I know. But your duty to your family, to your sister, comes first."

Lukas silently agreed, as he glanced toward Kassandra who rode at Sir Garrik's side.

"One day I will see you again, brother," he continued. "Of that I have no doubt."

"The sands of time flow ever fast." Sakkar held up an arm, as Sabra soared down from the heavens and landed gracefully upon it. "I shall await the day that we ride together again." With that he was gone. His flamboyant robes swirled as he mounted his desert horse. The Larissan rode to Bellec's side. He rode to the side of a man who was an outlaw in Annora. A man who his father would kill if he got his hands upon.

After two years of brotherhood, Sakkar's oath was fulfilled. Lukas felt a deep hint of sadness as he rode away. He was perhaps Lukas' only true friend, and his loss would be keenly felt.

Cailean placed a hand on his shoulder. Together, they watched the mercenary company embark on their passage west, until Cailean broke the silence.

"For what you have done here… I will not forget."

"I only wish that more had come."

"But you did," Cailean told him, "and for that, you will always have a place here, brother."

"Then we will share drink again upon a day."

Cailean bellowed with laughter and slapped a meaty hand onto Lukas' back.

"If you can hold it," he replied.

"When next we meet, I hope it is under better circumstances."

"It will be."

The pair embraced. Lukas nodded to his friend as they parted, before he took a deep breath and made his way over to his horse. The prince pulled himself up into his saddle and spared a final glance at the mercenary company, as they rode from sight. The bond that Annoran, Larissan, and Aedei had formed would be strong until the day they died. Of that Lukas was certain.

He swept his gaze around the trees. Here, he had known a freedom that was impossible to find in Annora. Here, there was no judgement, nor foolish laws, that bound man and religion. Here he could do what he wanted to do. Be who he wanted to be. Regardless of his rank. A thing that he longed for and desired above all else.

He clicked his tongue and, with a flick of the reins, rode over to join the Káli and Annoran contingent. He angled his mount toward Eirian, who rode halfway down the column.

"We are ready, Prince Lukas," the Káli general told him.

Lukas gazed into the distance, his mind lost in thought. "Mmm."

"Embrace the day," said from his side. "They will find your friend and bring her back to her people. The spirits will not abandon one of their own."

"I hope you're right," was all Lukas said.

Kitara was good. What had happened, how she had been taken, the thought angered him. "And now…" Lukas muttered and kicked his heels in.

He rode down the Annoran line, with Eirian hot on his heels. Lukas reached Kassie's side and gave her a smile. She returned it.

"Lukas, I'm glad you're here."

Few enough words, but ones of great comfort. The prince knew exactly what she meant.

"We ride west!" Sir Garrik roared from the head of the column.

With that, it began. The Annorans taking the road to Oryn. Sakkar and the mercenaries parting from the column and taking the path southwest.

The sun had gone down, and the company had stopped for the night. They took rest beneath those same trees that had once terrified them. The children of the Raynor clan sat alone, for in this moment, neither cared for the seriousness or the crude banter of the knights.

"When we get back and Father finds out what you did… there will be the devil to pay," Lukas said quietly.

"I suppose that makes two of us," Kassie replied, and shared a glance with her brother.

"I do not care for myself," Lukas told her bitterly. "But they want to ship you off north to marry some arrogant boy, a child who–"

"Lukas!" the princess cut in. She rested her hand atop his and gave him a soft smile. "It's alright… it's alright. If it is indeed Father's wish, then I will marry Emilian Aloys. For the good of the realm."

"Damn the realm," Lukas growled. "You do not have to do this."

"I am a princess of the blood. This is my duty," she replied. "You may not like it – *I* may not like it –but it is the right thing to do."

Lukas snorted and leapt to his feet. He could feel his anger burning now. It flooded his veins with fire. If Aloys was in front of him in this moment… steel would taste blood.

"Do you know what?" Lukas snarled. "I am *sick* of doing the right thing!"

Kassandra rose to join him as a hint of desperation slipped into her voice, "Then you do this now, for me. Please."

"I cannot just stand by while you are sold… and for what?" Lukas snapped. "So that Father can add to his legacy? The man who united Annora is not enough for him? Now he wants Medea as well?"

"Lukas, your hand is at your sword," Kassie said quietly.

Lukas tore his gaze from her pale face and glanced down. His knuckles had turned white, for his grip around the pommel of his blade was tight. He took a breath and closed his eyes. "I'm sorry," he murmured, releasing the blade. "I'm sorry."

"It's fine," the princess told her older brother, as she squeezed his hand.

Lukas sighed.

"I am just so *angry* all the time… and I do not know why."

"Listen to me," Kassandra said. She pulled him into a hug, wrapping her arms so tightly about him, as if at any moment he would be blown away. "Everything is going to be okay. I promise you."

Lukas returned the embrace and placed a gentle kiss on her forehead.

"No," he said, "I promise *you*."

"What happened up there?"

Morlag's quiet voice broke the silence. Kitara didn't turn to face him.

"Nothing."

The attack had passed, and once more she could see clearly. She was in control.

A thin layer of sweat still covered her body. She raised a hand to her temple and took a deep breath. The attacks were few and far between, but when they came, they ripped her apart. Here in a ship, held in such a cage, they grew worse. Her nightmares had begun to return, pulling her from sleep.

Kitara ran her thumb over the arm ring that Aeryn had given her. It gave her strength, as did the thought of the moonseer.

The memory of her face and smile suddenly made things less dark.

"Are you alright?"

A small hand reached through the steel bars and gently touched her arm.

Kitara glanced at the young girl who sat at Morlag's side. "It's okay. I'm fine."

"We will all make it. Together," the young Káli told her.

"I know," Kitara said with a smile and placed a hand atop the girl's. "What is your name?"

"Sereia."

"Sereia," Kitara echoed quietly, and her smile grew into a grin. "That's a pretty name. I'm Kitara."

Sereia's matching grin reached up to her emerald eyes, before it shifted into somewhat of a frown.

"Are you the one who came all the way from Miera to help us?"

"Just so," Kitara told her.

She could feel a coldness begin to edge its way into her voice now. In her mind, Kitara could still see Silas' heartbroken face filled with anger and rage. The day that she had made her choice. That had been over a month ago. Before Salvaar. Before the war. Before Aeryn. Before it had all been ripped away once again.

Kitara released Sereia's hand and looked away. She would not show weakness again. Not here.

"Then you—"

"Sereia, leave her," Morlag cut in, and he squeezed the young girl's shoulder.

His voice was kind, and Kitara knew that he must have seen the slight paling of her face. "Leave her to her thoughts."

Kitara closed her eyes, and she felt the girl's fingers brush her arm as she pulled her hand away. She set her jaw and clasped her arm ring tightly. She would *not* let this place, and her own memories, destroy her.

"Sereia," Kitara said, "we are going to get out of here. I will protect you. I swear it on my arm ring."

Darkness filled the brig, as the sun fell beyond the horizon. It slid beyond the waves to the west, as the Lioness cut through the waves. Sereia and many of the other Salvaari had long since drifted off to sleep, yet Kitara could not find herself among them. She had slept in worse places, but she could not find the comfort of rest in the prison. She shifted unconsciously as she let her head come to rest against the steel bars at her back.

"You are stronger than you know," Morlag whispered to her through the cage. "Do not be overcome with fear and doubt."

Kitara glanced over her shoulder at the chief's brother, as she felt an irritation begin to stir. "I told you before... I am fine."

"Something ails you. It has since you went above," he replied. "Do not think me blind."

"You know a lot about me, don't you?"

Sarcasm cut into her tone.

"You're a survivor, much like myself," Morlag told her. "That is how I know that we will not die here. Now we must act, and we must act quickly. I fear that if we do not escape by the time we land, our fates may be sealed."

Kitara met his eyes and saw the hope and passion held within them. The eyes of a leader. "There is an army of them up there. A dozen knights, maybe fifty mercenaries, and that number does not include the sailors. There are only a few of us, and how do you propose we get weapons?"

"I don't yet know," he said sincerely, "but I do know this... each day that we wait could be our last."

Kitara shook her head with a snort. "Absent weapons, absent plan, and–"

"Not absent hope," Morlag shot back. "I suggest that you find yours."

"Listen to me, and listen well," Kitara replied angrily, "I am not whoever it is that you think I am. I am not a good person. I have never been a good person, and I will never become a good person."

"If that is your choice," the Káli replied, after a moment, and a trace of sadness entered his voice. "But before you decide so finally, ask yourself this… what are you prepared to sacrifice for your freedom?"

They drifted into silence and, after a while, sleep.

Kitara awoke in the dead of night. Pain flared to life, as agony ripped through her mind like a hot knife. It seared and burned, as it turned her eyes from deep green to the fiercest of violets. Then she saw.

She saw everything.

She *felt* it.

The waves beneath the prow of the ship, and the men who slept in its bunks. The Salvaari, and the Medeans. Those who rested, and those who patrolled the decks.

Kitara bit down and gritted her teeth against the pain, as she fought. It sought to control her. To destroy her. She remembered the words spoken by Aeryn. Words that had once ended the nightmare. Kitara's lips moved and from them came the tongue of Salvaar.

"Remember the sea… remember her voice."

The pain began to fade, as Kitara held onto the words that gave her strength. She took a slow breath. The last of the agony fell away, allowing peace to fill her. She emptied her mind of all else, casting her thoughts deep into the visions for the first time. Then she could see. *Truly* see.

She could feel everything happening in the Lioness as it happened. All of it was in shades of grey and black, from bare skin to the flames of candles. She clung to this sight as she looked around and allowed her mind to fly through the brig and crews' quarters. Her mind moved from the deck to the food store. She could see the patrols, and the chests in which the captives' weapons were held. Sweat rolled down her face as she fought to hold onto the vision.

Something called to her. It was close. So very close.

She turned her head and ran her gaze along the metal bars of her cell. The vision faded, and with it the purple in her gaze. Kitara barely felt the sweat that coated her skin, nor the dull ache in her brow. Pain was covered by excitement. She reached out a hand and ran her fingers along the steel bars where they met the wooden flooring. They brushed bar and nail.

Nail.

The first nail she tried was fastened ever tightly, and its tip driven down deep into the bowels of the timber. Kitara extended her hand once more and tentatively went for a second nail. She pushed, and it *moved*. It was a slight movement. No more than the smallest of wiggles. A smile played across her lips, as she wrapped a single finger around its head and twisted. Again, it moved. Though slightly more than it had before. Its rounded head protruded no more than an inch. She hit it with the palm of her hand. Once. Twice.

The nail wobbled.

Again, she grasped it, and again, she pulled. It protruded the breadth of a finger. Again and again she hit it, and with each blow, her excitement grew. At last, Kitara gripped the nail and, with a strong tug, ripped it from the wooden floor. Her green eyes sparkled as they ran along its metal length. It was around six inches, and its tip was reasonably sharp. Sharp enough to pierce skin and flesh. A plan began to take form. Kitara slid the nail up under the bracer of her right arm, hiding it from sight.

SIX

Darkness wrapped around the great city like a cloak. The large silver moon shone down onto the tiled rooftops and cast its rays through the city streets below. Braziers burned atop the walls and in the homes of nobles and merchants alike. Banners bearing a fragmented silver star over a field of black and gold fluttered gently in the cool sea breeze. Steel glinted as men, clad head to toe in embellished plate armour and purple gambesons, strode atop the vast walls and through the quiet streets. The guardsmen held their halberds close and kept their eyes ever watchful.

Calm ocean waters lapped at the docks of the arsenal. The great river was still. Atop the flat rooftops of wealthy lords and merchant kings were men armed with Aureian crossbows. They had orders to kill any who attempted the climb.

Few enough dared.

Only one succeeded.

Only the Nightingale.

Only the one who had gained access to Lord Redmier's study within the arsenal keep.

The nobleman's guards, who watched the keep and patrolled its long corridors, knew nothing of the intruder. They knew nothing of the Nightingale clad in black who, even at this moment, was sifting through his lordship's papers. Redmier and his family slept quietly, as the phantom read every single word on every bit of parchment. Redmier was Master of Ships and as such kept record of every last vessel that came within the great city. Records of ships entering and *leaving* Elara. Even those of the magister's own fleet. A powerful man was Redmier, even as he slept so deeply. His guards were hawkeyed and fast, yet the Nightingale was faster still. The ghost had slipped past them unnoticed. Even those people in the streets, who caught a glimpse of the dark figure that flitted from rooftop to rooftop, saw nothing but the shadow of a phantom. Hooded and masked, it left naught but a pair of deep blue eyes exposed. Lips pursed behind the mask as those same eyes washed over the contents of a book. Upon its pages, written in dark ink, was a record of the trade fleets between Aureia and Elara. Each trade fleet was accompanied by one of the magister's own vessels. It was always the same. For the better part of two decades, silks, furs, jewels, steel, and coin were traded each month. Yet no cargo was listed aboard the magister's ships.

Strange. Elara was a colony forged by the blades of the empire.

Why would its leader send a single ship without cause?

What did Magister Imrohir have to gain?

The book ended there. It was just a record of trade. It did not mention to whom it went to, nor what it was used for. The Nightingale closed the logbook and placed it back from whence it had come. No one would ever know that its pages had been disturbed this night. The dark figure's eyes darted around the room and took in all the luxury and wealth that Redmier had gathered in his time serving the city. Jewels from every corner of the empire. Pearls and ivory from Tarik and beyond. Pouches laden with great sums of gold and silver lay within the drawers the intruder opened.

All of it was snatched up and shoved into the satchel that the Nightingale wore. A fortune of coin and jewels, enough perhaps for one to live in wealth for decades.

The phantom glanced back at the locked office door and smirked beneath the mask. The window from which the Nightingale had gained access would serve as an escape route onto the rooves, and none would be the wiser until morning. The dark figure vanished into the night and left naught but a gift atop Lord Redmier's table. A single brown feather. That of a nightingale.

The Nightingale's name came from an old Aureian tale of a thief. One who stole from the nobility and gave them nothing but blood in return. One who left the feather of a nightingale at the scene of every crime. As the story went, that old Aureian nightmare rebelled and took everything from the nobility who plagued its city. The Nightingale of Elara had taken the name and built upon it. It had struck fear into the hearts of those men who sat in their golden thrones and walked the corridors of power.

Screams came from below.

The Nightingale glanced down into the streets, blue eyes searching. A glint of steel was all it took to catch the Nightingale's gaze. The screams came from a woman who had been chased into an alley by a pair of hooded men. In a heartbeat the phantom flew across the rooftops and leapt down the fifteen-foot drop.

The two men turned as the Nightingale's gaze burned toward them. Shrouded half in darkness, the figure appeared as a monster conjured from nightmare. The men's eyes widened as they recognised the creature who gazed toward them. Fear followed in its wake. All it took was for hand to brush against the hilt of a wicked kukri knife and a slight shift in posture. The silver moonlight lit up the steel as the Nightingale half drew the blade.

The men ran and left their would-be victim free, alive, and without so much as a scratch. For the phantom's name was a thing well known. The Nightingale was a legend in Elara. It was spoken of only in hushed tones. No man was willing to risk its wrath. Was it the Aureian nightmare reborn? Was it that thing that had plagued the great empire's capital for near a decade?

"Thank you," the woman called out, as tears ran down her pale cheeks.

The Nightingale turned away.

No sound came from the phantom's lips.

Not even acknowledgement of the words.

"The Nightingale struck again last night."

Elise Delfeyre glanced over her shoulder as her companion spoke.

"Did he?" she replied.

"Yes, lady."

The young maid met her friend's gaze and briefly stopped helping Elise into her red and white corseted dress. It was the latest fashion in Elara, and Elise *hated* it. The garment pulled and pressed her body, yet only one thing made her more uncomfortable than the dress. The fact that she had a maid to dress her. Elise could barely contain her grimace as Halina continued her work. Two years in wealth and she still hated it. The clothing of the rich merchants itched more than any flea-bitten rag ever would. At first, Elise had complained about the need for a maid when she had been thrust into the halls of the aristocracy. Her words had fallen on deaf ears. Now her protests came in the form of eyerolls and grimaces. Elise rolled her strong shoulders back as Halina finished tightening the infernal contraption that was a corset.

"You mentioned the Nightingale?" Elise asked.

"Somehow, he gained entry into Lord Redmier's own house," Halina told her.

"The shipmaster?"

"Made away with quite the fortune, too."

"Redmier has all the gold and all the guards in the world, and yet it could not protect him," Elise told her. "If such a man is not safe... are any of us?"

"The Magister will catch that criminal soon enough, I have no doubt." Halina stepped back and ran her eyes over Elise. "There you are. Beautiful."

Elise smirked. To many – most, in fact – dresses such as these were graceful and glamorous. They showed elegance and poise. Both were necessities in the noble and merchant classes of Elara. However, it was overly tight for Elise's liking. It dug into her shoulders, upper arms, and back. She liked to be able to be free and to move. Somehow, the women east of the river had learnt not to breathe.

Elise spread her arms.

"I look like a doll wrapped up in this," she said.

"Lady Elise!" Halina chortled, as she tried to look horrified and failed. "You should not tease about such things."

Elise snorted in reply. "Another of my rough lowborn mannerisms, no doubt."

She gave Halina a wink before striding from her bare but dainty chamber and into the lustrous hallways of her uncle's home.

Despite being adopted into higher classes by her ever-doting aunt and uncle two years before, Elise still bore the rough hands and broader shoulders of one raised in the streets. She had barely seen her twentieth year when her father had been taken so cruelly from this world. His brother, Lord Rafael Delfeyre, had seen fit to take her under his wing and pull her from the murky depths of the Pits. Together Lord Delfeyre and his beloved wife, Claudia, had clawed their way up from the merchant class by trading in silk, a luxury good even in Elara. As such they had earned their way into the corridors of the city's elite. They had clothed, fed, and sheltered Elise ever since that dark day when a vagabond belonging to one of Elara's gangs had taken a knife to her father. It had only been a mere six months after her mother's sickness had claimed her last breath. Elise owed her uncle and aunt everything, even for the red and white dress that she hated so. They had given her wealth and position. Yet she would have given anything to have her former life back. Her *real* life. Not the one filled with fancy balls and pontificating nobles. A world in which lies were a common currency.

Elise glanced toward one of the windows that lined the corridor as she made her way through the house. For a brief moment, she could see a shimmer of her reflection in the glass. Middling height, with a little too much muscle for the liking of her fellow nobles. Her hair was of copper, while a pair of braids on either side pulled it into a bun at the back. Her fingers and ears were adorned with rings. Bracelets wrapped her wrists, and a necklace hung at her throat as was befitting her station. Gold, jewels, and trinkets she despised.

"My lady?" Halina called from behind.

Elise turned to face her maidservant and confidant.

"Sorry... lost in thought."

"Your uncle calls."

The once commoner nodded.

"Best not keep him waiting," she said.

Raphael Delfeyre's office was small, but embellished with glorious tapestries and a grand oak desk. It was a chamber befitting a wealthy silk merchant. It was there, at the desk, that the head of the Delfeyre family sat. Raphael had the grey streaked hair of one just shy of fifty, while his beardless face was covered in a patchwork of wrinkles. A sheet of parchment sat atop his desk, upon which he had begun to write the beginnings of a letter.

"Uncle," Elise said, as she entered the small room. "You wanted to see me?"

"Come in," Raphael replied, as he completed the final stroke of his letter.

With a sigh, Raphael pushed the parchment before him aside and finally glanced up at his niece. Elise could see the slightly frustrated frown on Raphael's face, even as he gave her something of a smile.

"How goes business?" she asked.

"I tell you, Elise, I am at my wits end," Lord Delfeyre said as he rose to his feet. "The gangs have been stirring in their boroughs of late, and there are those who refuse to go anywhere near the lower districts because of it."

"You speak as though anyone but soldiers and tax collectors cross the bridge anyway," Elise replied with a sigh.

Those were the only Riversiders that Elise could remember from her childhood. The rest held their chins so high in the air that they couldn't see what was right in front of them.

Raphael took up his silver jug and poured himself a glass of wine. He glanced at Elise to offer her the same, but she shook her head. If her uncle was drinking this early, then he was bothered indeed.

"This is different. They are shrouding the city in a web of extortion, bribery, thievery, and murder." At last, his lips twitched into a proper smile, as he raised his glass. "No better than the nobility among which we find ourselves."

Elise nodded. The Elaran gangs had *always* ruled the underground and sought control over the lower districts. They were growing stronger by the day. They were more impassioned and bolder than they had ever been. Though so far, at least, the city watch could keep them at bay.

"A bad time to be a merchant," Elise replied.

"Indeed." Raphael took a sip from his glass. "And then we have that intolerable Nightingale flitting around. I tell you, ever since he appeared, the nobles have been holding their coin ever more tightly."

Elise clasped her hands. "I am surprised that he has lasted as long as he has without finding the hangman's noose."

"Six months." Raphael grimaced. "Far too long for such a criminal. Though the politics of this city are not why I wanted to see you. It is your friend Tariq that concerns me. I heard that you wish to see him."

Elise frowned at the mention of her father's closest friend. A man who had helped raise her.

"I haven't seen him since I waved goodbye on the bridge two years ago," she replied sadly as she remembered the day and the reason why she had left the Pits. "He's family."

"Ever since we took you in and brought you into our house I have loved you as my own," Raphael told her. "When my brother was murdered in those streets, I swore that no harm would befall his daughter, and I would like to believe that I have made good on that promise. Tariq is a good man; from me you will get no argument in that. However, it is the borough in which he dwells that causes me concern."

Elise rolled her eyes. She understood him completely.

"Uncle, I will be fine. I grew up on those streets."

"As did your father."

She bit her lip. Barely two years on, her father's death was still an open wound.

"I am aware of that," Elise said.

"Elise, the Pits are *dangerous*," Raphael told her, as his voice grew loud.

He was worried, and perhaps he had the right to be so.

"The Pits are in my blood," Elise shot back.

Raphael sighed. "Elise... I know it's been hard for you," her uncle said. "Your new standing has driven you away from your former home. Too wealthy for the Pits, too lowborn for the aristocracy. I understand."

Elise snorted. He was right. It had been hard. She had no place in the Pits anymore. She would be treated like any noble who ventured into those streets... yet among the wealthy she was treated with nothing but disdain and disgust.

"That has not been hard," Elise lied, as she placed her hands upon the desk and stared at her uncle. "The people of your class, they can sneer and complain. That is nothing. What happened to my family, that was hard. Tariq is my family. The *last* family that I have across the river."

Sadness entered Raphael's eyes as he looked at his niece. "I have heard that he still fights, that he still wins," Raphael told her. "The people who fill those dens… the men who fight in them. They would take your life as easily as they would take your purse."

"Then it is a good thing, uncle, that I do not take coin. I was born in the Pits. It is in my blood. That is what keeps me safe across the river," Elise replied desperately. "Please Uncle… it's been years. I have to see him."

Raphael met her eyes and gave a slow nod. "I can see that there is no stopping you."

"I will be fine… and besides, you cannot keep me locked up forever."

"No, I cannot," Raphael said, with a chuckle. "And that is why a pair of my men shall accompany you."

Elise grimaced. Irritation flickered across her face. "Uncle, I–"

"This is not a debate," he cut her off. "I merely wish to protect you."

"I do not need it."

"No… but please do this. For me."

He gave her a smile, and Elise could see the pain etched in his gaze. She knew that he could see the ghost of his brother in her. Despite the class divide, they had been close.

"Alright," she conceded, with a sigh. "I'll do it. Tell them to get ready. The Pits await."

Raphael summoned his household guard, and then Elise made her way from her uncle's home. The finely cobbled streets of the merchant district were filled with life. Lords, ladies, merchants, and dainty citizens laughed and joked as they walked freely. They wore frocks as vibrant as the grand buildings all around. Their jewellery worth more than any kingdom. Those with wealth were not afraid to show it for there were no thieves this side of the river. Noblewomen carried fans and wore such dresses that made Elise's look common. They walked with an aloof arrogance that only those born into wealth would ever know. Even the common citizens wore clean clothing of vibrant colours.

The great buildings were pearl-white with tiled roofs of scarlet. They drove high into the heavens, sometimes three or four floors tall. Plants covered the grandiose balconies. Above all else, it was clean. Elise saw it all as she waited for her uncle's carriage to emerge. She could smell air cleaner than any she had ever known across the river. It tasted sweet upon her lips. Her eyes picked up on the glances thrown her way. Disdain. Disgust. The looks varied, yet it all felt the same. She had made the mistake of being born across the river, not just in the lower districts, but in the Pits. Elise was Elaran, the same as the lords and ladies who despised her so, yet to them, she was as foreign as any Salvaari. She was dirt to these people, regardless of her new standing.

Hooves clacked upon cobblestone as the grand carriage arrived. The two guards upon its back wore armour of the finest steel, that shone beneath the sun. Like all household guards in Elara, and the rest of the League of Trecento, they were mercenaries. They wore swords at their sides and had fought in wars for the aristocracy for years. Elise rolled her eyes as she climbed inside the carriage. They had seen battle, yet had not ventured across the river. The Pits would swallow them whole.

The crowds thinned as the carriage neared the river. Elise stared out the window. Few souls moved by the buildings that rose upon the stone bridge. Those who did were, more often than not, from the other side. Her uncle was right; it had worsened. Even with the growing numbers of soldiers, few Riversiders dared venture to the edge of the water and the bridge that crossed it. Those who did had fear in their eyes.

Without a thought, Elise pushed open the carriage door and

dropped down onto the cobblestones. A smirk graced her lips as she heard the two guards cry out and hurry after her. She strode toward the river and made her way down the stone stairs towards its bank. With a scowl, she tugged at the uncomfortable tightness of her sleeve.

"My lady!" one of the guards cried out. "Where are you going?"

"I am going to the Pits," she replied, without even looking over her shoulder. Instead, her eyes scanned the stone walkway that ran beside the river. So far below the streets a murkiness had set in, and Elise was searching for something.

"This only leads to the river," the guard continued as he caught up.

"Does it?" Elise replied as at last her eyes caught sight of a man sitting next to a small shanty. Netted cages for fishing stood against its walls, and a boat was tethered to a mooring post nearby.

"My lady, I do not think that this is a good idea."

Elise whipped around to face her *protectors*. "You don't want to go to the Pits, do you?"

"Lady Delfeyre, the people across the river–"

"Captain, you forget," Elise raised her brows as she cut him off. "I *am* one of those people. Now, I am crossing the river with or without you. The choice is yours."

The guard bit back a retort. He clenched his jaw tightly. Elise doubted he had ever served a charge who would question him, least of all a girl.

"Yes, my lady."

"We are not taking the bridge," Elise said, as she turned back toward the shack. "Because if we do… well, you will no doubt have heard stories about what happens to the *fine* citizens east of the river when they enter the Pits. This way, you might make it out alive."

Elise could almost hear the racing hearts of her companions. Like all those who called the east side of the river home, they had likely always never given thought to why their fellow citizens lived in such poverty. Riversiders, the people of the lower districts called them. Those with more coin than sense.

A man emerged from the darkness by the shack. Elise tossed him a coin purse as he approached. The unmistakable sound of a sword being half-drawn came from behind her. She shook her head. The guards were frightened.

"Clothes and safe passage across," Elise called to the man.

"Yes, Lady," he replied, as he tested the weight of the purse.

Within moments, ragged garments were tossed to the three companions. Elise took shelter in the shack as she changed. The infernal dress that tugged and pulled was cast aside. In its place she pulled on the filthy rags that clothed the people of the Pits. A rough cloak was wrapped around her shoulders. She barely noticed the foul odour given off by the rags, for she had grown up wearing just the same. When she exited the shack, she could see the looks of disgust upon her guards' faces as they ran their eyes over their own rags. No longer were they clad in their fine armour. Like her, they wore dirt-stained clothes of black and brown. Unlike her, they were not accustomed to the stench.

The boatman gestured to his small vessel, and then they were off. While they rowed, Elise's gaze was fixed upon the distant shore. She had not been to the lower districts, let alone the Pits, since she had been taken from that life by her aunt and uncle. That had been two years ago. Two years and mere days after her father's murder. Elise looked to the bridge above where she had waved goodbye to Tariq. That had been the last time she had seen her friend. Her family. Elise closed her eyes and took a breath. The foul smell of the Pits reached her nose. The guardsmen curled their lips in disgust and pulled their scarves over their mouths and noses. To her it, smelt like home.

The boat touched the western bank.

"Double if you wait," Elise told the boatman.

He replied with no more than a nod. Elise led her companions up the filth-stained steps and into an alley. The muck was so thick upon the ground that no one in the Pits knew how far down the cobblestones were, or if they even existed. The buildings were dark and gloomy. The air was thick. Elise turned to face her guards.

"Welcome to the Pits," she told them, as she pulled her hood up.

She led them into the alley without a backwards glance. The Pits had long ago been dubbed as such by those east of the river. The lowest of the poor boroughs, the name was a cruel joke among the nobility. Instead of wallowing in the shame, the gangs had united behind the name and turned the district into something more than an amusement of the Riversiders. They had turned it into a place so feared by those beyond the lower districts that even soldiers gave pause before entering.

The alley opened up into a street. There, the underworld known as the Pits truly began. There were no bright colours or horses. There were no silver-clad soldiers or banners bearing the sigil of Elara. Men, women, and children wore rags, with their hoods pulled low. None cared about the filth they walked in even as it splashed across their boots and clothes. The foul stenches of mud and piss were joined by those of sweat and alcohol. People drank and gambled openly on the streets. The smoke of their pipes hazed the already dreary air. Beggars sat against buildings, knowing full well that none of the people hurrying by could spare them any coin. Even after the years that had passed, Elise could spot the men of the gangs. They carried themselves more proudly than most of the people around them. Scarves hung at their throats that could easily be turned into masks.

The Pits. Here was the home of the forgotten, the broken, and the damned... yet they were as Elaran as those across the river. With every step she took, Elise felt it all coming back. She felt more at home here among the dirt than she did in silk sheets. She knew that if she looked back at the guards, she would see the horror in their faces. Even the poorest of souls across the river were clean.

Elise led her companions through the mire until they came to a huge wooden building. The doors were wide open. Candles and torches flickered through the smoke within. A great ruckus of roaring cheers assaulted Elise's ears as she let the way inside. They slowly made her way down the gnarled wooden staircase and into the underworld of society. The stench of sweat, drink, and blood washed over her like a wave and filled her nose with the grotesque. Dozens of people crowded the lower level. They were packed tightly, shoulder to shoulder, all the way up to the low wooden walls of the arena. They cheered for blood. Above them was a roughly hewn balcony, upon which Elise now stood alongside her fellow denizens of the Pits. Only a small wooden railing, and an eight-foot drop, separated them from the howling mob below.

Men and women lined the stands. Elise placed her hands upon the railing and cast her eyes down into the dimly lit chamber beneath. Her gaze was drawn into the ring. The floor of sand was ringed by wooden walls. The earth was disturbed. Small patches of crimson could be seen from the balcony. The sand was watered with the blood of the men who walked its sacred ground.

The first man to enter the ring bore the tanned skin of one native to Elara. Elise could see how massive he was from as far back as the balcony. He was the kind of man who could crush bones with his hands. His head was shaven bald, while his muscled torso covered in a thin layer of fat. He, like all of the fighters who entered the sands, fought topless. Loose pants covered his legs while his feet were as bare as his chest. Strips of white cloth were wound around his wrists and hands, protecting them from what came next. The Elaran raised a clenched fist to the great roaring of the crowd.

Then his opponent entered.

Skin black as the night sky. Dark hair neatly cropped and shaven at the sides. He could only have been Berenithian. He stood nearly as tall as the Elaran, though his body was more akin to an Aureian statue. The kind of man you looked at and knew that even his piss had muscles. He raised a wrapped hand to the heavens as he entered the ring, and the cheers grew deafening. He appeared around forty, while his opponent was near ten years his junior.

The chorus of cries grew to their peak as the two men began to stalk each other. The Elaran threw a jab while the Berenithian swayed back, watching his opponent closely, then flicked his left hand forward. A feint. The Elaran slid back in the sand as a cross followed.

Thud.

The sound of the blow washed through the pit, as the punch met a hastily thrown block. The Berenithian swayed back from a counter, and let the closed fist brush the air a hairsbreadth from his face. His arm straightened as he returned the strike and caught the Elaran hard in the cheek. The man stumbled. A flurry of blows followed in his wake. He swayed away from a vicious hook. His back met the fence. The Elaran sent a cross toward his foe's chin.

Too late. The Berenithian avoided the blow. He stepped to the side, as he loaded his hips for a counter. His uppercut slammed into the Elaran's jaw. The man's eyes rolled back as he fell into the wooden fence. Blood erupted from his ruined lips. His limp form crashed to the ground in a spray of sand. Just like that, it was over. The crowd howled their approval as the dark-skinned man raised his fists and strode into the centre of the sacred pit. Elise grinned as she saw the man cast his searching eyes up into the stands. His lips curled into a smile as he saw her; the same smile she had known her whole life.

Elise glanced at her guards.

"Come, let's go and see Tariq."

SEVEN

Road to Oryn, Forest of Salvaar

"Sir Elion and the other scouts have not yet returned," Lord Harold Robare of Aethela said, as he glanced to his prince and tried to read his face.

Dayne Raynor gave him nothing.

"We waste time," was all the prince said.

Dayne turned his gaze down the line of horsemen that had begun to form. Fifteen hundred Annoran knights joined with their Medean allies. A great wall of steel and horses.

"Every moment we delay brings closer our discovery," Dayne continued. "We can await Elion no longer."

Dayne rolled his powerful shoulders back and unslung his shield. He tightened its leather straps over his left arm. The sigil of his family sat emblazoned upon its surface. A red eagle was perched atop an ivory field. The prince's surcoat and cloak were equally as red. A second great bird flew upon his coat. Beneath, he wore a padded gambeson and shirt of mail, while atop his coat was a gorget of the finest steel and a chain coif pulled over his ears. His sword arm was covered in steel. Dayne took up his helm and placed it over his brow.

"Lord Robare, follow my banner down the centre, and then take your company south," he commanded. "Lord Aloys, lead your men to the north and cut off their retreat."

"It will be done, Prince," Emilian Aloys replied, and pulled his visor down. The young lordling hefted his spear and began to circle back to his own troops. The commander of his guard, Sir Berwin Isandro, rode at his back.

Dayne closed his eyes. "Durandail, Father of all Fathers, grant me victory this day. Durandail, Father of all Fathers, let me lead my men well."

Everything grew still. The wind and the leaves in the trees. Oryn sat barely half a mile from their position and knew nothing of the storm about to descend upon their heads.

Dayne reached up with his gauntlet covered hand and pulled his visor shut. He took the spear offered to him by one of his guard. He raised the weapon and drove its bladed tip skyward.

No words were uttered. No horns blown. The Káli would not know of their arrival until the line of horses cleared the trees.

Dayne kicked his heels in.

Maevin knelt beneath the trees. Her eyes were clamped tightly shut as her lips moved. Words rolled down her tongue quieter than any whisper. Words spoken in the tongue of Salvaar. The northern breeze ran through her dark locks and tickled her pale cheek, yet the Káli woman paid it no heed. The trees began to sway as the wind grew stronger, and the first hint of rain began to descend from the darkening clouds. Still Maevin never wavered. Her words, quiet as they were, traversed from this plane to the next.

She was calling him. The one for whom she had donned the garb of a priestess. The words were for he, the lord of twilight. The Dark One. They were for Tanris. Maevin's eyes, shut tight, could see ever clearly, and in that sight arose the spirit plane.

The bright glow of the silver moon. The purple light dancing through the sky. The vast shadows ever black. The dark form creeping beyond. She had traversed the plane before, and her faith, her sight, had grown stronger for it.

Her brow furrowed and her hands gripped her amulet tightly, as a wave of pain rolled through her. Maintaining a connection to the spirit plane took its toll. Even a glimpse at what lay beyond the veil would drive most men insane.

She saw a dark figure shrouded in shadow. His single eye burned with violet flame, as he turned toward her. Hooded and cloaked in pale robes was the dark spirit Tanris. He said not a word. Instead, he extended a hand toward her, and his fingers curled into a claw. Maevin heard a great flutter of wings. A screech came from above. That of a great eagle.

Maevin's eyes burst open as a branch snapped behind her. Footsteps crunched on the forest floor. Her lips curled dangerously as she heard them approach from behind. Slowly, she released her grip on her amulet. Closer came the footsteps. Maevin rose to her feet, not yet turning to see the newcomer. She knew that there was only one. His loud, stomping footsteps betrayed that he was not one of the Salvaari.

"You disturb my prayer," she said, and her voice was cold and loud.

"A dangerous thing to be so alone," came the reply. Gruff. Commanding. *Annoran.*

Still Maevin did not turn, as the man drew nearer.

"And yet, here you are," she said. "Alone."

He would have been little more than two paces from her now.

"Come quietly. I do not wish to harm you," the Annoran said.

"Your presence here speaks otherwise, and for this, Tanris will judge you."

Maevin's hand slowly dropped to the bone handle of her small dagger, a thing beyond sight of the Annoran. She was no warrior, but she was fast. The Annoran did not expect an attack. Maevin twirled. Her dark skirts waved around her as she lashed out.

The man leapt back. Steel met flesh as the dagger grazed his cheek. A gauntleted hand slammed into the side of Maevin's head and sent her crashing to the mud. The dagger flew from her fingers. Her dark hair streamed around her. The Annoran's hard leather boot connected heavily with her stomach. Air fled her lungs.

Maevin's head pounded, yet her lips twitched into a smirk. She could see the Annoran now, clad in steel scale armour, his cloak the colour of fresh blood. He could only have been a man of the royal guard.

Why was he here and not with Prince Lukas? Better yet… why was he attacking her?

The Annoran reached up and wiped a bead of blood from the thin scratch, as he glared down at her. He drew his sword in a single fluid motion.

"You will die for that, pagan."

Maevin met his eyes and stared deeply into them. She searched inside those blue orbs, as he approached.

There.

A hint of fear.

Her smirk grew, and he came closer. He knew nothing of the Salvaari. Nothing of the Káli. He knew not of what they were capable, or how they had held their own for so long in last war. He was too young for that.

He coughed.

In that moment, Maevin knew that it was over. Blood drained from the Annoran's face, and his sword fell from his fingers. He gasped for breath and clawed at his throat, for he was suddenly unable to breathe. His bloodshot eyes went to Maevin's dagger as he fell to his knees, and then he knew.

Poison.

Maevin snatched up the cold blade and stood over him, watching the last of his strength flee his shaking body. Then she heard the screams. They echoed over the rain that fell all around her and chilled her to the bone.

The screams came from her village. They came from Oryn.

Mud splashed as Emilian Aloys slid from his saddle. The battle, for as long as it had lasted, had been ferocious but decisive. The Káli had not been expecting them. The rain had helped to conceal the sound of a galloping army, and they had hit the pagans hard before they could react.

The duke's son still kept a tight grip on his crimson-covered sword as he began to make his way down the street. His spear was lost in the chest of one of the Káli warriors. He pushed his visor up with the crossguard of his sword. His left hand was covered by a golden shield bearing the image of the white lion of his family. The young lordling swept his eyes around the village. Annorans and Medeans alike still rode and walked through the town. Their eyes were wary, and their weapons held at the ready for any last resistance. The streets ran with blood, which mingled with the rain and the sludge created by hooves and armoured boots.

"Check the houses," Emilian called out, and he gestured toward one of the buildings with his bloody sword. "The battle is over. Round up any survivors."

"Lord!" one of his men called out.

Emilian turned as his soldiers began to scurry off toward the pagan hovels. The man who'd called to him was pointing down one of the streets. A dark figure was walking toward them, barely visible through the rain. Emilian frowned and adjusted his grip upon his blade. It was a woman who approached, and she held something large in her right hand.

Horror gripped him as he saw the head of the Annoran knight. The one who had stood as a brother to Prince Dayne.

"Elion," he breathed.

Maevin's face was covered in a savage smile as she slowly made her way toward the gathered horde of soldiers. They wore the yellow and white colours of Aloys. Annora had not come alone. She held the head of the man she had killed by the hair, and took joy in the horror that flashed across the faces of her enemies. Her hands were covered in sticky gore, her cheek split and bruised from the knight's armoured hand. Upon her face she wore a red mask. A mask of Annoran blood.

Around her, lying in their own entrails, were the ruined bodies of her people. Some she had known her whole life. She had no way of killing another of the invaders, for surprise was no longer on her side. There was only one thing left to be done.

The rain had long since soaked her clothing and stuck her hair to her face. It washed over the bare skin of her arms, down to the bloody head she held ever tight. Maevin did not feel the cold, for she had long since gone numb.

Too many dead, and yet the invaders, clad in their shining armour, stood in a pool of the slain's blood.

"Tanris, I come to you," Maevin murmured in her own tongue, as she approached. She saw the man in the yellow surcoat emblazoned with the lion, the visor of his silver helm pushed back. No doubt he was their leader.

"Tanris, I come to you," she repeated.

The man raised his sword toward her.

"Hold!" he cried.

She did not. Twenty paces became ten.

"Tanris, I come to you."

Without so much as a glance at the dead man's head, she tossed it toward the Medean's feet. All eyes went to the bloody and ruined face, that she had roughly hewn from its owner's neck. Then she stopped.

"Get on your knees!" the Medean leader roared, over the pouring rain.

She did not move. A pair of rough hands wrapped around her arms, while a hard boot was driven into the back of her legs.

Her knees hit the mud and a heavy fist connected with her jaw. Maevin fell to the side with a grunt as pain flared to life. Only her hands stopped her fall. The slurry of gore and filth splashed through her fingers and washed over her face. It mingled with her own blood. It filled her senses. Its taste and stench overpowering, but the blood of her people gave her strength. Maevin turned her gaze up once more, as she looked to the Medean, who had discarded his shield.

"You killed my friend," he told her, as he pulled off his helm.

One of the soldiers took it from his outstretched hand. Rage filled his eyes. He looked young, barely over twenty summers by Maevin's count.

"You took my village," she replied, and bared her bloody teeth as she pushed herself back onto her knees. "Slaughtered my people. The spirits are watching, Medean, and as night turns to day, you and all your kind will be held accountable. Tanris does not forget, nor does he forgive. That I swear."

The man snorted and shook his head. "You heathens need to understand, there is no place in the world for you anymore. You are a blight upon the gods' world, and one day soon you will all pay for the Medean blood you have spilt."

Maevin let loose a malicious laugh. "My gods smile upon me, Medean. Can *you* say the same?"

The man placed his sword upon her neck and rubbed its bloody length upon her skin. She felt filth drip onto her shoulder. The lifeblood of her people so cruelly taken from this world. Yet she did not let her gaze waver from his own. She would not give him the satisfaction.

He turned his sword, letting the edge of the steel blade come to rest upon her skin, as he spoke. "In the name of Durandail, Father of all Fathers. In the name of Azaria, Lady of Silver. I, Emilian Aloys, heir to the east, sentence you to death."

Lukas cursed the rain for the thousandth time as it cascaded down from the heavens and soaked the great column of riders to the bone. The only thought that warmed him was that the town in which they would take refuge was less than a mile from their position. Oryn, a village that he had once helped to liberate from the Catuvantuli, would return the favour and free him from this blasted weather. He exchanged a smile with Kassandra, who rode at his side. No doubt she was having the same thoughts.

Then he frowned. His horse stirred uneasily beneath his weight as, like its rider, the mare heard something through the rain. Its high pitch was barely audible over the downpour. For a moment, Lukas believed the noise no more than a distortion of the wind, a phantom sound. This forest was old. Very old. It held many strange secrets.

He heard it again. The sound tormented his mind.

"Screams," Sir Garrik muttered. He dropped a hand to his sword and stared out into the woods. "Oryn."

Lukas nodded. The shouts had unmistakably come from the village to the west. The prince shifted in his saddle and placed a soothing hand on his horse's neck as she whinnied. "Shh," he whispered.

The sound of galloping hooves reached their ears moments before one of the Káli foreriders cleared the trees. He charged straight toward his commander, Eirian.

"Myrdren," Eirian called out as the moonseer angled his mount toward him, "What is it? What did you see?"

"Soldiers," Myrdren cried out. "Hundreds of them."

Anguish illuminated Eirian's dark eyes. "Who would dare break Sylvaine?" he snarled.

"Medea," Myrdren replied.

Confusion ran through the ranks as the word spread. Without hesitation, Lukas led the column forward. What Medea was doing here, he dreaded to guess.

The rain grew into a downpour as Lukas and his companions rode into the streets of the Salvaari village. The prince felt his blood freeze as he looked around at the destruction. The ground beneath had been churned into a slurry of blood, bone, and filth. Doors had been torn from the ramshackle houses, and muddy footprints vanished into their depths. Lukas shared a glance with his sister as they rode through the debris.

He felt his heart nearly stop as he saw what lay ahead. Bodies were strewn all around the town. The bodies of the villagers left to rot in the mud. Elders, women, and children joined the fallen warriors. None had been spared. Some he could remember from that night in Oryn, a night that now seemed a distant memory.

The murmuring in the company died away as they slowly made their way through the village. Hands went to sword and spear. They gripped steel tight and watched the streets with wary eyes. The Annorans rode in silence as their faces paled. Despair washed through the eyes of the Káli warriors.

What happened here?

Lukas brought his mare to a halt and dismounted. A few of the knights followed his lead and dropped down onto the road, before they took up arms. Lukas handed the reins of his horse to one of the men and moved towards one of the burnt houses. He could barely feel the rain on his face anymore, as the true extent of the horror before his eye was unveiled. An old man lay face down in a pool of his own blood. Lukas felt bile rise in his throat as he took in the young, gore covered woman that lay in the arms of slaughtered old man. Lukas knelt beside the Salvaari and pushed a lock of hair away from her face. She was still young. Her whole life cut short by a butcher. Lukas closed her eyes, and felt a hand touch his shoulder. He glanced up to see the numb expression on his sister's face.

"Who could have done this?" Kassandra asked, her voice little more than a murmur. Her eyes never left the young girl's body.

Myrdren had told them that men bearing Medean colours had led the massacre, yet who had given the order?

"My prince," Sir Landon Montbard called, and gestured down the street. "Rider approaching."

A single mounted soldier bearing the colours of Aloys approached.

"Eirian, stay back," Lukas said. "Let me handle this."

Eirian did not say a word as he gripped his axe tight. Lukas could see the torment that had seized him like a glove and prayed that the general would hold his blade, and his tongue.

"Who goes there?" the Medean rider called out. "You bear the colours of Raynor, but did not travel with us."

"Sir Garrik Skarlit, commander of the king's royal guard and master at arms of Palen-Tor," Sir Garrik nearly spat. "I ride with Prince Lukas Raynor."

"My prince." The Medean offered a bow. "I am Sir Berwin Isandro of Duke Aloys' private guard. We came all this way to find you, and in so doing, helped deal a blow to those Káli devils. But I see some pagans in your company."

Lukas gritted his teeth, as he felt anger begin to surge through his veins.

"Indeed, you do," he growled.

"You had best come with me," Sir Berwin told him.

Lukas rose to his feet and glanced down the road towards the knight as his hand curled around the pommel of his sword. He had to force down the sickness in his stomach as he offered the man a nod. Aloys' soldiers were gathered in the town square. Their gazes were drawn to something in their midst. Every last man was covered in mud and blood. They had done this.

EIGHT

Fortress of Kilgareth, Valley of Odrysia

"Do you feel any pain?" Lysandra asked, as she ran her keen gaze over Kyler's chest. Where once his lifeblood had flowed from a fearsome wound, there was nothing. Not even a scar.

"None," Kyler said, as the arc'maija examined it closely.

"Curious." Lysandra pursed her lips for a moment, before she stood back from him. She turned her eyes toward one of the windows as if lost in thought.

"So far as I can tell, you are perfectly healthy. I had heard stories about the healing properties of ruskalan blood… but I had not thought to believe them. It truly is remarkable."

Kyler took up his shirt from where it lay and pulled it back over his head. "Can I resume training?" he asked.

Lysandra's lips twitched upward. "You soldiers, always coming to me with a broken arm or leg and wishing to be back in the field by midday."

"Best to be back in the fight." Kyler shrugged. A dark thought came into his mind, the image of Elena. "Less time to think."

"Nightmares trouble you?"

"By day and night," Kyler admitted, and tapped his chest. "About this… about *her*."

Lysandra made her way to the hospital bed and sat beside him. Her voice was quiet and measured, yet it held a deep sorrow.

"You miss Elena dearly, just as I do. She was as a daughter to me, and now they say that she is some kind of monster. Twisted and grotesque."

Kyler rolled his sun-and-moon amulet over in his hands, and let his eyes traverse its perfectly carved metal length. It gave him strength.

"The ruskalan are evil," he murmured. "They caused so much suffering. So much *pain*. And Elena may be one of them."

"There are stories about what happened. They have been passed down through the years," Lysandra said. "Stories from Bailon, Salazar, men of this very order. Yet this history is written by the victorious."

"Alarik told me that all of the old writings about ruskalan were destroyed by Duran Cormac."

"Did he?" Lysandra raised her brows. "Well, Duran did give that order not so long after the ruskalan were destroyed. To purge their evil from the histories. All such writings were lost, save a handful that were rescued from the flames by Stephanos of Delios. Hidden until their discovery by my predecessor. Those we keep close."

"So, they faded into myth," Kyler said quietly as he realised.

"To the outside world they do not exist and never did. To those here… many do not believe, for all they have are stories based on stories. Maybe not all of the ruskalan were as bad as we supposed. Elena was kind. She was considerate."

"But not human."

"Indeed," Lysandra told him.

"You speak of history and the Inqusition. That the ruskalan, if they ever existed, may not have been evil," Kyler said. "Yet they and their allies *started* the war, with murder and assassination."

"The Fiodine tells us that faith is the light that guides you through darkness, and so far as I have seen it does. True, Durandail may have given us this task in repelling those demons that once haunted these lands. But as the Silver Lady teaches…

there cannot be light without dark. Perhaps there is some of the gods' light in the ruskalan, or perhaps they are indeed creatures of shadow."

"I wish we knew," Kyler said, with a sigh, "so that I could put an end to these dreams."

Lysandra gave him a kind smile. "An old friend once told me something. Fear has two paths. Run from it all, and let it destroy you, or face it all and rise. The choice is up to you."

The sun blazed in the sky above, and its rays lit up the sands of the training yard. Sir Alarik and his instructors walked the lines of initiates as they sparred. Their voices loud and booming. War was at their doorstep and every man, from initiate to knight, *had* to be ready. That was Alarik's task, and by the gods he would see it done.

The battlemaster let his eyes wash over his trainees. He was searching for faults in technique or lack of will. His gaze was drawn to one man in particular. The Annoran highborn lad, Hugh Karter. He had survived being shot in Odrysia. Alarik could see a hint of pain in the young man's eyes, as he drove his opponent back with sword and shield. The lordling would not let it so much as slow him. As for Alarik's own wounds, the ones received at the hands of Wa'rith in Durandail's Vault, they were merely cuts and bruises. Ones that he would repay in deadly fashion.

He heard the knight approach long before the newcomer spoke.

"Sir Alarik," came the strong voice.

"Master." Alarik nodded as Sir Corvo Alaine, the new acting commander of the garrison, joined him.

"How are they?"

"Stubborn, complainers, lack discipline." Alarik snorted, as he tightened a hand around his gnarled cane. "The usual."

Corvo chuckled softly, watching the initiates train. "Do you have a moment?"

"Of course," Alarik replied.

He glanced at his friend for the first time and finally saw what he carried. Wrapped in a fine blue cloak was the unmistakable shape of a sword.

Corvo unbound the blade and pulled the thick cloak from its steel length. It was a hand-and-a-half sword, and by the look of it, the blade was as perfect as could be. Somehow, Alarik recognised it.

"This belonged to Wa'rith," Corvo told him, as he passed the sword to his fellow knight.

Alarik placed his cane to the side and took it up. He ran his eaglelike gaze across the steel. "Elaran make," he said.

"Aye," Corvo replied thoughtfully. "It may not be much, yet it is a start, and we should not let such a chance go to waste."

"I agree," Alarik said, and handed the blade back, "but who would go? Until such a time as a new grand master is chosen... you lead us. Now, more than ever, you are needed here, brother."

Corvo clamped his hand down upon the pommel of his own blade. He knew it to be true, however, it pained him greatly.

"It must be you," Corvo told him seriously. "We can find others to train these men while you are gone, yet only you have the will strong enough to bring that heretic to justice."

"Heretic?" Alarik murmured and gazed out across the sands.

Corvo glanced at his companion with the same distant expression mirrored on his face. "You know who he is, don't you?"

"I don't know for certain," Alarik said.

"No," Corvo cut him off. "You know him. Just as I do."

Alarik could remember that day in the Vault as clearly as when it had unfurled around him. He could remember the shouting and the smoke. The screams and the demon that stood before him.

"I find myself thinking of it again and again," Alarik said. "His face I could not see, but the way he moved... I have only seen two such as that before. You stand as one, and the other... a memory from a lifetime ago."

"A memory made flesh," Corvo said quietly. "And in this dark time, he chooses to reveal his hand." The master let his eyes sweep from one initiate to the next, as he continued to speak. "Who is your best sword?"

"Hugh Karter."

"That highborn lad?" Corvo asked. "Send him to me after midday meal. It seems that I am in need of a new apprentice."

An apprentice?

The meaning of this was clear. The greatest warrior in their order was looking for an apprentice. A man to train day and night for the sole purpose of one day bearing the mantle of Sword of Kil'kara.

"You wish to train him as your own?"

"I do," Corvo replied. "Whatever happens in the days to come... it will be in men such as Karter, and your boy Landrey, that we must place our faith."

The pair drifted off into silence; their thoughts taken. It had been not so long ago that Corvo had been squired to his predecessor. It had not been so long ago that Alarik had been a mere soldier in the imperial legion.

"Has Aureia sent reply?" Alarik said at last.

"It will begin with two legions, followed soon after by the full might of the empire, and then..." a slight smirk graced Corvo's lips, "then, there is an old friend of yours."

A flick of the wrist and a kick of the heels turned canter into racing gallop, as the glistening black stallion flew across the desert plain. The warm Larissan sun cast down onto the rider's skin and coated it in a layer of sweat. The man barely noticed, for he had long since grown to love the climate. The sleeveless purple tunic left his powerful arms and legs bare, while no more than Larissan sandals covered his feet. His dark hair was short and cropped, while a layer of stubble covered his strong jaw. He was proud enough to let the world see the web of scars that covered his skin. They told his story, and yet he did not care.

Strong and dignified. Aureian to the bone. The rider let his eyes follow the sun as he rode. In little over an hour, it would retreat behind the horizon. So, he had to return. The great city Danakis called. Reshada called. He clicked his tongue and angled north.

Sir Velis Demir, Knight of Aureia, Commander of Horse and Hero of Irene, slid from the saddle. He ran a weathered hand down the horse's powerful neck, and with a smile, he pressed his forehead to his mount's. They were bonded closer than brothers. From Aureia to the bloody Irene Mountains, with tribal screamers closing in around them, to the open sandy plains of Larissa, they had travelled a long way. Had it been Velis' choice, he would have remained no more than a humble knight of the empire, but fate and his emperor called his name.

He had been a champion of the joust at but seventeen years of age and had been knighted barely a year before that. He loved horses, loved the freedom of riding from horizon to horizon, but the gods had other plans for him. When he had entered the Irene Mountains fifteen years before, everything had changed. He had been given command over a force of four thousand heavy cavalry, and then barely two years ago had been sent here, to Larissa. The then newly crowned queen, Reshada, wished to enter negotiations with Emperor Darius. That was why he was here. Velis and his men now stood as Darius' hand here in the desert. They were shoulder to shoulder with their newfound Larissan allies.

"Sir?" a voice called out and broke the silence that the empty stable offered.

Velis turned to see his second hurrying toward him. A friend and brother who had stood by his side in the hellhole that was Irene.

"Ah, Jasir," he greeted his friend.

"Queen Reshada wishes to see you," Jasir told him. "Says that it's most important."

Without another word, Velis made for the palace.

He found her in the Lotus Garden. A great garden of ponds filled with blooming lotus flowers, weeping trees, and crystal-clear water. A large pavilion stood at the garden's centre with a grand white linen sheet which served as a roof. A pair of long reclining chairs sat atop the wooden flooring. A single banner flew at the pavilion. The image of a blue lotus flower atop a pale white field was emblazoned upon it. The symbol of Larissa.

Velis barely noticed the sole Tariki man who stood guard with his hand clamped down firmly on the dao sword at his hip. It was not the warrior that Velis saw, nor did he spare more than a glance at the beautiful lotus ponds. They were nothing compared to the woman who gazed out over the water. She wore a light linen dress that left much of her tanned skin exposed. A band of gold ran through her midnight-black hair, and another adorned her wrist. The Tariki gave Velis a glare as warning, for none could approach without the consent of his lady.

"It's alright, Palagius," Reshada said, as she turned to face Velis. "Let him pass."

"Yes, my queen," replied the warrior they called the Stormslayer.

Velis joined her by the edge of the pavilion. Together, they looked out across the shining water lit by the red light of dusk. Reshada, with charm, grace, and pride, had grown to be loved by her people: northerners and southerners alike. Through her, and the newfound alliance with Aureia, peace in Larissa had become a reality.

"You come too slowly," Reshada told him.

"Forgive me, Queen Reshada," Velis said. "I was riding."

"Forgive you? Perhaps."

Reshada allowed a smile to grace her lips, before just as suddenly it vanished. Something was hidden in her dark eyes.

Sorrow, perhaps?

Velis wasn't sure. The queen held out a letter with a broken seal.

"Disturbing news from Rovira," she told him.

The Aureian took the letter and slowly scanned the words written upon parchment. His heart skipped a beat and horror flooded his breast. He turned to face Jasir, who stood by the Tariki's side.

"Jasir, rouse the men. We're going to war."

"War?" Jasir stared at him. "Where?"

"Salvaar," Velis replied. He fought his instinct to tear the letter up. To rip the cardinal's words into pieces. "Now go. See it done."

"Sir." Jasir slammed his hand to his chest, before he spun around and marched from the gardens.

Reshada glanced from Velis to her guard.

"Palagius, leave us," she commanded.

"My queen." The Tariki bowed, before he departed in Jasir's wake.

Velis found his hands balling into fists before the Stormslayer had gone ten paces. He crushed the letter.

"Have I not given enough?" he growled. "Have my men not bled enough?"

Now that they were alone, Reshada placed a comforting hand upon his wrist and let a flicker of concern cross her elegant features.

"Did you know that the lotus seed can survive hundreds of years in desert or in drought, and yet still can finally bloom?"

Velis finally looked up from the crumpled letter and into her eyes. Eyes that knew every part of what he was. Eyes that had captivated him from the moment they met two summers past.

"Resilience," Reshada continued softly. "A resilience of near impossible nature. A thing that you can go centuries without so much as hearing whisper of. Yet when I look at you... that is what I see."

"I never wanted this," Velis sighed, and he let the parchment fall to the wooden decking. "I never wanted rank nor position. I am just a simple soldier."

Reshada shook her head.

"You are *much* more than that. A lowly stableboy who rose to prominence. Knighted in his seventeenth year. A man who *earned* the title of commander and gained a far greater reputation than any man who came before."

"I did not want it," Velis repeated sadly.

"A man will often meet his fate upon the path that he took to avoid it."

"And now, as always, I shall meet it," Velis replied, as he felt a fierce drive awaken inside him.

The same drive that had once led him to take command of his overrun and devastated legion in Irene. They had struck down their enemies, and then he had brought them home.

The queen pulled her golden ring from her thumb.

"Hold out your hand," Reshada murmured.

Velis did so. The queen slid it onto his right hand ring finger.

"You cannot give me this," he breathed, as he took in the snarling chimera carved upon it.

"My ancestor's ring," Reshada's words brought Velis' thoughts to life. "That of Nykalous Gaedhela, the greatest, and last, hero of Delios. The man whose empire once stretched from Delios to Aureia, to Larissa, and beyond. Until it was washed away like tears in rain."

"You are the *last* Delion," Velis murmured in disbelief. "The last of the Gaedhela line. The blood of Larissan kings flows through your veins. It is because of you that this country knows peace."

Reshada clasped his hand between her own.

"Indeed. And our friendship holds the alliance between our nations together," she said.

"Before long, we will both be gone, as will any descendants that follow. Larissa will pass to Aureian rule, and my people will be made safe from jealous kings. It is legacy that will remain when we leave this life. Be it in the form of deeds, children, a ring. Look after it until you return. That is an order."

"Yes, my queen."

Reshada reached up and pulled Velis' head down toward her own. She kissed him deeply, and he kissed her back. Advisor and ally had become more than such for over a year now. Slowly, hesitantly, they broke apart the embrace. Their eyes were drawn together, as unspoken words passed between them. Powerful words that neither Velis nor Reshada could bear to speak.

He turned to leave, for the war drums called. No matter how he longed to stay, how he longed to ignore their call, he could not forsake his duty nor betray his men. Fingers ran through fingers as the last of their touch fell away. The dream that they had long found themselves in was cast off.

"Aureian," the queen called after him.

Velis spared her a final look.

"Return with that ring," she said. "Or bury it with your blood."

"Yes, my queen."

Mud squelched as the thick wheels of the cart trundled down the road. To either side of the path, the great forest of Arzarlan spread for miles and all but blocked the light of the sun. A man held the reins sat at the head of the cart, while a woman sat to his side. Like him, she was Medean. Like him, she wore the clothes of a commoner. Theodore Landrey couldn't help his lips from twitching into a smile, as his wife's voice carried to his ear. They had met so long ago that to many it was a distant memory, but to him it was as if it were yesterday.

"Isleen was always a lovely girl, although the clowning she did… once she stayed up with the town drunkard and tried to match him drink for drink. Found her passed out in the goat pen," Maria

Landrey chuckled. "And then there was that time the taxman came to collect. Many of the families had no more to give, and so when the collector wasn't looking, she untethered his horse with his sacks of coin now freshly opened and sent them both galloping down cheapside. And Isleen, she just gave him a wink. I can still hear gold ringing upon the stones," Maria smiled as a new memory entered her mind. "Of course, it all changed when Lord Delmaigyr of Elara rode into Saragoza with his son. Isleen was introduced to the lord's son, and well, that was that."

"Who's Isleen?" Theodore frowned.

"Isleen Delmaigyr. My cousin in Elara," Maria raised her eyebrows as a hint of exasperation entered her voice. "Did you not listen the first *three* times?"

The corners of Theo's lips curled as he met her eyes, then a grin stretched across his face.

"You… you…" Maria slapped his arm as annoyance turned to laughter. The joyous sound rose to the heavens, as husband and wife let their hands interlock.

"Just a few more miles, and then we should reach Ilham," Theodore said with a sigh. "Be good to see…"

He trailed off as a new sound hit his ears. A familiar sound. He glanced over his shoulder. "Rider," he said warily.

It did not take long for the sound of clinking mail to join that of galloping hooves. Silver flashed as streaks of sunlight danced across the steel armour of a sole knight. Theodore recognised the blue cloak, as he did the sapphire crest and white sun emblem. This was a Knight of Kil'kara.

"Greetings, sir knight," Theodore called out, as the rider cantered up beside them.

"May the gods light your way, friend," a Medean accent replied. "Where are you headed?"

"Elara, by way of Palen-Tor," Theodore said and gave the man a nod. "What brings you this far south, brother?"

The knight shrugged. "I am looking for someone."

"Who might that be?"

"Perhaps you can help," the rider replied. "Tell me, do you know Kyler Landrey?"

Theodore glanced at his wife.

"Aye, sir," he replied. "He's my son."

"Then the gods have truly blessed our crossing," the knight grinned and pulled his helm from his head.

He pushed his coif back to reveal his face to the pair. Shrouded eyes, a weathered face.

Yet it was not the face of the warrior that drew Theodore's eyes. It was the scar across his lip.

NINE

Village of Faolan, Forest of Salvaar

"We're here," Aeryn called, as the humble village came into sight.

Only a fool could have missed the joy in her voice, as the words rolled across her lips.

Faolan was a small town with no more than two dozen thatched houses sprawled around somewhat of a clearing. A narrow river ran through its midst, and thin tendrils of smoke arose from the village's cooking fires.

"This is your home?" Sakkar asked her.

"Yes," Aeryn replied with a grin.

The moonseer let her keen gaze wash over the town as its people begun to notice their presence. Curious eyes turned their way and greetings were called. Aeryn waved a hand in reply as her company rode closer.

"Aeryn!"

The girl who watched from the doorway of her house suddenly barrelled toward them and ran as fast as her simple dress would allow. The moonseer laughed and slid from her saddle. Her boots hit the soft earth just in time to catch the girl who threw herself into Aeryn's waiting arms. They held each other tight, and Aeryn could not stop her grin from spreading ear to ear.

"Vanya," she said happily, as she stepped back to take the girl in.

Wild dark hair that she knew so well streamed down the girl's shoulders. Playful blue eyes flashed with joy, and that mischievous grin still graced her lips. A crown of wildflowers sat atop her dark tresses.

"Look at you," Aeryn placed her hands on the girl's shoulders as she spoke, "you've grown."

Indeed she had. Aeryn had not travelled home in over a year, and when last she was here Vanya had just passed her sixteenth birthday.

"I'll be as tall as you soon," Vanya told her. "Mother says…"

Her eyes flicked over Aeryn's shoulder as Sakkar dismounted. She pursed her lips, and her brow slightly furrowed. She was unsure what to make of the foreigners who rode with Aeryn.

"Vanya," Aeryn said as she gestured to the Larissan, and for the first time Aeryn's joy faltered. "This is Sakkar of Larissa."

Sakkar gave a small bow.

"Charmed," he greeted her and placed a hand atop his heart in Salvaari fashion.

Vanya smiled in reply and returned the gesture.

"This is my sister," Aeryn told her companions.

"We cannot delay," Bellec's rough voice cut through the air, as he dropped from his saddle and bundled the reins of his horse in his hand.

His tone held the same urgency that Aeryn felt grow by the second. It threatened to consume her. She set her jaw and buried it.

"Peace, Bellec," Aeryn told him. "The sun draws low, and we can get what supplies we need here. We rest in Faolan tonight."

The orange light of the dusk sun shone through the streets as Aeryn led the company through Faolan. The curious eyes of the villagers followed them as they made their way through the small maze of simple wooden houses. Like the rest of the Salvaari, the Aedei of Faolan had little to do with outsiders. Much of their experience with foreigners came from the wars that they had lived through. They were suspicious and a little on edge, but the fact that the newcomers rode with Aeryn was enough.

"They're watching us," murmured one of the mercenaries.

Galadayne snorted and gave him a knowing look.

"They're trying to figure out what you are, Jaimye," he said.

"Aye, that be it," Jaimye grinned in reply.

Aeryn brought them to a halt before a house. It was no different from any of the others within Faolan. A humble dwelling ringed with a small, thatched, fence. A large barn stood at its back alongside a fenced paddock. A small herd of horses was gathered within.

Bellec handed his reins to one of his men, as he watched the moonseer simply flick hers back over her mount's powerful neck. Aeryn allowed her hand to caress the dark mare's side. The hide of her horse was soft beneath her fingers. Aeryn let her hand fall before she made her way up to the door of the house with Vayna at her side. The entrance flew open before she could even think about raising a hand to knock, and out rushed a woman. Her lined face was lit with joy as she pulled Aeryn into a tight embrace. She squeezed her tightly as if the moonseer would blow away at any moment. Aeryn couldn't stop the grin as she gripped the dark-haired woman tight. Just like that, she was enveloped in a warm hug that said more than words ever could. She felt safe.

"Aeryn," the woman's muffled voice called happily.

"Mother." Aeryn felt nothing but joy as she said the word. It had been so long.

Her mother finally released her.

"We were so worried," she said in Salvaari. "When word of Caelis reached us, we *knew* that they would call your name."

"The spirits kept me safe," Aeryn told her.

"We thought–"

"Corre," a gruff voice cut in.

There, behind her mother, stood a man. His face weathered and his black hair wild. His clothes were as simple as any others, and his frame strong beneath them. His dangerous blue eyes washed over the foreigners before flicking to his family.

"It's about time you came back," he said simply.

"Father."

Aeryn gazed up at the man who stood in the doorway. Eivor, her father. As a young man, he had taken up his spear for his people. Now he raised the finest horses in all of Salvaar. It was times such as this that Aeryn felt her gift, her *burden*, grow heavier.

"I am moonseer," she told him.

"I know," Eivor said and took a step toward his daughter.

"I had no choice."

"I know," he repeated, as he placed a gentle hand upon her shoulder.

It was all that he needed to say, and all that he would say. Her father was not one to show emotion in front of strangers. Eivor had fought against Annora all those years ago. He had the scars to prove it, and though he had replaced the sword with a plough, it would take time to heal the past. He watched the mercenaries cautiously.

"Who are these men that ride with you?"

"Friends." Aeryn bit her lip. She knew that her next words would break the hearts of her family, yet she was determined. Nothing could stop her. She had made her choice. "Father, I'm leaving."

"Faolan?" He frowned.

"Salvaar."

Confusion turned into sorrow, for his eyes could not hide everything. A moonseer leaving the forest was unheard of, and now, they were about to lose their daughter again. Aeryn could not bear to look at her mother or Vanya. She watched as her father fought back the feelings that threatened.

"You there," he called to Bellec. "Your men can stay in our barn tonight."

"That is kind, but—"

Eivor held up a hand to silence him and gazed up into the sky. Clouds loomed overheard. Dark clouds.

"There is a storm coming. I can feel it in my bones. You would do well not to get caught in it."

"Gratitude," Bellec bowed his head in thanks.

Eivor shared the nod, before he turned to Aeryn. He could see the war being fought in her silver eyes. He could see it all.

"Aeryn, tell me everything."

Kitara rubbed her thigh with a grimace, as she rose to her feet. She had taken far worse injuries in days long gone, but it still itched painfully when she put weight on her leg. She fingered the nail that she had secreted up her sleeve. Finally, she had some luck, and perhaps this could be her chance of escaping from this stinking cell. It could be her *only* chance. Not just to save herself, but the Salvaari held prisoner with her. She glanced down at Sereia, and the mere sight of the girl hardened her resolve beyond contestation.

Kitara would not fail. She could not.

Taking a long, slow breath, she closed her eyes. Slowly, calm encompassed her. She stretched down. The muscles in her arms, back, and legs flexed upon command. The sinews stretched and loosened as she moved from position to position. Her body freely obeyed her instruction. Her boots slid atop the wooden flooring, barely making a sound as her form changed. Each move was as perfect as the last, allowing her strong muscles to loosen. Her body had seen, and been through, so much. She felt the scars beneath her shirt stretch as she moved. She felt her wounded leg offer a hint of protest. Each injury was a story, and the stories had made her wise.

Kitara rested her elbows upon the door of her cell as she stared out into the narrow walkway that ran through the centre of the passage. There was little enough room to move, to use the skills that she knew so well, yet she would make do with what she had.

"Guard," she called out.

Heavy boots thudded, and after a moment, a pair of armed Medeans strode toward her.

"What do you want?" one of them asked, irritation clouding his face.

"Tell Sir Rowan that I have reconsidered," she said. "Tell him that I wish to talk."

"You plan to go after her?" Eivor said.

They sat on a circle of roughly hewn chairs that surrounded a cooking fire. Its warmth should have chased off the cold, yet Aeryn's blood was as winter ice.

"We do," Aeryn told her father.

Eivor's eyes had not left those of his daughter for some time. The story she had told him had been long, yet he knew that his daughter had failed to mention one thing.

"You care for her, don't you?" he stated.

Aeryn nodded, and barely trusted herself to speak.

"She's special."

"She is *my* daughter!" Bellec exclaimed. "And I will not fail her."

"Were our places reversed, I would do the same," Eivor replied.

Aeryn leaned forward and placed her hands upon her thighs. "Then you know why I must leave," she said.

"And so, you travel west." There was a spark of anger in Eivor's gaze now as he spoke. He glanced from Bellec to Galadayne to Sakkar before he switched tongues to that of Salvaar. "West, Aeryn. Once you leave these trees, every one of those devils beyond will seek your blood. The further you travel, the weaker the spirits grow. Out there they cannot protect you. Death will stalk you the moment you cross into Medea. And it will find you," he jerked his eyes toward the foreigners as he spoke. "Their gods are cruel. I have seen it."

Aeryn ground her teeth, and she replied in the language of her forefathers. "I do not fear them."

"You would abandon the vow you swore as moonseer? You would betray the very gift that the spirits blessed you with?" Eivor countered incredulously. "And for what?"

Corre clamped her hand down on her husband's wrist.

"Eivor!"

Aeryn set her jaw as she fought to hold back the anger that threatened to erupt. She felt Vanya's fingers brush her own. The feeling calmed her. She took her sister's hand.

"I only say this because I love you," Eivor muttered. "We all do. I would not see you go to your death."

"Then do not watch," Aeryn said slowly through bared her teeth.

The moonseer rose to her feet and gave her father a venomous glare. Her snarl was as fire as she shifted once more back into the common tongue. For a moment the pain she felt was made bare.

"I will *not* abandon her."

With that, she stormed out of the house; silver eyes blazing with fury.

The gentle wind caressed Aeryn's cheeks and blew through her hair as she stalked away from her family's house. The moon was hidden by clouds, but her keen gaze allowed her to see as if she was in the clearest of days.

Aeryn made her way out into the paddock that ran behind the village. Step by step, the anger fled her body. Step by step, the calm returned. She closed her eyes and took a long breath, allowing the cool breeze to fill her. A familiar whinny broke the silence, and something soft touched her fingers. Her hand instinctively reached out and brushed the horse's nose.

"Hello, girl," Aeryn murmured.

She spoke in the language of the people. The language of the forest. The language that all born beneath these trees could understand. Something bumped into her back, and that was all it took for a smile to appear upon her lips. Her eyes flicked open, and there she was, surrounded by three of her family's forest horses. They had raised and bred the animals since she was a child. Now they were like family.

Aeryn brushed a hand down the powerful neck of the white mare before her, while she rubbed the nose of a chestnut filly. The third was a bay broodmare whose long dark mane hung low. Aeryn cupped its cheeks with a grin, as the other horses moved around her.

"Did you miss me too?"

Slowly, Aeryn leaned forward and pressed her forehead to that of the mare's, and once more, she closed her eyes. She could feel the horse's breath upon her chest and its soft fur upon her brow. Its long lashes brushed her cheeks.

"I missed you."

Here among the horses, each she had known for years, Aeryn felt at peace. The cool air was all around her. The sounds of birds and other animals echoed through the trees. One day she would bring Kitara here, of that she was certain.

She sensed a presence by the slight sound of footfalls upon wet grass, accompanied by the brush of cloth.

"I can hear you," Aeryn called, without even bothering to turn. She knew who it was.

"I am not surprised."

Aeryn glanced over her shoulder as Sakkar approached.

"What is it?" she asked.

Sakkar shrugged. "The children have been saying things, and though I cannot speak your tongue, I cannot help but assume that it is about me."

Aeryn raised her eyebrows and held back her grin as she replied. "They wanted to know if the spirits painted you."

Sakkar blinked at her. Aeryn's lips twitched into a smirk, and then Sakkar roared with laughter.

"And what did you tell them?" he asked, when at last he had composed himself.

"Told them that you were a demon from the Westlands. That you would eat them whole if you caught them staring."

Sakkar smiled at that. Cheers erupted from the barn, and the pair turned to it as the sound of a lute spilled from its open doors.

"Looks like Kompton is up to his old tricks," Sakkar chuckled.

"Aye."

He glanced at her, and Aeryn knew what he could see behind her smile. Perhaps he was the only one who could. He had seen much through his lifetime.

"We will get her back," Sakkar told her.

The moonseer paused. Perhaps he understood. Perhaps he could see the hint of fear in her eyes. Fear for Kitara. Aeryn nodded and pursed her lips. They were only words, but to her they meant everything.

"I know," she replied gratefully.

They settled into silence, staring out into the forest beyond the village.

"Aeryn," Eivor's gruff voice broke the quiet. "A word?"

Aeryn glanced over her shoulder as her father approached. She dipped her head. It took but a glance from Eivor for Sakkar to make his leave, and he waltzed off toward the barn. No doubt he would be deep into the mercenaries' wine stock by morning.

"You're still leaving?"

Aeryn's eyes drifted westward. Somewhere out there, Kitara was on a ship bound for the empire. Aeryn knew in her heart exactly what was going through Kitara's mind. Not so long ago, she had spoken of her demons, and monsters like those were not so easily vanquished.

"Kitara is out there somewhere," Aeryn said. "She's alone. She will not think that no one is coming for her. She will *know* that no one is coming for her. That is what she has been taught since the beginning. She has suffered enough."

Eivor nodded. "Forgive me. I was wrong to challenge you."

"There is nothing to forgive, Father."

"Stay vigilant out there," he warned. "I have fought the West before. I know what they are capable of. No matter what happens, I will always follow whatever course you charter. I hope that you know that."

"I know," Aeryn replied quietly.

He placed a hand on her shoulder. "May the spirits go with you and watch over you whenever I cannot."

"Thank you," she murmured, as he pulled her into his arms.

The morning came around all too soon, and just as quickly Aeryn was forced to say her goodbyes to her parents and beloved sister. She checked that the steel of a Tariki sword, Kitara's sword, was still under her saddlebags. Aeryn brushed its hilt gently, as she swung herself up into the saddle. Despite the forces that sang to her, willing her to stay, she had to follow her heart.

The riders travelled west with the dawn sun hot upon their backs.

"I have been to Aureia many times," Bellec said, when the company had made camp for the night. Before them, he had laid a map of the northern empire and the Larissan border. "And the city for which they are bound, Vesuva. I have walked those streets before."

"I am told it is a city of great appetites," Sakkar added.

"Indeed," Bellec chuckled. "Its aristocracy and merchant class live as kings, while its arena champions stand as gods."

"Slavery," Aeryn grimaced distastefully.

"Now," Bellec let his finger slide along the map, "they travel by ship, and the fastest route to Vesuva is from the north. They shall pass Larissa, and by my guess, dock at Belona. A port town barely half a day's ride from the city itself. But that is of no consequence, for hey will be in Vesuva long before we reach Larissa."

"We cannot afford delay," Galadayne cut in. "The Aureians have a voracious hunger, and each day a slave survives in that city is a blessing."

Luana Marquez gazed out over Laykos Island and the blue seas beyond. The mountain on which she stood gave her clear sight of Mykos Island, along with the fallen isles of Ephileon, Androna and Famier. If the captain looked close enough, she could *almost* make out Sacira, the first of their paradises to fall to Elara and the League. Her unwavering gaze found nothing moving on the ocean before her, yet behind, the entire island was filled with activity.

Luana heard the light footsteps of a man approach from behind.

"Calvillo," she called out, "how goes the evacuation?"

"The last of the boats are almost ready, Captain."

She pursed her lips. "And the people of Mykos?"

Luana glanced at the Tariki. Mykos, sister island of Laykos, was smaller, poorer, yet just as important. All life was important to those who were truly free, and now Elara had come to snuff out that freedom.

"All are assembled," he said. "The fleet is ready."

Luana allowed herself a brief smile.

"Teague's little trick with the boy worked. Gave us time. No doubt when the nobility of Landonsport heard the tale of us sailing north they panicked. Should been here days ago… but now we get away without a single scratch and in so doing save hundreds of lives. Garrett's plan worked."

"Shrewd bastard, he is," Calvillo smirked, before he turned to look down over the township. "This alliance, as impossible as it once seemed, has proven to be the very thing we needed."

"Unity was the only way," Luana said softly. "All it took was

Teague's leadership and Laven's guile."

"And your tongue of silver," Calvillo told her. "Don't forget who started this. No one but you could have convinced these people to abandon their homes."

"For better or worse."

"For better or worse," Calvillo agreed.

Luana let her gaze sweep back over the Sacasian. No gulls flew above, nor did any sound carry across the waters far below. It was too quiet. Far too quiet. Then it caught her gaze. A shimmer upon the horizon.

"They're here," she breathed, as she felt the icy cold tendrils of dread wrap around her heart.

Dozens of ships filled with heavily armed soldiers.

Elara had come.

TEN

City of Elara, the League of Trecento

"I see that age hasn't caught up with you just yet," Elise Delfeyre smirked, as she made her way through the tavern toward the seated fighter.

Tariq glanced up at her from where he sat at the crude wooden bench. A silver jug and a series of cups sat atop its rough surface. The fires of the nearby torches danced through his dark eyes. Tariq snorted, as he pulled his rough white shirt over his head. "Just as your people still do not know how to fight," his voice was deep and rugged.

For the first time in longer than she could remember, Elise felt true happiness. Her lips curled into a grin. A laugh left Tariq's lips as he rose to his feet. He pulled her into a deep bear hug, and his powerful arms shrouded her from the outside world. Tariq was the closest person that she had left, and the only one that she truly felt safe with.

Here in his arms, she felt at home. He brushed a stay strand of hair away from her cheek as he stepped back. Tariq's gaze darted over her shoulders to where it locked with the two men watching them closely from the door. Elise nearly chuckled. Her friend could see beyond the filth covered disguises and saw the guards for what they really were.

"It seems that someone has grown wary of these parts," Tariq stated.

"My uncle insisted," Elise grimaced. "Everyone across the river is getting nervous."

A dark look crossed Tariq's face. "We are cut off here," he told her. "You have seen the streets… the poverty. The Riversiders leave us further and further behind every day."

Elise could hear the anger in his voice, and it made her blood boil too. Here, in the mud, her father had been murdered, but at least in the Pits everyone was equal. At least in the Pits people confronted you with knives, they didn't stab you in the back.

"Word on the street is that the gangs are growing restless," Elise said. "Starting to seek control over more than the boroughs."

Tariq sighed. "It is a good deal worse than that," he told her. "Bhaltair and his gangs keep the people alive, yet he has started to extend his arm across the river. The Riversiders send soldiers across the bridge every day to hunt him, and those soldiers have become nervous. They lash out at any in their hunt for Bhaltair without care. The people are angry. They want to fight back. Not to mention that the Stentor family is not happy with the magister's rule. They say that he has forgotten his people, and judging by their actions, I would suggest that the gangs agree. Your uncle has good reason to be nervous."

Elise raised her eyebrows as she waltzed past her friend. "Lord Priamos Stentor, ever the voice of the people," she said. "Sometimes I wonder how the nobles became noble anyway." Leaning against the bench in a most unladylike way, she took up one of the cups waiting upon its rough surface and filled it with wine from a silver jug.

"Wealth and heritage, you know how it is," the Berenithian smirked. "Stentor says one thing, Magister Imrohir and his family say another, and then before you know it…"

"Chaos in the streets," Elise concluded.

"Precisely," Tariq took the cup that she offered. "The families were always clawing at each other, and too easily do words and anger turn to action. This war in the Sacasian has sheathed their swords for now, but make no mistake, without it we would be up to our knees in blood. There is a war coming."

Elise snorted. "The nobles were never much good at peace, were they?"

"No. No, they were not."

"Between them, the war, and now this deviant thief, it's a wonder that the city hasn't descended into utter madness."

"Hasn't it?" Tariq shrugged. "This so-called Nightingale, the shadow of a story cast from Aureia, has our *great* leaders up in arms. Robbing and stealing at will, leaving nothing but the feather of his namesake."

Elise rolled her eyes. "A ridiculous notion, and one dangerously arrogant," she said. "What kind of fool leaves behind evidence to tie each crime together?"

"A fool," Tariq agreed, "and a killer."

"Oh?"

"One of the lads heard that the Nightingale stopped a pair of would-be thieves last night. Let them go free, before later hunting them down like dogs and butchering them in the street."

"So, he's drawn blood?" she murmured, as a chill crept through her bones.

"And not for the first time," Tariq told her. "There are stories, the streets are full of them. Just like the Nightingale that once laid siege to Aureia. This impersonator does not shy away from blood and that makes the madman ever more dangerous. Though why take on the same name? I dread to guess. Perhaps he wishes to use the Nightingale's legend to add to his own?" Tariq paused, and sighed, his expression grim. "In this city, one thing is certain. He will be caught, and he will pay for his crimes. Gods willing, before he claims another life."

Elise was quiet for a moment. She let her eyes drift to the red wine that filled her cup. "How things have changed," she said.

"And yet, they have not changed us."

"No," Elise smiled sadly. "Though what could have been. Two years… two years in my uncle's house, and I am still not used to the title, nor the dresses or the maids that come with it."

"We wanted to keep you safe," Tariq murmured. "After what happened…"

He trailed off. Elise could only watch as her friend lost himself in the same ghosts that haunted her mind. The same ghosts that she saw every day. Tariq had been her father's closest friend… his brother. Being here brought those memories back. Memories of happier days.

"Do you think that things could ever go back to how they were?" Elise asked.

Tariq slowly shook his head.

"No," he said. "That life is long gone."

In her heart, Elise knew as much. Her father's circus troupe, travelling band of misfits that they were, had long since disbanded. The deaths of her parents had seen to that.

"You still put your strongman skills to proper use," she said and nodded toward the door that led to the fighting sands. "Though I am no acrobat. Not anymore." She studied his face. "Do you ever wonder about that dream you once had? A simpler life. A family. Will you do it?"

"Perhaps one day I shall take a wife, and father children," Tariq said, after a moment. "But there is still much to be done. I made a promise to your mother, and I intend to keep it."

"You're a good man, Tariq," Elise told him. "And a better friend."

"You're family," Tariq said simply. "How goes your painting?"

He spoke of the pastime that Elise had taken up recently. It was calming and let her mind have focus.

"Passes the time," Elise took a sip from her cup and swirled the liquid around her tongue. A smile played across her lips, as she recognised the familiar and most enjoyable taste. "Honeyed wine."

"Your favourite, aye," Tariq gave a growl of a chuckle. A sparkle entered his gaze. "A few more fights, and we will have enough coin to leave this wretched city."

Elise's smile faded, as her thoughts turned to a future outside of Elara. Though it was something that she greatly desired, she was not sure that would ever be rid of the tragedy that had once struck her family. Then there was something else. Those few she would be leaving behind.

"Just as we promised," she replied.

"I know that look," Tariq said quietly. "You have not yet told them, have you?"

"No," Elise admitted. "My aunt and uncle took me in... gave me a home, a family. After so much tragedy, so much pain, if I left I fear that it would break them. And yet I have to leave. I *can't* stay here. Every day I see them," she told him before touching a hand to her head, "in here."

The thought of her parents brought everything back. It threatened to engulf and crush her.

A warm hand was placed upon her arm. "Those we love never really leave," Tariq told her. "They will live forever in memory. All we can do now is honour them."

"I have missed you," Elise said, and squeezed his hand.

The hustle and bustle of Elara's great markets drowned out the sound of the outside world. The voices of bartering shopkeepers and their clientele filled the streets and market square, while fruit, clothing, jewels, and exotic goods lined the stalls. The Elarans were garbed in fine, richly coloured cloth and silks, embellished beyond reason, bearing self-satisfied expressions. They spent their coin without care and sated their every appetite. In a city of gold, where those who worked hardest were greatly rewarded, they stood as the upper echelon of civilisation. Even the armour of the halberd-wielding city watch was as highly decorated as the wealthiest knight's.

"What do you mean, you *lost* her?" the big man seethed, as he waved his huge arms.

Cleander glared at the blacksmith, as he replied. The gruff voice of an Annoran graced his tone, "An unfortunate circumstance soon to be rectified."

The smith cursed and turned back to the weapon racks that stood behind him. They were laden with the finest swords, spears, and halberds that money could buy. Nicolo was a proven master of his trade. He snatched up a sheathed hand-and-a-half sword, before he handed it to Cleander with a shake of his bald head.

Cleander felt its perfect weight. He half-drew the blade and ran his keen gaze down its shimmering length. It was already sharp enough to shave the hair of a pig in a single swing.

He pushed the blade back into its sheath. "This is a good sword."

Nicolo glowered. "And it will be the last."

"One can but pray," Cleander replied with a shrug, and held out a small coin purse.

As Nicolo took it, he glared into Cleander's eyes. "Misplace another of my children, Cleander, and perhaps the next one will find your throat."

Cleander belted the sword to his waist and gave a theatrical bow. "As always, Nicolo, a pleasure."

He strode away into the square, vanishing in the great crowd of people. Losing the sword in that gods-forsaken vault had cost him dearly. Not so much in coin, for he had enough to live a life of luxury until the end of his days. The blade, like its forger, was Elaran, and men such as the Knights of Kil'kara would be able to trace its providence.

It was only a matter of time, and he had much left to do. Elara had never heard of Markus Harvarder. Cleander, the name he now went by, would delay them for a time, yet he could only hope that it would be enough to secure the future he craved. Not just for himself, but for the city.

His left hand wrapped around the pommel of his new sword as he navigated the crowds. His dark attire and gambeson gave him the appearance of a mercenary in the employ of a merchant, while the half-cape over his left shoulder showed that he had rank. His brown hood was pushed back, freeing his mid-length hair and baring his weathered face. A few pouches and three small silver orbs hung from his waist, alongside the two knives that adorned his belt.

Thud.

Someone bumped into Cleander's side. A woman. Dark of hair, olive of skin, and her lips full. Eyes the colour of sapphires flashed over him. Her equally blue dress had a low front and a lower back, while a golden necklace adorned her throat. A courtesan. One of many who worked the Elaran streets.

"How clumsy of me," she said, and gave him a seductive smile. "My apologies."

"Not at all," Cleander replied, as his gaze was drawn in by her ocean blue eyes.

She leaned in closely. "Allow me to make amends," she whispered, before she took one of his hands.

The courtesan led him through the throng of people toward a thin alley. None paid them heed, for courtesans went about their business freely in the streets of Elara. She turned to face Cleander and kissed him deeply upon the lips, as she pulled him into the alley. Her lips were soft and smooth, her touch gentle. One of Cleander's hands went to her lower back, while his other ran through her long, rich black tresses. She pulled back from the kiss yet remained ever so close.

"Cleander," she whispered.

"Mistress Emberly," he said, and his voice was as quiet as her own.

Emberly kept her lips close to his ear. He could feel them brush his skin.

"M'lady Mellisanthi sent me to find you," she told him.

"Did she?" Cleander smiled and ran a hand down her cheek as she drew away from him.

"Been looking for you for some time." A flicker of fear danced through her eyes. It was well hidden, yet Cleander knew fear when he saw it.

"And I'm not the only one," she continued. "We're being watched… me and the girls… the gangs. I think the magister suspects something."

Cleander let his gaze wander back toward the town square. People hurried by the alley's entrance without sparing a glance down its dark corridor, yet eyes were everywhere in this city. He kissed Emberly's cheek. "What message did your madam give you?"

"There is an important meeting happening tonight," Emberly breathed, "below."

"With whom?" Cleander replied with a frown. It was not unusual for the gang to have meetings, yet rarely was he called upon.

"M'lady would not say. Only that your patron wishes you to attend."

"I will be there," he said, as he stroked her cheek and pulled her closer. "You're afraid."

"Yes," Emberly murmured.

Cleander felt a slight tremble run through her frame. If something had the courtesans spooked, then whoever was watching them was more dangerous than a mere spy.

"Tell Mellisanthi that I will join her when I can. I will see no harm befall you."

Emberly kissed him deeply again. When she broke contact, she said, her voice rising back above a whisper, "Amends have been made." She gave him a smile and fluttered her lustrous lashes. "You know where to find me if you wish for anything else."

Cleander grinned and tossed her a coin. "I will see you tonight, my lovely."

Emberly gave him a wink, and then with a swing of her hips and a twirling of skirts, she was gone.

Mellisanthi's girls were more cunning than the wiliest fox and twice as deadly. The perfect spies. They were invaluable, and their madam was his closest friend and companion. He would not see them undone.

The sewer system beneath Elara stretched for dozens of miles and created a great network of tunnels for those brave enough to enter the dark. Its stench was enough to drive away even the strongest of men, so now only the gangs dared walk its stone corridors. Those tunnels beneath the lower districts and the Pits had been transformed into a base for the gangs. Cleander kept to the narrow walkway that ran along the water's edge as he made his way through the dark. *Water* was a strong word for the filth that flowed through the tunnels. Even the warrior himself was near turned away by the smell. He kept his facemask up over his nose and his hood pulled over his head. It was not enough. It never was.

Cleander followed the passageway for some time without so much as thinking about which passage to take, for he knew every crack and crevice that the elaborate maze had to offer. He rounded a bend, walked up a few stone stairs, and then knocked on the heavy door that appeared before him. A square of steel bars was built into the centre of the door. A wooden hatch was pulled back and a pair of eyes appeared beyond the bars. Cleander pulled down his mask and revealed his face to the man on the other side.

"Cleander," the man on the other side greeted him.

The eyes disappeared, and the hatch was closed. Cleander heard three distinct clinks before the door was pulled open.

"Right this way," the roughly garbed man said.

Cleander was led through a series of rooms, each as embellished as the last, until they reached a large hall. Great tapestries hung from walls, while huge fur carpets were draped upon the floor. Massive tables of the finest oak and redwood, where dozens of men sat, stood throughout the hall. The room was lit by candles and torches, and it had something of a smoky haze to it. The men were as rough as the one that led Cleander. They were all drinking, laughing, and gambling. They had dangerous expressions, and they could turn violent at a moment's notice. Savage knives adorned their belts, while golden jewels hung from their ears and necks.

"Through there," Cleander's guide grunted and nodded toward another closed door.

Cleander said not a word as he walked past and pulled it open, before he strode into the small chamber beyond. Two men stood around a small desk, and they could not have been more opposite.

The younger of the two, a man not much older than Cleander, was dressed in black. A thick duelling cape was wrapped around his body, its rope fastening circled from his left shoulder to under his right. A wicked sidesword adorned his belt, and his face was rugged. Short greying hair sat atop his head, while his beard was dark and pointed. A pair of shining rings pierced his left ear, and his eyes glinted dangerously. That was Bhaltair. Leader of the gangs.

The other man was clothed in fine silks, with a thick fur-lined cloak at his back. He wore an embellished steel breastplate, while braces and greaves of their equal were clasped around his arms and legs. Like Bhaltair, he wore a sidesword at his hip.

"Ah, Cleander," Bhaltair said. "I was beginning to worry."

"Bhaltair," Cleander clasped arms with the gang leader.

He turned to face the other man, who carried himself with the pride and dignity of an aristocrat. Yet there was something stronger about him. Cleander had seen him before; however, he could not put a name to a face.

"Cleander, you may recognise Lord Priamos Stentor," Bhaltair told him.

Cleander barely stopped his eyes from widening. Of all the things he could have been summoned for, this had not been what he was expecting. A lord from across the river standing in the depths of the Pits? His fellow nobles would have spat upon him for even thinking of such a thing.

"Lord Stentor," Cleander greeted the aristocrat.

The noble held out a hand. Cleander took it.

"You may be wondering why I am here, of all places," Priamos said. "It is no secret that my family has never seen eye to eye with the gangs… and yet fate, it seems, has brought us together. Times have changed, and if we are to survive so must we. Our great leaders have forgotten the principles for which we stand, and now the people suffer for it. I would not have it so."

"It is getting worse," Cleander told his companions truthfully. "The soldiers who cross the river in search of us are as scared as cornered animals. That fear makes them turn to steel before words, and they have begun to lash out. Four men died today at Riversider hands. The people cry out for justice."

Bhaltair grimaced.

"I know," he muttered. "Do you know, Lord Stentor, that Imrohir has extended an offer to me? The magister says that this war will be over if I simply hand myself to him. That it will end the moment I hang in the square. This is something other than the truth and we all know it. If I believed that my people would be made safe, then I would gladly pay that price. My life for theirs. An easy choice. It would not stop him. It would not stop his soldiers from crossing that bridge. The lords across the river would rise themselves high and crush my people further and further into the ground. So, I am resolved. I will deliver my people into something better."

Priamos Stentor crossed his arms as he glanced from Bhaltair's impassioned face to Cleander's stoic one. "No lords will stand against the magister," he said. "He is too powerful now."

"You want Imrohir gone," Bhaltair said. "So do we."

"Then we are agreed. The magister will die," Priamos replied.

Cleander looked from the gang leader to the noble. They stood as two sides of the same coin.

"If the man is to die then it must be done in the right way," Cleander said. "A knife in the dark will serve no purpose save to enrage the people. It could start a war."

"No," Priamos shook his head as he spoke. "There is no time for that, I fear."

Cleander crossed his arms and frowned.

"Then explain," he said.

ELEVEN

Village of Oryn, Forest of Salvaar

"Move!" Lukas snarled, as he pushed his way through the ranks of Medean soldiers, with Sir Garrik and a dozen of his guard at his back. The soldiers did not know him, yet he spoke with the authority of a king. Slowly, they began to make way for the prince.

At last, the ring of steel broke and Lukas' eyes flashed over the unfolding scene. He took in the warrior first. A surcoat of gold, and chain armour of silver, with the great white lion of Aloys upon his chest. In his hands the man held a longsword of the finest steel; a blade which he now had pressed to the neck of an unarmed woman. Lukas knew those eyes for he would never forget their owner. Maevin, the Káli seer, priestess to Tanris. By her side lay the ruined ball of a blood covered head. That of Elion Montbard, a man he had known since he was but a child. He recognised the warrior as well, for they had met, once upon a time. He remembered the arrogance and cocky swagger of Alejandro's heir all too well. Emilian Aloys.

"Aloys!" Lukas growled, as he slowly walked towards the Medean lordling. He struggled to hold back the anger that threatened to engulf him. "Stay your blade!"

Emilian turned to face Lukas and the retinue of guardsmen at his back. "By the gods," he said. "Prince Lukas?"

"I said stay your blade," the prince snapped, as he stepped toward Emilian.

"I—"

Lukas glanced down at Maevin, saw her face awash with blood, and it made his blood boil. He glanced up and met Emilian's eyes with a dark glare.

"Let the girl go," Lukas commanded.

"She killed Elion."

"And you took her village," Lukas shot back, waving his arms in frustration. "Let the girl *go!*"

Emilian bit his lip and let his eyes wander to the knights at Lukas' back. He was greeted with dangerous expressions and hands ready to let loose steel. Emilian slowly nodded and stepped back, as he gestured to Maevin.

"Aye, *Prince.*"

Lukas ignored the tone and stepped past. His shoulder connected heavily with the lordling's. Lukas held out a hand to Maevin and looked into her green eyes. He saw no trace of fear. She took it and rose to her feet. No words were spoken. None were needed. Lukas turned on Emilian, and let his body create a wedge between the Káli woman and the Medean boy.

"What have you done?" Lukas growled.

Emilian frowned, unsure at the anguish in the prince's tone.

"We rode out to find you. Bring you home."

"WHAT HAVE YOU DONE?" roared Lukas, as a fire awoke in his chest. He could not help it now. He could not hold back the ever-burning rage.

"I do not understand," Emilian said, as his face paled ever so slightly. "The Káli are our enemy. Your brother told me so."

Lukas' blood froze. Months ago, when Cailean had rode into Palen-Tor and greeted the Annoran council, he had said as much. That Vaylin and her people were the enemy, but times had changed, and alliances with them.

"These people are our allies!" Lukas snapped, as he gestured around at the village.

"These people are savages!" Emilian countered. "To trust in them is folly. How many years have they plagued our border, Lukas? How many? Perhaps there could have been peace, but this is the time for war. And if we holy men must act, then we will be the wrath of the gods."

So that was it. Emilian did not care for any newfound friendships; not with the Salvaari. The same sentiment was written on the faces of his men. A thing that no doubt would be felt by many Annorans. Perhaps some of them were here. Perhaps some of them rode with him. To such people, the pagans from the east would never be welcome.

Lukas shared a glance with Maevin. At last he understood. He remembered every word that she had told him, and they came to him now.

"Remove the mask," he murmured, and in that moment, Maevin's lips curled.

"Prince?" Emilian questioned as he heard Lukas speak.

"You say you are a great warrior. Yet you butcher women, children, and old folk. People who trusted us. And you did it for what? Your faith?" Lukas' words started as a low growl that grew stronger with each word. The Annoran prince reached up and took hold of his sun and moon medallion. He gripped it tightly.

"Now you speak of making war in the gods' name. Listen to me, Emilian. We can end this now, and we can end this peacefully."

"The time for peace is over."

Lukas stepped forward. His face was barely an inch from Emilian's.

"Put an end to this god-fucked lunacy!" Lukas snarled.

Aloys said nothing. Instead, he met the stare head on. He set his jaw as the Annoran prince challenged him in front of his own men.

"Now it makes sense," Emilian said with disdain. "You fled your own people to be here. You side with the Salvaari and now spare the life of a savage. You may wear that amulet, you may be the blood of the eagle, but you are not your father. You are nothing more than a heathen."

Lukas could see that Emilian's hand had adjusted its grip upon his sword. He let his hand fall to his own.

"Go for your sword, boy," Lukas goaded him. "Go on."

Emilian began to raise his blade.

"Stop it!" a girl's voice cried out.

Both men turned. The woman pushed back her red hood and let her roughly hewn shoulder length brown hair spill free.

"Kassandra, stay out of it," Lukas said, as his little sister strode toward them, pushing through the Annoran guard.

"No!" Kassandra shot back. "Everyone here is on the same side. Haven't enough people died already?"

Emilian glanced from the princess to her brother; anger replaced by shock.

"What is she doing here?" he asked incredulously. "I was told she was in Palen-Tor."

"Well, here I am," Kassie said, as she spread her arms. "And I will not be spoken about as if I am not."

"She came without my knowing," Lukas told Emilian. "And you will show her respect."

Emilian turned on him as anger laced his words.

"You knowingly endanger your sister. My betrothed."

"I knowingly endanger myself," cut in Kassandra.

"War is no place for girls, least of all the princess of Annora," Emilian replied. "You will accompany me back to the border where it is safe."

"No… not after what you have done," she shook her head sadly. "You are a murderer, Emilian. No more than a butcher of children."

"Do not test me," Emilian warned, as he looked to her. "I do the gods' work. It is enough that you are here… yet now? Now you dress like a savage and champion their cause. Your blood is tainted."

Lukas nearly spat. How dare Emilian turn his anger upon

Kassandra? Lukas could no longer control himself. He placed a hand upon Emilian's shoulder and gripped it tightly. "You do *not* insult my sister," he snapped. "Apologise to her, *now!*"

Emilian brushed the hand off and straightened his back. "No."

Lukas' fist smashed into Emilian's chin. Steel cut through the air. Lukas danced back as the Medean's sword sliced toward his chest. It missed by a fingers' breadth. The prince snatched out his own blade with a flourish, as Annoran and Medean soldiers alike tried to intervene.

"No!" Lukas roared. "Do not come between us!"

The men halted upon his command, for when a prince made his will known, it was honoured. A square was formed around them. Rain lashed Lukas' cheek and thunder crackled overhead as the two men circled each other. The prince felt not the deluge nor the chill, for his blood ran as fire. He stilled his breath. Just as he had been taught long ago. Steel came flashed toward him as Emilian attacked. Lukas deflected the blow and replied in kind. Anger fuelled him. He did not care for the alliance between Annora and Medea, between Raynor and Aloys. He aimed to take off the boy's head.

Emilian blocked and countered. He angled his sword down Lukas'. Steel slid down steel and forced Lukas to leap back or be skewered where he stood. Chainmail and gambeson protected his chest and would stop even the sharpest of swords, yet like Emilian's, his head had no such defence. The clash of blades rang over the sound of the storm and echoed through the streets of Oryn, as the two lords sought to claim blood.

Prince Dayne glanced to Lord Harold Robare, as a new sound greeted them through the rain. Steel upon steel. Dayne snatched out his sword once more. There must be some kind of resistance left.

"With me!" he shouted to the fifty who stood with him.

He would prefer to leave some survivors who he could question, yet not if it came at the cost of his Medean allies. Through the streets of Oryn, the Annorans ran. Dirt and blood splashed over their boots. Bodies of Salvaari, Annoran, and Medean alike were strewn across the ground. Far fewer of the attackers were among the fallen.

The first Dayne saw of the duel was the yellow coats of Aloys men. But why were they not fighting?

His eyes swept the crowd barely fifty paces from them. He saw the red colours of the royal guard, and then he saw Sir Garrik Skarlit. The master at arms had ridden ahead of him to Salvaar. The crowd was quiet, and all eyes were fixed to its centre. Dayne exchanged a look with Lord Harold and made toward the body of men.

It started as an itch and clawed at his stomach like a talon. He tasted blood.

The sickness had returned.

Dayne's sword fell from his fingers. He began to shake. His body spasmed as every fibre of his being contorted in pain.

"Prince Dayne?" Lord Robare turned to see his prince turn deathly white.

Dayne's hand went to his stomach, as he fought to stay standing. It *burned*. Agony ripped through his body like a hot knife. He screamed. Dayne crashed into the mud as the sickness took over. His body fought to stay alive.

"PROTECT THE PRINCE!" roared Robare, as he dashed to his lord's side. "PROTECT THE PRINCE!"

Blood flowed as the edge of Lukas' sword carved a line through Emilian's cheek. The duke's son ignored the graze and drove forward. His blade cut at the prince from a dozen angles.

Lukas blocked. Once. Twice.

The third broke his defence and sliced across his bracer. Steel glanced off steel. An opening presented itself. Lukas' impulse was to take it and open Emilian's thigh from knee to hip. His mind, forged by the likes of Garrik, Sir Tristayn, and his brother, urged him to lunge for the throat. He hesitated as Emilian stepped back and fought to overcome his impulse... and then drove his blade toward the boy's neck.

Emilian stepped to the side and deflected the blow. Too late did Lukas realise his folly. The hesitation had cost him. At first, he felt nothing save the wind upon his cheek.

The pain hit him like a hammer.

"LUKAS!" Kassandra's horror-filled cry filled the street, as she watched her brother fall.

His head erupted in agony as he screamed and crashed into the mud. Emilian's blade had cut through the edge of his left socket and sliced deep into the eyeball behind. Half of Lukas' vision went black as his sword flew from his grasp.

Pain. It was all he felt. He raised a hand to his ruined face and felt blood flow through his fingers. In seconds, it covered his hand. He could not stop the screams that erupted from his throat.

No, no, no, no!

Emilian had taken his eye. Little more than its destroyed remnant remained in his head. Lukas tasted blood as it spilled down his face and coated his lips. Bile rose in the back of his throat.

He saw tears spilling from Kassandra's eyes as she screamed. Garrik's strong grip barely held her back. He saw the bodies of the Káli lying lifeless in the mud. He saw the fire burning in Maevin's gaze. He saw Emilian turn away.

Emilian thought the fight over.

Lukas shoved off Kassie's hand as she dropped into the mud at his side. His hand moved on instinct; fuelled by rage. He took up his war hammer and charged at Emilian Aloys.

"Look out!" one of the Medeans shouted to his lord.

Emilian turned and raised an arm. The hammer came down and shattered his forearm like a twig. He screamed, falling to his knees.

Lukas raised his hammer. His near unseeing face was a mask of blood and filth. Emilian looked up at him in horror. Lukas made to strike. To *kill* his enemy. Rough hands took the prince from behind and viciously pulled the weapon from his grasp.

"Unhand my lord!" Garrik bellowed at the Medean soldiers, free hand ripping his sword from its sheath. Steel rang through the street as the guard followed their commander's call.

"HOLD!" Emilian staggered to his feet and cradled his wounded arm. "Or your prince's life is forfeit. One move against me, and he dies here in the mud. I do not wish to claim his life today, though he attacked me. I will not be challenged in front of my men. Nor will I be attacked from behind by cowards. Give me his hammer."

Emilian held out his good arm, as one of his men handed him Lukas' weapon.

"NO!" Kassandra cried, as Lukas was forced to his knees. Tears spilled down her cheeks as she struggled against Sir Garrik, who still held her tight. "Please don't do this, *please!*"

"Lord Aloys," snarled Garrik, as he pressed Kassandra into the hands of Sir Edward. "Think about what you are doing."

Emilian set his jaw and raised the hammer. The air grew still. None felt the cold of the rain or the lash of the wind.

He brought the weapon down. The steel head smashed into the side of Lukas' knee.

Lukas screamed as his bones were smashed. Ligaments and cartilage splintered, ripped apart, as the hammer was driven deep into flesh. The Medeans threw the screaming prince down into the mud. He was barely able to hear his own cries. Unable to see. Unable to rise. Unable to think.

Mud splashed on his face when Emilian tossed the hammer to the ground. Then he saw black.

"What the hell is going on?" Prince Dayne's voice rolled through the crowd as he forced his way through Annoran and Medean alike. His stomach still burned, and his body still shook, but the screams haunted him.

His heart froze in his chest as at last he saw. Lukas was lying in a pool of his own blood. His face was a ruined mess. Kassandra was holding him tightly in her arms, as tears spilled down her face and sobs rocked her frame. How she had got here, Dayne did not know. Now was not the time to ask.

"Emilian, what did you do?" Dayne shouted, as the blood drained from his face.

He could see the guilt in the young lord's eyes, and the prince did not care that he cradled a wounded arm.

Emilian dropped to his knees. "Prince Dayne, he attacked me twice."

"Lukas, Emilian," Dayne growled, and he crouched beside his brother's body. Lukas' left eye was all but destroyed, and only a fool would be blind to the fact that his knee was irreparable. That was if he could survive at all. "My brother… how dare you."

"It's true, prince—" one of the Medeans began.

Dayne Raynor turned on the man.

"You will be silent," he snarled. "Your lord has his own tongue, and he will use it or I will cut it out. I have half a mind to order my men to kill you now."

"He forced argument," Emilian spluttered, as he saw Dayne's fury ready to be unleashed. "He struck the first blow, and we settled it like men. Then he attacked me when my back was turned. It was he who caused grievance, not I."

Dayne growled. He knew his brother was both reckless and

impulsive, but he could not believe this.

"Why would he start the fight?" Dayne asked.

"For the pagan witch, lord," Emilian said, looking to the black-clad Salvaari woman who now crouched beside Lukas. "She killed Elion, and I wished to claim her blood in payment."

A great sorrow hit the prince, as at last he saw the ruined head of his friend lying abandoned in the mud. It was a sight that drove a great chill into his very heart. His stomach still ached but he set his jaw and forced his emotion aside. Medean, Annoran, and Salvaari all watched him grieve in silence, for many present knew of his friendship with Elion. He refused to show weakness. He was the crown prince of Annora. He would not allow these people to see anything but strength.

The prince turned to the green-eyed woman. The one who had slain his friend.

"Why would my brother risk his life for a Káli woman?"

"Did you not know, Dayne of Annora?" the woman replied dangerously. "We are allies, Káli and Aedei. We joined with Chief Cyneric. We fought beside Chief Cyneric. We shed blood for Chief Cyneric."

Dayne held back a grimace. No longer could he taste the blood in his mouth. Now all he tasted was horror. Now, he understood; there had been a deadly mistake. One that had already claimed so much.

"When we left home, it was known that your people fought against the Aedei."

"Everything changes," the Káli woman replied with a dark voice, "like the wind. One day we are your enemy, the next we are your friend. As for your brother, we are bonded, he and I."

"We have made a grave mistake."

"Prince Dayne," Emilian spoke up, as he saw a small band of Káli arrive. They walked beside Sir Garrik and his guardsmen as if they were friends. Perhaps they were, yet only a fool could not see the look of violence that threated, "We have to leave."

The leader of the Káli glared toward the young lord, and his eyes spewed pure hatred. He gripped his axe tightly and stepped toward Emilian.

"You will not leave," Eirian snarled. "You and your Medean filth will burn for this desecration."

"Eirian, no," Garrik planted a hand on the Káli general's chest. "Enough blood has been spilt."

"Get out of my way," Eirian knocked the Annoran's hand aside. "I have enough men to take his life and those of his people."

"At what cost?" Dayne muttered, as he rose to his feet. "At what cost? Though I know it will never be enough, I am sorry for what happened here. But the Medeans are my allies first. Raise a hand to them, and I will show no mercy. Maybe you have the strength to kill him, but if you attack now… you will all die here."

Eirian spat to the side and glared down at Dayne.

"Then perhaps I should take your life now, prince," he said. "My people *long* to travel the Veil."

Dayne met his stare and did not turn away.

"Sir Garrik," Dayne said. "Prepare your men to ride. We return home. Kassandra, you travel at my side. Find my brother a horse. Strap him to it if need be."

"No," Kassandra snapped, as she turned her tear-streaked face up to her eldest brother. "In his condition, Lukas will die."

"We can't leave him here. They will kill him for this."

"He stopped you from claiming the life of one of my kin," Eirian snarled. "He fought at my side once before. Of all your people, he alone knows honour."

"They will not harm him," Kassandra told Dayne. "Here he will be safe. And I am staying."

Dayne snorted and shook his head.

"No. You ride with us. Garrik, take her up."

Garrik looked from the heir, to Lukas, and back. Finally, he nodded.

"My prince," he said.

With that, the knight reached down for the princess. She looked up at him and tears begun to flow again.

"No!" she cried.

"Lady Kassandra, please."

"No."

"Take her," Dayne said again, his voice growing loud as he watched the Káli closely.

They could attack at any moment.

Sir Garrik reached out and wrapped an arm around Kassandra's waist, before he hauled her up and turned to leave.

"No!" she screamed, as she kicked and pulled at him. "No! Lukas!"

"What of Prince Lukas?" Lord Harold Robare asked, looking to Dayne.

Dayne gritted his teeth. Once again, he was forced to choose between impossible choices. If he took Lukas, then more likely than not his brother would die in the saddle. If he left him then Lukas would be at the mercy of the Káli. They could stand and fight yet he could not endanger his sister and wounded brother.

Freezing rain lashed him as he made his choice. It was warm in comparison to the anguish he felt.

"We have to leave him," he said. "It is the only way."

The guard began to disperse and made their way back toward their horses as the rain grew heavier.

"Emilian, out," Dayne commanded, and his tone left no room for question. "Now!"

They left as suddenly as they had come, a great mass of horses made stronger by Sir Garrik and his three hundred men. Annoran and Medean alike vanished into the darkness, galloping westward, leaving the streets of Oryn red with blood.

Few remained. Eirian and his anguished warriors. A small gathering of Káli survivors. The priestess, Maevin, and the broken man she knelt beside.

Eirian did not shift his gaze from the horsemen as they rode away. The moonseer, Myrdren, stood at his side. His silver eyes were filled with agony.

It was the general who broke the silence.

"Only the warriors," he growled.

A simple command. Myrdren gave a silent nod in reply, before he turned to his horse.

TWELVE

Isle of Agartha, the Valkir Isles

Astrid stood before the table for the thousandth time. Her deep amber eyes scanned the large map sprawled atop it. She let her gaze wash across the empire, from the northernmost port of Valentia to its most southern tip and the city of Nardisium. Beyond lay that very thing she longed for. The undiscovered lands to the south. Any seafaring captain's dream.

"Jarl Astrid, it is nearly midday."

The captain looked up as the words broke the silence. A weathered face and grey streaked hair greeted her. The face belonged to a veteran of many raids. A man who had sailed with her father upon a day. She must have lost track of time again.

"Is it, Jarl Ulfric?" Astrid gave him a short smile. "Of late, this map and riddles have kept me quite occupied. Tell me… I look flat, but I am deep. Hidden realms I shelter. Lives I take, but food I offer. At times I am beautiful. I can be calm, yet furious. I have no heart but offer pleasure as well as death. No man can own me, yet I encompass what all men must have. What am I?"

The old warrior frowned for a moment as the riddle took him by surprise. Finally, his lips broke into something of a grin.

"The sea," Ulfric said.

"Precisely," Astrid chuckled. "The very thing that has captured my heart."

Ulfric glanced at the map as he entered the room. "The uncharted south, a place often spoken about in fear."

"And it calls to me… Imagine, Ulfric, undiscovered lands, great cities, strange people… new gods," Astrid's voice trembled as she spoke, for she was unable to suppress the passion that flooded her veins. "Even now, I can hardly believe that I am about to embark upon this journey. This *dream*."

"The preparations, how do they fare?" Ulfric asked.

"We have a ship, a crew, supplies. Now we just await Arndyr."

A shadow crossed Ulfric's face. "Are you sure that you want to do this?"

"With all my soul," she told him sincerely.

"But if you fall, what then?"

"What is this, Ulfric?" Astrid asked, as she folded her arms.

"Astrid, Agartha *needs* you," he told her.

"I choose my own path, not you," she waved a hand toward the door as she hissed. "Not *any* of them."

"And yet, those who you so swiftly dismiss need you," Ulfric growled. "The jarls cannot rule for long. Already they shout and bicker among themselves. They need leadership."

"So lead them."

"It is not me they look to. When they seek council, they come to you. You started this, Astrid," he ground his teeth. "You killed the earl and set Agartha upon a path of your choosing… and now you seek to abandon her."

"You think I wanted this?" she snarled venomously as her fists curled. "You think I wanted my father to be murdered? That I wanted to watch my friends and family be butchered in the street? Our city was under the rule of a madman and *none* of you had the spine to end his cruelty. Oh, it must pain you greatly, Jarl Ulfric, the noblest of warriors, that the one to slay the demon was anything but."

Ulfric's eyes blazed as he gripped the table with his weathered hands, "This has nothing–"

"I nearly lost *everything*, and now you say I wanted this?" Astrid interrupted as her rage grew. Finally, she could feel something again, feel the semblance of emotion. It felt *good*. "You coward."

The air grew still as her words hit the old warrior, and a blind man could see how they cut him.

"Coward?" he spat. "You should choose your words with care. I may be old, but my resolve has never been stronger, nor does my axe grow dull."

"Yet you come to me for help."

"I have made many mistakes in my life, but coming to you now is not one of them. The people, the jarls, respect you. Many love you for casting off their shackles. If anyone can unite them, if anyone can lead them, it's you."

Astrid turned her back on Ulfric.

"You seek to give me a crown, yet I do not want nor desire it," she said.

"Astrid…"

She held up a hand to silence him as she took a breath, forcing the anger back. "Jarl Ulfric, friend to my *father*, I do not want it. Leave me."

Ulfric glanced over his shoulder as he strode toward the door. "Be careful of this path you walk," he warned. "Too easy it is to lose your way."

The words echoed in Astrid's mind as Ulfric left. Crowns, thrones, and power meant nothing to her.

The sun burned brightly and cast its light down on the dragon banners of the three ships easing into port. The men of Vay'kis had come.

The southerly wind brushed through Astrid's dark hair as she watched on. Her keen eyes flicked between the sailors who stood above deck. To her right stood Erik. He was calm and relaxed yet strong and unyielding. His hands were loosely clasped behind his back, a long way from the axe at his side. Torben, ever vigilant, stood at her left, though his untrusting gaze never left the newcomers. The old warrior's hand nonchalantly brushed the weapon at his hip.

"Torben," Astrid hissed, without so much as a glance. "Your axe."

Slowly, the bloodsworn's hand dropped. It was no secret that her mentor held a dislike for the western Valkir, yet it was Earl Arndyr Scaeva that he distrusted most of all.

The first ship reached the dock. The vessel was larger than its companions and with the carved head of a dragon upon its prow. The gangplanks were lowered, and the first of the men of Vay'kis descended.

A shining steel cuirass marked with the griffin sigil of Aureia was strapped over the warrior's large frame. Beneath it sat a thick violet gambeson, while silver bracers and greaves covered his arms and legs. A shortsword sat at his side, and a magnificent crested helm adorned his head. His long purple cloak blew in the breeze. He reached for his helmet's rough buckle as the second of the newcomers joined him. The man took a long breath as he pulled the steel from his head and passed it to his companion. A long dark braid fell behind his shoulders. Brown eyes and a bronzed face were revealed by the sun. The face of a man beloved by half the Valkir, yet hated by many. Fighting for one not of their kind was a thing that the seafarers greatly despised. It was the face of a man who had helped free Agartha from the clutches of Magnus.

Arndyr Scaeva, Earl of Vay'kis, once the commander of the great Arkin Garter, had come.

Arndyr spread his arms with a grin as he approached. "Jarl Astrid!" he called.

"Earl Arndyr, you and your people are most welcome," Astrid replied, as she stepped toward her friend.

They clasped arms and pulled each other into a one-armed embrace. The people of Agartha roared their approval.

Within an hour, the longhall was filled with revelry, as the people of Agartha greeted their western kin with open arms. Drink flowed and laughter grew. Great mountains of food filled the bellies of the Valkir.

"My men tell me that they call you the Raven Jarl now," Arndyr said, as Astrid gestured to a pair of stools by a roaring fire.

Astrid let her hand drift to the carved amulet at her throat. "Many names I have been given of late, each more ridiculous than the last, and yet people will give life to such words so long as they have tongues to speak them."

"That is true," Arndyr's lips curved slightly. "Though there are worse names to be given."

Astrid smirked.

"Devious creatures, ravens," she said. "Intelligent. Adaptable. Like us, they can live long lives and survive almost any place. The bird is my amulet, my symbol, and now my name."

"And you have earned it."

"Time will tell," Astrid shrugged. Her deep amber eyes stared into the flames of the fire as she continued, "I have heard rumour that there is a man, a captain of the empire, who once sailed south… and survived the journey."

The sound of the hall seemed to fade away, as Arndyr ever so slowly nodded.

"In all my travels, in all my time in Darius' court, I have only heard mention of it once," he replied.

"Tell me."

The earl leaned forward as he spoke, and a shadow flickered across his face.

"Many years ago, long before my time in the Garter, there was a sailor who rose through the ranks," Arndyr began. "A common seafarer who served as a privateer under the employ of Emperor Neimon. He sailed with the imperial fleet and watched over the Elaran passage, often guarding treasure ships as they went from port to port. One day, he took his ship and made for southern waters.

Mad, they called him, insane. Yet he was anything but. He returned within a month... but he had changed."

"How?" Astrid asked, her curiosity growing with every word that Arndyr spoke.

"No longer did he care for the empire, nor did he follow its law. He freed all his galley slaves and sailed from those shores. His crew, ever loyal, stayed by his side... and yet upon their lips were tales too fantastical to be true."

"What tales?" Astrid's eyes turned to Arndyr as her breathing slowed. A chill ran through her blood.

"A week into their journey, they came across a deep mist," Arndyr said. "So thick that you could barely see the man beside you. It was in this mist that they heard it first... the enchanting voice of a woman whose singing brought them to tears. It was alluring, and soon the crew were diving overboard to their deaths. The nightmare grew as the ship ran aground on an island. The captain, brave man, went ashore alone, despite the pleas of his crew, to end this madness. There he found a cave, a rare chasm that changed everything. The singing stopped, and with it this dark dream. Whatever happened in that cave turned him from his own people. They say that he found the sirens... they say that one even graced him with a kiss."

Astrid shuddered, though why, she did not know. "This captain, what was his name?"

"They called him Teague," Arndyr told her, "Captain of the Oridassey. A man who now sails deep within the Sacasian and plagues those waters from shore to shore."

"I have heard the name before," the jarl replied, "though never that tale."

"He left no stories, nor drew any maps," Arndyr said. "And so, the way is still closed. Those waters still lie uncharted and dangerous."

"Tell me, Arndyr," Astrid could not help the thin smile as it spread across her lips, "is there any truth to the tale?"

"In the empire, as it is here, a man's truth constructs itself," he said. "Though the man who told me the story saw no lie in the sailor's eyes. I wish to see the south… to know what truly lies there. Why do you?"

Astrid looked deep into the fire as she replied, "Monsters and nightmares, Arndyr. Monsters and nightmares."

The sword whistled through the air as Erik lashed out with steel. Wood shuddered as blade was met by shield. The bloodsworn skipped to the side and threw his left arm up to catch the counter upon his own shield. His eyes flashed and muscle tensed. Erik lunged forward as his boots twisted on the ground. Steel met steel and the fighters disengaged. A bead of sweat slid down the side of his face as Erik's gaze narrowed. His shield came up before him as his fingers flexed upon the hilt of his training sword. The sun blazed ferociously. He took a breath.

His opponent came at him, a snarl hot upon his lips.

Erik parried. Once.

Twice.

He planted his feet as a third blow came. Steel met steel as he knocked the sword to the side and drove forward with his shield. Erik fought Torben until the day turned late. Knowledge and the testament of time were Torben's allies. Speed and youth were Erik's.

When at last teacher and student completed their training, Erik sucked in a mouthful of air as he tossed his dulled blade and shield to the side. Sweat covered him, from his head to his toes, and his muscles had long since grown heavy. He pulled his sweat-stained white shirt free of his body and cast it to the side. Erik poured the contents of his waterskin over his head. It cooled the warrior and helped to clear his mind. The burn in his arms felt a distant memory, as he sat upon the massive trunk of a fallen yew tree. Erik gazed up at the sun and took a long draught from the skin.

"You moved well today," Torben said from his side, as the old bloodsworn joined him.

"You never stop learning," Erik said and clapped his mentor on the shoulder, "if you do, that will be the day that you begin to die."

Torben took a sip from his own waterskin. "You remember it all, don't you?"

"Every word. All of your teachings… I remember it all. From the first," Erik told him sincerely.

The older warrior had always been there for both him and Astrid. He had taught Erik nearly everything he knew about honour and the sword. Torben nodded before he turned to face the open sea.

"How is the arm?" Torben asked.

The itch was slowly beginning to fade, though the pain of a freshly inked tattoo was a distant memory. More lines had been added to the fearsome mark of the bloodsworn after Magnus had fallen.

"Eighty marks… thirteen since we returned with father," Erik said as he gazed upon the tattoo. "The serpent grows."

"And with it, your strength," Torben told him. He sighed, "It feels as a lifetime ago that we returned from the summer raids. Sven was just the first to fall at your hand."

"Another four when they attacked in the night," Erik said as his hands balled into fists. He could remember it all. The night that Magnus and his men had come for Astrid and her crew. Swords blazed with the light of torches. Gritted teeth and lips curled into snarls. Flickering shadows and the screams of the dying. Blood as it flowed in the streets.

"I had no choice but to join Magnus then," Erik murmured. "But when I saw them kill even the old, I could *not* just stand by. I followed them, the ones who had killed Raol and used his head as a trophy. And I killed them all, every one of them."

"What is it that grieves you, lad?"

Erik closed his eyes. "I know that it was the only way. The only way to see that murderer to his end, yet having to look into those eyes... the ones that ordered those of my father closed forever... to serve such a man was a hard thing, Torben. And then Hélla..."

"A good woman," the old warrior murmured sadly. "The daughter I never had."

He saw the golden-haired shield maiden whenever he closed his eyes.

"She was bound to you as much as she was to me," Erik continued. "She was the brightest of flames and, like so many candles, *he* snuffed her spark out. When Magnus fell to the knife, I felt *great* joy and yet great sorrow. For it had not been me to wield the blade." Erik glanced at his mentor and gestured toward the town by the bay as he continued. "Some of them now look to me for leadership, did you know that? But I am just a sword. That is all I know."

Torben met his companion's stare with his own. Though they were not of the same blood, the same fire that flowed in his veins ran through Erik's.

"No Erik, you are more than a sword, more than a warrior. You are a serpent. It is time that you knew that."

THIRTEEN

Coast of Medea, the Mithramir Sea

"He will see you now," the mercenary said through the bars of the cell.

Kitara watched the guards closely as the steel door was unlocked. One of the two men entered and bound her hands with a rough rope. The other stood outside the cage, ready to slam the door closed if she so much as thought about trying anything. Kitara was shoved from the cell and into the narrow walkway, barely six feet wide. She silenced her mind as the Salvaari waited. One of the guards walked before her, no more than two paces ahead. The other stood the same distance behind, and his hands tightly clutched a vicious wooden club. Kitara flexed her wrist and brushed her fingertips across the head of the nail shoved up her sleeve. Slowly, without lifting her hands from level with her hips, Kitara pulled the nail forth. The guards did not fear a bound enemy. A mistake that would be their undoing. The Salvaari were ready.

Flow like water.

She had no sword. No tarkaras. She was *more* than that though. She tightened her fingers on the nail.

The man behind her posed the most danger as she could not see him. He had to die first. Kitara spun. Her feet slid atop the wooden flooring. Hips and shoulders rotated as her arms straightened. Kitara drove the point of the nail forward. The guard moved.

Too slow. Kitara's hands glanced off his shoulder and steel drove deep into the side of his exposed neck. Blood flowed as she ripped the nail free. The wound was deep and wide. His would be a slow death. The man snarled and lashed out with his club as a crimson tide erupted from his lips. The blow cracked into her cheek as she tried to avoid it. It slammed Kitara into the steel bars of another cage. Pain lanced through her face as her skin split under the club's weight. Kitara gasped as she swivelled back. She heard the familiar rasp of a sword being drawn. A powerful Salvaari arm reached through the bars of the cell and wrapped around the guard's throat. A second hand joined it and clamped down firmly over the guard's mouth to prevent the screams.

Instinct told Kitara to duck. She obeyed, as the second man's sword sliced over her head. Kitara jammed the bloody nail into his exposed thigh and drove it down into flesh with the full weight of her body behind it. She twisted and pulled it free with a snarl. The heavy crossguard of his sword met the side of her head and nearly drove her to the ground. Kitara danced back and fought off the daze that clouded her vision. The steel blade ripped through the sleeve of her left arm and sliced across her flesh beneath. Kitara gritted her teeth as blood begun to flow across her pale skin. She had but a nail and her hands were bound. Her leg had begun to ache, for it was not yet healed. The guard levelled his sword.

A hand shot out from the cage to his side and clamped tightly around his wrist. The Medean glanced down in disbelief before he was wrenched to the side. His head slammed into the steel bars, and in that moment his fingers loosened their grip on the sword. Kitara dashed forward and shoved him back onto the cell wall.

His hot breath filled her senses as her muscles tightened. She drove forward with all her weight and pushed the nail up. The steel was hungry for blood and she would oblige. The Medean grabbed at her arms with his spare hand, but he could not stop her. The nail was slowly driven up inch by inch. Horror filled his eyes as he made to scream. The nail drove up into his throat. Steel cut through skin and his defence crumbled. Kitara pushed with all her might as blood poured from his wound, and she forced the nail up behind his chin. Kitara did not stop pushing until the light finally fled his eyes.

She stepped back and at last the body crashed to the ground in a lifeless pile. Her breath was ragged, and her body ached, but she felt alive. Her blood burned with fire as she snatched up the cell keys from his belt and tossed them through the cell bars to Morlag. The Salvaari fled their prison, as one by one the doors were forced open. Kitara severed her bonds with one of the dead man's knives before she handed the weapon to Urlaigh. Morlag took up the club and met her eyes as he handed her the final weapon. The Medean sword. She flicked her wrist and tested its weight. Perfectly balanced. It was slightly longer than her dao, yet it would do. She gestured down the narrow walkway toward the closed wooden door. The three armed Salvaari led the way as they prepared to make their escape. Their eyes were hungry and full of vengeance.

These people had caged them like animals. For that, there could be no forgiveness.

Slowly the Salvaari crept through the bowels of the ship. Their eyes flicked from shadow to shadow as they searched for the first hint of their discovery. Only the golden light of the sun that shone through the small cracks and crevices in the side of the Lioness lit their way. They reached an open doorway. The flickering light of candles glowed beyond. Morlag held up a hand as he stopped and glanced back at those who followed him. He must have heard something.

The sound of footfalls reached Kitara's ears. She took a deep breath. This was it. The moment that they had all been praying for. She took a second breath and Morlag gestured to Urlaigh. The Káli warrior flipped his knife so that he held it backhanded.

With that, he slipped passed Morlag and through the entrance to the ships hold.

There was a muffled grunt followed by the sound of a struggle. Something heavy hit the ground. A moment became an eternity as they waited. Kitara's knuckles grew white on the hilt of her sword.

Come on.

Urlaigh's hairy face appeared through the doorway. Streaks of blood covered his skin. Medean blood.

"This way," Urlaigh hissed.

Kitara joined him in the hold and crouched behind a large crate. The warm body of a sailor lay lifeless upon the ground. She glanced over the top of the wooden box and allowed her eyes to take in her surroundings. Empty hammocks lined the hold, for most of the crew were on deck. Boxes and crates laden with all manner of goods filled the room. Other oddments hung from the wooden ceiling, while further into the hold stood four men. A combination of knives, vicious war hammers, and steel swords adorned their belts. They stood between the prisoners and the stairs that led to the deck. Kitara met Morlag's eyes. There was no way of getting to them before the alarm was raised. They had to move now, and they had to move quickly.

The Káli leader raised his club ever so slightly as he gazed around at his people. They would fight and die for their freedom. With a roar Morlag vaulted over the crate and charged toward the Medeans. The fire in his eyes was as bright as any burning flame. Kitara barrelled after him as the rest of the Káli took up his cry and surged across the hold. Surprise turned to horror on the faces of the Medeans, as the Salvaari crossed the distance between them.

"ESCAPE!" one of the Medeans yelled as weapons leapt into their hands.

Kitara pushed all thought of her companions from her mind as she reached the first of her enemies. He swung his hammer, its deadly spike aimed to skewer her skull. Kitara slid to the side and allowed her body and muscles to flex as she swivelled. She blocked the hammer overhead and deflected it. It swung by her shoulder harmlessly. Her wrists used the momentum of the hammer to flick around as she stepped forward and inside his range.

Her form was perfect. The steel edge of her sword parted shirt and flesh as if it were nothing. She cut him from right shoulder to left hip and spilled his blood upon the ground as he staggered back. Her arms came around, elbows straightened, boots slid atop the wood. Kitara took his head from his shoulders with a single swing of her sword.

A pair of Medeans emerged above, at the top of the stairs. The first angled a spear toward her. He launched it as she threw herself to the side. Kitara barely felt the steel graze her ribs as she charged up the stairs. She *could* not let them shut the heavy door.

The spearman stepped back and hastily reached for his sword as his companion swung an axe toward the golden-haired woman. Kitara leaned back and let the axe pass within an inch of her chest. She countered, and her blade sliced across his exposed forearm. The Medean cried out and aimed his backswing at her head. Kitara caught it with her sword and the weapons locked for a fleeting moment. Kitara pressed her advantage and leapt up the stairs. She drove forward with all her strength and slammed the crossguard of her sword into the Medean's jaw. He fell back as Kitara spun. Her sword came up once more to block the second warrior's blow. She crashed back into the stair's railing as steel came together. She raised her blade, and then the Medean was gone.

Urlaigh's huge body barrelled him down even as the Káli's knife slid between his ribs. Kitara leapt to her companion's aid as the axeman lashed out. She knocked the axe aside and slid steel across the back of his leg. He dropped to the ground with a scream and was silenced, as sword drove through throat.

Kitara took in a deep breath as the Káli flooded the deck. Some held the newfound weapons of the slain, while others had naught but their bare hands. Two of their number had fallen in the hold. The Medeans charged at them from every angle as they spilled from the hold and fought to confine them to the centre of the deck. The pain in Kitara's leg and face was long forgotten as her instinct took over.

She sliced a sailor's arm as he charged at her with a hammer. The hammer fell from his grasp as her backswing opened his cheek. Kitara drove forward. The muscles in her legs and back added power to her thrust. The steel tip of her sword ripped through his chest and pierced deep into his heart. With a snarl she ripped her blade free as he toppled over and sent his lifeblood splashing onto the deck. The unarmed Káli at her side fell to the thrust of a spear as he tried to tackle the Medean who wielded it. He dropped to his knees as the blade tore through his stomach and emerged from his back. The spearman released his grip on the shaft and ended the Káli's life with his dagger. Steel glinted in the sunlight as he drew his wicked longsword. It matched his chainmail armour and helmet clad head.

A knight.

Kitara raised her sword to greet him. She had killed one knight in Salvaar. She had shattered his collarbone and forced his companions to leave him to die. Maybe the eyes behind the helmet were filled with the longing for revenge.

Bows sang in the distance and their song carried across the deck. A pair of Káli fell as shafts tore through their bodies. A third man howled and staggered as an arrow ripped into the back of his shoulder. Urlaigh. The archers stood above them on the quarterdeck and picked shots that they could not miss.

"Tanris," Urlaigh managed as he struggled to rise, "I come to you."

With that he charged toward his attackers with his axe held high and a great battle cry upon his lips. Kitara's attention flew back to the knight as he aimed his sword at her chest. She parried the blow and countered before flicking her sword toward his wrist. He blocked and levelled his blade.

He was armoured and she was not. Any blow to her body could be fatal, yet if she struck him, she would leave nothing but a thin scratch on the mail. His hands and legs were exposed. Perhaps she could time a blow and skewer his neck. All of this Kitara could see. She moved and angled her wrists and sword up. He raised his blade to counter. A feint. A quick change of posture brought her blade down diagonally. It glanced off his shoulder as he stepped back. She slipped his counter and drew a thin line of blood along the inside of his thigh. A scratch. The Medean's sword darted her way. Steel met steel as she blocked. Kitara danced backwards and slid to the side as his sword sliced where she had been. Kitara lunged. Her aim was true and deadly. The knight flicked his sword skyward at the last moment and sent her sword up. Steel rang as blade met helmet. Kitara saw his next move coming before he made it. She leapt back as his sword came down through her defence.

The air rushed by her face as the blade missed by a hairsbreadth. The knight followed through and she deflected the blow. His armour made him fearless. The knight barrelled into her with the momentum of an enraged bull. Kitara flew back a step before her boots hit the ground and she slid to a stop.

She reacted instantly. His guard was off centre. Kitara swept inside his guard and struck hard. Her hip and shoulder rotated, muscle tensed, and her two-handed blow caught the Medean hard in the back of the thigh. He fell to a knee with a scream, as his leg would no longer take his weight. He raised his sword weakly, as she pivoted. Kitara sent it flying from his grasp with a second strike. Kitara'sright boot slammed hard into the man's helmet.

He fell onto his back.

Kitara stood over him, covered in the blood of her enemies. Her green eyes were wild as she prepared to strike the Medean down.

"I HAVE THE GIRL!"

The shout ripped her back into the present as it boomed down from the quarter deck.

The fighting stopped as all eyes went to the voice. There he was, Sir Rowan of Patchi, one hand clamped down on the shoulder of a tearful Sereia. His other hand held a knife to her throat.

"Stop this madness!" he roared with voice full of venom. "Lay down your arms or she dies."

Kitara grimaced and let her gaze wander to the carnage that covered the deck. Many had fallen, both Medean and Káli alike. The deck was covered with the blood of friend and foe alike.

Morlag and a small group of his people had *almost* reached the longboats that they had fought so hard to get to. His arm wept from a jagged slash. Rage flashed across his face. He was torn. After a moment, he tossed his club and axe to the side. He was enraged yet looked like weeping. They had been *so* close.

One by one, the Káli threw down their arms with a deep pain etched in their faces. That was when Kitara saw him. Filled with arrows and bleeding from a hundred wounds. Urlaigh. He was on his knees before the steps that led to the quarterdeck. He had fought hard to try and get to the archers, and yet it had not been enough. A knight stood over him with his sword pressed to the defenceless man's neck. Kitara closed her eyes and cast her blade down.

It was over.

"I thought so," growled Rowan from above, as he handed Sereia to another of his knights.

He started toward the steps and slowly made his way down them until he stood before Urlaigh. "He who tries to touch the stars stumbles at a simple step. You fought hard. You killed many, but ask yourselves this. Was it worth losing so much? Your people are half dead, yet still you fought. You could not bear the thought of a lifetime behind bars and so you rose." He reached out his free hand and took Urlaigh by his long hair. "And for that I honour you."

Rowan drove his dagger forward and slid it deep into Urlaigh's throat. The warrior did not cry out, nor beg for mercy, as the life left his eyes. Sir Rowan shoved his body to the side and watched, as the deck was watered with his blood.

"NO!" roared Morlag.

The hands of his people seized him, stopping their leader from charging into the ranks of their enemies. He struggled for a moment, unable to take his eyes from bloody and broken body of his friend.

Kitara felt her face pale as she watched Urlaigh fall. Her gaze flicked up to the knight captain, as he spoke once more.

"Raise a hand again and the girl dies," he warned the Salvaari. "Consider this mercy."

FOURTEEN

Fortress of Kilgareth, Valley of Odrysia

"You sent for me, master?"

Sir Corvo glanced up from his sword, as Hugh Karter made his presence known. "Aye, Hugh, come in," the knight said, as he slowly eased a whetstone down the blade before giving it a satisfied look and sheathing the steel. "I have a proposal for you."

"What kind of proposal?"

"I have been watching you." Corvo rose from his chair as he spoke. "You have shown aptitude and great promise with the sword that I have not seen in many years. Tell me, what do you know about the way of the sword?"

Hugh frowned. Was this some kind of test? Hugh thought for a moment before replying.

"Swordplay is like a conversation. You must listen to your enemy. Without listening, a man is doomed."

Corvo nodded and ran a hand down his scabbard.

"I have travelled much in my life," Corvo said. "Studied with blade masters from the deserts of Larissa, the savage Valkir of the Arkin Garter, mercenaries and knights from Medea and Annora both. Even the famed bladesmen of Tarik. Just as in life, each style has beauty just as it has flaws. Tarkaras, the swordsong, a way of fighting created by the great duelists of the far north. It is as graceful as a dancer and flows like a river. In open combat, where you are free to move and dance like water, it is unparalleled. But in the chaos of battle when you cannot move, you cannot flow, the swordsong ends. And that, Hugh, is why the Tariki have not yet conqured the world. Absorb what is useful, discard what is not. Forge your own path. This is the way of the sword."

The master extended his blade toward Hugh Karter and offered the initiate its hilt as he continued to speak. "Darkness has begun to fall upon the Order, and it needs able men to lead it back into the light. There are those who have forgotten that we answer to Durandail, just as we fight for Durandail. I called you here today because it is time I took an apprentice of my own. Take this sword and help me lead the Order into the light."

Hugh looked into Corvo's eyes and saw the raging inferno within. He saw the embers which lit a fire in his own mind. For many years he had been without purpose. A sword without an edge. It was time he changed that. Hugh took the blade.

Glistening rays of light shone through the stained windows of Durandail's temple and painted the stone floor of the great hall in a riot of colour. The church was empty save for one lone soldier. He knelt with his head bowed before the great carved statue of the warrior god.

Though the image was marble, it had power beyond contestation. Clad in armour and bearing the symbol of the sun, the statue of Durandail stood with its hands outstretched. Held aloft by the god was the most holy of relics, its length glistening of the purest silver. The god's fabled spear.

"Durandail, Father of all Fathers," Alarik's murmured, his hands clasped tight around his amulet. "The time is now that I, your servant on this earth, ask for your guidance. Through your infinite wisdom I have known a world of true freedom. A world of remarkable spirit and danger. I have followed the path you laid for me and recovered that which is most sacred. But now I come to the crossroads of destiny. Do I stay? Make safe the city, protect my brothers, and lead them in a time of great uncertainty? Or do I leave? Abandon all that I know in the chance that I can bring an enemy, greater than any other, to justice? A man who I once called brother. What would you have me do? I swore a vow to defend this Order, but now I stand upon the precipice. Grant me a sign, Lord. Show me your will, and I, your ever faithful servant, shall see it done."

Akarik opened his eyes. The dark hazel gaze that had seen horrors beyond count flicked up to the face of the idol, and for the briefest of moments he thought he could see a tear run down the cold marble cheek. Alarik rose to his feet and slowly, almost tentatively, reached out a bare hand. Weathered skin met with the silver spear. Duraindail's Spear. The knight's eyes widened as images exploded though his mind.

A long corridor shrouded in darkness. Water underfoot. A hooded man standing in shadows tossed a sun and moon amulet into the mud. Kilgareth was in ruins and its streets ran slick with blood. A city burned under a moonless sky. A great tower stood sentinel... the belltower of Elara. Eyes blazing the colour of flame. The cry of a bird. A nightingale.

With a gasp, Alarik staggered back. The vision faded, yet it was branded upon his mind.

"So, it will be decided in Elara," Alarik murmured as he stared deep into the face of Durandail. "The fate of the Order rests in my hands. I will not fail you, Lord. By your blood, by your name, and by its power, I shall continue the search for truth. No matter what road it leads me."

The gates of Kilgareth shuddered to a halt, as the party of steel-clad knights rode through the doorway and into the courtyard of the great fortress. Shields were slung across backs, while heavy spears were gripped tightly in hand. There were fourteen in the party, with one of their number wearing the loose robes of the maija. Kyler couldn't help his eyes from flicking around, as the townspeople looked to them. They looked nervous; tense even. He couldn't blame the fear and shadow that he saw in their faces, for it was something that he felt too.

Everything had changed when the cardinal had sent forth the call, and only time would tell whether it was for the better. Initiates hurried over to the party of horsemen and took the broad spears from their hands. Sir William Peyene, the newly minted warden, slid from his saddle and took his mount by the reins. Kyler swung a leg over Asena's flank and dismounted in the wake of his leader. He unbuckled his yet untarnished helm, and pulled it from his head, before he pushed back his coif. Kyler nearly sighed as the cool breeze brushed against his cheek. The patrol had given him the chance to adjust to his new kit, and gods, it felt good to remove it.

"Brother Landrey," the warden called, as he made his way toward the knight. Kyler glanced to his commander.

"Sir?"

"Your chest, how did it fare?"

"Well enough," Kyler said with a shrug. In truth, the wound hadn't so much as itched since he woke from his sleep after the battle in the vault. The warden clapped a hand on his shoulder, as the pair led their horses toward the stable.

"Good man. In a few days I will be leading a patrol north through the Twilight Pass."

"You would leave the valley?" Kyler asked.

William nodded. "We have remained silent long enough. Those bandits tarnished our reputation in days past, and I would not have us appear weak. We must show ourselves to be more than just watchers. The Order must be strong, now more than ever."

"When the fires of the Citadel burn, the knights of Kil'kara shall ride again," Kyler murmured.

It was an old saying, yet one powerful beyond measure.

"And I tell you now, that time is fast approaching," Sir William told him. "The gods have made their will known, and we shall honour it. So, we ride for Cacera to safeguard the realm from all those who would cross the Rift."

Azaria's moon had begun to rise when Alarik came for Kyler. He woke the boy from his sleep in the dead of night.

"What I am about to tell you must not leave this room," the battlemaster said. His wary eyes bored into Kyler as if they could freeze his soul.

"I understand," Kyler told him.

Alarik took a step toward him as he spoke, "Swear it on your amulet."

Kyler looked to his mentor and saw a storm brewing in his eyes. If Alarik was worried about what he had to say, then it was grave indeed. Kyler wrapped the fingers of his right hand around the sun and moon.

"I swear by Durandail the warrior, I swear by Azaria the healer, that I shall keep this oath until death take me."

All was silent for a moment.

Alarik set his jaw. "I am leaving," he said.

"You're leaving?" Kyler replied, as his eyes widened.

"Only the Circle know. There is a task now to be done. One of paramount importance," the battlemaster said. "The gods came to me… and I fear for the Order if it is not completed."

"What task?"

"Questions come later. I ride for Elara come first light."

"You would cross Miera? Those savages would tear you limb from limb." Kyler was aghast. To even consider it was insanity. Alarik withdrew a token from his satchel.

"Not if I carry one of these," he replied.

Alarik handed the token to the boy. It was bronze and shaped in the figure of a phoenix emerging from flames.

"King Zoran's mark," Kyler stated. "How did you get this?"

The battlemaster waved the question away. "Will you ride with me?" Alarik asked.

"You ask this of me when—"

The door shook as a fist pounded against oak. Kyler saw Alarik's hand drop to his sword out of the corner of his eye. Alarik was nervous, even here, even in Kilgareth. Something, somehow, had gotten inside the battlemaster's head.

"Landrey?" a voice called.

Kyler pulled the door to his room open as he recognised the voice, "Sir Peyene?"

There was something hidden in the warden's eyes.

"What is it, William?" Alarik asked.

It was sorrow. Something had changed in the night. The warden looked from one man to the other.

"Kyler, you had best come with me." With a flash of his blue cloak, Peyene vanished into the corridor.

Kyler exchanged a glance with his mentor before he followed the knight into the depths of the castle.

Stone rang underfoot as they reached the courtyard. Five men stood around a horse drawn cart. Four were knights, while the fifth wore the poor clothes of a farmer. Nestled tightly against the farmer's leg was a child, a girl, no more than six or seven summers. A thick blanket covered what lay within the cart, but it was not the faint smudging of blood upon canvas that drew Kyler's gaze. It was the dark bruising upon the famer's face. He had been attacked. A swirling of faded purple and blue robes hurried into the square. The arc'maija. Lysandra. Another maija, the librarian, Rene Aristo, was with her. All eyes went to the woman as she crouched in front of the girl. The lips of Lysandra's kind face twitched into a friendly smile.

"I am Lysandra, I am here to help you," she said softly. "What is your name?"

"Ivana," the girl replied hesitantly.

"Such a lovely name," Lysandra told her. "Are you hungry, Ivana?"

The girl glanced up at her father before she nodded slowly.

"Come," the arc'maija said and extended a hand, "let us see what we can find."

Ivana bit her lip, before slowly reaching out and taking the kind woman's hand. She turned back to her father.

"Go on," he told her and stroked his daughter's dark hair. "I will be with you after."

It was the only push Ivana needed, and within moments she was walking toward the castle with Lysandra's arm wrapped around her shoulder. The farmer waited for her to be out of sight before he spoke. His voice was quiet; fearful.

"Are you Kyler Landrey?" he asked.

"Aye," Kyler replied with a frown. "You know me?"

"No," the farmer shook his head sadly. "I am Mateja of Ilham. I have a message…" He trailed off as his face paled whiter than the moon above.

"What message?" Kyler asked. "Do not be afraid. You're among friends."

Mateja wrapped a hand tightly around his amulet of the Twins. He was petrified. Kyler could feel it chilling his blood. "I am so sorry. He came in the night, armour wet with blood. Said that it was for a brother, slain by your hand. I… I tried to refuse, but my daughter… Ivana…" The man's voice grew panicked. His eyes widened as fear took over. "I couldn't… he…"

Kyler's eyes narrowed. Someone had sent him a message, someone who knew his name. A man who had threatened Mateja and his daughter.

"A brother slain by my hand?" Kyler replied slowly. "I have only killed as many who tried to kill me."

Rene began to make his way around to the back of the cart.

"What man?" Sir Peyene asked, "A knight?"

"He wore your armour," Mateja took a breath, "but he was not of any god."

Rene locked eyes with Alarik as he pulled the canvas back. Kyler saw the glance pass between them. What blood drenched gift had been sent for him?

"What did he look like?" Kyler demanded, as his heart began to race. His eyes went to the cart as a limp arm fell from beyond the canvas. It dangled mere inches from the ground. A silver ring adorned a man's finger.

He knew that ring, as he knew its bearer. His heart broke long before Mateja spoke again.

"A scar ran across his lip."

Kyler pushed the farmer to the side as he ran to the cart.

"Kyler!" called Alarik in warning, as he stepped past Rene to face the broken Medean. "KYLER!"

Kyler barely felt the strong arm grab him as his gaze went to the cart. His blood froze and tears streamed from his eyes as knees hit stone. "No..."

Sobs began to roll though Kyler's body.

His scream was long and loud. It tore at his throat and ripped through his body. The pain grew too much. His fist slammed into the stone paving. He could barely look at the mangled corpses covered in dried blood. Kyler took his mother's lifeless hand.

"I am so *sorry*," Kyler cried as his soul tore. "I should never have left you... I should never have left."

Alarik's hand dropped to his shoulder, as Kyler fought back the screams that threatened.

"I am sorry."

It was all Kyler could manage to say as the tears took over.

A great pyre was erected as the maija cleaned the bodies of Kyler's parents, Theodore and Maria. They were washed and clothed, before their caskets were joined with the pyre. The congregation assembled to give strength to Kyler. The Circle were there, and Hugh Karter as well. The maija who had taken care of the bodies stood with Rene and brother Lorencio. Gaius Aureilian had come, fetched by Haylin and Evander. Yet Kyler felt alone. His mind was clouded by the ghosts of his family and memories from Odrysia. The man with the scar lip had attacked him, Hugh, and Elena. Hugh had been wounded and their assailants had been slain; all but one. All but the man with the scar lip. All but the one he had told his name. All but the one who had hunted and killed his parents.

"Grant them eternal rest, Silver Lady," Lysandra's voice was strong and filled with compassion. "Guide their souls to heaven and let your light shine upon them, as they journey from this life to the next. Cuun'ecta hěy'læn."

"Cuun'ecta hěy'læn." The words were echoed by all.

Kyler froze as he looked down at the burning torch held in his hand. He could not do it.

A hand lightly touched his back. By his side, Sir Alarik gave him a nod. The simple gesture spoke volumes. He was not alone. Kyler squared his jaw and walked toward the pyre.

His mind played across the fight in Odrysia. Many times, he had been given the chance to kill the man with the scarred lip, yet he had not. His knuckles grew white upon the handle of the torch. He had failed his parents. Kyler extended his arm. The pyre caught. He remembered waving goodbye to his parents when he had left Adrestia. That had been the last time he'd seen them alive. The flames flickered across the caskets. The torch fell from Kyler's fingers as the fire burned. A tear ran down his cheek as the pain tore him apart.

Kyler barely remembered leaving the pyre. He now sat in the Twins Cathedral with red-rimmed eyes, staring toward the stone figures of the gods. He had finally been left in peace.

His gaze barely saw the carved faces of Durandail and Azaria.

Instead, his mind was filled with memories. He had been so *sure* that he had needed to leave Adrestia all those months ago. Now his family were gone. Kyler held his amulet tightly before rising from the pew and walking toward the great marble statues. He wasn't sure if he had decided to drop to his knees of if they had given way beneath him. He stared up at the cold faces of his gods. A tear ran down his cheek.

"I chose to leave Adrestia," Kyler muttered. "I chose to... to abandon them. And now they're gone. I killed them. I CAME TO SERVE YOU! I let you guide me and set me upon this path. They were innocent. They were kind. They were *good*. But I left them for *you*. And you did not save them. Were they destined to be butchered? ANSWER ME!" he roared. Grief flowed through him like a river. He was greeted only by silence.

"Lords, I swore an oath to you. I gave you glory, and for what? For what? Your teachings? They say that a man will not know how strong he is until he has sacrificed for his faith. Is it wrong then, that I feel so weak now in this moment? Elena, Torin, my family. All gone. Father of all fathers, Lady of Silver, help me now. Show me your light, give me your strength."

He gripped his amulet evermore tightly. "Must I lose everyone I love for my faith?" Kyler closed his eyes. He did not know how long he was there. All he felt was cold. All he felt was dread.

"Pisspot," the voice echoed through the church.

Kyler looked to Alarik as he walked through the doors.

"Get on your feet," the battlemaster growled as he approached.

"Sir," Kyler muttered, and he rose as instinct kicked in.

"Are you going to sit there and grovel all night?"

The boy glared at the veteran. "Sir Alarik, I–"

"You think you're the first one who has seen death, Pisspot? It happens to us all," the knight told him. "Feeling sorry for yourself? By all means... stay here and fall apart if it will make you feel better. Or you can get up and do something about it."

"They're dead," Kyler hissed. His hands curled into fists.

"Aye, they are. And there is nothing that you or I," Alarik nodded to the statues, "or they, can do about it. You stay here, Pisspot. Let it destroy you, and you will join them. You think you're the only one who's had people die? I have lost friends, brothers, blood. But I will be damned if I let a dead man drive me to ruin. How would they feel if you gave up after they were gone?"

"How do we move on?" Kyler forced his hands open, and he met the intensity in Alarik's eyes with his own.

"We fight for them, Kyler, in their name," the battlemaster told him. "We honour them."

"Then I will do whatever it takes."

"I know, lad, I know. In a few hours I ride. If you are not at the city gates by then, I will leave without you. Stay or leave, the choice is yours. I know how you feel," the battlemaster continued. "Truly I do, and I am sorry. A man grows with the greatness of his task."

Anger rolled through Kyler. His pain, his sorrow, his *rage* burned. His lips drew back as he bared his teeth. Alarik knew *nothing* of his pain. A cry left his throat as he threw his first punch. His fist slammed hard into Alarik's cheek. The battlemaster staggered back and shook his head. He met Kyler's eyes.

"COME ON!" Alarik shouted. Kyler struck him again as the ghosts haunted him. As the man with the scarred lip tormented him.

"HIT ME!"

Kyler roared as he hit his mentor again and again. Blow by blow, his punches grew weaker. Blow by blow, the bellows of rage turned into tears which ran freely down his cheeks and splashed upon the cold stone floor. Kyler shuddered and fell to his knees. Alarik knelt before him and gripped his shoulder tightly. Blood trickled from the battlemaster's nose, yet he said nothing.

"I'm going to kill him," Kyler managed between sobs. "I'm going to kill him."

Alarik led his apprentice to the boy's chamber and helped him to his bed. The night grew late, yet Kyler would find no solace in sleep. It would not come. He was exhausted and all he felt was pain.

He found Lady Lysandra in the aviary. Pigeons flew and roosted all through the great stone room. Nests of straw filled the square holes in the walls. The arc'maija stood alone as she slowly stroked the feathers of one of the grey birds.

"Kyler," the woman smiled, as she saw him enter.

"My lady," he dipped his head.

Lysandra put the bird down and rose from her stool. "What is it?"

"I am leaving with Sir Alarik."

"Ah," she pursed her lips.

"You don't approve?"

"What I think does not matter. You have been given a choice, and you have made it. I only wish that I could accompany you in case anything happens with that chest of yours. You will be careful, won't you?"

"I promise," he said.

"Don't make a promise that you cannot keep," she told him. Lysandra gently touched his arm as sadness entered her eyes. "I need you to do something, and I think you may be the only person that I can trust."

"Even the Circle?" *What was going on?*

Lysandra snorted, "It is about Amaris."

"The grand master?"

"I don't think he died in his sleep. I think he was poisoned."

Kyler's eyes shot open.

"What?"

"Think, Kyler. He died so suddenly with no cause. He was not a sick man, nor did he have any symptoms. He just fell ill one night and passed. I have tended to many patients in my time, yet none of them were like this."

"What can I do about it?"

"Bludvier, an *extremely* rare plant, found only in the mountains near Rovira and worth more than any kingdom. Its flower is more deadly than all the swords in Miera. It causes a quick and painless death while leaving not a trace."

"How can I be of use? I am no healer nor herbalist!"

"Kyler, I am sorry to force this task upon you."

"You cannot trust the Circle, yet you trust me?"

Lysandra pursed her lips. "I know that I am taking a risk," she told him. "Yet Elena trusted you above all others. She believed you could become the best among us. I trust her judgement."

Kyler clenched his jaw at the mention of her name. Another one he had lost.

"The only place outside of Darius' palace that *may* have some traces of bludvier is Elara," Lysandra explained. "When you are there speak to a trader named Arntair. He will know if even a whisper of the plant has been made known. Find this and report back to me. No birds. No writing. This has to stay between us. Do you understand?"

"Yes my lady, but—"

"There is no time," she interrupted and gripped his arm more tightly. "The sun draws near. I am sorry for this… for Elena… for everything."

"But there is no other way," Kyler told her, as he struggled to comprehend what she had told him. Amaris had been murdered, and by one of his own brothers.

Lysandra pulled him into a hug. "Take care of yourself," she told him. "Know that you will be in my prayers."

"Light of the gods be with you," Kyler said as they broke the embrace.

"And always with you."

The first hint of the sun's rays cleared the horizon when Kyler rode to Sir Alarik's side. Both wore unmarked armour and cloaks to help them slip through Miera unnoticed.

"Wasn't sure you would come," Alarik told him, as he extended an arm. Kyler took it.

"My father once told me that even in the darkest times the sun will keep rising. I think now I finally understand what he meant. Life goes on. You can either keep up with it or be swept away."

"A wise man," the battlemaster replied with a hint of pride in his voice.

Alarik kicked his heels in, and the pair rode forth. The light of Durandail's sun guiding their way. One thought gave Kyler strength. He would honour his family. Honour his name. That is what he fought for.

FIFTEEN

Káli Lands, Forest of Salvaar

"How are you?" Prince Dayne asked as he approached the sentry.

The knight looked over his shoulder as his leader approached. The light of the fires danced along his steel armour.

"Lord?"

"Your cousin," Dayne said, as he felt a twinge of sorrow. "Elion was a brother to me and shall always stand as such."

"We broke bread with them, lord," Landon Montbard said darkly. "*I* broke bread with them… and they killed him."

Anger turned to rage as the knight bared his teeth. "They took my cousin's head," the knight continued, and his voice grew louder still. "How does that make you feel?" Dayne asked, as he gazed out into the forest.

What lay beyond each tree, he wondered. *What new threats did this beautiful, terrible, land hold?*

"Like killing them," Landon told him.

"Aye," Dayne replied, and he let his hand brush against the pommel of his sword. His voice was quiet and calm, yet as strong as stone. "There will be a tide of killing to come. Where and when I know not, but it's coming."

The sound came quietly at first yet grew into a gentle rumble. It was a familiar sound. Hooves sinking into mud, and a lot of them.

"Riders approaching!" the call echoed through the trees.

"TO ARMS!" Dayne shouted. His sword was halfway from its

sheath, as he began to charge back across the campsite. He made for Kassandra. "TO ARMS!"

Steel rang as Annorans and Medeans rallied. Soldiers reached for the nearest weapon and jammed helmets upon head. The royal guard materialised around Dayne. No matter what came through these woods, they were prepared.

"It's Lord Hornwood!"

The shout sent relief coursing through his veins. The prince shoved his sword back into its sheath as the first of the Annoran riders materialised from the dark.

"Prince Dayne, thank the gods your men found us when they did," Lord Edmund Hornwood called, as he dropped from his mount's back. "Would have ridden into Oryn and some kind of Salvaari ambush."

Dayne clasped the noble's arm. "I trust that Sir Duncan told you everything?" he asked.

"Aye, Prince," Hornwood replied, as he unbuckled his helm. "In war, one does what one must. There is no reason to regret the past. Salvaar is a cursed land ruled by monsters. We will be well rid of it before it grows into the nightmare that plagues my rest."

The nobleman looked around the camp, and for the first time noticed the tense look in the eyes of the armed men.

"Did my scouts not warn of our approach?" Lord Hornwood asked.

"We have seen no one," the prince told him.

Dayne was quiet for a moment as Hornwood's eyes closed. The prince understood as well as any. Lord Hornwood knew as well as he that if the scouts had not arrived, then they were almost certainly dead.

"Something draws near. I can feel it in my blood. My father once told me that in Salvaar one would be wise to fear the dark," Dayne said, as he remembered every lesson that Dorian had passed on.

"There is no lie," the older lord told him, as his eyes watched the trees. "There is no salvation here. It is to the Twins that we must look."

Dayne saw the shadow pass beyond his companion's eyes as he spoke.

"Your ride north. Did you succeed?" the prince asked.

"Yes, Lord," Hornwood replied, as his fingers unconsciously reached for his medallion. "We found the shrine. The one that the heathen call Yorath. They say he is the spirit of the sun. That he is a great warrior who gives his followers the strength beyond that of their greatest enemy. We tore down the false idols and burned what was left."

"Then you played your part well," Dayne murmured. "Though now this attack upon their towns, on their *faith,* demands response."

The prince found Emilian Aloys sat atop a log with one of his men strapping a splint to his forearm.

"My Prince," the Medean greeted the prince as he approached.

"Lord Aloys," Dayne returned. "How bad is it?"

"I believe it to be fractured," Emilian replied. "Though pain is irrelevant."

Dayne allowed himself a hint of satisfaction. Lukas had got him good.

"I am torn, Lord Aloys."

"Torn?"

The Annoran let ice creep into his eyes as he spoke. Calm, slow, yet strong.

"On what to do with you," Dayne said. "My men tell me that your words rang true. That my brother started the fight… and yet he is my blood. If we were not so allied, then I would kill you now, no matter the consequence. On the day we rode into Salvaar I gave command that the only people to die were those who took up arms against us. Do not think me blind, Lord Aloys. I saw women, children, and elders slain by your people in Oryn. That leads me to question your intentions."

Dayne watched his companion carefully. He could see the first traces of fear begin to enter the young lord's eyes.

Emilian frowned, "My intentions?"

"You see, Lord Aloys, the only reason we stand shoulder to shoulder is because I allowed this alliance to be. It now stands upon the edge of a knife, and the only thing holding it together is her," Dayne said and gestured toward where his sister sat. Kassandra was young. She was scared, but she was stronger than most. "And you spurned her in front of your men. In front of *my* men."

"Lord, I did not–"

"Do not lie to me," Dayne cut in loudly. "You do not want to play games with me, Lord Aloys. Make things right, for I warn you… the lion may be strong, but the eagle *does not* perform at the circus."

Kassie pulled her cloak tightly about her shoulders. It was cold here at night. Especially without fires. She knew that she should be sleeping, yet sleep would not come. The one person she loved more than anything in the world could be dead. She had seen him lying in the sludge covered in his own blood. His leg ruined and his eye destroyed. All by the person that she was supposed to one day marry.

"Kassandra?"

She glanced up as she recognised the voice. It was Dayne. Kassandra, he said, always Kassandra. Never anything else. Not Kassie or even Kass.

"Mind if I join you?"

Kassie bit her lip. "Would it make a difference if I said no?" she replied.

Her brother sat down. "I am sorry," he said.

She froze. She was barely able to look at him as anger rolled from her tongue.

"You're sorry? Lukas is your brother... our brother. And you left him in the mud."

"Kassandra–"

"You left him," she snapped as the anger grew. "He was nearly killed. He was alone. And you left him. Our brother!"

"I had no choice," Dayne replied.

"There is always a choice."

Her brother did not react. He showed nothing, as always. "What would you have had me do? Strap him to a horse? He would have died within hours. There was nothing any of us could have done. He chose his own path, and now he must travel down it."

Kassie shook her head bitterly. "You are cold," she said. "Sometimes I wonder if you feel anything at all."

Dayne was quiet for a moment before a sigh escaped his lips. The first emotion he had shown her in a long time. "I do love you. I love Lukas. Everything I do is for my family," he said as he rose to his feet. "I hope one day that you will see that."

Then he was gone, and the princess was left alone with her thoughts.

A longbow's song rang through the trees. The arrow carved a path through the blackness of night. It hummed as it flew. Moonlight glinted upon its steel bladed tip. Its aim was true. It was beautiful and deadly. Steel ripped through the flesh of an Annoran sentry's throat. He fell. A garbled cry erupted from his lips.

"SHIELDS ON ME!" Prince Dayne roared, as a second man fell.

Annoran and Medean alike huddled together and interlocked shields in an unbreakable cocoon of wood and steel.

"Salvaari night raid," hissed Sir Garrik from his prince's side.

"They will be gone soon. They will slip away into shadow as if they were never here."

A Medean fell with a scream as a shaft sprouted in his thigh. He made to rise, but a second arrow claimed his life. Prince Dayne gritted his teeth as he stared over the rim of his shield. He saw nothing. He heard nothing, save the gentle caress of the eastern breeze.

"Damn the dark," he cursed.

Light flicked across Lukas' face as his eyes opened. He was on a makeshift bed inside a thatched hut. Light crept through the cracks around the door and danced through the shutters. Half the room was dark. He glanced down at his legs. Then he remembered. He remembered *everything*. The pain hit him like an avalanche.

No, no, no.

Lukas cried out in agony. A splint was strapped tight around his right leg. He reached up to his face. A rough bandage was wrapped over its left side, while something thick was beneath. Lukas bared his teeth as an animal like growl came from his lips. The wooden door opened.

"Lie still," a woman's voice commanded. The voice was musical and soft, enchanting. It was enough to pull him from the nightmare. The dark-haired woman sat upon the edge of the bed and held out a wooden cup.

"Go on," Maevin told him, and she placed a calming hand upon his arm, "take it."

Lukas winced as he took the cup. The motion sent pain lancing through his skull. The liquid had a faint pink tinge to it and appeared as thick as milk.

"Drink it," the priestess said. "It will make you feel better."

"Smells of strawberries," Lukas replied, as he raised it to his lips.

Maevin smiled. Her emerald green eyes sparkled as she watched him. The prince frowned as he tasted it, before draining the contents in three draughts.

"Tastes like strawberries."

"Dulls the pain," Maevin replied.

Lukas leaned back. "How long was I asleep?"

"Two days."

"Two days?" Lukas let out a long breath. "Then they're gone."

Darkness ran through those green eyes. "Leaving nothing but carrion for crows," Maevin murmured.

The pain began to fade as the brew worked. Finally, Lukas took her in. She was as enchanting as he remembered, yet he could not help a frown from distorting his brow. The small movement sent a lance of pain through his left eye socket.

"Your face."

There was a small, yet dark, bruise covering her cheek.

"It is nothing," she said sadly. "My people suffered a far worse fate."

"I am sorry." It was all he could say. What Aloys had done to Oryn, what his brother had done, chilled him to the bone. "What happened here is unforgivable."

"The spirits are old, Prince," Maevin told him. "The deep magic that courses through the forest is their lifeblood. They know all. They *see* all. This bloodshed shall receive their reply."

Slowly, tentatively, Lukas reached out gently and placed his hand over hers. Maevin barely reacted. Her skin was cool beneath his touch.

"I wish that I had been here sooner," he said sadly. "I wish that I could have stopped the attack."

"You did what you could."

"But it was not enough."

"You speak the impossible," Maevin replied. "No one has the power to turn back the sun and rewrite the past. What has been written is written, prince, and it is written in blood."

"It will never be enough," Lukas continued quietly.

Shadows crossed his thoughts and stole into his mind. He released her hand and stared up at the ceiling.

"And now?" Lukas growled as anger crept into his voice. "Look at me... I am *broken*. The shadow of a man."

"You yet live." Maevin looked at him with newfound intensity.

Fear gave way to doubt. Anger. It was all he felt. All he ever felt. Now he was all but ruined. A soul that longed to be free, trapped within the crumbling remains of a man. He would never walk again. Never truly be able to see again.

"I am *nothing* without my leg, without my sight," he snarled. "I wish that I was dead." Maevin clamped a hand around his wrist and stared deep into his face. Her gaze pierced through to his heart.

"You could have died," she said. "You would have died save for Sylvaine. Save for Tanris. The spirits see something in you and the Dark One has whispered your name. I told you once that greatness only comes to those who are free. Truly *free*."

"How can I be free if I will never walk again?" Lukas hissed at her. "I am *broken*."

"Ask yourself this, Prince, were you ever free when you were whole?" Maevin's lips curled as she spoke. "I believe that to be something other than the truth. And you know that in your heart. Once you know who you really are, this path you are destined to walk upon will make itself known. The spirits have a plan for you, Lukas, son of Dorian. Yet it is up to you to discover it."

"You place too much faith in your gods," he growled, pulling his arm from her grasp, "and I am done. I am done." He glared up at the woman as his blood boiled. "Leave me! I am nothing but the ruined remains of a ghost. Haunting a world that has grown forever dark." Hands clenched into fists as teeth were bared. Tears flowed from his remaining eye, only adding to the agony that lay beyond his face.

"Leave me…"

Maevin met his glare with her own blazing gaze. The emerald of her eyes ignited like flame as she looked down upon Lukas.

"You are changed, lord. That will not make you weak."

"Weak? Look at me, priestess. I am *crippled*. I am broken. I am shattered. What use am I to you now, to any of them?" Lukas bit down on the sobs that threatened. They were not from pain, nor sorrow. Only the building fury that arose within. "I am no more than a lame beast and a burden."

"You are *much* more than that; in time you will see," she told him.

"Go!" he said, malice lacing his voice. "Leave!"

"No," Maevin said. "I will wait by your side until the final dusk. And I will follow you now until whatever end."

The Salvaari priestess sat by his side for days, leaving only to bring him more of the potion that took away the pain. When the sun rose on the third day, she came to him with a crutch, and she was not alone. A second Káli, a man carrying an assortment of blades and tools, came into the hut. There he set to work measuring Lukas' knee and gathering wood, iron, and strips of cloth from his packs. The craftsman worked tirelessly and by noon had created something that Lukas had never seen before. It was a kind of brace. The man took apart Lukas' splint, and then Maevin cleaned the wound yet again. It had been her who had first cleaned it after the attack, before she had sewn it back together as best she could. They strapped the brace to his leg. A pair of long nails were driven down the sides of the brace to hold Lukas' leg in place.

"When the time is right, remove these," the man tapped the side of the brace. He ran his finger up to the top of the device, "You will never walk unaided again, that much is certain. But use this handle and with the strength of your arm and a crutch, perhaps you will be able to walk."

Maevin wrapped Lukas' arm around her shoulders, and then together they slowly made their way from the hut. Lukas winced as the sunlight hit his eye. He leaned heavily on the crutch and raised a hand over his face.

"I had almost forgotten what the sun felt like," he murmured.

He closed his eye and turned his face skyward. A long breath left his lips. The warmth of the sun kissed his cheeks while the breeze gently ran through his hair. The blood had been cleaned from the streets while the bodies had long since been burned. Much had been repaired, though the scars remained. Tracks could be seen upon the earth and deep ruts where horses had churned it into mud. He had one eye, but Lukas could still see.

Any fool could see the destruction that had been brought down upon the village. Doors had been splintered and houses ransacked. He could still remember the girl. The one that he had seen face down in the mud, next to the body of an old man. Had he been her grandfather, or just a friend trying to protect her from the onslaught that followed? Pain drove through Lukas' face. It ripped through his skull like any axe would. The purple and grey bruising had grown worse upon his swollen face, while the flesh was still tender. In time it would heal, yet the scars would remain, and he would forever be half sighted. No medicine, no man, and no god would ever change that. A horse's whinny came from behind. The sound of hooves crunching upon the earth. Lukas gripped tightly onto Maevin's shoulder as he turned toward the noise. He gritted his teeth and bit back the ever-constant pain. He was already exhausted from moving.

A group of Káli rode past the pair. Thick white grease pushed their wild hair back, while their faces were painted black as night. Spear and bow were held tightly within their hands while the only thing that their cold faces showed was fury.

"Your people are on the warpath," Lukas murmured as he watched them pass.

"They ride west," Maevin told him fiercely. "What happened here will not stand. It *cannot* stand. All those lives lost… the dead will be avenged."

SIXTEEN

City of Elara, the League of Trecento

Brush met canvas, and pale white was turned to the richest black. Stroke followed stroke, and slowly the image began to take form. Elise had already spent days on this one picture, and with each flick of the wrist she came closer to its completion. Upon the canvas was the image of a woman. A pair of blue eyes blazed upon the woman's face, while her brunette hair was all but hidden by a white cloth. Her nose was small, and her lips formed a straight line. The woman wore a free moving costume of velvet, broadcloth, and a hint of leather. The outfit, covered in deep blue and ivory stripes, fell from her neck to her hip. A sapphire shoulder length hooded cloak was clasped at her neck. The sleeves of the tight tunic were as pale of snow, though intricate tendrils of blue ran down their length. They flared outwards before meeting with thin gloves the colour of the sea. The hood was trimmed with silver lining. Elise reached out with her brush and slowly ran it across something held within the woman's left hand. A glorious silver mask. Had it adorned the woman's pale face, it would have covered her skin from the tip of her nose to her brow. Elise could not stop her gaze from being drawn to the dark eyes. They called to her. They spoke her name.

"Begging your pardon, my lady, but you should not leave the shutters so open at this hour," Halina's voice cut through Elise's thoughts like a blade. "You'll catch a chill." Elise glanced up as her maid hurried through the darkening room to close the shutters. A thin tendril of silver light came through the wide-open window, though the cold would never brother her. She had slept in mud with no more than a flea-bitten rag to warm her. Riversiders did not understand what cold was.

Was it that late already? "The sun has set? I must have lost track of the time."

Halina pursed her lips as she reached Elise and saw the image upon the canvas.

"She is as beautiful as I remember," Halina said with a smile. "And you are her image."

"This was the last night she performed," Elise replied, and she smiled up at the maid as a sad edge entered her voice.

The last night before her mother had been taken ill. She remembered it all. Her mother's shining blue costume, her father rich ruby clothes, and her own violet ensemble. The cheers of the crowd as they had spun and twirled, flipped and rolled. That was the life of an acrobat.

How she had loved it.

"And she was magnificent, lady," Halina said, placing a warm hand upon Elise's shoulder before hurrying to the open window. "You all were."

"You know," Elise said as she glanced across the room to her friend. "I miss it. Performing. The fire burning in your belly that only grows stronger with the roar of the crowd. The feeling of peace and serenity that comes with the most dangerous of tricks… when the distance between life and death is not so great. When one misstep can end it all. Even now, it calls to me."

"Will you ever go back to it?"

"Maybe I won't go back. But going forward isn't an ending."

"Right you are, my lady. The days grow shorter. Winter is well on the way," Halina said.

She bolted the shutters closed and that was when Elise saw it.

The slightest flicker of anxiety upon the maid's face. She looked worn. She looked thin.

"You look tired," Elise said, and rose to her feet.

"I've not been sleeping well," Halina sighed.

"Tell me," Elise said.

"Each night it grows worse... the fear. The sound of flapping wings... of bumps in the night," Halina murmured. "I fear that dreams and promise of better days won't come until that madman is caught... until the city no longer sleeps under the shadow of the Nightingale."

"He is as cruel and heartless as he is cunning, and I pray for the day he falls," Elise told her. "But we cannot let this monster destroy us... if we do, he wins. Do you know that I once feared water?"

"Truly, my lady?"

"Truly," Elise grinned. "Whether it be pond, lake, or river. I feared the deep and the monsters within. And you know what my mother told me? Even the bravest among us know what it is to fear. Even they know what it is to be hopeless. The trick is, she said, was knowing how to blunt your demon's teeth. Once fear is unmasked... it cannot hurt you. And then she sang to me... of the waves and the ocean. Not of calm and gentle waves, but of a storm. Do you know what? Once she had sung of the thing I feared most strongly, it did not frighten me. Strange, don't you think?"

Elise drifted off for a moment, barely noticing the fact that her eyes had wandered to the half-finished painting of her mother.

"Do you know that poem? The one about the Nightingale?" Elise asked.

"Yes, lady."

Elise looked her in the eye, deadly serious.

"Sing it. Unmask your demon."

Halina bit her lip as her friend spoke. Then she began to sing. Her voice soft and slow yet strong and measured. The sound of the song echoing through the small room was almost haunting.

"A bird is crying in the night,
A city sleeping in his sight.
Souls are lying wide awake,
Anxious for the dawn to break.
For the bird, silent, cold,
Comes to haunt your own threshold.
When the demon hunts his prey,
Blood and tear will mark his way.
A single feather will be left,
Amidst the house of hope bereft.
Coffers will empty,
Blood will flow,
Under the Nightingale's shadow."

The Nightingale, silent and cold, gazed down from the rooftop of a wealthy lord's villa. The phantom's eyes scanned the large walls that surrounded the magister's palace. The information the thief had gathered from the shipmaster's log had only served to arouse the Nightingale's suspicion.

What was the magister up to? Why did Imrohir send all those ships to the empire with the trade fleet absent reason?

What the magister was planning, the Nightingale dreaded to guess. Perhaps something as sinister as the thief feared, or perhaps nothing but harmless trade to strengthen ties. Either way it would be discovered, and it would be discovered tonight. The Nightingale waited. Seconds passed. Then the opening came.

Seven armoured guards walked by in the streets below, halberds and torches held close. A patrol, one of many, that the Nightingale had watched for untold hours. The phantom knew their every step.

They passed beneath, their heavy iron-shod boots echoing on the paved stones. The Nightingale rose to full height, and the gentle breeze rolled through the thief's dark cloak. It took three steps to reach the edge of the roof, three steps to accelerate, and then leap forth.

The Nightingale flew through the night.

Boots touched red tile lightly as the Nightingale landed on a lower rooftop. Dark eyes washed over the vision before the bird. The slanted roof of the next house shrouded the thief from what lay beyond. The wall that surrounded the magister's palace. The Nightingale peered around the slant, lost in the shadows as watchful eyes gazed at the steel-clad sentry who stood atop the wall. The man looked back, but saw only darkness watching him. He turned and began his slow walk down the wall. The Nightingale almost smiled.

Almost.

The phantom vaulted onto the slanted roof and broke into a sprint. The tiles gave way into nothing as once more the bird took flight. Feet came forward and hands extended. Boots touched the wall and then fingers wrapped around the edge of the gap in the merlons. The Nightingale did not make a sound. The Nightingale waited.

Nothing.

Hands pulled and muscles tightened, and the Nightingale launched up onto the wall. The bird crouched as it crossed the wall and barely spared a glance at the guard who walked away, suspecting nothing. More soldiers scurried about the yard below. The Nightingale watched as they passed before dropping down from the wall and vanishing into the shadows. Leather boots made barely a sound upon the stones as they dashed across the small walkway and vaulted over a small wall.

The Nightingale landed in a corridor lit by torches hung from the walls. The phantom strode down the outside hallway, head on a swivel, eyes searching for the first hint of a guard.

Footsteps rang. The Nightingale leapt over the short wall and crouched beyond it. The iron-shod boots drew near. The thief waited with bated breath. The guards passed by. The thief waited.

Three seconds.

Five seconds.

The Nightingale's eyes turned to the side of the inner wall. A small warehouse stood against the stone. Its flat roof rose halfway between the courtyard and the ramparts. A pair of the magister's soldiers stood sentinel across the bailey with vicious tipped halberds in their grasp.

This would have to be quick. The Nightingale took a breath before breaking into a run toward the wall beside the warehouse. Leather hit stone as the thief flew two steps up the wall and then kicked off its surface. The Nightingale spun toward the edge of the warehouse. Fingers found a hold and then the thief vanished over the top. Sound hit the Nightingale's ears.

Soldiers.

The Nightingale dove into the shadows of the wall, as the guards atop gazed down into the bailey. Seconds stretched into an eternity as the voices from above died off. The sound of footsteps faded. Up the wall the Nightingale flew. Over the ledge and the merlons, and then the thief dropped onto the ramparts. The Nightingale scanned the wall and took in the sight of a dozen armed soldiers carrying halberds and crossbows. None stood before the tower that arose further down the wall. The thief dashed toward its cover. The inner bailey appeared before the Nightingale. The *last* thing that stood between the thief and the magister's keep. Barely fifty feet away. The Nightingale entered the tower and took the stairs two at a time. At any moment a soldier may enter and draw steel. The bird glanced out of the empty doorway into the night. Ever vigilant guards patrolled in force. Across the courtyard, a staircase led up the side of the keep to an outside corridor. A pair of guards stood before the great doors. The Nightingale ducked behind cover as a group of guards walked by.

Eyes closed.

A breath taken.

Four seconds passed.

The thief walked out into the courtyard, dashed across the paved surface, and hid in the shadow of the staircase.

Three seconds.

The Nightingale followed the staircase and strode passed its length. The thief pressed its back into stone. The patrol rounded a bend and slipped from sight. They walked beneath an arch. Their eyes wary, yet unsuspecting. The Nightingale's gaze swept over the arch. Above was an overhanging section of the keep, complete with an empty window as if it were a lookout station.

An opening.

The patrol once more vanished from sight. The Nightingale accelerated. Two steps up the wall. The thief kicked off and turned. Fingers latched onto the edge of the sill. There were no footholds, nor a lower wall to push against. The Nightingale swung under the ledge and heaved as momentum carried the phantom back. The thief flew up and over, and landed gracefully in the corridor beyond.

Torches lined the wall of the magister's keep and cast out the darkness of night. The Nightingale strode down the hallway. A door arose before the thief. The Nightingale had never seen it before, yet it was well known. The map that the Nightingale had committed to memory told of the room that lay beyond.

The magister's private chamber.

The lockpicks were in hand before the thief reached the door. The Nightingale glanced over their shoulder and drove metal home. Teeth were gritted behind the mask as the thief went to work. Seconds grew into moments. Moments grew into an eternity. Something clicked.

Close.

So close.

Sound came from behind. The hooded head turned. The thief's gaze flicked up. Straight into three armed soldiers. The guards eyes widened. The Nightingale snatched out a short knife and launched it toward the men. The blade glanced off the stone walls and missed by a finger's breadth, as the guards moved. Halberds lowered as they charged. The shadow vanished out onto the ramparts, as the cry went up.

"NIGHTINGALE!"

Soldiers along the wall charged toward the keep, as the bird left its confines. Halberd and crossbow turned toward the thief. The great bell atop the palace began to sound and it echoed through the night. There was no time to look and little time to react. Crossbows sang as the Nightingale leapt from the ledge. Steel tipped bolts filled the air and sliced past the falling bird. They glanced off tile and stone. Fragments exploded all around. The thief landed with a roll and rose into a sprint. Moonlight danced on the silver edge as a halberd was swung toward the phantom. It missed by a hair's breadth, as the thief ducked to the side. Soldiers cried and their shouts filled the yard. The tolling of the bell grew louder. The Nightingale charged toward the castle walls and the stairs that led to salvation. Two guards came at the intruder with steel raised in defiance. There was no way around them.

None that any normal man could see.

Muscles tightened. The Nightingale feinted left and leapt right. The thief kicked off the wall and soared into the air over the soldiers. The Nightingale landed and began to sprint into the night. Something heavy hit the Nightingale's upper arm. Blood flowed as the tip of the halberd ripped through flesh. The Nightingale didn't make a sound. The thief angled for the stairs that led up onto the wall. Instinct told the bird to duck. A thrown halberd carved a path through the air above. Steel hit stone as the wall sent the weapon glancing away. More soldiers came sprinting from the keep. They came from in front. They came from behind.

Every direction was cut off, save one.

Up.

The Nightingale accelerated and reached the stairs of the wall, just as the men in front of the thief arrived. The thief leapt as a sword sliced forward. The bird's shoulder slammed into stone as the Nightingale jumped to the side. Sparks flew as the blade struck the stairs behind. The thief barrelled upward. The soldiers reached the stairs. An archer appeared above. His hand tightened upon his crossbow's trigger. The Nightingale launched a knife into the air. The guard cried out as the blade struck his crossbow. It turned the weapon as the trigger was pulled. The bolt soared down into the courtyard below. The Nightingale shoved the guard aside and made for the ramparts. Soldiers rushed forward, weapons leaping into their hands. They came from both sides and from the stairs. Archers raised their crossbows. The Nightingale accelerated into a sprint and charged toward the edge of the wall as the pursuers closed in with a web of steel.

Crossbows sang.

The Nightingale flew from the wall.

Tariq ran a cloth across the knuckles of his left hand to rub away the blood as he walked through Elara's streets. The fights, lucrative as they were, took their toll. The Berenithian had begun to amass a tidy sum of coin in recent days, and it would not be long before he could buy passage from this wretched city. For him and for Elise.

The Pits, the place he called home, were filled with neat streets and houses that had begun to fall into disrepair. The magister's ever-growing taxes had slowly become an intolerable burden, and many were struggling to make ends meet. There was unrest and discontent. Any fool could see it in the eyes of those who lived in these streets. Tariq took out a key as he reached his house. He reached for the door, key met lock, and then he pulled it open.

The fighter walked into the darkness and bolted the door behind him.

The house was simple, yet well maintained. A stone floor ran beneath his feet while a pair of chairs sat before the empty fireplace. A small bed ran parallel to the far wall, while a plain chest sat at its foot. The smell of smoke reached his nose. One of the candles upon the table had been knocked over. Sound hit his ear. It came from the depths of the room. He knew the sound and he knew it well. The pain filled breathing of a wounded man.

"Who goes there?" the fighter growled, as he snatched up a small knife.

The only answer was another groan. Tariq slowly began to walk through his house with his blade held before him. That is when he saw it. A figure clad in darkest black sprawled against the back wall. Tariq was too startled to react. He recognised the shadow before him from the stories.

"You!" Tariq snarled.

He turned on the Nightingale and levelled steel toward the fallen thief. The criminal said not a word. He could see the end of a bolt protruding from the thief's side. Blood dripped upon the floor. A second wound was visible upon the villain's arm.

"You made a mistake coming here," Tariq told the Nightingale. "I am going to call the guards, and you will hang for your crimes."

He went for the door.

"Wait!" the Nightingale gasped, as it clutched at the arrow.

Tariq stopped, his hand inches from the latch. The voice was muffled behind cloth, but he knew the voice belonged to a woman. "Who are you?" he asked.

The Nightingale's blue eyes shut as a wince rolled through the thief's body. Gloved hands pulled back the ebony hood, before wrenching off the cloth that covered nose and mouth. Last came the mask that covered the woman's upper face.

Copper hair and pale skin filled Tariq's gaze. A pair of thin lips pulled back into a grimace, while pain was shown clearly in those sapphire eyes.

"Elise," he breathed.

The knife rang as it hit stone.

Elise bit back a scream as the sharp blade of a needle was driven through muscle and flesh. In one hand she held a half-emptied wine skin while in the other she held the hem of her shirt up, as Tariq worked with needle and thread. Her cloak and jacket lay abandoned to the side. She had been close…

"Done," Tariq said, as he stepped back after tying off the wound.

"Thank you," Elise said, closing her eyes and taking a breath. "Tariq, I–"

"How could you?" the fighter snapped, as he stared at her wide eyed. "Everything that you have done."

"I have done nothing."

"Then what is it that you are doing exactly? Lying, stealing, killing," Tariq waved his arms as he growled. "You're a *murderer*, Elise."

She leaned forward on the table and met his glare with her own. "I have *never* killed anyone!" Elise countered.

"The stories–"

"Are no more than that," Elise told him, as her eyes willed him to believe. She needed him to believe her, nothing else mattered. He was the last person she had left. "A word here, a tale there, whispered in the right ear will spread like any fire. Growing more embellished with every telling."

The fighter was silent for a moment. "This crusade against the nobility," he said. "You risk your life and hopes of a better future for what? A few handfuls of coin? What if they kill you?"

"They can *try*," Elise smirked, as she snatched up a strip of cloth. She bound it tight about her arm, covering the wound the halberd had given her.

"I am serious," Tariq told her in exasperation.

"As am I."

"What if you get caught?"

"I am an excellent thief. The best in the city. I won't get caught," she said fiercely.

"Aye, until you do," he turned away. "So what? You gallivant in the night risking everything, and for what? Pleasure? I do not know you at all, do I?"

Guilt shattered the pieces of her broken heart even more. Only her drive was holding those pieces together, only a very thin thread. "This has nothing to do with gold and jewels," Elise snarled as she felt the cracks within her heart begin to grow. "Beyond these walls there is no justice. You can see it yourself."

"Elise–"

"The Riversiders… I grew up *believing* that I am less than them!" she cried desperately. "Despite being a Delfeyre, despite living in my uncle's house, across the river I am treated with nothing but disgust and scorn! Can you not see how the soldiers and their lords treat those from the Pits and the lower districts? The people want to fight back!"

"That fight would only end one way," Tariq countered. "If we cross that river we will be killed. All of us."

Elise knew that truth in her heart, yet it only made her more desperate. "I hate them for what they have done to us," Elise snarled. "Driving us into the dirt. Forcing us to grovel and kneel." She reached out and gently touched her friend's shoulder. "You are the only person who truly knows who I am," Elise pleaded. "Perhaps I do gain pleasure taking from those who live on the backs of the poor. Yet that is not why I steal, nor the only reason that I wear my mask."

"Then tell me," Tariq said, the first hint of desperation edging itself into his voice. "Help me to understand."

"Silver, gold, jewels, they're all just means to an end. To see us far from this city."

Tariq bared his teeth as he spoke, "Elise, I fight so that you do not have to."

"I know," she said quietly, yet she was unable to meet his sad eyes. Elise gestured to the costume as she continued, "But this *illusion* is about more than just coin. Until recently, I had almost given up hope. That is until I uncovered a letter. Written by the banker, Ilario. It spoke of a gift granted by Magister Imrohir to Lord Renardo Redmier. I broke into Lord Redmier's vault inside the arsenal and read the shipmaster's logbooks. Tariq, the magister sends a single ship to Aureia with the trade fleet every month." She held up a finger as she continued, "A single ship. Strange, don't you think? Stranger still that its cargo is not logged, while that of every other vessel is. Silk, cloth, steel, gold. Yet upon the magister's ship, nothing."

The fighter snorted and shook his head.

"Conspiracy, Elise," he said as he waved his hands incredulously. "This is madness. I hold no love for Imrohir, yet he is our leader. We are naught but a colony of the Empire. No doubt the magister is merely keeping our bonds *strong*."

"No, he is up to something," Elise replied fiercely. "I'm sure of it." She had found the first end of a ball of string, and she would never stop hunting what lay at the other. " I believe this is the secret that my parents died for."

Tariq stiffened. Elise saw the fury sweep through his eyes long before he spoke.

"A *secret* they died for?" he snarled as his voice rose. "Can you not hear yourself? They were not killed by an order or a lone man's whisper. Your mother, she was taken by the sickness. The physician came every day. I was there when she breathed her last breath. Your father was killed in an alley by thieves in pursuit of coin. All you do now is cling to a false hope and use it as a weapon to strike against those whom you have turned your anger upon. They were my closest friends. They were my family. I swore to your mother that I would watch over you. I swore it! But do not ask me to stand by and watch you die as you pursue this fool's crusade that will only end one way. With your death."

A tear ran down her cheek. Whether it was caused by guilt or sorrow or anger, she did not know. Perhaps it was all of them. A piece of her heart broke. Elise had hoped... she had *prayed* that Tariq would understand. He did not. Elise hid her pain behind a mask. All of her arrogance, all of her drive, it all came from the agony within.

"The night he died, my father came to me," Elise told him. "It starts with the gold, yet the griffin's seal casts a long shadow, he said. The magister's seal, that is what he spoke of. That and the banker. What he meant I dread to guess, yet it was the last thing he said before he died."

Elise pulled her jacket on. She snatched up her cloak and mask. "Why would he say that without cause? So I will do all in my power to find the meaning behind his words. Stay or leave. With or without you. I will do this."

SEVENTEEN

Coast of Larissa, the Mithramir Sea

The blood upon her face had long since dried. Her wounds still ached, and bruising had begun to stain her cheek. Yet still Kitara heaved her body up with the strength of her arms. Urlaigh and thirteen of the Káli had fallen and their lifeless bodies had been unceremoniously thrown overboard. Kitara ground her teeth as she lowered herself back down. Her arms strained. She pushed herself through the motions again and again. Sweat rolled down her warm skin and dripped onto the wooden boards below.

"You continue to fight," Morlag muttered through the bars of the cell. "Even after all this loss. Why?"

Muscle tightened as she heaved. It was a lesson that she had learned a long time ago.

"You must have a fire inside you when it is time to let that fire out," she said. "I have been a slave before. I will be *no* slave again."

The soldiers came for her when the noonday sun burned bright. This time they took no chances. This time she was clapped in chains so tight that iron cut into the flesh of her wrists. She offered no complaint and merely granted the Medeans a smirk in reply.

Kitara squinted as she was led out into the light. She had been below for days, caged and given barely enough food and water to live. She ran her eyes over the deck. The blood had long since been cleansed. Chips and furrows covered both railing and deck. Kitara was led toward the quarterdeck. Her gaze was drawn to the foot of the stairs where Urlaigh had fallen. The guard behind shoved her in the back and forced her onto the steps.

She climbed.

Sir Rowan of Patchi stood at the edge of the Lioness, staring out portside across the waves. His hands were clasped tightly behind his back. There, at the edge of the sea, was a city. It was distant, yet shining beneath the sun's rays.

"Laeonidir," the knight explained as she approached, "the northernmost city of Larissa. Do you see the mountains it is nestled against? Great waterfalls, pure, clear water. It is a magnificent city."

Kitara frowned before she replied, "We have travelled far."

"Passed Danakis two days ago," Rowan told her. "I have been there once. The Queen's city, made famous by the lotus gardens."

"What do you want with me?"

"What do you want for yourself?"

Kitara glared at his back. "We attempt escape, kill your men. Yet now you bring me up here to talk of cities?"

"You are many things, yet a fool is not one of them." Finally, the knight turned to face her. "You fought well. Outnumbered, surrounded, against a stronger and better equipped foe. You nearly killed a knight absent your own weapon. Absent armour. Absent hope."

"Beneath the armour of a knight stands a man like any other." Kitara shrugged. "You say I was absent hope for the advantage lay with my enemy. Yet strength and reach are advantages that can be overcome with superior training and skill." They were words she had once been told. Words that in time had been proven true time and time again. Tarkaras, the swordsong, had given her a strength that she had never known she possessed.

Rowan slowly nodded. The knight pulled something from his belt and held it up. It was a nail. The same one that she had used to kill those two men below.

"Recognise this?"

"I will not apologise for what I did," Kitara growled. "I have seen slavery before. I have seen those bound in chains lose everything. Even their desire to escape from them. As for your men, they would deny freedom to those who are born free. They did not deserve to be free themselves."

Rowan ran his eyes over the nail before he spoke. "Pelayo Aranoea. He was born in Valengos, a small fishing village in Bailon's territory. He had a wife, Luanana, and two children. The youngest of them, Catalina, would be but six months old now."

"Why do you tell me this?"

Rowan's fist tightened around the nail as he looked into her face. "There it is. I can see it in your eyes," Rowan said. "Death. The pale horseman in your gaze. Everyone that you have killed is nothing more than a stroke upon your red canvas."

"You know nothing," Kitara told him.

Her hands curled into fists and the shackles cut deeper into her wrists. She did not care. The list of people she had killed was long and there were countless names upon it. Such was her fate.

"Pelayo, you, your men, you're all the same. You caged me like an animal, beat me, took away my freedom and slaughtered my people. You intend to sell me to the highest bidder, yet you summon me and wish to speak. You once said that you wished to help, so listen to me now. No matter what anyone says, no matter the excuse or reason, what a person does in the end is what he intended to do."

The knight met her storm filled gaze and tossed the nail out into the ocean. Kitara could see a darkness reveal itself in his eyes. She had awakened the beast.

"Know this," Rowan hissed. "If you attempt escape again... the girl will die a swift death... but you? You will be chained and beaten. You will be a slave beholden to the will of another. Once you have lost everyone and everything that you hold dear, you will die to the roar of the crowd. This will be your fate if you fail to cooperate."

Dusk arrived at the border of Salvaar. Through the trees, within eyesight, were the lands of Medea. What would await them beyond the woods, Aeryn did not know. Like the rest of her kin the moonseer had never left her homeland, let alone drifted this far west into the Káli lands. She took a slow breath as she waited. The cool southerly breeze brushed upon her cheek. Her silver eyes gazed north as she clutched her longbow tight. It was an old trick, to lie in wait downwind of your quarry. Here, she was alone. Here, she was at peace. Her silver gaze caught sight of the pigeons roosting high above in the canopy. The feathers of the arrow brushed against her cheek as she drew her powerful bow. The strength of arm and back took the weight of the draw as if she were lifting an empty cup. The weapon sung and her aim was true.

It *always* was.

The smoke reached her senses long before the camp came within sight. The mercenary company had set up barely a mile from the edge of the forest. They would begin their crossing into Medea as the sun rose upon their backs.

"The mighty hunter returns," called Jaimye, as Aeryn walked into the camp with a brace of birds swinging from one hand.

The moonseer smirked as she saw the Annoran sitting on a fallen tree trunk by the fire. She approached Jaimye as amusement danced across his face. She pushed the birds into his chest without a word, nearly shoving him off his makeshift stool as the pigeons dropped into his lap. The mercenaries roared with laughter.

"Then you will cook them for our pleasure, no?" Aeryn grinned, "As I caught them."

"Girl's got you there, Jaimye," Galadayne chuckled. "She is the best shot we have. Try not to upset her."

Sakkar glanced up with a frown.

"She's the best shot?" he chortled.

Aeryn raised her eyebrows as she replied, "You scare away all the food when you stumble around these woods clumsy as a child."

"Wait just a minute. You want him to cook?" Kompton asked. He gave his companions a horrified look as he turned toward Jaimye. "We all know what happened last time."

"What happened last time?" Aeryn asked mischievously, as she sat beside the men.

"Bard, don't you dare," Jaimye growled and sent a vicious glare toward his friend. Kompton's grin widened as his fingers began to strum the string of his lute. His eyes sparkled as he started to sing.

"Fifteen sat beneath Miera's skies,
Soon enough wind was filled with their cries.
Young Jaimye of Ilham,
Said he could fill 'em,
Yet now there's nothin' but ash for the flies."

They all set about their own tasks after they had finished eating. Some sparred, while others sharpened blade and spear. Some polished armour, while others tended to the horses. Aeryn watched on curiously as Sakkar snatched up three cups and moved to sit opposite Jaimye.

"How is your memory?" the Larissan asked.

"Good enough," Jaimye raised an eyebrow.

Sakkar smiled as he produced a small pebble from his sleeve. He placed it upon the ground and turned the three cups upside down. The pebble disappeared under one of the cups. One by one, the mercenaries begun to turn toward the show. They watched on expectantly as Sakkar started to move the cups. He weaved them in and out and made them dance upon the earth. Finally, he brought them to a halt.

"Three choices," he said. "Right, left or middle."

Jaimye leaned in with a frown. Aeryn watched closely as she saw the thoughts wash across the Annoran's face. Slowly, almost hesitantly, Jaimye pointed toward the cup on the right. Sakkar placed a hand upon it.

"You're sure?" he asked.

The mercenaries stared with bated breath, as their man nodded. The Larissan took ahold of the cup and flicked it up to reveal… *nothing*. Laughter filled the camp as Jaimye stared dumbfounded at the cups. He grabbed the left hand one and raised it. Nothing. His frown grew with the laughter. The third cup came up.

Nothing.

He looked from the ground to Sakkar with hard eyes.

"You cheated," he growled.

The Larissan stared at him blankly and extended an arm. He reached out past Jaimye's ear and flicked his wrist. His hand balled into a fist. Aeryn pursed her lips as she watched the man retract his arm. Jaimye growled and snatched Sakkar's wrist.

"What are you playing at?" he swore.

Sakkar, saying nothing, merely opened his hand. Eyes widened and there was a sharp intake of breath. There, in the palm of his hand, was the stone.

"A humble trick." A smile broke Sakkar's lips.

"Pah!" Jaimye snorted, as he pushed his companion's arm away. "Devil's magic."

The moon had risen higher when Bellec came to find Aeryn. She glanced up as he sat at her side.

"We're going to need to pass through Bandujar," Bellec said. "It's a small town barely a mile from the edge of the forest. We can gather supplies there. Though there is another reason we must go."

"Why is that?"

"Your clothing… any fool could see that you are not Medean by your appearance alone. We will have to find you something more suitable and pray none see your face."

Aeryn ran her fingers along the iron length of her arm ring. "Whatever it takes," she said.

Bellec was silent for a moment before he pulled a small knife from his belt.

"Here," he said, holding its hilt toward her.

The moonseer took the blade and washed her gaze over its length. It was no larger than two fists, with a plain wooden hilt. Yet there was one thing that set it apart from any knife that she had seen before: a series of notches, carved into the blade's hilt.

"It belongs to Kitara," Bellec told her. "You should have it."

"You are her father," Aeryn replied, turning the dagger in her hands.

"Perhaps," he said. "Kitara trusts you more than anyone. A blind man could see that. She cares for you as much as you care for her. I spent little enough time with her, though I can see what goes beyond words. Whatever her demons, whatever she suffered, I can see how it forged her. You might be the first person to have seen her as anything more than a tool, a sword, or someone who has every answer even when there are none. She needs you. She is in love with you, I think. I know you feel the same."

Aeryn glanced at Bellec. She knew the truth of his words, yet to see it in his eyes went beyond that.

"I can see it in the tensing of your jaw and furrow of your brow when her name is spoken," Bellec continued. "I can hear it in your voice and see it in your eyes. You have the look of someone who would travel to the ends of the world to save her."

He had guessed true. He had seen the truth. Aeryn knew that the mercenary captain spoke from experience.

"When she told me about her past, about what she had suffered," Aeryn told him. "I promised her I would stand by her side, however long it took to slay these demons that haunted her. That is my oath."

"You have a good heart," Bellec said. "Don't ever lose it."

Aeryn gave him a nod as she held his gaze. She sheathed Kitara's knife.

"Tell me something," Aeryn began. "You say the passage to Belona is two months' ride, yet not half that by ship. Why do we not just *take* a ship from the Medeans?"

Bellec gave a growl of a chuckle.

"The thought did cross my mind," he admitted. "Yet none of my men are sailors. Say we commandeered a vessel and its crew and made it to Belona... within hours, if an hour, the soldiers would be onto us. Word travels in Aureia faster than anywhere else. We may make it out of Belona, only to be set upon long before we reached Vesuva. At least if we travel by land then we can approach the city unnoticed."

"I will pray to the spirits that you are right. Just as you should pray to your own gods."

"I have no gods." The mercenary stared out into the forest and a dark look crossed his face. "The spirits, the Twins, the Sea-Father... they're all the same. The same wolf in sheep's clothing. When I look around and see what religion has done to people... I am glad to have no part in it."

Aeryn looked to him. The idea that one could be without faith puzzled her. *Did not all Salvaari serve the spirits? Did not all outsiders follow their own gods and ways?*

"A sellsword who fights for coin without religion or purpose. I wonder: do you believe in anything at all?"

Bellec rose to his feet and let his hand fall to his blade.

"I believe in my sword," Bellec told her. "I believe in my brothers. I believe in family. That is all a man needs."

Then he was gone. Aeryn had seen the sadness in his eyes. "Where does he go?" Aeryn asked. She looked across the camp to Galadayne who, like her, had watched the mercenary leave. "Each night it is the same."

"Ghosts haunt him here," Galadayne replied. "They haunt all

of us… but they nearly broke him."

"What happened?"

Galadayne let his gaze flick from mercenary to mercenary, yet he said nothing. The sellsword did not want to speak. That much was clear.

"Tell her. Tell them both," Jaimye said as he glanced at Sakkar. "They ride with us now. They deserve to know."

Galadayne ran a hand through his short hair and across the runes that covered the shaven sides of his head. "Alright," he murmured. "Years ago, long before any of this, many of us served in the Aethelan Royal Guard. We were young men then. Bellec was our captain. When the newly crowned *Dorian* Raynor," Galadayne nearly spat the name, "joined with King Balinor of Laeoflaed, and King Galan of Torosa, and marched north against your people, we rode with him. A few weeks into the campaign we were attacked by your people. We were unprepared and outnumbered. I remember looking up at the sun as a warrior stood over me. I should have died then. Bellec saved my life that day. He saved many of us. He stood in the middle of the river, sword in hand, screaming for us to retreat as he alone held the line. When the smoke cleared Bellec was gone. Your people, the Aedei, had taken him. A year passed before Chief Raywold sent a delegation to treaty with us. Bellec rode with them, and before long our king met with your chief. There was a truce, and finally we may have been going home. That is when he came to me."

Galadayne looked into Aeryn's silver eyes. "Bellec had found love in the arms of an Aedei woman. She was special, he said, not like the others. Her hair was like gold and her eyes… I only met her once. Oriana. She was strong and fierce, compassionate and loyal beyond reason. And then all came to an end."

He spoke the last words as a whisper. Galadayne set his jaw as anger rose from within. "An ambush in the dead of night. The screams of the dying. Eldred Raynor, brother to Dorian, was slain. One man alone escaped. He had been cut badly and left for dead. The men of Laeoflaed found him and they alone heard his last words. They say that he spoke of treachery within our ranks. They say he said that Dorian's own captain was the one that struck Eldred with the mortal blow. They said that Bellec killed him. A lie, yet one that took root."

Galadayne winced almost as if he had been struck. His hand curled tightly into a fist.

"Dorian banished Bellec and sent his dogs after him," Jaimye began. "They chased him into Medea, but he was not alone, for they hunted Oriana as well."

"And the child she carried," another of the mercenaries muttered. "Bellec's child."

"Eventually the hunters found them trying to hide in Sevillona. Oriana was taken. Bellec never saw her again," Galadayne continued and his voice rose. "He chased them down. Tracked them to a port. But it was too late. His woman was gone. That is when we found him. He was standing over the corpse of the harbour master, screaming at us to try and take him. But he was my friend, my brother. I could not kill him. None of us could. Aiding him was treason and that cost us everything. But ask yourself this… would you have killed a brother, a man who had saved your life countless times, if your king had commanded it? No." Galadayne shook his head.

"In that moment, we all became outlaws. To be hunted and killed should we so much as step foot upon Annoran soil. In the years that followed we searched for Oriana day and night. We fought against the dogs that Dorian had unleashed against us. Men whom we had once fought beside. For decades we searched for Oriana and her child, yet we heard nothing. We found nothing."

"Eventually we took up the sellsword trade," Jaimye spoke up. "Fighting in hellholes from Idrisir to Berenithia and beyond. Slowly our band grew… outlaws, knights," and he nodded toward

Kompton, "even bards. We were in Medea when word came to us of a golden-haired woman, an outlander in Miera who swung a sword. Her hair, and the rumour that she had Salvaari heritage, was enough. It was the only shadow of a whisper that we had heard in many years, and so we rode east toward Carlian. Had Kitara not been in Chausac when we were passing, we may never have found her."

"I knew who she was from the first," Galadayne said. "She looks just like her mother."

"That is enough ghost stories for one night," Bellec's growl cut through the air like a blade. "We rest now. We ride before daybreak."

Aeryn could not stop her eyes from flicking to the sellsword as he walked back through the camp. She would never understand the pain that he felt, yet now at least she understood the reason for it. Love, loss, and betrayal had forged the man.

"Prince Dayne, you had better come quickly," the outrider called as he approached his prince.

Dayne glanced at Lord Hornwood, who rode by his side, before he kicked his horse into a gallop. The two lords led their men in the outrider's wake. The sight that lay at the edge of the forest paled even the most hardened of faces. Many clutched at their amulets and whispered prayers to their gods.

"Your scouts," Dayne said to Lord Hornwood as he gazed upward.

Hanging in the trees were the bodies of a dozen men. They were strung up by rope wrapped around their broken necks. They' were stripped half naked and left to rot in the sun. Symbols had been carved in their chests, and their bodies were awash with blood. This was the Káli reply.

EIGHTEEN

Moonwatch, Valley of Odrysia

They rode hard. They barely stopped long enough to catch a breath. They ate in the saddle, and they drank in the saddle. They would rest only for a few hours each night. On the third day, at the setting of the sun, Moonwatch arose before them. A great tower drove into the sky like a spear, ringed in a wall of stone, and atop its pinnacle sat a pyre. Garrisoned by two hundred knights of Kil'kara, the watch stood sentinel over the Steppe of Miera. Kyler clicked his tongue and begun to angle Asena toward the garrison. The thought of a warm meal and soft bed called to him.

"Not that way, Pisspot," Sir Alarik's voice crushed the boy's hopes. "No one knows where we travel. I would rather not be seen this far east."

"Aye, sir," Kyler replied with a grimace, running a hand down his mount's neck. Kyler scanned the horizon and watched as the sun vanished. "It's getting late."

Alarik nodded and pointed to the base of the mountains in the north. A forest covered the floor of the valley, before it rose up the mountainside all the way to its pinnacle.

"We rest here tonight," Alarik said.

They reached the woodland in moments.

"Something on your mind, boy?" the battlemaster asked as his companion slid from his saddle. "You have barely spoken a word since we left Kilgareth."

Kyler looked to his mentor. The man he trusted above all others, yet Kyler was almost scared to speak his mind.

"Before I arrived at Kilgareth with Torin we were set upon by bandits," Kyler told him. "One, their leader, was marked with a scarred lip. Months later in Odrysia, it was he who attacked us in the streets and nearly killed Hugh."

Kyler ground his teeth. He could feel guilt and anger wash over him. His knuckles whitened as he gripped his reins. "He asked for my name, and I gave it," Kyler continued. "That man alone survived. When Mateja spoke of the man who murdered my parents, he spoke of a man with a scarred lip. A man whose brother I killed. It can only be the man from the road. The man from Odrysia. He stood before me *twice*. If I had killed him, my parents would still be alive. If I had not given him my name, my parents would still be alive." His voice broke as the words left his mouth.

"It is my fault that they're dead," Kyler snarled.

Alarik froze. He glared into Kyler's eyes. "Don't you ever say that," he said. "There are monsters out there that go beyond the ruskalan. There are monsters out there like the animal who murdered your parents. If you give into despair now, then he wins. I will make you this promise. When our business in Elara is done, I will help you hunt down and kill the one who took your family from you."

Kyler did not look away from his mentor's hard stare. The words did nothing to cast aside his guilt and his anger, yet the promise of vengeance stirred something within. "After Elara then," Kyler growled.

"You will have questions," Alarik said as they continued into the woods.

The boy looked skyward as they walked beneath the trees. There was so much that he needed to know. So much that he needed to learn. There were times that he felt as helpless as a baby.

"Why Elara? You spoke only riddles in Kilgareth. Yet there is a look in your eye, a look that I have seen in men's faces before. We're hunting something, aren't we?" Alarik brought his horse to a halt and reached beneath his saddle rug. He withdrew a sword wrapped in cloth.

"A shadow," Alarik told him as he extended the sword.

Kyler took the proffered blade and his eyes widened. "I know this sword," he murmured.

"It belonged to Wa'rith," the knight told him. "Look closely at the steel. It speaks of a story. One that began in Elara."

Kyler unwrapped the blade and let his eyes wander its length. This was the weapon that had claimed Matias' life and the lives of so many in the Vault.

"Then he is our prey," Kyler said. He set his jaw as he looked to his mentor. "Good," Kyler continued. "After what he did to our brothers… to Torin… we will bring him to justice."

He remembered the smoke that had filled the chamber. He remembered the blood flowing from the bodies of his companions. He still felt the power of the bolt as it was driven through mail. Alarik nodded slowly.

"And if in the pursuit, you have the chance, you *must* take his life," Alarik commanded. "We cannot afford mercy. Not now. Not with him."

"You speak as if you know the man."

"He was a knight once, a brother," Alarik ran a hand over his amulet as he softly replied.

Blood drained from Kyler's face. "That murderer was one of us? How does a holy knight fall so far as to kill his own brothers?"

The Aureian took a breath and looked to the rising moon.

"Markus Harvarder came to us long ago in search of purpose," he began. "He was an Annoran knight, trained in the art of war from the time he could walk. Markus was the best pupil that I had ever had. A man whose spirit was matched only by his skill and dedication to the sword. Loyal, reckless, and naïve. He quickly rose to prominence within the Order."

"What happened?" Kyler asked.

"Within months of his joining, Markus, along with another initiate, was apprenticed to Sir Edwin Vuliir, the Sword of Kil'kara. The two young men grew closer than any brothers by blood. They trained together, ate together, fought side by side. They saw Edwin as a father… and then a few years later it all changed. Sir Edwin led a company of knights north to Cacera. We had received word of a druid inflaming the tribes. The village was attacked, and in the fight that followed Sir Edwin was killed. They said that when the Sword fell to the pagans his apprentices finished what he started. To them killing was an art form, and they painted Cacera in a sea of red. Markus avenged his mentor and took the druid's head." Alarik did not show emotion as he spoke.

"Upon their return, a great pyre was lit, and we sent Edwin into the heavens. Yet the mourning for our fallen brother would be cut short. It started with a dream. Or a dream of a dream. Lysandra, then just a maija, was granted a vision by the Silver Lady. Azaria told her of a staff; *her* staff. An artefact, they say, that could cure all ills. We rode at dawn with Edwin's chosen. The journey served another purpose. To see who was best suited to taking upon the mantle of Sword. Far to the west, to the Silver Tower, we travelled."

"Azaria's Rose," Kyler breathed. "I know that tale." He had heard of the Tower and what had become of it. Travellers passing through Adrestia had often told him of the magnificent tower that drove up into the sky like a lance. A great window in the shape of a rose imbued upon it. Once a great beacon of their faith, now it was a tragedy that brought many a tear to the eye of believers.

"No," Alarik told him. "You *think* you know it. You weren't there. Lysandra's vision led us to a cave that drove deep into the heart of the mountain. And then we found it. The staff. It was atop an altar of stone. Silver with a ruby that blazed like fire. The legends spoke that it could cure all ills. Harvarder took the staff from its pedestal, removed it from its clasp, and the cavern, ancient and old, began to tremble. Stone and earth began to fall around us. We escaped the cave, yet the Tower… the Rose… fell. The screams of the people dying. The dust in the air that took our senses as we fled blindly. A pillar came down, trapping me beneath it. Lysandra came to my aid with our other companion. But Markus, he could only stare at the ruins of the town. He looked to the staff."

Alarik gritted his teeth as he remembered.

"He walked to the edge of the cliff face… and then cast it into the ravine. He turned on us, on his brothers, even as the city fell around us. He ripped the sun and moon from his neck and cast it down… and Harvarder, staunch warrior of our faith, drew steel. Brother turned on brother. As the last of the city was ruined, as the two knights crossed blades, Harvarder fell, following the staff into the ravine. No one could have survived that fall. We searched for days. Yet the man and the artefact had long been taken by the river."

"You saw him fall, and thought him dead," Kyler said, breaking the silence that followed Alarik's tale. "Then how do you know Harvarder and Wa'rith are the same man?"

"Listen to me, Kyler. Harvarder is one of the best swordsmen that I have ever seen," the battlemaster growled. "The way he moves, the way he *fights,* I have only seen in one other."

"Who?"

Alarik snorted. "The one he trained with. The one he held closest. The one he turned on. A man of equal skill and deadly zeal. A man who stands above all others yet would gladly die for any beneath him. Corvo Alaine."

Cleander waited until midnight had long passed before making his move. He pulled his hood high up over his ears to shroud his face and kept his hand clamped upon the hilt of his sword. There could be no mistakes. If Emberly was right and the courtesans were being watched, then their alliance was compromised. Mellisanthi's girls provided more than just warmth on cold nights. To Bhaltair and his gang, they provided something worth far more than all the gold in Elara.

Information.

The girls told them which lords could likely be swayed to their cause. The girls told them everything from whisper to rumour, and the gangs reaped the reward.

Cleander knew these streets well. In the years since his arrival the warrior had learned every shortcut or hidden passage, every secret that Elara had to offer. It did not take him long to lose the man who had begun watching him two streets back. Nor did it take him long to locate the man who watched the brothel from the shadows.

He was alone. Men such as him always were. Cleander backtracked and took a shortcut down an alley. With each step he made less noise upon the cobblestones. As a knight his footwork had always been his greatest strength and it had not taken him long to learn to walk as silently as a cat.

His right hand curled back, and he flicked his arm to allow the hilt of a small dagger to emerge from his sleeve. Cleander's left hand wrapped around the spy's mouth as his right planted the dagger upon the man's neck. The spy rose to his feet without so much as a word, as Cleander walked him back into the empty alley. He spun the man around and even in the darkness he recognised the face.

"Scream and I will open your throat." With that, he removed his hand from the spy's lips.

The man said not a word, meeting Cleander's dark gaze with a withering glare.

"I saw you days past, tailing the courtesan in the market," Cleander growled. "Who sent you?"

Nothing.

Cleander flicked his wrist and a line of blood appeared upon the spy's cheek.

"I won't ask again," he said through bared teeth. He wrapped a hand around the man's neck and pushed him hard into the wall. His knife lowered to the man's crotch.

Cleander could see the man breaking as he stared into his eyes.

He applied pressure with the blade.

"Lord Daivin," the spy spluttered as he squirmed in Cleander's grasp. "Says you're mad, the lot of you. You have plagued this city for too long and deserve the end that is coming for you. The hangman does not forgive."

"Thank you."

The knife vanished from the spy's crotch. An ember of hope sparked in the man's eyes. Cleander released his tight grip. The spy's lips twitched. The blade was driven up into his throat. The ember vanished as he crashed to the ground at Cleander's feet. He cleaned steel on the dead man's cloak and then made his way from the alley.

The side door to the brothel opened before Cleander's fist could knock for a third time.

"Welcome to the Star of Elara," a scantily clad, red headed, beauty whispered seductively. Her eyes widened as he pulled his hood back.

"Cleander?"

He pushed past her and walked into the smoky room. "Your mistress here?"

"She's upstairs in her study," Emberly's voice cut in.

Cleander glanced up as a new woman descended the stairs and made her way toward them. The skirts of her blue dress swayed as she moved.

"Is she expecting you?" the red-haired woman frowned.

"No," a thin smile flashed across his lips. "But I am sure she knows that I am here."

Emberly bit her lip and looked to her companion, "That will be all, Julia."

Julia nodded and left the room leaving the pair alone.

"I have something for you," Cleander said, as he procured a coin purse and tossed it to Emberly.

Her eyes widened as she looked within the pouch. "How did you…?"

"It wasn't a gift," he replied. "And that man from the market… he won't bother you again."

Emberly's lips trembled as she walked toward him and slowly pulled him into a hug. "Cleander, thank you."

He gave her a squeeze and gently ran a finger across Emberly's cheek. He could see something more than friendship burning behind her eyes.

"Forgive me, but I must see Mellisanthi."

"I understand."

"I will see you after," he said. Cleander made his way upstairs to the madam's study.

"I expected to see you sooner," Mellisanthi said, a hint of amusement in her voice.

Cleander grunted, taking her hand and planting a kiss upon her soft skin.

"I was delayed."

"Delayed?"

The gangman glanced from his friend to the closed door. "We are compromised," he said.

"I am afraid you're speaking in riddles."

Cleander reached into a pouch and pulled forth a coin, covered in blood. "This belonged to the man sent to watch your girls," Cleander said as he held it out.

"He's dead then?" Mellisanthi took the coin and ran her gaze across its surface.

Cleander nodded. "Not before he talked. Said he was under the employ of Lord Daivin."

"Daivin Aillard? The magister's nephew... then we are betrayed."

"So it would seem. The man was always a friend to the people. He was even willing to turn from Imrohir in the hopes of saving this city," Cleander said.

He walked through the room and looked to the painting of a Larissan man. Mellisanthi's father. He had once been a slave, yet the laws evoked by the magister of days long gone had freed him and his kin of chains. That magister was gone now, and Mellisanthi's father along with him.

"He will need to be dealt with, or we will all be undone," Cleander added.

"I agree, but it must be done correctly," Mellisanthi told him. "We cannot risk turning the people against our cause."

Cleander closed his eyes and a sigh slipped through his lips. "I do not know if there is time to do it the right way," he murmured.

"Explain."

"When I met with Bhaltair, he was not alone."

"Your leader has many friends," Mellisanthi shrugged. "Not–"

"Not Priamos Stentor," Cleander cut in.

"What?" The words came as a whisper.

The gangman placed his hands upon the desk. "The gangs are restless. The people want justice. The Nightingale is out there stirring up the nobility... and Lord Stentor... it is no secret that his family were disillusioned of the magister many years ago. The taxes grow each year. The merchant's guild begin to fight among each other like rabid dogs, not caring for all those caught between. And what does the magister do? Beats the people into submission. Treats them as serfs and then wines and dines. Priamos came to us for help. Wants to set aside the past and work with the gangs."

"Then it all makes sense," Mellisanthi said. "Word on the street is that there is a fight brewing. The people are close to riot, and if a high lord casts in his lot with them… this city could burn."

"I fear that fate is unavoidable now," he said quietly.

"What is it, Markus? There is something else. Something you're not telling me." She placed a hand upon Cleander's arm.

"Markus?" he murmured, and he offered her a quiet smile. "I had almost forgotten the sound of my own name."

"You should not be so swift to cast it aside," Mellisanthi replied. "You cannot escape the past. No matter how fast you run from it. Now tell me."

Cleander was silent. He remembered the intensity of Priamos' words that day in the tunnels. *Was he fanatical? Maybe. Yet perhaps that was what they needed.*

"In two weeks, at the high mass, the nobility will gather in the senate house. They move to propose new laws that will, without the emperor's blessing, enable the magister to seize land."

"Then that means… that means that once the Sacasian threat is no more, our armies will not disband."

"That is not all," Cleander continued as he repeated the same words that Primoas Stentor had told him. "The accords struck with Miera thirty years ago will be abolished, and yet the horsemen will *not* be warned. With this new crusade against the Salvaari, the armies of Aureia will march. Imrohir wants to seize this opportunity to lay claim to the lands of Miera with not just the League, but with Aureian legions at his back."

"And who will suffer the most," Mellisanthi gritted her teeth. "Many of the lords still stand with Imrohir, thanks to the Nightingale."

"The vote will be unanimous," Cleander nodded. "When the vote is cast and counted, Imrohir will stand as a king. We have no time. Not to deal with Daivin. Not to sway the lords. Not even to fully prepare. We must act."

"What has been planned? What do you know?"

"Powder," Cleander said, and he pulled one of his smoke

bombs from his belt, "the same kind that I use for these... but so much more. Dozens of barrels, if not more, stored in the sewers beneath the senate house."

Mellisanthi's jaw fell.

"That is murder," she hissed. "There are those in the senate who are good people. Kind, considerate. And Stentor would kill them all."

"Bhaltair has agreed. There is nothing to be done."

"There is *always* a choice," she said as she looked at him in horror.

"Then what would you have me do?" Cleander snarled. "Let the magister and his kind send our people to be butchered? Let everything that we have worked so hard to build crumble?"

Mellisanthi gave him a sad look as she replied, "What happened to you, Markus? When you first came to Elara you were so full of hope. What would your benefactor say if they saw you like this? They risk death in Kilgareth for *you*. You once told me that the only reason that you still have purpose is because of them... yet now what? Killing wicked men is one thing, yet burning the senate house? How many would be killed in the blast? How many afterward, when the riots begin. There would be chaos in the streets. Rivers of blood. How much of Elara would burn?"

"The price of freedom is high, Mellisanthi, you should know that best of all."

Her hand slapped his face, whipping his head to the side. Her teeth were bared, and her eyes wild. "Damn you, *Cleander*. I followed you when you asked for help against the Order. I joined you without question when you asked me to inform the gangs. But I will not follow you to murder."

Cleander turned to leave. "You are my closest friend," he said. "The debt I owe you is one that I will never be able to repay. I am sorry."

He reached for the door handle when Mellisanthi's voice stopped him.

"You can't tell Emberly. It will break her heart. Do you even know that she loves you?"

Pain came from his tightly balled fists. He took a breath. The man he had once been, Markus Harvarder, a man of hope and pride, was gone. Only Cleander remained.

He left the room.

NINETEEN

Lukas hissed as he made his way from the house. He clamped his jaws together to bite back the pain that surged through his leg. His head still ached and burned with each passing day. It was an agony only lessened by Maevin's brew. Dark thoughts still plagued him day and night, threatening to drive him to insanity. Lukas made his way over to the stump of an old tree and gently lowered himself onto its surface. He winced as a sliver of pain ran through his knee. Maevin saw him in the yard for the first time and approached with a cup in her hand.

"You begin to heal."

"All I feel… all I *see* is pain," he said bitterly.

The priestess placed a hand on his shoulder and held the cup out. "Drink."

Lukas took it and raised it to his lips. The rage came from nowhere and it burned within him like a great fire. With a snarl he threw the cup to the ground and sent its contents splashing across the earth.

"Am I weak?" he snapped. "Tell me true, am I weak? Answer me!"

The emerald of her eyes blazed as she met his glare. Maevin crouched before him and took his head in her hands.

"Tell me, what do you dream of?" she asked.

"I dream of darkness, of a world fallen to ruin. I see the

hammer as it descends. I see everything turn black… and then I dream of before, my life in Palen-Tor. In those dreams I am not a cripple. In those dreams I dance."

"And so, you shall dance again. I promise you that," Maevin said as a tear rolled down Lukas' cheek. "I once met a man who was led by his heart. A man who knew who he was. A man who rode hundreds of miles, alone, to save a people that he did not know. That man saved my life, saved *many* lives. Now you ask me if that man is weak? You, who pulled the blade of a sword away from my neck. You, who stood between me and death… and smiled at it. You are not weak, and nor is your story over."

"I'm just so… helpless," he muttered, "So angry. I feel so much pain."

"What you need is a purpose," Maevin told him. "A reason to fight."

"My father once told me that all soldiers fight for a cause. I always knew exactly what I needed to do, until now. Now I am lost, adrift. A cripple."

"You are never crippled, Lord," she said as she stroked his jaw. "Not until you lose hope."

Lukas' gaze did not waver from hers as she rose to her feet. Her hand fell from his chin, and she took his hand.

"Come," Maevin told him, as she pulled the prince from the stump, "get on your feet."

Kitara started and woke from her sleep. She blinked and shook her head.

"Kitara?" Sereia's soft voice came through the bars. Kitara gave the girl a smile and reached through the bars, to rest her palm upon Sereia's hand.

"It's nothing," she said. "Get some rest."

"As long as you do."

"Always," Kitara lied and gave Sereia's hand a squeeze.

The Káli girl, satisfied, leaned back into Morlag who sat at her side. Kitara closed her eyes and let out a breath.

In truth, sleep would not come to her. The nightmares had returned and the peace she had found for a moment had been torn away. She looked around the brig and glanced from face to face. These people were all she had left.

Who would come for her? Theron Malley… Bellec? The man who stood as father in name only and had abandoned her as a child. Aeryn? The one that she had mistakenly let through her armour. She had probably already forgotten her.

Kitara squared her jaw. She was all but alone again, and she would survive. She *always* did. Kitara frowned as a new sound came to her ears. It grew louder and pulled the Káli prisoners from their slumber.

"What is that?" one of the men called.

Kitara bit her lip. It was a sound she would never forget. One she had awoken to each day for nearly eighteen years.

"Gulls," she said, as a sickening feeling roiled in her stomach. "That means only one thing. Land."

"And where is land exactly?"

"The port of Belona," Morlag answered.

Kitara turned to face him. "Welcome to Aureia."

The sunlight was blinding as they were led out onto the deck, hands chained tightly, while the mercenaries watched them closely, steel in hand. Kitara squinted as she took in the town that arose before them. The Lioness had docked in the harbour against a great stone pier. A bustling market sat at its end, while a great sea of red roofed houses ran all the way to the wall that encompassed the city. An older man met with Rowan and handed the knight a coin purse. By the look of him the Aurean was a slaver. His men joined with the Medeans as they made the prisoners ready. They were led along the pier under the gaze of the people of Belona.

The Aureans stopped and stared in curiosity and disgust. Few, if any of them, had seen the pagan barbarians before and knew them only by tale and song. Kitara's boot caught upon the pier, and she stumbled into an Aureian lady. The woman screamed and then the rough hands of a slaver pulled Kitara away with a snarl. It was all she had the chance to see before Sir Rowan and his men led them from the ship and threw the prisoners into the back of a caged wagon. The canvas was unfurled and then the Salvaari saw nothing of the outside world.

Kitara heard the sound of hooves and the whinnies of horses as they were brought to the convoy. The knights and their mercenary soldiers mounted up. There was a crack of a whip, and then the wagon begun to move. Kitara nudged Sereia who sat at her side.

"Do not fear," she said. "There is still time."

They would reach Vesuva tomorrow. That gave them one day. One last chance.

Moonlight shone down on Oryn when the druid appeared from the forest. He was hooded and cloaked in gnarled robes. He walked alone through the village. All was quiet. Maevin stood at Lukas' side, as the dark robed man approached. There was no fear in Maevin's eyes, though it was something that the prince keenly felt.

"You are summoned," the druid called, his voice light upon the wind.

"Whose summons do you bring?" Maevin asked.

"It is not your name that has been called, priestess," came the reply.

Chills rolled down Lukas' spine. It was to him that the druid now beckoned. Maevin looked to the prince and he saw a flicker of surprise in her face. Lukas turned from her to the druid as cold seeped into his bones. He said not a thing and leaned on his crutch as he began to hobble toward the man.

The druid led him deep into the forest, to a place so dark that even the light of the moon was extinguished. Mist rolled over the earth and covered all in white. There was no sound. Not even a breeze. There was nothing, save the ever-growing chill in the air.

"I make my leave," the druid intoned.

Lukas looked over his shoulder as his companion vanished into the darkness. He was alone, save for the whispering of the wind. He turned back as his hand tightened upon the handle of his crutch. The shadow of a man appeared before him. The fog shrouded his features and revealed nothing but the blackness of his clothes. A raven cried out.

Lukas spun toward the sound. His knuckles grew white, and his blood grew cold. More of the phantoms appeared all around him as he turned. They were distant, wreathed in darkness. He could see six. Whether there were more, he knew not. The fear inside began to grow. Lukas looked back to the first man. The figure stood before him. He was barely ten steps away. The prince had not heard him approach.

The man's pale skin seemed stretched across the sharp bones of his cheeks. His nose was thin, and his ears narrowed into points as sharp as any dagger. Black runes covered his beardless face, while his dark hair was thin and hung down to his neck. The only imperfection in his pale skin came in the form of a long scar that stretched from temple to chin. It was not the scar, nor the worn black clothing, that drew Lukas' gaze. Fangs lined the man's maw. His eyes blazed with light; his irises burned crimson as they stared deep into Lukas' soul. They froze his bones, his blood, his breath. He could not move, nor tear his gaze from the blazing inferno.

"Why are you here?"

The voice was cold and measured, yet strong. It spoke as if in a slow melody.

"I came here to–"

"You came as Annora's lackey," the man growled, as he approached, "and now villages burn."

The man begun to circle him as if he were prey. "I did not wish harm to befall your people," Lukas replied.

"And yet it did."

"They were good. They were kind," Lukas could not stop the pain from entering his voice.

"This pains you, does it?" the man said as he drew near to the Annoran's back. He walked like a dancer; his feet barely disturbed the soft earth below.

"Aye," Lukas told him.

The pale face showed no emotion. "Everyone is born to die. Everyone is a sacrifice."

"Who are you?" the prince asked. "When I look at you, I see darkness."

The man's piercing gaze turned to him once more.

"Can you not see, broken man? Can you not hear? Listen… the spirits' voice is in the air, in the earth and water. I am the blood of Tanris, second child to Sylvaine. I am the firstborn. A whisper in the wind. A song long forgotten. An echo of the ashes. Look me in the eye, broken man. Do you not know who I am?"

Lukas' heard began to chill. It froze as the fear took hold. He knew what the man was. A myth that even the scholars thought was nothing but a tale. Yet here he stood, one hundred years since the Inquisition purged his kind, alive.

"You are ruskalan," Lukas breathed.

The phantom before him bared his teeth as if to smile. "That I am," he said even slower. "Do you fear the spirits?"

The prince gritted his teeth. The ruskalan would see the lie if he spoke it. "Yes," Lukas told him truthfully.

"Good," came the vicious reply. "Then let's begin."

Lukas finally tore his eyes away from the man and swept his eyes toward the others. They did not approach. They only watched silently from the shadows. They were ruskalan too. That much was certain.

"You are all that remains of your kind," Lukas said as he finally understood.

"Very good," the ruskalan told him with something of a sneer. "We are the last of the old blood."

A frown crossed the prince's brow as his mind worked. "And only the druids know of your existence."

"A thousand questions in your eyes I can see. I am called Harkan. You wish to know why I summoned you here this night. It is whispered in the stars, in the sky, in the trees, that the broken shall reply to the bloodmoon."

"What meaning do you carry?"

"Your fate has been written," Harkan intoned. "A curse stalks you, Annoran, and a choice must be made. The spirits gaze upon you... the Dark One gazes."

"If they are here, and if they watch, then perhaps they will answer me this—"

"The spirits do not deal, Annoran," Harkan cut him off with a growl. "The spirits do *not* deal. Know this: Tanris has sent a guide, and it is this guide who will give you what you seek."

Lukas' skin crawled. It was not from the freezing wind, nor the ruskalan's heavy voice. It was the words he spoke.

"And what is that, exactly?" Lukas asked.

"In your heart of hearts, you know. You must awaken," Harkan said.

"And this guide?"

Harkan gazed out into the trees. He closed his eyes. "You know of whom I speak. She follows the snake's path," he said.

Maevin. It could be no one else.

"Why me?" Lukas murmured. He could feel the power of the ruskalan's words. He had seen the spirits light up the sky and had seen the hope that they had born for their people. The ruskalan were supposed to be gone, destroyed. Yet here they were. His own people would cast aside a cripple as if he were a burden. Just as Dayne had done to him. The Salvaari, the spirits, had given him a new chance. Maybe he did not believe in the gods, in Durandail and Azaria, but perhaps if he followed this path, in time the spirits would heal him of pain and grief. He had seen how the Salvaari lived, how they loved, and it was a thing he longed for.

"When the spirits choose," Harkan began, "they choose the forsaken. They choose the broken and the lost."

"Then what must I do?"

Harkan turned back to face him and stepped close. The fires of his eyes were blinding like the sun. "Will you be Tanris' messenger? Will you be the wind?"

Lukas did not hear Maevin's words as he returned to the village. Harkan's face was fixed in his mind. What the ruskalan had told him echoed down into his heart. Only when Maevin spoke again did her voice pull him back to the present.

"Lord?" Maevin repeated. "You are pale."

The warmth had not yet returned to his body, but the fear was long gone. "Tanris came to me," he murmured.

"And what did he speak?"

Lukas looked into her eyes. "I am the messenger... and you my guide. The broken shall reply to the bloodmoon. Those were his words."

"I see." The priestess did not argue, nor question.

"The chiefs ride north to Aildor in Conclave and now Tanris has come to you with a purpose," Maevin said.

"What lies in Aildor?"

"A village sundered by the fire and steel of Annora. A sacred place burned. Many were killed," Maevin looked out into the night as she spoke. "A time of choosing has come, Prince. If you wish to return to your people, it must be now. It must be today."

Lukas looked down without reply. He looked at the ruined

earth beneath. He remembered the face of the young girl slain by the Medeans. He remembered Emilian's smirk. He remembered the boy standing over him. He remembered his sister.

The cool weight of the silver amulet hung beneath Lukas' shirt. The sun and moon, gods he had never truly believed in.

"I cannot abandon my sister," he whispered.

"Greatness only comes with great sacrifice," Maevin nodded slowly. "Family is much more than blood. As are your people."

"Do you know something?" Lukas said after a moment. "I resent them… they are no longer my people. I am not sure that they ever were. I cannot abandon my sister, Maevin, but that does not mean that I will ever go back. If I do it shall be on my own terms. Here, in Salvaar, for perhaps the first time, I have been free, and I would like to remain as such."

"Then what do you decide?"

"You offer me a choice that leads me to a fork in the road. A decision where going left means following my father blindly, and where going right means forfeiting my past. A decision which will cost me every desire, and force me to a life of servitude, yet one that will keep my family together. Where the other road leads, I do not know. Yet it is the path to freedom at the cost of my sister and my life. One leads away from home. This place is peaceful… it is a place that a man could grow old and remove all else from concern. A simple life. That is what I truly long for. And I cannot get that in Annora. I have obeyed the will of the council and held my tongue. And it has cost me. No longer."

He could feel it in his heart, in his very bones. "Aye, I made my decision a long time ago."

"Are you certain, Prince of Annora?" Maevin asked of him. "If you make this choice, there is no going back."

Lukas pursed his lips before he replied, "I am no longer Lukas Raynor, son to Dorian, and Prince of Annora."

"Then who are you?"

"I do not know," Lukas said. It was the truth. "Yet I am willing to find out," Lukas continued. "I will return to Palen-Tor, yet not as a prince, and not alone." Lukas looked down the road. He looked to the south-west. He looked to Annora. "My path leads south, and wherever this fate leads… you are my guide."

"Then at dawn we at last leave Oryn."

A dozen Káli, faces awash with black, pulled themselves into their saddles. Bow, spear, and axe were held tightly within their grasp. Passion lit their eyes as they turned to the south. They had fought beside Lukas against the Catuvantuli. They had seen him save what remained of their village. They knew what he was willing to sacrifice, and they would follow him without question. Lukas placed a foot in the stirrup before, with a snarl, he heaved his crippled leg around his horse's flank. He grimaced, biting back the pain, as Maevin rode to his side. She believed in him with all of her heart. They exchanged a look. Lukas had made his choice. He no longer felt caged. Maevin had freed him. Lukas clicked his tongue. The column moved.

TWENTY

City of Elara, the League of Trecento

Elise rose early to do what so few noblewomen could. Dress herself. She pulled on the emerald and ivory dress, before tightening the loose corset. She winced as she pulled on the strings. Even though it sat loosely, it still brushed against her fresh wound. The puffed shoulders and long sleeves of the dress covered the bandaged gash on her arm. Elise took a breath, straightened her back and pushed back all thoughts of the night. Instead, she flung open the shutters of her window and closed her eyes. She let the morning sun wash over her skin.

"Good morning, m'lady."

"Good morning, Halina," Elise replied and gave her maid a smile.

"You're dressed?"

The noblewoman snorted. "Yes, well, I am not quite as helpless as those other fine ladies."

"Right you are, miss."

Halina returned the smile and gestured to the stool that stood before a mirror.

Elise flicked her hair behind her shoulders as she sat, allowing the maid to begin her work. She had long since stopped her complaints. They had never worked and her uncle had insisted that she had a maid. Elise already felt her discomfort settle in. Halina started with the jewel embellished comb and ran it through the long chestnut locks. Next, she began to braid it up behind Elise's head. The long braids were then curled up into a bun. The maid pursed her lips.

"We will have to think of another way to put this for the celebration," she said.

"The celebration?"

"The magister's party, m'lady," Halina reminded her. "In six days' time."

Elise stiffened and looked up at her friend. "So soon?"

"Yes, lady, the same as last year and–"

"The year before that," Elise finished for her. Elise bit her lip. Already ideas began to spring to life. "My mind has been taken of late," she said.

It was true. Her days were spent surviving and navigating the pathways of the nobility, while her nights were spent on the rooftops. She was more tired than she would care to admit, yet she could see a faint light at the end of the tunnel now. It was the only thing that kept her going. This fight, to her it was more than that. If the party was in only six days, then...

"They say that it will be a ball far grander than any before. A masquerade," Halina told her with a grin, as she placed her hands on her mistress' shoulders.

"A masquerade?" Elise replied with a chuckle. "All of Elara's nobility hiding who they are for a night of revelry and debauchery. I suppose it does sound more enticing than the usual pontificating of senile old–"

"Elise!" Halina chortled, as she struggled to withhold a laugh. Halina stared down at her lady in horror, and Elise felt her lips curl upwards.

"I had best find a mask, I suppose," Elise replied. Thoughts already clouded her mind. This ball could give her the opportunity that she needed. If the Nightingale could not infiltrate the magister's palace, then Elise Delfeyre would.

"Something red. It will accentuate your eyes," the maid said with glee. "And a dress. We can..." Halina gasped.

"What is it?" Elise said with a frown as she rose and turned to face her friend.

"M'lady... your arm."

Elise glanced down and for the first time noticed a small dark stain upon the inside of her sleeve. It was clearly blood. A gift from the magister's guards.

"Oh that? It's nothing, Halina. A small scratch from the Pits."

"I will call the physician."

"No!" Elise's hand shot forward and latched onto Halina's as she spoke. "I'm alright. Truly."

"But–"

She held up a finger to silence the maid. "I'm fine. A little blood never hurt anyone. I have seen far worse than this *flesh wound*. There is no need to worry a doctor or physician."

"I... right you are, m'lady." Halina nodded but displeasure was still written across her face.

Elise gathered up her dark green sleeved cloak and pulled it on. "And what my aunt and uncle don't know, won't hurt them. Do you understand?"

"Yes m'lady," Halina sighed.

Elise let the chamber and started to make her way through her family's villa. Claudia Delfeyre's kind–voice echoed through the house as she spoke to servant and guard. The lady treated all beneath her roof with the same compassion, for her blood ran with kindness.

"Ah, Elise." She smiled, as her niece descended from the stairs.

"Aunt Claudia," Elise greeted the lady, before she took her aunt's hands and exchanged a kiss on the cheek.

Raphael Delfeyre's wife had been with the merchant for longer than Elise had been alive. They had been married at sixteen and, as Claudia had told Elise, had been madly in love since. Like all of

Aureian heritage, Claudia's hair was dark and her skin olive. Her amber eyes glowed and her smile was full of life. She had a big heart and, although they weren't bound by blood, Claudia had treated Elise as if she were a daughter.

"I'm off to the market. Would you care to accompany me?" Claudia asked Elise, as she brushed a lock of her niece's hair back behind her ear. "We can find some masks for this exquisite ball, and perhaps," her eyes sparkled as she gave her niece a wink, "some honeyed wine."

"You had to mention that, didn't you?" Elise raised her eyebrows as she spoke.

"You are just like I was at your age. Always chasing the sweeter things in life."

"There should *always* be a time to smell the roses, or taste the honey, as it were." The girl shrugged. She took a step toward the door. "Well, are you coming or not?" Elise asked, as she turned back toward her aunt.

Claudia grinned and gestured to one of the household guards. "Let's go, Marshall," she told the soldier. "See what new delights we can find."

Elise walked side by side with her aunt through the throngs of people at the merchant district's bazaar. Six strides behind was the captain of her uncle's guard, Marshall. His eyes were hawklike, and his armoured hand never left his sword. He had been one who had accompanied her to the Pits.

Like most noble ladies, Elise walked with posture and elegance. Unlike other noble ladies, Elise saw *everything*. From the children accustomed to finding marks for their thieving fathers, to the upper-class aristocracy who held their purses a little too loosely.

"How is your friend? The strongman?"

"Tariq?"

"Yes. Nasty business with the gangs down there," Claudia said darkly. "I hope he keeps out of it, for your sake."

"He's not one for politics," Elise snorted. "Nor anything that requires deep thought."

Her aunt pursed her lips. A deaf man could have heard the sarcasm. "Something has happened?" her aunt asked.

"Nothing of consequence," Elise replied as they walked. Just ahead walked a noble dressed in *very* flamboyant clothing. A pair of armoured guards were stationed at his back. A heavy purse hung from his belt. Elise could feel her blood boil as she looked at the man. He was fat and lazy. A pampered parasite living off the backs of the poor.

"Just the sound of opportunity passing by," Elise said.

"Keep your friends close, Elise. Now more than ever."

Elise did not reply. She knew that her aunt spoke true, but Tariq, long-time friend to her family, had turned his back. He was the last person who tethered her to her old life, and perhaps it was time to let that rope go. She looked down as the nobleman walked by and gently bumped into him. It was a light touch and to all else it would have looked like nothing in the hustle of the bazaar. You did not come here without being bumped, after all. Not a soul saw her hands snake out as she hit him. Her shoulder covered her work. In less than a second the purse was safely within the pocket on the inside of her cloak. The guards saw nothing, and the noble *felt* nothing.

"Ah, here we are," Claudia said, and she indicated a small shop ablaze with colour. Masks of all kinds and hues hung from large racks. Full faced and half faced. Some were plain, while others bore the likeness of animals and beasts.

"Lady Claudia Delfeyre!" A voice boomed from the back of the shop. A man dressed in fine silks hurried toward them. A grin was half hidden by the bristles of his moustache and beard.

"Hello Ettore," Claudia said, as she returned the smile and allowed the merchant to kiss her hand. "It has been too long."

"And this is?" Ettore asked, as he looked to Elise.

"Elise," the girl cut in. "Elise Delafyre."

The man nodded, "Your ward."

"My niece," Claudia corrected.

"That I am." Elise cocked her head and fought back the urge to smirk. Ettore took her hand and placed a kiss open her skin.

"Charmed. I was sorry to hear about your parents' passing."

"Thank you," Elise replied. "And you are?"

The merchant took a step back and gave a theatrical bow. "Ettore Leonora, at your service," he introduced himself. "Purveyor of fine gowns and costumes, games, and masks to astonish."

Elise ran her hand along the edge of a stall as she made her way deeper into the shop.

"So I see," she said. "Tell me, Ettore, were you aware that there are two men watching your shop?"

The merchant's eyes widened as his gaze went from niece to aunt. "Oh, she's good," Ettore said with a grin. "They're mine. Mercenaries from Kiriador. Battle hardened against those dreadful pirates. Can't be too careful these days, not with the Nightingale flitting about."

"I take it that you are not inspired by him then?"

"What I think does not matter," Ettore shrugged as he replied. "The truth of it is that our ever-loving aristocracy are nervous and with good cause. They hold their families close and their purses closer still. The thief has created a spark among the poorer of our city, and their blood had warmed. What the future holds we do not know. As long as he stays clear of me and my customers… everybody's happy."

Elise bit her lip as she took up a black half mask. It was one with a long beak protruding from its front. She held it in front of her face. Nothing but her eyes and chin peaked out from behind the mask.

"And what if I am the Nightingale, come to deceive you?" Elise told him.

Ettore blinked and then roared with laughter. He turned to her aunt.

"I tell you Claudia, she reminds me of you at her age."

"That's what I'm scared of," the lady replied, and graced her niece with a wink. "Why do I have the feeling that your flare for the dramatic will get you killed?"

"Well I did grow up in a circus," Elise scowled, and rolled her eyes as she put the bird mask back.

"I take it that you're here for the magister's masquerade?" Ettore asked.

Claudia nodded.

"Well then," he said and clapped his meaty hands. "I have no doubt that you are prepared. However, I may have something for your niece."

"Oh?" Elise looked up as Ettore vanished into the back of the store.

The merchant returned after a few moments with a small lacquer box. He placed it on the bench and opened its lid, revealing a beautiful half mask within. Brilliant red coated its top half and nose, while ivory shone below. Gold ringed the eyes and ran around the mask's edges in swirling patterns.

"The red will bring out the blue of your eyes," Ettore told her.

"It's magnificent," Elise breathed, as she gazed at it.

It was elegant, graceful, a far cry from the simple black mask that she wore as the Nightingale.

"Let me see you put it on," Ettore said, as he gestured to his creation with a smile.

Elise bit back her grin, as she placed the mask over her face. It fitted perfectly, with its lining soft upon her skin. Claudia bound the red, white, and gold ribbons behind her niece's head. Elise turned to face her aunt.

"Perfect," Claudia murmured. "In every sense of the word. You have outdone yourself, Ettore."

The sun was low when Elise and her aunt returned from the bazzar. They dined, and then Elise found her bed. She feigned sleep until Halina had left. The moon had risen to its peak when she rolled from her bed. The orange glow of a freshly lit candle broke the darkness. She made her way over to her green cloak and withdrew the nobleman's coin purse. Elise tossed it upwards and caught it in a single hand with a satisfied smile. It was filled with gold and silver. Not as much as she had taken from the shipmaster's house, and the banker's before that, but each coin raised her coffers.

Elise took up her candle holder and walked to the far end of her room. She crouched by the wall and ran her hand along the wooden boards that ran along its bottom. One of the small planks was loose. Elise placed the candle to the side and pried off the loose board with a small knife. She reached within and pulled forth a small chest. It was nearly full. Gold, silver, jewellery, and gemstones lay within. A small fortune. Enough to get her far from this city. She poured the coin purse into the chest. It had been meant for her and Tariq to escape Elara.

Now, it seemed, she would be alone.

Why would he leave the city with a criminal who hid behind a mask? What kind of sane person would wear the costume of the Nightingale?

A tear rolled down her cheek. It splashed onto a silver coin. First her parents and now Tariq. Elise bit her lip and brushed the tears away. She shut the chest.

It took Kyler and Alarik nearly two weeks to cross the steppe of Miera from west to east. They had been met at the border by a small company of horsemen with great suspicion. The Mierans, ever eager for bloodshed, had gone for sword and spear. Alarik had flashed the king's mark and granted them safe passage.

They were tracked from the border. A small force of horsemen never far behind. They rode from town to town on their passage east, never sparing more words than necessary with the locals. The Mierans, ever distrustful of outsiders, had no words to give anyway. Even with the phoenix mark, the two men preferred not to spend their nights in taverns and alehouses. Instead, they slept under the sky far from towns and hungry swords. By night Alarik continued to train the younger knight. They trained for an hour before first light and an hour after they stopped for the day. Kyler's skills grew, and Alarik's remained sharp.

"Master," Kyler nodded over his shoulder. "They've stopped following us."

"I know," came the reply. Alarik gestured ahead of them to the great mountains that arose. At their base sat a large fortress of stone. "And that is why. Even the pagans know that this is the arsehole of the world. They watch from their fortress in case of attack but rarely venture into the mountains. The Iribian Alps. The great gateway between Miera and the lands of the League. It was here, many years ago, that the accords were struck. The only thing that saved the imperial foothold on this end of the world."

The great wall of earth drove skyward from horizon to horizon. The sight took Kyler's breath away.

"I had not realised that mountains could grow so tall."

"That, Pisspot, is why they serve their purpose so well. The Iribian Alps are hard to cross at the best of times. In winter, the passage is unpassable. It creates a natural barrier of earth and stone between my kin and the pagans."

It took a day and a night for the companions to cross the alps, as they rode upon the narrow trail. They began to find the outposts built by the League and manned by the men of Tallis. There were patrols watching over the plains below; wary of Mieran attack. It was an exhausting ride for man and beast. Relief hit Kyler when they finally descended, but they did not stop.

Alarik wanted to push to a place of safety. One that could provide them with thick walls and a warm bed for the night. Barely a mile from the foothills, nestled against the sea, was the first of the three great cities founded by the Aureians decades ago.

"Welcome to Tallis," Sir Alarik grinned as they rode through the city gates. "Sister city to Kiriador and Elara. Sixty years ago, there was nothing here save a fledgling colony of Aureians. Now look at her. Through trade Tallis has grown strong and bears wealth beyond measure. A city to rival even the silver halls of Aureia.

Traders and merchants filled the streets and paid no heed to the two mounted warriors. Banners bearing the colours of the league blew in the breeze; three silver bands over a purple field.

Kyler's eyes showed him no lie to the boast. From the huge houses that spread for miles, to the massive keep that stood in the centre of the city, Tallis was far grander than Odrysia or even Kilgareth.

"It must be fifty... no... a hundred times the size of Adrestia," Kyler told him with an open mouth.

"At least," Alarik said, and he clapped a hand on the boy's back. "Come Pisspot, let's find a place to get *moderately* insensible around here."

The two men dismounted outside the first tavern that they found. A stableboy appeared moments later to take their weary horses away.

"So, what now?" Kyler asked, as he pulled his sword from his saddle and buckled it on.

Kyler nodded to the boy and tossed him a coin. Alarik turned to Kyler as the boy left, his teeth bared into a grin. He slapped Kyler on the cheek with a gloved hand and pointed to his pupil's face.

"Now we get a drink," he said. "And then... then we charter a ship to Elara."

TWENTY-ONE

Duchy of Salazar, Medea

Sakkar Alsahra ran a finger down Sabra's soft neck. The hawk made not a sound as the Larissan stroked her. They had been in the saddle for two weeks now and, under Bellec's lead, had kept a constant pace. He knew these lands well, as did those among his company.

They rarely travelled down main roads, riding across the countryside instead. It was faster, and spared them questions that would come with the frequent patrols. Their journey though Medea had begun well enough. Upon leaving Salvaar, Jaimye and a pair of the Medeans had ridden for Bandujar to gather supplies and, more importantly, new clothing for Aeryn.

The raven-haired girl had once worn the pelts and furs of her people. She now wore leather boots, dark breeches, and a white shirt. She had rolled up the sleeves and wore a sleeveless brown gambeson over the garb. Kitara's knife was sheathed through her belt, while a long, hooded cloak of dark green completed the look. The moonseer, now clean of woad, had tied her hair back loosely. With her bow strapped to her saddlebags alongside Kiatar's sword, to the untrained eye she no longer looked Salvaari. Instead, she appeared as nothing more than a companion to the mercenaries and would perhaps pass as one from a distance. If need be, she could pull up the hood to hide her face.

Sakkar raised his arm and sent Sabra soaring into the sky high above. The land before them was beginning to paint itself orange as the sun dipped.

"We have just crossed into Salazar lands," Sakkar said.

"Aye," replied Bellec. "In fourteen days, we will reach the crossing at Sadsworth. That is our road."

"Then Larissa," Sakkar murmured, stroking his mount's neck. "Home."

"Each step we take is the furthest I have been from mine," Aeryn said. "I am glad that you will soon be reunited with your own."

"Two years. Two long years," Sakkar replied. "An eternity."

The company found a place to camp and soon fires sparked to life.

"When we cross the mountains and make for Larissa, what road do you suggest?" Bellec asked, sitting beside Sakkar. "I have travelled in your land many times, yet I have only known the north."

Sakkar thought for a moment. "To travel the northern roads would be to risk rebel attack," he said.

"The rebels we have fought before," added Galadayne.

"Perhaps," Sakkar replied. "Yet now they are a dying breed. Queen Reshada and her alliance with Darius of Aureia has all but broken them. They are cornered dogs and have become more potent because of it."

Aeryn's silver eyes flicked up at the mention of the emperor's name. She bared her teeth. "Your Queen knowingly has forged ties to the empire?" she said. "The same empire that now marches on my home? My people?"

"You don't understand. Reshada does not crave war," Sakkar told her.

Aeryn stared at him, anger burning brightly in her gaze. "But the empire–"

"But the empire," Bellec cut in, "for all its evils, has a hundred times as much good."

"How can you say that?" the moonseer snarled.

"I can see how easy it would be for you and your people to hate them all," the mercenary said. "Believe me, I do understand after everything they have done. The silver army, their emperor, all of it. Much can be said about the empire, but they are not the bloodthirsty conquerors that many believe them to be."

There was pain in the moonseer's face as she replied, "Much of my forefathers' blood was shed when the empire came to destroy us and cast us from our land."

"Was it not the assassinations which led to the inquisition which became the war?" Galadayne questioned. "Mathias Bailon. Solan Aloys. Dozens more. Not to mention the emperor's kin. All dead. All killed at negotiations that would have stopped the war before it ever began."

"I do not believe that," Aeryn replied. "The man who sat upon your southern throne was a demon haunting this plain."

"There is rumour that it was not Cardinal Octavan who sent the southern armies to the north," Jaimye added. "That Emperor Janus was blinded by grief and rage. That he commanded the bloodshed that followed. But Darius, on the other hand, is a different animal all together. Under him, the empire is peaceful."

"Its people are no better or worse than any of ours," Kompton added. "They love and hate, laugh and dance. And the festivals, ah! A glorious place is Aureia."

Aeryn ground her teeth, "And yet now they march on my home. Many thousands of them."

"They follow orders," Bellec muttered. "Like all good soldiers do."

"I am sorry," she replied bitterly. "But that is not enough."

Sakkar looked from face to face. Pain, anger, tension; he saw it all.

"Pah!" the Larissan clapped his hands. "We dwell on darkness too long. My wife, Senya, though her mother was Aureian, has more of the desert in her veins than most who were born in my country. In just a few weeks you shall enjoy the hospitality of my kin, feasting and dancing under a sea of lights."

He turned to Aeryn. "You are in for a grand spectacle. At night the stars illuminate everything from horizon to horizon, and the sands come alive with song."

Jaimye leaned forward, grinning. "What of the women?" he asked. "Tell us of them as well."

Sakkar chuckled. "Where I come from, the southlands, there are women of such beauty that you would be willing to die for them."

"Then I should like to meet them all," Jaimye replied.

"But would they want to meet you?" Kompton said.

"Piss yourself, bard," Jaimye clapped his friend on the shoulder.

Sakkar raised his eyebrows, "Not interested, friend?"

"Far from it," Galadayne answered for Kompton. "Our bard here is in love."

"That so?"

The bard grinned, "In love, spellbound, ah, the heart yearns!"

Aeryn glanced at the musician. "How does a bard join paths with soldiers of coin?" she asked.

"Those stories are both one and the same," Kompton told her. "Though I am as Annoran as my brothers, it may surprise you that we first crossed paths a little over a year ago in the court of the Larissan queen."

He started to pluck the chords of his lute.

"It is quite a merry tale," the bard said.

Kompton stamped his foot and clapped a hand on the side of his lute three times. His fingers moved, and then its music began to echo across the Medean plains.

"Summoned west by the Lotus Queen,
a humble bard for all to be seen.
With revelry and much delight,
was the court at once set alight!

By song and tale and a cup of ale,
the queen did astound at the bard's travail!
In the lotus court did I sing,
while noble lord and queen were revelling!
Kings and dukes from afar did gather beneath the
　　desert stars,
to witness the union of north and south,
whose tales of romance would spread from mouth
　　to mouth.

Though the queen and the griffin did dance,
the bard spared them both not a glance!
Through the night of revelry,
his eyes were taken by a sight to cure his soul's
　　disease!
From Torosa did the minstrel hail,
of copper eyes and a face of art,
with a smile that shone, and hair o' gold,
the woman sang and captured my heart!

Then we shared a cup o' wine, her laugh of beauty
　　and smile so fine,
I looked her in those eyes that night and said that
　　she was my heart's delight!
A scream came, a woman's plight, as the queen was
　　captured in the night!
Knights did rise and swords were drawn, as the
　　griffin blew his mighty horn,
they rode beneath the stars above in pursuit of the
　　lotus dove!

In the lotus court did we sing,
while noble lord and queen were revelling!
Kings and dukes from afar did gather beneath the
　　desert stars,

to witness the union of north and south,
whose tales of romance would spread from mouth
    to mouth!

A saviour's song begins this night
as the hero of Reyna heard the plight!
He followed bard and minstrel both
as the songmakers heard the sound of an oaf!
With devil's horns and eyes of fire, did the captors
    state their desire,
or the romance of griffin and lotus to expire!

They captured me as I tried to free the queen, with
    swords of steel and faces mean,
tied me up and sent me forth, falling for the deep
    ravine!
It was then that the hero's bow did sound,
sending the devil to the ground!
He caught my hand and stopped the fall,
freed the queen and sounded his call!
But the captor took his back,
drew a knife and with a whack,
the minstrel's lute resounded from its head and
    sent the devil to its bed!

In the lotus court did we sing,
while noble lord and queen were revelling!
Kings and dukes from afar did gather beneath the
    desert stars,
to witness the union of north and south,
whose tales of romance would spread from mouth
    to mouth!
Bound together were bard and mercenary,
until the day they would escape the shackles and
    be free!

For a desert oath chained the bard to a life of
   swords and travels hard!
Back to Torosa did the minstrel head,
a kiss so sweet that tears were shed.

She'd wait for me is what she said,
yet still I ride with the hero
until I stop his blood from being shed!"

The men cheered their approval as Kompton's song ended. The final sounds of his lute faded into the night.

"A great tale!" Sakkar roared. He had heard tale of the celebration that had marked the alliance between Queen Reshada of Larissa and Darius of Aureia. He had heard how the rebels had attempted to abduct the queen to stamp out the idea of friendship between kingdom and empire. "I have shed my own shackles weeks past, friend," Sakkar continued. "Soon enough you will be able to follow your heart's desire and find your minstrel."

"What is her name?" the moonseer asked. "The woman with copper eyes." Kompton gave a smile as he looked to the stars above.

"Her name is Bryanna."

Aeryn nudged Bellec, her silver gaze not leaving the bard, as she whispered, "Is it true? The song?"

"Perhaps half, but it didn't happen like that," he chuckled, and handed her a drinking skin. "Here."

The Salvaari grinned and took the drink. She raised it to her lips and barely noticed the eyes of the mercenaries flick to her. Her eyes widened as the foul taste hit her. Aeryn spat the vile liquid into the dirt, and the mercenaries roared with laughter.

"What was that?" Aeryn coughed.

"That was wine," Bellec explained with a chuckle.

"That was foul," she snapped, whacking the wineskin into Bellec's chest. She raised her eyebrows at her laughing companions.

"How do you drink this?"

Jaimye snatched the skin from his leader and downed its contents in a single draught. "An acquired taste," he laughed.

Out of the corner of her eye she saw some of the mercenaries exchange coin. *Had she been part of some wager?*

Bellec turned to Galadayne and sent a nod toward his second. The other former royal guardsman rose to his feet with a clap.

"Alright lads, that's enough for tonight," Galadayne told them. "We could all do with some sleep. Bard, since you have energy to spare, you have first watch."

They rose before the sun and ate a breakfast of salted meat and bread. Dawn's first rays had begun to creep over the horizon, when they mounted their horses and began their journey west.

The shrill cry of a hawk came from above as Sabra circled high in the heavens. Sakkar frowned. The bird had been his companion for many years. He knew that cry and the warning that it foretold.

"Something is wrong," he called down the line, angling his horse toward the slope of a hill. He kicked his heels in and galloped up onto the ridge. He raised an arm as his eyes widened. Sabra dove from the sky and landed upon the proffered roost. Sakkar felt a familiar chill run down his spine.

"What is it?" Bellec shouted as he charged up the hill with Aeryn and Galadayne hot on his tail. Sakkar pursed his lips as they joined him atop the ridge. His eyes stared far into the distance.

A great line of soldiers and steel marched westward across the plain; standards fluttering in the wind. There were *thousands* of them.

"Salazar is on the march," Aeryn murmured. Sakkar could hear the agony in her voice, though he knew it was about more than just the host that lay before them.

"No, not just Salazar," Bellec said. "Those banners bear the black tiger of Reyna. See there," he said and gestured to the head of the army, "the stag of Salazar. A welcoming party for Duke

Anejo Reyna. The houses are uniting."

"So it would seem," Aeryn murmured, and she bit her lip. She was unable to tear her eyes away from the terrible sight before them.

"Where do they march?"

Bellec shrugged before he replied, "By my guess they will be headed for Sergova and an alliance with Alejandro Aloys."

"Medea is come," the moonseer said, and she looked from the soldiers westward toward Vesuva and Kitara. "My people must be warned... they will expect to face Aloys and Bailon alone. But not this. In this land I am torn. My heart, my *soul*, call me west. But my people... they cannot go unwarned."

It was Bellec who spoke first. A reply fell from his lips less than a heartbeat after Aeryn had spoken.

"Nor will they. Though I was not born in Salvaar, though I do not share your blood, those trees are more my home than Aethela ever was. Anejo Reyna is my friend, but this goes beyond friendship."

His fingers drifted to his own sapphire ring. The mercenary did not mention the jewel, but its meaning was clear.

"If I have to choose between helping a friend and honouring the memory of Oriana, then that is an easy choice."

Bellec turned in his saddle toward his men.

"Hadwin, Layan, our paths split here. Ride for Salvaar. Tell them what we have seen. Tell them that the might of Medea is marshalling against them."

The pair of Annorans looked to their leader.

"And after that?" Hadwin asked.

"Find the chief of the Aedei. Stay at his side..." Bellec again turned his gaze to the sea of steel. The mighty horde would only grow. "... and pray."

Kitara's arms ached. For the better part of a day she, along with her companions, had been hauled through the Aureian wilderness by cart. The road was full of bumps, and they felt *everything*. Having their hands tied behind their backs only made the journey worse.

The Salvaari talked quietly among themselves. They did nothing to arouse suspicion or provoke the lash of a whip, yet they were anything but resigned to their fate. There was still fire in their eyes. They would not be slaves. They would not bow and scrape at the whim of another. The canvas covering the wagon shrouded them from the sight of their captors. All Kitara knew of the outside world was that their guard had almost doubled thanks to the slavers from Belona.

"When we reach the city," Morlag muttered, looking from the face of one kinsman to another, "we may have but one chance to be rid of these binds. We are not slaves who obey the will of our master. We are free men. The lifeblood of Salvaar roars through our veins and burns deeply in all of us. I say that we cannot be tamed or broken. Sylvaine made us strong, made us who we are. We are wild. We are strong. Káli to the bone. Once the outside world feared us, and so they will again. It is time that we remind them who we are, and why they are right to be afraid. No matter if Tanris greets me through the Veil... I will be free of chains. In this life or the next."

The Káli grumbled in agreement.

"We are with you, Morlag," one of them spoke. "For the spirits. For freedom. To the death."

"Then it *will* be death," Kitara muttered, leaning forward from the bars of the cage. "They are the many. We are the few."

"Are you afraid?" the Káli man asked.

Kitara shook her head and bared her teeth. When she spoke her words were as true as her heart. "No. I do not fear them. I do not fear death. I would live, and not fight when there is only one outcome. We will be unarmed, our hands bound while they have sword and spear. It will be the end."

"And it will be glorious," Morlag grinned savagely.

Kitara wiggled away from the bars. "And what if I was to give you another solution?" she said. "One that would stop you from recklessly throwing your lives away?"

"Explain," Morlag frowned.

The woman shuffled and showed her back to the Káli. She almost smiled at the silence that followed.

"How?" one of the Káli breathed, as he saw the brooch in her hand. It was long and sharp, and now she slowly edged it through the rope that bound her.

"In Belona," Kitara replied. "From that woman at the dock."

"The spirits have smiled upon us," Morlag said. "And I for one will *not* turn my back on them."

"Then tonight we at last meet our fate," Kitara said.

TWENTY-TWO

Isle of Agartha, the Valkir Isles

"War?" Astrid frowned, as she spoke to the messenger. "With whom?"

"With Salvaar," the man replied, glancing from the jarl to Earl Arndyr. "I trade in pelts and furs. Each year I travel to Valentia upon the coast. Two legions were passing through, headed north. Another has left Larissa, while a fourth will travel by sea. They say that the cardinal has called the faithful to arms. They say that Annora and Medea stand ready. That the Order of Kil'kara will soon leave their mountain fortress."

Astrid let out a breath, before looking to her companion as he spoke.

"That is not all, is it?" Arndyr asked.

The man clasped his hands behind his back. "No, it's not," he said. "His Imperial Majesty, Emperor Darius, leads them. I saw him myself, mounted on a stallion black as night, his armour silver and gold. Surrounded by a sea of silver and purple."

"The Arkin Garter," Earl Arndyr murmured.

"Yes lord, hundreds of them," the trader replied. "There are rumours that Cardinal Aleksander himself has left Rovira with a company of knights." He fell silent as he looked around the hall. His eyes flicked between the faces of all present. Erik, Torben, Nenrir, and Laerke watched on, their faces awash with emotion. Pride, anger, sorrow, but not fear. Never fear. Arndyr turned to Astrid.

"If the cardinal rides, then the southern Order rides with him," he said. "Not just his guard, but Grand Master Bavarian himself."

"Bavarian?" Astrid asked.

"I met him long ago when he was merely a knight," the earl told her. "Even then he was a great leader and a cunning warrior. His brothers loved him, as did the man who sat on the silver throne before him. Astrid, the master of the south commands the entire Order. And you say that they march for Salvaar?"

The trader nodded as he spoke, "They say that an artefact has been found. The blade of one of their gods. A fairy tale. Aureian madness."

Chuckles echoed through the great hall. Astrid held up a hand to silence the raucous.

"All superstition, every fairy tale, has some truth to it. Do not be so fast to dismiss it," she said, as she rose to her feet and looked to the trader. "Thank you, my friend. My hearth is your hearth. Eat and drink your fill."

The man bowed in gratitude before he made his way from the hall.

"What are you thinking?" Erik asked Astrid.

"The south is united, and with their northern allies at their side Salvaar will fall," Astrid told him. "That much is certain. I have never met any of the Salvaari, nor even stepped foot on land more than a mile from the coast, yet I have heard tell of their bravery. But bravery alone cannot win a war. Not against such odds."

"Ever since the fall of Delios none have been able to resist the silver army," Torben replied with a snort.

Arndyr Scaeva curled his lips as he countered, "Perhaps if Gaedhela's sons had not been so war hungry, then Aureia would not have been forced to intervene."

"Intervene?" Torben's replied. "When the Delion armies tore each other apart it was only then that Aureia got involved and took their land. Just another piece for the empire."

"Oh enough," Astrid sent a glare toward the two old warriors as she spoke. "We are not here to talk about a nation that fell a century ago. Empires rise and fall, but the Valkir, we survive."

"If we are to survive then we should fight," Erik started as he walked into their midst. "If Salvaar falls, how long will be it before the swords of Aureia turn to us?"

"Darius would not bring war to our shores," Arndyr retorted.

"And why is that exactly?" Torben cut in. "Because you once stood as brothers? We all know how the empire treats its neighbours. Like Salvaar, we are no more than pagans to its leaders."

"Then we must show them that we are not what they fear us to be," Arndyr replied with a shrug. "What do you say Astrid? It is to you that Agartha looks, and if you choose war many of the Isles will join you."

Astrid closed her eyes and turned away from her companions. She had long since stopped caring for the outside world, yet now the world called to her.

"Can I not have peace?" she murmured. "After everything that has happened, everything we have lost, I don't want to raid. I don't want to fight. I am tired. I have seen enough bloodshed to last two lifetimes. Now I am asked to take up axe and shield. I am done with that. All of you do what you will. If the sword calls to you then take it. But I will sail south nonetheless."

The wagon rolled slowly down the road, heaved on by the slavers' horses. Mercenary, knight, and slave master talked absentmindedly as the hooves of their mounts churned the ground, adding to the crunching sound caused by the heavy wheels upon the earth. Kitara worked the brooch; it slowly picked apart the rope that bound her hands. Fibres split and her hands burst free. The Káli looked to her with hope in their eyes. They talked as if nothing had changed, adding to the wall of sound that masked Kitara's work. She slid across the wooden surface of the wagon and turned her attention to her companions' bindings. One by one, they were freed. Still, the Káli did not move. Morlag's bindings fell away. He rubbed his wrists and gave Kitara a nod as she moved to Sereia. Kitara smiled at the girl as she freed her.

"When we get out there will be fighting," she whispered. "Find someplace to hide. I *will* find you."

The girl met her eyes and gave a solemn bow. She was brave and strong. Stronger than any child should ever have to be. Her parents were gone and these few in the wagon were all she had left. Kitara brushed Sereia's cheek and pushed back a lock of dark hair. If she died for this girl then so be it. In this moment Sereia was all she cared about.

"Now hold me," Kitara said and pulled her into a hug. "Like a sister."

Sereia wrapped her small arms around the older girl. She squeezed tightly, as if she were afraid Kitara would vanish. The wagon shuddered to a halt. Kitara took a breath and released the girl from her embrace. Her green eyes flicked to the entrance of the cage.

She set her jaw.

Be like water.

Kitara slithered to the end of the cell and jammed the brooch into the lock. She pursed her lips. There was a click. The Káli made ready. Their faces were still marked with black, just as they had been when they were taken. They were ready to die for their freedom.

"Tanris, I come to you," Morlag murmured in his own tongue.

The canvas flap was pulled open.

Before the mercenary's eyes could widen, before his face could pale in surprise, Kitara was on him. She leapt forward and drove her full weight into the man. He stumbled and they crashed to the ground. Kitara tore the warrior's knife free from his belt and drove it deep into his heart. A scream left his lips as he died.

The Káli charged from the wagon with savage cries upon their lips. Kitara didn't hesitate. She ripped the dagger free and launched it into the chest of the next man. He cried out as she rose to her feet and took up the second man's mace.

The steel ball crushed the next man's skull and the slaver fell. He was dead before he hit the ground. Kitara freed his sword of its sheath and pulled the bloody knife from his body. She took a breath as her trained senses took in everything. It was nearly dark, and the setting sun painted the land orange. They had taken their guard by surprise, and now many of the Káli stood armed. Mercenaries and slavers on foot and horseback swarmed them. Kitara saw Morlag leap into the air and barrel into a mounted man. He tackled the slaver to the ground and took his life with a dagger. She swivelled as she heard heavy boots upon the earth. A mercenary came at her, the blade of his spear driving toward her face. Kitara slid back and parried the polearm with her sword. Anger lit his eyes as he came at her again.

Kitara slipped to the side, deflecting the blow and stepping inside his strength. The mercenary tried to move aside, but he was too slow. Her dagger came down. It ripped through the flesh of his neck and drove deep into his body. The spear fell from nerveless fingers as blood washed over Kitara's hands, then she was gone. She twirled away as a new opponent came to avenge his dying companion. His sword came toward her as she moved. She parried the blade with her dagger and forced it aside, as her own sword came around to carve a path through the second man's jaw. Her knife left his blade and slid across his throat. Another spear came at her as she spun through the carnage. She blocked once, twice. Kitara switched her knife to a backhand grip. The man barrelled into her and tried to send her off balance.

Kitara skipped back lightly, and her stance could not be broken. She leapt to the side as steel was thrust toward her chest. Her hands came together, locking her sword and knife as she deflected the spear. The backhanded dagger drove forth as she countered. Her backswing turned into a thrust and the knife was embedded in the slaver's neck. He crashed to the ground in a pool of his own blood. A Salvaari slammed into her side with a cry and heaved her out of the path of a thrown spear. The steel blade sank into the Salvaari's chest and ripped out his back. The force of the blow sent him crashing to the ground.

He had saved her life.

There was no time to think as a sword was drawn by the man's killer. A knight. Kitara met his eyes. Beneath the helmet and armour stood the same man from the Lioness. The one she had nearly slain. He wanted revenge. The longsword came toward her, but she was ready. Kitara slid back and knocked the blade aside before she thrust at the man's eyes. He turned his head to allow steel to slide harmlessly across his helm. The move saved his life but took his vision. Kitara danced forward as the sword came up blindly. She ducked and parried the blade over her head as she moved, stepping in close as her sword met with his. She slid inside his reach long enough to slice the edge of her blade across his unprotected thigh.

Kitara danced back as he countered and raised her blade. Steel hit steel. The knight levelled his sword. She followed his every move, matched him step for step. He lunged to the left. She moved to counter, sliding back as he came on. It was a feint. The knight changed direction, flicking his wrists and thrusting away from her defence. Kitara read him like a book. Her arms moved and her muscles tightened. Steel rang as she parried. Kitara spun inside his reach as he swung. She ducked the blade as it sliced over her head. Her dagger came up. Steel glinted in the orange light, and then it drove deep into the knight's jaw. The man had no time to shout or scream. Bone splintered and then the steel slid into his brain. Tears of blood poured as Kitara tore her blade free.

The knight's sword fled his nerveless fingers as he crashed down into the mud.

Out of the corner of her eye, she saw a mercenary hurling a halberd. It was sharp and its aim true. Kitara threw her arms up to defend herself as she leapt aside. Her sword deflected the weapon from her chest, but it cracked hard into her wrists. The blades missed, yet the halberd tore her sword from her hands. Then the man was on her with a sword that longed for her blood. He snarled and drove his weapon toward her. She had no time to think and lashed out with an arm. She hit the shaft of his blade and forced it to the side. The blade missed by an inch. Kitara heaved with her aching arm and dove toward him. Her dagger found his leg as he moved to avoid her. The slaver topped over with a scream and then she was upon him. The blade drove down between his ribs. Blood splashed across her face. It was all she could smell. All she could taste.

Kitara rose with ragged breath, clutching the crimson-stained knife tightly. The ground was covered in the bodies of the Salvaari and their enemy, abandoned in the mud. She saw Sir Rowan cut down one of the Káli before thrusting his sword toward the wagon.

"TAKE THE GIRL!" he cried.

NO! Kitara turned to the cart as Rowan and a pair of his knights charged toward the wagon.

"SEREIA! RUN!" she screamed.

The knights closed in. Morlag appeared before them, a bloody spear in hand. He thrust steel toward them, but the knights did not fear it. The spear was blocked twice; before Sir Rowan deflected it into the mud. Sir Rowan stepped forward and his sword sliced across the Káli's chest. Morlag fell to his knees. Sereia jumped from the wagon. Kitara's legs burned. One of the knights turned to her. Rowan's shield smashed into the side of Morlag's head. The Káli's limp form toppled over as darkness took him.

"Take her!" Sir Rowan roared, charging after Sereia.

His companion reached out with an armoured hand. There was a scream. Kitara reached the first knight. Steel came toward her. Kitara danced to the left and sent a feint his way, sliding to the right. The knight made to thrust. She had one opening.

One chance.

Kitara took it. She hurled the knife at the man's face. He turned away on instinct and raised his sword to block. It was enough. The blade glanced off his pauldron. Kitara dashed passed him and skipped aside as he lashed out blindly.

"CAPTAIN!" he bellowed.

A cry lit the air as Sereia was caught. The rough hand of a knight held her tight by her hair. Tears streamed down her cheeks as she was tossed to the ground. Sir Rowan, warned by his companion, turned to her. He tossed his shield aside.

Kitara, armed with nothing but her bare hands, charged him. If she died here, so be it. She ducked beneath his thrust. Her every thought turned toward Sereia. She had promised to protect her. The thought gave her strength.

Sir Rowan braced as she tackled him into the side of the wagon. The cart stopped his fall, yet Kitara was ready. She tore the knight's knife free from his belt. The steel was hungry for blood as Kitara drove it toward its master's throat. He did not hesitate, nor try to free the blade. Rowan jammed his chin down into his chest. The knife glanced off the knight's helmet. The hilt of Rowan's sword crunched into the side of her head. Kitara staggered. His left hand grabbed at her throat, and with a heave, the knight slammed her into the wagon.

Kitara's vision blurred as her head cracked into the bars. The knife fell from her fingers. A trail of blood rolled from the corner of her lips as she felt the sticky edge of his sword come to rest against her neck. Her hand snatched feebly at the arm that held her. She bared her teeth as Rowan drew closer. His blazing eyes were reflected in her own.

"I warned you," he snarled.

Kitara grimaced as she tried to turn to Sereia. "I will *not* die a slave," she swore.

Sir Rowan roared and cast her down onto the earth. Kitara looked up from the mud to see what remained of her people. Only seven still drew breath. They were surrounded by the slavers, bereft of weapon and hope. Morlag had regained consciousness, yet he still lay in the earth with blood weeping from his body. A knight stood over him, pressing a spear to his chest.

There was still fight in Morlag's gaze. Kitara gritted her teeth and struggled to rise. She swayed and felt blood flow through her teeth. She met Sereia's eyes. The girl trembled in her captor's grasp, but the fear in Sereia's face was gone and the tears had stopped. Her cheeks were wet and there was a dagger at her neck, yet she stood with pride. Kitara glared at the knights. Her anger fuelled the fire that burned in her veins.

Hands grabbed her arms and she was driven to her knees. The mercenaries held her tight as she struggled. Sir Rowan looked to the man who held Sereia and nodded. Kitara's blood froze. Her heart stopped. Sereia did not look away from her face. The knight adjusted his grip on the knife.

"No!" shouted Kitara. She fought against the men who held her. "Please! PLEASE!" She was unable to control the emotions that burned within. She had failed the Káli. She had failed Sereia. A tear spilled from her eye.

"Halt!"

The voice stopped the hungry knife. A man rode over. The rich clothing of an Aureian covered his body. He held a bloody shortsword in his hand. He slid from his saddle and strode toward the knight that held Sereia.

"Release the girl," he commanded.

"Master Ilario," Sir Rowan began, unable to hide the bitterness in his tone, "I warned them–"

"I said release her," the older man snapped. "Or would you kill a child? A child that *belongs* to Magister Valliro. I would not see my employer's coin so easily thrown away."

Rowan grimaced.

"Aye, Sir," he said and nodded to his man to put down the knife.

"Now make them ready," the slave master growled and gestured to the Káli. "And this time, *captain*, do not let them escape. The magister has lost enough gold on this venture."

The knight released Sereia as Kitara was shoved into the dirt. The girl barrelled across the open ground toward her friend. Kitara pushed herself to her knees in time to throw her arms around Sereia. She felt the girl tremble in her grasp.

"I'm sorry," Kitara murmured, as she held Sereia tight. "I'm so sorry."

TWENTY-THREE

City of Palen-Tor, Aethela, Kingdom of Annora

Dorian Raynor, High Lord of Aethela and King of Annora, walked slowly through the palace gardens. It was the afternoon, and the birds were singing. It only added to the beauty and serenity of the colour that stretched around him. All the flowers, shrubs, and trees had been meticulously looked after by the palace gardeners. What had once been bare stone and earth, was now a place of peace and contemplation. No soldiers or servants were in sight, and so he could at last shed the mantle that weighed so heavily upon his shoulders.

"Tell me, my king–" the woman at his side began.

"No," the king cut her off. He turned to the Medean woman at his side. The sun glistened on her ebony hair and made her hazel eyes dance. "Here, I am just Dorian."

Eveline Ayria, friend to prince Dayne's wife, Sofia, and now confidant to the Annoran ruler, smiled. "Dorian," she said, as she allowed the name to roll from her lips.

Eveline ran a thumb across the bright scarlet petals of a rose. "This place has many pleasures, yet when one walks though the stone corridors of Palen-Tor... a garden as beautiful as this is most unexpected."

Dorian chuckled softly as she turned back to him, and the skirts of her yellow dress brushed the soft earth beneath. For the hundredth time he wondered how she was not cold. For like the rest of her people, the light cotton dress that Eveline wore was sleeveless and backless. It was as though their land had nothing but summer.

"When I was a boy, this garden did not exist," Dorian said.

Eveline gave him a sidelong glance, "Oh?"

"My father, gods rest him, was a simple man who needed nothing," Dorian said, plucking a rose from its bush. "You see, a rose, for all its beauty, has no practical use. You cannot use a flower for a sword. For many years, I believed him. Yet as I have grown older, I have come to find a kind of serenity within the beauty of it all."

He held the rose out to his companion. She took it and ran her gaze over the flower.

"I find that their short-lived beauty holds more than that. It reminds me that we are no more than human," Eveline said. "We, like flowers, are born, live, and die far more swiftly than we intend. I believe that in the brief time we walk this earth we are here to do more than just exist. We are here to *live*. To enjoy all the fruits within the gods' garden and to sate each and every desire that you feel."

Dorian met her eyes as she slowly, almost tentatively, placed her hand upon his arm. Her smile faded, but there was something else in her gaze. Something that called to Dorian. She was young, and strong, and *filled* with life. Just as he had once been.

"My king!" a man's voice broke the silence.

Eveline's hand vanished from his arm as Dorian turned to face the newcomer. The rough voice belonged to the Annoran general, a man whom the king had known since boyhood.

"What is it, Tristayn?" he asked with a frown.

"They were spotted at the edge of the forest."

"Who?" Dorian squared his jaw as his peace was shattered. The king had once more returned.

"Your son," Tristayn Martyn told him. "Prince Dayne has returned."

"Mother!"

Dayne willed his lips to smile, as his sister leapt into the queen's waiting arms.

Riona hugged her daughter tight. "Kassandra," she whispered.

"I'm sorry," the princess cried. "I'm so, so sorry."

"You have *nothing* to be sorry about," Riona said, as she cupped Kassie's cheeks in her hands and stared into her daughter's eyes. "You're home now. Everything will be alright."

The queen hugged her again and looked to Dayne. "Thank you," the queen murmured.

The prince nodded to Riona as he watched the reunion. He loved them both dearly and would die for either of them and yet, as always, he struggled to show that emotion. The prince had thought to take his sister straight to the king and his court, yet she was just a child. Her mother and the comfort of her room was all she needed.

"My queen," was his only reply, as he bowed to his stepmother.

Riona kissed her daughter on the cheek as they broke apart. Tears of joy threatened to spill from her eyes. She looked Kassandra up and down and noticed for the first time the rough, travel-stained, Salvaari garb.

"What happened, Kassie? Where did you go?"

The prince left before words could leave his sister's mouth. He had seen to his sister and delivered her safely to her mother. The corridors and walls of Palen-Tor seemed out of a story to the prince as he wound his way through them. For over a month he had seen little more than forests, plains, and green grasslands. Now all he saw was cold stone.

Yet he had grown up in the castle and could navigate it blindfolded. He had not yet seen his father, the king, nor changed from his armour. Yet before he could, there was something he needed to do. The prince pulled off his rough leather gloves and shoved them into his swordbelt as he walked. The oaken door arose before him, and with a turn and a push, the prince flung it open.

"Dayne…"

There she was, sitting at the end of the bed, her eyes shining with happiness. Sofia shot to her feet and was in his arms before her name had crossed his lips.

"Sofia," he murmured, as he squeezed his wife. His love. The curls of her dark hair tickled his cheek, and her scent filled his breath. The scent of flowers. It *intoxicated* him. They broke apart and he kissed her deeply.

"I have missed you," she said and placed her hands upon his armoured chest.

"You have been in my dreams," Dayne told her, as finally his lips twitched into a smile.

Her hazel eyes met his sapphire gaze. Longing, love, desire, joy… it was all written in her face.

"There is something I must tell you," she said, taking half a step backward.

Dayne's hands did not leave her own.

"What has changed?" Dayne asked.

Sofia said nothing. Instead, she placed his hand upon her belly. His gaze drifted down and flicked straight back up.

"You're…"

"I'm with child," she laughed and dragged him back into an embrace.

The prince said nothing. He just held her. He could feel her smile against his cheek. Fire entered his belly and he felt alive.

"Say something," Sofia said, as she closed her eyes and leaned into her husband.

"I did not even know that I could be this happy," Dayne told her and ran a hand through her hair.

"Forgive me, Prince Dayne," Tristayn's voice came from the passage. "The king demands your presence."

Dayne bit back a retort as he broke off his embrace. Irritation wormed its way into him. He did not so much as look to the man. Instead, his gaze was fixed firmly upon his wife.

"Thank you, general," Dayne said before stroking his wife's cheek. "I will see you soon."

Sofia nodded as their hands held for but a moment more, before the prince followed Tristayn Martyn into the corridor.

"I am truly sorry, my prince," the general began.

Dayne held up a hand to cut him off as they walked. "No, it's alright," he replied.

"Welcome home."

It was time for Dayne to see to his duty as a prince... and as a son. They did not go to the courtroom, nor the great hall, nor even the king's chamber. Instead, it was to the castle courtyard that Dorian Raynor beckoned his son. Dayne took a breath as he descended the stairs into the yard and pulled his gloves back on. He knew what would come next. His father, king of all Annora, stood opposite with his arms crossed over his powerful chest. Only the roughly hewn band of gold atop his head separated him from the three veteran soldiers who stood with their liege lord.

"Your sword," Tristayn said as he turned to Dayne.

The prince obliged. He unbuckled his sword belt and handed it to the general.

"Welcome home, my son," Dorian called.

Dayne dropped to a knee. "Light of the gods be with you, my king."

A wooden sparring sword was thrust into his arms as he rose back to his feet. Dayne rolled his shoulders back and unclasped his scarlet cloak. It fell down onto the cold stone beneath.

"Begin," the king commanded.

The first soldier came at him. Dayne slid to face the man, and his sword flicked up into both hands. He mirrored the soldier's steps as they circled. Dayne saw the move coming before it was made.

A thrust drove toward his head as the man attacked. Wood struck wood as Dayne deflected the blow and countered hard. It forced the soldier to block and retreat as his sword was forced to the side. The blade came up and then an overhead cut came at him.

The prince deftly moved forward as the swords met. He pushed the soldier's arms to the side and slid inside his reach as his wrist rotated. The blunt edge of his blade came to rest on the man's neck.

"Begin!" the king roared for a second time.

This time it would not be one man. This time it would be both. Dayne turned and ducked as a sword drove over his head. He grabbed the blade of his weapon and sliced it *hard* across the exposed chest of his attacker. The man fell back with a grunt; the tip of Dayne's sword cracked into his shoulder. The prince moved like lightning. He spun just in time to knock the second man's blade aside. They exchanged blows. Once, twice, three times.

Dayne switched back to halfswording and held his weapon both by the hilt and blade. He caught the next attack with the blade as he stepped forward before. He spun and cracked the hilt into the soldier's jaw. The man stumbled with a shout as Dayne's weapon found the soft flesh of the back of his leg. Then it was over. Prince Dayne cast his sword aside and tossed it down onto the stones. The test was passed, as it always was.

The council chamber was cold, yet Dayne did not notice the chill. His travel-stained armour kept that at bay.

"Your skill with the sword and mind remains sharp," Dorian mentioned, as he looked to his oldest son.

"Steel hones steel," the prince replied, as he glanced down at the great table and the map upon it. "Discipline begins with the mastery of your mind. If you do not control what you think, how can you then control what you do?"

The king clapped his son on the shoulder as they walked.

"How was your journey?" Dorian asked.

"Salvaar is strange," Dayne replied with a shrug. "Those trees are silent, yet full of memory. Being there is like being trapped in a bottomless pit, unable to climb out. It truly is godless."

"Tell me of Lukas. The rider you sent spoke of a fight with Emilian Aloys."

The prince clasped his hands together.

"We had just taken Oryn from the Káli when he found us," Dayne started. "My *affliction* took my mind and body as Lukas met the boy. You once told me that alliances in Salvaar change as easily as gold changes hand, and that is a thing now known to me. In the weeks following Cailean's arrival at court, the Káli had allied themselves with his tribe. We were misled to attack the village, and Lukas took that to heart. The men say that Aloys insulted Kassandra, and that was when Lukas attacked him. They fought and when the dust settled, Lukas had lost more than just an eye… his leg as well. I had no choice but to leave him. If blood loss had not killed him on the ride, then sickness surely would have."

"He is with the Káli then?"

A shadow crossed Dorian's face. "Yes father." Dayne's gaze swept across the map and came to rest upon Salvaar. "For all their faults, honour is not one of them. They will not harm him," Dayne said.

"I know," the king sighed, as he gripped the edge of the table. "Lukas you damn fool… what have you done?" His hand went to his sword and lingered upon its hilt. "Beware snakes in the grass. Trust no one. Everyone who is not family is an enemy. Alejandro Aloys and his son chief among them," the king said.

"A necessary evil that must be endured for the greater good," Dayne nodded slowly. He thought to bite his tongue for a moment, but there was a question that had slowly seeped into his mind. It had begun to consume him in recent days.

Dayne placed a hand upon the map and moved it as he spoke, "A great many people love and respect you, Father, yet there are those who would consider you a conqueror. And while I do not believe this so, there is something that I do not understand. The three kingdoms, Caspin, Aloys… I know you well enough to know that you do all of this for more than just prize and possession."

Dayne gauged his father's reaction before he had the chance to speak. He saw the glint of pride and strength flicker across the blueness of his eyes.

"Many years ago, long before all of this, before I started down this path…" the king murmured as he planted a hand atop the kingdoms of Annora, "… I fought for glory and the reputation that came with it. I was no more than a warrior, and warriors crave war."

"What changed?"

"I married Elodie," Dorian said, and gave him a sad smile. "It was your mother who taught me that the most important thing in the world, far greater than any glory, is family. When Eldred died to a traitor's sword, when Balinor murdered my wife, my brother, and took my sisters from me… darkness came. And in that darkness, blood and fire were born. I avenged myself upon him and sat atop the throne of Laeoflaed covered in the blood of my enemy, and there at last I understood. The wars of men are meaningless. I do not care about wealth, nor even legacy. Everything that I do is to ensure that such a tragedy never occurs again. Everything that I do is to ensure that our family remains strong."

Cailean's heart broke as he walked through the ruins of Aildor. It was once a peaceful town and spiritual centre. Now it lay sundered. Houses had been torn down and burned, while the people had been left to rot in the street. As for the stone shrine to Yorath, great spirit of the sun, nothing remained but shattered rock and scorched earth. A tear slid down the chief's cheek as he saw the destruction. All among the company of Aedei and Icari were silent as they walked through Aildor. Etain placed a comforting hand upon his arm, yet the same grief was clear in her eyes. An unspoken pain.

"Annora has betrayed us," Cailean growled, and his hands whitened as they grew tense.

"The forest rages," Etain said. "I can feel it in my bones."

"After everything that we did for them, everything we suffered..." Cailean murmured. "We gave them a king."

"The spirits do not forget, my love," Etain's hand dropped to her sword as she spoke. "And soon they will send reply."

Together they waited, for *all* the chiefs were coming. A conclave would arrive with the moon.

The twelve chiefs gathered as night descended before the fallen shrine. Their anger burned so bright that it could only be dimmed by their pain. Henghis of the Catuvantuli had the fury of a wildfire within him, yet he held his anger in reserve.

"Annora shall bleed for this," cried Balor of the Sagailean, and his lips pulled back into a vicious snarl.

"They desecrated this place," Vaylin murmured, her face streaked with tears. She rose from a crouch and let a handful of ash fall from her fingers. "So many lost. Two villages sundered without cause. The spirits are in turmoil, and Yorath"– the Káli chief turned to the fallen shrine – "great spirit of the sun, weeps. The west is come."

"I fear that it has gone beyond that," Morrigana, Chief of the Belcar, growled. The wind howled and whipped through her blonde hair, as she hurled an arrow to the ground. "This was found in one of my warriors," she spat.

Cailean's eyes were drawn to the shaft as he picked it up. It was shorter than any arrow, and its tip was of broad bladed steel. He knew what it was.

"Crossbow," Cailean said.

"How?" Etain asked, as she took the bolt from Cailean and ran her eyes over it.

"Who attacks to the east?" Henghis frowned.

"*Merchants* from Tallis met our traders at the border," Eira,

Chief of the Niavenn replied. Like Morrigana, she wore crude armour over her furs.

"Many were lost," Morrigana continued, as she stepped to Eira's side. "My people, my sister's people, cut down like beasts."

"We are attacked on all sides," muttered Henghis as he finally spoke. "And not only do they kill… they come to make slaves of us all. Medea showed us that."

"They took my own brother," Vaylin bared her teeth. The chiefs turned to her. Morlag, her brother, was well known to them. He was a man of honour and fierce pride.

"I do not know if Morlag is alive or dead. That is the truth," Vaylin continued as her fingers brushed her snake fang necklace. The necklace was the twin of her brother's. Henghis placed a comforting hand upon her shoulder. Vaylin reached up and placed her own upon it.

"I shall tell you another truth," the Catuvantuli leader said, as he walked into the centre of the circle and gestured from the bolt to the ruins. "The outside world is marshalling against us. They have grown strong while we have been bickering among ourselves. They will come to Salvaar but not to take. They come to destroy us. And they will. Tribe by tribe." He raised a clenched fist to stop the outraged cries. "In the old times we were strong. We were united as one people. Catuvantuli and Aedei stood as brothers. Káli broke bread with Sagailean. So it must be again if we are to survive. We must stand together with one purpose; one army."

There was silence as his words echoed through Aildor. They could all feel it in their bones; in their very blood. The heartbeat of the forest stirred within them all. Cailean closed his eyes. He could feel the strength of his brothers, Cyneric and Malakai, flowing in his heart. He knew what he had to say.

"With one king," Cailean said as he strode forth.

"Yes," Henghis nodded. "One king."

"Then here and now, before Yorath's shrine, beneath the stars of the Veil, and under the gaze of the spirits, we must choose," Cailean's voice was strong and loud. "There is one among us who has been tested by the spirits. One among us who is ruled by his head, not his pride. He who has been willing to sacrifice his own life for honour. He whose blood bleeds with the forest. He who walks the spirits' path."

Cailean looked to the man that he spoke of and raised a hand toward him. Henghis of the Catuvantuli nodded back. His eyes blazed with light as he turned. He took in the faces of each of the Salvaari leaders.

"If it is your will, and that of the spirits, then I will make you no promises save one," Henghis said. "Those leeches have gorged themselves on our blood long enough. I will bleed Medea from Palanza to the Western Mountains! I will burn Annora from the waters of the Eretrian to the walls of Palen-Tor itself! If their rulers do not bow, then I say we drench the spirits with their blood!"

The Salvaari roared, and the sound of their cheers echoed through the forest.

Cailean drew his knife and sliced it across the palm of his hand, before he tossed steel to the ground. He wrapped his bloody fingers around his arm ring and bowed his head.

"I, Cailean of the Aedei, pledge my life, my blood, and my sword to you."

"I, Etain of the Icari, pledge my life, my blood, and my sword to you."

"I, Vaylin of the Káli, pledge my life, my blood, and my sword to you."

One by one the chieftains followed suit. The fire that had been started would now burn beyond control.

TWENTY-FOUR

Island of Vieara, Gulf of Lamrei, the Sacasian Sea.

Luana Marquez sat with her feet resting upon the wooden table before her. Her eyes were half closed as a dagger danced between her fingers. The room, an office on the second floor of the island's main tavern, was empty save for the captain of the Emeralis. A jug of ale and a mug half-drunk rested beside her feet on the table. She was tired. The days since Elara and the rest of the League had come had been exhausting. In rare moments such as these, when she was *finally* alone to her thoughts, the captain lowered her façade and allowed herself a few moments peace.

The door opened with a thud.

Luana's eyes shifted to the entrance, as the hulking mass of the newcomer made his way over to the table. His coat was midnight blue and a vicious curved sword hung at his hip.

"You seem awfully pleased with yourself," Luana muttered, as Captain Teague took up the jug and poured himself a drink.

"This has never been about my happiness," Teague replied, as he sat opposite his fellow captain. "The trick with the boy gave us time to act, and now Captain Laven leads the Elarans on a merry chase around the Sacasian. We can finally charter our next course."

Luana glanced back at her spinning knife as she spoke, "Tethys and Illarys are evacuated. Haevara and Tira as well. The rest will be here in days. Giving up the land we fought for; the land we *built*. You're right, my friend. I am not happy about this either.

But our survival depends on it."

"Do you have any regrets?" Teague asked after filling her cup and extending it.

Luana slid her knife back into its sheath and took the tankard. "I have lived a full life, Teague," she said. "You opened my eyes to all of this, and because of that I have known true freedom. What has it been since that day in the Lupentine? Eighteen years? More?"

"Twenty," Teague smiled beneath his beard.

Luana sighed and took a draught of ale.

"Twenty long years we've been friends," she said. "I was barely twelve summers then. So much has changed... but do I regret anything? For so long, I have had the freedom to choose. I have known a life of the sea. I have known blood and sweat and tear," she smirked. "I have known many men and women, aye. I have plunder and position. Yet when I look at the course I have run, I have but one regret. No child to call my own. The one who was as a daughter was torn away."

"Kitara?"

"I gave her my heart," Luana said. She remembered the girl that had been her friend, her confidant, her *daughter*. "Taught her everything I knew."

"And Barboza died for it," Teague murmured.

"Had I not fallen ill... no matter. You know, I often wonder if the stories his crew told were something less than true," she shrugged. "But that is of no consequence. What is done is done, my friend."

Teague nodded, "It would be good to have her sword now. Anyone trained by the Jade Queen and Calvillo would be a great asset."

Luana Marquez snorted before replying, "What about you, Teague? Do you regret anything?"

The Aureian met her eyes and ran a hand down the three scars that covered the side of his weathered face. "None, not even these. This place, what Lamrei has become, is my life's work. It *is* my life. Until my last breath I will fight to defend it no matter the cost. Once, a lifetime ago, when I sailed for Aureia, I was yet to be awoken. I killed who they told me to kill. I burned rebel towns to ash and took many slaves. I didn't care who I hurt or what lives I destroyed."

"And then you sailed south beyond Aureia," Luana said absently. "I know this tale."

"No," came the reply. "You *think* you know it. Here, now, we are at the precipice of death and salvation. We have the chance to rewrite history… or become no more than a page in someone else's book. I will not fall without seeing all this through, Marquez. Destiny may side with us."

Marquez raised her eyebrows. In the past she would have called him for a jest, and yet she could see more than just passion in his eyes. She could see truth.

"Spare me the riddles and this talk of destiny and fate. Speak normally."

"A month into our voyage we were running low on supplies," Teague started. "The crew begged me to turn back and return home. We could still make it if we went to half rations. But I couldn't. Somehow, we had survived this far when no one else had. The mist came from nowhere; enshrouding us in the night. We could not even see the water. Then we heard the singing. It was a woman's voice. I had never heard anything so beautiful. She swam before us in the water, her face that of a goddess. She beckoned to me as she sang her song. It reached into my heart; into my very soul. It called me down toward the water. Some of the men began to jump. They hurled themselves out into the mist. They were never seen again. Somehow, I found the will to tear my eyes away from the woman and bound cloth around my ears. I don't know what gods were watching, nor who sat in judgement, but somehow we survived the night. We were run aground on an island wreathed in fog. It was then that the siren's song returned, yet now it only came to me. My men urged me not to go, not to seek that which called to me... but I could not resist. I left my brothers and my ship and followed the voice in the wind. I found a cave, a rare chasm, that led me deep underground. Beneath rock and stone there was a pool. Its water was clearer than any crystal. Within the pool there were three. Hair of ebony, blazing fire, and shimmering gold rolled down their shoulders like waves, caressing their bare skin. Eyes deeper than the ocean and as mesmerising as sunrise. Now, as before, they beckoned. A hundred words they said to me, each branded in here," Teague touched his brow. "They spoke of destiny, my destiny. A destiny that can cut two ways. I will liberate the broken and the damned; free men of chains. The world will begin anew. An age of freedom. But if I fail, if I stumble in my path, my life will be claimed in payment and the world shall fall to the silver empire. I should have left then; turned away. I couldn't. She of the dark hair looked into my soul, as she reached up and placed a hand upon my cheek. *They will come for you*, she said. *Warrior, emperor, the kingdoms of man, and try to take it all. But you cannot let them*."

The pirate ran a thumb across the edge of his cup as he relived the memory. It was so long ago, yet it felt clearer than yesterday. Teague lifted a hand and pressed it to his mouth.

"I knew, when she kissed me, that my fate did not lie with the empire. I can still feel her lips... then they were gone... leaving me alone in the darkness as if awakening from a dream. I freed the slaves aboard my ship. Then we returned but not to the empire. Who I was before *died* in that cave. Yet one day I will return, and I will remember. Not just in the saying of our words."

Luana could not help but say them. Those words that had become more than just a saying; a prayer as well. "Rest easy now," she murmured. "Drift deeper and deeper. The sirens are calling your name."

The room grew silent as the pirate captain trailed off. Luana could not help but stare. The storyteller, if anyone else had spoken it, she would have called them a liar. She knew what Teague's lies looked like. She could see them in his eyes. What he said was true and it scared her.

"So what happens next?" Luana asked after an age.

Teague slowly nodded. "You know what happens next. It is time for us to meet our destiny. Tonight you must leave these shores and make contact with our man."

Lukas watched from the distance, as Maevin knelt on the earth. In her hands she clasped an amulet bearing the image of a viper. He saw her lips moving yet could not hear the words spoken under her breath. Her emerald green eyes, that could see into souls, were closed. Suddenly she stiffened and let loose a scream that shook the prince to his core. Lukas winced as he hobbled toward her. Pain burned through his leg. He could see Maevin's hands clawing at the earth as she gasped for breath. Worry filled him with dread as he reached her. Her eyes were open, yet she could not see him.

"Maevin," Lukas called, as he reached her and tossed his crutch to the side. He dropped to his good knee and bit back the scream that threatened. "Maevin," he repeated, as he took her shoulders in his hands. "Look at me… look at me."

She turned to him and grabbed at his arms. Her grip was strong. Her mouth contorted into a grimace as she closed her eyes once more. Maevin's breath began to slow. She leaned in and planted her forehead against the prince's.

"Lukas," she murmured.

"What is it?" he asked, and he felt her begin to relax in his grasp.

"I see the death of kings and the fall of cities," Maevin bared her teeth. "The Dark One comes to me in my sleep. He calls to me, but I cannot hear… I felt his power grow when we crossed the river last night. Now I hear his voice once again."

"What did Tanris tell you?" Lukas asked as her eyes opened. He could see the blazing green fire within as she could at last see him.

"He spoke of the Whisperer. He said that the heartbeat of the forest burns bright even as it wanes. Times are changing," Maevin said with fervour. "The Whisperer is about to sing his song."

Hesitantly, the prince reached up and stroked her cheek. Her skin was cool to his touch. She did not recoil nor look away. Instead, something of a smile slid across her lips.

"The Whisperer?" Lukas questioned.

Maevin took the hand that stroked her jaw. "A harbinger of the end times," she said. "The prophecy into the blood of this land. There will come a time after the sun falls. A time of darkness and blood and steel. A time when the old ways begin anew. A time that the wind and the earth and the trees will whisper *the moon will not rise*. In this time a conqueror reborn will emerge from ice and snow. A conquer scarred by the blades of his enemy. A conqueror shackled by lineage and who shall be called the Whisperer. When steel shatters and the winds howl, darkness will spread, and the world will kneel before the Whisperer," her eyes blazed and her words were spoken in deadly reverence. "He is a man whose voice has the power to turn enemy to closest friend. A man who can cause both chaos and peace with but a word. A man they say who is descended from the spirits themselves."

Lukas bit his lip. The spirits, the Veil, indeed all the Salvaari beliefs, were still very much unknown to him. Yet he understood faith and the strength and power that could come with it.

"What meaning did you take of it?"

"He walks among us now, Prince," Maevin told him. "And for good or evil, when he makes himself known, great change will be upon us."

They returned to the company of Káli together.

"Tell me about Tanris," Lukas said in Salvaari. His words were crude, and yet the language of the forest had started to reveal its secrets to him.

One of the Káli glanced at his companions with a grin and spoke in his mother tongue, "The Annoran begins to learn our words."

"Soon they will flow from my lips," the prince smirked, as he switched back to the common tongue.

The man who had spoken was known as Rodion. He was a skilled marksman and a cunning warrior. It had been he who had first answered Maevin's call when the priestess had asked Eirian for a company of warriors. He, and the eleven others of their number, had sworn blood oaths to avenge Oryn in the days after its fall. The twelve men would be instruments of Salvaar's wrath upon the westerners.

"The story of Tanris is rarely spoken of," Rodion said and looked to Maevin. "Perhaps you would be best suited to its telling."

The priestess looked slowly from the warrior to Lukas before she reached into a pouch and pulled forth a small handful of powder. The prince watched as Maevin cast the powder into the fire.

The flames roared and the blazing red turned to emerald light.

"It began five thousand years ago with the birth of Sylvaine, the Great Queen," Maevin began, as the Káli warriors stared into the flames.

Maevin's eyes did not leave Lukas. She opened the palms of her hands as if gesturing to everything. "The First Woman created all of this from the darkness that came before," she continued. "The rivers that run wild, the trees that sing in the wind, the mountains that soar high into the heavens... and it was all her domain. The only thing that Sylvaine lacked was someone to share this new paradise with. A child... and so she created a one. Yorath, the sun, was her firstborn. Tanris, the Secondborn, followed. He became a prince to this new world. Kerrigan. Lycan the great hunter. The rest of the spirits followed. The Great Queen created man to fill this world, and white-haired elves to guard the sacred forests. They were warriors. Tanris, wanting to please the First Woman, set about using his own gifts. He created dragons from fire and phoenixes from ash. Great creatures spilled forth at his whim. Creatures of magic. The temptresses were sent to the ocean, while the ruskalan, created from Tanris' own blood, emerged from their caves," Maevin's teeth flashed as she spoke. "The Dark Ones, those who came before, those who inhabited the darkness long before Sylvaine, grew jealous of Tanris. One night they disguised themselves as elves and brought the spirit prince a gift of fruit. A single bite was all it took and sleep enveloped Tanris. He awoke in chains forged in the blackness, chains that could not be broken by any spirit. The Dark Ones kept him in the bowels of the world tied to the Black Stone, and in that darkness they tormented him with torture and slavery. By day beasts would feast on his flesh, while by night the tormentors would heal his wounds. They took his eyes, his ears, and his tongue... only to return them. He whispered to the Dark Ones secrets that he knew and secrets that he did not know to begin with, and after an age finally his chance came. But Tanris was not so easily defeated. It is written in the stars that when one reaches his lowest point he is open to the greatest change.

As Tanris' power waned he reached out beyond the Veil with his mind and called upon the strength of the dead. The spirits were forbidden to cross the Veil into the ancestral plain beyond, and in the shadows Tanris was consumed. He gave an eye to aquire their power. One of the Dark Ones ventured too close, corrupted by greed as the prince spoke of unimaginable power, and removed his blindfold. When at last the Dark One looked into Tanris' eye, the Secondborn had won. He succumbed to the prince's will and, using a knife of carved from the Black Stone, the Dark One shed its own blood upon the chains. They shattered and Tanris was free. Those who came before awoke to see the prince no longer in his shackles. They panicked and attacked with knife and spear to no avail. Tanris turned them against each other with his gaze and took on the form of a serpent. In the bowels of the world he slaughtered them and claimed their power as his own. He swore that he would be no slave again. That night, beneath rock and mountain, before the Black Stone, Tanris became the Dark One. The one who rules the Veil and commands the dead," passion ran through Maevin's words, and she clasped the snake amulet at her throat. "When the darkness encroaches once again Tanris' eyes will open. It is written."

Lukas shivered, though not from the cold. It was not fear that gripped him. No, fear did not send fire surging through his blood, nor did it awaken the hunger that lurked within.

"And the eyes?" Lukas asked.

"Many moons ago the druids spoke that the time is near upon us," Maevin said with fervour. "A time that the eyes of Tanris will open. What form they will take? I do not know... but the spirits have spoken of a prophecy as old as time itself. When darkness falls and balance is undone, the Whisperer shall rise and Tanris' gaze shall burn, casting aside the steel of the sun."

Lukas let out a breath. He had never put faith in any god or religion. As a boy, myths and superstition had done nothing but humour him. That time had ended, and it had ended in Salvaar. Now he believed. The prophecy spoken by Maevin chilled him. He bit his lip. He could see something awaken in the Káli, as if a great beast stirred inside their very souls.

"I have never heard such a thing," Lukas said.

"There are few who have," Maevin told him. At last she broke her stare as the fire flickered and the emerald flames shifted.

Once again the forest was lit by orange flames.

"You have heard our story, prince," Rodion spoke up after a moment, "tell us yours. What is it that you want from this life?"

Lukas snorted and flicked his gaze up. The Salvaari had only ever given him the truth. Perhaps it was time for him to speak his own.

"What do I want?" he muttered. "When my brother was fifteen

my father sent him to the court of Aureia. He grew up with the emperor's son, Darius. For five years he learned the teachings of great lords and kings, renowned philosophers, politicians, and artisans. He and Darius became as brothers and when he returned, Dayne had become more than just a master of war but a keen intellect. Wiser than any three mentors I had as a boy. By the time he was my age he had already won battles and toppled warlord and jealous king alike. Ah, the poets and bards already sing great songs about the great Eagle of Annora. My father... they call him the Uniter. The first man to ever bring the three kingdoms together in a sacred union. Under my father Annora is strong. The famous Dorian Raynor, the greatest king that Aethela had ever had, rose above all who came before with but a single act. By thirty he had achieved more than entire bloodlines of kings ever achieve. As skillful with the sword as he is in politics. Stories of the great king swept the land from Tarik to Berenithia. When my father was adding to his kingdom, and my brother was winning battles, I, the *second* son to the crown, was dealing with outlaws and renegades that ran wild in the forest. No songs bear my name, nor tales speak of my great deeds. I am a cripple. What do I want? I want everything."

"You want to be greater than your brother? Your father?" Rodion asked.

"Far greater," Lukas told him fiercely. "I shall compose a ballad that shall reach the stars."

Maevin reached out a hand and let the flames kiss her skin, yet it remained unburned. The priestess' face spoke before the words left her tongue. It was a story that blazed like the sun; a story that enchanted Lukas.

"You are led by your heart," Maevin said. "You feel it all... all of the anger, all of the rage. Use your emotions wisely and one day the world will kneel at your feet."

TWENTY-FIVE

City of Elara, the League of Trecento

The doors to the magister's palace were thrown open. The last rays of the sun's light had faded, and great torches had been lit. Halberd wielding guards stood at every entrance, patrolling hall and corridor alike, as the guests began to stream in. Noble lords and ladies, wealthy merchants, and foreign guests from afar filled the palace for the magister's ball. They were richly clad in a vast array of colour. The only thing that united the aristocracy were the flamboyant masks that hid their faces. The music was loud, and the tables were covered with great platters of food and jewelled jugs of wine. The great hall, transformed into a ballroom, was filled with people as they danced and swayed across its marble floor.

Her dress was fiery scarlet and ivory white to match her mask. Gold trimmings ran around the gown. No longer was her hair tied back in a pair of braids. Her brunette locks fell down her shoulders like a gleaming waterfall, caressing the soft skin of her neck. She moved around the ballroom as if it were made for her and navigated the throngs of dancers with grace. Such was the skill of an acrobat.

Elise Delfeyre's eyes danced around the room, taking in everything. Elaran merchants in their fine silks, Medean traders in their cotton gowns, Annorans, Aureians, Larissans, and even those from the recently landed Landonsport delegation. They spun and twirled atop the marble. In their disguises, all could pretend to be something that they weren't. In the dimly lit corridors, hidden in the shadows of pillar and doorway, some were making their desires known. Lord and lady exchanged kisses, before they vanished into the dark recesses of the palace. Elise's eyes were not drawn to the debauchery this night, instead they followed the guards as they made their rounds. Elise had come here for a reason. If the Nightingale could not infiltrate the palace and slip into the magister's private rooms then Elise Delfeyre would. She saw an opening through the crowd and began to weave through the dancers toward a closed wooden door. A single guardsman stood by the door, yet every so often he would leave to make his rounds of the ballroom.

That was her target.

A hand shot out and latched onto her wrist. Elise spun toward its owner as she fought to retrieve her arm. A pair of brown eyes greeted her. A man stood opposite her, his greying hair the only thing that gave away his appearance. His garb was that of a noble, perhaps even a councilman.

She gave him a sweet smile as she greeted him, "My Lord."

"May I have this dance?" he replied with a smooth tongue. His voice gave away its Aurean origin.

Had he been here when the Elaran colony had been founded? Elise bit back a grimace. There was no way she could refuse him without drawing the gaze of many. She nodded as once again the guard returned to his posting.

"They say that eyes are the windows to the soul," the man said, taking her hand as a new song began to play. "And in yours I see the eyes of a woman I knew."

Elise nearly froze at his words. She willed her body to move with the melody and followed in the steps of the nobleman.

"And whose eyes might they be?" she asked.

He leaned in close, and his lips nearly brushed her ear. "Those of Catinya Delfeyre," he whispered.

Her breath caught as the man whispered her mother's name. He had guessed her right.

"And who are you to say so?"

"A friend. Cirillo Eris," he replied. "I grew up with her father."

Lord Cirillo Eris was a name she knew well. He had been one of the first men to sail from Aureia. His family's trade routes stretched from Tarik to Berenithia and had earned him great wealth and granted him entrance to the council.

"I know that name," Elise murmured as they spun around the floor. "What do you want with me?"

His hazel eyes swept to where a pair of armoured guards stood. The magister's men.

"I am dying," the lord told her.

"What do you mean?"

"I know too much," Lord Cirillo said quietly. "Poison. Small doses in my food and water. I do not know how. I may be old, but I am not blind. I have seen it before. I thought I had been careful. Imrohir wants me gone, and my tongue silenced. I have but months... perhaps less. Even if I were to root out the cause of the poison, it will be steel that finds me. And so I am leaving this wretched city. But before I depart, there is something that you must know."

"Why come to me now?" Elise asked with a frown.

"I am being watched. It was never safe. Even now, I fear it may be too late. Eyes are everywhere, and the risk high, yet I could not leave without first honouring your mother's memory," Lord Cirillo stepped in close as he spoke. "Your parents' deaths were no accident, nor were they natural. They were ordered."

Elise's heart skipped a beat. She felt her face pale as he spoke those words. She had been right. If her mother had been murdered then, more likely than not, the same fate had been given to her father. Someone had taken her parents, her childhood, and cast her into a world that despised her.

"But why?" Elise managed.

The last notes of the song echoed throughout the hall. The dancers cheered, and Cirillo leaned forward.

"Meet me at the eastern docks after the council session in two days," he told her. "There I will explain. The magister's shadow is vast."

With that, he kissed her hand and vanished into the crowd, leaving nothing but questions in his wake. For the first time Elise felt the tremble that ran through her body. A surge of hope ran through her despite the sorrow that she felt at Lord Cirillo's words. She had been right. Her parents *had* been murdered. The purpose that had born the Nightingale was true.

Elise glanced toward the door again and waited as a plan started to take root. She made her move, gliding across the ballroom floor. Her confidence grew with each step. She reached the door mere moments after the guard had begun his round and snatched out the lockpick hidden up her sleeve. Within moments there was a click and she slipped inside, unnoticed.

Elise strode down the corridor, her light steps barely made a sound on the stone beneath. The sounds of the festivities behind her began to grow faint, yet she kept her mask on. If soldier or noble saw her then her face would be unknown to them.

Footsteps.

Elise ducked behind a pillar and held her breath. The sound drew closer. The ironshod boots of a pair of soldiers echoed on the floor.

An eternity passed.

The two guards strode by with their hands tightly gripped around their halberds. Elise watched their backs as they continued down the corridor, oblivious to her presence. She took a breath and resumed her course. The passages were long, and every sound made her skin crawl. To be caught was to be killed. That much was certain. Yet Elise revelled in it. She flew through the corridors and passageways of the palace, memorising each turn she took through the labyrinth. Elise climbed stairs and hid behind pillars.

Occasionally she saw soldiers or servants in the distance, but for the most part she was alone. Imrohir's ball she had to thank for that. She came to a final turn. Elise peered around the corner of the passage. Her eyes locked on an all too familiar door. The entrance to the magister's rooms. This time four soldiers stood sentinel. They had not seen her watching in the shadows.

How would she get past them? She could not be seen, and she carried no weapons. She heard the echo of boots once again. Her heart dropped. The guards were coming back. Elise was trapped. She could not move forward. The magister's door guards would see her. Nor could she move backward. There was no place to hide. No place to run. Elise glanced around frantically. Her gaze swept from pillar to door.

To door.

She ran over and frantically tried the handle. It was locked. Shadows flickered upon the ground as the guards closed in. She pulled the lockpick from the inside of her sleeve and drove it into the lock. The light of torches glinted upon their armour. Elise worked the pick faster and faster. The boots drew closer. The door clicked. She ducked inside and gently eased the door shut as the guards walked by.

Elise leaned on the door for a moment before she turned to investigate the room. It was a bedchamber that, by the look of it, would serve a high-ranking friend or ambassador. The wooden posted bed was nearly as big as Elise's own room. Books filled the ornately carved shelving and fine rugs adorned the floor. A set of closed doors led out onto a balcony that overlooked the palace grounds.

Elise dashed across to the doors and slipped outside into the cool air. The silver moon shone high above. The breeze ran through her hair and caressed her cheeks. She gazed out over the courtyard and watched as soldiers patrolled the grounds. Finally, she looked to the walls of the keep itself. The balconies were large and many. Each room had access to the outside world. Indeed, only a few feet separated each of them. Elise let her eyes wander again as she bit her lip. None of the soldiers below could see her, nor did any along the wall look inward to the castle. She was alone, save for the moon. With a grimace, Elise hopped up onto the balcony railing. The damned dress that made her look like a doll would make this far harder than it needed to be.

Slowly, she extended a toe over the void and leapt onto the next balcony railing before she dropped onto the stone flooring. She could barely hear the noise that her shoes made, but every small sound made her wince. Jump by jump, balcony by balcony, she edged her way closer to her destination by following the keep's wall around. Elise made her final leap and landed on the final balcony of the guestrooms. She peered down into the gloom, At best, to fall was to break every bone in her body, and at worst...

Elise felt not an ounce of fear at the thirty-foot drop. She dropped down into the balcony and looked out across the wall toward the magister's balcony. It was nearly fifteen feet from her position and impossible to jump in her dress. She ran a hand across the stones of the wall. They were mostly smooth, but there was enough room to jam the tips of her fingers into the gaps of the stonework. A thin stone lip ran level with the top of the balcony railing which led around the building. Elise pursed her lips. It was the only way.

She pulled herself up onto the railing and hugged her body to the wall. Her fingers dug into the edge of the stonework and latched onto any crevice that she could find. She stepped a foot out onto the lip and slowly began to edge her way around the building. She was exposed here and had no place to turn to if she was seen. Elise half expected to feel the blinding pain of a crossbow bolt sliding into her back, but she felt nothing but the cool kiss of the wind. Finally, she dropped down onto the magister's balcony and allowed herself to breathe. The doors to his chambers were bolted with no lock for her to pick. Instead, she reached beneath her skirts and pulled forth a dagger. Elise jammed it between the doors and pushed it upward.

The latch lifted, and she was in.

Hangings shrouded the massive wooden bed frame while lavish chairs sat by a huge oaken desk covered in carvings. Tapestries covered the walls alongside a banner bearing the Aureian griffin. Books and scrolls filled the shelves and covered the tops of bookcase and bench alike. There were great paintings and displays holding swords, and even the lowliest candleholder shone of gold. Elise took a second to take in the majesty of Imrohir's chamber and wondered just how much it was all worth. She took up the candleholder and sparked a small flame to life, before she made her way over to the shelves. She ran a finger across the volumes.

Histories and works of culture, religious scripture and even journals of great kings filled the bookcases. Elise made her way over to the shelving behind the desk. More of the same. Then she saw them. A series of captain's logbooks. Elise frowned.

Why would the magister hold onto the logs of seafarers? Logs always sat within the cabins of their writers.

She snatched one from its shelf, placed it upon the desk, and flicked it open. Her eyes widened as she read. This book belonged to Captain Odile Nilsine of the Andromakei. The ship had been among Imrohir's private fleet.

On the eighth day of summer, last year, the ship docked in Aureia and exchanged two dozen livestock for eighteen *thousand* crowns. The sum far exceeded the value.

Elise kept reading.

The thirtieth day of winter... the fifth of spring. It was all the same, varying amounts of livestock exchanged for coin of nearly unimaginable value. *What was Imrohir up to?*

Elise grabbed a second log. It was more of the same. Then she read one of Nilsine's notes written at the bottom of a page: *Fourteenth day of summer. Docked at Palen-Tor for resupply. Upon paying the harbour master, one of the stock tried to escape and screamed. Cost five hundred crowns to seal the harbour master's lips. Upon returning to sea, the stock was flogged to ensure obedience of all at the port of Valentia.*

Elise's jaw dropped.

The stock was flogged to ensure obedience.

Now she understood. Her anger rose. Now all the secrecy made sense. The magister was dealing in slaves. Yet slavery was outlawed in Elara. That meant only one thing. Elise swallowed the bile that threatened. Imrohir was trading in his own people for coin. She slammed the book shut and shoved it back into its shelving as her heart raged.

What kind of monster was he? What kind of a man could do this?

Imrohir was a beast, a base animal at best. Elise gathered up what gold she could as she fought to compose herself. She filled a small pouch before she took up one final item. The magister's seal. The seal of the griffin. She left one thing for him. The feather of a nightingale.

The corridors of the palace were cold as she made her way back through them, though it was not the cool air that chilled her. A war raged within Elise.

Had her parents discovered the magister's sick trade? Was that why they had been murdered at his command?

If the people ever found out, Imrohir was finished. So angry was she that Elise rounded into a new passageway without checking. She heard the thud of a knife being driven into a body before she saw it. Before her, not twenty paces away, were two men. One clad in the fine attire of a noble. His black mask fell from his nerveless fingers as the blade tore through his heart.

The other wore the garb of some kind of mercenary. His clothing was dark, the cloth bandana that covered his nose and lips darker still. A half cape hung from his shoulder. A hood was pulled up over his ears while a padded gambeson protected his chest. A pair of bracers armoured his arms, and a hand and a half sword hung from his hip. Silver orbs hung from the belt that ran around his waist, and blood dripped from the dagger that he had plunged deep into the noble's chest.

Elise bit back a scream as the dark clad man tore his blade free and watched the dead man crumple into a pile at his feet. She recognised the noble. Lord Daivin Aillard, nephew to Magister Imrohir himself. Elise thought to shout, thought to cry out for the guards, but then she would be found here at the scene of a murder with a lockpick in her possession on the very night that the Nightingale had returned to the palace. Calling for help was impossible.

The killer heard her sharp intake of breath and turned to her. They locked eyes. Elise felt them swallow her as she froze to the spot. It was like staring into the gates of hell.

Thud.

They both swivelled to the sound of ironshod boots. *Guards!*

Elise leapt back and ran for the closest door. She slipped inside just in time. Elise peered through the thing gap between door and wall as a pair of soldiers marched around the corner.

"Lord Daivin?" one of the guards called as they sprinted toward the body. "Lord Daivin!"

She heard the clang of a halberd striking the stone as its bearer tossed the weapon aside. The last she saw before easing the door closed was the two soldiers kneeling by the body of their lord as they screamed for aid. Elise fled. She flew from room to balcony and then hurried back down the corridors from whence she had come. Whoever the dark clad man was, he would be hunted for the rest of his days for this. How had he gained entrance to the palace, how had he gotten so close to Daivin? Perhaps they had been friends once, allies even. The killer would bring down the magister's wrath upon him. The wrath of a man who enslaved children. Whatever came next, blood would follow. But one thing was certain; in two days' time she would at last have answers. At last she would know why the nobility had murdered a common family from the Pits.

TWENTY-SIX

Isle of Agartha, the Valkir Isles

Astrid awoke to the soft feeling of a finger tracing the raven tattoo on her shoulder. She smiled, her eyes still closed, as Arndyr followed the dark lines around her skin.

"Finally awake," the earl murmured.

"Mmmmm."

"This is new," he said as he traced the ink.

Astrid rolled over to face him. "I thought it fitting."

The jarl slowly opened her eyes and drank Arndyr in. The long braid he wore fell down across his strong shoulder, while the bristles of his stubble covered chin tickled her hand as he planted a kiss upon her palm. He watched her with a contented look as she entwined his fingers with her own.

"The Raven Jarl," he said as he looked into her eyes. "It has a nice ring to it."

"Tell me," Astrid said and bit her lip, "that I am not crazy for this voyage that I am about to undertake."

"Your madness is as untameable as the sea," his smile widened into a grin, "and I revel in it."

The jarl snorted as her lips curled. "Madness… a thing somewhere between insanity and a dream. And it is in this madness that I have found freedom."

"And happiness?"

Astrid sighed. She was not sure of the last time that she had truly been happy, not since her mother had died.

"Happiness… no. Satisfaction, maybe. I have taken what joy I have found, yet true happiness has eluded me. Perhaps I will find it in the south or perhaps we will sail off the edge of the world," she chuckled. "It is the one riddle that I have not yet been able to make sense of."

"I hope you find what it is you seek."

"I know," Astrid gave him a quiet smile and stroked his jaw. "The future is shrouded to me and filled with uncertainty."

"I will stand by your side, whatever that future holds," he told her. "When we return, you know what will happen."

Astrid let out a deep breath and gazed up at the ceiling of her chamber.

"Ulfric and the other jarls will demand I take upon the mantle of earl," she said. "Do you know something? Even after everything that I have suffered, everything that I have lost, it is that which fills me with dread. The thought of command."

"There is no one they would rather follow. No one that I would rather follow," Arndyr said with a shrug. "You know that. It is to you that they will look to lead them though the chaos that will undoubtedly spill across from the mainland. I have marched from Aureia to Berenithia and back and let me tell you; our fears do not stop death. They stop life."

Astrid gripped his hand and placed it over her heart.

"What a pair we make. Both trying to run from our responsibilities, both unable to do so. I want peace, Arndyr. I want to build a future here that will last without the constant fear of death on the horizon. The raids have made us strong but keep us from ever truly living. Perhaps the same as you, I will open up trade with the empire and forge a long-lasting peace with its people. We could farm, just as my father once did. We could sail across the seas forever and grow fat and old without the need to take up arms."

"There are those who would wish to fight, those who believe that if Salvaar falls, that we will be next," the earl said.

"There are those who believe that a race of giants created the stars with the embers of their forges," Astrid retorted with a grin.

"Maybe they did."

Arndyr touched her chin, turning her face toward him. "You deserve to be happy. You deserve the right to choose your own path. Do not let others make you forget that."

For a moment, her heart softened as her smile began to fade. She felt something new as she looked into those shining eyes. Joy. Astrid leaned toward Arndyr and kissed him deeply. Perhaps it was possible for her to find some happiness after all.

"Come," he said, "There is something I want you to see."

They walked through Agartha side by side without a care. If either of them harboured any doubts about the voyage none were spoken. Astrid felt nothing but longing when they reached the harbour and the Ravenheart appeared before her eyes. Men scurried about the deck and filled the rigging, while the last of the cargo was being taken deep into the vessel's hold. Beside the Ravenheart sat the Draekor, Arndyr's flagship. It would be with this mighty vessel that she would sail. A warship even larger than the Ravenheart, with a crew one hundred strong and marked by the dragon banners of Lumis. Fargrim glanced toward the pair as they walked down the pier.

"How is it?" the jarl called to her helmsman.

"We are almost ready, Astrid," Fargrim replied. "The last of the food is being loaded as we speak. We will be ready to sail with the dawn."

"Yah!" Astrid exchanged a grin with her friend and clapped him on the back, before she followed Arndyr toward the Draekor.

The ship's deck thudded as Astrid dropped down from the boarding plank. Arndyr exchanged greetings with his men as he led her down to the main deck toward a series of wicker cages sitting by the entry to the hold.

Astrid frowned as she heard a strange but not unknown noise.

"Do you keep birds?" she asked.

"Birds, yes," Arndyr chuckled as he opened one of the cages and withdrew a grey bird barely larger than his hand. "Pigeons."

He stroked the bird's small head, before he held it out. "Go on, take it."

Astrid took the pigeon tentatively. Its feathers were soft and delicate to her touch. She gently wrapped her fingers around the bird's small body, careful not to hurt it.

"Ask away," Arndyr said. "I can see the question in your eyes." Astrid stared at the bird for a moment as it cooed.

"Why pigeons?"

"A little trick I learned in the empire. There they use the birds to send messages across land and ocean far faster than any rider or ship," the earl told her. "They can find their way back anywhere, even from distant places that they have never been. And besides, a pigeon cannot talk or read so it cannot divulge the true nature of the writing that it carries. A rather ingenious method of communication founded by the Aureians, don't you think?"

Astrid dipped her head and ran a thumb over the small messenger's head.

"Genius indeed," she admitted. "I have to know how they do it."

"To this day no one really knows," Arndyr shrugged.

"Really?" Astrid handed the bird back.

"Priests, scholars, handlers; they all have their theories," the earl replied as he took the pigeon from her. "Some believe that the gods granted them some kind of map or compass, allowing them to determine their location. Others believe that they carry the memories of their ancestors inside their heads, and through them have charted the world. There are some that believe that it has something to do with their mate."

Astrid smirked. "Their mate?"

"Aye. Like us, pigeons mate for life." Arndyr did not shift his gaze from the bird. "They can always find their way home and cross thousands of miles in search of the one that they love. Thus arose the belief."

"Is that true?" Astrid asked as her companion put the pigeon back in its box.

"You may as well ask the stars."

The jarl smiled as she felt her curiosity grow, "I should like to find out this secret."

"One day perhaps you will," he replied. "Yes, I have no doubt."

A whistle came from the quarter deck, followed by the booming cry of a sailor who gestured out to sea.

"Earl!"

Astrid's gaze swept the ship, before her eyes followed the man's outflung arm. Soaring down toward them was a small grey speck that grew larger by the moment.

"A message from Lumis," Arndyr said without looking at her. "It will be from Jormund."

"Go," Astrid said, nodding toward the quarter deck. "See what your brother wants. I will see you at the celebration tonight."

Arndyr chuckled and planted a kiss upon her hand, before he dashed up the stairs toward the pigeon as it flew ever closer.

She did not return to the town or her hall. Instead, Astrid made her way deep into the wilderness and up the surrounding mountains.

"Knew I'd find you here."

Astrid glanced at Erik as his voice broke the silence. *Here* was the top of the cliff upon which Astrid now sat. From the cliff top she could see it all. The blue waves of the ocean lulling against the harbour and beach, the tree covered slopes of the mountains that surrounded Agartha, and the eagles that floated high in the breeze. Ships at anchor filled the bay, while thin tendrils of smoke arose from chimneys and if one looked close enough, one could almost see the specks of the villagers in between the houses.

"It's beautiful," Astrid murmured as her brother approached.

He sat beside her, overlooking the bay as she spoke.

"Up here, it is untouched by the troubles of men. There is no fighting, no war… no judgements. Only peace."

"There is no place finer to watch the sun slip behind the horizon," Erik agreed.

"When I was a girl, mother used to bring me here," Astrid said, letting her hand brush against the raven amulet. "She would sit me on her lap and run her hands through my hair. She told me that serenity is found somewhere between the ocean and the heavens. I did not understand her words and it would be many years before I discovered her meaning. Chaos. It resides all around us; in the sky, in the land, in the sea. When you find the calm in the chaos, when you exchange your expectations for acceptance; that is when you will know inner peace. That is when you will know serenity."

Astrid looked to Erik. She could see her mother's face clear as anything. From the feel of her hair to the colour of her eyes, the caress of her touch, to the sound of her voice. She could still hear Lief's booming laugh and his warm embrace.

"I miss her, Erik. I miss them both. Do you feel it too?"

Erik placed his hand atop hers and gave it a squeeze. "I do," he said as he stared out over the bay. "Gods curse me, I do."

Astrid closed her eyes and leaned against her brother as they drifted into silence. He was her last family, her last true family. After everything that they had been through together, they were bonded closer than by just blood.

"The moon rises," Erik said at last. "You're missing your own feast."

"I know," Astrid replied quietly. "Let's just stay here a while longer."

Her brother's arm wrapped around her shoulders.

The blazing light of the fires cast great shadows around the hall, shadows of the crew, shadows of their families, shadows of the people of Agartha; for all had come this night to bid the sailors of the Ravenheart farewell. Astrid and Erik were greeted with cheers as they entered through the doors.

"Come, drink," Nenrir the archer roared and shoved a tankard into the jarl's hand.

"And how many have you had?" she replied as she downed a mouthful of mead.

"Lost count after twenty!"

Astrid laughed and tapped his chest with her fist.

"Best you have some before he drinks it all," Laerke Redleaf chuckled and draped an arm around the drunken warrior. Redleaf had always been the more reserved of the brothers. His mind was quick and tongue unmoveable and that was precisely why it had been in Laerke that Astrid had entrusted to bring Magnus to heel.

"Oh my brother, forever worrying," Nenrir said, before thrusting his tankard to the heavens, his voice rising in song. "The moon was shining high above when I heard a call to heed!"

"To slip into the sea that night and down a cup o' mead!" Astrid bellowed along with her crew.

Tankards were slammed together and they all drank heartily. Astrid shook her head and grimaced as she swallowed the last of the alcohol. The Valkir filled the hall with their merry cheers as Nenrir went in search of another drink. Laerke rolled his eyes with a laugh and followed in his brother's wake to make sure he did not get *overly* drunk.

"Fargrim!" called Erik as he saw the helmsman, and with a grin, sauntered through the crowd toward his friend.

Astrid made her way through the hall. She navigated throngs of her people, exchanged greetings, clasped arms and clapped hands upon backs. She came to rest against one of the large carved pillars of the hall and leaned back against it with a laugh.

Even two days ago it would have been all but impossible to take much comfort from this night... the thought of laughing would have been foreign. Astrid looked around the hall as the sound of singing and dancing, the laughter and song began to fade.

She saw Arndyr through the crowd and the pair exchanged a smile. He sat with his own crew as they joked and sang the night away. It was in his cool eyes that Astrid saw a mirror of her own soul. They were both sworn to their people, sworn to their crews; yet they both shared the same curiosity and longing for adventure free of the shackles that bound them.

"Not drunk yet, are you?"

Astrid tore her gaze from the earl as Torben reached her side.

"Some of us have to remain sober, sadly," she replied, looking him up and down with a raised eyebrow. "Though you should be more careful. Wouldn't want to pass out and make a fool of yourself in front of the *younger* men, eh, old man."

"Pffft," Torben snorted. "Beardless boys the lot of 'em. I could still show them, and you, a thing or two about drinking. *Girl.*"

"On another night I may take you up on that."

"And on the day that you do, you will find yourself awoken by a bucket of water held by this *old man*," he said with a growl of a chuckle.

Torben met her glance with his own, before flicking his eyes around the hall. "You did all this Astrid. Brought them all together. And now you are in pursuit of the grandest prize of all, a thing worth a hundred times more than any amount of gold. After this you will be famous. The world will know your name."

"I don't care." Astrid sighed. "This is not about legacy, nor about songs that may one day be sung. I just want to sail, Torben, to know true freedom. I do not know what lies to the south, yet it is *not* the only uncharted sea. What lies beyond the Sacasian, well east of Idrisir? I want to go there. I want to see it all. I want to live this life how I see fit. A life of peace, a life of choice... a life of *adventure.*

Though some day, someone in another life will remember us. Not as raiders, not as the scourge of the Lupentine, but as free people."

Torben nodded his great mane and placed a hand on her shoulder. "What you're doing here, seeing the woman that you have become… I am *proud* of you, Astrid. Never forget that. Never forget that you stand as my daughter and will always be as such."

Emotion stirred in Astrid as she looked to her friend. The man who had been by her side since the day she had entered the world. The man who had been her father's closest friend.

"There is no way that I could ever tell you how much you mean to me, nor thank you for all that you have done," she said, giving his arm a gentle squeeze. "You are my dearest friend and I hold you to heart as a father."

Torben smiled, placing a tender kiss on her forehead. "Go," he said, and gestured to the dancing with a grin. "Enjoy this night. It is for you."

Astrid spun through the hall, her hair twirling in her wake like a black wave. The light tunic and dark breeches she wore allowed her to freely move across the wooden floor. Her heartbeat flew and a layer of sweat covered her body when at last she left the dancing in search of another drink. She reached the long table just as another woman did. Clad in a dress of burgundy, with wavy brown locks tumbling down her shoulders, was Mayrun.

"Here," the woman said and held out a cup. A smile flashed across her lips as she saw Astrid's furrowed brow. "Don't worry; it's water."

The jarl took the cup from her friend. "Thank you."

"No, it is I who is in your debt," Mayrun said quietly. "When Raol died, it almost broke me. Astrid, my world was on fire and no one could save me. No one but you. And you did."

"Mayrun, I did nothing."

"You saved me," the woman said, meeting her gaze with one of strength. The girl who had been so afraid, so ruined, was gone.

"I grew up with Raol. He was my brother, nothing will ever change that," Astrid placed a hand on her friend's cheek. "Scâldir... family, they are everything to me, sweet Mayrun, and you stand among them."

Mayrun smiled as Astrid withdrew her hand. "I am going to miss you when you sail."

The jarl spread her arms and laughed. "Whatever for?" she said. "You're coming, aren't you?"

"What?" Mayrun breathed. "I am no warrior nor sailor."

"You're a friend, a sister, and I want you to come. Will you join me?"

The woman shook her head and grinned, joy radiating across her face, "Of course I will."

"Good," Astrid replied. "Then I have one last question."

"Hmmm?"

The jarl nodded over her shoulder toward her dancing crew. "Shall we?"

TWENTY-SEVEN

City of Vesuva, Aureian Empire

The darkness of the forest and the bodies of the fallen were the last things that Kitara saw beyond the sheet that covered the cage. The stench of dried blood, stale sweat, and mud filled her nose, covered her clothing and clung greedily at her hair. It turned her golden locks to murky brown. She was in pain; they all were. Yet none offered complaint. They were too proud for that.

Blinding light assaulted her eyes.

The canvas was wrenched aside by Sir Rowan and then the surviving prisoners were pulled from the wagon. The Salvaari were separated and then one by one were tussled to an Aureian bathhouse. Where they were exactly, Kitara did not know. By the look it was the inside of some wealthy lord's house. They were now in Vesuva, the great northern city of the empire, that much was certain. Household slaves scurried around the villa and acted at every whim of their master, while soldiers and guards clad in silver and purple watched her every move with hawklike eyes and sneers. The Aureian guards shoved her into the large bathroom and closed the doors behind them. Four remained with her, hands tightly gripping spear and shield. Her bindings were removed.

"You, bathe," one of them commanded and nodded toward the clear waters of the pool before them.

A slave deposited a white garment on the small bench beside

the bath, before she vanished from the room. The guards did not look away and barely reacted to Kitara as she glanced back at them. There was no way out, not yet at least. One against four would not have been difficult for her, yet when the one had no weapon to bring against spear, shield and steel armour… all thought of escape fell away. Kitara gritted her teeth and with a sigh pulled her once white shirt up over her head and tossed it to the side. She took some satisfaction at the intake of breath as the guards saw the white scars that ran across her muscled back. Boots, pants and bracers followed in the wake of the soiled shirt before she walked down the stone steps and into the water. The only things she still wore were the wolf's head arm ring at her wrist and the sapphire ring that swung at her throat. They were too precious, and she saw the way that the Aureian's eyes lingered.

The bath was warm thanks to the ingenious heating system the Aureians had invented decades ago. Kitara felt her eyes close as she eased herself into the water. The mud and blood began to slide away from her skin. The warmth gave her strength and, as the filth begun to fall from her hair, she began to feel reborn.

A towel was tossed to her by a soldier as she left the bath, and with no surprise, she noticed that her clothes were gone, the emerald sash from her time in the Sacasian as well. In their place was the ivory garment left by the slave. Kitara pulled on the sleeveless white tunic that hung to mid-thigh, before she followed the guards from the room.

She met with the Salvaari in the corridor, each and all scrubbed clean, each and all garbed in white. Their hands were bound and surrounded by Sir Rowan and his men, along with a contingent of the Aureians.

"So what now?" Kitara hissed at the Medean as they began to move down the marble hallway.

"Now you are to be judged," the mercenary replied as they walked into a square yard within the villa. A small pool sat at its centre, while the roof above was open to allow the sun's warm light into the palace.

Kitara glared at her captor.

"If I was your judgement, you would already be dead," she told him.

One by one, the prisoners were lined up before the pool. Kitara took Sereia's hand and gave it a squeeze. Then the massive bronze doors flew open. In walked a party of men. The leader was unmistakable as the master of the house. A second, younger man strode at his side, while at their back walked half-a-dozen heavily armed soldiers. The leader wore a clean white robe with a violet band wrapped around his body from shoulder to hip. Golden rings adorned his fingers, and yet he did not seem a man who played the part of self-serving, overindulgent fool. His jaw was as strong as his arm, his chin covered in little more than a thin layer of stubble. Thinning black hair streaked with grey covered his scalp. His posture, even his eyes, bore great strength. The Aureian looked around forty summers, maybe more.

"Magister Valliro," Sir Rowan bowed to the noble. "It is a great honour to finally meet you."

The senator waved the words away and clasped the knight's arm. "Save the sentiments, captain. It is to you that I am indebted," the magister replied. "Now come, show me these savages you have procured from the edge of the world."

Kitara let her gaze linger on the noble as the men came her way. He was a soldier, or at least, *had been* a soldier. His hands were calloused from the sword, shield and spear of the legions: few nobles would ever greet a mercenary with such familiarity. Least of all with respect. The younger noble stood just as proud, just as strong. He shared the same dark eyes as the senator. A son perhaps?

"Your *new* master," Rowan indicated the Aureian as he spoke to the prisoners. "Valliro Nilor. Former commander of the Ninth

Legion, senator to the empire and magister of Vesuva. And his son, Arias Nilor."

Valliro had been a soldier then. A good one at that. Only the best rose to prominence in Aureia while fewer still ever attained the rank of magister. His son, Arias, looked no more than in his mid-twenties. Such a young age to achieve his rank. Maybe it was due to his father's position; maybe he forged the path himself. Valliro Nilor walked the line of prisoners, and let his gaze move from face to face. His eyes ran up and down Kitara as he came to a halt before her.

"Rather muscular for a *woman*," he said, before looking her dead in the eye. "You are not Káli."

Kitara stared back and let him see the storm that blew within. "I am Aedei," Kitara said.

Valliro turned to Rowan as he indicated to her wrist. "I see that you let them keep their arm rings," he said.

"Gave them something to believe in and gave me no harm, sir," Rowan shrugged.

"Nonsense," Valliro Nilor told him. "There is no greater force in this world stronger than the power of belief, Captain. Remove their rings."

Anger rippled down the line of Salvaari as they struggled against their captors, some even trying to lash out. The Aureians showed no mercy or remorse as they beat the malcontents down and took the arm rings anyway. Kitara merely rolled her eyes as her own was roughly pulled from her wrist. There was no point trying to resist the impossible. It was then that the senator noticed the band at Kitara's throat for the first time. His hand snaked out and he tore the ring and it's binding from her neck.

"No," she snarled, fighting against the hands that clasped her as the one thing that she held to heart was torn away.

Rage boiled to the surface and she spat in the Aurien's face. A heavy fist connected with her stomach and nearly sent her to her knees, yet she did not care. Her eyes did not leave the ring that dangled from the senator's hand. Valliro wiped the spit away as his rage turned into amusement.

"What is your name, girl?" he asked.

"They call her Kitara," Rowan said. "Caused quite a deal of trouble on the road."

"Better to die on your feet than live on your knees," she snapped back.

"Indeed," Arias Nilor smirked. "She's a fighter then?"

"I don't know how, I don't know when, but somehow the girl knows tarkaras," Rowan told him.

"The swordsong," Valliro said slowly and almost in admiration. "I have heard stories about how the Tariki fight. Is it true what they say?"

"Killed over a dozen of my men… including two knights," the mercenary replied.

Kitara smirked at the anger coming from her captor.

"Indeed," the Aureian raised his eyebrows. "I have always admired the Tariki yet have never had the chance to see one fight. Perhaps then it would be more entertaining to see this one compete in the games than it would be to simply send her to Theon's whorehouse."

"What games?" Kitara demanded as she watched him turn away, taking the sapphire ring with him. "What games?"

"The arena," Arias replied absently. "The place where even lowly slaves can become gods. Sildari, that is what we call them."

Kitara felt the blood leave her face. "You want me to fight and kill for the sake of sport?" she asked.

"And a great deal of coin," Valliro chuckled.

"I will *not* kill for your entertainment."

"Then you will die where you stand," Valliro stopped before Sereia. He reached out a hand and lifted the girl's chin, "Such a little dove. It would be a shame to lose something do innocent, and yet Theon must be paid. Many would pay for an eastern savage. Have her made ready for transport."

"No!" Sereia screamed as a guard grabbed her shoulder. She looked to Kitara, her eyes wild. "No!"

"Stop!" Kitara roared and thrashed free of the soldiers. She could not let Sereia be destined to a life in a whorehouse, a life on her back.

"Please! Valliro, take me instead. Do not send her there, not to that darkness."

The magister stepped back and spread his arms. "Such fire, such passion. See how it burns? You want to save the girl? Well then, let's play a game. So long as you win in the arena, the girl will stay in the villa as my daughter's house slave. But if you fall... so to shall the girl fall."

"For how long?" Kitara felt hate harden her gaze.

"As long as I so command," Valliro gestured to the Salvaari prisoners. "The games begin this evening. Make them ready."

Kitara had seen the fear in Sereia's eyes as they were ripped apart. From there she, along with the Káli warriors, were trussed into another cart and sent forth. They barely talked in the back of the wagon and what little was said came in hushed whispers. Kitara's hand itched to reach for the arm ring that was no longer there, just as it longed to clasp her mother's wedding band. There would be no comfort in the caress of bronze, silver or sapphire. Instead, her hands clenched into fists. Whatever fate awaited her, she was prepared. Flickers of light assaulted their eyes as it slipped through the cracks in the wooden walls of the cart. The only thing she could make out from the world beyond the wagon's confines was the sound. It started soft, yet the closer they got to their destination it grew into a deafening roar.

From what she knew of the arenas those few slaves who survived time and time again received glory, wealth and more; the love of the crowd. A love that could just as easily turn. Some called it art, others blood sport, yet it was all the same. Sildari. Condemned slaves, forced to fight for the entertainment of their masters. The wagon was halted, and the prisoners were once more separated. They were in a small, fenced room that stank of sweat, puke and piss. There was another smell too, one that Kitara knew all too well. One that reeked of blood and death. They were in the bowels of the arena, that much was certain. A pair of Aureian soldiers escorted her through the tunnels beneath the spectators, while dozens more watched on as sentinels.

There would be no fight beyond the sands of the arena. The ceiling thundered as the stomps and raucous cheers of the mob grew ever louder. Through the maze of earth and wood was she led, until at last, a barred door was opened and the guards led her inside. Two more of their number stood within, their faces showing nothing. A stand stood at the back of the cell and strapped to it was armour of boiled leather and bronze. Kitara glanced at one of the soldiers who indicated the garb. He said nothing, yet the purpose was clear.

The greaves came first as she buckled them over her shins. The lining was white, like her tunic and added padding to the bronze. Grand etching encompassed the armour, its likeness adorning the bracers that she strapped to her arms. Like the greaves, they too were lined with ivory padding. Then came the cuirass that covered her from shoulder to hip. A strand of cloth she used to tie back her waves of golden hair, before at last she took up the great helm, its bronze shimmering in the torchlight. It had both nose and cheek plates and stood just as embellished as the rest of the suit. A magnificent plume of white horsehair sat atop it.

Kitara slid it under an arm and then followed the guards out of the cell, through the great maze and to a second cage. She was roughly pushed inside and then the steel door was bolted behind her. A shower of dust came from above as the crowd grew into a frenzy. Something was happening outside. She placed the helm on the long bench that ran the length of the room, making her way over to the second door, one that looked into the arena itself. She was about to peek when the bolt was drawn, and a second person was thrown into the cell. With a crash it shut behind the man as he bared his teeth and roared in defiance.

"Morlag?" her green eyes widened as she saw her friend.

He still wore nothing more than his white tunic. No armour and certainly no blade.

"Kitara," he took her proffered arm and the pair embraced. He pressed his forehead into hers, "Are you afraid?"

She looked from him and then to her hand, for the first time noticing the tremble that ran down more than just her spine. She forced her hands into fists with a grimace yet did not let her stare leave that of the Káli.

"I don't know if I can do this. I swore I would never fight for entertainment. I swore… and they have taken away my choice. I had killed before, and it is not death that I fear, and yet here, now, I tremble as a child."

Morlag opened her fists and wrapped her hands with his own. "Be strong, the spirits are with you," he said. "Sometimes we must show strength no matter the pain we harbour beneath. Now more than ever it is you who must be strong. After this day, you will be all that Sereia has."

Kitara's breath caught in her throat as she replied, "What do you mean?"

"Beyond this cell," Morlag gestured to the door and the arena beyond, "My people are being slaughtered one by one. I am to be executed next. I heard the soldiers laughing. While we have been bound in chains, a great war has begun. An army marches upon our homeland. Not just the legions of Aureia, but all of Medea is mustered. The knights of Kil'kara have ridden out from Rovira and the kingdoms of Annora gather their strength."

Horror filled Kitara. Another crusade against the pagans, just as there had been a century ago when they had been wiped from Medea. Morlag placed a hand upon her cheek before she could speak.

"They shed the blood of me and mine in the sands as a spectacle for the people. An offering to their gods. Do not despair," the Káli man told Kitara as he saw the sorrow rise within her. "And let no tears fall. I have known much happiness in my life, and the world will not end when I give my last breath. If you want a happy ending, it all depends when you end the story. And yours is not over yet."

"Morlag, I–"

He cut her off and gripped her shoulder. "I have seen my last day, that much is certain. But you must live. It is to you that Sereia will look. It is to you that she will place her hopes. She believes in you, as do I. Get her home."

Kitara took a deep breath, pushing back the turmoil that raged within. This was her friend's goodbye, his last words. She would not let him see her be weak.

"I do not know what strength I have," Kitara told him fiercely, "but I swear to you that I will watch over the girl, protect her, and reunite her with Salvaar once again. She will be as my own. By the spirits I swear it."

Morlag stepped back and reached to his throat. He still wore his snake tooth necklace. For some reason, the Aureians had left it. Perhaps a parting kindness for one so condemned. He pulled it up over his ears and held it out. Kitara bowed her head as her friend placed it around her neck. She ran a finger down the tooth, feeling the strength that lay within.

"May the spirits always watch over you," Morlag murmured as the door was thrown open and the guards poured in.

Kitara stepped back, fists rising in defiance. Her stance was light. The soldiers saw her poise and the darkness in her eyes. Spears were levelled and swords drawn as they eyed her, daring her to make a move. She tensed, her gaze flicking from one man to the next. She would fight them all if need be, with nothing but her bare hands.

"No," Morlag whispered from her side. "If you do then we both die here. Sereia dies."

Kitara closed her eyes and slowly lowered her fists. He was right, she knew it in her heart. There was nothing she could do; this fate was inevitable.

"I am ready," Morlag said louder, and his words were directed at the soldiers.

It was time. The Káli straightened his posture and squared his jaw. The Aureians led him to the wooden door as it opened. "Tanris, I come to you," he said for the second time in days. It would be the last. Then Morlag was gone, vanishing into the light. A deafening cheer rose to meet him. The door shut.

She never saw her friend again.

The last she heard of him was the great cheer that erupted followed by the roar of an arena fighter. Morlag was dead. The brother to the Káli chief was dead.

The loud voice of an Aureian echoed through the arena but she could not make out the sound. Kitara forced back the trembles that threatened and the emotion that surged. Pain, anger, sorrow, hate, rage. Confusion. She had to go now and fight for entertainment or lose the one person that she had left in this world. If she did not fight, if she *refused* to fight, Sereia would die; or worse. She would be whored for the rest of her days until age took her youth and she found a knife in her heart. She held Morlag's necklace tightly as a sword was thrown through the barred door to the tunnel.

Steel landed at her feet as the soldier's voice broke the silence, "It is time."

Kitara closed her eyes, feeling the strength of the spirits fill her with fire. She had never prayed to any god or spirit before but somehow the amulet comforted her. She placed the bronze helm over her head and took up the blade. It was straight and unembellished, the Aureian style. No longer than her own sword was, now so far away that it was a memory. Golden light flooded the cell as the gateway to the arena opened. She took a breath, and then walked out into the sun's gaze.

The sands beneath were coarse, perfect for her boots to grip on. She stood in a great wooden square that soared skyward on every side. Hundreds of people packed the stands. The sound, the smell. It was overwhelming. She could almost *taste* the blood and sweat in the air.

She was not alone. A man stood opposite her. Greaves covered his shins and a sleeve of armour ran down his right arm. A shining pauldron adorned the same shoulder, and his helm glinted in the sunlight. His chest was bare and well-muscled. Yet it was not to the armour, nor the vicious spear he carried that she looked. It was to the fresh blood that covered his form that drew her gaze. It dripped from his helm and ran down the blade of his lance. Her eyes went to his armoured right fist. Steel and flesh were covered in blood.

Morlag's blood.

It had not been quick.

It had not been painless.

That much was certain.

Rage burned beneath her skin. It was hungry… it wanted to be unleashed.

She was so engrossed in her enemy that she did not notice the silence that gripped the crowd. A silence only broken as the magister spoke from the stands. His strong voice gripped all of his people.

"A hundred years ago our ancestors marched east with a single purpose, to free the land of Medea from the tyranny of the Old Religion. Much of our forefathers' blood was shed to save the once ruined kingdom, and that distant land was strengthened by their sacrifice. The war was won, my brothers!" Valliro bellowed and raised his hands aloft.

He waited a moment as the cheers that followed fell silent once again.

"And yet that same enemy was not defeated. Now they rise again. Now, as before, they spread their dark magic. To make safe our great kingdom, his imperial majesty, Emperor Darius, has called upon our sons, our fathers, our brothers, to follow him east. May the sacrifices I gave you this day serve as harbinger to the fate that the emperor shall inflict upon the savages himself!"

More cheers resounded through the stands. Kitara felt her heartbeat begin to slow as the great beast within her stirred.

"And now, a final offering of blood," Valliro gestured down to the sands. "Entering the arena stands a man above all men, a titan of death. A sildari whose blade still runs with the blood of our enemy! I give to you Scarpa!"

The man opposite Kitara thrust his lance into the sky and let loose a war cry. He sounded more animal than man, and spirits, did it make her skin crawl. The crowd screamed their admiration as their champion slowly turned in a circle, taking it all in. Kitara bared her teeth as he turned to her. Scarpa took up the spear in both hands as Kitara's own fingers tensed on the hilt of her blade.

"His opponent hails from the distant lands of Salvaar. A warrior who has slain man and beast, a warrior whose tale is of blood and whose song if of the sword," the magister's voice echoed down to Kitara as his arm followed it. "People of Vesuva, I give to you Alessandra!"

Kitara frowned as the new name reached her ears. This was just a game to them, she realised. No more than a pastime... yet it was not their lives that were played with, nor their bodies toys in their bloody games. Jeers showered down upon her, yet she ignored them. They did not know her. She was not sildari. Not yet.

Scarpa levelled his spear toward her and gave the slightest nod. It was a gesture that she did *not* return. He had killed Morlag and countless others. She took a breath and allowed her feet to slide upon the sand. Her body was loose, her form perfect, as she clasped the sword with both hands. Everything faded from her vision save Scarpa. He filled her senses. She felt his breath, his speed and strength. She saw the confidence in his eyes and the lightness of his step as he came toward her. He had been in the arena many times. Had fought countless times. Had killed countless times.

But so had she.

Kitara had one advantage: she knew what it was like to lose. If she lost here, then Sereia would die.

"BEGIN!"

The cry came from the stands and the crowd erupted into a frenzy.

Sun glinted upon spear as it darted toward her throat. Kitara slid back and allowed the tip of the lance to miss by an inch. She did not move her sword to deflect, for it was too soon to give away her speed. Instead, she read his movements. Kitara slid to the side and feinted high. Scarpa barely reacted. He was good, he was very good.

He grasped the spear like a staff and turned thrust into cut as he came at her again and again. Kitara began to move as if in a dance as the swordsong began to play. She drew first blood and left a shallow line of crimson upon his bare left arm. Scarpa did not even grimace, instead he marched forward. Kitara blocked once, twice, three times, never staying still long enough to be hit. The spear added to his reach, and one false move would be the death of her, but the swordsong had enveloped her. He came close, the spear missed its mark by an inch as she moved. Instead of driving through her skull, the steel glanced off her helm. Her head rang as the blade left a furrow in the bronze. He had been fast, precise. And it was enough. She could read him now.

The spear came around, angled to skewer her like a boar. Kitara shifted, this time she took the blow with her sword as she moved. A slight flick of the wrists sent it out of harm's way. A second thrust followed the first and carved a path toward her throat. Kitara leaned back and rolled her shoulder to the side even as she stepped forward. Sword moved in unison with her body as muscle stretched and flowed. The blade came up inside Scarpa's guard and slid across the flesh of his side. The fighter barely grunted as blood was drawn; instead he turned with the blow and brought the shaft of his weapon around like a staff. Wind was driven from Kitara's lungs as the hard wood slammed into her back. She gasped even as her armour took the brunt of the blow. Kitara spun with it. She pirouetted and shifted her posture. Her sword came up and blocked the blow aimed at her head as she dropped to a knee. Steel slid down the spear's shaft where it met with Scarpa's fingers.

The man howled and stumbled back. Blood spewed from his hand. Kitara followed him back, deflected his hastily thrown thrust and then countered. The tip of her sword found his shoulder and staggered him. The blade ripped free of flesh, before it flashed across the muscle of Scarpa's opposite arm.

The spear fell to the sands and the crowd cheered for blood. Kitara stepped forward and pressed her advantage. Her first stroke sliced across his chest and sent him to his knees. She held her form, her stance was wide as she looked down at her defeated enemy. The crowd began to chant.

"Kill! Kill! Kill!"

Kitara gritted her teeth as she saw the fear enter Scarpa's eyes.

I will not kill for your entertainment.

She thought of Sereia, of Morlag's last words. Of her promise.

Kitara brought her blade down with a scream.

Blood flowed and the crowd roared. Scarpa fell beneath her sword.

TWENTY-EIGHT

City of Elara, the League of Trecento

Gulls cried high above as the shouts of 'landfall' came from the crow's nest. Kyler exchanged a grin with Alarik before he dropped from his bunk, snatched up his sword belt and charged up the steps that led to the deck. Merchant traders, passengers and sailors alike crowded the ship's railing as the great city of Elara arose before them. Dozens of massive cargo ships lay at anchor in the harbour, red roofed houses spread out as far as the eye could see, and the streets were swarming with townspeople. The city walls that wrapped the city were impenetrable. Glints of silver armour came from atop the stone as soldiers patrolled wall and rooftop alike.

"Welcome, my lords, to Elara," the captain called from the quarterdeck with a toothy grin.

Alarik clapped a meaty hand on Kyler's shoulder as he spoke, "Magnificent, isn't she?"

"I've never seen anything like it," the Medean breathed as he took it all in.

It was as beautiful as the songs described. A city of such wealth and prosperity that it could withstand not just empires, but the master of all things, *time*.

They made landfall and disembarked. The horses were brought up from below and, once they were safely stabled, the knights found lodgings in a tavern. The price was good, and if the innkeeper was to be believed, the wine was better still.

Alarik carefully closed the door behind them and dropped his packs on one of the beds. Kyler glanced out the shutters into the street a floor below, watching as the people of Elara hurried down the paved streets. Merchants and craftsmen alike seemed to be at every corner, while some of the buildings had been likewise transformed for trade.

"Here," Kyler turned back as Alarik spoke. The battlemaster held out Wa'rith's sword, now wrapped in a faded cloak.

Kyler took it with a raised eyebrow.

"You want me to have this?"

"Don't lose it," Alarik chuckled, reaching back into his pack. "There is a task now to be done: find the man who forged that sword."

Kyler nodded and flipped back a piece of the cloak to allow his eyes to wander the sword's hilt. "This is good steel. I imagine that even here there are few men who could forge its likeness. The soldiers here I would imagine get their equipment from whatever lord pays them. So a few coins and I'd wager that any of the mercenaries or hired swords here would be able to tell of its providence."

"And you got all that from looking at the blade?" Alarik said as he withdrew a small pouch.

Kyler shrugged before he replied, "When I was a boy, I spent a few summers apprenticed to our town blacksmith, Gascon. He was renowned for being one of the finest smiths north of the empire. Sellsword and duke alike would pay fortunes for his work. It was he who forged my own blade."

"Full of surprises aren't you, Pisspot?"

The battlemaster ran a thumb over his pouch. Kyler grinned and took out some thin rope from his own bag. With it he strapped the cloak to the sword and left naught but its hilt free. He took a second length and used it to create a makeshift bandolier, slinging the sword across his back securely.

"And while I am playing tracker, what will you be doing?" Kyler asked as he tightened the rope.

Alarik raised the pouch. "I have here the remnants of one of those little smoke bombs. There are men here, apothecaries, foreign traders and dealers of the so-called *mystic*, that I think may be able to give some answers. Whether by the sword or the powder in this pouch, we will find Harvarder. Meet me back here at nightfall, no matter what you find. If you discover anything at all come back here without delay. Am I understood?"

"Yes, sir."

"It is a dangerous game, hunting shadows. Don't stray too far from the light."

Clad head to toe in chainmail, sturdy bracers, greaves and a gorget of steel, matched by the sword and knife at his waist and blade upon his back, Kyler had no difficulty making his way through the packed streets of Elara. Despite moving out of his path, few people gave him a second glance for he looked no more than a hired sword.

"Excuse me," Kyler called out as he noticed a four-man retinue of plate clad soldiers walking down the street.

The men turned as they heard his voice and watched his approach. The leader, sporting embellished steel plate, ran his wary eyes over Kyler.

"Aye?"

"Could you perhaps point me toward the arsenal?"

"Looking for work?" the soldier replied and fingered the hilt of his sidesword.

"Something like that," Kyler said.

The man nodded thoughtfully before he gestured back down the road from whence he had come. "Follow the street until you reach the harbour. Look south to the belltower, you can't miss it. There you'll find what you seek."

Kyler dipped his head in thanks before he headed down the

road. His path through the maze of streets, alleys and markets led him to the city arsenal; a place where armour, arms and other implements of war were forged, maintained and repaired. As the soldier said, he could not have missed the belltower if he had tried. It stood as a great pillar of stone, lancing over a hundred feet into the sky. Atop it was a huge bell of bronze. Its ringing could be heard from anywhere in the city and was loud enough to awaken even the deepest of sleepers from their slumber. The perfect warning tool.

The arsenal was built all around it. Huge walls surrounded the district and cut off its private docks from the rest of the port. Warships lined the harbour, while crossbow wielding soldiers lined its walls. A company of guards stood at its massive gates. By day, people could pass through freely. By night, entry without permission would cost their life. The few inns in the arsenal were for housing mercenaries, sellswords and providing food and drink to their ilk. Kyler made his way inside, and his eyes slowly adjusted to the dim light of the inn.

Around half the tables were filled with warriors of all sorts. Some carried swords, others axes or vicious war hammers. Many regarded him momentarily, before they turned back to their drink or games of chance. Kyler made his way over to the counter and bought a drink, turning to examine the room fully. Few of the clientele sat alone. One man caught his eye, a man with the olive skin and dark hair of an Elaran. Kyler made his way to the table and sat opposite the warrior.

The Elaran looked up with something of a glare. "Can I help you?" he asked warily.

"Perhaps we can help one another," Kyler replied and pulled the wrapped sword from his back. He placed it on the table between them. "I am looking for the man who forged this blade. I thought that a man in your position might be able to offer some assistance."

"Might be able to," the mercenary gave him a suspicious look and pushed back the cloak to reveal the steel beneath, "You said something about helping me?"

Kyler grinned. As he had thought, the sellsword only thought to procure coin. Though men of his station were tight lipped about their employer and true nature of their work, asking for something like this and offering coin... well, that tended to yield far better results.

"I'm willing to pay," Kyler told him.

The mercenary returned the toothy smile and pushed the sword back toward Kyler. "Perhaps then we can help each other," he said. "I know this smith's mark as most know their own hearth."

Without another word, Kyler snatched a few coins from his purse and placed them on the table beside the sword. When the sellsword reached for them, the knight curled his fist around the gold and gave the Elaran a withering look.

The mercenary snorted. "The man you seek is Nicolo," he told Kyler, "and if it's more steel that you seek there is no one better in these parts."

"How do I find him?"

The mercenary's directions were precise, and it did not take Kyler long to locate the blacksmith.

"Nicolo?"

The bald blacksmith turned toward Kyler and ran his shrewd eyes over the Medean. He was a big man, broad of shoulder and strong of arm. Kyler could not remember seeing anyone so large, even among the Order.

"Aye," the Elaran replied gruffly.

Kyler glanced over the racks of sword, spear, halberd and shield. It was as the mercenary had told him: Nicolo's craftsmanship was remarkable.

"I hear that you are the best smith in the city," Kyler told him.

Nicolo grunted. "And who are you? You don't strike me as a

common soldier or one of the magister's knights."

"I ride with Malius O'Lacey," Kyler replied. O'Lacey was famous throughout the kingdoms, a true son of Medea. His skill as strategist, warrior and businessman had attracted many, many men to his company of mercenaries. His name and deeds only rivalled the Annoran sellsword Bellec.

"O'Lacey? Even here that name has power," Nicolo nodded. "When last I heard your master thought to make his way to the far north. What brings you here so far east?"

"I am looking for a friend of mine. Saved my life in a battle not a month back and in so doing lost his sword," Kyler pulled the blade from his back. "I owe him my life, and thought that if I returned the sword, I could thank him properly."

Nicolo took the proffered blade. His eyes widened when he saw the steel beneath and let out a long breath.

"I thought she was lost forever," Nicolo breathed. "When Cleander came to me for a new blade I nearly refused him. These swords are my life," his lips curled upward for a moment before he handed the weapon back to Kyler. "So why come to me?"

Cleander. So that was the name he used. It made sense for a man such as Markus Harvarder to take an alias. If the Order had learned of his survival he would have been hunted down and killed as a traitor many years ago.

"I am new to the city," Kyler admitted. "All I have to go by is this sword and my friend's name. I thought perhaps that a man such as yourself might know how to find Cleander."

"I cannot help you, my friend," Nicolo sighed. "Cleander keeps to himself for the most part. You might try your luck with Mellisanthi, though."

"Mellisanthi?"

"Larissan woman, runs a brothel in the merchant district. The Star of Elara. Seen Cleander with her girls from time to time." He gestured down the street toward the district.

Kyler slung the sword back across his shoulder as anticipation burned through his veins. He thanked Nicolo and began his walk back to the tavern and Alarik. They had found him. They had found Wa'rith, and soon they would burn the nest down around him. For Matias and Emir, Neph and Quinn... for Torin, and all the others that Harvarder had slain.

Elise spun the magister's seal in her hand. After the ball last night, she had hoped to have found answers, and in some cases she had. The magister was dealing in child slaves and her parents had been murdered by his hand. Somehow the two were connected, yet she would not know why until she met with Lord Cirillo. Then there was the issue with the dark clad man, the one who had so viciously killed the magister's nephew. *Inside* the magister's palace. She gazed at the seal, a signet ring of silver bearing the griffin symbol. Elise would get answers, and then Imrohir would pay a heavy price.

Elise rolled from her bed. Bare feet touched the ground as she lightly began to walk toward her hidden chest. The night air was cool against her cheek, and her pale nightdress did little to keep it at bay. Elise took her kukri knife out from under her bed, slid it in between the boards in the wall... there was a faded hiss and then the light of the candles fled. She shot to her feet as she heard boots cross her room. The kukri came up as the dark figure lunged. A hand muffled her shout while a second latched around her wrist and stopped the kukri in its tracks.

"Scream and they will all know your secret," a man's voice growled as he used his strength to turn the kukri against its owner.

Elise stared into those eyes, those dark pits that bored into her. It was the man from the ball, the one who had killed Daivin. She nodded as he took the knife from her grasp. He stepped back and lowered the kukri. Elise ran her gaze over him, looking for some kind of clue… yet he wore a mask and a hood. All she could see were his eyes and even then, absent the light of the candles, she could not get a read on him.

"Lady Elise Delfeyre," the man said at last. "The Nightingale."

"I have no idea what–"

"I saw you at the ball, slipping though the magister's palace unattended. I will admit I harboured my doubts, that is, until word reached me this morning that a feather was found in Imrohir's rooms," he replied. "I came here this night to talk, nothing more. Now, if you do not lie to me, I will not lie to you. I am sure that after last night you have questions."

Elise straightened her nightdress and clasped her hands. She met his stare with her own, she would not show him fear. Gods, she had been careless. This man, this killer, had so easily tracked her here, to her family's house.

"You killed a man," Elise stated.

"Lord Daivin, the magister's nephew. And you wish to know why? Very well. I work with the gangs and for some time Daivin did as well. He was our ally among the nobility… or so we thought."

The dark clad man offered the kukri back to Elise. "But while we were planning on toppling Imrohir, Daivin was spying on us, plotting against us, waiting to strike. I first learned of this through one of his agents tasked with finding where we ran our operation. I followed the trail he left in death, and as I sought out Daivin's men one by one, it became readily apparent how deep his treachery ran. Daivin had to die."

Elise fingered the blade. It all made sense.

"You have me at a disadvantage," she said.

"Pardon me?"

"You know who I am, what I am," Elise sneered to show that she was not afraid. "Seems only fair that I know your name."

The man snorted, as if amused. "Cleander of Annora," he told her.

"Well then, *Cleander*, what do you want with me?"

He turned his back on her and crossed his arms. "For many months now you have vexed the nobility of Elara," Cleander said. "Breaking into their chambers and strongrooms like a devil and leaving without a trace."

"I'm an excellent thief," Elise offered. "The best in the city."

"A fact that gives me some kind of peace of mind."

"What makes you think I care about your *peace of mind*?" Elise bit back a laugh.

"You have courage, Elise, but that will not save you," Cleander said. "If I can find you, so can they and while I am sure that this quest of yours is about more than just gold and jewels, it leaves too much to chance. I think this dangerous game that you are playing with the magister will lead to only one place. I think that it will claim your life. And I think you know that."

"He is dealing in child slaves," Elise blurted.

She was not sure why she said it, perhaps it was because she knew that Cleander spoke true. Perhaps it was out of spite toward the magister. If such a man knew of his crimes, then he could be toppled.

"Imrohir," Elise muttered.

Cleander's eyes shot open. "What did you say?" he asked.

"Last night when I was in his rooms, I came across the logbooks of Odile Nilsine."

"Captain of the Andromakei?"

Elise nodded. "The same. I thought it odd that the magister would have such books in his possession, the private logs of a captain in his employ. So, I had a look, and it was all there, written neatly upon its pages. He sends children to the empire, and Nilsine brings back great quantities of gold."

Cleander's hand fell to his sword. "That explains it then," he said. "How he has been able to bribe the council so easily for all these years, how he has garnered enough power to call for a vote to rescind the accords."

Now it was Elise's turn for surprise.

"The accords have kept us at peace for nearly three decades," she started, "have stopped the fear of war with Miera becoming a reality… and Imrohir wants to cast them aside? No, that cannot be true."

"Look around, Elise. The city is divided now more than ever. The empire has sent forth legions to bring Salvaar to heel. Now think, with tens of thousands of allied soldiers mere days from Miera's border, what would Imrohir have to gain?"

"Gods," she murmured. "The city states would unite against the horsemen, and if he wins in battle… if the League does what has long been thought impossible and defeats Miera, then the man who sits at the helm would be untouchable. Imrohir would not just be magister, he would be one of the greatest leaders outside of the empire."

"And now you tell me of how he has gathered such great wealth," Cleander said.

"This is not about the slaves, it never was," Elise closed her eyes. "This is about Miera and the power that would come with it."

Cleander looked to her with intensity burning in his gaze. "Then help me stop him," he said.

"How do you intend on doing that?" Elise asked. "The council is firmly in his pocket. Of the lords I only know perhaps *three* who would stand against him. If such accusations were brought to life it would be us at the hangman's noose."

Cleander ran a hand across the top of a flameless candle, allowing his fingers to slip through the smoke that still hung above.

"I do not believe that the mask you wear is the disguise. I believe that Elise Delfeyre is the illusion, and that who you are, who you truly are, is the Nightingale."

"You can tell that, can you?" Elise raised her eyebrows sarcastically,

"After one conversation."

"The Nightingale has become a symbol," Cleander continued. "Symbols mean something. They are all that give some people hope. People need something to believe in, something greater than their own lives. The people of this city, those the aristocracy drive into dirt for their own gain, they believe in you. It is this belief that gives them the power to achieve the extraordinary, and for what comes next, that is what this city will need."

"No," Elise shook her head in horror. "I am no saint for people to put their hopes into, nor symbol for them to follow. I never wanted this. All I ever wanted to be was Elise."

"It is too late for that now," Cleander told her. "You may not be looking for war, but war is *looking* for you. This fight has become bigger than either of us. The people will need guidance. When their leaders fall, it is to you that they will rally."

"Why will their leaders fall? What have you done?" she asked.

"It will happen tomorrow evening," Cleander told her. "When the masters of the city gather to vote and rescind the accords, when the magister's voice echoes through the council chamber, the lords of this city will die. The plans have been laid and we stand ready to move. The time is now, Elise, for us to take back Elara."

Elise paled as Cleander spoke. She was a thief chasing the man who killed her parents and destroyed her life, but this was something else altogether.

"You speak of *murder*," Elise growled.

"New growth cannot occur without first the destruction of the old," Cleander explained as he looked her straight in the eye.

Elise thought of Lord Cirillo, the man who had asked her to meet with him *after* the council meeting. She fought to stay composed and barely noticed the anger that seeped into her voice.

"Not all of the lords are bad. Imrohir rules with fear, and they are forced to obey. Others are beloved by the people and champion their causes. Priamos Stentor is a good man, Armorgas of Valentia,

Lord Cirillo Eris... you would destroy everything they have built."

"It was different in the beginning," Cleander told her. "It was never about destruction, it was about redirection. This vote changes everything. How many will fall in battle? To fight the Mierans in their own land is insanity. With the legions of Aureia at his back, Imrohir may triumph, but at what cost?"

"And how many will die in the streets when those men who provide them with food and shelter fall to your desires?"

"Great achievement is born out of great sacrifice," Cleander said.

Elise glared at him and her voice twisted into a snarl. "You are heartless."

"Heartless, no. I learned a long time ago to use my heart less."

"My parents were killed by the tyrant. It is cruelty that has taken so much and destroyed so many lives. And do you know why it still lives? Because of men like *you*," Elise spat as a tremble ran through her body. "I will *never* join you."

Elise knew that he could see the rage in her face, the pain that had frozen her to the spot. Nothing would ever persuade her to murder of innocent people, no matter whom they served. She had never killed, never shed blood; not even that of the most vile of men. She would not start that today.

"You're making a grave mistake," Cleander muttered.

"I don't think so."

"So be it," he said, and stepped toward her, malice filling his voice. "I should kill you now. My every instinct tells me to do so. But I won't. Tell yourself that the Nightingale isn't a symbol, tell yourself that you don't move against the magister out of a sense of misguided naivety if you must. But know this: if you move against me, if you so much as try to stop me, the street will know your name. When they come for you, when the magister's men bind you in chains and take everything from you, you *will* hear from me again."

TWENTY-NINE

City of Palen-Tor, Aethela, Kingdom of Annora

Lukas' lips twitched as the shouts began. Cries of panic and confusion came from atop the walls; screams of fear came from the people below. He saw the gates of the city begin to close. Lukas exchanged a look with Maevin, flicked his reins and led the company of horsemen toward the city.

"Stand or we shoot!" The shout came from above, accompanied by the sound of longbows being drawn.

Lukas held up a hand to stop the Káli riders as he brought his own mount to a halt. He looked up to the gatehouse and swept his gaze over the Annoran soldiers. In the months he had been absent, Lukas had become all but unrecognisable to those who had known him at Palen-Tor. His hair was longer, and his jaw covered in the beginnings of a beard. In place of armour and fine clothing, he wore the pelts and furs of a Salvaar warrior; to say nothing of the ragged cloth that covered his empty eye socket. His father's soldiers could only witness a band of pagan savages at their gate.

"Open the gates," Lukas called.

The gate captain glared down while his hand brushed the sword at his hip. "You are in no position to give commands here," the soldier replied.

"Oh, I am," Lukas sneered.

"What is your name, Salvaari?"

"Lukas Raynor, son to Dorian Raynor and Prince of Annora," he roared, and his voice was filled with the authority of one born into royalty. "Now *open the gates.*"

Within moments the doors boomed open.

"Prince, forgive me," the captain stuttered as Lukas met him within the walls. "If I had known–"

"Makes no difference," the prince replied from his horse. It was then that he saw the look in the captain's face, in the faces of *all* the soldiers and people nearby.

Fear.

They paled as they glanced at the Káli warband. Yet there was something else in their eyes, a thing that Lukas had seen before.

"You look at my companions like they are your enemy," Lukas said quietly.

The soldier frowned for a moment before he replied, "Then you don't know?"

"Don't know *what*, exactly?"

The captain looked at the Salvaari and regarded them with the same wary eyes that they now turned on him and his own men. Hands drifted close to weapons.

"The Spear of Durandail has been recovered," the soldier said. "Cardinal Aleksander has called for the holy army to assemble. The legions march here even as we speak... Emperor Darius is with them."

Lukas looked to Maevin and squared his jaw. He said not a word, knowing that she could see it all in his eyes. The Káli stirred as if a great beast had awoken inside of them.

"I see," Lukas replied, loud enough for all to hear. "I trust then that no harm will befall my companions today. If it did, the man responsible would pay a heavy price."

"By your order, my Prince."

It was only then that he saw it. The ruby eagle flags fluttering above the street... and they were not alone. Banners bearing the image of a silver lion over a great yellow field flew with them.

"Tell me, Captain," the prince said, staring at the flags, "why the sigil of the Aloys clan flies here."

Lukas felt anger roil within. He knew the answer before the captain spoke. He felt the emotion begin to take control.

"The betrothal, my Prince."

"What betrothal?" Maevin asked as she stared down at the captain.

"That of the Princess Kassandra and Emilian Aloys," he replied. "Duke Alejandro arrived here shortly after your brother's return. The king commanded it be done before the bells of war ring. Annora and Medea must stand shoulder to shoulder."

"Then there will be no justice here," Maevin hissed.

The Káli remembered Oryn and Aildor. The bodies of their people strewn though the streets, left to rot.

Lukas clicked his tongue to command his mount to walk.

"Not unless we take it," he said.

He led them deep into the city and through the throngs of people in the market. There were screams at their approach, mixed with cries of dismay. They fell upon deaf ears. The people scattered as the Salvaari rode through their midst. The many who could not flee into the cover of their houses crowded the edges of the street and prayed that the pagans would not attack. Lukas did not let his head so much as swivel as his own people cowered.

They made their way from the lower city into its wealthier districts, and then finally though the gates of the keep itself. Lukas and his companions dismounted under the watchful gaze of Annoran soldiers. He could see the hatred clear in their eyes, a hatred reflected in those of the Káli.

"Rodion," the prince turned to the warrior. "You and eight others remain here. Stay with the horses." Lukas placed a hand upon his shoulder. "Be wary, I do not expect a warm welcome."

"We are ready," Rodion grunted, his hand flexing upon the

shaft of his spear.

Lukas untethered his crutch from saddle and allowed his free hand to brush the sword and hammer at his side. Lukas exchanged a nod with Maevin, before he started toward the castle steps with the priestess and four armed warriors at his back.

The corridors were colder than he remembered. They seemed closer, as if they wished to suffocate the prince. He felt strangled here, as if the shackles and the mask that he had shed were screaming to be returned. Two royal guardsmen, clad in steel scale armour and blood red cloaks, stood at the entrance to the great hall. Shields were strapped to their left arms and bladed spears were grasped in their right hands.

"Stand aside," Lukas called out as they approached.

The guards shifted, lowered their stances and levelled their lances.

"Who goes there?" the lead guard commanded.

"Your *prince*," Maevin answered for Lukas.

The man hesitated for a moment. "Prince Lukas?" he called.

Lukas smirked. He recognised the voice as he recognised the face beneath the armour. He came to a halt, placed the crutch before him and rested both hands upon it.

"Did you not recognise me, Sir Landon Montbard?"

The knight looked from him to the Káli beyond. "Why are *they* here?" Landon asked.

"Oh," Lukas grinned savagely, "My friends and I have come to pay our respects."

"That witch took my cousin's head," Landon snarled as his hand tensed on his spear.

Maevin stepped to Lukas' side. "Blood for blood," she growled.

"Stand aside," Lukas commanded and nodded to the closed doors.

"My prince," Sir Landon grimaced and gestured from the weapons Lukas carried to the Káli at his back. "I cannot let you in so armed."

Lukas knew of the law, they all did. None could bear sword, axe, spear or any steel while a religious ceremony was taking place. Even in court it was forbidden without the permission of the king. The prince's grin faded.

"I gave you an order," he said.

"Prince Lukas—"

Lukas flicked an arm toward the two guards without a word. The sound of steel being drawn echoed through the hall. He met the Annorans' gazes with his own of fire.

"Stand aside, Sir Landon," Lukas ordered.

All conversation ceased as the doors to the hall crashed open and the armed Káli strode in. Two held Sir Landon and his companion at swordpoint while the other pair stalked behind the priestess. However, it wasn't to the Salvaar that the congregation looked, it was to their leader.

They saw his one eye; they saw his crutch and ruined leg.

Gasps filled the hall, a sound Lukas revelled in. He saw Father Bardhyl at the altar with King Dorian and Alejandro Aloys. Queen Riona stood with Dayne and Lady Sofia, her face paling. He saw Garrik Skarlit and Tristayn Martyn gazing wide eyed toward him, while Edmund Hornwood, Harold Robare and the other lords who had destroyed the Salvaari towns wore expressions of anger. He saw Kassandra garbed in a turquoise betrothal dress and at her side stood the duke's son, Emilian Aloys.

"Hello Father," Lukas began with a bitter smile.

"Welcome home, my son," Dorian replied coolly. If he felt any shock or surprise, he did not show it.

"Lukas!" Kassandra flew down the alter steps and threw herself at her brother.

The prince did not tear his eyes from the king as he wrapped an arm around his sister and held her tight. He had missed her more than he could say. Lukas took her cheek in his hand and placed a gentle kiss upon her forehead.

"You desecrate this sacred ceremony with steel," Father Bardhyl growled. "And worse, it is *pagans* that defy the gods' law. My king, take measure here."

Lukas waved a hand. "Priest, you will be silent," he said.

Bardhyl stared at the prince and visibly recoiled, as if struck.

"Prince Lukas, do this for me," the priest begged. "I have known you since you were a boy, taught you as best I was able. Yet this is sacrilege. You break the gods' peace by bringing heathens here. Blood and bone you are Annora, have you forgotten?"

"It was your *gods* that saw my village burn and my people murdered, holy man," Maevin spat as she stepped to Lukas' side. "And there you stand speaking of breaking peace? Your words are false."

Father Bardhyl gestured toward the doors, rage flashing across his eyes.

"I see your forked tongue, snake. I see the poison lies you spread. Remove yourself, or the gods will."

Maevin looked him up and down with a sneer and ran her tongue across her lips. "Remove me then. Show us the power of your *gods*." The priest did not move from the alter steps. "I thought not," she said.

"Enough of this," King Dorian snarled. "We will not exchange base insults like animals. We are all of us civil and shall act like it."

The hall grew silent as Annoran, Medean and Salvaari eyed each other dangerously. The Káli possessed all the weapons yet the delegation outnumbered them severely. If it came to it much blood would be shed. Lukas watched as his brother exchanged a look with his wife Sofia, before he hurried down the steps toward him. Dayne nodded to Lukas and held out an arm. The younger brother took it and pulled him into a one-armed embrace.

"I am sorry for leaving you, my brother," Dayne said. "Had we stayed the streets would have run with blood. I feared that to take you with us then would have been the death of you."

"I understand," Lukas replied as his brother stepped back. He looked to his father, the king, and his heart hardened. "And I thank you for it. But what I do not understand is how you have allowed my sister to be betrothed to that bloodthirsty, warmonger of a half-wit lion cub. A half-wit boy who takes pleasure in the slaughter of women and children. A half-wit boy who cost Annora an ally."

Emilian stepped forward, "You forget–"

"A half-wit boy," Lukas cut him off as his voice rose, "who knows *nothing* of the ways of men."

"You forget your place!" Emilian shouted. "First you side with the pagans and then you bring them to the heart of Palen-Tor. These people have no respect, no loyalty."

"These people know more about honour then you ever will," Lukas countered, planting both hands upon his crutch.

"Prince Lukas," Alejandro Aloys spoke up, words flowing from his silver tongue. "You will forgive my son for his indiscretions and the injuries that he has inflicted. He is young and has much to learn. But I ask you now, as friend and ally to your father, to apologise. See it done, let us move on."

Lukas said nothing, simply glared up at the duke. They were trying to speak to the *prince* that they all thought he was. That man, if he had ever existed, was gone.

"My son," Dorian walked down the steps toward him. "We stand side by side with our Medean brothers. Any other lord would demand your life for such an insult. Instead of blood, Duke Alejandro has given you a way out. I suggest you take it."

Lukas bit back a chuckle, though was unable to stop the sneer from contorting his lips. "You think you know me," he said. "You think that an apology will solve everything. It will not."

"Lukas, you will–"

"No," he growled and cut off the king. "I will not. I will not apologise for my words. I will not apologise for who I am. Even now your eyes betray you." Lukas looked around the hall and turned his gaze from lord to lady, knight to duke.

"Do you think that I cannot see the pity in your eyes? You are all looking at me like I am a cripple. I am *not* a cripple. I am not broken. I am a normal person, yet even before I lost my eye and leg you never treated me as such."

"My son," Dorian fought back the temper that flared. "Self-pity does not become you."

"Just as self-importance does not become *you*."

The king's furious glare met Lukas' icy gaze.

"You carry the eagle sword, act like it," Dorian said.

Lukas snorted and fingered the blade at his side. The blade bearing a hilt in the shape of the eagle. The symbol of Annora. The Raynor symbol.

"I am *done* following your commands, father," Lukas told him.

"You are a prince of Annora," Dorian said furiously. "Being prince is not a pastime, it is calling. It is a *duty*."

His voice was not filled with emotion; it was slow and measured. He was enraged, they all knew it. The hall had grown quiet as all watched with dread as father and son spoke.

"A duty forced upon me," Lukas replied.

"Then what are you going to do, *boy*? You can bleat or you can make a decision."

Lukas straightened his jaw before he replied, "You offer me a decision now? Decisions have never been mine to make. My eyes are open now. You do not know me, father, you never have. But now I know you. You take and you take and you take. First the three kingdoms, now Medea falls in line, and then what? Salvaar? What have they ever done to us? Was Annora not enough? And you would march on them, burn their villages, kill their people. And for what, father? For what? Greed? Religion? Yes, I have heard of this crusade, of how willing you were to join with the cardinal and his madness."

"Brother," Dayne placed a hand upon his brother's shoulder as he spoke. "Think about what you are saying. I implore you."

"He can speak for himself," Lukas shook the hand off. "For once, I want the truth."

"So this is what it comes to? There is much that you do not know, and perhaps some of the blame lies with me," Dorian clasped his hands behind his back and furrowed his brow, "Yet it would appear that my fears about you were well founded. I have placed far too much trust in you. You want the truth, my son, then listen well. If I was distant, it was because you refused to listen. If I was hesitant to give you command, it was because you are reckless. If I was hesitant to place my confidence in you, it was because you were naïve. A hundred times you would have fallen prey to your heart, and a hundred times you would have driven the world to ruin." Dorian's voice softened. "Lukas, you are my son." He extended a hand toward the prince. "Come. Let us speak as men. Perhaps when you have heard me, you will at last understand."

Lukas felt his heart being pulled in opposing directions. Here he found himself at a fork in the road. The sword of destiny cut both ways; he had been told. Perhaps this is what was always fated to be. He knew the path he had to take. Lukas glanced to Maevin, to the one person who had seen him for who he truly was, and she had not been afraid. Harkan had told him that she was his guide, that she would give him what he most desired. The spirits were with him.

"I refuse," Lukas said through bared teeth. "I will not stand by men who see me as anything but. I will not stand by those who have shown me little more than mockery and scorn. Perhaps I am not ruled by my head, perhaps I am not the son that you craved, father. Yet I will not silence my tongue and turn from myself any longer. You never trusted me, never saw me as an equal."

"And do you know why?" Dorian snarled, no longer able to hold back his anger. "You are a *jest*. A boy playing at being a man."

"We shall see," Lukas replied with a savage grin.

Father Bardhyl gazed down at the prince sadly. "Do not turn your back, Lukas," he implored. "Do not forsake the gods."

Lukas looked to the priest and withdrew the sun and moon amulet from beneath his clothes. A necklace he had worn since he was a child. He stared at the metallic surface and ran a finger over the iron. Then he raised it over his head and cast it onto the stones for all to see. Horror and stunned silence filled the hall. None spoke. None knew what to say.

"Lukas," Kassie said quietly and reached out to take his hand. "Please."

He could see the sorrow in her face, feel the pain in her eyes. He gave her a thin smile and clasped her hand. "It's okay, sweet sister. It's all okay."

Lukas placed a second kiss upon her brow, before he turned to leave. Her fingers slid from his own.

"Go then, leave," called out Emilian. "You tell your heathen friends; tell them we're coming."

The prince stopped and looked back to Aloys. "What did you call them?" he growled.

Emilian stared at him with venom as Lukas approached him. "*Heathen*," he repeated.

Luke stopped before the Medean, one hand rested upon his crutch while the other fell behind his back. "Say that again," Lukas goaded.

Emilian grinned. He leaned forward, his lips inches from Lukas' ear.

"Heathen."

The Medean lord gasped as air suddenly fled his lungs. Lukas wrenched his hand upward with all his strength and drove the knife deeper into Emilian's stomach. Blood spilled from Aloys' mouth as he fought for breath. He grabbed the prince's knife arm and he struggled to stand.

"Go to your gods," Lukas bade him as he twisted the blade deeper. "Tell them that they hold no power in the east." He pulled the blade free and sent a tide of blood pouring from the wound. Emilian Aloys fell, his eyes wide as if he had expected to live. The boy was dead before he hit the ground. A crimson pool stained the stones.

"What have you done?" Dayne shouted as cries began to fill the hall. "Lukas, what have you done?"

"What was necessary," Lukas spat.

Alejandro surged through the crowd and dropped to Emilian's side. Lukas stepped back from the body as the king roared for order. Duke Aloys placed a hand over his son's blood covered chest and closed his unseeing eyes.

"Light of the gods be with you," he whispered, before he turned his enraged vision to Lukas. His lips twisted into a violent snarl as he thrust his arm toward the prince.

"He murdered my son. *Kill* him!"

The Medeans in the crowd charged forward.

"NO!" cried Dorian, but it was too late.

Aloys' men leapt at the Káli with their bare hands to avenge their lord's death. Salvaari axes flashed as light glinted upon steel before the silver was stained red.

"STOP THIS MADNESS!" the king bellowed, and his command echoed around the hall.

His gaze swept the room. Three Medean lords lay dead alongside Emilian. Aloys' surviving men encircled the Káli with their Annoran allies. Thirty of them against Lukas and four armed Káli warriors.

The prince looked up from Emilian's corpse and stared at his father. He felt the blood upon his hand and the fire that had come with it. He felt alive. Dayne stood with Kassandra, an arm thrust protectively in front of the princess. She did not tremble, nor shed tear. She was strong, no matter the heartbreak Lukas knew she felt.

Sir Garrik and Tristayn stepped alongside their lord and king as his voice filled the hall, echoing out into the palace, "GUARDS!"

He met Lukas' eye. Royal guards descended upon the room, shields and spears held at the ready. Steel dipped toward the Salvaari. Lukas adjusted his grip on the knife, unwilling to look away from Dorian.

A cry came from the altar. "Lower your weapons or the holy man dies." Maevin's voice cut through the air like a sword.

They all turned to the priestess. She held Father Bardhyl's robes tightly in one hand, while with the other she pressed a knife into his neck.

"Throw down your weapons!" King Dorian shouted without hesitation. "Do it now!"

The guards complied and tossed spear and shield onto the hall floor. Maevin pulled the distressed priest down from the altar into the midst of the Káli. She had given them a way out.

"Goodbye, *father*," Lukas spat. He spared Kassie a final glance, before he led the Káli from the hall.

Maevin brought up the rear, her blade resting on Bardhyl's back as they made their escape. Lukas heard the king's shouted orders as they fled the hall. Soldier and guard sped through the castle. Dayne and Sir Garrik followed barely twenty feet behind, swords in hand, with a company of armed royal guard. Soldiers flooded the courtyard to either side, and those few in front scattered with a glance from Lukas as he gestured to his hostage.

Rodion and his people still watched over the horses. They saw Lukas and his company coming and swiftly mounted before they brought steel to bear. Rodion snatched out his bow and nocked an arrow as he turned to the gate of the keep.

"Form a circle!" Rodion roared. The Káli rode forth and created a wall of horse and man between their companions and the pursuit.

Lukas heaved himself into the saddle and snatched up the reins of Maevin's mount. She needed both hands for the priest. One to clutch his robes, the other the knife at his throat. They made for the gate and walked out into the street beyond. Lukas looked back to Dayne.

"Remove your men from the wall and shut the palisade," Lukas called. Maevin pressed her knife into the priest's back ever more to prompt a cry from his lips.

"Do as he says," Dayne said.

Lukas watched the wall. They did not have much time… if but one man had fled the keep before they had reached the gate they could still be undone.

The Annoran archers left the wall, reaching the older prince's side just as the palisade thundered down. Lukas waited a moment as the last of the soldiers left the gatehouse; the man who had brought the palisade down. He let the reins of Maevin's horse fall to the stallion's neck and looked to his brother. Dayne looked back with a squared jaw and ice-cold eyes.

There was a gasp and a scream. Father Bardhyl toppled to the ground. Blood turned his white robes red. Maevin leapt into her saddle as the first of the cries left Dayne's lips. The Káli surged down the street with Lukas at their head.

Dayne reached the top of the wall a step behind his men. Bows came up as arrows were turned toward the retreating horsemen.

"No," commanded the prince as he watched his brother ride away. "You could kill Lukas. Let them go."

King Dorian raged as he stormed into the council chamber. He tore the crown from his head and cast it aside.

"My king," called Tristayn, hurrying to his lord's side.

"Get out," Dorian roared, turning his furious eyes on everyone.

Knight, general and lord hurried from the room without a word. He looked to his wife, Riona, who stood with an arm around Kassandra.

"All of you."

Riona nodded and took her daughter's hand before she led her from the chamber. Dorian waited until the door closed behind them and then he grabbed at the edge of a small table and wrenched it over with a bellow that shook the heavens. Map, scroll and gold scattered all over the ground. The king clenched his hands until they hurt.

He felt the hand gently take his arm before he saw it. Dorian spun around, a roar upon his lips. Then he saw who owned the hand and the shout died.

Eveline Ayria.

"My Lord," she started.

"Did you not hear me?" he said quietly.

"I did," Eveline replied. "But some burdens you should not bear alone."

The king felt a tremble roll through him. It was strong and burned far brighter than any flame. It was a thing he had not felt since Aspasia's death.

"I am *enraged*. I grow weary of this... so weary."

"Let me help you, Dorian," Eveline said tenderly, and she reached out slowly. Her hand found his cheek. "Let me help you carry it."

Dorian met the Medean woman's eyes. His gaze softened in those pools of shining hazel. They burned softly like a candle at first, before that flame grew. His lips found hers. The kiss was deep. Her breath, her touch, intoxicated him. She was all he could feel, all he could taste. His hands went to her back as their bodies pressed together. Dorian gripped her tight as she pulled him backward. Eveline was on the council table, her strong legs wrapped around the king's waist as her hands sought his belt.

THIRTY

City of Palen-Tor, Aethela, Kingdom of Annora

Kassandra bit her lip and fought back the turmoil of emotions that raged within. She stilled her trembling hands as she closed the door to her room behind her before she leaned heavily against the sturdy oak. A single tear spilled from her eye and rolled down her pale cheek. It had been a day since Lukas had returned. Kassandra had thought her prayers answered when the hall's doors had been flung open and in walked her brother. She had thought that when he returned, all her problems would have been solved.

Now Lukas was gone. Now Emilian was dead.

Lukas. The one person aside from her mother who she dearly loved, the one who had been as her closest friend, was gone; disappearing back into the shadows from whence he had come. The sight of his crippled leg and one eye had torn at her heart yet what he had done threatened to shatter it.

Kassandra wiped away the tear and dropped to her knees by her bed. She reached under and pulled forth a long chest. Kassie lifted the lid to reveal the wooden practise sword within. The tool that Lukas had given her when they had trained together. A knock came from the door. The princess glanced up and was just about to shove the box back under her bed when she heard a girl's voice come from beyond.

"Princess?"

Kassie bit her lip as she recognised the voice. "Come in," she said.

The door opened and in came her handmaiden, her friend, her confidant, Marian Martyn. The girl's eyes widened as she saw Kassandra and the wooden sword. Without a word she turned, shut the door and drew the bolt.

"You need to be careful," Marian hissed as she came to Kassie's side. "If anyone *else* had seen–"

"Please don't tell," Kassandra murmured.

"I would never," the maid kneeled by the princess as she replied.

Kassie took her friend's hand and pulled her into a tight hug. "Thank you," she said.

"I am so sorry," Marian whispered. "I know how close you were."

The princess broke off the embrace. She ran her fingers down the smooth wood of the sword.

"Before he left, Lukas gave me this," Kassie said. "He would take me down to the castle cellars and give me lessons. Against tradition I know, and many would have called it sacrilege... but in truth I never much cared for those. I have been raised to look to knights for salvation. I would rather learn to use a sword myself. Do you understand?"

"Yes," Marian replied as she looked to the blade. "I think I do. For so many years we have been friends and you have never been one to follow, to watch. The day you returned from Salvaar, what did you do? You did not hide yourself; you did not lock yourself in your room like you had every right to do. You walked through the streets and greeted the people as friends. You danced with the children. You smiled. You have a good heart, a willing heart, and the people love you for it. We all love you for it."

"People paint the world with shadows," Kassie said after a moment. "They tell you what is right and wrong, who loves you, who hates you, who deserves to live and who deserves to die. If the world was meant to be painted so, then would it not have collapsed a long time ago? There is hope in this world, there is joy. Your spark, my dear Marian, burns ever bright."

The maid placed her hand atop Kassie's and pressed it into the wooden sword.

"You have always been strong, even without this," Marian said.

"Do you know something? It is not anger, nor even sorrow that I feel for my brother," Kassie told her. "I am worried that he has lost his way."

The city bells tolled, and their song resounded through Palen-Tor. Shouts filled the hallways. Kassie exchanged a look with Marian. A fist thumped into the door.

"Your highness, you had better come quickly," a guardsman called. "The king awaits you in the courtyard."

Prince Dayne watched from atop the walls of the keep as rank upon rank of soldiers marched through Palen-Tor. An ocean of violet and steel. The great silver army had come. Ahead came a company of mounted knights led a pair of finely clad griffin standard-bearers. They held aloft the griffins to the cheers of the crowd. Behind them flew another two banners, one with the Aureian griffin over a purple field, the other bore the sun and moon of the gods to remind the men why they fought.

For their gods.

For their people.

For their emperor.

Then came the legions. Dayne recognised them by the marking on their flags. They were the men of the fifth legion, hardened veterans who had served in every corner of the empire. They were of the seventh legion, soldiers who had marched north in the pacification of Irene. With the griffin standards rode the leader of this force, a man whom Dayne knew by name and deed. General Ilaros Arran.

Though the prince had never met the man, the general's reputation had spread far and wide. Ten thousand of Aureia's finest marched under his command. A great line of silver shining beneath the gaze of Durandail's sun. Then he saw the sea of blue riding in the column's midst. Cloaks and plumes of sapphire, armour that shone brightly in the sun, lances held tightly in steady hands and heater shields slung across their backs. The banner of Durandail and Azaria flew in the breeze above them.

The knights of Kil'kara, and they were not alone. A pair of men rode side by side at their fore. One wore steel plate, etched with Durandail's sun. His cloak was trimmed with white fur, while atop his head sat a magnificent helm. The other man wore an embellished cuirass matched by his bracers and greaves. His cape was of violet while an equally coloured sash ran from shoulder to hip. His plumed helm bore a crown of gold, while the hilt of his sword bore a pair of entwined griffins. Now there was a man that Dayne knew, a man he knew well.

The prince hurried down the stairs and crossed the courtyard. Ranks of brilliantly clad royal guardsmen filled the castle steps, while Dayne joined the company before them. His family.

Five heavily armed men rode into the courtyard. Bands of violet adorned their left arms, while their armour had a pair of griffins carved upon it. They were of the Arkin Garter. The emperor's private guard. Strong men that hailed from the Valkir Isles. Then came the griffin and banner bearers, followed by five more knights of Kil'kara.

"Make way for the King of Kings," one of garter roared. "His Imperial Majesty, Darius the third, Emperor of Aureia and the free cities, High Lord of Berenithia, Conqueror of Irene and Heir to Larissa."

The company parted and three men rode through their midst. One bore the colours of the knights, another, those of the legions, while the third man, the lead rider, was Darius. In unison they dismounted.

"Welcome to Annora, your majesty," King Dorian called before he bowed to the emperor.

Dayne followed suit, they all did.

Darius spoke, his accented tone as smooth as silver, "Rise. I will not be bowed to by a king in his own kingdom."

"You do me a great honour," Dorian replied.

"Come now," the emperor extended a hand. "You and my father were great allies, friends even. I would have us stand as such."

King Dorian clasped the Aureian's arm. A great roar filled the courtyard as people cheered.

Emperor Darius let his gaze move to the woman at Dorian's side.

"Queen Riona," Darius greeted her. "The rose of Torosa some call you. I can now see why."

"You are too kind, my lord," Riona smiled.

Darius looked to the girl at the Queen's side. "Let me guess, you must be the princess, Kassandra."

Kassie nodded, "Yes, Lord Emperor."

"I have heard tell of the princess that so gallantly rode to Salvaar with three hundred hardened men to find her brother," Darius said. "I should very much like to hear the tale from your own lips."

Then Darius saw the eldest son of Dorian. He stepped in front of the Dayne and looked him up and down.

"Prince Dayne."

"Emperor."

The emperor grinned and pulled his friend into an embrace. "It is good to see you my brother," Darius said.

Dayne grinned and clapped a hand on Darius' back. "Likewise, my friend. It has been far too long."

"Five years? No, six," the emperor stepped back. "Not since Ventos. But tell me, where is Prince Lukas?"

"There were complications yesterday," King Dorian told him. Neither voice nor face betrayed emotion.

"Nothing bad, I trust."

"It will soon be made right," the king replied.

"Ah, I have been remiss," Darius turned to the two warriors at his back and gestured to them in turn, "You will not have met my companions. General Ilaros Arran, commander of the northern armies, and Bavarian of Rovira. Grand master of the south and leader of the Order of Kil'kara."

"Light of the Twins be with you my brothers," King Dorian said in greeting.

The general thumped fist to heart and dipped his head in salute.

"And with you, my king. The gods have shown you their favour here in the north, and I pray that same strength remains with us on the road we walk," Bavarian replied. "You will have heard that his holiness, Cardinal Aleksander, travels with us."

"Indeed," Dorian nodded.

A rider had been sent well in advance of the great silver army to forewarn the Annoran court.

"The cardinal will join us this evening," Darius informed them. "He brings with him a mighty gift. One that been in my family for a hundred years."

The Nightingale watched silently from the rooftop as Lord Cirillo Eris moved about his house. Elise watched as he walked into the Aureian styled courtyard within the very centre of the villa. A pair of sellsword bodyguards strode behind their lord as he entered the roofless room.

He came closer and faced his men. His words were lost on Elise as she made her move. The Nightingale dropped down from the tiles and landed at Cirillo's back. The kukri flew into her hand as the guards cried out. The knife was at Cirillo's throat before the two sellswords had freed their blades.

"Send them away," she hissed into the lord's ear and her voice was barely loud enough for him to hear.

"Leave me," Cirillo ordered. "Bar the door."

"Lord?" One of the warriors took a step toward them.

Elise moved the kukri ever so slightly and tightened her grip.

"Do it now!" the lord growled.

The guards fled the room and heaved the doors closed. Elise spun Cirillo around, knife still at his neck. "If you are here to kill me, I am ready," he said, and his eyes burned with anger.

The Nightingale stepped back and sheathed the knife. Her gaze did not leave the lord as she reached up and tugged the scarf down. The mask came next. It fell to her throat as she loosened its ties. Only the hood remained, but that was enough.

"Elise?" Cirillo gasped. "What are you doing here? It is too dangerous… we were supposed to meet tonight."

"I had no choice," she replied and moved back into the shadows. "There is going to be an attack tonight. The gangs move against the council. They want to stop the vote."

"How do you know of that?" Cirillo frowned.

"What difference does it make?" Elise said and spread her arms.

"None, you are right. The gangs would not be so reckless," Cirillo gritted his teeth. "Does anyone else know."

"I am not sure," Elise murmured. "I only found out last night. I came here to save your life."

"Then I am indebted."

"Tell me about my parents," Elise bade him.

The lord let out a long sigh, before he turned to the small table that sat beside the pool. He took up a jug and poured wine into a glass. Cirillo looked to Elise and indicated a second cup. She shook her head in reply.

"When I met Catinya's father many years ago, the world was a different place," Cirillo began, "Elara was a different place. It was he who saw what could be gained from ending slavery here in the states. He had a great gift you see. When Aillard Viorica spoke, everyone listened. His words could grip you by the ears and reach deep into your heart. He was a visionary, a man who thought that there were too many laws that enslaved the people to their leaders. People came from the far corners of the empire just to speak and argue; some just to listen. In a few hours he could take everything that you knew and held dear and turn it on its head. Aillard was a great man, a brother. His ideals were soon taken up by many. His daughter, his students, and the brightest of them all, was Imriel Delfeyre, your father."

Elise felt a shiver run down her spine.

"I didn't know," she said.

"They were entangled in the most dangerous of games, Elise," Cirillo said quietly, "A danger that they wanted to spare you from. After Aillard died, it was Imriel and Catinya who took up his cause. They worked in the shadows to keep you safe, they had to. Slowly people were coming to hear them as well. Not just the poor of the city, but some lords and councilmen as well. Two years ago they came to me for help. They discovered a secret kept by the magister himself. A secret that could see the city undone."

"The slaves," Elise told him as she slowly pieced the puzzle together.

"So you know then?"

"Two nights ago, at the ball," she confirmed. Then Elise froze in place and stared at Cirillo. "If you knew, then why was Imrohir not charged for treason? Why is he *still* magister?"

"Think, Elise, through the deal with Aureia, Imrohir had *bought* most, if not all, the council," Cirillo said quietly. "Any attempt to remove him from power would have failed, and the perpetrators would have found the hangman's noose. By the time your parents came to me, Imrohir was more than just untouchable, he was invincible. I tried to warn Imriel and Catinya. I tried to tell them to forget Imrohir and leave their course before it was too late."

Elise felt anger surge through her like a raging fire. She fought to hold it back, but it grew strong.

"You *coward*," she spat.

"No," Cirillo shook his head. "You weren't there. If it had just been my life in peril, perhaps I would have joined them. But tell me, if the lives of your family, a wife, children, were at stake, would you have stood against such a man? A man who would have killed them all had I acted? I tried to save your parents that night. I tried. I couldn't."

Elise's knuckles whitened on the hilt of her kukri.

"What happened next?" she asked.

"I do not know how but the magister learned of what your parents knew. He feared what they had learned, and who they might tell."

Cirillo placed the glass upon the table and ran a finger across its lip. "He dealt with Catinya first. She was the daughter to Aillard Viorica, a man whom Imrohir feared and despised. The poison was given to her in small doses at first, and then when she became ill, the physician gave her more. Then they came for Imriel. The magister's men disguised in the rags of gangmen were ordered to make it appear as a brawl."

"How do you know about the physician," Elise growled in anguish. Tears filled her eyes.

"After Catinya's death, he came to me, confided in me," Cirillo said. "When the time is right, I believe he will give testimony against Imrohir. Until that day comes, I have waited and prepared. I have been biding my time, watching for the day that Priamos Stentor at last makes his move. I suggest that you do the same."

"His name," Elise hissed.

"Who?"

She took a step toward him. "The physician. Give me his name."

"Casimir Dusan," Cirillo told her.

He looked to her with sad eyes. Could he see even a hint of what she felt? She had barely been nineteen when her parents had been killed. The whole world had believed in the sickness and the gang violence, yet thanks to her father she had guessed the truth. For two years she had searched and hunted in the dark alone while being treated as less than dirt by the people that she walked the streets with. She had uncovered the lies and now she knew that none who had known the truth had stood up to their monster of a lord.

"I beg you, do nothing rash. The fate of the city depends upon it," Cirillo bid her.

Elise blinked back the tears and closed her eyes. She took a breath; at last she knew the truth. Her parents' deaths had been no accident. Everything that she had worked for, everything that she had fought for had been no illusion. Then she remembered Cleander.

"Did you say Priamos Stentor?"

"Yes?" Cirillo frowned.

Dread filled her. "Stentor is on the *council*," Elise breathed.

"The gangs," the lord's face paled as they both understood. "If Stentor dies, everything will have been for nothing. Your parents will have been for nothing. Elara will be enslaved by the next tyrant awaiting his crown. What did you hear? Speak!"

Elise turned her mind back to her conversation with Cleander. She remembered his words and the passion of which he delivered them.

"Some kind of powder. It will turn the council into ash."

"I know of the powder," Cirillo cursed. "In enough quantity it can sunder ships and destroy stone. But where could you store enough to destroy the hall?" He looked up and met Elise's gaze. "The tunnels. They run beneath Elara for miles... from the magister's house to the Pits, even beneath the council chamber."

Without a word Elise pulled the scarf up over her nose and lips, reaching for her mask.

The feasting that followed Darius' arrival in Palen-Tor had been magnificent. No expense had been spared, and even the emperor had brought gifts. The great hall had been filled with song and dance, merriment and no shortage of wine. Yet when the celebration had at last come to an end, Darius ushered King Dorian, Prince Dayne and a company of Annoran, Aureian and Medean lords and knights down to the castle courtyard. Dayne watched on as the first of the Cardinal's guards rode through the gate in his garb of white. There were twenty of the ivory knights in total, riding in formation around a pair of wagons. One was a magnificent carriage fit for any king or emperor, the other a caged wagon covered in canvas sheets.

The first man to dismount introduced himself as Farris Quinnal and then turned to the first of the carriages. A guardsman opened the wooden door and then their charge stepped down onto the paved stones. His wizened face was covered in wrinkles. His thinning grey hair was neatly cropped. A pair of amber eyes shone brightly, while his lips were twitched into a kind smile. His long robes were whiter than ivory and shimmered in the torchlight. The wide sleeves of the garment were trimmed in silver, embellished with symbols. The medallion at his throat was of the finest silver and gold.

"In all my travels, I have never seen a city so beautiful, your highness," the cardinal said as he approached.

"Your Holiness," King Dorian kissed Aleksander's ring. "You are most welcome."

"I apologise for my delay," the cardinal said. "Yet the gods spoke to me and in the vision they revealed a sacred truth that may prove useful in the wars to come."

Dayne's gaze wandered to the second wagon. Farris and another of his men had untied the canvas. He glanced at his father and then to Darius. The emperor stared at the wagon with an intensity that the prince had seen only once before. The same look had crossed his face when he had ridden to Berenithia to take its crown.

The canvas was drawn and at a gesture from Aleksander, it was pulled free of the cage.

Dayne saw the silhouette of a person beyond the bars. A woman crouched alone. Cardinal Aleksander held out a hand to stop them approaching the wagon, and reached for his medallion.

"We must not fear those who can burn the body but cannot burn the soul, rather, be afraid of those who can sunder both," the cardinal began. "May Durandail's strength flow through us and may Azaria grant us her shield against the darkness."

He gestured to Farrius Quinnal and the man took a torch from Sir Garrik. Dayne stepped toward the cage first and shared a glance with Darius as he did so.

Was this woman the mighty instrument that he had spoken about? The one that had been with his family for generations?

The light of the flame flashed across the woman's face and revealed her. Dayne gasped, unable to stop the shock that spread through his body. He reached for his amulet and muttered a silent prayer, unable to tear his gaze from the prisoner. Her eyes were bluer than any ocean and more dazzling than the truest of sapphires, though they were cracked with a web of white lines. The woman stared through him, as if she could see past his heart and deep into the depths of his soul. He could not look away.

Her skin was pale beneath the rags that she wore, lines and swirls of back tattoos etched upon her skin from her right temple to her throat and beneath her clothes. They swirled across her face from the side of her eye to her ear beyond. Her ragged hair was as white as fresh snow, and as it shifted, he saw the thing that sent a tingle of fear down his back.

Her ears were sharpened into points.

Dayne felt his breath catch.

"Is she?"

"An elf," Darius told them, "the last of that ruined kind. Make no mistake, my lords; this is no mere woman to love and hold dear. She is a demon made flesh. A monster that a century ago nearly brought Medea to ruin. I brought her here today to show you not the death that they once cast upon our world, but to serve as a warning to all that would seek to destroy us. Now as before we stand united. Now as before we will cast aside the shadows. By the gods' will it shall be done."

THIRTY-ONE

City of Elara, the League of Trecento

Elise's lungs burned.

She forced her legs faster as she flew across the rooftops. Screams came from all around as the people below saw her. Archers atop the rooftops shouted and crossbows were brought to bear. Elise ignored them all. She had no time to move about the city unseen, nor the chance to fear the steel tipped bolts. The Nightingale leapt across a narrow street and soared through the air, as the clack of a crossbow sounded. Her boots touched down and her hand brushed the tile as she pushed herself forward.

A bolt sped past her face and smashed into roof. Clay shattered beneath its power as the bolt ricocheted by. Elise ignored it. All her focus was on the council house that drew ever closer. All her thoughts were on Priamos Stentor. She leapt another gap, charged across the next roof, and flew into the air. Bolts rained down around her and created a web of steel, splintering wood and chipping brick and tile alike.

The hall drew closer.

Elise gritted teeth beneath her mask and accelerated. Her right foot came down, muscles tightened. The steel of a bolt sliced across her thigh.

The force of the blow tripped her, and before Elise could so much as cry out, she fell from the building. The wind howled all around her as she descended toward the hard stones thirty feet below.

Only her reflexes saved her.

Elise lashed out with her hands and caught the ledge of a lower roof. She smashed into the side of the building hard and the air was driven from her lungs. Her ribs screamed from the impact, and the tile she held was sliding free. Elise watched it cascade down into the street where it shattered across the stones. With a grunt she reached up, took hold of the roof, and heaved herself up. Shadows flickered as the bowmen drew closer.

Elise bit back the pain as she forced herself into a run. Blood dripped from her leg as she leapt from ledge to ledge, dancing across carved stone and clay. Cries came from behind as the archers caught sight of her. Elise charged toward the edge of the house and cast herself into the abyss.

Steel flashed by.

Elise curled and angled her shoulder forward. She smashed into wooden shutters. They splintered and she hit the ground beyond. The Nightingale rose to her feet and forced her aching body to obey. She staggered through the room, opened the shutters at the opposite side, and vaulted out. Her boots touched down on a long corridor that ran along the outside of several buildings. People in the open hallway cried out as they saw the Nightingale materialise before their eyes. Elise grimaced and slowly started to run. Run became a sprint as she saw the council hall dead ahead.

There was still time.

Elise shoved people aside as she barrelled down the corridor. She reached its end, vaulted the small wall, and dropped down into the open plaza that surrounded the hall. Elise saw soldiers at its doors. If she could get to them, if she could warn them, she might save hundreds of innocent lives. The soldiers turned her way as townspeople screamed and fled her path. Halberds were levelled and they cried out for her to halt. Elise reached for her hood.

A faint roar came from below.

The earth shook.

Elise was blasted from her feet. She hit the ground hard. Her ears rang like bells. Bricks and mortar flew through the air. Ash filled her lungs. Elise pulled the mask from her face and ripped her scarf down. She coughed and gasped for breath as she staggered through the great dust cloud.

Elise saw the bodies of the two fallen soldiers first. Both had been caught by the razor-edged stone splinters that had flown from the hall. Blood soaked their shredded clothes, staining armour and cobblestone. Through the dust she saw the ruins of the hall. Much of the massive building had been destroyed. Its stone walls lay all round her. Though the grey mist she saw half-a-dozen men emerge from the remains. Their steps were hobbled, and their breathing came in ragged gasps as they fought for breath. Dust and blood ran through their hair, covered their faces, and ruined their fine clothes. One of them was screaming. A long shard of wood was embedded in his stomach. Elise fell back as she heard soldiers run into the plaza. She hid in the shadows as she looked to the survivors. A noble gestured frantically to the guards.

"Go to the arsenal!" he shouted. "Take however many men you need. Stentor was not here. Bring him to me. I want him alive."

Elise could barely make out the soldier's reply as he ran from the plaza. So Priamos Stentor had not come after all. That meant he was somehow involved in the attack, and what was worse, it had failed. It was Imrohir commanding the soldiers. The magister turned to another company of his men.

"Find horses," Magister Imrohir ordered. "This treachery must be answered. Lord Cirillo Eris was not here as well."

Elise ran through the city. This time most of the people barely spared her a second glance, for the smoke and dust of the hall could be seen for miles. The ash had filled her lungs, yet she kept moving. Through the adjacent streets she saw Imrohir and his soldiers riding toward her friend's house. Elise climbed up onto the rooftops surrounding the villa and leapt across.

The sounds of fighting filled her ears. Steel met steel and the screams of the dying echoed through the streets. Elise sent a silent prayer to the gods as she reached the roof of the courtyard. She saw Lord Cirillo below, standing by the pool with a pair of his soldiers at his side. The guards went to the closed door as something heavy smashed into it. Elise looked to the lord and saw him looking back. She made to leap down.

Cirillo slowly shook his head. Elise froze. He did not want her to help him.

The door crashed open, and the lord's men fell to the spears of the magister's men.

Imrohir strode into the courtyard and drew his sword. Lord Cirillo Eris, unarmed, stepped toward the magister with hands clasped behind his back. No words were spoken. None would have made a difference. Imrohir drove his sword though Cirillo's chest. Steel speared through the nobleman's heart and tore out his back.

Cirillo cried out.

The magister wrenched the blade free. Lord Cirillo Eris fell backward into the shallow pool and the crimson of his blood turned the water red.

They had left the celebration early, abandoning Prince Dayne to deal with the cardinal and foreign emperor. Each time Dorian took his mistress to his chambers he vowed it would be the last. Maybe it was the long raven black hair, enchanting hazel eyes, and olive skin. Perhaps it was her keen intellect that allowed her to manoeuvre arrogant lords and aid with both politics and the wisdom of life. Maybe the king had spurned his wife in favour of the dark haired Medean beauty for all those reasons and more. Dorian shut the door to his chambers and turned to speak. Lady Eveline planted a finger on the King of Annora's lips to stop whatever he was about to say, before she planted her lips hard and urgent on his. The king felt heat rise in his body, as he wrapped his Eveline tightly in his arms and kissed her.

The lady shoved the king onto the bed and climbed on top, straddling him between her strong thighs. Eveline ran her hands up his sides and kissed him again. The king felt her hips as she reached up and unpinned her raven locks. Her hair cascaded down her shoulders in a wave that shimmered in the candlelight. Dorian paid no attention to the razor-sharp edge of the hair pin. He was too besotted with the one who made him feel alive again. The woman his soul yearned for.

She brought the pin down hard. It slipped between his ribs and into his heart.

Darius the Third spun around the hall as the music played. He had spent much of the night drinking and talking with King Dorian and his friend Dayne, yet now he desired a moment away from politics. A final moment of peace before the bells of war that would consume them all rang. So now, as he glided through the hall, the emperor had the chance to enjoy a thing he loved more than most others. Dancing. He had never met, nor had he seen, many of the Annoran and Medean congregation but he embraced them all as friends, as brothers and sisters. Despite their separate kingdoms, they were one faith, one people.

Partners were traded as the tempo increased.

The music grew louder.

A woman as beautiful as any he had seen paired with him. She was strong and lithe, Aureian to the bone. Her dark hair whipped through the air as they moved, the light of the torches reflecting in her eyes. They spun together, bodies moving in unison. Darius looked to the heavens, a laugh upon his lips.

A laugh broken by the spray of blood that spewed from his lips.

The world blurred as he reached for his throat. The blood ran through his fingers as he fell to his knees. Screams filled the hall. The woman who had slid the knife across his neck was gone, vanishing as if she had never been there. As if she were a dream. Ilaros Arran ran to the emperor's side, his voice roaring for the guards. One final rasping breath fled the body of Emperor Darius the Third.

Imrohir gazed out across the small courtyard that was within the arsenal gates. Hundreds of soldiers stood atop the walls, their keen eyes searching the streets and crossbows held at the ready. The magister stood atop the long wooden platform of the gallows. His face and body were still covered in dried blood and dust. His hand tightly gripped the hilt of his sidesword, as he let his eyes move between the faces of those present. Some were nobles, many were craftsmen, and others innkeepers. His words, whatever he spoke, would reach friend and enemy alike.

"Eighty-seven," he said with a growl, and his voice carried across the yard. "Eighty-seven innocent lives were taken this night. Eighty-seven people had their futures taken from them. Eighty-seven families weep and my heart breaks for them. There are no words to describe what happened this night. No words that can change the horror that we have witnessed. I am drenched in the blood of my people, in the blood of my *brothers*. It would appear that the death of my nephew was merely the precursor to this attack upon us all. But my friends, even in this dark time, I offer you no hope or promise for better days. I am here to offer you vengeance. For one man, one man *alone,* a sworn councilman of this city, did not attend this night. It took but a word to identify the architect of this crime and it is to him I send this message. Priamos Stentor," the magister bellowed for all to hear. "You are a coward who hides in the shadows playing this dark game. You are a murderer and a monster, and one day soon your blood will run through the streets!"

Imrohir gestured to the two people who stood atop the platform with him. Two people who wore necklaces of rope. "Yet this will not be the fate of your wife, your father. If you wish to continue upon your present course, then allow me to offer you an invitation from my family to *yours*."

Magister Imrohir raised his arm high.

The hangman took ahold of his lever.

The arm came down and the bodies fell.

Astrid strode from her great hall. Her blood ran warm and a layer of sweat covered her skin. She felt the breeze on her cheek and through her hair. The wind was cool. The cold would have frozen a lesser person from the mainland. But not Astrid Farrin. She was Valkir. To her, the breeze was as soft as a tender kiss.

The jarl's hazel eyes swept over the bay and took in the assembled ships. In a few hours, when the sun rose beyond the mountains and laid claim to the sea, the Ravenheart would sail with the Draekor as consort.

Astrid crossed her arms as she looked to the south. She had spent so long fighting for her people, for her crew, and then for her father's memory. Now, at last, she could do something for herself. Perhaps more than just the unknown lay beyond Aureia. Perhaps it was there that she would find what she sought. Astrid glanced to her side as footsteps crunched on the dry earth. She nodded as Earl Arndyr stood to her side. No words needed to be spoken as the two Valkir leaders looked out over the sea. Any fears were quenched by the warmth that Arndyr brought with him.

Astrid turned to her lover, and met his eyes. They were filled with the same curiosity that was reflected in her own. A curiosity that had made them more than partners. They were kindred spirits. She reached out and stroked his bearded jaw. His forehead met hers, and then Astrid kissed him. It was a gentle kiss, filled with the emotion that had for so long been hidden from her.

Astrid couldn't hear the rustle of fur over the roar of the icy wind. She didn't see the broad knife in the earl's hand. She didn't feel the pain as Arndyr drove the blade into her stomach.

For the first time, Astrid shivered.

She stared wide eyed at Arndyr and grabbed at his arms.

It was not the blade that she felt first, nor the agony that came with it. What she felt was pain, not from the knife, but from the betrayal. Astrid looked into his eyes, unable to speak.

Why?

The question branded itself in her mind as the first of her tears began to spill. Astrid cried out, as he stabbed her again and again. Blood filled her mouth and dripped from her lips, but still she could not feel it. She could not feel her legs. Astrid fell to her knees with a groan, breath fleeing her lungs. She could not move. She could barely see.

The doors of the hall boomed open. Erik's roar was long and loud. The warrior charged from the hall with Torben at his side. Astrid bowed forward and crashed to the ground. She fought for breath, willing her lungs to work. She was close, so close to achieving her purpose. Erik and Torben surged toward Arndyr.

"For the empire!" Arndyr bellowed and raised the knife to his own chest.

He hit the pommel and drove the blade deep into his heart. The earl staggered with a grunt and then toppled to the earth. Astrid barely heard Erik call her name as he dropped to her side. Her brother took her hand and held her tight. In the encroaching darkness she saw Torben and Mayrun fall to their knees with Erik.

"Astrid," Erik shook her. "Astrid!"

"It's alright," she managed as the coldness drew near. "Don't be afraid."

Nenrir, Fargrim, Laerke, all of the crew had gathered now. A cough ran through her body.

"Remember," she murmured and gazed up into Erik's tear-filled eyes. "Remember *why*."

The last of the light in her eyes faded as the warm shroud of darkness took her. Astrid Farrin, the Raven Jarl, passed into the realm of the Sea-Father.

THIRTY-TWO

"Come in," Senator Valliro Nilor called, yet did not look up from his scroll.

Kitara fought back the urge to use the chains that bound her hands to strangle Vesuva's magister. The two soldiers at her back shoved her into Valliro's office. The magister sat behind a plain wooden desk covered in books and quills. He glanced up as she entered the room and then rolled up the scroll. Kitara said not a word, instead she glared down at the man. Her armour and sword had long since been taken and the Aureians had once again forced her to bathe. The sweat, blood, and stench from yesterday's games had been washed away, yet the memory remained.

"Sit," Valliro said, beckoning to the chair opposite as he at last looked to her.

Kitara remained standing, her hands curled into fists. "Where is she?" Kitara asked.

"She's safe," the Aureian replied.

"Where?" she asked louder.

Valliro met her glare without emotion. "Nowhere that concerns you," he said.

Kitara gritted her teeth as the impulse to strangle the man grew. She cared not that the soldiers would kill her in reply, only that it would cost Sereia her own life.

"I fought for you," Kitara growled. "I killed for you. Now tell me where she is, or I will shove a sword so far up your back that you will be spewing steel at the gates of the afterlife."

Finally, Valliro showed emotion. He *laughed.* He had all the leverage.

"Such ferocity. You do not command me. You do not hold power here. I am a magister, and you are a slave. It is true that you have experienced hardships these last weeks, and so I shall let your lack of manners and decorum go this once. Speak out of line again and I will not be so merciful. Now," Valliro once more indicated the empty chair, "sit."

Resigned, Kitara slumped into the chair. "Alessandra?" she smirked.

"Yes, I thought it fitting," the magister nodded. "Alessandra Gaedhela, sole daughter of Nykalous Gaedhela, the *only* woman from Delios to ever wield a sword. Trained in the art of war from a young age by her father, taught to fight and taught to kill. They say she was the only one of the conqueror's children to remain loyal after his death. They say her skill was only matched by her courage. A great many Aureians died in the attempt to capture her."

"What happened to her?"

"She fell that day," Valliro explained, "awash with the blood of my kin."

Kitara leaned forward on the table. "And what is that to me? What is her name to me?"

"Alessandra, that is *your* name now."

"No," she growled. "That is *not* my name. I am Kitara of–"

"Who you are, the lands from where you hail, do not matter," the magister cut her off and rose to his feet. "Here, your slate, your sins, will be washed clean. You will be forged and moulded into something greater. The people will chant your name in the stands, and one day perhaps you will be as a god to them. A sildari."

Kitara bit her lip and placed her chained hands on the table. "I don't want that."

"Perhaps today, perhaps tomorrow," Valliro shrugged. "But the wheel of time is always turning. Things change. The arena changes you."

"I am no beast to fight in your blood games," she snarled through bared teeth.

"Have you not killed before?" he asked rhetorically.

"Oh yes," Kitara shot to her feet and her eyes blazed with emerald fire. "I have killed as many who have tried to kill me. I fight and kill to survive: not for sport, not for entertainment."

Valliro stared at her as he replied, "And what of the survival of Sereia? Will you let your pride lead to her death?"

"What do you want with me?"

"What do you want for yourself?"

"Freedom!" Kitara snapped. "For myself and for Sereia."

Valliro watched her curiously as he ran a finger through a small pile of coins. "Then perhaps we can help one another," he said.

"How?"

"It cost me a great deal to keep you and the girl here," the magister replied. "The slavers had wished for me to send you both to Theon the whoremonger. In choosing not to do so my relationship with them has been frayed. It is clear to me that a woman with your skills is more suited to a life of blood rather than a life upon her back. Just as it is clear that if the girl had gone, you would have turned. The cost of blood would have been high on both sides, and that is an outcome that I would rather avoid."

"So, you want me to believe that I am here because of what?" Kitara shook her head incredulously. "My skill with a sword?"

"You rose against your captors *twice*. You nearly escaped *twice*. You were a slave with nothing. No hope, no weapons, yet still you rose. Courage, will, loyalty. I can think of no three things more deserving of admiration. For those qualities alone it would be enough, yet you also know the swordsong. And so, *Alessandra*, I will offer you a deal. More than that, I give you my word that it will be done."

"I have heard stories about those who deal in slave warriors," Kitara said as she looked him up and down with a wary eye. "That there are some that will let others *use* those slaves for other amusements in return for coin. That there are some who will use their position to take advantage themselves."

"I am not one of those men," Valliro told her without breaking his gaze. The truth of his words was mirrored in his eyes.

"What is this deal?"

"Fight for me, win for me, become sildari, and we will both rise," the magister said. "In time, when the cost of the coin I paid the slavers to repair our relations has been met, when the coin you win for me pays this debt, then I shall give you and the girl, your freedom." He held his hand toward her. "You have my word."

Kitara squared her jaw. She *knew* that the choice had been removed yet if what Valliro said was true then perhaps this was not the end. Perhaps this way she could get Sereia home unharmed. The cost would be her pride. The cost would be heavy burden. She would have to fight for the entertainment of her enemies, time and time again. Yet if Sereia was made safe, the deal could save them both.

Kitara took Valliro's hand.

"We do what we must to save those we love, even if it means appeasing those whom we despise. You're making the right decision," the magister said as they shook.

"Did I have a choice?" Kitara muttered.

"No," Valliro shook his head.

The soldiers entered the room; it was time to go. Kitara turned to the open door without a word, without resistance. This was the path she now walked, and she would see it through.

"Before you leave, Alessandra," the magister's voice halted her. "If you are to take on this role, then you should look the part as well as you play it."

Kitara's chains had long since been removed by the time she entered the training sands. Her sleeveless white tunic showed the strength of her arms, while her bootlike sandals gripped easily on the shifting earth below. *'Looking the role'* as Magister Valliro had said, had meant dealing with her wild blonde hair. The golden mane bearing small braids that she used to tie back was a thing of the past. Now her long hair was pulled tightly into braids, so tight that no strand of hair hung loose. Down both sides of her head and behind her ears were a pair of small braids, creating a weave that hung down beneath her shoulders. A fifth braid, larger and wider than the rest, was woven from temple to neck, falling down her back with the others. Even in combat, her hair would cause her little distraction.

Sildari sparred all around with wooden sword, spear, axe, and shield. Their sweat covered bodies were filled with lean muscle, while their eyes were fixed dangerously upon their opponents. Some were clad in basic armour of plate leather, steel and bronze, while others wore nothing save faded tunics. These were no mere soldiers or warriors. These were true blooded fighters who spent every waking moment training for conflict. To a man they were masters of death. Another of the sildari, older and wiser than his brethren, let his gaze wash over Kitara as she leaned against a pillar belonging to the balcony above.

Like the other slaves, his scar-covered physique was built of rippling muscle. Like them he had fought atop the sands of the arena, that much was certain. It was not the cane that he carried that gave Kitara pause. It was the way he carried himself. He did not seem to have the bearing of a slave, sildari or no. He carried himself like one of the Sacasian pirate captains.

"CEASE!" his bark carried across the training ground.

The response was instant. The fighters all turned as the old warrior began to move toward the villa steps. They formed up faster than any soldier. There were more than twenty of them, each and all watching Kitara with the hungry eyes of a wolf stalking its prey.

"Today our number grows," the man with the cane said, and he gestured toward Kitara.

"What is this, mentor?" one of the sildari frowned with disgust clear in his voice. "Instead of a fighter we're sent a little girl?"

Kitara smirked as a wave of chuckles ran through the men. She had heard it all before, and the anger that she had once felt at the insult had long since turned to amusement. Kitara crossed her arms and glared at the man who had spoken. A sneer curled her lips.

"This is Alessandra of the savage lands of Salvaar. Supposedly she is Tariki-trained," the mentor replied. "Supposedly she can fight. Indeed, Magister Valliro had her tested in the sands at yesterday's games. Her being here with breath in her lungs tells me that she passed the test. That she won. But to say that she stands as one of you, to say that she is any kind of sildari... I find the thought far removed."

Kitara snorted. She had known men of his ilk many times. For them respect was earned, not given. One had to prove themselves as an able warrior to even gain consideration. Kitara pushed herself from the pillar and was down the steps in two strides. She did not let her eyes waver from the mentor as she walked right up to him.

Kitara gave him a dangerous sneer. "Is that so?" she said.

The old warrior took her words as they were meant. A challenge. She could feel the amused eyes of the warriors boring into her back. She knew cocky smiles adorned each face. The mentor stepped closer. He was tall, at least a head taller than her. His glare spoke of a storm.

"I have met many like you before," the mentor said. "You think that bold words and a quick sword make you a fighter, but that is not so. Every man here has bled upon this sacred sand. Every man here has lost brothers to the arena. We are, all of us, born for this. Each day brings new pain and torment, yet the reward is so much more than victory. We walk between the heavens and hell. We walk between a nightmare and a dream. Many crumble, many fall, and you will be among them."

Kitara smiled up at him without mirth. "Underestimate me if you will. You would not be the first, and you will not be the last. But you will be wrong. Give me a sword and I shall prove it."

"Are you so eager to die?" the mentor sneered to the amusement of his brothers. He raised his gnarled cane and placed it upon her shoulder. He pushed it into her neck. "Beg for it, claw for it, perhaps you will survive. Until then, learn your place, *Alessandra*."

Kitara did not flinch as the wood forced her head to the side. To show weakness in front of these men was to ask for death. Had she a knife, it would already be in the mentor's heart. Yet she was unarmed.

Or so they thought.

Sword and knife were not her only weapons. She moved fast. She moved with precision. Her left hand knocked away the cane as her right shot up and latched onto his shoulder.

The mentor moved and grabbed at her arm. Kitara's forehead smashed into his face. Blood erupted as the cartilage shattered. She felt it upon her skin, tasted it upon her lips. She grinned as the cane came around and drove into her stomach. A second blow rang her head and split her cheek. Kitara staggered back with a grunt and fell to a knee. Her gut screamed as she sucked in a deep breath. It took everything to not collapse, to not clutch at her aching body. Her fist wiped crimson from her mouth before she spat blood onto the sand. Kitara stared up at the mentor and into his emotionless eyes.

"You may have won yesterday," he said. "But one victory doesn't make you sildari."

Sadsworth, a city in the western reaches of Torosa, sat within the embrace of the mountains that bordered Larissa. The paths beyond the Annoran town that ran through gully and over peak would take two days to traverse if everything went perfectly. The tracks beyond Sadsworth were one of the only crossings to Larissa north of the Annoran pass nearly a week to the south. As such, the city had become a trade hub for the desert people of the west and their Annoran allies.

Sakkar could not help but feel a warm shiver run up his spine as the companions made their way through the town. The closer toward home he rode, the greater he felt its pull. Under the setting sun that washed Sadsworth with orange light, he saw them, mingled with the Annorans. A small band of Larissan traders, their skin dark and their clothes flamboyant, walked the streets. It was a sight that he had not seen in years, and even the thought of the traders made him smile. He was so close to the desert that he could *feel* its warmth upon his skin. Bellec turned from the front of the column and nodded toward an inn.

"We rest here tonight," he told them. "Tomorrow we make for the mountain pass."

"I'll meet you there," Sakkar said and glanced back at his kin.

"Where are you off to?" Galadayne asked.

"Ah, you easterners," the Larissan grinned as he snatched his coin purse from a saddlebag,

"if we're to make it through the southlands at this time of the year, there is something we will need."

Sakkar made his way back into the town. He approached the Larissan traders and raised a hand in greeting. They clasped arms and exchanged names.

"Whereabouts are you headed?" Jaheira asked as he took the proffered coins.

"South," Sakkar replied as his kinsman reached for a sack.

"Toward Amari."

"Good land and better people," the trader nodded. "What takes you there?"

Sakkar clapped Jaheira on the shoulder as he took the sack of scarves, "Family calls me home."

"Then may Amkut ride with you brother, and speed you on your way."

Like any other, the tavern stank of sweat and ale. People drank and ate around tables in small groups while others stood by the bar. Some were soldiers, but most were just the townspeople enjoying a cup of ale in the inn. The warmth of the establishment washed over Sakkar as he entered. Bellec's company were gathered around a few large tables enjoying the last Annoran drink they would taste for many weeks. Some were gathered around Jaimye and another of the mercenaries as they played a game of cards. Judging by the shouts and cheers of the men, the game had become intense. Kompton played his lute absently while Bellec and Aeryn talked in hushed tones by the bar. The Salvaari moonseer kept her hood up as to avoid unwanted attention. Her face was as much a giveaway as her pelts and furs had been and Sadsworth, though far from Salvaar, was *still* Annoran. As such, if anyone saw the face belonging to those silver eyes, the night could end in bloodshed.

Bellec snatched his cup from the counter and sauntered over to Galadayne. While held in high regard in Medea, if the people here knew their real names, if they knew that Theron Malley and Galadayne Eralys stood in their presence, then the outlaws would be hung, drawn, and quartered by morning. It had been a risk coming here. Sakkar knew it as well as they, yet the mercenaries talked and laughed without care. The Larissan did not know if those he rode with were brave or stupid, perhaps a bit of both. But what he did know is that they were good, honest, men. He moved to join Aeryn at the bar, but he was not the first to do so. Another man bearing the gambeson and sword of a soldier reached her before Sakkar.

"May I buy you a drink, my lady?" the Annoran asked, leaning against the bar. He looked to Aeryn. He placed his own full cup on the counter's rough surface. "My lady?"

She snorted without turning.

"Just so," the soldier continued. "I am Warrick Kathan and it is unthinkable to me that a fine lady such as yourself should be so unattended."

Aeryn glanced at him from under her hood. "Thank you for the offer," she said. "But I am sorry, I must be going." She turned to leave, but Warrick's hand shot forth like a snake and wrapped tight around her wrist.

"Now wait just a minute," he said with a frown. "Your voice... you're not from around here."

Sakkar heard the man's tone change. Where there had once been kindness, now was replaced with suspicion.

Aeryn's silver eyes blazed into a fiery glare. "Take your hand off me," she commanded.

Warrick's grip tightened and his free hand fell to his sword.

"Did you not hear the lady, friend?" Sakkar asked and his hand clamped down on the man's shoulder.

"I think I have heard enough." Warrick let Aeryn's arm go and pulled forth steel. He levelled the sword at her throat as all eyes turned toward them.

Kompton's music stopped.

Men leapt to their feet and many hurried toward the confrontation. Sakkar had half drawn his khopesh when Warrick held a hand up to stop him. The Annoran's blade was already pressed to Aeryn's throat.

"Think about what you are doing," Sakkar said and removed his hand from his weapon.

Aeryn did not flinch as Warrick's sword slid inside her hood and flicked it back. Gasps filled the tavern as the Annorans saw the face revealed by the light. Moonlike eyes, pale skin, and wild black hair. Yet most disturbing of all, the sharp features of a Salvaari.

"A heathen walks among us," Warrick Kathar breathed.

The inn was filled with the song of shouts. Soldiers' hands fell to swords while the menfolk of Sadsworth let their hands curl into fists. They gathered in a ring around Warrick and Aeryn. A ring broken only by Bellec and the mercenaries as they shoved their way through the crowd.

"As does a man so brave as to draw steel on one without a weapon," Aeryn smiled. She raised her hand to the sword and ran a finger along the steel. "What do you intend now?" she said without fear.

Warrick twitched his wrist, pressing the sword ever so slightly into her neck and brushing her hand aside. "Quiet yourself, pagan," he growled.

Aeryn said nothing and instead replied with a deadly smirk.

"Steady now, you wouldn't want to do anything rash, would you?" Bellec called as his left hand dropped to his blade, while his right rested atop his wrist.

"You are Annoran," Warrick snarled back. "Yet you side with this pagan. Who are you to do so? Who are you to stand against your own?"

Bellec stepped to Aeryn's side with a sneer dancing across his lips. "You may be from here. You may even command respect here. But I, I am in charge. Now lower your sword before I paint the floor with your blood."

"And who are you to say so?"

"Who am I?" The mercenary took half a step toward the soldier as he growled. "I am Bellec."

Warrick took a breath. "I have heard the name."

There was something new in his voice. Fear. Bellec was famous even here. His deeds from Tarik, to Berenithia, to Medea and the

Valkir Isles were legendary.

"Good," Bellec said dangerously. "Now listen well. Stay your blade and walk away. Do not leave this place until we have, do not call for soldiers. There is no reason for this to come to blood."

Warrick looked from Aeryn to Bellec and back. The Annoran grimaced and sheathed his sword.

"Very well," he said at last.

Hands left weapons as Warrick turned from the mercenaries.

"One more thing, before you go," Sakkar said, unable to stop himself. "You'll be owing the lady an apology."

The Annoran froze. He glanced over his shoulder at the Larissan, hatred burning beyond control. "No."

"No?" Sakkar grabbed Warrick's full cup from the counter. "You misunderstand me my friend. That was not a question."

"You do not command here."

"You would do well to learn some respect," Sakkar replied as the Annoran stepped opposite him.

The Larissan was ready for what came next. He could see the flicker of anger contort Warrick's face and before the Annoran clenched his fist, he knew the punch was coming. He took a long draught from the tankard. "Such a waste," he said, grinning.

Sakkar ducked the fist that drove toward his face and slammed that cup into the side of Warrick's head. Wood splintered under the impact as the Annoran crashed to the floor in a senseless heap. An angry growl came from the men of Sadsworth as they watched their friend go down. Cups were put aside while soldier, mercenary, and peasant alike rose from their chairs. There was only one way this would end now. The thought filled Sakkar with fire. Bellec's company came to his side, as the Larissan let the broken tankard fall from his fingers.

With a roar the Annorans charged them, snarls upon their lips and hands curled into fists. The first man came at Sakkar with a right hook. The Larissan smiled as the punch came toward him, remembering the brawls he had been involved in… ones he had *caused*. Sakkar slipped to the side and smashed his elbow into his attacker's face. He felt the man's nose shatter under the blow as he pivoted and followed with an uppercut. The Annoran's eyes rolled back as the punch sent his gaze skyward. He joined the first upon the ground.

Sakkar raised his fists as a third man came at him. He slid back, blocked the first blow, and then countered, driving the full weight of his body behind his fist into the Annoran's stomach. As he doubled over, Sakkar grabbed his opponent's shoulder and neck, and pulled him down into a vicious knee. Blood flowed as the blow connected with the Annoran's face.

He fell. The Larissan stepped back as Jaimye sent another of Warrick's men to sleep. Then it was done. Over a dozen of them lay flat on their backs at the hands of the mercenary band.

"The fuck was that?" Bellec grumbled as he turned to Sakkar.

"The man needed to learn respect," the Larissan told him.

"What a bloody mess," Kompton chuckled as he wiped crimson away from his split cheek.

Galdayne prodded Warrick Kathar with his boot.

"I would suggest that our stay here is no longer welcome," he sighed. The Larissan let out a breath. No more warm bed for the night. They would have to take refuge in the mountains.

"Time to go."

THIRTY-THREE

Isle of Agartha, the Valkir Isles

The hall was quiet. The ever-bustling market and port was devoid of life. Agartha was silent. Its people were in mourning. They had loved and admired the fierce Raven Jarl and her loss was a blow keenly felt. Astrid's wooden coffin was befitted the greatest of heroes. Its carved sides were covered in soaring crows, dancing around the dawn sun. The gentle waves of the sea swam across the wood, so beautifully crafted that they almost seemed to move. Only the wooden cover was removed.

Erik Farrin sat by his sister's coffin, his face as pale as it had been when she had breathed her last. He felt nothing but pain. The last of his family was gone. The last of his family was dead. His sister, his older sister…

"By now she will be drinking and feasting with the Sea-Father in Ra'Haven," Torben murmured, and his voice echoed the pain that Erik felt.

"No," Erik glanced at his friend, the only companion he had in his family's house, "Astrid will be sailing through the great silver sea above. She will write an odyssey across the stars just as she dreamt."

"Aye," the old warrior quietly agreed. "That she will. And it shall be a grand tale."

Erik looked down at the carved raven amulet in his hands. The empty eyes of the skull stared back at him, its eyes as unseeing as Astrid's.

"Such a small thing to have known so much pain," Erik said, running his thumbs across the wood. "My mother carved this amulet long ago... when she died it went to my father, then in turn to Astrid. Now it is mine. Will I be fated to follow my family in death?"

Torben reached out a hand and gripped Erik's wrist. "Your mother was the greatest shield maiden of her generation. Your father was Lief Farrin, scourge of the Mieran coast. And your sister, Astrid, she was more than just the slayer of tyrants. She was a dreamer. She was a woman who would have discovered the *world*. The great adventurer, the Raven Jarl, they call her. Your blood is the blood of heroes. Blood that the priests say is descended from the Sea-Father himself. Whatever your fate, whatever our god has in store for you, you can change the world."

"The blood of heroes... do you believe that?" Erik glanced at his friend.

Torben nodded. "That I do. I know that you will not grieve until the battle is won. I know right now your path is joyless, yet heroes are not born out of happiness."

Erik curled his hand tightly around the amulet as Torben rose to his feet.

"Then may the spirits of my ancestors envelop me," Erik murmured.

The old warrior clapped Erik on the shoulder as he spoke, "I will give you a moment alone."

Then he was gone, slipping through the doors to the hall. Erik sighed and glanced at the coffin. He would not grieve, not yet at least. His sister needed to be avenged, and yet he knew that Astrid would not want him to shed tears. She would want him to laugh. She would want him to sing and dance.

"Who would have thought that the voyager would go on this last grand adventure before the warrior? The fates truly curse us," Erik chuckled.

He placed a hand upon the coffin.

"Remember, you said. Remember why. What meaning did your words carry? You were always the wise one. Smart enough for the both of us. What I do remember is you running along the beach as a girl. Father had warned you that the sea was ever changing and the waves treacherous. And you laughed, before racing across the sand and into the water. You were not afraid. You never were. When mother died it was you who held me in your arms. You stroked my hair and told me that we would be alright. Your belief was so strong that it willed me to fight against the encroaching demons. I wanted to be as strong as you, I wanted to follow in your footsteps. I became a great warrior as you navigated the seas. I spent my whole life learning the axe and shield. I took the serpent brand... I can kill a man with my eyes closed. But the truth is that you were always stronger than me. It is your strength that guides me now and I know what I have to do."

Erik rose from his seat and looked to the still body of his sister. She wore a fine sapphire dress, and her dark hair was unbound. Her hands were clasped peacefully over her chest as if she were but sleeping. A wooden shield painted midnight blue covered her hips. A shield bearing the symbol of a raven.

"You are my closest friend, my dear sister. You are the captain that I would have followed to the ends of the earth. It was you who brought our family to glory. Never forget that."

White flowers crunched underfoot as the procession marched toward the harbour. Flowers thrown by the hundreds of people that had come to bid their beloved jarl farewell. Fathers and sons, mothers and daughters, warriors and farmers; all had come. The silence was broken only by the tears of the Valkir.

The coffin was carried by half-a-dozen of the Ravenheart's crew. Men who had sailed with Astrid since she had been but a girl. Men from the Wind Rider, the ship that had been with the Farrin clan for generations. Erik walked at the head of the procession, with Nenrir at his back. The archer carried his aulos reed pipe and its haunting sound carried through the streets. Behind them came Laerke and Torben, Mayrun and Fargrim. The rest of the crew and their families walked not far behind.

The column followed the path formed by the townspeople and slowly made their way down onto the beach. They stood by the edge of the waters, six acolytes to the Sea-Father clad in their grey robes. The priests of Ra'Haven parted and revealed the small boat in the water.

It was lined with offerings: shining jewels, silver weapons, rich cloths, and vibrant silks.

Erik felt his heart churn at the sight of the vessel. The last ship Astrid would sail. Slowly the coffin was placed within the boat, and at a nod from Erik, the vessel was cast off. Nenrir, Laerke, Fargrim, and Mayrun walked out into the sea with the boat until the water washed against their chests. With a mighty heave they sent the vessel and their jarl, into the bay.

Erik watched his sister drift further and further away. His hand trembled against the raven amulet and for the first time he felt a tear roll down his cheek.

Torben sparked a flame to life upon the tip of an arrow.

It had been he who had sent his friend and shield brother Lief to Ra'Haven. Now he was duty bound to do the same to Lief's daughter. The woman he had held as close as any child.

The bloodsworn drew back his powerful bow and sent the shaft forth. The orange light shimmered through the sky, arching up over the bay, before it plunged down into the vessel.

Flames burst to life around the coffin as the arrow ignited the flax oil. Erik could not tear his eyes away. He saw nothing, heard nothing, felt nothing. All that mattered was Astrid.

He swore that he would one day take the Ravenheart south beyond Aureia. He swore that he would fulfil her dream.

A dozen burning arrows flew out across the water as the Valkir gave a final salute to their hero. Still Erik did not notice.

He gripped the raven head so hard that a tendril of blood ran down the palm of his hand. He would see Astrid's last wish through, no matter the cost. Yet first, someone had to answer for his sister's death. Arndyr Scaeva was dead. His last words spoke of the empire. What he meant, Erik dreaded to guess. Yet he would find answers from one person. Jormund Scaeva was very much alive. Jormund Scaeva was still on the Isle of Vay'kis.

Lumis would *burn*.

They arrived at Valham two days after fleeing Palen-Tor. Lukas had visited the small town before, a few years back. The king had tasked him with a pilgrimage when he had been but ten years old. A pilgrimage to the most sacred site in Aethela, the Temple of Saint Daleka.

"Why do we come here?" Rodion asked as the company brought their horses to a halt atop a small hill overlooking the walled town.

"The Temple of Saint Daleka, the first man to bring the religion of the Twins to Annora."

Lukas stared past Valham toward the church not half a mile down the road and remembered everything that Bardhyl had taught him. "Many years ago my father sent me here. The priests gave sermon from dawn until dusk. Every waking moment was spent praying and meditating. They tried everything to indoctrinate me into their faith. The faith of my family, the faith of my people. I tried for so long to be a part of it… I couldn't. Even then I did not want to bow and scrape to the whims of pious old fools. Now I am returned and not as my father's well-heeled dog. Why are we here, Rodion? I don't yet know. Something calls to me, that much is certain."

"I feel it too," Maevin said from his side. "In the wind and in the earth. In my blood. Tanris wants us here this day."

Lukas glanced at the priestess; his guide. "Then it is probably time we find out *why*," he said. "My father's men will not be far behind us. We should seek sanctuary here tonight."

He clicked his tongue and urged his horse into a walk.

"Who goes there?" a priest called down from atop the wall, as the Salvaari made their approach. The Káli halted before the closed gates as a pair of Annoran holy men looked down from their perch.

"The man before you is your prince," called Maevin, her voice strong and loud. "Lukas, son of Dorian. He bears the blood of the Eagle of Annora."

The priest who had spoken hesitated, as if unsure. To him they must *all* look like Salvaari barbarians.

"Is that true, Lord? Are you who she says you are?"

"I am," Lukas replied as he looked the man directly in the eye.

The priests exchanged glances. A prince of Annora had come to their house, yet he looked nothing akin to the Raynor clan. Why would Annoran royalty be garbed in Salvaari pelts and furs?

"The Temple of Saint Daleka welcomes you back, my prince," the man replied after a moment.

Cobblestone clacked under the weight of hooves. The Káli looked around almost anxiously as they rode into the small courtyard. They shot anxious glances at the stone statues of the Twins in the yard's centre. Yet it was not priests that came down from the wall that made the Salvaari nervous. It was the great temple at their back. A giant structure of marble, stone, and wood soared high toward the heavens. A huge round window adorned the temple atop its door. A window of magnificent stained glass bearing the sun and moon symbol of the Twins. Lukas leaned heavily on his crutch and stared toward the doors as they boomed open. Out poured three priests garbed in white robes. They were old and weathered, yet their eyes were kind and their smiles genuine.

"Prince Lukas Raynor," the lead priest called out as he descended the stairs into the yard. "It has been many years."

"Just so," Lukas replied.

The priest reached out and took the prince's shoulders in his hands. "Let me see you, my boy."

"I trust you are well, Father Gennady," Lukas resisted the urge to shove the old man off. Months ago, he may have embraced the priest, but all things had changed.

"Ah," Gennady smiled. "The sun rises and falls, the moon shines ever bright, and time passes like sand through an hourglass. We grow old yet the gods provide for us. Their light guides us, and I pray that it guides you too."

Lukas snorted and touched the cloth covering his empty eye. "Their light, if it *ever* shone upon my face, has long since abandoned me," he said.

A sad look darkened the priest's expression. He lowered his hands. "You have had a hard road, Prince Lukas, yet the gods turn from no one. I will pray for you, and the sun will shine upon you again." Gennady looked over Lukas' shoulder to the Káli that stood tall, hands never straying far from steel. "Why are you here, my Prince? With *them?*"

"Forgive me, Father," Lukas turned to the Káli as he spoke. "My companions from the east lands. They saved my life and as such are as blood to me."

Gennady gave the Salvaari a kind smile. "Then they are our friends," he said. "Welcome to our home and hearth."

The Káli gave no reply as they dismounted and stood beside their horses. Only Maevin moved. The priestess glided across the cobblestones toward the two statues. She reached out a bare hand and ran it across the cold stone arm of Azaria. One of the Annoran priests hissed; which Maevin noticed. Her lips curled as she stared up into the goddess' eyes.

"Tanris is here," she breathed. Maevin looked to Lukas. "The spirits are close."

"My child," Gennady said with a frown, "your spirits are not here in the Twins' house."

"You are wrong, holy man," the priestess replied. "The spirits are everywhere. They are in everything. They see everything."

The priest ran a hand over his medallion. "Azaria's moon shines above us and lights our way, just as it has for generations. The goddess burns as a great beacon and nothing can pierce her flame. It is she who watches us, it is she who protects us from the evils within and without. She is the *true* goddess, and your spirits hold no power here."

Maevin made to reply, but Lukas spoke first.

"Father Gennady, we fear that men follow us upon the road, men who wish us harm. We seek sanctuary this night. Will you help us?"

The priest looked from Maevin to the prince and his expression softened. "Of course I will, Lukas," he said. "This temple is open to all, and the Silver Lady's word is to protect pilgrims and travellers, no matter their allegiance."

The company were fed and watered in the shelter of the temple. Despite the priests showing nothing but the kindness in their hearts, they and the Káli still watched each other with unease. A blind man could have seen the visible tension in the eyes of holy man and Salvaari alike. Soon enough the gates were closed and bolted and one by one the Káli fell into slumber. All but Rodion. The warrior was restless and committed to standing watch, even under the protection of the most holy church. It was his voice that woke the Annoran prince in the dead of night.

"What is it?" Lukas muttered, as he sat up from his resting place on the ground.

"I heard something," Rodion breathed in his mother tongue.

He glanced toward the temple doors. "Out there."

Lukas' skin crawled. The Salvaari were skilled hunters and scouts. They were not easily turned in the night. He heaved himself to his feet and took the proffered crutch. The two men slowly made their way to the bolted doors, and listened. Ears went to wood and breathing was stilled.

Nothing. Nothing save the quiet breath of the wind.

Then something creaked. It was the gates of the church yard. Lukas limped toward the closest window. Footsteps rang atop the stones. The Salvaari horses grew skittish. The prince gazed out into the night and his eye widened.

"What is it?" Rodion called.

Lukas saw the priest first and then the shadows at his back. "Soldiers. We are betrayed. Wake them up, Rodion, in silence."

The Káli nodded and jogged through the room. He shook his people awake and hushed them with but a word. Lukas ambled back into the heart of the temple and pulled his war hammer free. Maevin stood to his side and withdrew her long knife.

"Arrows and spears," Lukas murmured to his companions.

Without a sound, the Káli snatched out their bows and raised their wicked spears over their shoulders. The door thudded and the locking plank cracked. Arrows were pulled back as the Káli bows came up. The temple doors crashed inward and, with a great roar, the Annoran soldiers spewed inside. They charged forth forwards into the storm that the Káli unleashed. Arrows and spears cut through the air and sliced deep into the bodies of the soldiers. Eight men fell within three steps. Three more joined them in death before the two sides collided. Lukas roared as one of his kinsmen came at him with a sword.

He planted his feet and drove his weight into his good leg, before he swung his crutch up. The sword was deflected to the side and Lukas' hammer split the soldier's helm. The attacker fell with a cry and crashed to the ground. The soldier's hand reached for his sword. Lukas jumped on him with a snarl. The soldier went for his knife, ripping it free and driving it toward the prince. The blade sliced Lukas' cheek. Then he had him. The prince grabbed the soldier's knife wrist and heaved down. He slammed it into the floor. Lukas' elbow found the man's face once, twice, before he raised his hammer.

With a scream, Lukas brought the weapon down spike first. There was a dull crack as blood exploded from the wound. The soldier's hand grew limp, and the knife fell from nerveless fingers. Lukas panted as he tasted the man's blood upon his lips. He rose to his feet, his clothing painted red, and started to limp toward the temple doors. The Káli cut down the last of the Annorans as he reached the steps leading to the yard. There were nine priests including Father Gennady gathered.

Lukas tossed his bloody hammer at their feet, as the Káli stalked from the temple and surrounded the holy men.

"I came today here under the banner of friendship," Lukas began as he made his way down the stone steps. "I came here today seeking sanctuary in your house, a sanctuary that you granted us freely. We showed you respect, we showed you honour, yet in turn you saw fit to betray us. You see me as you see them," the prince said, gesturing to his companions. "To you they are all the same. To you they are nothing but heathens and barbarians. You do not know the mothers. You do not know of the fathers and sons. You do not know of the friendships and peace."

"If you wish to take my life then take it. I am ready," Father Gennady said. "The pale horse comes for us all. Yet before I die, know this. Your murder of Emilian Aloys has cost you greatly. The crown has named you an outlaw and you are banished from Annora. You are a prince no longer."

The feeling that came to Lukas was almost unexpected. He felt as if a great weight had been lifted from his shoulders; it made him smile.

"And what is that to me, Father? Though I was born in this land, Annora is not my home, nor its people my own. The home I seek is not in this place that enslaves me. It is in here," Lukas placed a fist over his heart as he spoke. "If this is my fate, then so be it. But remember this, Father, it was not I who slaughtered an innocent village. It was not I who was praised and honoured for the deed. And it was not I who betrayed those who sought sanctuary."

"Aye, we all have sins, my boy," Gennady said, his words strong. "I have no doubt I will be judged by the gods. I can only pray that in their infinite mercy, the gods see fit to forgive me. There is always a way back Lukas, a way back to your family, a way back from this dark path. The gods are merciful, let their light guide you. Come with me now, come to Palen-Tor. Everything will be as it should be."

Lukas gritted his teeth and shook his head. He thought of His father and Dayne. He thought of Kassie, the one he loved over all else. Even now, his heart yearned to be by her side... and yet it could not be so.

"Family? My own family declared me an enemy."

"Lukas, your family love you. Let me help you–"

"No, Father," Lukas cut him off as he moved to stand before the priest. He drew his eagle handled sword. "Today you have shown your true colours. Today you have proven that there cannot be peace, and do you know why?"

Gennady said nothing, yet the fear was clear in his eyes.

Lukas leaned in, his lips nearly brushing the old man's ear as he spoke, "Because of men like *you*."

Horror filled the priest's gaze and then light left it. Lukas' sword was driven so far through his chest that the steel blade ripped out his back. Gennady screamed as his once pupil wrenched the sword up through his body. With a snarl Lukas ripped the blade free and turned away. The lifeless body of the priest crashed to the cobblestones behind him.

It was all the Káli needed.

The eight holy men met the same fate as their leader as the axes and spears of the Salvaari descended upon them. Lukas ran his gaze across the eagle on his sword. The eagle of Annora. His *father's* eagle. With a savage cry he drove the blade into the ground between the stones before the steps of the temple. Lukas looked to the Temple of Saint Daleka as a great rage awoke within him.

"Burn it," he growled.

The flames scorched the heavens as the fire sundered the once great building. A very real smile etched itself across Lukas' lips as he felt the heat of the blaze. He watched from the temple gates as the Káli mounted up, leaving him alone with Maevin. He had left his sword at the bottom of the steps where it would be found before the ruins of a sacred church. It was one of only three such blades.

His father would hear of this.

His brother would hear of this.

Lukas had made his choice.

"I now know why you're here," Maevin said at last. "You were sent by the spirits to save us." Her words were full of fervour, full of passion. They reached deep into Lukas' soul.

THIRTY-FOUR

City of Elara, the League of Trecento

The cloud of smoke and dust rose from the remnants of the council house. It started with a small spark; an ember. The Stentor family still hung in the gallows, blowing in the wind. The ember grew into a flame. People of every class flooded the streets with harsh words upon their lips. Then the fire started to burn. Soldiers had been sent into the lower districts. The fighting had begun. It spilled from the Pits to the rest of the poor's boroughs. It spilled to the bridges. Those men who had forced the poor into the dirt with their taxes and laws were all but eradicated. The family that had championed them swung in the arsenal. The gangs had taken advantage and emboldened the lower districts. The poor began to cross the bridges.

Kyler had left the inn when the explosion had shaken his room. He had run through the city toward the blast and had seen the wreckage that the gangs had left in the wake of their dark deed. Word of the eighty-seven deaths had spread fast, riling rich man and beggar alike.

News of the Stentor executions had only emboldened passions. Soldiers armed to the teeth with steel patrolled the city in growing companies, while great hordes of townspeople began to march through the streets.

Kyler had found himself caught in the crowds as the sun began to lower. He shoved his way through the jeering throngs and noticed the assortment of spear, knife, sword, and hammer carried by the peasantry. Kyler tried to force his way through the people, but he was swept up in it as if caught in a rip. Through the crowd he saw the glimmer of silver helmets. Soldiers. There were six of them. Their hands tightly wrapped around their halberds. Behind them was a richly garbed man. He must have been a noble of some kind. The noble's words were lost as the horde noticed him and jeers echoed down the street.

"DEATH TO THE MAGISTER!" one of the peasants bellowed and thrust a smith's hammer toward the group.

The crowd surged forward like a great wave and crashed into the helpless soldiers. They vanished beneath the might of the horde. Their screams rose to the heavens before they were forever extinguished. While they were distracted, Kyler shoved his way through the throng and heaved himself into the empty confines of an alley. He glanced back into the street with a racing heart. The last thing he saw was a spear being driven skyward, the noble's head jammed upon its tip. A sickening feeling chilled the young knight to the core. He had seen blood and battle. He had witnessed the deaths of friends and family alike, yet this was different. This was the basest of animal passions made real. He had known that the people of Elara had been on edge for many months, and now it seemed that the destruction of the council hall and the public execution of a beloved family had driven them to madness.

Kyler ran through the alley. His hand never strayed from his sword. Shouts, screams, and vile chants spread through the city as the riots grew. Kyler kept to the backstreets as he made his way through the alleys toward the tavern. He hid in doorways and behind corners as angry mobs and steel-clad soldiers passed by.

He heard the screams of a woman echo down the alley. Kyler turned toward the horrified cries for help. He saw them on one of the main streets. A gang of four armed peasants. They stood outside the smashed in doors to a merchant's villa. Clearly the trader had chosen the wrong side. The bodies of two guards lay at the entrance and the ground was wet with their blood. The woman's cries came from inside the building. Kyler had but moments to act. The knight ripped his sword free as he left the darkness of the alley and walked out into the light. He was barely ten paces from the men when they noticed him. The first of the peasants turned to Kyler and ran his gaze over the mercenary styled garb.

"Who goes there?" the Elaran called as his hands flexed upon the crude spear.

"A knight," Kyler replied.

The man levelled his weapon, suspicion clouding his face. "And, sir knight, are you with us or *them?*"

Kyler looked from the peasant to his companions and then to the villa. "Liberty or death," Kyler said.

The Elaran lowered his spear and chuckled. It was the last sound he would make. The laugh turned into a gurgle as a tide of blood spewed from his lips. Kyler ripped his knife free from the man's throat. As the first man fell, Kyler lashed out with his sword at the second.

The blade caught the second man across the face; biting through skin and shattering bone. The third man swung wildly. Kyler deflected the man's sword and stepped in close. He drove his dagger between the Elaran's ribs and sent steel into the man's heart. Sword dropped from nerveless fingers as Kyler slammed his shoulder into the dying man and sent him toppling over. Kyler's sword flashed across his chest as he fell and carved a bloody red line from hip to shoulder. Kyler spun lightly upon the cobblestones and barely avoided the final man's makeshift club.

He blocked the first strike and switched his grip on his sword. One hand stayed at the hilt while the other gripped it halfway down the blade. A second overhead blow flashed toward Kyler's head. Steel rang as the club thudded into Kyler's raised guard. The knight lunged forth, spearing his sword into the Elaran's throat. Kyler drove the blade forward until crossguard met neck before he tore his sword free.

The last man fell to his knees and then crashed to the ground. Kyler brought his weapon up into guard and looked around the street. It was empty. No more weapons came toward him with hungry intent. Another scream came from the villa. He heard a man's cry, followed by the sound of steel striking flesh.

Kyler barely spared the bodies a glance as he ripped his knife free from the third Elaran's lifeless body, before he charged into the merchant's house.

He had no time to take in his surroundings.

A woman knelt in the house. Her face was wet with tears. Her hands were pressed tightly to the bloody body of a man who could have only been her husband. Two others stood over her. Both were armed with wicked clubs. The first raised his weapon over his head and angled it toward the merchant's wife.

Kyler launched his knife across the room. It spun though the air and then stabbed into the Elaran's lower back. He turned with a surprised shout.

Kyler's sword sliced through his stomach and then across his chest. He deflected the second man's club, countered, and took his head. The two corpses hit the ground. The merchant's wife stared up at him in horror. She was unable to stop the sobs that rocked her body.

"Do not fear me," Kyler kneeled by the pair and met the woman's eyes. "My name is Kyler Landrey. I am a knight of Kil'kara."

A flicker of relief flashed across her face. She said not a word.

Kyler slowly reached out and closed the dead merchant's eyes. "Cuun'etca hěy'læn," he murmured. Kyler did not know the man, nor did he ever know of his deeds. He probably never would and yet the merchant had been so brutally murdered in his own house.

He deserved some respect at least. Kyler glanced up at the woman.

"There is chaos in the streets," he said. "The people have risen. There will be more coming." He rose to his feet and took up his dagger, wiping the blade clean on the dead peasant's clothes. Kyler sheathed the blade and extended a hand to the woman.

"We have to go," he told her. "I am sorry."

They ran through the maze of alleys together. The sun had begun to lower, and the streets were lit with the burning brands of the mob. Some of the noble and merchant houses had been engulfed in flames as the crowds grew emboldened. A shrill scream came from behind.

Kyler whirled around, his eyes scanning the alley.

Nothing.

He allowed himself a breath and then glanced at the merchant's wife.

"Don't look back," Kyler said. "We're not going that way. Stay close."

She followed him without a word, her hands clutching at her dead husband's ring. Kyler peered around the corner of the alley and gazed into the street. They would have to cross it. There was no other way. No mob was near, yet further down the street there were armed rioters. They were far enough away to not notice the knight and his companion. Dead bodies filled the street. Men and women alike. Poor and rich alike. All would fall as the madness took hold of the city. Kyler turned to the lady.

"Look at me. Don't look down. We will make it."

"Where are we going exactly?" she whispered. It was the first time she had spoken.

"The arsenal, my lady," Kyler replied. "We will be safe there."

She nodded and then followed him into the street. The knight's boots lightly thudded upon the cobblestones as he carefully navigated the maze of bodies. He looked back on occasion to make sure that the woman's gaze was fixed firmly on him, and not the dead below. Kyler offered her a smile, and then they were through.

"Cross the square at the end of the alley," the knight told her, "and the arsenal awaits. We should be–"

"Oi!" the shout came from the shadows. Two men stepped in front of them, both armed with steel.

Kyler raised his sword with one hand and used his other to shield the lady. "Let us pass and there will be no trouble," Kyler ordered.

"Her dress is too fine to be anything but that of nobility," one of the men growled as he stepped closer.

"And you're too well armed to be with the mob," Kyler replied and levelled his sword.

"The gangs have grown strong while those who sit in their ivory towers have grown complacent. One word from us and the ground shifts beneath your feet," the man flicked his spear up as he spoke. "For too long they have taken everything from us. Now we take from them. Soon the city will be ours. This is but a taste of what is to come."

"Step aside, sir," Kyler commanded. "I will not warn you again."

The gangman came at the knight just as Kyler knew he would. He strode forward to meet the Elaran.

Steel kissed steel.

The knight blocked once, twice, and then caught the third blow on his bracer as he lunged. The gangman's spear slid off his armour and Kyler's sword found his chest.

He stepped back as the second man came forward. The knight blocked the sword overhead, spun to the side, their blades still locked, and delivered a kick to the man's stomach. He fell backward toward where his prey had come.

The first man attacked again, and his spear carved through the air. Kyler launched himself forward. He blocked the man's weapon and then shoved him into the alley wall. Shouts came from where they had entered the alley. Men poured toward them. He did not know if they were the mob or gangmen. It did not matter. They were all the same.

"RUN!" roared Kyler. "RUN!"

The lady needed no further motivation as the newcomers surged toward them. Kyler heaved with all his might. His muscles ached. His sword rose, still locked with the other man's spear. Kyler twisted savagely and sliced his sword across the man's neck. He fell with a spray of blood.

Kyler had no time to breathe as the other man attacked again. He leapt back and lashed out. The gangman's sword sliced into the knight's thigh. Kyler's blade drove between his ribs and took his life. He took a step down the alley against the will of his protesting leg. His thigh screamed as blood began to stain his trousers. Kyler snatched up the dead man's spear and used it to take his weight. He turned, staggering toward the arsenal square as the mob charged. He saw the lady cross the yard. He heard the roars at his back grow and the footsteps close in. The lady reached the gates of the arsenal.

Kyler hobbled into the square as fast as he was able. The shaft of his spear thudded against cobblestone. His leg felt like it was on fire. He clutched at the wooden shaft with both hands, driving his full weight into the spear as he struggled to stand.

The horde closed in. Kyler turned back as the first of his pursuers reached him. He spun without warning and caught the man unawares. Kyler's spear carved through his face and put him down. The knight skipped aside from a second man and then stepped toward the arsenal. He heard a cry. A man leapt at him and grabbed his foot. Kyler fell and his spear flew from his grasp.

He hit the ground, rolled onto his back, and then the man was on him. His stench filled Kyler's mouth. His bared teeth mere inches from the knight's. A knife drove down toward him. Kyler blocked it with his bracers and then grabbed the man's arm. A shadow came over Kyler as second man arrived. He saw boots begin to surround him. The song of crossbows filled the yard.

He heard the screams as his attackers were caught in the storm of steel. The pressure vanished. Kyler shoved the man to the side, and only then did he see the pair of bolts embedded in the man's back. They were all around him, sprawled from the shadows of the alley to the centre of the yard. A dozen men riddled with arrows. The soldiers atop the arsenal walls had greeted the rioters with death. Kyler heaved himself to his feet and snatched up the spear.

The arsenal was warm. Braziers and fire burned brightly while hundreds of crossbow armed men patrolled the walls. Thousands of their kind, along with many more mercenaries, filled the streets. The magister, for all his sins, was not stupid. He had brought his whole army to bear. They were ready for anything. In the morning they would sweep through Elara from east to west and deal with whatever remained of the rebellion.

Kyler was alone. He had been granted a room for saving the merchant wife's life and had been implored that if an attack was made on the arsenal, he would man the walls. Though he had agreed, he had not told them of his creed or of his allegiance. The knight still wore his armour, though his sword belt was placed upon the table before him. A length of cloth was bound tightly around his leg and the bleeding had long since stopped. It was a shallow wound and caused him no concern.

He was not prepared for the pain, for the agony that ripped through his body. Kyler fell against the table with a gasp. Sweat coated his brow and he gritted his teeth against the scream that threatened. Everything burned. It was as if he was being ripped apart from the inside. He clawed at the table as the pain worsened. He saw the veins of his hands bulge and felt the rest follow suit. Kyler's eyes widened. The veins were *black*. He did not see them etched across his face. He did not see his eyes turn red. Then he saw nothing.

Elise had been compromised after the death of Lord Cirillo Eris. The city was alert and the soldiers had seen her. She had made for the only place that she could hide. The only place that would give her the cover she sorely needed to patch her wounds and remove the Nightingale garb.

Tariq's house.

He had made no mention of her appearance nor asked any questions. He had instead enveloped her in a bear hug. Tariq managed to find her a dress from a neighbour while Elise washed her hair and scrubbed her body clean of dust, ash, and blood. The dress itched and was a little too big, yet she did not care. Tariq had wrapped her in a cloak, bagged her Nightingale attire and then led her out into the street. They took the back roads, crossed the bridge, and, after what seemed like an eternity, they reached the Delfeyre house. That was when the riots had begun. The first of the mob's howls filled the air when the doors were thrown open and Marshall led the pair inside. Raphael met them first. He took one look at Elise and then pulled her into a hug.

"Where have you been?" Raphael murmured as he squeezed her tight. "I've been so worried."

"I saw it fall," Elise said quietly.

"You're safe now," came the reply. "You're safe." Raphael broke off the embrace but kept an arm wrapped around her shoulders as he turned to the fighter. "You would be Tariq?"

"That I am, sir."

The merchant nodded. "Then I am in your debt. You are welcome in my house and may stay as long as you please. Something tells me that we won't be getting much sleep tonight."

"Thank you," Tariq replied. "Sir, if I may. How are your men?"

"What do you mean?" the merchant frowned.

"How are they in a fight?" came the reply. "Will they stand and fight in the face of ever-growing odds?"

Raphael beckoned to the closest guard. "This is Marshall, the captain of my household guard. He spent ten years in the navy and achieved the rank of captain. A further five were spent training soldiers in Kiriador. He and his men are as strong in battle as they are loyal to a fault."

Tariq glanced at the guardsman as he spoke, "Then you understand what it is that we may face?"

Marshall looked the Berenithian up and down. "Those are men beyond those doors," Marshall said. "Men who right now are angry at those who stand above them. Right now, that anger has turned to madness and the beast that lives within is awoken. It is that beast that can be the architect of untold horrors. And yet they are flesh and bone, just like the rest of us. I know how to fight them, and I know how to kill them."

Elise found her aunt in the villa courtyard. A small flight of stairs led up onto the balcony that overlooked the pool, where Claudia Delfeyre sat with a great length of material in her hands.

"Aunt Claudia," Elise called as she reached the balcony.

"Elise," Claudia's face lit up like a beacon as she leapt to her feet. The dark green material was left on the reclining couch, all but forgotten as the woman embraced her niece. "You had me scared to death."

"I'm sorry."

"I am so glad you are home."

Claudia stared in her eyes and placed a kiss upon her brow. She stroked a stray strand of brown hair up behind Elise's ear. "When we heard the explosion, I feared the worst," Claudia said.

Elise smiled to hide her pain. The memories were still fresh, and she could still taste the dust in her throat. Her body ached. She had seen death before, but not like this. What Cleander had done was the act of a monster.

"I am fine," Elise lied.

"I know, my love, I know," Claudia's lip trembled, and a tear rolled down her pale cheek. "It's just that after everything that has happened, everything that you have lost, I love you as if you are truly my own. But you were never mine."

"I have rebuilt my life from the ashes, and you were there the whole time," Elise said as she placed a gentle hand on her aunt's arm. "You have only ever loved me, and if there was nothing else that would be enough. You may not be my mother by birth, but you are by deed."

They embraced for a second time. Elise stepped back and gestured to the material and the sewing tools that sat beside it on the couch.

"What are you making?"

Claudia led her over to it by the hand and picked up the green length, "I made this for you."

Her aunt let the wool unfurl, and then there it was, a magnificent sleeved cloak.

Elise's eyes shone as she took the garb, "It's beautiful."

"Let me see you put it on."

Elise grinned and slid her arms into the cloak. It was not too heavy, nor too light. It warmed her, casting off the chill that had clawed its way into her body.

"Perfect," Claudia Delfeyre said.

The house was still awake when the moon reached its highest peak.

There were still shouts and screams echoing through the city streets. Fire burned bright and the sound of fighting echoed to the heavens. Despite this, Elise said her goodnights to her family and Halina, before going to her room. The city would not sleep tonight, and even without the riots, she knew that slumber would never have taken hold. Elise bolted the door, removed her cloak and began to pull on her dark garment. Black boots and pants matched by a shirt, vest, and short hooded cape. A knock came from the door. Elise said nothing. She hoped that whoever it was would think she was asleep.

"I know you're awake," Tariq's voice came through. It was a hissed whisper. The fighter did not want to draw attention, that much was certain.

"Let me in."

Elise grimaced and strode to the door. She unlocked it, let her friend in, and then swiftly bolted it behind him. "What do you want?" she asked.

Tariq looked her from head to toe. "I had a feeling that you would do something rash."

"And you came to stop me?"

"Aye, that I did."

Elise snatched up her scarf and bound it around her neck as she spoke, "Let me save you your breath. You can't."

"And what is it that you intend on doing, exactly?" Tariq frowned. "You can't stop a riot. No one can."

"And that is why I will not be trying something so impossible," she replied. "I am an acrobat, not an idiot."

"Then what?"

Elise picked up her ebony mask and faced her friend. "Before he died, I met with Cirillo Eris," Elise told him.

"Lord Cirillo Eris?"

She nodded and stared at the man. Her eyes filled with the purpose that she now held within her heart.

"Tariq, I was right. He killed them. Magister Imrohir killed my parents."

"*What?*" the fighter's face paled.

"Do you remember Aislinn?"

"The girl who joined us five years back? I remember."

Elise folded her arms. "She would have been what? Eight? Nine? Aislinn was with us for a few months before one night she vanished in the dead of night. My parents searched for over a year but found nothing. We were all she had, and it always struck me as strange that she left without a word. That is until a few nights ago when I broke into the magister's chamber and uncovered the secret that he had my parents killed to hide. He deals in slaves, Tariq, child slaves."

Tariq let out a long breath, "By the gods… if the people knew…"

"Exactly," Elise said. "When my parents found out they went to the nobles, the ones that they trusted. Imrohir found out. He may be a tyrant, but the Magister is no fool. Gang violence and sickness, the perfect ways to deal with dissent without harbouring blame. It was poison that killed my mother, not some illness. The physician was in Imrohir's pocket the whole time. It is to that same healer that I intend to pay a visit this night."

A dark look crossed Tariq's face.

"But what if it's a trap?" he said. "What if somehow Imrohir knows that he is compromised?"

"If I do nothing, what's the point?" Elise replied desperately. "I have to know the truth. I have to know all of it. Casimir Dusan is the *last* person that can help me. The rest are gone, dead. I have to do this myself."

"Elise, please," Tariq extended a hand. "Wait until morning. You need to rest. Wait until the riots are over. It is too dangerous out there. Please, I beg you. For our friendship I beg you."

Elise pulled the scarf up over her mouth and nose. She knew he was right. She had been fighting without respite for two years. She was exhausted, and now she was heading into a fight far greater than any before.

"Please, do not do this," Tariq pleaded. "We have the gold. We can leave this city tomorrow. Just as you wanted."

"I'm sorry," Elise said as she tied on her mask and pulled her hood up.

The Nightingale left through the window.

Kyler's eyes flickered open.

His head still ached. The knight looked to his hands first and heaved a sigh of relief. They were normal. Had he not woken up on the floor, he would have thought it all a dream. He rose to his feet and ran a hand through his hair. It took him a moment to realise that he felt no pain in his leg, pulling off the bindings he looked through the tear in his trousers. Where there had once been a ragged slice, now there was nothing. Not even a thin white scar.

What?

The knight reached for his medallion and uttered a prayer. It made no sense. A cut, no matter how shallow, would not heal so fast. Kyler buckled his sword on and made for the door. The walk back to the tavern was long. Though the sun was beginning to rise, the streets were all but empty. Empty save the bodies left for the crows, empty save for the smoke that hung in a haze, and empty save for the sound of marching soldiers. Whether by the sword or the regaining of sense, the mobs had dispersed. Still, Kyler's hand stayed atop his sword and his eyes remained ever watchful.

Alarik met him at the door. "Pisspot. Where in the hell have you been?" the battlemaster asked as he stepped aside to let his companion in.

"Good to see you too," Kyler snorted as he entered. "I got caught up in the mob. And when I made it out, this place was too far off. I spent the night in the arsenal."

"Lucky that the horde did not sweep you up," Alarik muttered. "I have seen these before. They are not pretty, and what comes next more so. The fact that you made it out in one piece, despite holding no allegiance to those animals, proves that you are a troublesome man to kill."

"And you?" Kyler glanced at his mentor. "When I left to investigate the explosion, you had not yet returned."

"I found my trader of rare goods in the bazaar, and we had a long conversation. Said that the man who purchased these,"

Alarik tossed Kyler the pouch of fragments, "is called Cleander. A false name is a thing that comes as no surprise. Harvarder works with the gangs... and that was all Arntair knew."

Kyler's breath caught. Arntair, that was what his mentor had said. The man bore the very same name Lysandra had once mentioned. It was Arntair that the arc'maija had wanted him to seek out.

"What about you, Pisspot?" Alarik asked. "Did you find the man who created the sword?"

Kyler took up the wrapped sword from his bed. "Better," he said. "I have a name. Mellisanthi." The battlemaster shrugged and gestured for him to continue. "It would appear that Harvarder is known to spend time with courtesans," Kyler told him, handing over the blade. "Mellisanthi is the madam of the particular establishment that our man likes to frequent. The blacksmith suggested that we speak to her."

Alarik clapped him on the shoulder with a grin, "You've done well, Pisspot. Tonight, when the cesspit storm outside dies down, we should go pay this Mellisanthi a visit."

"And until then?" Kyler asked.

The battlemaster nodded toward the shutters. "The joys and pleasures of Elara are all yours."

The only life in the bazaar was that of the soldiers who patrolled its streets. Some of the shops had been looted or vandalised, others left untouched. After getting directions from guards and merchant's voices from behind doors, Kyler found the shop belonging to Arntair. It was closed, as expected, yet a few knocks later the lock was pulled back.

The door opened slightly and a bearded Elaran face poked out.

"What do you want?"

"Are you Arntair?"

The trader frowned as he spoke, "I am."

"I am told that you may know something about the bludvier plant. I can pay," Kyler reached for his coin purse, "handsomely."

Arntair flicked his gaze left and right, down the street. Kyler was alone.

"Come in. Few men know of the bludvier, fewer still that I have on occasion procured it," Arntair said as he led Kyler into his shop.

Plants and herbs filled shelves, while trinkets, clothes and even some weapons adorned tables and benches. "It is an incredibly rare plant with the most dangerous of toxins, and as such demands great expense," the trader continued. "You mentioned coin."

Kyler tossed him the pouch. "Should be enough for what I seek."

Arntair tipped its contents out onto a bench and ran his greedy gaze over the gold. He pursed his lips and turned to Kyler. "Enough for henbane or valerian perhaps. But for bludvier? Not nearly enough."

"I am not looking for bludvier," Kyler said.

"Then what do you want with me?"

The knight crossed his arms. "These riots may have left your shop undamaged," Kyler told him. "Yet its aftermath will affect all, I am sure. Coin will be hard to procure from even the most loose of purses."

"Go on," Arntair waved a hand as he replied.

"It is no secret to me that you control the trade of bludvier, not just in Elara, but everywhere east of the empire. From what I am told, kings have traded daughters, land and even castles for the toxin," Kyler said with a shrug. "As such, few men would have the means to buy such a rare plant. A few months, perhaps even a year ago, you procured bludvier for a buyer. I want to know who."

"I am not in the habit of selling my clients to the highest bidder," Arntair growled.

"Indeed," Kyler nodded. "Though after last night's events those clients will be few and far between for many months. Who knows how long this will last or which establishment will fall next?"

"Are you threatening me?"

The knight shook his head. "No, I merely speak the truth and you know it."

Arntair glared at Kyler, and it was in his eyes that Kyler saw the war raging. He was teetering on the edge of a knife, unsure which way to jump. The riots could continue, and many could fall. Most of his buyers were among the nobility and it would not take much for him to lose everything. The trader sighed and closed his eyes.

"Your words are true, gods curse me," Arntair said at last. "He came ten months ago and gave no name. His tongue was that of Aureia. He wore a hood and I only saw his face once. It is a face that I will not soon forget. Lined and scarred it was. The kind that had seen much conflict."

"A soldier then?"

"Aye," Arntair replied. "That is all I know."

The trader's words had given more questions than answered. Amaris' killer was a knight, that much was certain, but who? Who would have wanted the grand master dead? Better yet, it was now certain that a traitor lived among the Order. It would appear that Lysandra had been right.

THIRTY-FIVE

Palen-Tor, Aethela, Kingdom of Annora.

The strand of cloth was yellow and it shimmered in the light. Dayne held it in front of his eyes for a moment before he handed the golden material to General Tristayn Martyn.

"You're sure of it?" the warrior murmured.

"Aye," Dayne replied. "It matches nothing that belonged to the king, yet I came across it in his chamber the night of his death. I had my suspicions about them, but now I know that I was right to harbour doubts. You know what must be done."

"Yes, my Prince."

"Do it discreetly, do it quietly," Dayne told him. "If you are discovered then we are all undone."

Deep into the night, Prince Dayne stood in the palace cathedral alone. His hands were clasped at his waist. The sun and moon medallion hung from his fingers. Dayne's eyes were closed, yet the stone statues of his gods that arose before him were still clear in his mind.

"Durandail, Father of all Fathers, Lord of Justice, Lord of Wisdom, I am in such need of your wisdom now," the prince said quietly. "The days grow dark. My father's torch has passed to me, and it is a brand that I shall carry high until my last. So many words were left unspoken and yet fate is fickle. Can you see the coming flood, Lord? The warring about to be done in your name? Violence without purpose makes the noble man flawed, yet my purpose is clear. I have spent my entire life training for this moment in which I find myself. Yet here upon the precipice I find myself, for the first time, afraid. Will I lead my people well? Father of all Fathers, grant me your light, and grant me victory. Help me save my people, Lord, and if the cost of salvation is my life, it is a cost that I shall gladly pay. This is my kingdom, this is my crown, and I shall defend it to the death."

Dayne opened his eyes and stared into Durandail's stone gaze. The prince bowed his head to the god before he placed his amulet around his own neck.

The doors boomed open.

"I arrived in Palen-Tor expecting the emperor to be standing before a great silver army," a very Aureian voice broke the prince's silence. "Instead, I find that the king is dead, and my emperor murdered. I had thought that The Eagle's son would have been doing all in his power to bring the culprit to justice. Yet here you are, praying."

Dayne ran his eyes over the Aureian soldier. His silver armour and purple cloak were travel-stained, while the bare skin of his face and arms skin was a patchwork of scars. He would have been little over thirty summers, with a strong jaw covered in dark stubble and eyes that betrayed a darkening storm. By himself, the Aureian would have made for an imposing figure, yet at his back walked an equally as strong Larissan warrior.

"Yet here I am," Dayne replied. "Let me guess, you would be Sir Velis Demir, the man they call the Silver Horseman."

"I am a knight, Prince Dayne," Velis said. "No more than that. I believe only in titles earned."

"You earned your position in Irene, did you not?" the Annoran glanced at man who had achieved more renown in *one* campaign than most could ever achieve if they lived two hundred years. "I have heard the stories."

"Not all of them," Velis growled. "You weren't there."

"Indeed," Dayne nodded.

He had heard the Aureian's tone before in other men. The knight was not a man to be pressed.

"Have no fear, General, the wheels are in motion. The murders will be answered soon enough. But now is not the time to grieve or seek vengeance upon the shadows. War is upon us. We leave at dawn."

"The cardinal has made his will known," Velis said, brushing the sword at his side. "And we shall honour it."

The prince glanced back at the statues. "The gods are with us."

"Never been much of a churchy man," Velis replied with a snort.

"Interesting, for a man in your position," Dayne stated. "An Aureian knight not beholden to the faith of his people, of his forefathers."

"In Irene it was not the gods who did the fighting, not the gods who did the dying. Their light was not our saviour on the day that thousands of my brothers died. The earth was covered in rivers of blood, and the gods never got their feet wet."

"And yet there is no thing stronger than the power of belief," Prince Dayne replied as he looked at the soldier with a newfound curiosity.

A man such as Velis could have been arrogant, and a man with his reputation could have stood as a king. Yet the knight seemed to want no part in glory.

"The Knights of Kil'kara have an age-old saying 'Areut talc cuun'etc'. Blood or immortality," Dayne continued. "Their belief in the gods, in the heaven that awaits them should they fall in battle, grants them a power even above their greatest enemies."

"Pray to your gods then, Prince, if you wish," Velis told him. "I have fought many tribal leaders before and these men of Salvaar will be no different from those demons in Irene. Many suffered at their hand. Never again."

"How many are you?" Dayne asked.

"Four thousand horses," the knight gestured to his Larissan companion. "Another two thousand of Queen Reshada's own. This is Chiher who leads them."

"Prince Dayne," Chiher bowed.

The prince dipped his head to the Larissan. Six thousand skilled riders under the command of the greatest horseman the empire had ever known.

"We leave for Kilgareth come first light," Dayne told them. "General Ilaros and Grand Master Bavarian ride at my side. We will meet the sons of Medea in the north and then begin our attack."

"Forgive me, my Prince," Velis said. "But we will not be travelling with you. Darius was your friend, I know, but he was my emperor, and I *will* honour his last command. I ride for the Rift come break of day. We will drive our spears into Salvaar from west to east and see this war to its bitter end."

"Fortune favours the bold, my brother," Dayne extended an arm. "I pray that we live to see its end."

Velis clasped his wrist firmly as he replied, "My life is but one of many hundreds, Prince Dayne. The world will not suffer if it ends too soon."

Both men turned as another entered the temple. Dayne knew why he was here, yet let his eyes betray no emotion. "Sir Tristayn," he greeted the man.

"My lords," the general offered a bow.

The prince could see the unspoken words in his friend's gaze. His command had been carried out to the letter, just as he knew it would have been.

"Forgive me, General," Dayne said to Velis as he made his way toward his kinsman. "I must make my leave."

Princess Kassandra found Dayne at the city square. He stood alone atop a raised dais beneath the dawn sun. Her brother watched from the balcony as rank upon rank of soldiers marched through Palen-Tor. They were the stalwart men of Annora, Kassandra's own people. Next came the hardened soldiers of the fifth and seventh legions, veterans who had served in every corner of the empire. Blue and silver clad knights riding beneath the banner of the sun and moon came next. Aureia's finest, the great southern Order of Kil'kara, rode atop their great steeds. A line of colour shining beneath the gaze of Durandail's sun. At the fore of the army were the griffin standards, held aloft by their bearers to the cheers of the crowd. Behind them flew another three banners, one with the Aureian griffin over a purple field, another the eagle of Annora. The third bore the sun and moon of the gods to remind the men why they fought.

For their people.

For their country.

For their gods.

Kassandra wrapped an arm around her brother's waist and gently placed her head upon his arm. Soon he would mount up on his horse and lead them into battle. Such was the fate of princes. Dayne's arm came down around her shoulders.

The Vesuvan sun burned high above. Even the air was sweltering. Beneath her cuirass, Kitara's tunic was soaked through from sweat. Even her well moulded muscles ached from the training she had been subjected to for nearly two weeks. Despite the blood that she had shed upon the sand, despite the bruises that covered her skin, the weights and hard exercise had slowly gotten easier. The mentor walked the yard giving out sage advice on technique, inspiring the sildari to train harder. Upon occasion he would use his gnarled cane on those who ignored him, spoke back, or did not push themselves.

The sound of wood striking wood echoed around the yard as

many of the fighters sparred. Kitara slid back as Shaye's staunch came at her. She parried the strike and lunged. The dark haired Aureian deftly skipped aside and caught the sword upon his own. Kitara moved. Her feet glided upon the earth as she circled her opponent. Sweat dripped from her brow. She ignored it. To raise a hand to wipe it away was to invite death. Kitara saw the look in Shaye's eyes and the angle of his body. She saw his attack coming before he made it.

Kitara caught his blow as he stepped in. It was high, aimed to carve her from shoulder to hip. Kitara changed angles as the weapons came together. She let her crossguard catch on the blade of Shaye's sword, and then slid her own down between his arms. With her spare hand she caught the blade of her stanch and then viciously wrenched her sword. The Aureian's arms twisted, and then the sword flew from his grasp. Kitara's blade came around with a flick of her wrist and she brought it to a halt upon the side of his neck.

"What did I do wrong?" Shaye growled.

"You attacked," Kitara shrugged.

"Pah!" Shaye shoved her sword from his neck. "Just you wait. One day I will catch you."

The Salvaari woman snorted and at last wiped the sweat from her brow. "I welcome the attempt," she said with a smirk.

"DRINK!" the mentor's voice ripped through the yard like a needle through cloth.

Almost as one, the sildari downed their wooden weapons and weights and moved over to the well. They were all weary, yet none would ever complain. Every hurt was a lesson, and the daily torments made them strong. As Kitara reached the water and went for a cup, the mentor's strong arm thrust out, halting her in her tracks.

"Not you, Alessandra," he said.

Kitara rolled her eyes. She had grown accustomed to the name, yet even after two weeks it felt foreign to the ear. "Mentor?"

"You are summoned."

Two soldiers led her through the villa and into Valliro's office. The magister's words had barely reached Kitara's ears before she replied. "What do you mean they *want* me?"

Kitara frowned as she stared at Valliro Nilor from across his desk.

"Ceolsige Teora, the slave master of Vesuva has asked for you personally," the Magister told her. "It would seem that because you cost him a good deal of gold at least you can compensate him with blood."

"He wants me to fight?"

"He wants you to *die*," Nilor replied.

Kitara glared at her master. "I don't die easily. Not despite your fighters' lack of trying."

"You will not earn their respect until you are tested."

"And what test might that be?"

"This is your test!" Valliro snarled, "Listen to me, Alessandra, the man you will be fighting is named Taliskar."

"What is that to me?"

"Taliskar is no mere sildari. The man you killed, Scarpa, is nothing compared to Teora's champion. He has killed many, many men and strikes fear into the hearts of a great deal more. He is fast, strong, and completely without mercy," the Magister told her. "Teora wants you dead and knows of your knowledge of the swordsong. This will be no arena fight, for his games take place inside the most deadly of cages. There is no room to move, no room for you to sing your song of steel. This way he can be certain that your head leaves the ring far in advance of your body."

Kitara squared her jaw and folded her arms. "Are the stories of Taliskar as exaggerated as I have come to expect?"

"No," Valliro shook his head. "His reputation is well earned. No man has ever stood against him and lived."

"And when I win?"

"Beat him and glory beyond measure will be within our grasp," the Magister said with a smirk. "Teora was once the empire's greatest seaman, yet now he rules an empire of his own. An empire of slavery. He believes himself a god and is so rich in coin that the man pisses gold. I would end that flow and with your help, bring him to heel."

"And our deal?"

"You will be one step closer to achieving your end. Kill this man for me, Alessandra, and we both grow stronger."

Kitara sighed, "It is all anyone can do."

Valliro nodded. "There is no greater glory than standing victorious in the sands," he said.

The Magister's words echoed in Kitara's mind as she made her way through the roaring crowd of Aureians. A steely calm came over her. All eyes were fixed upon her, a leanly muscled girl of twenty-five, with long blonde hair and sporting a suit of bronze and hardened leather. Yet it was not the armour that caught the crowd's eye, nor was it the crested helm tucked under her arm.

It was the white scar running from above her left eye to her cheekbone.

Kitara lightly tugged at her bracers as she strode toward her destination: the large cage that stood in the very centre of the crowded room. A cage where two people would enter, but only one would leave. The fights that took place in the cages were dirty, brutal, and without honour. Fights where only the strongest survived. After growing up with a band of bloodthirsty pirates, where betrayal and backstabbing were rampant, along with years on the streets, Kitara had learned every dirty trick that there was. In order to survive, she had been forced to turn her entire body into a weapon. She had learned to react instantly to any situation and to win, no matter what. The cell was small, granting her little room to move or use tarkaras.

Behind her walked Arias Nilor and a pair of the Magister's

soldiers. In his hands the young noble carried the blade Kitara would wield. It didn't take long for the crowd to turn against Kitara. Here she was the *challenger*. Here she was the prey. She had cost these people valuable coin, and now would pay with blood. Kitara was used to every obscenity hurled her way and blocked them out.

"Quiet!"

The crowd instantly froze, and all turned to face Ceolsige Teora, slave master of Vesuva, as he rose to his feet. At over six feet tall and covered in muscle, Teora made for an imposing figure. As a brilliant, if theatrical leader, and one of the greatest sailors in the known world, Ceolsige had all the appearances of the captain that he had once been. He bore a dozen rings at his fingers and ears, a shortsword at his side, and a savage glint in his penetrating brown eyes. Valliro Nilor stood at the slave master's side. His gaze was fixed firmly upon Kitara. He gave her a nod.

Ceolsige's mouth broke into a toothy smile as he waved a hand over the crowd. "I believe it's time to bring on the entertainment," his voice echoed around the room. "Enter our champion, Taliskar of Vesuva!"

The crowd cheered as the warrior entered the cage and returned the crowd's roar. Kitara ran her gaze over her opponent. If there was a weakness, she would find it. Taliskar swung a longsword around as he strode around the edge of the cage. With a leer on his face, he used the crowd to fire himself up. His head was shaven clean, his muscular arms bare. He was a head taller than Kitara and carried himself with the ferocity of an enraged wolf. His garb was that of chainmail, while his silver helm was crestless.

"Bring on the challenger!" Teora bellowed as the crowd grew quiet.

The jeers grew into a deafening crescendo, battering at the golden-haired woman. All eyes turned to Kitara as she took a deep breath and entered through the open door of the cage. The cell was filthy and might have been fifteen feet long. Little enough room to move and swing a sword. The bars and nails that held the walls and roof were rusted. It was a true slaver's cage.

Kitara placed her helm over her head. Arias Nilor presented her with the same sword that had taken Scarpa's life in the arena, and then left the sands. The door closed and she flexed her hand upon the weapon's hilt. She blocked everything out but her opponent and the cage itself. Kitara brought her sword into a light two-handed grip and bent her knees slightly to centre herself. Her eyes locked with her opponent's as he entered his own fighting crouch.

The sildari shot her a withering glare and spat at her feet, his eyes glowing with contempt. Kitara stood lightly on the sand covered ground as she carefully watched her opponent. She could sense everything going on about her as she readied herself for the fight.

She didn't turn her head as Teora leaned over the table before him and roared, "Begin!"

The crowd cheered as Taliskar charged toward Kitara, his sword swinging into a diagonal slash aimed at her neck. Reacting instinctively, Kitara moved her right boot back and slightly changed the angle of her body, even as the sword whistled down. With a flick of her wrist, she angled her blade and deflected Taliskar's weapon before spinning aside as his follow through came at her stomach.

Steel struck steel, and then they flitted apart.

Their blades clashed together again and again in a deadly melody. The sound of sword striking sword was barely audible over the sound of the crowd braying for blood. Kitara didn't give the man time to pause before launching herself at him. Her blade became a blur as it cut through the air. The swords rang as they collided. With a roar, Taliskar put his weight behind his sword, pushing it closer and closer to Kitara's neck. Suddenly she ducked, flicking her wrists and deflecting Taliskar's sword to the side. She didn't hesitate as she slipped inside her opponent's reach and hammered her pommel into his chin. Kitara danced to the side. Her sword changed angle. The cage cut her movement off.

Fast as lightning, Taliskar barrelled forward. Kitara thrust at his face as she leapt aside from the cage wall. The man switched his grip, one hand grasped the hilt of his sword, the other its blade. He knocked the thrust aside as he erupted toward her and brought the crossguard around. Steel smashed into the side of her helmet. The pain of the blow hit Kitara hard as she stumbled backward. She blocked once, twice, as she backed up, trying to escape his onslaught. She stayed calm and kept her breath steady. The sweat rolling down her cheek beneath the helm was forgotten as the crowd screamed. Taliskar drove his sword at her.

Kitara angled her sword, twisted, and lunged.

A lesser man would have been caught.

A lesser man would have died.

Taliskar was fast. He turned his head and allowed the blade to scrape along his steel helmet. Kitara ducked his counter and pirouetted away. Taliskar came at her like a bull, first stepping to the right, before charging left. His step cut her off from the centre of the cage. He blocked her first strike and then exploded forward. Kitara had nowhere to move. She was trapped in the corner. She slid away from his attack and lashed out, catching him across the arm and chest. Blood poured from his exposed bicep and the mail turned her steel aside. He barrelled into her. Kitara got her sword up just in time to save her head from his blade. The weight of his body drove her hard into the steel bars of the cage. Air was driven from her lungs. Her back screamed. He grabbed her wrist with his bearlike hand and wrenched it to the side. Gods he was strong. She could see the rage in his eyes; taste the stench of his breath. The hilt of his sword smashed into her head twice. The world blurred. Their swords locked together as he pressed forward. Steel sliced the flesh of her arm as he heaved forward and crushed her against the cage. Then Kitara's blade was ripped from her grasp.

She went for his wrist and pushed with all of her strength as Taliskar drove his weapon toward her throat. Steel glanced off the cage bars. It nicked her neck and drew blood. Kitara roared defiantly and wrapped her fingers around the blade. Blood flowed yet she clung to the sword in desperation. Her second hand came up and latched onto steel as it edged closer.

Kitara felt it brush her neck. She bared her teeth and strained with all her might. Yet against such a foe her strength was not enough. Her arms began to burn, her muscles screamed under Taliskar's weight. Kitara twisted her left arm up and found the bars of the cage with her boot. She released her grip on the blade with her left hand and erupted. Kitara drove herself forward and heaved from the cage with her foot as she sliced her elbow up.

Taliskar's sword speared through the bars at her side as her movement caught him by surprise. Kitara's elbow crunched into his unprotected jaw. She felt something break in Taliskar's mouth. Blood spewed from his lips. The pressure vanished as he staggered back. He released his grip upon her and his weapon. She had but moments to find space. Kitara's foot came down and she pivoted, following Taliskar's movement, and launched a body kick. Her greave connected heavily with chainmail as she sunk the blow in hard.

Taliskar winced and almost doubled over. Almost.

Kitara angled her body and skipped to the side. He saw her eyes go to her fallen sword. The fighter charged her, not fearing the power in her hands. Taliskar barrelled into her side and tossed her into the cage bars. Pain flared to life in her side as Kitara hit the steel.

She blocked the first punch, parried the second, and then his armoured fist cracked into her head. Taliskar lashed out with his left fist and Kitara ducked… straight into the path of his right hook. The blow caught her in the stomach, and she staggered backward. Now he was on the attack. He rained down blows mercilessly, and

Kitara was barely able to keep out of range. She moved to counter as Taliskar made to move, but it was a well-timed feint. Before she could act the back of his right fist slammed into her check and sent her crashing into the wall of the cage. Then he was on her. Taliskar shoved her up against the bars and hammered another punch into her stomach. His power buckled her legs, and then he grabbed her shoulders and slammed her into the cage.

Her head met steel.

Kitara fell.

She hit the ground. Sand washed through her fingers and filled her mouth. Kitara heaved herself back as Taliskar's boot bit into the ground beside her face. Her helmet was ripped from her head, spilling her golden braids all around. She moved on instinct, blocking the kick aimed at her face, before a second slammed into her ribs. Taliskar hammered his boot into Kitara's prone form again and again. She felt something crack beneath her skin. Pain ripped through her body like a spear through water. Kitara cried out in agony as she rolled to the side and barely avoided the next blow. Then she was up against the wall of the cage again. Taliskar saw her trapped and sent a vicious kick toward her head. Kitara saw an opening. She rolled toward him and pushed off the steel bars of the cage. Taliskar's boot sailed over her head as she crashed into his leg. Kitara wrapped her arms around his ankle and lashed out with her feet. They caught his hips hard. His balance fled.

Taliskar fell.

Kitara rolled once, twice. She leapt to her feet and launched a kick toward her rising foe.

Taliskar stumbled back a step as her shin connected heavily with his head. Blood poured from his shattered nose. Kitara had space. She dove for her sword, and it eagerly flew into her hand. Kitara turned as Taliskar spun to face her, steel in his grasp. He hastily blocked Kitara's sword as it sped toward his neck. Taliskar knocked it aside with a roar and took a step back. He watched

Kitara as she gazed at him with her emerald eyes blazing like fire. She twirled her blade and brought it back up into a two-handed grip, its point levelled toward Taliskar's neck. Sweat trickled down her cheeks and mingled with the blood that covered her skin and armour. She watched and waited, until finally, Taliskar made his move. With a vicious snarl, the man charged toward her, a wall of muscle twice her size. Kitara slowly moved her right foot back and angled her body.

Taliskar's sword came up and flashed toward her neck. His weight and momentum made the man almost unstoppable as his sword sped closer. Kitara's eyes blazed as she started her move. Fast as lightning, Kitara's blade came up and deflected Taliskar's sword even as she spun to the side. Taliskar had barely enough time to show his surprise as his movement carried him past Kitara. His sword missing her by a hair's breadth. Without pausing to think, Kitara flicked her wrists and slipped her sword inside Taliskar's defence. Her first blow sliced across the side of his unprotected leg. As the man sped past, Kitara's foot flashed across her opponent's ankles, and in an instant he started to fall toward the ground. Taliskar bellowed as her second blow came down. It sliced through skin and muscle between shoulder and neck.

In a few heartbeats it was all over.

Taliskar lay face down in the sand. His sword lay just beyond the reach of his outstretched fingers. Kitara strode toward the fallen man and kicked his blade aside. He struggled to rise.

Blood seeped from his wounds as Taliskar knelt before her. His whole body shook. The crowd watched in stunned silence as their champion barely held himself up and all could see that he was finished.

Kitara didn't take her eyes off Taliskar as she raised her blade. Her whole body burned. Kitara's skin was a canvas of blood, sand, and sweat. The tip of her sword touched the point between Taliskar's neck and shoulder. Her hands wrapped around the weapon's hilt. The champion bowed his head. Kitara drove the sword down. Steel slid through his body and cut deep into his heart. Taliskar groaned.

Kitara wrenched her blade free. Blood erupted from the champion's mouth. He toppled forward, dead before he hit the sand. The sword fell from Kitara's hand. She closed her eyes and looked to the heavens as the cheers began to wash over her.

THIRTY-SIX

The Southlands, Kingdom of Larissa

Sabra soared high above in the morning breeze and her joyous cries echoed across the desert that spread before them. The hawk's call reached Sakkar's ear as he raced down toward the foot of the mountain and leapt from his saddle. His boots found the sand and he dropped to his knees. Sakkar's fingers brushed the sand before he gathered a handful. A grin broke across Sakkar's lips as he held the sand before his eyes and watched as it drained through his fingers.

Home.

The Larissan let loose a laugh as he spread his arms and breathed his land in. He felt the warm sun of his homeland upon his skin. Sakkar took a deep breath… he could almost taste it. The blood of the desert ran through his veins and made him feel truly alive. With a cry, Sabra dove from the heavens and alighted upon her bearer's forearm. Sakkar's smile grew as he ran his fingers across the hawk's feathers.

"You feel it too, eh, girl? We're home. We're home." The Larissan turned as his companions arrived at the foot of the mountains.

"Here we are, lads," Galadayne nodded out across the dunes, "the golden sea of Larissa."

"Ah, the sands welcome us, my brother," Sakkar replied. "Soon you will be enjoying the hospitality of the southlands. A warm hearth, a full belly, and song echoing across the sands beneath a great ocean of stars."

"Never been in the south before," Jaimye said. "How far is the crossing?"

"From where we stand?" Sakkar glanced out across the sands. "Thirty days and thirty nights. We will take the pass at Talisier."

"This land," Aeryn spoke up and was unable to tear her silver gaze from the desert. "Is it all like this?"

"More or less," Kompton told her.

The Salvaari pursed her lips as she replied, "I have never seen such sights."

"Did I ever tell you about—"

"Bard, no singing," Bellec cut him off with a growl. A smirk betrayed the mercenary's menacing tone as he spoke, "It's a long ride to Talisier. Don't push your luck."

The horses thundered across the desert sands kicking up a great wall of dust. It had been twenty days since the company had arrived in Larissa, and for the most part the journey west had been uneventful. They had stopped at Kianakis to gather supplies before continuing on their way.

To the north lay the Scoran Mountains. They rose tall and stretched for days in every direction. The mountains, it was said, were home to the last of the rebels who had once tried to claim their young queen's life. Sakkar felt the chill in his bones before the hawk's screech reached his ear. The Larissan brought his mount to a halt and stared to the west. He squinted and raised a hand above his eyes to fend off the sun's burning light.

"What is it?" Bellec called as the company stopped behind their guide.

Sakkar's face paled as he saw it. A faint brown smudge upon the horizon that stretched from the desert to the heavens. "Sandstorm," he muttered.

"It appears far off. We could make for the mountains," Aeryn said from his side.

Sakkar stared at her, and a laugh threatened to pass his lips. Of course, she had never seen a desert or its treacherous storms. "Only a Salvaari would think that you could flee a sandstorm," Sakkar said with a grin. "It would catch us *long* before we got anywhere near the mountains."

"Then what do we do?"

Sakkar pulled out a bag and reached for the masks he had bought from Jaheria in Sadsworth. He tossed the large pouch to the moonseer. "You will all need one of these and we must set up camp now," Sakkar told them.

The Larissan pulled the orange cloth of his headscarf tight to cover his mouth and nose. The storm had doubled in size as the company pitched their tents. Sakkar called Sabra down and wrapped her in a cloak. The winds grew and dust began to swirl around them. The skies were painted dark as the sun was blotted out. The air grew cold and it drove the warmth from their bodies. The great wave of sand and dust surged toward them. Sakkar whispered to his horse and gently stroked the mare's powerful neck. She grew calm under his touch and slowly took a knee beside the tent. Slowly Sakkar tugged on the reins and pulled the horse's head beneath the rim of the canvas. One by one, the mercenaries followed suit. The wind began to howl, contorting both yells and shouts as the men ran through the makeshift campsite. Sakkar ducked inside the safety of his tent as the storm hit.

"The shifting sands arise, churning the heavens and painting the world with shadow," he murmured. "May the spirit of the Desert Lord protect us."

The Valkir warriors filled Agartha. They were quiet, reserved, yet filled with hate. Erik's face was pale but devoid of emotion. He tightened the buckles of his lamellar armour and strapped sword and axe to his side. The bloodsworn tied his long hair back, where it fell down behind his shoulders. Next came the white ochre; cool and gritty upon his skin. It painted him like a demon from the surging maelstrom that was Skûra. He took up his shield and ran a hand across its surface. The image of a mighty snake was upon it. The symbol of the bloodsworn. The symbol for battle.

Erik looked out across the bay as the wind caressed his hair and kissed his cheek. He stood atop the hills overlooking Agartha, the same place that he had sat with Astrid not so long ago. As soon as his sister's last ship had burned, as soon as her soul had been taken by the Sea-Father, the bloodsworn had sent forth the call. They had all answered. Man and woman, warrior and shield maiden, farmer and jarl. Now he watched as all the ships of Agartha made ready to sail. He wished that he had time to mourn, wished that he had time to properly say goodbye. Arndyr had forced his hand. If Erik did not act in this moment, the world could lose more than just one captain. One jarl. One sister. So, he had prepared.

"Are you sure about this?" Torben asked from his side. "What we're doing here could cause a great calamity."

"I have never been more certain," Erik told him. He looked to his old friend, "My sister was murdered in cold blood. My sister was murdered by a friend, an ally, a lover. My sister was murdered, her song, her light, never to shine again. I hunger for blood and answers, Torben. You are my greatest friend, the last person that I can truly trust. Be my friend now and do not try to dissuade me."

"Dissuade you?" Torben frowned with pain clear in his eyes. "My heart aches with loss. I have lost two daughters in as many months. One to the sword and her death has been answered in kind. The other to a traitor's knife. What you feel, I do not pretend to understand, but my heart is broken. An empty vessel that only Scaeva blood can fill."

Erik bared his teeth and the emotion that he keenly felt entered his voice.

"Your heart is empty," Erik growled. "Mine has been *filled* with rage. Arndyr stole my revenge, stole the justice that he so deserved. I can feel Skûra's demons stirring inside me, awaiting my call. Waiting to be unleashed. When I am done the only thing that remains will be a tomb."

Torben gripped the head of his axe. "This battle will be swift and without mercy. They started this war, and they started it without honour."

"Arndyr made a grave mistake," Erik told him. "He started a war his people cannot win."

The old warrior nodded. "Our people will follow you as they followed her. Bloodsworn are forbidden from taking command above that of jarl, yet in this fight they stand with you. What are your orders?"

"Our fleet shall divide and lay at anchor beyond the horizon. A single boat under the cover of darkness shall descend upon Vay'kis from the north. Nenrir shall lead our greatest warriors and slay the watch at the river mouth leading to Freydis' Tears. Two ships, a hundred men, shall sail the river upon Nenrir's signal. The main fleet will attack Lumis from the sea to the south while a second attack shall come from the land to the north."

Torben turned to his younger companion. Erik knew what the old warrior saw, for the time of hiding emotion was done. His face was weathered and drawn. His gaze spoke a hundred stories and burned with ferocity. Erik was barely keeping his anger in check, barely keeping the jar shut. What would happen when they reached Lumis, when the jar was opened, Erik did not know.

He extended an arm. "I am with you, brother. For Astrid. To the death."

"For Astrid," Erik said and took the older man's arm.

Their grip was firm and strong. The grip of warriors long beholden to the axe and sea.

"Jarl Erik," Nenrir's voice came from behind. "The ships are ready."

The young bloodsworn looked to the archer and gave him a nod. "Then we sail for Vay'kis," he said at last. "We sail for Lumis. We will find Jormund Scaeva and I will rip the answers from his tongue if I must."

Erik stood at the prow of the Ravenheart as it soared across the waves, cutting its way through the ocean blue. He took up the raven amulet and held it tightly.

"I hope one day that you will forgive me, my dear sister," he said quietly. "Forgive me for what I am going to do to Scaeva when he stands before me. I know that you never wished anyone dead. I know that you never wished to kill. But some people do not deserve the life that they have been given. I know that you may never forgive this deed, Astrid, but it is to an end that I am committed. I am sorry."

Lukas sat by the Eretrian River, watching the current as it slowly made its way downstream toward Ilham. The Annoran town rose barely a few miles to the west. They were completely unaware of the small band of Káli camped at the border. Rodion and a few of the others had vanished into the wilderness to keep watch, disappearing like ghosts in the night. Lukas had offered to take a watch but, as the Káli had told him, his days of approaching anyone unnoticed had come to their end. A bad thing if an Annoran wandered too close. So here he sat, alone, watching the waters run. It had been a month since he had been injured at the hands of Emilian Aloys, yet his injuries had not fully healed. His leg still protested though the day and his head constantly ached. Yet he would not let these afflictions truly cripple him.

"Here," Maevin's smooth voice broke the silence.

Lukas glanced toward the priestess. He had not heard her approach. The happiness in Maevin's slight smile was reflected in her gaze. Her eyes were the colour of forest leaves with speckles of sunlight shining through. Lukas took the proffered cup. It was filled with Maevin's brew. The drink that dulled the pain and helped him heal. He took a sip, savouring the taste of strawberries as it rolled down his throat.

"The pain," Maevin said as she sat beside him. "How is it?"

Lukas shrugged. "Each day it lessens. What you have done for me I may never be able to repay."

"You being here is enough," Maevin told him. "You led us to that city. Answered injustice with justice."

"I am torn," Lukas said. "To choose between family and honour is a hard thing, Maevin. I had to act on what I knew was right, no matter the consequences. Now I am Lukas of nowhere, son to no one."

"All sons are born in the shadows of their father, but the day will *always* come when they must step out into the light," the priestess replied. "You chose a different path to the king, and that took great strength."

"He is a man that I both love and despise, but I am not my father," Lukas told her. "I will not make the same mistakes that he did."

"Since the day we met in Oryn, I knew that there was a strength in you," she replied. "A strength that even you may not have known."

"What has changed since I left changed since I left Palen-Tor all those months ago?" Lukas asked absently. "What has been my purpose?"

"You are what you always have been, yet now you are awoken to it," Maevin replied. "You are both saviour to my people and a friend to those who live free. You were not born in the great forest, but blood and bone you *are* Salvaar."

"Then I am of two peoples but belong to neither."

"You are an Annoran who is also Salvaari. Perhaps one day you will rule them all."

"What a tale that would be," Lukas chuckled.

"The spirits' will is seldom known," the priestess said. "Trust in it, trust in me, and strike all else from concern."

He leaned forward and rested his forearms upon his knees. He had a question, one that he had been almost unwilling to ask for the longest time.

"Do you know who I am? Who I truly am?"

"Of course," Maevin replied. "You are Lukas the One-Eyed. You are a man born of the heart, and that is no bad thing. I can see the chaos in your mind and the wildfire burning in your soul. I see you now and I see what you can become. You have lost much but let me tell you something. Your deformities mean that the spirits favour you, that they guide your path."

Her words warmed his blood; they always did. When she spoke, he felt as strong and alive as a stag in the spring. Lukas stared at her for a moment.

"Do you want to know something?" he said.

"Tell me."

"Somehow I feel as though I can trust you, perhaps even more than anyone before."

"The spirits brought us together," she said and gently stroked the snake pendant that hung from her neck. "We are bonded, you and I."

"That is a thing known to me," One-Eye replied, and let his gaze wash over the priestess. "I felt it ever since I knew your name."

The corners of Maevin's lips twitched. The moonlight kissed her pale skin, its rays danced across her cheeks as she turned her head to face him. Her voice was strong yet soothing like gentle waves upon a beach.

"I would give my life for you if you asked me to," Maevin said.

Lukas met her stare, barely able to speak. It was as if she had placed some kind of spell upon him. Try as he might, he could not tear his gaze from Maevin's.

"I would miss a thousand sunsets just to look into your eyes," he said softly.

The priestess leaned toward him and placed her forehead upon his own. Lukas' hand went to her cheek. Her hair tickled his jaw and sent fire roaring through his veins. He could smell the trees in her breath, feel the warmth of her skin. Then he felt the taste of her lips. His hands ran through her wild obsidian hair as he kissed her deeply.

Maevin's arm wrapped around his neck as she pressed her lips against his own.

THIRTY-SEVEN

City of Elara, the League of Trecento

Dawn was only a few hours off when Casimir Dusan finally returned home. Cries for healers and physicians had been plentiful during the chaos that had unfolded in his fair city. Casimir was old, drawing close to sixty summers, yet the lifelong physician had done what he could for all that had been caught up in the Elaran madness. He was a healer and had sworn an oath a long time ago. Man or woman, no matter their allegiance, if they so needed it, would receive Casimir's treatment.

The old physician locked his door behind himself, before he flared candles to life. Casimir placed his satchel upon his desk with a weary sigh. He had grown old a long time ago and healing was a game for young men. He reached for a candle holder.

"You are the healer Casimir?" a voice came from the shadows.

Dusan's breath caught as he turned toward the back of the room. He squinted into the darkness, barely able to make out the form of a person.

"I am."

"Then you will answer me."

"Who are you?" Casimir asked as he took up his candle holder and held it toward the shadows. "I hear the voice of a woman."

He lifted the flame, only for a hand to snake out and smother it. A thin tendril of smoke arose as the dark figure emerged from the shadows, gliding forth like a wraith. The woman was hooded and cloaked while a mask obscured her face. What little Casimir could see vanished as she extinguished the rest of the candles.

"Do you not know?" she asked.

"You are the Nightingale."

Elise stared at Casimir Dusan from behind her mask as the smoke from the smothered candles filled the room. He looked as she had expected, yet one thing surprised her greatly.

"Are you not afraid of me?" she asked.

"I am too old and too weary to fear the dark," Casimir told her. "If you have come to claim my life then it is yours. I have lived a good life and shall go to the gods without regret."

"The gods?" the Nightingale growled. "The gods do not welcome oathbreakers and murderers."

She did not even turn to face the physician, instead slowly walked through the shadows.

Casimir said nothing, yet even in the dark Elise saw his face pale.

"Catinya Delfeyre," the Nightingale glanced back at him. "I believe the name holds meaning."

"I don't know what you are talking about."

"Don't lie to me!" Elise snarled. "Two years ago, you were welcomed into the Delfeyre house to tend to Catinya were you not?"

Casimir's eyes flicked shut and a long sigh came from his lips. The old healer slumped into one of his chairs. "Aye… that I was."

"What was her sickness?"

"Some kind of fever. A contagion contracted through–"

"A fever?" the Nightingale cut him off with a malicious laugh. "Your lies today may be your undoing. You don't want me as your enemy, Dusan. A woman died in your care. We *both* know how. Tonight, I want the truth."

Casimir ran a hand through his thinning hair. "The truth… the truth is a game most dangerous. Already many have died for the answers that you now seek. I am the *last* of what once was."

"Then help me."

He looked up at her with great sadness. "All I ever wanted was to help people. A healer, they call me. Yet you are right, I did betray my oath that day. This path you now walk will not end how you think it will. Life is not a fairy tale and there are no happy endings."

"What makes you think that this has anything to do with my happiness?" Elise told him as she leaned upon the table. "Now speak." She forced herself to keep the desperation from her voice. Her jaw was tense behind her mask. Her gloved hands curled into fists.

"When I was first called upon by Imriel Delfeyre to help his wife, I was resolved to do so. She was very sick, that much was certain. In the beginning I was at a loss for what could have caused it. There were no signs, nor traces that a contagion would leave. I started to ask questions, and that was when they came to me."

"Who came to you, Casimir?" Elise asked. "Who convinced you to aid in their murder? What did they promise you?"

"Each day I was to secrete a small dose of poison in her medicine," the physician murmured sadly. "In exchange for her death I was to be rewarded with a great fortune."

"You broke your oath?" the Nightingale seethed as anger contorted the lips behind her black mask. "You murdered an innocent woman, a kind woman, for the promise of coin?"

"No," Casimir cried. "They had my grandson. A life for a life, he told me. Do this dark deed, and I would die a wealthy man with a home and a family. In time I would find forgiveness in the arms of the gods."

"And the man who promised you this fortune?" Elise pressed.

"Imrohir."

The Nightingale gave away nothing, not even letting the relief show in her eyes. Her heart beat ever fast as the ray of hope that she had long since fed upon grew stronger. So, it had been the magister after all.

"Before he died, Lord Cirillo spoke to me in confidence," Elise told the man. "He said that when the time was right that you would speak out *against* Imrohir."

"Cirillo is dead?" Casimir murmured.

"The magister killed him," Elise said. "He took your friend's life for the secrets that he held close. He feared what he knew and who he might tell."

The physician looked up at her and clasped his hands together upon the table. His face had paled. If Cirillo was dead, was he to be next?

"Would that our places had been exchanged. That I had died and Cirillo had lived."

"Lord Cirillo was waiting until Priamos Stentor moved against Imrohir," Elise continued as she stared at the man. "You heard the crowds in the night. The people want *justice*. They need leadership and now Lord Stentor has given them that. He can bring the gangs and the people together like no other. Priamos is powerful, now more than ever. This is the moment that Cirillo spoke of. The moment in which a word could bring Imrohir to his knees."

Casimir Dusan rose to his feet and his gaze fixed firmly upon the black clad woman.

"What would you have me do?" he growled.

"I would have you *speak*," the Nightingale nearly begged, no longer able to keep the emotion from her voice. "Please, will you help me?"

He said nothing, yet Elise could see the scales tipping in his eyes. The choice was no easy one, for to help her could invite death to him and his family.

At last Casimir nodded.

"Aye. I will," he said.

Elise could not stop the grin from spreading under her mask as they clasped hands. Finally, after all the pain, after all the years of sorrow and anguish, a time bereft of hope and filled with emptiness, she at last had a way out of the dark. At last she could bring justice to the man who had torn her from her home and slaughtered her parents.

The door crashed in.

The pair spun toward the entrance as a roar met their ears. Steel-clad soldiers poured into the healer's house. Men bearing the magister's mark.

"What is the meaning of this?" Casimir shouted.

The blow came without warning. A soldier's sword drove deep through the physician's chest. Casimir Dusan cried out as the blade's tip pierced his heart.

"NO!" Elise screamed as the soldier kicked the healer to the ground and bathed the floor with his blood.

The Nightingale ripped her kukri free from its sheath and leapt at the old man's killer. Her heart shattered as she lashed out in desperation. The knife came up. One of the soldier's caught her in the temple with the guard of his sword. She stumbled. Another grabbed her arm and twisted. The kukri was wrenched from her fingers and sent to the floor. Steel had not finished ringing upon wood before they had her locked in the embrace of two men. The Nightingale struggled against the arms that held her and screamed at the men as she watched the light leave Casimir's eyes. The pommel of a sword stopped her cries but not her tears. The soldier who had so assaulted her stepped back to allow another man to take his place.

This one wore finely embellished plate armour over chainmail and a rich gambeson. A sidesword swung at his hip and a half cloak was drawn across a shoulder. The man pulled his crested helm from his head and revealed the face of the magister.

Dark, cropped hair, a clean-shaven jaw, and lips curved up into a mirthless smirk greeted her. His eyes were pale blue, almost the colour of ice. Magister Imrohir.

"You know who I am," he told her. "You know my face. Now the world will know yours."

Imrohir reached out a hand. He pulled her hood down first. Elise gazed up at him as a glare hardened her red rimmed eyes. This man had murdered her parents and ruined her life. This man had been the harbinger of so much pain. Imrohir pulled the scarf away from her nose and lips.

Elise bared her teeth. She was scared of no man, least of all the one who stood before her. He ripped the mask away.

"Elise Delfeyre," he breathed as he stared into her eyes.

She spat into his face, unable to control the rage boiling inside her. There was no word for the hatred she felt. She screamed and struggled, trying to push the soldiers aside so that she could get at their master. The magister wiped the spit from his skin and then lashed out. The back of his fist cracked against her cheek. Elise barely felt the tendril of blood roll down from her split lip.

"I expected nothing less from a traitor sired by traitors," the Magister said as he cupped her chin with rough hands. "This day will be your last. This day you will hang. Take her to the dungeons."

"You are the traitor, Imrohir, and a liar," Elise cried as the soldiers dragged her from Casimir's house. "One day justice will find you, I swear it will!"

The way back to the inn was as dreary for Kyler as the journey to Arntair's shop. Some of the townspeople had slowly begun to emerge, though usually in quiet groups. Some had begun to repair their homes while others flocked to Elara's churches. Physicians and healers wound their way through the streets, for untold hundreds had been injured in the riots. Twice people called to the knight and twice he stopped to listen. He offered his advice and prayers to those in need. Kyler tried to show nothing in his face, yet the pain that others felt, the despair in their eyes, chilled him to the core.

He saw a small girl sitting on the steps of a hovel. Her dress was little more than rags and her hair was unkempt. In her arms she hugged a doll close. Beside her was an old man. What little hair he had left was grey and his tired skin was covered in a web of wrinkles. The child's grandfather, Kyler guessed.

"Her parents? Are they?" the knight looked from the girl to the elder, and the old man sadly shook his head.

Kyler pulled his coin purse from his belt and handed it to the grandfather. "Take care of her. May Azaria's light guide you and Durandail give you strength. I will pray for you both."

"Gods bless you, sir," the man said as tears filled his weary eyes.

Kyler knelt before the girl. "My name is Kyler. What is your name?"

She looked up at him with wide eyes and trembling lips, "Layana."

"A name as pretty as its bearer," the knight gave her a smile and placed a comforting hand upon her shoulder. "Are you scared?"

Layana nodded.

"So am I," Kyler admitted as he looked into those big eyes. "But let me tell you something. Fear is nothing more than forgetting that everything is alright. You will be alright. Don't be afraid, the sun will shine on you again."

He gave her shoulder a squeeze and with a glance at her grandfather, Kyler continued on his way. There was nothing else to be done, nothing else to be said. All wounds would heal in time. Something in the distance caught his eye. Between the flashes of people walking down the street Kyler saw the unmistakable brown robes of a maija. Beneath the large hood the healer's shrouded head nodded toward an alley. Kyler frowned, clearly the maija knew him. Yet he knew nothing of the Order sending another of its creed this far from Kilgareth. Whoever it was wanted something. Kyler followed the hooded figure.

Down the alleys and streets they went, as if in a dance yet

separated by twenty feet. Finally, the maija strode to the entrance of a small house, unlocked its door, and vanished inside. In moments the knight reached the threshold and then pursued his summoner within. The room was dimly lit by candles and all the shutters were tightly closed. Kyler shut the door as he walked inside.

"How did you find me?" Kyler asked as he looked toward the maija.

She stood with her back to him, hands lightly resting atop the table. They went to her hood. "I followed you from Kilgareth," she replied, and turned to face him as her hood came down.

Ebony hair cascaded down her shoulders in a dark wave while her copper eyes danced in the candlelight. Kyler's jaw fell as he heard her speak. He knew her name long before he saw her face. His heart cried out.

"Elena," he breathed.

She took a hesitant step toward him. A smile curled her lips. "Kyler."

He wasn't ready for the wave of emotion that hit him. Joy, sorrow, love, anger, and above all else, confusion. He didn't know what to feel.

"I thought you were…" his tongue stumbled upon the words.

"It's good to see you," Elena said, her words as soft as her expression. She held out a hand. Kyler looked at it and felt his heart lurch. He longed to take it, to pull the one he loved into his arms, and yet he could not.

"What are you?" he murmured. He could only watch as her face fell.

"Kyler, I am as human as you," Elena told him.

"The men tell me that you are a monster," the knight grimaced. "A demon of the old world."

She clasped her hands and stared straight into Kyler's eyes.

"Why? Because I have a thimbleful of ruskalan blood? Does that make me evil?"

"A hundred years ago your kind led Medea to ruin," Kyler muttered.

"A hundred years ago *humans* slaughtered the ruskalan," Elena growled back. "An entire race all washed away like nothing. For what? For what?"

"For the countless lives that they stole," the knight countered. "The graveyards they filled. Your kind poisoned Medea."

"You are wrong," she said. "You are wrong about so much."

"The Order made a vow, a solemn pledge that suffering like that would *never* happen again. That if any of those creatures of shadow still walked among man, they would *all* be dealt with."

Elena bared her teeth. They were just like his own. No fangs, nor even tapered points. She spread her arms. "Then what are you going to do about it?" she asked.

Kyler bit back the pain that threatened to consume him and break his voice. His hand fell to his sword. "I try to do what is right for my order and for my gods. They would have me kill you for the path that you now walk."

"The *path* I walk?" Elena seethed. Her voice cracked as the cry left her lips, "I WAS *BORN* WITH IT! When you fell in that cave, when I held you in my arms… I should have let you die. I couldn't. In that moment, between life and death, I was given a choice and I made it. The price of saving your life, of using my blood to save yours, was great. I lost the life I had built to save yours. In that moment when you fell, when the one I loved *fell*. When the fates demanded that I choose between your life and my own, there was no choice at all."

Kyler staggered as if he had been struck.

"All this time you've been–"

"You know who I am," Elena said gently, "Who I have always been."

The knight looked toward her as she approached slowly, once again extending a hand. This time he did not move, did not flinch. It was as if he were rooted to the ground. "But you…"

"I'm Elena," she hushed him and placed her hand upon his arm. "I'm *your* Elena."

Her touch crumbled his walls. Kyler nearly collapsed into her embrace, wrapping his arms around her tightly as if scared she might disappear. It all came at once. Everything that he had felt since he had first arrived at Kilgareth all those months ago came back. His exhaustion from training. His weeks of sleepless nights. The bloodshed in the Vault and the riots in Elara. The deaths of his parents. His guilt for having not slain the man with the scarred lip.

"After the cave when I dreamed, I dreamed only of you," Kyler whispered as he fought against the tide of emotion. "But when I woke you were gone."

"I know," she breathed as she held him. "I know."

"Elena, they're dead," the first tear ran down his cheek and then the dam broke. They flowed in an unbroken stream as his body began to shake, "My parents are dead."

"I am so sorry," she murmured.

Elena held him tight in her arms as for the first time he fell apart.

THIRTY-EIGHT

The Southlands, Kingdom of Larissa

The storm seemed to last an eternity. When the sands finally stopped shifting, Sakkar left the confines of his tent. He squinted as the harsh glare of the Larissan sun assaulted his eyes and slowly began to seep its warmth back into his frozen bones. One by one the mercenaries begun to emerge from their shelters and get their horses back to their feet. Sakkar unwrapped Sabra from the cloak and stoked her feathers gently.

"The sands welcome us home, my girl," he murmured.

Aeryn was the first to pull off her headscarf and let her dark hair fall free. The moonseer placed her forehead against that of her mount, before lightly running her fingers down the mare's jaw. The horse shifted and Aeryn whirled around, eyes sweeping across the dunes. Her brow was furrowed.

"We're not alone," she called out before snatching up her bow.

Rebels.

Sakkar sent the hawk skyward and strapped his small buckler to his forearm. The song of swords being drawn echoed through the camp as steel leapt into the hands of the mercenaries. Sakkar nocked an arrow in his powerful bow as Sabra's cry came down from the heavens.

They appeared from every side. Mounted men with hands clasping spear, khopesh, and bow. They wore loose flowing robes. Their faces masked by scarves of every colour. Some wore pieces of steel armour. There might have been fifty of them. Sakkar raised his bow as one of the riders approached. Feathers touched his cheek.

"No further, horseman," he called.

"You would kill a man in his own land, hawk-bearer?" the Larissan rider replied.

Sakkar's hand twitched on the bowstring. Though the man's scarf distorted his voice there was something about it. Something familiar.

"Show yourself," Sakkar called out.

The rider brought his mount to a halt and dismounted as gracefully as one born in the saddle. He unwrapped his headscarf and pulled the cloth from his face. His skin was dark and his eyes darker still. His rich black hair was thick and coarse, pulled into rough locks that appeared as braids. A short beard graced his jaw and a moustache wrapped around his upper lip. The desert warrior glared toward Sakkar and began to walk toward him. The mercenaries all watched on with bated breath. Their hands itched at their weapons even as their companion lowered his own.

The newcomer's glare broke first.

Sakkar's lips curled into a grin.

Then the two men laughed.

Sakkar pulled the other man into a hug. His heart soared in his chest.

"At last we are reunited," the warrior told him.

"Sakkar, you know this man?" Bellec called out as he warily approached the pair.

Sakkar stepped back. "Ah, but it is good to see you, little brother," he said.

"Little?" the warrior snorted and clapped a hand on his brother's back.

"You've grown strong," Sakkar wrapped an arm around the

young man's shoulders as he spoke. "Everyone, come. Meet my brother, Zahiir."

Zahiir beckoned to his men. "Sakkar is returned to us!"

The Larissans cheered as they descended upon the company. They tore free their scarves to reveal their toothy grins. Sakkar Alsahra greeted his kinsmen with open arms.

The ride to Amari was long, yet felt as if no more than a passing moment. The town appeared in the distance, a village of clay and brick pressed tightly against the bank of a large clear water lake. The people walked the streets in their flowing garb, while children ran and played by the lake. Every step that their horses took brought back Sakkar's memories of his home. With every breath he felt as if a burden upon his shoulders began to fall away. Sabra soared overhead and her cries filled the sky with song. Zahiir led the company into Amari and the townspeople stopped and stared. First at the two dozen foreigners, and then to the man who rode beside Zahiir. A crowd began to gather as the riders came to a halt deep in the heart of the Larissan town. Zahiir leapt from his horse and took the steps three at a time until he stood atop the stone dais.

"Come on," Zahiir said as he beckoned his brother. With a grin Sakkar followed him up onto the stand. Zahiir grabbed his arm and thrust it into the air. "My brother is back!" he roared.

"Welcome home!" the first cry washed over Sakkar as the crowd cheered and clapped.

The hawk-bearer held up a hand to silence the people. "Friends," Sakkar called. "Tonight, I will tell you of my travels, but now... now we drink!"

The Larissans roared their approval.

Sakkar jumped down from the dais to embrace his kin. Someone passed him a wineskin and he *gladly* took a draught. A pair of small arms wrapped around his leg. He looked down to see a boy of ten summers smiling up at him.

"Uncle Sakkar," the boy cried happily.

"Zadkiel." The hawk-bearer dropped to a knee and hugged the boy. "Look how big you've grown!"

"Father says that one day soon I'll be big enough to ride with him to Danakis."

"You'll be tall as a mountain, taller even than your father," Sakkar grinned back and glanced at Zahiir as he approached.

"Though I pray not as ugly," Zahiir laughed before he swung his son up onto his broad shoulders.

Sakkar rose back to his feet. His brother was here, his nephew was here, as were his friends and kinfolk. Yet one was missing from his sight.

"Where is she?" Sakkar asked.

"Down by the lake," Zahiir replied, and he looked up to his son and then the crowd, "Go to her, we will hold them off."

Sakkar was already gone by the time the final words left his brother's mouth.

She stood at the bank, gazing out across the water. The gentle waves kissed her bare ankles just shy of the pale white shoulderless dress that hugged her lean form. Beads ran through the midnight-coloured hair that hung down to her shoulders in tight braids. A bracelet of gold adorned her left wrist while a ring hugged her finger. Her skin was a shade lighter than that of those born of Larissa, for her blood was mingled with that of Aureia. Sakkar could not see her face, yet the vision took his breath. He had never seen anyone or anything so beautiful.

"Senya," he called, his voice little more than a whisper.

She stiffened as the words kissed her ear. Senya slowly turned to face him. Her almond shaped eyes spoke of autumn, a melt of hazel and honey. Her face had a vulpine beauty to it. Angular and fierce, yet as soft as the water in which she now stood.

"Two years," she murmured with trembling lips. A fire burned in her eyes as she came toward him, "Two years!"

"Senya, I—"

First she shoved him back, and then she pulled him into her arms. He gripped her with all the strength that he possessed, drinking her in as she melted into his embrace. Her joyous tears wet Sakkar's skin as their cheeks pressed together. All he could feel, all he could smell, was her.

"I have missed your touch," she said.

"My wife... my love," Sakkar whispered as he ran a hand across her cheek and through her hair. He leaned back for a moment to gaze into the face that had captured his heart so long ago. Her lips were soft against his own and their taste consumed him, just as it had the first time. Senya broke it off and her smile lit up her face like the sun.

"How long as it been since you bathed?" she said with a grin, her arms still wrapped around her husband.

"I had not thought to count days," Sakkar chuckled.

Senya took his hand and nodded over her shoulder toward a cave by the edge of the lake.

"Come. I would not have my husband smell of *goat*."

The razor-sharp edge of a knife slowly made its way around Sakkar's scalp. He sat still in the waters within the cave, stripped to his loincloth. His eyes were wide open as he watched the vision before him work. Senya sat atop his lap. Her dress was gone and the lake's water gently brushed her bare midriff. Her body was that of a dancer, elegant and muscled from leg to neck. She squinted her hazel eyes as she worked and slowly slid the blade across her husband's skin.

"It was agony to leave you, my love," Sakkar said.

Senya looked at him with a scowl. "Every moment that you were gone I hated," she said.

"I had to stand by my duty. To my oath and to you," Sakkar squeezed her hand. "I could not bring dishonour upon us."

"You had to go on alone," Senya smiled sadly. "I understand that."

Sakkar brushed her cheek and gently flicked her chin up. They both chuckled. "I am here now," the hawk-bearer said. "I walk on your water; now and always."

"And I will always choose the course you charter, my love," Senya replied as she placed the knife upon the rocks to the side. She took his hand and placed it over her heart, "Your song is my own."

"I pray that we are never parted again," Sakkar told her and wrapped his fingers through his wife's.

Senya's lips curled as she ran her free hand across his bare scalp.

"Tell me of your friend. In your letters you spoke of the one you called brother. This Lukas Raynor, is he a good man?"

Sakkar gazed up at her. "After he saved my life Prince Lukas took me back with him to Palen-Tor. A hundred times he tried to grant me my freedom… he wanted me to return here, to be with the ones that I loved. A hundred times I refused. From the beginning, ever since he learned my name, Lukas treated me as a friend, as family. He is not like any prince or lord that I have ever met. He is not self-serving, nor does he believe himself above any other. He would not wish his crown upon anyone," the hawk-bearer trailed a hand through the cool water as he spoke. "Is he a good man? I will tell you that it was never anything less than an honour to serve him. You would like him, I am sure."

"Is that so?" Senya replied with a snort.

"Aye," Sakkar chuckled. "You can say much about the prince, but he was never much of a godly man. Once, after a particularly *dull* sermon, Lukas hollowed out an apple and placed a beetle within. After it was returned safely to the church it did not take long for the screams to start. The apple, it had begun to rock backwards and forwards, and the priests, ever superstitious, believed it to be possessed."

Senya's lips twitched, and then her laugh echoed through the cave.

"But what of you, jewel of my life?" Sakkar asked. "What has changed here? Though it has been only two years, everyone here seems happier… more content."

"Everything has changed," she replied with a shrug and gently placed her hands on his chest. "After Queen Reshada came into power it took but eight months for the empire to extend their hand. Our peoples were united and then shortly after they laid siege to the rebels. With Reshada coming from the north, and Aureia from the south, the rebellion was swiftly crushed. What little of them remain long since fled into the mountains. There is peace here now, my love. More than that, Tadira has been avenged."

"Tadira," Sakkar stroked his scalp. "My friend will finally know rest in Amkut's garden. It has been many years since his passing yet still I remember everything that he taught me."

"Those who we love leave us," Senya told him. She was quiet for a moment as they both remembered the old man's face. "And besides, at least Tadira gave you the sense to get rid of all this hair," she continued.

Sakkar gave a toothy grin and made to speak. Senya placed her finger over her husband's lips. "Stop," she said, placing her hands upon his cheeks. "I just want to feel you in my arms again."

They stayed in the cave for hours and when finally called, Sakkar hated it almost as much as he had hated leaving Senya all those years ago.

The sea of silver stars shone high above when the whole town gathered by the lake. They had come together beneath the moon and now they all waited with bated breath. No fire had been lit yet, and the only sound was that of the drums. Slowly the tempo began to ride. Senya walked out into the centre of the formed circle. Instead of the dress, she now wore a garment of ivory and red that left her arms and stomach exposed to the cool night air. A short skirt hung from her hips allowing her free movement. From each hand swung a rope, and from each rope hung a flaming dart.

Everyone grew silent.

The only sound was the ever-growing song of the drums. Senya moved slowly at first. Her body freely flowed from one movement to the next. Her muscles glistened as the light of the burning darts danced across her skin. With her wrists and arms Senya sent the flames circling through the air and left trails of blazing light. She danced through the web of fire she created, a master of the flame. She pirouetted and her bare feet slid through the sand. The balls of fire blazed around her as she spun forward. Her hair crashed around her like a wave as she flipped. Senya's feet kissed the soft earth. Sweat caressed her skin and reflected the magnificent light of the flames. The heartbeat of the drums quickened. Her movements followed the rhythm and increased with the speed of the melody. Her muscles flexed and curled almost at their own accord.

Her pace grew. The drums roared. Fire danced all around her. Her feet slid into the waters of the lake. The last of the melody sounded. Senya dropped to a knee and the flaming darts splashed into the water. There was a hiss and then smoke arose around her.

The people roared.

"Life is returning to Amari, brother," Zahiir grinned as he sat with the companions. "You returned to us and now everything is as it should be, eh?"

"Aye," Sakkar laughed and then the pair shared drink. The hawk-bearer sat by the lake, his legs stretched out and an arm draped tenderly around the shoulders of his wife. With them were Bellec and Aeryn. The other mercenaries had long since begun to mingle with the people of Amari. The tune of Kompton's lute and the song from his lips carried through the village streets and echoed to the stars.

"When I left home you were but a little desert rat," Sakkar looked to his brother with a grin. "And now dozens gladly follow you."

"To begin with, it was hard," Zahiir shrugged. "After you left, the rebels grew ever more brazen. Someone had to do something about it. If not me, then who?"

"I'm proud of you," Sakkar told him.

Zahiir clapped him on the shoulder. "Now tell me," he said. "I did not expect to see so many in your company upon your return. What has happened?"

"The rabble that ride with us belong to me," Bellec said as he glanced Zahiir. "But we are here in this moment because of my daughter. She was taken."

"How?"

"In Salvaar nearly two months ago," Bellec explained. "One of the tribal leaders had enlisted the aid of a few dozen Medean knights. They took her, had a ship lying in wait, and then sailed for Belona. They had planned to take their captives to Vesuva and sell them to the highest bidder."

"Slavery," Senya cursed. "If there was one evil I could purge from the empire, that would be it."

"The people captured. Were they warriors?" Zahiir asked.

Bellec nodded as he replied, "For the most part, aye."

The Larissan stroked his jaw. "If they were, and if *half* the stories that I have heard about the Salvaari are true, then they may have risen against their captors," Zahiir told them. "They may have captured the slave ship, or many may well have fallen to Medean steel."

"That is a lot of 'ifs', brother," Sakkar said.

"And I would add to them," Zahiir continued. "I have known slavers. I know how cruel and heartless they can be. We cannot know if she is alive or dead."

"Kitara is alive," Aeryn spoke up and her voice was as fiery as the burning brand in her silver eyes. "I can feel it. I would know if she wasn't."

"And so, we will ride for Vesuva tomorrow," Bellec told Zahiir. "We will find her, free her, or die in the attempt. I know what I am willing to die for, and I will gladly give my life for her to see another dawn."

"Just as I would do for my own child," Zahiir told him. "What can I do to help?"

THIRTY-NINE

Valham, Aethela, Kingdom of Annora.

The great army had left Palen-Tor days ago. So far, the march had been anything but simple. Despite the steady hands of Prince Dayne, General Ilaros Arran, and Bavarian, leading so many thousands was a hard task. Watches had to be kept and scouts sent forth. Food and water had to be supplied to the men and their horses. Hundreds and hundreds of tasks had to be completed daily.

Logistics, Dayne knew, were a devil's curse.

Not to mention the followers camp that had left the city in their wake. Despite the chaos of the civilians at their back, Dayne had little to fear. Kassandra travelled with followers camp and kept them in line easily enough. The prince gazed out across the countryside as he rode and took in every part of the land. His land. Though he did not yet wear the crown nor mantle of king, he held himself as one. He would be the king that his father would have wanted. His brow furrowed as the clean country air changed slightly.

"Do you smell that?" Dayne asked and turned to Tristayn.

"Smoke," the general replied. "And not the good sort."

Dayne clicked his tongue and galloped up the hill overlooking Valham. Tristayn and the guard followed in his wake. First, he saw the village. It was unharmed.

"How could the gods let this happen?" Sir Landon Montbard murmured and clutched at his medallion.

"The gods had nothing to do with this," Dayne told him.

Before them lay the Temple of Saint Daleka; charred and ruined. A lone horseman rode toward them from Valham. He bore the colours of the Annoran guard.

"My Lord, you had better come quickly," Sir Garrik Skarlit called as he brought his horse to a halt before them.

They rode through the temple gates and into the scorched courtyard. The ground was soaked with dried blood. Many had fallen here. The company dismounted and slowly began to make their way through the wreckage. Dayne bit back the wince as a flare of pain ran through his stomach. These days the ache was a constant companion and even the prince, as strong as he was, could feel it sapping his strength.

"This was a temple," Tristayn said quietly. "The only people who called this place home were priests."

"They are with the gods now," Dayne replied.

"Who could have done this?" Landon asked as he stared at the remnants of the temple. "This was a place of worship, a place of *peace*."

Sir Garrik looked to his prince and even the hard veteran could not keep the sorrow from his face.

"There," Garrik said and gestured to the bottom of the charred temple steps.

Dayne saw it standing tall. The golden wings of an eagle spread around the crossguard of a longsword. He knew the blade as well as he knew the one that hung at his own hip.

"Lukas, what have you done," Dayne whispered. "What have you done?"

The Annoran contingent said nothing as their lord pulled the sword free.

"What happened here will not stand," the prince told his people.

"What of your brother, Lord?" Landon said. "The people will

soon know of his deed. The people love their prince. He is a man whom many have fought beside. A man whom many admire. When they find out what that man did here it could tear our army, our kingdom, apart."

Dayne nodded and did not take his eyes off the sword in his hands. "It is clear to me that the heathens have poisoned Lukas' mind. That witch has wormed her way inside his heart like a snake and turned my brother against his own kind. The people must know the truth of what happened here."

"And what is that truth?" Garrik asked.

"That Salvaar is not as weak as we supposed. That the nightmares that they once conjured and the fear that they once instilled remains," Prince Dayne said. "Let the men see this place. Let them see the evil that the pagans inflict. The Salvaari are men not monsters. They fight like us, they bleed like us, and they die like us. They burned a scared temple and slaughtered unarmed, unarmoured men of the cloth. Soon we will see how they fare against a foe who can fight back. Soon we will see how they fare against Annoran steel. That is the truth, Sir Garrik."

Dayne walked into what remained of the temple. The roof had all but collapsed, taking much of the wall with it. Despite the fire that had ravaged and raged, despite the pillars that had fallen, the twin statues still stood. The stone was charred and marked by ash and dust, yet they had been immovable.

The prince pulled forth Lukas' sword and drove it into the floor at their feet. Next, he removed his amulet and wrapped it around the weapon's crossguard. He knelt before the statues of his gods and bowed his head.

"Silver Lady, forgive me on this day that I beg for your guidance. I fear that my brother is lost to darkness. I fear that this temple will not be the first that he so smites. Help me now. Help me save him. Help me bring my brother back into the light before it is too late," Dayne murmured as he gripped the pommel of the sword with both hands. "He has a good heart. A heart that I fear has been darkened. He has the potential to do so much good, but I am not blind in this moment. Give me the strength to do what must be done if it is too late. All those souls lost... I cannot, I will not, let that happen again."

The prince rose to his feet and stared up at the statue of Azaria. His faith made him strong. It always had. It called to him now more than ever before.

"This war will test us all, but the gods are on our side," the man's voice came from the temple doors.

Dayne glanced over his shoulder as Bavarian walked inside. The grand master clasped his amulet and moved to stand beside Dayne.

"Even here, even now, they give me comfort," the prince told him. "During my time in Darius' court I met Evalio. I was sorry to hear of his passing."

Bavarian slowly nodded his thanks. "The pale horseman comes for us all. It was his time to pass from this life and begin his journey into the next."

"He was a good man," Dayne said as he rubbed a hand over his aching stomach, before he clasped both together.

"Aye," Bavarian replied sadly. "That he was."

"We spoke a great deal about philosophy, history, and the gods. He told me that a man's deeds are meaningless unless they are for some higher purpose. I have tried to live by this creed my whole life. To serve my people and my faith as best I can," the prince said and he did not take his gaze from the carved stone.

"A creed to live by... Evalio was as wise as many who bear the title of philosopher," Bavarian replied. "But the words he told you were spoken first by another."

Dayne glanced at the holy knight.

"Who?"

"Zavian, the first king of Miera," Bavarian began. "When Idrisir came, when they conquered the steppe and filled Miera with rivers of blood, the Easterners claimed the lives of Zavian's wife and child. The farmer gathered a small company, stormed the Idrisian lord's castle and took his life. This started a war. A war that nearly ended in the first battle. Zavian was defeated, and his army butchered. He fled, barely making if from the field alive. He had no more than forty men to fight the greatest army the east had ever seen. Zavian was hunted like a dog for months. With each attack his number dwindled. His cause was in ruin and the man all but absent hope, yet he did not give in. He would not surrender. Zavian went from town to town, stealing inside in the dead of night. They began at Imalric, slaying the small garrison and killing their commander. News spread like wildfire, and on that day Zavian's legend was born. Using his knowledge of the land and the Mieran's superior skill with the horse and bow, Zavian slowly begun to fight back. They swooped down and stung like wasps from north to south. Stinging and then vanishing, and the Idrisians began to bleed. Zavian and his great army met the enemy upon the fields of Karlian, and there they defeated them. They cast them back into the east from whence they came. Though his purpose was not for any god, Zavian did not believe that the fates had cursed his people, his land, to an eternity of servitude. He dedicated his life to the freedom of Miera. That was his purpose. The creed in which we live was once his own."

"He made his people strong. He wrote his own destiny," Dayne murmured. "When all is said and done, will the gods be pleased with what I have accomplished? What I have sacrificed?"

"Of that I have no doubt, Prince Dayne, no doubt," Bavarian smiled.

"Perhaps, yet it is for my brother and his fate that I grow uncertain."

"I have seen this before," Bavarian told him. "I have seen men seduced by shadow. The darkness is within us all, Prince Dayne, yet we men must do what we can to keep it at bay. For in every shadow there is light, yet it is also true that you cannot have light without darkness. The moment a man chooses war over peace, chooses darkness over the light… chooses to walk into the abyss… that is the moment a man ceases to exist. That is the moment that the beast is born," Bavarian told him. "That is what they will tell you, but it isn't true. The flame can always be tendered and brought back. Even after the darkest night, the sun will return. There is light in everyone even if you cannot see it. Have faith."

Then Bavarian was gone, leaving nothing but the words ringing in Dayne's mind. The prince pulled his amulet over his head and took up his brother's sword.

"A light in the dark," Dayne's eyes went to Azaria's cold face as he spoke. "I may never succeed. I may struggle for the rest of my life trying to bring my brother back in vain, but I will not stop."

Kitara allowed her face to contort with a grimace for the first time. Though still in Teora's pit, she was alone. After the fight she had been taken to a small empty cell and left to her own devices. Her neck, her arm, her hands, were all covered in her own blood. Aches came from a dozen places, but adrenaline masked most of the pain. She knew that in the morning it would return tenfold along with a great deal of bruising. Kitara placed her helm upon the small bench and leaned her elbows on it. She stared down at the cuts upon the palms of her hands. Beside her there sat a small water bowl and some rags.

"You fought well, Alessandra."

She glanced up as the mentor entered the cell. There was no anger or malice in his expression, nor a taunt upon his wizened lips. She nodded and curled her hands into fists to cover the bloody furrows in her skin.

"Here," the mentor said and handed her a bowl.

"Taliskar. His reputation was well earned," Kitara said as she took the bowl.

"The fights in the cage are bloody, brutal, without honour," the mentor told her with a hint of disgust in his wise voice. "They lack the nobility of the arena and its history. Many of those who fight beyond the steel bars are driven to madness and become more animal than man."

Kitara gently washed her hands in the water. "Will I have to fight here again?" she asked.

"No," he replied. "You are sildari now and deserve more than a cage to die in. What you did, defeating Taliskar, earned you that respect. He was a man many feared. He was stronger than you; faster. He came at you time and time again, yet you did not give up."

Kitara winced as she rubbed water into the tender cut along her neck.

"Two times down, three times up," she said quietly.

Those words had kept her alive. The mentor gathered up a strip of cloth and glanced at the wound on her arm. Kitara nodded.

"I have seen the swordsong before, yet what you did was more than just that," he told her as he began to wrap the strip around the cut on her arm.

"Tarkaras has many weaknesses," Kitara replied. "I learned that long ago and so I adapted. Had I not, I doubt I would be standing before you in this moment."

"You are more than just a sword," the mentor said. "You proved that tonight. You proved yourself to be sildari. More than that, you have shown promise, both here and in the sacred sands of the arena."

Kitara said nothing.

"Yeomra, our champion, a man who is uncommon among uncommon men. Unbeaten in the sands"– the mentor clasped his hands behind his back as he spoke –"I knew from the moment I laid eyes upon him, that Yeomra would rise to the pinnacle and stand as a god of the arena. He has the blood of a champion. I see that in you, Alessandra. I hope you find it."

Kitara nodded and gave him something of a smile.

"Well, in the meantime, I have a request," Kitara said.

"What's that?"

"When next I fight, give me a knife," she told him.

Cheers greeted Kitara's ears as she returned to the yard. The sildari chanted her name and clapped their strong hands on her back. Her wounds from her fight with Taliskar had been patched, yet his blood, and hers, still covered her armour and skin. Despite the initial misgivings of her fellow slave warrirors, after this fight, it appeared to have been forgotten. Yeomra was the first to extend an arm. Kitara looked up at the champion. He was a man whose reputation alone would cower cities. His skin was unmarred by scar or wound, yet you could see the monster stirring in his dark eyes. He was a man resolved not to be trifled with.

She clasped the champion's arm.

The sildari filled the small hall, laughing and drinking. The room was little more than clay brick with a few crude wooden tables lining its interior. It served as a place for them to eat and rest during breaks in the day's training. Before being locked away in their cells for the night, often they would come and jest, wrestle, and drink. Though to a man they were some of the most skilled warriors that Kitara had ever seen, they were like any group of soldiers. Kitara had bathed upon returning from the pit and cleansed the blood and filth from her skin and hair. She sat alone; lost in thought.

Thud.

A wooden cup was placed on the table before her. It broke her peace.

"Mind if I join you?" the man asked with his own cup held tightly in his hand.

His hair was long and shaggy. His beard short and thick. Vidarr his name was. A man who had once been a sand miner. He was broad and strong, yet his eyes were brimming with mischief and his grin was ever present. Kitara pushed the cup he had given her into the centre of the table.

With a shrug, Vidarr joined her. "You don't drink?"

"A lifetime ago," Kitara replied. *Not since Salvaar, not since…*

"This is your new life," the man told her, his eyes sympathetic. "I do not mean to offend. Far from it. Once, a long time ago, I was very much like you."

Kitara snorted. "I doubt that."

"I was once free. Now I am a slave," Vidarr said. "I was once condemned to die at the will of the Aureians. I once believed of a life outside these crumbling walls. You are adrift, like I once was. You do not need to say anything to tell me that I am right or say that I am wrong. What you now feel, I once felt."

Kitara leaned forward over the table. "How did a free man become so enslaved? How did he rise to prominence in such a place?"

"Stole from the wrong man I suppose," Vidarr replied with a chuckle.

"For what purpose?"

The man spread his arms and gave a wide grin. "For the same reason that any man does anything. Because I *wanted* to."

"Ever the fool then," Kitara replied.

"So I have been told on many occasions," he laughed. "This place grows on you, does it not? With every drop of sweat, with every tear you shed, this place will become a part of you as much as flesh and bone. Garnering my reputation was no easy thing. With my sacrifice comes the blood, sweat, and pain that I took to get it. Look at Yeomra. A man equalled by none, marvelled by all. Before his time is done a thousand, thousand pages will be written about what that man has achieved inside the arena. The people cheer our names, they sing songs about us, write poems about us… but they know *nothing* of the sacrifice. Already they begin to talk about your legend. Already they begin to talk about Alessandra."

"And what do they say about me?" Kitara resisted the urge to roll her eyes as she spoke.

Vidarr liked to talk, and he was good at it. Yet she could see the truth in his words. No matter how ridiculous they sounded.

"The same thing being said inside these very walls. Yesterday you were but a dog who defied death. Today you proved yourself one of us. As for tomorrow? Who knows what the sunrise shall bring." Vidarr rose to his feet with a smirk.

"Outside they call us slaves, but here we are truly free. Already you begin to feel it, that stirring in your blood. The roaring of your name. The glory… there is no greater glory than to stand victorious upon the sands."

"I can think of a few things," Kitara said, glaring up at him.

Vidarr let loose a great laugh and gestured to her cup as he sauntered away. Kitara closed her eyes with a sigh. Tentatively she reached out and her finger curled around the wooden handle. It was almost an instinct; an action that she could not control. Kitara raised the cup to her lips.

She drank.

FORTY

They arrived at the brothel as night fell.

"Do you have any secrets, Pisspot?"

Kyler frowned and glanced at Sir Alarik. *Did he know about Kyler's meeting with Arntair? Had he seen the boy meet with Elena?* The young knight merely nodded in reply.

"Then don't give even one of these girls a second glance. They have a way of getting into a man's head and loosening his tongue," Alarik grinned and clapped Kyler on the cheek.

A pair of guards stood at the whorehouse entrance, eyes wary and hands tightly clasped around sideswords.

"Evening, friend," Kyler called out as they made their approach.

"We are here to see Madam Mellisanthi," Alarik told them. "We are not expected."

"Seems everyone this day is after an audience with the lady of the house," the guard frowned. "She is indisposed."

"Indisposed?" Kyler retorted, and he looked to his companion.

"Is that so?" Alarik growled. He stepped closer to the door guards as a glare darkened his face. "I have no argument with you, friend," Alarik continued, "but lie to me again and I may just have cause for grievance. We're here to see the lady."

The guard puffed up his chest and fingered his sword. "No."

Kyler glanced from the guards to his mentor. A blind man could have seen the storm brewing. He stepped between them.

"Wait… wait!"

Kyler reached into his coin purse and pulled three silvers from its depths. He pressed them into the hand of the guard. "We mean no offence, yet we *must* see her. It's about a friend of hers. Don't let us pass if you wish, but your lady will know why."

The Elaran remained expressionless as he stared at the Medean. He was weighing his options. In that moment Kyler *knew* that he had him.

"Weapons," the gruff voice said.

One of the guards led them through the brothel. The house was dimly lit with candles, and sweet-smelling smoke wafted through the halls and rooms. Scantily clad courtesans walked through the establishment or lounged upon couches. Some shared drink and laughter with clients, while others gazed at the newcomers with lustful eyes. One of the women called to them and beckoned mischievously. Alarik grinned and gave her a wink as they followed the guard up a flight of stairs. The courtesan laughed and watched as the men walked down a long corridor.

"Wait here," the guard told them as they reached a wooden door. He vanished inside.

After what seemed like an eternity, he returned and ushered them inside. The door closed as the guard left.

"My man tells me that you bring word of a friend of mine," the Larissan woman said.

Kyler ran his gaze over the madam. True to her kin, she had dark skin, a darker gaze, and thick ebony hair. Her voice was as smooth as her skin looked, while her dazzling copper eyes blazed with intelligence. Mellisanthi watched them from behind her desk, her hands clasped at her stomach. Her dress was emerald and gold and left little to the imagination.

"Aye lady, more or less," Alarik told her.

"More or less?" She smiled, gracefully moving around to their side of the table with a swing in her hips. She leaned back on the desk and placed her hands on its edge. "And would that be more more or more less?"

"That depends."

Her eyes flashed. "Depends on what?"

"On if you can help us locate an old friend of *ours*," Alarik replied. "Of yours."

"And you believe that the humble owner of an establishment such as my own could help you find this mysterious man?"

The battlemaster smirked as he replied, "Oh, I believe that this place is far more than that. That you are more than just the madam that you appear to be."

Amusement burned in her rich eyes. "Well sir, I must say that that is quite an interesting tale."

"I know it to be true."

"Tell me," Mellisanthi's smile grew, "Do you enjoy sparring with words as much as you do with swords, sir knight?"

"Upon occasion." Alarik shrugged and returned her grin. "Though where you heard such a story that my companion and I are knights. I must say, that is quite the rumour."

Kyler said nothing. Alarik had once been a soldier of the legions and no doubt had spent his share of time in establishments such as these. He knew how to talk to the courtesans. He was now playing a game with one well versed in it, and he was *enjoying* it.

"Oh, I hear whispers from time to time," Mellisanthi told him and glanced down at the jug beside her. "Would you care for a drink?"

"Perhaps *after* we are done here."

The madam's lips curled up. "Well then, the sooner we get down to business, the better," she said. "This man you seek, what is his name?"

"His name is Cleander," Kyler spoke for the first time. "We were told that he frequents your establishment."

"Were you just?" The madam gave away nothing in her voice or expression.

"We were also told that he meets with your girls upon occasion far from the brothel walls," Kyler said.

"Now, that is an interesting story," Mellisanthi replied coolly.

Alarik took a slow step toward her. "One that bears merit, as I am sure you would agree," he said.

"Would I just?" she said, staring deep into the battlemaster's eyes. "And if I knew such a man, if I had such a friend, why would I be so inclined as to tell you his whereabouts?"

"I owe him my life." Alarik did not look away, did not tear his gaze from Mellisanthi's. "I owe him a sword. His sword. I have it in my possession and wish to give it back."

"You fought by his side?"

"I did," Alarik nodded.

Mellisanthi rose from the table and stood directly before the veteran knight.

"Well then," she murmured as she glided around Alarik slowly. She did not shift her eyes from his face, nor remove the gentle tone from her voice. "If I did know this Cleander, perhaps then I would be able to arrange a meeting."

"If you did, we would be indebted."

"What if I were to tell you that there is a place not far from here, a place where in three nights you could meet with this man, your friend?"

"And where would this place be?" Alarik murmured as the courtesan circled him.

"The inn of the Red Rose, do you know of it?"

"Aye."

Mellisanthi stopped before him. "On the third day, at dusk, speak to the innkeeper. Tell him that I sent you, and then perhaps he will take you to the man you seek."

Alarik gently took her hand and placed a kiss upon it. "My lady is most generous. Thank you."

Mellisanthi waited until her guests had left her house before she donned her cloak, pulled her wide hood up, and made her way into the establishment's cellar. Below ground, beyond the reach of all but her, was a hidden entrance to a hole in the flooring. She gathered up a torch, pulled back the doorway, and then descended the ladder into the bowels of Elara.

Mellisanthi scrunched up her nose at the stench that greeted her. The tunnel led into the sewers. A network of stone passages that ran from one side of the city to the other. Here, you could navigate unseen to the eyes far above. The gangs had made good use of this place. They knew the sewers like they knew the back of their hands. She followed the maze until she came to a crude door well beneath the Pits and knocked three times. The steel bolt was drawn, and then the oaken door was pulled open.

"Didn't expect to see you again," Cleander said.

Mellisanthi strode into the small room and looked back at the man. "Loyalty means something, Markus. At least to me."

"Even after what I did?" he asked.

For the first time since she had met him, Markus looked tired. His face was drawn and his eyes distant. Mellisanthi placed a hand upon his arm. "If I thought you got any kind of enjoyment out of it, I would have turned you over to the guards long ago."

Cleander sighed and ran a hand through his dishevelled hair. He sat down upon a table and looked at the ground.

"You were right," he murmured. "You were right. I cannot shed my past like a snake sheds its skin. I grow weary, Mellisanthi. I grow weary of this fight. I grow weary of this *name*."

"Tell me," she soothed. "Let me help you."

Emotion filled Cleander's tired eyes. "Cleander was born out of great tragedy; out of great darkness. I created him as a means to an end. Without Cleander, without this thing I have become, I would have died a long time ago. The path I have walked would have been impossible as Markus Harvarder. Markus Harvarder had given too much; lost too much. And so, I conjured Cleander. This man who I both created and feared. I feared that a man born of such darkness... I know the art of the sword... I know the art of war. that is all I have ever known. It is what I was born for. That is why they fear me. That is why I fear Cleander. I knew that when he came out, hell was coming with him. I am *scared* of Cleander."

Mellisanthi knelt before her friend. She placed her hands upon his own.

"You could let him go."

The man snorted. "I have tried... he bites and scratches, refusing to be dislodged."

"Then we will find a way," she told him. "Together."

He gripped Mellisanthi's hands. "Thank you for not abandoning me."

She rose to her feet and cupped his cheek. "You are my friend. You cannot escape who you are, and who you are is Markus Harvarder."

Cleander stood up from his seat and the weariness fled his face. The Annoran made his way through the room toward his small alchemy table and gathered up a small vial.

"What's that?' Mellisanthi frowned as he peered into the yellow contents.

"It's a herbal extract," he explained. "I learnt how to make it a few years ago. A clever little potion that enables its user to see and breathe more easily through smoke and mist."

"And how did you become so well versed in alchemy?" Mellisanthi asked with folded arms as she moved to stand beside him.

Ingredients covered the table. Plants and herbs, vials and pots. Books and small silver shells that Cleander used as his smoke bombs were piled alongside. "One of the maija," Cleander told her. "When I fell from the cliff, it was she who saved me. She healed me, taught me a few tricks, and taught me to stay alive."

"And this healer, is she the one who feeds you information from the Order?" Mellisanthi asked as she ran her fingers across the cover of a book.

"She knows of the Order's evils as well as I," he replied. "Knows what they hunt, and what they are capable of. When I turned on the Order she was there."

"And so, she risks discovery by secreting herself with them, knowing it could mean her life?"

Cleander frowned at her. "Lysandra knows what she is doing."

"Men came looking for you today," Mellisanthi told him after a moment.

The Annoran froze.

"Who?"

"They didn't say. They somehow knew that we were in some way connected," she replied.

"What did they want?"

Mellisanthi pursed her lips as she replied, "They wanted me to arrange a meeting. One of them, the older man, claimed to have fought by your side in days gone. While I have no doubt that this is the truth, it was not all of it. They were reserved, never saying more than they intended. Half-truths if you will. Though both stood as knights, I am sure of it."

"Knights? You're certain?"

"I would bet my life on it," the madam told him. "One, the older man, was Aureian. The younger, Medean. The older struck me as more of a common soldier than a knight. Perhaps he served in the legions?"

"They've found me," Cleander whispered, and he placed the vial back on the table, "I could guess the Aureian's name, for the Order would not be so naive to think that a common knight could stand against me."

"And the younger?"

"I'm not sure," Cleander shrugged. "And this meeting?"

"I told them of the Red Rose," Mellisanthi said. "Told them in three days at dusk."

The Annoran nodded. "Gavril will show them the way... I will prepare."

Cleander made his way through the labyrinth of stone that was the sewers. He had long since become accustomed to the darkness and the smell, yet even still he kept his scarf pulled up over his mouth and nose. The sewers, though controlled by the gangs, occasionally played host to uninvited guests. Stoneworkers and architects mainly, yet soldiers too upon occasion. Cleander found his way to Bhaltair's hall easily enough. Once it had been a huge storage room for the original workers and builders of the tunnels, now it played host to the crime lord of Elara. Roughly clad gangmen filled the rooms and halls of Bhaltair's keep. Each and every man was armed. Each and every man wore the same dangerous expression. Cleander pulled his scarf and hood away from his face as his all-seeing eyes navigated the rooms.

"Welcome back, my friend," Bhaltair called out as he approached.

"Bhaltair."

Cleander clasped the man's proffered arm.

"Look at them," the leader muttered. "They drink and jest, celebrating a victory that we have not yet won."

Cleander glanced at his companion. "The world has shifted beneath their feet. The council that has ruled this city for decades. The only leadership they have ever known has fallen. They are not men to be governed. They take what they want, and they live heartily. That is the world you are building. That is why they celebrate. They know nothing else."

"They will be tested in the coming days, Cleander," Bhaltair told him. "We all will be tested. I can only hope that my men are up to the task."

"And Stentor?"

The crimelord shrugged.

"He mourns his family's passing, yet he is no fool. He knows that now is our best and perhaps our only chance at ridding this city from the yoke of its tyrannical leader. He is prepared and his soldiers are ready. When the time comes, when we rise, so too will Stentor."

"How can you be so certain?" Cleander asked with a frown.

Bhaltair reached into his cloak and pulled forth a wicked kukri knife. "Word just reached us that the Nightingale has been captured this night. I sent my people to find out the truth and we found his blade where the magister took him. In the morning the Nightingale will hang. There can be no denying it. And when that nightmare swings from the gallows, the people will have their martyr. You saw them after the council hall, after Cirillo Eris and the Stentor family were butchered. They were angry then. They are angry now. After a lifetime of servitude drowning in filth… what will they do when their hero falls?"

Cleander took the blade. So, Elise Delfeyre had been caught. He had expected it to happen, yet not so soon. The girl was but a child still. A child who had suffered greatly at the magister's hand.

"I often wonder what the Nightingale's game was," Bhaltair continued. "I suppose we may never know."

"Justice," Cleander told him.

"There is no justice," the crimelord snorted. "Not in Elara."

Cheers cut off the reply as it left the Annoran's lips. The gangmen leapt to their feet as a man swaggered into the hall. A longsword hung from his hip and a small shield from his back. He wore a shirt of chainmail beneath a travel warn cloak. His hair was long and his beard unkempt.

A scar was carved across his lip.

It was a face that Cleander knew all too well. Olivera. A man who had grown to prominence with his skills as a cutthroat. The Medean was more than just a knife in the dark. He had the intellect to match. Despite Olivera's thirst for blood and lack of empathy, these traits had earnt him a place at Bhaltair's table. Theatrical, brutal, and completely without mercy, Olivera was the kind of man needed when the gang's primary weapon in their war was fear.

Bhaltair grinned and clapped Cleander upon the shoulder.

"Our odds grow better by the moment it would seem," he said.

The pair pushed their way through the crowd until they arrived before the Medean.

"Olivera," Bhaltair greeted the man before he took the Medean's arm and pulled him into an embrace. "It is good to have you back!"

"It's good to be back, Bhaltair," Olivera replied as they broke apart. "Cleander."

"Olivera," Cleander greeted him. "You travel alone?"

The Medean's face darkened. "My brother is dead, killed by a knight," Olivera told them.

"I am sorry," the Annoran told him. "Julio was a good man."

"I will avenge him upon a day," Olivera replied and brushed his sword's hilt. "Until that time I will take comfort knowing that the man's family lie as a feast for the crows."

"You killed his family?" Cleander asked, as he tried to hide the distaste that threated to turn his voice.

Olivera had little use for the word honour. "An eye for an eye, brother. Wouldn't you agree?"

"Indeed," Bhaltair cut in. "You return at the turning of the tides, brother. You and your sword have been dearly missed in days past."

"It is a curse having so much to offer," Olivera called loudly with a grin. "I heard about the council... it would seem that I missed out on the fun."

The crowd cheered as he spoke.

"How was Medea?" Bhaltair asked him.

Olivera shrugged. His lips curled into a smirk. "Killed a few knights, spilled some blood, took some coin. Enjoyed the company of virtuous women… I would say my time there was well spent."

"Well now that you're back, I have a task for you," Cleander said.

Olivera grinned and spread his arms theatrically. "See my friends, so much to offer," he said. "And what can the best cutthroat in the city do for you, Cleander?"

"In three days, we will be playing host to some guests," the Annoran told him. "Knights. Gavril will make the introduction. Capture them if you can. Kill them if they resist."

"A proper welcoming indeed," the Medean smirked. "I will see it done."

Cleander did not tarry with his companions for long, instead he retreated to the confines of his own dwelling. He needed to think. Cleander wasn't sure if it was late or early. The Annoran would be getting no sleep this night, that much he knew for his mind was taken. He sat in his chamber by the fireplace and slowly turned the Nightingale's kukri in his hands.

Bhaltair was growing ever more daring, and his game was growing longer and more dangerous by the day. Why he had sent Olivera to the valley of Odrysia, Cleander wasn't sure. Though it had been to do more than help the Annoran in his attempt to claim the Spear, that much was certain. Now, as Bhaltair's plan navigated its way through the streets of Elara, he was committed to allowing the death of one who could not only be an ally, but their saviour as well.

Elise Delfeyre, the Nightingale.

A girl from the Pits, whose parents had been killed by Imrohir. A girl who had been thrust from her home into the arms of people hated her for being born across the river. A girl who had lost everything. A girl who was about to die for her quest. She would not see the justice that she so desired. It was as Bhaltair had said. There was no justice in Elara. Magister Imrohir and his ilk had seen to that a long time ago. If the Nightingale fell it could well ignite a spark inside the people. A spark that could bring the magister down. It could also add to Imrohir's legend and only serve to add more fear to his name. The people would be cowed into submission.

Cleander ran his keen gaze along the edge of the curved knife.

Even if Elise chose not to help him, help his cause, she did not deserve to die at the hands of her parents' killer. She did not deserve to be a pawn in this political game. A piece to be used and then discarded at a whim. Cleander stared into the flames of the fire, watching as they danced in the light. A light that he had seen in Elise's eyes. Despite everything she had suffered, she had not let it destroy her. If she died in the morning that same light would be forever extinguished.

Markus Harvarder rose from his chair.

FORTY-ONE

The cell was cold. A cage of steel and stone deep within the bowels of the arsenal keep.

Elise had been deprived of her mask, her daggers, and her tools. Absent these tools meant absent hope as well. She sat on the icy stone with her back pressed against the prison bars as she stared absently toward the sole window. It was still dark outside, yet Elise had spent many months flitting among the shadows of the night. Dawn was not far off.

The cell door rattled as a key turned in the lock. There was a click. Elise glanced up as the magister entered. He was alone, save for the sword swinging at his hip. She rose to her feet and glared balefully at her captor. Her hands balled into fists as she stepped away from him. Elise expected an attack. She had grown up in the Pits. She did not know how to swing a sword, yet she knew how to swing a fist. It was the only way to survive. Elise could see the violence in the soldiers' eyes. Anything she attempted would be met with far greater force.

Her hands uncurled.

"No," the magister began as he saw her move. "You will not be harmed tonight."

"Not tonight, no," Elise snorted as she donned her mask of arrogance. "In the morning perhaps. What is this all about, your *Lordship*?"

Imrohir reached into his cloak and pulled forth a strip of black material. He held it up into the torchlight. It was the Nightingale mask.

"Elise Delfeyre, the Nightingale," he said, opening his hand and letting the mask fall to the ground. "You have vexed this city for many months."

"As you have for years," she told him. "I did not want to get drawn into this, did not want to don the mantle of an Aureian fairy tale and live my life as a thief in the night. You forced my hand."

"I gave you the means, no doubt. But it was you who accepted this fate and now you will be destroyed by it," Magister Imrohir clasped his hands behind his back as he spoke. "In the morning you will hang, and we will at last be rid of each other. I see no reason why we cannot have a few moments of honesty."

Elise chortled and shook her head. "Honesty? A word you are most unfamiliar with."

"You have a sharp tongue," Imrohir stated.

"So I am told."

The magister gestured to her, and his face betrayed no emotion. No anger nor irritation. "You have questions?" he said.

Elise met his stare with her own. This was one battle that she could fight, and she would not back down from it. "How did you find me?"

"I will admit, it was difficult," Imrohir shrugged. "There was no pattern to your targets. Nothing to link them save their wealth in coin. You are quite the thief, I will give you that. However, you do not last long as magister without being careful. I spent many hours mulling it over. How were the victims related? And then there it was, laid out neatly before my eyes. Banker, shipmaster, magister. The three men at the heart of it. After you paid a visit to Lord Cirillo I knew that it was only a matter of time before the healer was next, and so I prepared."

"And all this death, all this slaughter… the war you plan upon Miera, the slaves that you have captured, the lies that you have told," Elise said in disbelief. "What was it all in aid of? Adding to your name? Your wealth? An empire?"

Imrohir paused. "It may come as a surprise, but all I have ever wanted is to make my people strong. To make my people flourish."

"That cannot be," Elise snarled. "You lie!"

"It is not a lie!" he shot back and stepped toward her, his voice strong and loud. "Look at Elara, Elise. We are *surrounded*. To the north lies an army of heathens who would all too gladly see us dead. To the south the Sacasian pirates come and go, picking at the wound they inflict upon us each day. Elara is bleeding. Elara is fragile. Now more than ever. While those too blind to see the end that is coming stand against me and divide what resources I have, our enemies have been growing bolder and more daring by the day. Our coffers have been all but depleted by this endless debate that has all but seen our city to ruin. It may not be this year, or the next, but the end is coming. And I swear that all I have done has been to stop the tide. I have only ever wanted the strength to defend my people."

"What?" Elise nearly choked. She blinked at him, unable to comprehend what he had told her. "And you would do this through murder, through war?"

"Yes!" he roared.

His tone almost made her flinch. *Almost.* Imrohir sighed and ran a hand through his hair. "Many years ago," he continued, "Delios was on the brink of collapse. They were besieged from north and south, east and west. Nykalous Gaedhela rose to meet the coming storm and forged an empire greater than any before. He was no saint or good man. He was a warlord who did what needed to be done to ensure the survival of his people."

"And where is Delios now?" Elise countered.

"The great conqueror made one mistake… I will not make the

same." Imrohir glanced toward the window. A thin sliver of light began to emerge over the horizon. "The sun is rising."

Elise glared at him. "So what happens now?"

The magister glanced through the bars of the cell and nodded to his guards. They vanished from sight, as if an unspoken order commanded them. "Now?" he replied. "Now I am forced to kill someone that I greatly admire."

The cell door opened and the magister's soldiers dragged in a third person. A woman. Elise's eyes widened. Tears were in the woman's eyes and her face was white with fear.

"Halina," Elise breathed as she saw her friend.

One of the soldiers held the maid, while the other stood between her and Elise. His sword was drawn and levelled.

"You must fall, and with your death so will it be the death of the rebellion," Imrohir told her. "For that, I thank you. At the gallows you will be given a chance to speak… to sing your song."

The magister looked to the man who held Halina. Without a word the soldier drove a knife into the girl's back and plunged it deep into her heart.

"No!" Elise screamed, "No!"

She leapt at the guards as her friend fell. Halina's blood watered the cold stone. The sword wielding soldier grabbed Elise tight in his strong arms as she fought. He was too strong. Elise was overcome as she stared down at Halina, once so full of life, and now without breath. Halina had been the one person who had not treated her as dirt. Elise's cries echoed through the dungeon as her tears began to fall.

"Your aunt and uncle will follow if you speak at the gallows. This is my word."

They gathered at sunrise. Hundreds of them. Men and women, young and old. Soldiers and civilians, alike.

"Miera is at our gates," the magister's voice boomed across the courtyard. "A phrase often used to inspire fear. We have known fear. We have known suffering and we have known loss in recent days. Here now, I give you a harbinger of chaos and anarchy. A thief of more than gold and silver, but one who had stolen lives as well. One who has tormented this city for too long. One that we must now bring to justice. I give to you the Nightingale!"

Despite the Nightingale mask and hood, despite the scarf that was pulled up over her mouth and nose, Elise heard it all.

The slow beat of the drums, the jeers and screams of the crowd. She could see the hatred in their eyes. She could feel their hunger for blood. Her blood. There were hundreds of them. A sea of men and women. All had come to cheer her death. She shivered as the cold claws of fear began to freeze her blood. Her hands were bound tightly behind her back, while six armed soldiers surrounded her. They pushed her toward the gallows that arose before them. The magister stood upon the platform with four of his men and a black clad executioner.

Only the thought of her aunt and uncle kept the pieces of her broken heart together. Her mother was dead. Her father was dead. For two years she had waged a war from the shadows to uncover their killer. This drive was the only thing that had kept at bay the exhaustion and kept her moving forward. It was the only thing that had shielded her from the mockery and disgust of her peers, despite how it had torn at her. Living among the very same people who saw her as less than them. Now those few that had tried to help her had been killed. Halina was dead because of her. Everything that had happened was because of her.

The soldiers forced her up the steps and shoved her toward the gallows. Elise was turned to face the crowd.

The crowd longed for her death, and it terrified her. Her breath grew short as the dread set in. Cold sweat covered her skin. She felt frozen; desperate. Elise had never been so afraid.

The magister held out a hand to silence the crowd.

"This nightmare goes by another name, wears another face so that it may walk among us," he said as he looked to one of the men who held her. With a savage tug, the guard pulled down her hood and then tore free her mask and scarf. "Those belonging to Elise Delfeyre," Imrohir cried.

The screams and cheers of the crowd filled the arsenal with a great roar. Elise shivered, barely able to keep standing against the gale. The world knew her secret and it hungered for her blood.

"If you have something to say, say it," the magister intoned. "Tell the people of your crimes. Tell us, Nightingale, what do you have to say?"

Her heart pounded. Her breath grew ragged. She thought of Raphael and Claudia; her aunt and uncle. The people that had given her a second chance, a second family, and she had betrayed that trust.

Elise said nothing.

The executioner grabbed her and pulled her back. The noose was lowered over her head. The rope was pulled tight. Her breath was cut off. She saw the executioner move over to the lever that would send her plunging down. The magister turned to face her. The crowd looked on as their cries grew louder.

Imrohir raised an arm.

She saw it fall.

The ground shifted beneath her feet.

Elise dropped.

The rope tightened.

The man began to ease his way through the baying crowd. He was slow at first, yet with each step his pace quickened. He saw the Nightingale fall.

Cleander ripped his sword free and shouted. The people around him screamed and leapt aside from the steel. Two soldiers came at him with cries upon their lips. They fell in a heartbeat beneath Cleander's blade. He ran through the parting crowd and charged toward the gallows.

The magister pointed toward him.

Weapons leapt into soldiers' eager hands. There could have been twenty. There could have been fifty. Cleander did not care. He pulled silver capsules from his belt and launched them forth. They shattered upon the stone.

Smoke filled the courtyard.

The last thing Elise had seen, before the smoke came, was the brown clad man. Now she couldn't breathe, couldn't see, couldn't hear. The rope tightened. Her lungs were on fire. Her neck burned.

Then she was falling. Her boots hit the stones, and she crashed to her knees. Elise gasped for breath. Her throat screamed as she coughed. Her bindings were cut. The noose was ripped from her neck, and she was heaved to her feet.

Cleander was all she could see through the smoke. He shoved her kukri blade into her hands. Cleander spun back as a shadow found them. It was the executioner leaping down from the platform. Cleander grabbed her shoulders and threw her aside as the Elaran's axe descended. The steel flashed by her face, and then her saviour replied in kind. His sword tasted blood, and the executioner toppled to the ground.

"Imrohir has no intention of sparing your family! Go!" Cleander roared. "Go!"

Her eyes widened at his words. Elise rubbed her neck and managed a nod. She staggered away from her saviour as the smoke engulfed him. She found the edge of the platform. She saw black shapes amidst the smoke. She could hear the shouts of soldiers as they closed in.

The haze thinned and Elise stumbled. She crashed into the wall of a tall building.

A yell came from behind as a soldier saw her. He thrust his arm her way and called for his comrades. Elise glanced in every direction. She saw nothing but the magister's men. She was surrounded; alone. They came at her.

She flew up the wall.

Elise pulled herself onto the rooftop.

The platform roof was made of flat stone. Two crossbow wielding soldiers saw her. She heaved herself into a run as the deadly weapons turned her way. Her boots pounded upon stone. She launched herself from the rooftop, as the bows' song filled the air. A bolt sped past her head as she touched down on the roof opposite. Her hands hit the red tiles and she pushed herself up. The tiles rang underfoot as she flew across the rooftop. Shouts came from all around. More soldiers appeared atop the buildings. Bolts filled the air. Clay tiles shattered, wood was splintered, and stone chipped.

Elise dropped down a level and rolled as she hit the lower rooftop. She launched herself at a series of arches between buildings. Her boot hit the first and then she sprinted across them one at a time. Beneath her, soldiers ran through the streets in pursuit. Above, others tried to navigate the maze of rooftops. Bolts glanced off the arches underfoot as the men below attacked. Elise launched herself to the side and her hands latched onto a ledge. She threw herself up. Her feet reached for the ledge as her fingers searched for the tiles of the roof. She found them and heaved herself up. Elise barrelled across the rooftop. Soldiers descended toward her.

A gap in the roofs appeared. It was wide and the drop deeper still. Elise cast herself across it without a second thought. Her feet found the lip of the flat roof and she rolled forward across it.

Elise threw herself into a run. She leapt another gap between the rooftops. A soldier appeared before her. She had nowhere to go and no way to stop her momentum. Elise gritted her teeth and leapt at him.

Her knees found his chest and her speed sent them both falling from the roof. The soldier fell backward and landed on a lower platform with a sickening crunch. Elise's fingers found the sill of a building opposite. She sped up the wall and flew onto its roof. She ran.

Bolts flew at her from all sides. The magister's soldiers closed in. Shouts came from in front.

The arsenal wall rose before her.

Soldiers armed with spear and bow patrolled the walls. With cries upon their lips, they charged toward the section of the wall she had angled toward. Elise soared through the air, hit the wall, took two steps, and vaulted the merlons.

Once again she was airborne, barely avoiding the thrust of the soldiers' halberds.

She fell and her momentum carried her forward. She hit the slanted roof of a tiled building. Elise slid down its length and launched herself onto another roof. She flew across it, launched herself from platform to arch, to rooftop, never slowing. She dared not look back. Soldiers still hunted her from all sides. She could not escape the hungry, steel tipped bolts.

A man appeared at her side and charged toward her. Elise accelerated. The gap between rooftops opened before her. She leapt into it. Air kissed her cheeks.

Her boots caught the lip of the opposite roof and she fell forward onto the flat stone.

The man was not so lucky.

He crashed into the side of the building and tumbled down into the street below.

Elise felt blood on her hands as she vaulted a small ledge. She barely felt the pain. The magister had sent soldiers to take her aunt and uncle. The last family she had left. Elise changed direction as guards appeared before her. Bolts rained down.

She dropped onto a lower roof, rolled, and then jumped to another roof that was lower still.

A soldier charged across an arch at her as she ran. Another appeared in front.

Elise barely dodged the man on the arch's sword as it sped past. Clay shards exploded through the air as the blade smashed into the arch. The other soldier thrust his spear her way. She slid to the side as it flashed by her face. The man snarled and turned his thrust into a sideward cut. The shaft hit her hard in the shoulder and sent her flying from the ledge.

Elise crashed onto a lower roof. Her side screamed as it hit stone. The men jumped down toward her. She lashed out with a kick and slammed her boot into the first man's shin. He fell.

Elise rolled to the side as the second man descended toward her. Her feet found purchase, and then she was up. His sword grazed her arm, as she leapt to the side.

More shouts. More soldiers.

Elise ran.

She leapt from rooftop, to arch, to ledge, skipping across them like only an acrobat could. The guards were untrained and clumsy. Some slid to a halt while others fell.

She landed on the roof of a temple. Elise saw four guards appear on a roof opposite and level crossbows. The bolts splintered clay brick as she sped past a steeple. She ducked around the towers, as soldiers appeared around her in a swarm.

They closed in.

Elise quickened her pace. Her body ached and her lungs burned. She leapt into the air and curled into a ball. Her shoulder hit the closed shutters first. They shattered, and then she crashed inside a house. Plates and jugs fell as she pushed herself to her feet, vaulted a table, and ran out the opposite doors. Elise bit back the pain as she entered an open corridor. She sped along it. She had no time for the pain.

Shouts came from below as soldiers ran into the house. They looked up, saw her, and angled for the stairs. An opening appeared at the end of the corridor. She ran for it. The soldiers reached the hallway. They came from behind and from the side. She reached the opening and leapt through it, launching herself toward the wall of the building opposite. Her hands latched onto a sill, and she heaved herself up. She kicked off and spun. She found purchase on a ledge opposite. Again, she leapt and spun. This time her fingers reached the rooftop. Elise heaved herself up and all but staggered to her feet. They came at her again and again. Each time they drew closer. The rooftops flew by below as she retreated. Elise's eyes remained locked on what lay ahead.

She was over forty feet above the street now, yet she did not slow. Elise reached the final rooftop. It was flat and stone. She could see the river. She could see the bridge and the Pits beyond. She was halfway along when the first soldier reached it. Crossbows sang as she leapt into from the rooftop. A bolt sliced into the muscle of her left arm.

She turned her fall into a dive, splashing into the river.

Elise heaved herself from the icy waters into the darkness of an alley. The Nightingale had lost them after the jump, yet she could still hear the cries and shouts of soldiers echoing through the city. She had not gone to the Pits as the soldiers may have expected. She had doubled back and found her way to the merchant district.

She grimaced. Her hand went to the bolt that protruded from her left bicep. She had been lucky. It had only grazed the bone beneath. Her momentum and clothing had stopped it from cutting the whole way through.

Elise bared her teeth and snapped the shaft. She pulled both ends out and bound her wound with part of her cloak. Her hands were torn and bloody. Her body battered and bruised.

Yet she was alive. Against all odds she was *alive*.

Slowly, carefully, she began to navigate her way through the alleys and backstreets. She knew them all. She was only a few blocks from home. Only a few blocks from her aunt and uncle. She had to warn them.

It did not take her long to find the Delfeyre house.

She peered from the shadows. Soldiers stood posted at the front of the house. They did not belong to her uncle. Horror filled her as she saw the doors had been breached. Marshall and the other warriors would be inside defending her family; she knew it. Even Tariq would be with them. A man who was as hard as any to capture, let alone kill.

Elise used the shadows as she hurried across to the walls of her family's villa. She followed them around and entered through the shutters of a window on the second floor. The first thing she saw was the body of a fallen guard. Unlike those outside, he was bereft of life. Unlike those outside, he wore her uncle's colours.

Elise crept through the house as dread began to take hold. There had been an attack. More bodies. Both those of the magister's men and those of her uncle's. She reached the inner sanctum and entered the small courtyard. The house was in ruins. Couches and tapestries had been torn and broken. Blood covered the ground.

She found her family by the pool. They lay side by side. Their hands stretched across the floor; fingertips brushing each other. Tears filled Elise's eyes as she saw the blood that pooled around Raphael and Claudia Delfeyre.

They were dead. The *last* of her family.

She began to sob, and her hands went to her aunt's still arm. Elise screamed, and did not care that the soldiers heard. Her heart was *broken*.

She barely heard the footsteps. She didn't see the soldiers that approached.

There were three. She glanced over her shoulder with blazing eyes as tears soaked her cheeks. Swords came up, and in that moment she did not care if she lived or died. Her entire family was dead. Her friends were dead. Her only allies were dead.

This was her fault. If she had not been so reckless, if she had not taken up the mantle of the Nightingale…

There was a shout. One of the soldiers was sent flailing to the ground as a thrown spear ripped through his chest.

"DELFEYRE!" Marshall's roar filled the yard. The warrior bled from a hundred wounds. His blood, and that of his enemies, covered his armour. Sword and shield leapt into his hands as he charged the two remaining men.

Marshall was not alone.

Tariq was at his side and held a wicked war hammer in his hands. The fight lasted but moments. The magister's men fell swiftly to the blades of their foes.

"We have to leave, Elise," Tariq called as he reached down toward her.

"More come," Marshall growled as he barely held himself up.

Shouts came from the house entrance.

"We have to leave them," Tariq told her as he took her hand. "I am sorry."

Elise said nothing. She couldn't. Words would not come to her.

The Berenithian shoved her toward the stairs leading to the balcony as five more soldiers came toward them. The three reached the top of the stairs, as another of the magister's men appeared before them. Marshall leapt forward to engage him, while Tariq pushed his charge behind him and held an arm in front of her protectively.

The soldiers reached the top of the stairs and spilled onto the balcony. They were trapped.

Tariq raised his hammer and let loose a roar. Steel met steel as Marshall fought against his foe.

Elise drew her kukri.

He appeared like a demon, emerging from the entrance of a second floor's room, as if conjured from nothing.

Cleander.

He walked between the two sides.

There were five standing opposite him, but the balcony was narrow. Cleander drew his sword and levelled it at their enemies. He said nothing. He attacked. Cleander let the blades and spears of his attackers miss by inches as he wove through their midst. His sword creating a web of steel. It was as if he was in a trance; his blade hungry for blood. Each move was precise and done with meaning. The first man fell to a sword through the heart, and the second to a pair of strikes across the chest. Cleander's dagger found the throat of the third, and a backhand slice caught the fourth across the neck. He continued his dance and carved his steel across the fifth man's body from shoulder to hip. The soldier fell to his knees, and Cleander took his head.

A grunt came from behind as Marshall drove his blade through his enemy's chest and out his back. The household guard kicked the soldier to the ground and pulled his sword free with a gasp. Cleander wiped his blade on the cloak of a dead soldier before turning to face them.

"We have no time. Follow me."

FORTY-TWO

The silver moon burned high above when Nenrir's boat landed. There were eight of them. Clothed in black and their faces awash with dark coloured earth. They hurried across the beach and within moments had their vessel hidden within the foliage. Nenrir snatched out his bow, and then without a word the eight men separated.

Arndyr Scaeva had once told them that upon landing, his watchman had seen the Wind Rider enter the river mouth, and so Nenrir had landed his boat more to the north. The archer made for the river now, silent as the grave. He was a hunter. He had been since before he could walk. The men he had chosen to accompany him had been the same. Men skilled in both tracking and the bow. It did not take him long to find the first of Scaeva's watch.

There were two of them.

One stood with spear in hand and looked out across the sea. The other sat upon a log in their makeshift campsite. There were no fires and only a single small tent. The seated man fell when Nenrir's first shot sank in his back, pierced his heart, and punched out his chest. The standing man turned as he heard his companion hit the earth. He staggered as an arrow found his stomach and took the air from his lungs. He fell when the second arrow kissed his throat and took his life.

Nenrir glanced up at the moon as he entered the camp. It was a barely a few hours before dawn. If Erik was to attack, then it had to be now. The archer quickly put together a small fire using grass and his flint stone. He tendered the blaze to life and ripped a strip of cloth from his tunic. Nenrir wrapped it around the head of an arrow, and then plunged it into the fire. It ignited.

He nocked the arrow and turned his weapon skyward.

"The signal!" Laerke cried and gestured upwards. A sliver of orange danced through the night sky for a moment before it vanished down into the forest.

Erik gave his friend a nod. "Then it begins," he said.

Erik placed his helmet over his head. The Ravenheart surged toward Lumis with five other ships in tow.

They caught the city unprepared and unawares. The Ravenheart was well within the bay before the first screams echoed across the water. Small boats overflowing with warriors were launched. The larger ships found homes at the piers. Some were forced to board anchored ships and scurry across their decks to reach the dock.

Erik brought his massive round shield to bear as he strode down one of the piers. Fargrim and another warrior walked at his side. Together they blocked the path in an unbroken shield wall. Laerke's bow sang as the first of the defenders charged toward them. He crashed onto the wooden planks of the pier and then topped into the bay. The men of Lumis reached them. They streamed forth in a steady wave to try and contain their attackers to the harbour.

The first man swung an axe. Erik caught it upon his shield before he drove his spear through the man's neck. He ripped it free as the man gurgled and fell. Erik moved again and thrust his weapon into the heart of the next man. The bloodsworn adjusted his grip and launched the weapon forth. It drove deep into the raised shield of one of Scaeva's warriors. A man who was forced to cast the shield aside, and a man whom Erik sent to the halls of the slain with a swing of his axe.

"FORM!" Erik roared as his men reached the dock.

Their enemy had formed a wall of steel and flesh between the invaders and the city. Erik's warriors and shield maidens linked their shields three high to cover them. Step by step they closed in on the city. Step by step their ranks swelled. Arrows rained down upon them, yet the shield wall held.

"RELEASE!" Erik bellowed.

The shields opened and the rear rank unleashed a volley of spears and arrows. Many of Scaeva's people fell to the storm of steel. The shields closed and the wall remained unbroken.

"WE MOVE!"

They began to advance with chants upon their lips as they closed on their enemy. Erik bared his teeth as the distance between the sides closed. The men of Lumis charged. They crashed together in a song of steel. Erik's axe tasted blood as the defenders swarmed all around them. They were outnumbered, pushed back against the sea, yet a cornered dog was the most dangerous of beasts. The bloodsworn heaved with all his might and dug his boots into the earth in the attempt to stop the enemy's weight of numbers from pushing them too far. He strained, feeling the breath of his foe mere inches away. He tilted his shield, raised his arm, and brought his axe sharply down. Blood flowed and the man fell, only to be replaced by two more. More boats from Agartha began to land. Cries of triumph became screams of terror as the invaders' numbers grew. Their reinforcements crashed into the sides of the defenders' formation. Suddenly Erik and his crew were advancing. Horns blew and the people of Lumis began to flee into the streets. A roar came from an alley, and then dozens of warriors surged into the breaking lines of defenders. Torben led them, axe and sword in hand as he hacked and slashed amidst the enemy. A berserker.

Erik stepped forward and thrust his arm forth to send his axe spinning toward the retreating foe. It caught a man in the back and sent him crashing to the ground with an anguished cry. Erik's sword leapt into his waiting hand as he strode over to the fallen man, struggling to rise. Erik glared at the man and saw nothing but the image of the one who had killed his sister. Her voice. Her hair blowing in the breeze as the Rider drove through the Lupentine. His shield cracked into the warrior's head and sent him down into the dirt. Erik's sword found his throat.

Torben bellowed after their retreating foe and beat the flat of his blood slick blade against his serpent tattoo. "They were unprepared. Had no warning," Torben called to Erik.

"They have the advantage of numbers still, and a trapped beast may yet bare its fangs," Erik said to his friend as he retrieved his axe. "Join the wall, brother."

Torben nodded and shoved his axe into his belt. He took up a shield, and then together the warriors of Agartha began to march to the Scaeva hall.

Men charged at them as they made their way up the hill, and each time a wall of shields greeted their foe. Erik felt the hot blood of his enemies upon his face. He could taste its iron. His sword stabbed between the small gaps in the shield wall and found the throat of the man opposite. The warrior dropped with a scream as Erik tore his blade free. Blood for Astrid. That had been his vow. That had been his pledge.

One by one the warriors of Lumis fell to his blade, and yet the advance had been halted.

An arm grabbed him and heaved him back from the front line.

"Erik!" Torben called, "Erik! We are losing ground. They have rallied."

"Just a little longer," the younger man nodded and raised his sword, "Keep your shields up, we are a wall!"

His warriors roared in reply. They were pushed back an inch, yet the wall held. They were pushed back a foot, yet the wall held.

Erik wound his way to the front and shoved his shield into that of his enemy.

"BRACE!" he roared.

The warriors of Agartha dug their feet into the soil and heaved. Those behind drove their shields into the backs of their brothers and sisters. All movement stopped. Erik growled and his legs strained for all they were worth.

The shouts greeted his ears like music. Chaos rippled through the defenders ranks. A great roar came from the north.

"It's Nenrir!" Torben shouted.

The warriors of Agartha cheered as a newfound energy strengthened their arms. The people of Lumis began to back away as fear entered their ranks. Erik raised his sword and beat it upon his serpent painted shield.

"FOR ASTRID!" he bellowed.

"ASTRID!" Torben cried, baring his teeth.

The shout was taken up by the Valkir of Agartha as they surged forward in a wave of steel. They crashed into their enemy and tore through their ranks with no thought, nor fear, of death. Blood began to run through the streets.

"ASTRID!" Erik roared. A spear materialised from the chaos and sliced a bloody furrow across Erik's sword arm. The bloodsworn did not feel the wound. He countered and thrust his sword deep into his attacker's neck.

"ASTRID!"

A horn blew in the distance. Jormund Scaeva had sounded the retreat. They were completely surrounded, and they were pulling back to the hall. Their lines began to disintegrate. The shield wall broke. Warriors fell left and right. Erik lost his sword in the melee and pulled his axe free. It tasted blood as he buried it in the chest of a warrior.

Scaeva's men fled.

"ASTRID!"

Rank upon rank of warriors greeted them atop the hill. They stood before the great hall of Auraeva. There were hundreds of them. They were all armed with whatever weapons they had found. Some wore armour, others no more than tunics and breeches. All were ready to fight, and bleed, and *die*. They stood in a circle with their shields interlocked into an unbroken wall. Nenrir and his warriors appeared at the crest to the north, weapons stained with blood, and eyes blazing with passion.

The two armies surrounded the besieged warriors of Lumis in a ring of steel. Archers materialised through the front rank of Jormund Scaeva's men. Bows sang and arrows rose to greet the invaders. The man to Erik's right vanished, and a pair of shafts bit deep into the bloodsworn's shield. The defenders charged toward the broken shield wall with cries of triumph upon their lips.

The walls came together again.

Erik snarled as he heaved. His muscles burned as both sides fought for advantage. Men began to chant all around. Erik killed one man and then another. He saw a flicker of purple through the chaos. A man of the Arkin Garter; the emperor's private guard. Like the bloodsworn they were baptised in blood and battle. The warrior to Erik's left fell. Another joined him in death, sent there by the sword of the purple crested warrior. Erik lashed out and found nought but the purple warrior's oval shield. He caught the counter as it darted at his throat with his axe.

An unspoken word stilled the battle, and a ring began to form. The bloodsworn clashed blades with the man of the Arkin Garter. Erik watched him closely as the two men circled. They did not fear the blades at their backs. No man would break the sacred pact. Erik watched his eyes as they moved and looked for the sign of an attack.

When the blow came, it came hard and fast as lightning.

He caught the thrust on the rim of his shield and deflected it, countering with a diagonal cut. The warrior blocked the blow and danced back before he darted in again. Erik parried and replied with his own thrust. Steel bit into his foe's griffin embossed shield. He lashed out with the edge of his own shield and hammered it into that of his enemy. Erik forced him back, using both axe and shield as weapons, but the purple warrior had replies to every assault.

Erik drove forward. Axe and shield met sword and shield. The bloodsworn heaved and forced his enemy's weapons to the side. He angled his axe, brought it down low and then sliced it up under the warrior's shield. Steel slid across cuirass before ripping through the flesh and muscle of the man's shoulder. Erik leapt back and danced aside from the counter as it came. He watched cautiously as the warrior circled him with no sign of pain. Yet it was there, Erik knew it. No man, no matter how strong, could support the full weight of a shield with a wounded arm. Not for long. Erik lashed out with a vicious downwards cut. It wasn't clean, yet its purpose was clear.

The warrior caught the blade upon his shield with a grunt. Erik pushed his advantage and threw everything he had into his strikes with axe and shield. He battered away at his enemy's weakening defence. He pursued his opponent back across the ring. Erik was attacking and defending like a man born to fight. The man thrust with sword and shield. Erik brought his left arm down and forced the blow to the side even as he countered. His axe darted forward and found the man's exposed throat. Before weapons could fall from nerveless fingers, Erik's shield came up hard and hammered into the warrior's jaw. The man's feet left the ground, and then he crashed into the earth in a spray of dust and blood.

The warriors of Agartha cheered. Erik stood still for a moment. His chest rose and fell, slower by the moment. Erik rolled his shoulders back and beat weapon upon shield. He roared and rose his axe to the heavens as he strode toward the line of defenders.

"Is there anyone else?" he bellowed as he stalked down the line. "Is there anyone else? STEP FORWARD!"

Erik twirled his axe as he walked. He crossed the open ground between the two armies. He was closer now to the defenders than his own people. He had no fear. There was no time for fear. None stepped forward to face him.

"SCAEVA!" Erik shouted. "SCAEVA!" Movement came from the Lumis lines, and then a man clad in the silver and violet of the Arkin Garter stepped forth.

"You wish to talk?" Jormund Scaeva growled.

"It is far too late for that," Erik snarled.

Jormund adjusted his grip upon his sword. "And what is it you are doing exactly? You attack my people, invade my home, paint my city with blood."

"Your *brother* killed her. He killed Astrid. My sister," Erik's voice grew loud.

Jormund frowned. "What?"

"SHE'S DEAD!" Erik shouted. "ASTRID IS DEAD!"

The purple clad warrior nodded slowly. "And now you wish to kill me too?"

"She died on the cold earth, a knife between her ribs, because of your blood, your alliance to the empire. I will avenge her no matter the cost," the bloodsworn replied. "Of course I am going to kill you!"

"Then face me now. Champion against champion. One life in place of hundreds," Jormund told him. "When I kill you, your people will leave these shores. Never to return."

"You can try," Erik snarled. The bloodsworn turned from his foe and stared at his own people. He pounded the flat of his axe upon his breast and spread his arms with a war cry. A great roar greeted him. Hundreds of voices screamed. Weapons were beaten upon shield and chest.

Erik Farrin looked back to Jormund as an equal cheer went

up from the Lumis ranks. He lowered into a fighting crouch and brought his shield up. His heartbeat slowed. His breathing was steady.

Erik made the first move. He leapt forward and thrust his shield out. Jormund caught the attack upon his own shield and then swung it up to intercept the blow that followed. Erik skipped to the right and lashed out again. Jormund deflected the weapon and thrust his shortsword out. Erik slid to the side and the blade missed by a hair's breadth. The bloodsworn countered and bought his axe down hard upon Jormund's raised shield.

They broke apart.

Jormund came at him. His short blade thrusting again and again like a wasp. Erik drove his shield down, deflected the sword, and countered. Scaeva ducked low and the edge of his sword sliced across Erik's thigh. The bloodsworn's axe followed him down and caught the lip of Jormund's hastily raised shield. The axe head looped over the rim and crunched into Scaeva's shoulder. Steel sank into armour and bit into the flesh beyond. Jormund lost his balance and stumbled to a knee. Erik rammed his shield forward and caught his opponent across the chest. Jormund rolled backward and barely avoided the axe blow that followed. Earth sprayed into the air as steel crunched into the soil. Erik skipped back as the sword darted at his face. A line of red appeared across his thigh. Blood rolled down Jormund's arm.

The two men eyed each other as they circled. Jormund showed no pain in his eye. He cast his shield to the side. Erik did not hesitate nor question, instead he followed suit.

The bloodsworn's shield hit the ground.

Hate strengthened his arm as he moved forward. Rage gave power to his blows. He slid aside from a slice aimed at his neck. Jormund danced away from his axe. The weapons came together. Their deadly song filled the yard. Erik deflected a lunge with his bracer and sent his axe forward. Jormund ducked the blow and replied. Erik leaned back. The blade missed his chin by an inch.

Sword locked with axe.

The bloodsworn wrapped his second hand around the head of his weapon and viciously brought it down. He carved a furrow into Jormund's cuirass. The man of the Garter staggered back. Erik thrust the head of his axe up and caught Jormund in the jaw. Scaeva stumbled and fought to keep his footing. He sent a desperate stab toward his foe. Erik angled his shoulder and ducked. The sword flashed past his cheek. He knocked the lunging arm aside and brought his axe around.

There was a thud. The weapon buried itself in Jormund's side. The man cried out. Erik wrenched his weapon free. He leapt back as Jormund's sword sliced toward his stomach. It slid past. Erik grabbed Jormund's sword arm by the wrist and looped his axe around. Scaeva dropped to a knee and caught the axe by the shaft. Erik heaved. His muscles strained against those of his enemy. Jormund was more than a warrior. One could not become a man of the Arkin Garter by being a common soldier. He would not give up. With a roar Erik brought his knee up. It cracked into Scaeva's jaw. It stunned him for but a moment.

His grip slacked. The axe head came around and smote the side of Jormund's head. He fell and Erik followed him down. The bloodsworn took up the sword that had slipped from his foe's fingers. He cast his axe into the ground and held the sword above Scaeva's throat.

The warriors of Agartha cheered.

Jormund met his eyes. "Do it," he said. "Send me to the golden halls of our forefathers."

Erik gritted his teeth and raised the sword high. His knuckles whitened upon the hilt. Astrid's face swam before his eyes. Erik brought the sword down with a cry upon his lips. The crossguard crunched into Jormund's head. His eyes flickered and closed as consciousness left him.

Jormund Scaeva would live. For now at least. The bloodsworn needed answers. Erik rose to his feet with bared teeth and wild eyes. His chest was heaving and his breathing ragged.

He levelled the sword at the people of Lumis.

"It is over. Lay down your weapons."

FORTY-THREE

City of Elara, the League of Trecento

Kyler awoke with a start.

His head ached like it had for days now. It was hard to think or focus. He sat up and swung his legs over the edge of his bed. Kyler leaned forward and rubbed his temples with a sigh. The pain began to grow. A bead of sweat rolled down the knight's cheek. Kyler grunted and stumbled to his feet. The world spun all around him as his mind became a roaring inferno.

He staggered into the table and its contents crashed all around him. The exhaustion hit him like a hammer. He felt worn thin, stretched to breaking point. His veins ran black, and the irises of his eyes burned with crimson. Kyler collapsed, crashing to the floor as darkness took him.

Kyler groaned as he came to. His head rang like a bell and the dull ache inside his mind still burned. He rolled to his side and heaved himself up to his feet. The knight fought to focus as he made his way through the chamber and out into the inn. He followed the steps down and then strode out into the stables behind the tavern. Kyler snatched up a bucket of water from the well and placed it on the ground. He dropped to his knees and without hesitation drove his head within. He breathed out through his nose as he shook his mane. The icy water bit at his face. It did little for the pain, yet the cold forced back the weariness that fought to engulf him. Kyler shook his submerged head one last time before he pulled it free. Water cascaded around him. It calmed him. He closed his eyes and took a long breath. Kyler raised a hand to his amulet.

"What is happening to me?" he murmured absently. Kyler found his way into his horse's pen. He reached out a hand and stroked Asena's strong neck. The mare nuzzled his shoulder.

"You feel it too, girl?" Kyler said as the horse nudged his face with her own. "This place, this city, stands upon the precipice. The dice have been cast… I wonder which way they shall fall."

"Where they fall, what form they will take, we can only guess," Alarik's voice came from the gate to the pen. "The future is yet to be known, Pisspot. Do not waste thought and breath about what may be. We do not live in the future any more than we live in the past."

"It is sometimes hard to remember how easy life was," Kyler told his mentor. "Even in the Citadel… when we set out from those gates in pursuit of the Spear… our enemy stood before us. They did not hide in the shadows. They came forth in pursuit of blood or coin, and we did everything we could to deny them. Yet here… Elara is different. Who knows from which shadow the next adversary will emerge? This is a whole new war."

"The fear of the unknown is powerful." Alarik shrugged as he entered the pen. "Many men have been consumed by it. Do not fall prey to it, Kyler."

"Aye." The younger knight ran his hand down Asena's side.

"Is that what woke you?" Alarik asked as he glanced at Kyler.

The boy shook his head.

"Nor me," came the reply. The battlemaster gazed out into the distance. His eyes clouded over. "Some days I remember," Alarik murmured.

"Remember what?"

"The good. The bad. Memories from a lifetime ago," Alarik said.

Kyler looked to his friend, his mentor.

"Tell me."

"Many years ago, before the Order, before all of this, I served under the griffin standard. Twenty-three summers I had been with the legions when the call came to march west for Irene. When we set out from Aureia, we did so without question. After weeks on the march, we reached those trees. We had expected to face minimal resistance… instead they were all there. All the clans. The first we heard was the song of their bone whistles. The people of Irene carve them in such a way that they *scream* when blown. It came through the mist and fog. Thousands of screams crying out like beasts from hell.

They attacked the rear of the column when we were spread through the forest. We had no place to properly form up. No place to fight them upon open ground. By day they came at us again and again, whittling down our numbers, while by night the screams kept us from sleep. They sacrificed their prisoners upon altars of stone. I can still hear them even now. In those last days we turned to the gods for salvation. Our commanders had fallen. We had lost over half our men and those who lived were battered and broken. The army was split. We were cut off from the rest of the legion without hope of reinforcement. We fought our way to a hill and upon its peak we made our stand. Surrounded, outnumbered, yet we stood with the last griffin standard. We would not forsake it. We would not forsake the empire. The gods work in mysterious ways. Our prayers were answered. Aureia still remained. They appeared through the fog like demons, streaming toward our enemy without fear. A young knight had rallied what was left of his riders, and with them met the men of Irene head on. We fought until our weapons found no enemy, until the trees were painted with blood. The screams of the whistles met their end, and on that day, we knew that the victory was ours.

The knight led us from one battlefield to the next until all of Irene fell to our blades. In him there was a man we could follow.

In him there was a man who could have been a king. He was as close to me as family, more so. We were brothers. All of those who survived that hell were."

"And the knight, what happened to him?"

"After the war was won he gave up his command. He wished for no more than to return to his station as a knight," Alarik told. "Velis was sent to Larissa as an envoy. Emperor Darius himself named the man as commander of horse to *all* Aureia. Now I hear that he rides for Kilgareth at the Cardinal's request."

"So he will fight then?" Kyler asked.

The battlemaster nodded.

The sun had barely risen when Kyler wrapped himself in a warm cloak and made his way out into the city. He pulled the hood up over his ears to hide his face from the outside world. Perhaps he should have stayed back at the inn with Alarik. Perhaps he should have been training with his tutor or resting before his body fell apart from exhaustion. Yet there was something he needed to do. Kyler did not know the streets of Elara well, nor did he have a map, but the path he now walked was branded upon his mind. After what seemed like an eternity, he reached the oak door.

It opened at his knock.

"Kyler?" Elena said softly, a hint of surprise in her voice. She gestured into the house, welcoming him inside.

"I needed to see you," he told her as he pulled his hood down.

Elena closed the door and then the pair embraced. Kyler hugged her tightly. He was almost afraid to let her go. "Did anyone see you?" she asked.

"No." Kyler shook his head. "No, I was careful."

She gave him a tender squeeze and for a moment all his worries slipped away.

"I was worried for you," he told her and took her hand gently.

"I adapt, I survive," Elena replied. "I do not need protection."

"Aye, I know," Kyler chuckled and looked down at the hand he held. "Only those who get in your way do. All the same, no man ever lived who does not fear for those who he loves."

Elena smiled and planted a kiss upon his lips. He returned it, revelled in it.

Then it ended.

Elena placed Kyler's hand over her heart. She did not look away from his eyes.

"Kyler, I choose you. I chose you in Adrestia. I chose you in the cave. I will keep choosing you until the end of time."

Kyler entwined her fingers with his own.

"You are my heart," he told her.

"What is it?" Elena murmured with a furrowed brow.

"Hmmm?"

"You seem tired," she told him. "I have seen that look in your eye before."

Kyler stepped back with a sigh. "In truth I do not know."

He saw the worry in her face as she squeezed his hand and placed her other upon his arm. Her words were as soft as her eyes. "Tell me."

"During the chaos of the riots I was wounded. A blade cut my leg," Kyler told her. "I washed and bound it… that's when it happened. I felt this *thing* inside my mind. It ripped and tore… as if my mind itself was being torn in half. I saw my veins run with black blood… and then I woke up. When I woke my wound was healed. Since that moment there has been a dull ache in here," Kyler touched him temple. "It happened again last night."

"And now?"

"It is there," he said. "I feel spread thin… this curse, whatever it is, drains the strength."

Whatever it was that afflicted him, it exhausted him more than his sleepless nights. It exhausted him more than his guilt. Elena stepped back and something new entered her eyes. Sorrow.

"It is no curse."

"Then what?"

"Kyler, I am *so* sorry," she replied sadly. "This is my doing."

The knight froze. He could see pain in her eyes.

"What do you mean?"

"I only wanted to save your life," Elena said as she stared into his eyes. "Please believe me. Please." He heard the desperation in her voice, saw it in her face.

"Hey," he said and placed a hand on her cheek. "I believe you. It's alright."

"I caused this… I caused this."

"Be still, my love. I have known worse than this," Kyler pushed a stray stand of hair back from her face. "What did you do?"

"It is my blood, the blood of the ruskalan," Elena told him. "It saved your life in the Vault. I saved you. Maybe it had no time to complete its effect. Maybe I was interrupted too soon. Maybe—"

"Stop," Kyler interrupted her. "You saved my life. You were not to know what would happen if you did so. All we can do is find a way to stop it."

"But how?" Elena pursed her lips. "My mother. It was from her that my ruskalan blood came. She taught me the old ways. She taught me to use my gift and taught me the history of my people. You see Kyler, once a ruskalan has sired children with a human that blood stays with the lineage forever. We could never be fully ruskalan, nor could we be fully human. We are something different. Half-blooded. My mother taught me this… and then when she believed me to be ready, she tried to teach me to hate."

Kyler squeezed Elena's arm as he saw the look she gave him. She was scared. She thought that in his heart he believed her to be a monster. She thought he would leave.

"Hate?" Kyler asked.

"Hate humans." In dismay, she stared up into his eyes. "For what they had done to the ruskalan, to the elves. For a long time I believed her. I grew to hate and despise. And then it changed.

You changed me." There was a plea in her eyes as she spoke her heart. A plea for him not to leave, not to run. Kyler stayed.

"Now I fear that this blood that I bear is the very thing that is hurting you," Elena told him. "It is in you… coursing through your veins."

It was clear to Kyler that she had never spoken of her heritage before. Why would she have? Kyler was a sworn knight of the order that had once fought a bloody war against her people that had wiped them out. Or so the world thought.

"And if it is ruskalan blood, what next?"

"There is only one who may be able to help us."

"Who?"

Elena crossed her arms as she thought. "A scholar, a healer… one more skilled than any before. Lysandra. She may be our only chance to solve this puzzle."

"Lysandra? But she stands as maija," Kyler said incredulously. "She is with the Order. Even if you managed to get into the Citadel, would she not turn you away?"

"She will see me," Elena said with certainty.

Kyler thought back. Lysandra knew Elena's parents. The maija had helped with her father's pain and her mother's sickness. Did she know of their heritage?

"And if you are right and it is ruskalan blood coursing through my veins, what would stop her from turning me in?"

"Kyler, do you trust me?"

"Of course, but–"

"Then trust me," she told him. "Lysandra can help us. Lysandra will help us. She is as close to my family as anyone. She will not turn us away or betray us."

Doubt still plagued Kyler. All it would take would be one word from the arc'maija's tongue and she would see them both to ruin.

"But what if–"

"Shh." Elena cut him off and placed a finger over his lips.

"She won't. Trust me, as you always have. I want to make this right. I *will* make this right."

"I know." Kyler smiled.

Her passion burned more brightly than the sun. He knew Elena. He knew her heart. She was determined to fix this, to solve the puzzle that had been laid out before them.

"You have never let anything stop you before," Kyler told her. "This affliction will fare no better."

"Exactly." Her amber eyes softened as they looked deep into his own. They shone like starlight and burned the colour of autumn leaves, drawing him in as they always had. She took a step back and her fingers trailed through his own. Elena kissed him.

He tasted the joy on her lips. He felt it on his own. Despite the horror of recent months, despite the darkness, it was with her now that he truly felt whole. He did not care for anything beyond her arms. Her eyes enthralled him. Her soul tamed the restless spirit within.

He was hers.

She was his.

It was quiet in her house, far removed from the chaos beyond its walls. Here, they were alone. Here, there was no fighting, no war. Kyler felt her breath on his chin. Felt her hair tickle his neck. They lay wrapped in each other's arms. Kyler reached out and gently traced his hand along Elena's cheek.

"You came back. Followed me to Elara. Knowing it could mean your life," he murmured.

She smiled slowly.

"I could not leave without seeing you again," Elena said quietly. "Kyler, the fight that once was between your people and mine… we will overcome it. Together."

"You truly believe that?"

"I have to," she replied. "I have to believe there is still some good in this world. A dawn after the darkest night."

Kyler took her hand and squeezed it. "Then this dawn you speak of, I will give it to you."

Kyler stayed with her for as long as he could. Alarik would be waiting for him, and eventually he could not delay any longer. Kyler wrapped his cloak around his shoulders.

"I wish I could stay," he told Elena.

"I know," she replied. "But you are bound by your duty and will never turn from that. And that is no bad thing." Elena pressed the knight's sheathed sword into his awaiting hand, "Be careful out there."

"*You* be careful out there."

Elena smirked. "Me? I made it here from the valley without anyone holding my hand. Did you?"

"I was but another lonely traveller on the road, with nothing but a sword between myself and certain death," Kyler countered sarcastically. "At least you had that temper of yours… and well, who would stand against that?"

"My temper?" Elena scoffed and gave him a shove. "I would suggest that yours has been the cause of a good deal of trouble, *sir knight*."

"Sir knight?" Kyler smirked.

"Indeed, how remiss of me, not using your title sooner." She rolled her amber eyes and attempted a curtsey as she continued, "Forgive me, sir."

"I see that you have learned your place."

"I see that you haven't."

They laughed. Kyler said nothing as a smile curled his lips.

"What?" Elena chuckled, raising her eyebrows.

"Do you think things will ever go back to the way they were?" he asked. "Before all of this."

"No," Elena replied. "And that is no bad thing. Despite everything we have suffered and lost, we have not changed."

"And may what the dawn brings *never* change us."

Elena ran her thumb across Kyler's hand. "Alarik will be wondering where you have gone. You should go before you are missed."

"Alarik can wait," Kyler murmured and leaning down toward her.

Elena kissed him once. "There will be plenty of time for that later. Go."

"But–"

She kissed him again with a smile and pushed him backward toward the door. "Go."

Kyler looked back at her with a grin. She was dazzling. Her eyes were filled with joy.

He pushed the door open and backed into the street.

"Hurry," the dark clad man whispered.

Luana Marquez said nothing as she followed the man into a crevice carved into the mountainside. Three of the Jade Queen's sailors followed her into the earth. Their hands never moved far from their weapons.

Marquez herself wore a headscarf to hide her face from the man who led them. Calvillo walked before her and, as far as the guide knew, *he* was the leader.

It was a deception. A deception forced upon her. She knew those she was about to deal with would not take kindly to the ploy, however they would have refused to meet with a woman. These were dangerous times, and they knew no better.

She would prove their fears wrong.

Slowly, the crevice morphed into carved stone. A tunnel hidden deep within the bowels of the ground. Unlit torches adorned the walls. One of the sailors reached for one and was stopped when the guide's arm snaked out and latched onto his wrist.

"No," the man snapped. "No light. Death could be awaiting us around the corner. You don't want to bring it down upon us, do you?"

The four pirates followed their guide for miles. How many, Luana did not know. The tunnels wound this way and that in a labyrinth of stone. Countless paths could be taken, yet their guide never once looked back. The only break in the solid foundation was a deep stream flowing down its centre. The stream's stench meant only one thing. A sewer. Luana was suddenly glad for the headscarf, though it barely stopped the smell. After an eternity, the companions came to a door. The guide knocked and then they were ushered inside.

Braziers and torches lit the room from end to end. Luana swept her gaze around and took it all in.

The room was more of an abandoned warehouse than any kind of chamber. It had been filled with long tables, tapestries, and other oddments. They were taken to the centre of the room which had been cleared of tables. The men who filled the hall rose from their seats and made their way toward Luana. They surrounded the pirates. Some smirked while others showed no emotion at all. To a man they were ready to fight. Calvillo rested his right hand upon his dao and his left upon his opposite wrist. Luana placed her own hand atop her sidesword and watched as two men pushed their way through the crowd.

The first man wore a duelling cape over a shoulder and a pair of gold rings in his ear. A sword hung at his hip and his face was weathered. His eyes shone dangerously in the light, revealing a glimpse of the storm that lay beneath. The second man was clad in a dark gambeson and had his large hood pulled up over his ears to shroud his face. The first man ran his gaze over the pirates. After a moment he nodded, seeming satisfied.

"I hear that you wish to speak," he said.

"You are Bhaltair?" Calvillo asked, meeting his stare.

The man dipped his head. "Indeed."

"Then there is much we should discuss."

Bhaltair held up a hand to silence him.

"And your name?"

"Calvillo of Tarik," the pirate replied.

"Calvillo of Tarik," the gang leader said slowly. "Tell me, pirate. I have eyes and ears from Elara to Aureia, from the slums and pits to the council hall of the palace itself, yet I have not heard your name even once. When I was approached days past and given the letter that you wrote, I had expected to be speaking to someone with reputation."

"Aye, you may not know me, nor may you know my name, but in the stories you have been told, I was there in every one," Calvillo told him. "From the shores of Lamrei to the coast of Kiriador, I was there. Unwritten, perhaps, but I was there."

"Then why are you here?" Bhaltair said, "A man unknown to the pages of history, wishing an audience with me in my hall."

"The world changes," Calvillo shrugged. "My people are chased across the sea while yours live in servitude. Those with the will to fight back are imprisoned or worse. Alone we cannot match them but united we could—"

"Could what?" the gang leader interrupted. "Topple the magister? Free the city from his grasp? I've heard it all before. You are not the first to have believed it and you shall not be the last. Thousands look to me for guidance and sanctuary. You have what? Three men? Now, I took this risk in secreting you through those tunnels, in meeting with you in the hopes that we could broker some kind of deal. Yet now I am forced to concede that will never be. What is left of your kind is being hunted down, and those few who have not fallen soon will. If the great Cillian Teague is not here in your place, then no doubt your leader is resting in the dark depths of the Sacasian Sea. So, I ask you, why should I listen to a man with no reputation, a man with nothing to offer, a man who has done nothing save *write a letter*?"

"He did *not* write it," Luana stepped beside her companion as she spoke.

Bhaltair glanced at her. "And who are you to say so?" he asked.

"Who am I?" The pirate captain smirked beneath her mask. With a single movement, she pulled the scarf from her face, freeing the wild hair that fell down her shoulders in a dark wave. "Luana Marquez, captain of the Emeralis. I wrote the letter. I sent my man to arrange this meeting. I am the architect that brought us together."

Startled cries emanated around the hall. Men stared at the woman who stood in their midst. A woman, armed with a sword, who commanded a ship that struck fear into the hearts of many.

"Even here your name is known, *captain*," Bhaltair said. "But I do not take kindly to being deceived."

"Would you have met with me, had you known who I was?" Luana asked and turned so that she spoke to all the assembled gang men. "A woman who wields a blade is not seen so fondly in these parts."

"Are these few all that remain of your people?" the hooded man asked.

Luana glanced at him as she replied, "I do not recall your name."

"Cleander," he told her.

The pirate captain looked from face to face. "Well then, Cleander, we are far from the last. Cillian Teague lives. Garret Laven lives. I live. The League believes us broken. No more than a whisper soon to be spoken no more. It was they who sailed on my home. It was they who slaughtered my people," she beat a fist upon her chest as she spoke. "Yet my fire still burns. They have taken Lamrei from Sacira to Haevara, it is true. Yet my fire still burns. When at last they arrive at Tasir and Partharon, they will discover a most *unpleasant* surprise. We will *not* be waiting for them. Right now, Garret Laven is in the south, intent on keeping our enemy far from these shores. So, we sailed north. Right now, Cillian Teague lies in wait barely half a day from this city. And right now, twenty ships are at his command. For now, my people are safe, yet only a fool would believe that they can remain undiscovered for more than a couple of days."

Cleander and Bhaltair exchanged a look. All the experience in the world could not have masked the surprise on the gang leader's face.

"And what is your purpose?" Bhaltair asked as he gestured toward her.

"We cannot match the League in the sea. That much is certain. The old guard tried and they paid the price. They took my home, and in return I will take theirs. Whatever the cost," Luana said fiercely. "We have the ships. We have the swords. What we do not have is a way past those walls. A way to avoid the discovery of the bell tower. I am here today because we need one another. I am here today because we are both fighting a war that alone we cannot win. I am here today because together we can *win*."

Bhaltair pursed his lips. "If I were to ally myself with you and yours, I would be risking more than just my own life. Many of my own people would meet the same fate."

"Is living and dying in the shadows a better fate?" Luana told him. "Is watching your people suffer by the day a *worse* fate, than taking what could be the only chance that you may have in this lifetime? I have come too far and lost too much not to risk this. Can you say the same?"

Cleander looked at Luana, though when he soke his words were to Bhaltair, "It could work. With Stentor and the men the captain can bring, we could do this."

The pirate captain took a step toward the two men. "Only those who risk going too far can possibly find out how far one can go," she said. "Only those prepared to sacrifice everything will achieve *everything*. What you have done here, no other could have accomplished, but you cannot fight this war on your own."

Bhaltair strode toward her and halted barely a foot away. She could see his mind at work behind those dark eyes.

"The magister still has a tight grip upon Elara. He sits in the arsenal watching, while the last shreds of rebellion are crushed. He has thousands of soldiers at his command. Men loyal only to him," Bhaltair told her. "Between my men and Stentor's we could take the streets, hold them for a time even. But the arsenal? The belltower would see us to ruin."

"How many are you?" Luana asked.

"With Stentor? Maybe fifteen hundred," Cleander replied. "If we rose, the lower districts would rise with us. We would be thousands."

The pirate glanced at the hooded man.

"I can bring nearly a thousand skilled hands to bear," she told him. "And equal their number of free men and women. And they will fight. They have nothing to lose."

"Imrohir will expect an attack," Bhaltair said. "He is no fool. A plan begins to take root. However, with the belltower the city will be alerted and made impregnable before your first ship lands. Even if we herald a miracle and manage to unite our forces, we will be almost hopelessly outmatched. We may have the numbers, yet numbers do not win a battle. They have discipline. They have walls."

"And we have *nothing* to lose," Luana countered.

"Perhaps you do not," Bhaltair muttered. "But if we fail, everything we have built will crumble to ruin."

Cleander stepped between the two leaders.

"It is better to die on your feet than live on your knees. The pirate is right, brother. This could be our *only* chance at freedom. I will deal with the belltower. You have my word."

"And if you fail?"

"Then I die," Cleander shrugged. "But I am not prepared to sit idly by while this opportunity passes. The people are restless.

They crave justice. The Nightingale was but the first to step out into the light and stand against the magister, and that thief won't be the last. If we do this then the people will rise. We are not alone. We never were."

"Join me," Luana said and stared directly in Bhaltair's eyes. "Join me, and together we can take down Imrohir and give the city back to the people."

The gang leader gave away nothing. He looked from his people to the pirate, and then slowly raised his arm toward her.

She took it.

Their grip was firm and strong, as unbreakable as the unspoken pact that they forged.

"We are the same, you and I. Cut from the same cloth, and so what?" Luana swept her gaze across the faces of each man as she spoke, "They call us criminals. They call us monsters. We may have nothing to our names, no gold, no position, but I say we are *free*. Truly free. And one free man fighting for his liberty is more powerful than *three* Elaran soldiers. Lameri taught me that. You want your homes back? You want your lives back? Then we *have* to do this, and we have to do this now. In two nights, Teague will sail into the bay. What will you do? What would you give for this one chance to take back what is rightfully yours? What would you give to live outside of the shadows? Ask yourself, all of you, what would you sacrifice to know what each of us was born with: freedom. Because out there they seek to take that away. I will not stand aside and let them take it, will you? I will stand against Imrohir, will you?"

Luana drew her sword and beat it upon her chest. She saw the fires igniting in the eyes of those all around. She heard their cheers.

"We will fight and when we do, we will fight with one heart! With one *soul*! Don't fight for silver, don't fight for glory. Fight for your families. Fight for your homes. Fight for your liberty!"

FORTY-FOUR

City Vesuva, Aureian Empire

Kitara slid aside as the spear darted toward her. She stepped inside the fighter's reach, as he danced back. He did not counter with his spear. Instead he thrust the small buckler and sword held in his left hand at her. Kitara forced her blade up, intercepted the blow, and deflected it to the side. Her dagger leapt into her left hand as she moved. The spear came around. The knife drove up, slid beneath the fighter's ribs, and into his beating heart. Blood washed over flesh and steel.

The chants of *Alessandra* began before the body hit the ground.

Kitara parried the sword as it came to take her head off. She countered and carved her wooden staunch toward her sparring partner's chest. Nuallan caught the attack upon his shield and lunged. The tip of his blade drove toward her heart. Kitara had seen the blow coming before it was made. She twisted her body, stepped toward Nuallan, and swiftly brought her left arm down. It wrapped around the man's wrist as his sword drove past and latched it to her body.

The crowd roared as Kitara continued her spin. She ripped the man's sword from his grasp.

He stepped back as she came on, pressing forward and launching strike after strike. The fighter was quick and agile. They all were. He caught the blows one after the other upon his shield. The fighter suddenly halted and sent the edge of his shield forth. Kitara slid to the side, skipped passed the blow, and opened the man's thigh. He fell to a knee as she pirouetted. Her sword came around. His head hit the ground well in advance of his body. The people cried out her name.

The name given to her by Aureia.

Kitara arced her staunch. Its hilt cracked into Nuallan's jaw. He staggered and she pressed her advantage.

He danced back, blocking once, twice. Kitara knocked his shield to the side, stepped forward, and brought the edge of her sword to his throat. She grabbed the back of his neck, used her left foot to wrap between his legs and take his balance. The pair crashed to the ground. Sand and dust rained down.

The fighter was strong and tall. His vicious bearded axe was held tightly with both hands. He was faster than a man that size had any right to be. Kitara had to fight the perfect fight and so far, she had. One false step, one bad move, and she was dead.

Kitara dashed forward. He blocked the blow with the shaft of his weapon and countered.

Kitara leapt back and felt the wind slice by her throat as the axe flew by. The fighter swung back. Kitara ducked. The weapon carved a path over her head as she dove forward. Her aim was true, her form perfect. The sword sliced through muscle and flesh, drove through the man's chest, and ripped free at his back.

The crowd roared.

The dead man toppled over. Kitara spread her arms and raised her sword to the heavens.

The chants washed over her.

Kitara knelt above Nuallan with her knee pressed to his belly. Her hand held his wrist, and her sword was pressed to his throat.

"Dead," she told him as her lips curled into a smirk.

"Piss yourself, Alessandra," he growled back.

Kitara chuckled and petted his cheek. He pushed her hand away with a grin. In the weeks following Taliskar's death, the fighters had embraced her as one of their own. Instead of the taunts and slurs, they laughed and shared jokes. They were all sworn to the Nilor family, yet all had their own cause for fighting in the sands. Some wanted fame and glory, others wealth. Some just wanted a better life than that of house slaves. Most had been warriors and soldiers, but few of their number had been stone haulers, sand miners, or even prisoners of war. Some were Aureian, others Larissan, Berenithian, or from faraway Irene.

They had all come from nothing, but the sands had forged them into something new. Something better. Here they had found something more than just friendship. They had found a kind of brotherhood. Though doomed to live short lives, they revelled in it. When one returned victorious from the arena, they all celebrated for a whole night. When one fell, they all mourned together and would burn their brother beneath the moonlit sky. By day they trained and by night they slept.

Now Kitara, Alessandra, was one of them.

"Alessandra," the mentor's voice called. "Pair with Vidarr."

"Yes, mentor," she replied and walked toward her new opponent.

"One day I'll have you," Nuallan called out. "I'll put you on the flat of your back. What would that make me?"

"Dreaming," Kitara said without looking back.

The day wore on and the sun rose higher. The only respite the sildari received was when the mentor called for a water break. Nuallan and Vidarr were but her first partners for the day's training. It was aways a different face, a different style. In the sands the sildari had to be prepared for anything.

"BREAK!" the mentor's voice cut through the air like a whip.

The sounds of sparring, of grunts and groans, wood striking wood, and steel striking steel faded. Some of the younger house slaves scurried around the yard collecting the weapons from the fighters. A bead of sweat ran down Kitara's face and dripped from her chin. It splashed onto the rough sand beneath.

Her tunic was soaked through and her body weary. The aches that she had grown used to had all but faded after the first few weeks of training. Now she just felt the tiredness in her body. Her body that had been made stronger. She felt faster, lighter on her feet. As agile as a cat and more powerful than a spring stag. She was leaner now than she ever had been.

"You move well," Vidarr told her as he handed his sword and shield to one of the attendants. He gave her his lopsided grin, "Perhaps one day you may prove a challenge."

Kitara raised an eyebrow as she gave up her blade. She tugged at the bindings of her swordarm bracer. It was late and there would be no more training this night.

"I was the better sword today was I not?"

"You were not," Vidarr replied.

"She was," Yeomra said as he walked by and clapped the other man on the shoulder.

Vidarr glared at him. "She was not," he said.

Kitara's lips curled. She strode past Vidarr and smacked her shoulder into his arm as she did. "I was, and I enjoyed it."

Kitara made her way over to the water trough and filled one of the empty cups. She relished the cool water as it ran down her parched throat.

"Alessandra," one of the household slaves called as he approached.

She gave him a glance.

"The master wants to see you."

Kitara nodded and splashed a handful of water over her face to clear some of the sweat. "I'm on my way."

Soldiers led her up into the Nilor house as they always did. This time she was not taken to Valliro's office. This time she was taken to the courtyard of the villa. The Aureians surrounded her like hungry vultures.

"Quite the sculpture, isn't she?" a noble said as he circled her. His clothes were as rich as his smug look. By the look of him, he ate and drank too much.

Kitara stared directly ahead with her hands clasped tightly behind her back.

"Carved by the gods themselves," Valliro Nilor told the man.

The second man stopped in front of the slave and ran his eyes over her. "Who would have thought it, magister," he said, "that a *woman* would send so many men to the afterlife."

"Alessandra has proven to be quite the sound investment," Valliro replied.

"Eight fights, eight victories," the richly clad man said. "Tell me, slave, do you fear any man?"

Kitara did not shift her gaze from over the man's shoulder. It was as she had been taught. "No, master," she replied.

"Do you fear death?"

"No, master," she said again.

The noble gave a malicious smile and pulled a knife from his belt. An irritated look crossed Valliro's eyes but he said nothing. The household guards did not so much as flinch as the man raised the blade and put it to Kitara's throat. She did not move. She did not react. The urge to take the blade from his fat hands and jam it into his belly was hard to resist.

"Tell me, Alessandra, are you scared?" he asked.

"Everyone falls. Only the time and method change," Kitara

replied. "If you want to take my life, take it. But I can give you what so few can. A king's fortune."

The man pressed the blade closer. Its edge pushed against her skin.

"Brave, reckless, and arrogant," he said before finally lowering the knife. "She is everything that you told me she would be, Valliro, my friend. I can always tell when someone is lying, and she is not."

"She–" Valliro started.

"Let me fight in your games. Bet on me to win no matter the opponent," Kitara cut in. "You will not regret it."

The noble froze for a moment. Valliro Nilor had been about to speak. The magister of Vesuva had been about to speak, and a slave had interrupted him.

The noble let out a laugh and gave a mirthless smile. "We have a deal then," he said. "But as for regrets... well, we will see."

Valliro held out his hand. "A deal then."

The noble took it all too gladly. No doubt he could see the coin that he would be making soon. Most of it would be spent before he left the villa.

"My man, Bellon, will arrange the details," Valliro said and gestured to his aid.

"Indeed," the noble nodded. He gave the master of the house a short bow, "Magister."

"Senator," Valliro returned the nod.

And then the noble was gone, following Bellon into the heart of the villa. His footsteps had barely faded when the magister turned to her.

"Did you interrupt me?" he said.

"Master, if I–"

"What do you think you were doing?" Valliro snapped as he crossed the room in three strides.

She looked down. "Master, I overstepped."

"Yes, you did," he growled with a glare. "But now we have Senator Vulir's games. You truly have a mind for this."

The angry look shifted, and then a great laugh came from the magister's lips. He clapped Kitara on the shoulder. She allowed herself a smile as the surprise hit her. Of all the things she had expected, this had not been one of them.

"Thank you," Kitara told him.

"Ah, you played your part well, Alessandra," Valliro filled a pair of finely embellished cups with wine and handed one to her. "Drink. Your master commands it."

Kitara took the cup gladly and raised it to her lips. She sipped at the drink and savoured the taste that greeted her.

"Valentian?" she asked.

"A special occasion, wouldn't you agree?"

"Fighting in Senator Vulir's games... a great honour," she replied.

"The final fight of the games," Valliro told her. "You were chosen above all others. Over Yeomra, Vidarr... all the champions in the house... and Vulir wanted you especially."

Kitara frowned. "Why me?"

"Because the gods favour you," the magister smiled. "Vulir has all the guile of a mule, yet he has an outrageous amount of gold. Indeed, he stands as the richest man in the empire. Gain his support and we all stand to profit. One month from now, when the horns sound and the crowds cheer, when blood is spilled upon the sands, a fortune beyond imagining will be within our grasp. Fight, win, show Vulir what you can do. Songs will be sung about Alessandra. I will pay to have them written."

"You honour me, master."

"No," he said. "You honour yourself."

Kitara took another gulp of the wine. She watched as a slave entered the room and handed a letter to Valliro. The magister opened the scroll and slowly scanned its contents. A dark look crossed his face. He staggered as if he had been struck and slumped down into his chair.

"Master?" Kitara called out.

He held up a hand to silence her. "It appears that I am being recalled to Aureia," he murmured. "My beloved emperor is *dead*."

"Darius is fallen?"

"Killed by an assassin's blade," Valliro muttered. He rubbed his brow as if it ached. "Now we magisters have been called for a choosing. Darius' son is still young… he will need a steward until he comes of age. The magisters of our great empire will decide who sits upon the throne in Darius' absence. I leave at dawn."

"How long will you be gone?"

Valliro shook his head. "Weeks, months… I cannot be sure. My son, Arias, shall oversee the house while I am gone. I have said too much. Leave me. I must prepare."

Kitara bowed her head. "Master."

She left him to his thoughts. Kitara saw the girl, Sereia, as she made her way back through the villa. She walked alone and carried a jug of wine. Her clothes were neat and well kept, while skin and hair were just as clean. She was being well looked after. Kitara made to call out, she wanted to hold her and tell her it would all be alright.

A cane was shoved into Kitara's back to keep her moving. The soldiers said nothing, just gestured for her to keep walking. There was no compromise nor argument to be had. There was nothing. All of this was for Sereia. She had not forgotten her vow to Morlag. Kitara would get her home. She returned to the training sands without a word.

"I heard that Senator Vulir graced our house with his presence," Vidarr said as he handed Kitara a cup filled to the brim.

"The man is a leech," Kitara replied with a snort.

"One with a penchant for making coin," the man shrugged. "Each winter the senator hosts games to celebrate the new year. A time fast approaching."

"We will be fighting in his games," she told him.

"HA!" Vidarr leapt up onto one of the tables with a laugh. He spread his arms and pirouetted. The hall fell silent. "We will be taking prominence at Vulir's games!"

The fighters cheered as one.

Cups were emptied and filled and then emptied some more as the night wore on. Laughter echoed through the villa, as the men made merry. They sang and joked beneath the stars. Only one did not drink. Only one remained reserved. Only he, only the champion, only Yeomra.

Kitara's head had long since begun to pound when at last she stumbled out of the hall and made for her cell. She bumped into the brick wall and downed the last of her wine. She gave the empty cup an almost disgusted look and tossed it to the ground.

"You drink too much," Yeomra said as he stepped out from the shadows.

"Is that so?" She made to pass, but the champion blocked her.

"Magister Valliro did not summon me to speak of the games, and that leads me to the conclusion that it would appear to be *you* fighting in my stead."

Kitara nodded. "I believe something of the sort was discussed."

"Then I heed caution. The man you face, whatever form he takes, will be *far* greater than any you have faced before," the champion told her. "Let me give you some advice, Alessandra. You learned your craft and you learned it well, but there is *always* someone stronger of faster or more skilled. Ignore me if you will, drink if you must, but do *not* fall in love with your own legend. The cost will be greater than you imagine."

"There is more to life than just fighting," Kitara shot back. "You are a great warrior but if killing is your only talent then you are cursed."

The champion glowered and stepped closer. "There is no *talent.*

There is hard work," he told her. "There is obsession. In my heart I know that I am not the best, yet I have the potential to be something great. Think about that. Do *not* dishonour this house. Remember that when your time comes there is nothing after. Do not be so rash as to lose the fight before you step foot into the sacred sands."

Yeomra turned and began to walk away.

"He was right," Kitara called after him. "Valliro. He was right. There is no greater glory than standing victorious upon the sands."

"No there is not," Yeomra murmured.

FORTY-FIVE

Village of Amari, Kingdom of Larissa

Sabra's cries carried through the wind, echoing down to the streets below. Amari was quiet for the sun had risen, and with its rise their guests would depart. Their friend, their brother, would depart once again. The moonseer knelt by the lake upon a bed of stone. She gazed across its still surface and looked to the west. Looking toward Vesuva. Toward Kitara.

She rose to her feet, as the sun's light warmed her skin.

Aeryn slung her quiver over her shoulder and pulled the straps tight. The arrows she had checked to perfection in the night, fixed the flights, and sharpened steel. Next came her knife belt, buckled tightly around her waist. Aeryn ran a hand across her arm ring and closed her silver eyes. She spoke in her mother tongue. Her voice was soft.

"Lycan, Great Hunter, may you run at our side and send the winds to push us. Sylvaine, Spirit Mother, watch over us, watch over her."

Something cool brushed against her cheek as if the spirits were answering her prayer. She ran her gaze along the sword that lay before her. The blade usually wrapped in her cloak. Kitara's sword. She squared her jaw and nodded, leaving her words unspoken. The moonseer wrapped the sword and tied it to her saddle.

Aeryn met her companions in the centre of Amari. They were armed and armoured. They were determined. Little over a week separated them from Kitara and their fate. Bellec glanced over his shoulder and looked into the faces of all that followed him. Aeryn met the mercenary's eye and dipped her head.

"We move," Bellec cried, and with that began their journey.

The villagers watched in silence from the sides of the street and alleys, as the company rode toward the edge of the town. They looked sad, fearful even, as if they knew that many of the riders would not be returning. They knew the danger into which the mercenaries rode. Twenty against the full might of Vesuva.

Aeryn felt no fear, only a sense of anticipation. She did not know what the days to come would bring, what forces would oppose her, yet she would face them, nonetheless. The crowd that had formed in an intersecting street began to part. The first horseman appeared, clad in his flamboyant robes and covered by a layer of armour. Dozens followed in his wake bearing spear, shield, and bow. There would have been forty or fifty of them. Larissans armed for war. Bellec held up a hand to stop his party as the lead rider angled his horse to meet the mercenary.

"Zahiir?" Bellec called out as he recognised the rider. "What is this?"

"We cannot follow you to Vesuva, we cannot," the Larissan replied. "But we *can* see you through the mountains."

Sakkar approached, a grin baring his teeth. "You are most welcome, brother," he said.

The pair clasped arms and embraced. Zahiir said nothing and instead nodded over his shoulder to one the riders in his company. Unlike the rest she wore no armour. Unlike the rest she carried no sword or spear. The woman held out a hand as Sakkar approached. He frowned as he took Senya's hand.

"A long time ago, you rode into the east. You came back two *years* later," she said. "I am never leaving your side again."

Cheers rained down from the walls of Odrysia as the great army went by. Thousands of soldiers united in faith and marching with a single purpose. A city of tents materialised as the army set up camp in the valley. The griffin and red eagle banners flew high in the breeze and danced in the wind. Prince Dayne had left Tristayn in charge of his people before he had ridden for the fortress of Kilgareth with Sir Garrik, Ilaros Arran, Bavarian, his knights, and the cardinal.

The prince could not help his eyes running over the great stone walls that arose before him as they rode up the mountain. Ever since childhood he had been told of the impregnable fortress and the men who called it home. He had been told that it would have been impossible to take with the city an army of a hundred thousand. The sight before him proved this more than just a tale. Kilgareth lived up to its reputation.

The blue and silver clad knights stood sentinel through the fortress streets where they lined the road and created a path for the newcomers to travel. Cardinal Aleksander rode at the head of the column with a hand raised in salute to the men who greeted them. The knights cheered in reply as the leader of their faith passed by. A man clad in armour finer than his brothers, and a sapphire cloak trimmed with white fur, met them at the citadel gates. He wore no helmet, and his face was as hard and strong as the man himself. To his side was a woman equal in years yet clad in the robes of the maija.

The company dismounted in the courtyard and made their way toward the steps of the castle, while stable hands came to collect their horses. The finely clad knight dropped to a knee as the cardinal approached; the rest quickly followed suit. Aleksander held out his hand, and the knight kissed the ring without hesitation.

"Rise, my son," the cardinal told him.

"Your Holiness," the warrior said as he stood proud before the head of his faith. "Welcome to Kilgareth. I am Corvo Alaine, Sword of our faith and acting master of the citadel."

"Tell me, Sir Corvo, are you prepared?"

The knight nodded. "The gods have set me upon my path, and I will follow it."

"Everything said and done is in their hands," the cardinal told him. "If we commit ourselves to the gods and go forward bravely, if we trust in them, then there is nothing to fear. Their light shines true even in the darkest night. You have done good work here in the absence of Sir Amaris and should be congratulated for that."

"Thank you, Your Holiness," Corvo replied.

"Now tell me about the Spear."

Sir Corvo and Lady Lysandra led the way into Durandail's sacred temple deep within the citadel. Dayne shared a glance with Sir Garrik as the acting master opened the massive doors and walked into the holy church. The great statue of Durandail stood before them, carved from solid stone, and emanating pure power.

"Behold," Corvo said as he gestured to the weapon held within the stone god's outstretched hands. "The Spear of Durandail."

Dayne's hand flew to his amulet as the silver lance appeared before his very eyes. He felt something stir within his heart and the prince knew then that the gods walked among them. He could not tear his eyes from the weapon, for its pull was strong. For a moment he felt warm. He felt invincible.

"The blade that cut the skin of the pale horseman himself," Sir Garrik murmured.

Lysandra glanced at the knight. "They say that the spear can pierce the fabric of time and grant a glimpse into what will come to pass," she told them. "They say that the spear shows his truth."

"With this mighty instrument Durandail shows us the way," the cardinal said as he approached the spear. "He has granted us more than just a gift but the merit of being able to take it and hold it as well."

They all watched in silence as the holy man reached out a hand and placed it atop the sacred silver lance. Aleksander's eyes slammed shut and his fingers tightened around the weapon.

"Step forth, Dayne of Annora," the cardinal said.

The prince did as he was bid and Aleksander turned to him.

"Durandail has made his will known. Beyond these walls all the peoples of our faith stand ready for war. We need one leader to unite them. One leader to stare into the darkness that stands against us and reveal the light. It is time, Prince of Annora, to become who you were born to be. It is time for you to become king."

Dayne froze. His eyes widened as all within the chamber looked to him. "There must be a choosing," Dayne said. "By law the Lords of Annora must decide who will follow in my father's footsteps."

"The gods have chosen," the cardinal told him. "You are to be their king. This is their word and as such is above contestation. Hold out your hands."

If what the cardinal said was true, then there could be no refusing. Dorian had wanted his eldest son to succeed him. That much the prince knew, yet for the gods themselves to whisper in the most holy man's ears that they wanted Dayne Raynor as king… it became more than a title. It became a sacred duty. Prince Dayne stepped toward Aleksander, as the men extended the spear toward him. The light of the torches danced across the length of silver and brought the lance to life. Dayne reached out tentatively and placed his hand upon the spear.

A bolt of lightning ran down his spine.

He saw an army standing before a dark forest. He saw monsters beneath those very trees. A scarlet eagle soared above a great battle. The ground was soaked in a river of blood while the sky wept. There was a shrill cry, and then the eagle's black twin emerged from the forest.

The coronation had been small, with few more than the heads of the Order, the Aureian generals, and the Annoran nobility inside the great hall. Dayne had knelt atop the stone and made his vow to his people and country. Kassandra Raynor, who had ridden with the followers' camp from Palen-Tor, had watched on as Cardinal Aleksander placed a thin silver crown atop Dayne's head.

The hall had been filled with cheers and well wishes. Now he stood in silence, a hand pressed to his aching stomach. King Dayne was alone within the temple now. His eyes were closed as he relished the one thing he rarely had these days: quiet.

He bit back a wince as a flash of pain ran through his body. Dayne clutched at his belly. He closed his eyes and let out a slow breath. This thing that was consuming him more by the day had grown worse of late. Perhaps the gods were testing him, or perhaps it was as the healers thought: an unknown and incurable illness that may one day claim his life.

"Something troubles you, my son?" Aleksander's voice broke the silence.

Dayne shifted his hands from his belly. He would show no weakness. Not while he had the strength. He clasped his hands behind his back. "Already I feel the weight of the crown I bear," Dayne murmured, as the older man approached.

"This mountain that you carry, you must learn to climb," the cardinal replied.

The king turned to his companion. "I should not be king, and I am not worthy to lead this great army."

The cardinal frowned for a moment. "What is it, my son?" he asked. "What makes you doubt?"

"I am weary, Your Holiness, weary of this fight. Weary of standing against this affliction that so ails me," Dayne told him. "I have fought in many battles and am no stranger to death, yet now I feel its grip upon me. I have never been afraid, Your Holiness, never. Yet now I fear that I have no time."

"The pale horseman comes for us all. It is this unwinnable battle that we must fight and keep on fighting," Cardinal Aleksander said. "It is not in life but in our deeds that we must find some measure of peace."

"Indeed. One day I shall find that peace, of that I am certain. Until that day, I will continue down this path laid out for me without complaint," Dayne glanced toward the statues of Durandail and Azaria. "I will serve the gods as I always have. I have given them my life and even now, as mine begins to wane, my faith has never been stronger."

Aleksander stood to his side and turned his gaze to the carved stone. "What happened to your father was a terrible crime."

"To lose both he and my closest friend was a hard thing, yet to lose them on the eve of war was harder still," King Dayne admitted. "Yet my grief will not stop me from doing what needs to be done. It is better to suffer than to lose judgment. My people look to me now, and they will not see a weak man looking back."

"I hear that the killers vanished, like shadows, leaving no trace."

"None that need be spoke," the king told his companion. He had been far too busy than any could have imagined since the killings. He had barely slept.

"Whoever they were, they were artisans of their craft," the King continued. "I may yet have stumbled upon a trail, Your Holiness. The murders will not be forgotten, nor forgiven, you have my word. The inquiry continues and I shall see it to its bitter end. Justice closes in upon the assassins as we speak."

"Then say nothing more," Aleksander implored. "Even here the walls may have ears. Proceed with caution. Proceed with the gods, for they stand with you."

Dayne met with the council within the hour.

"Salvaari of increasing numbers have begun to raid across the border," Sir Corvo Alaine told the assembled commanders as they stood in council. "They swarm from the coast to Cacera in small war bands. Striking in the night and then slipping away like ghosts. Sir William Peyene left here some days ago with a company of five hundred mounted knights to keep the heathens at bay until we arrive in force."

King Dayne stepped up to the table that sat in the centre of the room. A large map lay open upon it. He gestured to the centre of the duchy of Aloys.

"As we speak," Dayne begun. "The Medeans assemble at Sergova. Not just Alejandro Aloys and his people. All of the houses are there. They plan to join us when we leave the valley and then march east as one army."

"We could be at the Salvaari border in a matter of days," General Ilaros said. "With the full might that we here muster, along with our Medean brothers, we could crush them."

Bavarian stepped up to the table as he spoke, "I am not so certain that it would be so easy to tame Salvaar. In Rovira we still have Duran Cormac's journal about his campaign. There were reasons a hundred years ago that Salvaar was not taken, and so I heed caution. We will proceed yet all options must be considered."

"You speak true. Many of my soldiers fought against the tribes not so long ago," King Dayne gestured to another man as he continued. "General Tristayn among them. If we fall prey to the same mistakes as Cormac, and as my father, many will die beneath those trees. The victory that we seek may escape us."

"The Salvaari do not like to fight in open battles, it is true, yet do not believe them to be cowards," Tristayn spoke up. "They attack in the night. They shower our ranks with arrows. They use poison and their knowledge of the forests to pick us off one by one. We could build marching camps each night as we did twenty-five years ago. It would slow our progress yet would save many lives."

"What if we divide our forces?" Ilaros suggested. "We could attack from a dozen points. Make them guess where we will be. Surprise them."

Dayne clasped his hands. "It would work for a time, I am sure," he said. "However, the further we march, the slower we march. The Salvaari would grow more daring by the day. If we could not force them into battle, then half our men would be dead in little over a month."

"Well then if we cannot stand as one army, and we cannot divide, then what do you suggest, King Dayne?" Ilaros asked.

"It is said that you can only defeat an enemy if you know him better than you know your own heart," Dayne replied. "I have studied Salvaari art and carvings for years. Ever since my father rode to war against them. I know how they think and, because of the writings of Dorian and Duran, we know how they fight. We need to force them into an open battle of our making, upon a field of our choosing, and in so doing win a single, decisive victory. They are no fools and will *only* face us if they believe that they have the advantage. We have the discipline that they do not have, and they know it. I suggest that we meet them north of Bandujar."

"I know the place," Corvo said. "The plains there are rugged and surrounded by small hills. It leads directly to the edge of the woods."

"Precisely," King Dayne told him. "The Salvaari will be watching our every step, and so I suggest we divide, at least for a moment. I have five thousand spears, equal their number in cavalry, and a further ten thousand bows. General Ilaros, I believe then that you may have as many as eight thousand men?"

Ilaros nodded. "Another two of horse."

"Join your eight thousand with my own soldiers. We will make no use of the griffin banner or standard, and so your men will be seen as Annoran. The Salvaari will have no way of knowing that the empire is already on their doorstep and so that is how it shall remain. With my men and yours, I will march beyond Bandujar."

"Your plan is deception?" Bavarian said. "With so few standing against them, all under the guise of Annora, the Salvaari could be lured into an attack."

"If only to eliminate one foe before the others bolster their ranks," Corvo added. "In the face of ever-growing odds, a wise move would be to attack. They will take the bait of that, I am most certain."

Iaros placed his hands upon the table.

"Yet what of my cavalry?" the Aureian general asked. "What of Medea and the knights?"

"With whatever horse that they can muster, the houses must ride for Palanza and there make ready," Dayne planted a finger upon the map. He looked up at Ilaros as he continued, "General, if your own cavalry could join with Master Bavarian and Sir Corvo south of Cacera… then we will be in position. When the Salvaari come, and they will come, they will find nothing but Annora waiting for them. When the battle is joined Medea shall come from the north and your own men from the south. We will surround them, break their will, and crush them all."

"You would stand as bait?" Corvo asked with a frown. "Knowing the risk?"

"Aye," the king replied. "Much has changed since the last war beneath those trees. They do not know of my men, of their courage. They do not know of the Aureian shield wall. They have never faced us, not united under one banner. Days ago, my father passed from this world, yet his memory lives on. His faith lives on. Now he is gone, and I stand as King. The gods work in mysterious ways. Ask yourselves: do you know their ways? Brothers, when I touched the spear, I felt their presence. I feel it now, here in this room. Their strength, their *light,* is with us. It guides us and flows through us. We will be their vengeance to fall upon those heathens who desecrate the holy places of our land. We will make them pay for the cruelty. *We* are the wrath of the gods."

Grand Master Bavarian glanced up at the pinnacle of the castle; watching, and waiting. He clasped his medallion.

"When the fires of the Citadel burn, the Order of Kil'kara shall ride again," he murmured.

The flames blazed to life as the fire keepers lit their mighty pyre atop the keep. For the first time in a century the Order was going to war. Then, it had been the pyres in the south that had been ignited, now the north was riding into battle against a mighty foe. Bavarian nodded to Corvo at his side. The two grand masters urged their horses forward.

Row upon row of mounted knights rode through the streets in an armoured column. Cloaks of the richest blue fell behind them like waves. Their lances, held ever tight, drove high into the sky, while shields were slung across their strong backs.

They were riding into battle for the first time in a century.

They were riding into *victory*.

FORTY-SIX

Arwan River, Forest of Salvaar

The day was young when Maevin led them across the border. The mighty Arwan River that ran from the edge of the Mithramir Sea to the great Lake, Thirlryda in Miera, cut through the forest at only one point. That point was beholden to the lands of the Káli, beholden to Vaylin. They were only a few miles from the forest when a whistle greeted them. It sounded like a bird's call. A cry that meant nothing, yet almost as one the Káli spun toward a small tree covered hill. A single rider emerged from its depths. His face was a canvas of black war paint and he clasped a powerful bow in his hands. Had they been anyone but Salvaari the archer could have turned them into pin cushions, before they had so much heard the song of a bow.

"Welcome back," the archer called in his mother tongue as he approached on horseback.

Lukas squinted and for the first time recognised the man's silver gaze and weathered face.

"Myrdren," he replied in the language of the forest as the moonseer reached them.

"I had not expected to see you again, Prince," the Káli told him.

Lukas shrugged before he replied, "I am prince no longer."

"We *must* see Chief Vaylin," Maevin said from the Annoran's side. "Take us to her."

The Káli were camped along the banks of the Arwan. A huge

village of makeshift tents sprawled deep into the depths of the forest had become their home. Dark painted warriors with their spears, bows, and horses beyond count, watched the mounted party as they rode through their midst. Blades were sharpened to perfection and arrows were fletched.

The Káli were ready for war.

Lukas knew it not by the blades in their hands or the paint upon their skin, but by the look in their eyes. A huge tent of pelts arose before them. The posts that held it tall were carved with coiled vipers. Outside the tent Vaylin spoke with a man that Lukas recognised all too easily. Eirian of Oryn, a general to his people. They glanced up as the small war band approached. Vaylin showed nothing, yet a hint of surprise could be seen on Eirian's face.

One-Eye dismounted and winced as his bad leg took his weight. He gathered up his crutch and then followed Maevin toward the Káli chief.

"You return to us, priestess," Eirian said with a frown. "I had not expected you so soon, nor to see the Annoran in your company."

I am Annoran no longer," Lukas replied, placing both hands upon his crutch. "I was banished. As of this moment I am a no longer a prince."

"Lukas avenged Oryn," Maevin told the Káli. "He killed the duke's son."

"Did he just?" Vaylin ran her gaze over One-Eye as she spoke, and her eyes ignited as if she saw something new in the crippled man before her. "And how does that make you feel?"

"I spent *years* living in the shadow of my father, the shadow of my brother," Lukas began.

He had spent a great deal of time trying to decide how he felt. In the end the reply came all too easily. "Now I am free. Free to forge my own path."

Vaylin stared at him for a moment.

"There is a change in you," she said. "As if you have discovered something once lost."

"I know who I am now," Lukas said, and his voice was filled with a beautiful certainty. "Walk with me."

One-Eye shared a look with Maevin, before he followed the Káli chief into her tent.

The makeshift structure was simple. No fine tapestries adorned the pelts. No shining armour was covering a wooden stand. There was no crown nor battle standard, no huge bed that the western commanders often kept with them, not even a thick rug upon the earth. Only a small table and a small bedroll of furs lay upon the hard ground.

It was basic, it was warm, and it was *pagan*.

"Tell me, Lukas," Vaylin murmured and brushed her hand along the table as she walked, "after Oryn, you were a broken man resigned to his fate. Yet here you stand. A cripple who is whole. What did the druids say to you, what did *Harkan* say, to cause such a change?"

"You know him?"

"Nothing happens within my realm that I do not know of," Vaylin told him. "The ruskalan were great healers and inspired philosophers. They counselled my forefathers, and they counsel me to this day."

Lukas watched the chief curiously, and she watched him back. "He told me that the broken shall reply to the bloodmoon, that if I follow that path that I now tread, that I shall get what it is that I seek most strongly."

"And what is it that you seek?"

"All my life I have heard the tales of my father's conquests and past glories... the songs and great ballads. I have heard them all. I have seen my brother wage war and make peace and crush his enemies without mercy upon the battlefield. Do you know that he once fought against a rebellion ten years ago? He had the enemy surrounded and outnumbered by many, yet still he gave the Outlaw King a choice. A duel. Beat him and the rebel would be granted his freedom. Lose and what was left of the insurrection would surrender. It was then that they crossed blades. My brother slew the Lord in single combat. Then his own legend began. By the time we returned to Palen-Tor, they were already singing about it in every inn and tavern, every house and hall. Dayne had done it to save the lives of his people; both his own men and the rebels. On that day all the fame, all the glory, fell to him. As the years went on his legend only grew, eventually rivalling that of our father. The whole time, in those songs and on those pages, I was not mentioned even once and yet I was there. On every battlefield. In this darkness I was blinded, eclipsed by their light. Maevin showed me this. Harkan showed me this. They told me of the spirits, of their power. Now my eyes are open."

Vaylin approached him slowly. The dark ochre around her eyes made her emerald gaze burn evergreen. The black war paint started on her face, ran down her neck, and spiralled along the bare skin of her midriff. She appeared unearthly. A demon witch from the night.

"What is it that you seek?" she asked softly.

"I wish for my name to be remembered for a thousand years. Long after our bones turn to dust," Lukas told her seriously. "I wish to carve it into the pages of history."

"My people know your name. You will be remembered as the man who stood against his own people to save an innocent village. As the sun rises it will be heard and known that your slayed the man responsible for the massacre," Vaylin told him. "A fine start to the tale."

"I only wish that I could have seen the look upon my father's face when he realised that it was all slipping through his fingers."

The Káli paused and her brow furrowed slightly. "Would it

grieve you then to learn that he is dead?"

"Dead?" Lukas froze. "That cannot be."

"And yet it is so," Vaylin told him.

One-Eye saw no lie in the woman's face. She had no reason to lie. Despite everything Dorian was still his father. Lukas had seen him weeks ago standing tall and strong as he always had.

"How?"

"I am told that it was by an assassin's blade," she replied.

Lukas bit back the warring emotions. His hands tightened upon his crutch. "Death comes for us all," he said. "He may be gone, yet the king's chronicle shall endure."

Vaylin nodded, as if satisfied. "What will you do now? Where will you go?"

"My fate is tied to Salvaar," Lukas shrugged. "My place is here. My place is with the spirits, with the Káli, and with Maevin."

"It is no lie that I am relieved to hear you say that," Vaylin said. "You are strong, and only the strong can fight this war."

Lukas could see the smooth smile upon her lips, and hear the slight edge of a seductive tone in her voice. The smell of wild berries was so strong that he could almost taste them.

"You have done a great deed for my people and for that I have a gift."

The chief slid a hand down her arm where it came to rest against three bands of silver. She pulled one of the arm rings from her wrist and held it out. "You are a friend to the Káli. Now, and always."

Lukas took the ring she offered. It was carved as to look like a coiled snake. A pair of fanged heads adorned the ends of the band while tiny emeralds shone in their eye sockets.

"Take it," she said and placed her hand upon his arm. "Wear it if you will. The spirits know what you have done. I know what you have done. Believe in Tanris, believe in me. Together, we can find our destinies."

"I believe," Lukas murmured as he pulled the arm ring on.

"I will *not* ask for your oath, for you have been beholden to the will of others for too long. I would not have it so again," Vaylin stepped past him, so close that he felt her breath upon his cheek. "When we ride, will you ride with the Káli?"

"I will," One-Eye swore, his gaze flicking from the arm ring to the chief.

"We will set the world on fire," she told him. "We will see the earth alight."

The words echoed in the tent long after the exiled prince had left the chief's presence.

Lukas tipped his head back and closed his eye. He felt the medicine begun to work as it forced the pain from his aching head and aching leg. He gritted his teeth, savoured the sweet tasting drink, and then the soreness was gone. For the thousandth time One-Eye stared down at the silver band that encircled his wrist.

The snake was a symbol of cunning and adaptability; this he knew. It was *also* the brand of Tanris; the dark spirit. He ran his thumb across the arm ring and felt the tiny coils against his skin. He had felt a charlatan when he had worn the sun and moon medallion, yet something about the snake felt right. Perhaps his great friend Cailean had been right. Perhaps the fairy tales that he had once been told of were more than what they appeared. The things he had seen beneath the trees... the sky painted violet, the changing of Sylvaine, and then the ruskalan, Harkan. Months ago, Lukas would not have believed it possible, and he would have called the man who did a fool.

"What are you thinking?"

Lukas glanced up as Maevin appeared. She gazed down at him curiously.

"I feel at peace here," One-Eye told her. "Not as if I wish to build a home and lay down my blade… far from it. I am at peace with myself."

"And you are stronger for it," Maevin replied after a moment. "You have a restless spirit. You are not one to settle down. You never were. There is always something better beyond the horizon and you will never stop seeking it. I saw that in you when we met, and I see it in you now. It drew me to you. Now that you have removed your mask, now that you are here with us, the greatness you seek will be yours in time."

There was something in her voice, something in the truth that she spoke that made Lukas truly believe. He felt stronger, as if the loss of an eye and full use of his leg could not stand in his way. As if his destiny was inevitable. He held up his new arm ring.

"Vaylin asked for my loyalty and gave me this. She made me swear no vow or oath, nor bind me to her service. I march with your people now."

"That is no mere trinket," Maevin breathed. "The ring that you bear once adorned Vaylin's arm. They say that she is descended from Tanris himself. That she has the blood of the ruskalan in her veins. And she did not ask for your oath? Then you are *free*. After what you did in Oryn, after what you did in Palen-Tor and Valham, many will follow you. Vaylin has granted you her friendship, and that is no small thing. If you fight with us, warriors will join you. Rodion and many others *will* join you."

Lukas' eye widened. A thin breath slid from his lips as lightning ran down his spine.

"A war band?" he said quietly.

"In time, yes."

"And so it begins," One-Eye smiled. Once again, he would be a leader. Once more warriors would fight with him, yet this time he would not be restrained. This time he would be beholden to no man or law.

"Wait here," Maevin told him, before she vanished into the

forest. Lukas watched her leave. His eye fixed was upon the future. What Maevin had said was true. The Káli chief had given him a great gift. A gift that he would use to find his destiny.

At last, Maevin returned with a small wooden bowl in her hands. She sat beside him and glanced at the strip of cloth that covered his empty eye socket.

"May I?" she asked.

Lukas bit his lip. To him, showing the ruined and empty socket was a weakness. It was scarred and grotesque. One-Eye could not stand the thought of revealing it to any other… any other save the priestess. He slowly nodded.

Maevin gently unwrapped the cloth. Lukas did not look away from her emerald gaze, nor she from his own stare. The priestess' dipped her hands into the bowl and when she withdrew them, they were masked with black paint. Lukas closed his eye as she tenderly began to smear the blackness across his skin. In moments she was done. The sacred rite of the Salvaari people was a part of him, as much as it was to any who bore the markings.

"May Tanris protect you, now, and always," Maevin murmured.

She ran a hand across his bearded jaw and kissed him hungrily upon the lips. Lukas kissed her back, feeling her fire. The priestess rose to her feet and extended a hand.

"Come. There is something that you should see."

One-Eye nodded and swiftly tied the cloth around his empty socket. He took her hand, and with the aid of his crutch, pulled himself to his feet.

They walked side by side through the forest. The Káli warriors spared them no look or glance and instead focused on their tasks. Some were being marked like Lukas had been. Their faces were being turned into canvases for the ebony paint. Others sharpened blades and spears, while some knelt and prayed.

Yet it was none of those men and women that drew Lukas' gaze. It was the groups that passed around bowls and used cloths to smear the contents upon their weapons. Arrow, knife, or spear, it mattered not. The liquid was clear to the eye, yet the Káli were most careful with its handling.

"What do they do?" Lukas asked, turning to Maevin.

"The serpent's kiss. It could fell even the greatest of warriors within moments," she told him.

"Poison?"

"Yes," Maevin replied. "We are at war. The Káli may not be the greatest warriors or riders yet we have one advantage over our enemy. It would be foolish not to make use of it."

Lukas frowned. "But do your people not fear the poison?"

"My people learned its secrets long ago," she told him. "Learned how to work it, how to become immune to it. There are many plants that can heal the sick and give life to those upon the threshold of death. Just as there are those that can take it away with but a touch. A kiss."

"You speak from experience," One-Eye stated.

"Many times. The most recent at Oryn," she told him truthfully. "When someone is trying to kill you, should you not rise and kill him first? He came at me with a sword while I was in prayer. I had one chance, so I took it."

"Then I am glad," Lukas replied. A slight smirk contorted his lips, "Do you know that where I come from, they believe that poison is the mark of a coward?"

"Where I come from, killing *children* is the mark of something far worse," Maevin looked to him. "Lukas, they come to kill us, to wipe out everything that we hold dear. It's us or them. I know that you are torn. I know that no matter what they have done to you, you do not wish to fight your own people. I know that. But when the time comes, when steel is drawn beneath the sky, will you fight?"

Lukas sighed and turned to his companion. He ran a hand along his arm ring. "I have the blood of the eagle flowing inside my veins. The blood of Raynor. The blood of Annora. A part of me will always belong there. And yet with each passing moment I find myself more certain that I am in the right place. I can hear the heartbeat of the forest in the trees, hear the voices of the spirits in the wind. Yes, my place is here. My place is with you."

"Not so long ago you did not put faith in god nor spirit."

"Things have changed," he replied. "I have changed."

Maevin smiled, "It lifts the heart to see you so strong, so *alive*." It was true, and he felt it.

A great cheer arose from the eastern side of the camp.

"What has happened?" Lukas frowned, flicked his head toward the sound.

"Come with me."

One-Eye's heart began to quicken with his pace as they made their way toward the growing chorus of cheers. He saw flickers of movement through the streets and heard the sound of horses. Hundreds if not *thousands* of horses. A great crowd had gathered around a contingent of mounted warriors.

Lukas saw blue woad.

With a grin he pushed his way through the horde of Káli toward the newcomers. He reached the horsemen as a huge Salvaari warrior dismounted. Lukas planted both hands upon his crutch and stared at the man's back, a grin spreading across his lips.

"Just in time, big man," the Annoran called.

Cailean of the Aedei spun around as he heard his friend speak. A great laugh left his throat as he charged at his former companion. He pulled Lukas into a bear hug. The Káli roared their approval. Cailean stepped back, a hand on One-Eye's shoulder as he properly took him in. The Aedei's eyes widened as he saw the crutch and brace, the black paint and the cloth covering the emptiness behind.

"Lukas, my brother, what has become of you?"

FORTY-SEVEN

Talismon Alps, Kingdom of Larissa

The ride from Amari had passed all too swiftly. Before long the company had ridden by the city of Talisier and reached the foothills of the Talismon Alps. The mountain range was higher and vaster than any other.

"I did not know that mountains could grow so tall," Aeryn murmured as they approached the Alps.

"They run from north to south for hundreds of miles," Zahiir told her. "Some say that you could fit the duchies of Medea within its range."

The moonseer glanced at the man in surprise.

"Where I come from, there are highlands and peaks that reach for the heavens, yet none stand half as tall as your mountains. How long is the crossing?"

The Larissan pursed his lips, "Two days and two nights. There is a path that leads through to the Aureian city of Baelvyr. From there, your journey will take you north."

Bellec joined them and ran his wary eyes over the mountains. Aeryn knew what was on his mind for she also felt it. Anticipation. What lay beyond the Alps in Aureia, they did not know. What awaited them in the empire? Who awaited them?

Kitara was close now. They were close.

"I would consider it as a blessing if you rode with us to Vesuva, my friend," Bellec looked to Zahiir.

"I know," the Larissan replied. There was no room for argument in his voice, nor thought to compromise. He was decided. "But I have a duty to my people, not just to Amari, but all Larissa. I cannot lead a company of soldiers across the border and fight the Aureians. We are no army, nor do we wish to start a war with a trusted ally."

"You are a loyal man," Bellec told him. "One of the last ones left."

Zahiir nodded. "Maybe I cannot go with you but what if I were to take only a few riders. We could make for Belona and find a safe house. You could meet me there after you find your daughter. You are friends to my brother, and I understand the love that a father has for his child. I will not abandon you."

Despite the countless paths and endless canyons, Zahiir led them true and without hesitation. They rode for miles and miles beneath the sun's light, along both track and goat path. Aeryn never looked back; her gaze was keenly fixed upon the horizon. Each step that they travelled, each peak that they climbed, she felt her blood begin to rise. She could not place it, but something pulled her toward the empire. Travelling into the realm of this enemy was not just a choice. It was a calling.

When at last the sun slipped beyond the hills and the company made camp, Aeryn clambered up a nearby peak and turned her eyes northwest. She stared out across the Alps yet barely saw the mountains. Aeryn stood higher than any other, yet barely felt the cool kiss of the wind upon her cheek or its caress though her dark hair. Footsteps upon the earth broke her peace. Even without turning she knew her companion by the scent that they bore.

"You should get some rest," Senya told her.

"Rest won't come," Aeryn replied truthfully. "Nor sleep with it."

The Larissan woman walked to her side. "You have been riding for two months."

"I could run for hours, ride for days without rest, and still have the strength to fight," the moonseer said. "There will be a time to rest yet it is not now. *Nothing* could keep me from her. Do you understand?"

"I knew that there was something about you. Something that went unspoken. I could see it in you burning like a bright flame, yet now I know. You care for her, don't you?"

Aeryn did not turn. She did not tear her gaze from the horizon. Her heart churned and roiled in a way that it never had before. She did not speak and instead gave a solemn nod.

"We will find her," Senya said.

"She is strong and her will greater than that of a thousand armies," Aeryn said and at last she looked to her companion. "But she has demons. I know that they will have returned to haunt her dreams, and now once again she is alone."

"She is *not* alone," the Larissan replied softly. "She knows in this moment that you, and that her father, will be hastening to her."

"If only she knew," Aeryn murmured. "But I fear she does not. You have no idea what she has suffered. How rudely she has been treated. Slavery consumes everything. It preys on the old and the young, the weak *and* the strong. That is why we cannot linger too long. I must find her. I *will* find her."

They travelled at first light.

"Hedvika Watch," Zahiir told the company, as the small fortress rose before them. Banners bearing the griffin of Aureia flew high in the wind, while silver clad warriors stood atop walls of wood and stone. "The Aureians built it as a way station between our two nations. Often used by traders. We will rest here for the night and then part ways come morning."

Bellec glanced over his shoulder at the mounted warriors. "Assuming that they let us pass *peacefully*," he said.

The Larissan chuckled and then led them toward the gates of Hedvika.

Shouts came from the fortress, and within moments an army

of crossbowmen stood atop the walls. The vicious weapons turned toward the horsemen.

"Hold!" an Aureian voice cried out.

Zahiir gazed up at the walls of Hedvika. "Is that you, Tulliro?"

"Zahiir?"

"Aye, my friend," the Larissan called back.

"The hour is late, and you come with so many armed soldiers."

Zahiir glanced back and waved his brother forward. Sakkar clicked his tongue and rode to Zahiir's side as he gently stroked Sabra's feathers. "The hawk-bearer is Sakkar. My brother," Zahiir told the Aureian, "newly returned to us from Annora. His companions seek mercenary work in the empire. I am their guide to the border. No more than that."

Tulliro pursed his lips as he stared down at the force before his walls.

"Oi, big man," Sakkar said loudly. "We're tired and hungry."

"Open the gate," Tulliro commanded.

Their horses were taken and stabled, and then the Aureians welcomed the companions into their hearth.

"I apologise for the welcome," Tulliro told the companions as he joined them at the table. "These are dangerous times and seeing a force such as yours arrive at my gates unannounced caused concern."

"Think nothing of it, my friend," Zahiir said, handing Tulliro a cup.

"Dangerous times?" Bellec frowned. "I had not thought that the war would trouble you this far west."

"It is not the war that has caused me sleepless nights," the Aureian replied. "The future of the empire is being decided upon. The magisters have been recalled to Aureia."

Bellec's eyes flew open as he spoke, "Recalled? But that can only mean—"

"Our beloved emperor is dead," Tulliro finished.

Aeryn froze for a moment. She looked around the table and took in the expressions that greeted her. Shock, curiosity, horror. A myriad of emotions. The moonseer felt relief. Without such a man to lead the great army, hope was kindled for her people.

"What of the war?" Galadayne asked. "Without Darius at their head, does the alliance stand?"

"Dayne of Annora leads them now," Tulliro answered.

"Prince Dayne?" Bellec frowned.

"He is King now," the Aureian told them. "King Dayne Raynor."

"Dorian is dead?" Aeryn asked.

"The world grieves," Tulliro nodded. "Already the alliance has been tested. We can only pray that it remains strong."

The moonseer glanced at Bellec. He had grown silent. All the mercenaries had. Kitara's father stared down at his hands as if unable to find words and speak them. His hated enemy was dead. The man who had taken everything from him was dead. The Annorans that followed him had lost much due to the King's greed and now Dorian was gone.

"Where do you travel?" Tulliro asked them.

"North," Sakkar replied. "We ride north."

"North? Then I have some news if you are to pass Vesuva. Senator Vulir arrived the city weeks ago to announce his games for midwinter," Tulliro told them. "He stayed to give the people comfort and hope for the promise of better days. He is bringing his games forward and adding to its magnificence. Instead of celebrating the arrival of midwinter, they will be to celebrate the life of our beloved emperor. A grand spectacle of blood I am told."

"I have seen the games before," Bellec muttered.

Aeryn could make out the faint sound of disdain in his voice. The slave fights were savage and cruel. To the moonseer they were barbarian, no doubt Bellec felt the same, especially after what had happened to his woman.

"Not like these ones," Tulliro smiled. "Starting tomorrow there will be fights from dawn until dusk for two days. The last of which to feature eight pairs from the greatest houses in the region. Yeomra will be fighting, Sloane and Zathrian. Even Alessandra of Salvaar."

Aeryn's breath caught. A slave fighter from Salvaar? How could the empire have come by one of her people? None of the imperials had ventured that far to the east, let alone taken slaves. That could mean only one thing. That Alessandra was captured by Medeans and from there sent to the flesh markets of the empire.

"That is *not* a forest born name," she said. "Who is this, *Alessandra?*"

Tulliro shrugged. "Valliro Nilor's most recent acquisition. A golden-haired demon from Salvaar. The way she fights, like the warriors of the far north, from icebound Tarik. Appeared not so long ago and has since painted the sands red."

Aeryn exchanged a look with Bellec. Alessandra had to be Kitara. There was no other explanation.

"You have piqued my interest," Bellec said as he leaned forward on the table and met the Aureian's eyes.

"If you leave at dawn and ride with haste, you may yet make the final day of the games," Tulliro told them. "It would be a shame to miss so grand a spectacle."

They stayed with the soldiers for a time. Bellec was the first to leave. Aeryn found him atop the northern wall. The mercenary stood alone by the brazier with his shrouded eyes looking across the mountains. The Salvaari did not greet him, nor he her.

"So, the man who banished you from your homeland is gone," Aeryn said.

"I can find no comfort in the words," he replied. "Dorian forced me upon this path. A path of blood and gold that I have known now for over half my life. The door homeward is now ajar and yet any thoughts of Annora are far removed. *She* is alive. We found her."

"We are mere days away," Aeryn replied quietly, yet full of conviction.

The mercenary sighed, "Kitara just needs to hold on for a moment."

"She will. She has to," Aeryn told him. She placed her hands on the parapet, "Are we agreed then that this will be the last night that we sleep?"

Bellec nodded. "Every moment we delay could be her doom. My men are ready to ride without rest for as long as necessary. When the sun rises, we do not sleep until my daughter is safe."

"If it is true what the Aurian says, that she does not sow the fields or toil in the mines, that instead she fights in the arena," Aeryn ground her teeth, "I fear that for her that would be a fate far worse than death. She who despises slavery, and those who kill for joy and entertainment, has now been forced into a life of both. I fear for her, Bellec."

The mercenary placed a hand upon her shoulder. "So do I, but we cannot let that fear control us," he said. "In the arena her face will be marred with dust and sweat and blood. A face that will at best know triumph through pain, and at worst fall to the cheers of the crowd. It is a place not for those of timid souls who know neither victory nor defeat."

"Her soul is not timid," Aeryn said. "It is a burning brand."

"Then you know she will not fall."

"She is a survivor. It is all she has ever known. That is why I worry," Aeryn told him. "Burn the ships after you have crossed the river and you shall take what lies beyond. You know as well as I that she thinks no one is coming for her."

"Neither will those who hold her," Bellec's expression hardened. "I feel pity for the man who first gets in my way."

Aeryn turned to him. Bellec had always been strong, yet after living so long as a man hunted like a dog by his own people, a man whom his own king and friend had betrayed, he had become capable of great violence. The sword was all he had known for decades. She met his eyes and let him see the emotion in her own. Where they had once been no more than travel companions, they were now friends. Aeryn had come to find affection for Kitara's father. It would pain her greatly if they came so far only for him to be lost.

"When we reach Vesuva, when we find her," Aeryn said, "we will stand at the crossroads. Do not take the wrong path."

The sun rose and the mercenaries with it. The word had been spread that they would eat, drink, and rest in the saddle. From now on they rode as if the dark ones pursued them. Aeryn stroked her mount's jaw. She had raised Heidrun from foal to mare, and the horse had been as a constant companion for many years and countless miles.

"Are you ready?" she murmured in Salvaari. Heidrun nuzzled her arm and then shoulder. Aeryn took the mare's head in her hands and placed her forehead to Heidrun's. She set her jaw, closed her eyes, and took a long breath. Nothing could keep Kitara from her arms. Not the Aureians, not their steel, not even their gods.

In a single motion, Aeryn swung her leg up and leapt into the saddle. She rode toward Hedvika's gates. Sakkar embraced his brother as they made their farewells, for the traveller would finish the journey that he started. Zahiir extended a hand toward Bellec. The mercenary took it.

"We will meet you in Belona," Zahiir Alsahra told him. They at last parted ways. One heading north through the mountains. The other westward, toward Baelvyr and the empire.

"The games have been brought forward," Arias Nilor's first words broke the silence. "You fight tomorrow at the going down of the sun. Both of you."

Kitara glanced at Yeomra who stood beside her. The two fighters were alone in the courtyard with Arias. Alone save for the soldiers who watched on.

"The games have been brought forward?" Kitara asked.

"Indeed," Arias nodded. "In honour of Emperor Darius, you are both to honour his memory with blood."

"We are to fight each other?" Yeomra frowned slightly.

Arias shook his head. "No, you will fight as one. Eight houses. Eight pairs. To the winner goes the glory, and by the gods it shall go to the house of Nilor."

"We will not fail you, Master," Yeomra told him.

Arias raised his cup, "See that you don't."

Kitara's eyes flicked to Nilor's arm as he raised his cup to drink. Bands of silver and bronze adorned his wrist. Silver arm rings belonging to the Káli and the lone band of bronze being of Aedei make. She remembered being given the arm ring by Aeryn, what it had once meant. Arias saw her staring and flicked his hand absently.

"Yeomra, you may go," he said.

"Yes, Master." The champion left the room with a pair of soldiers at his back. Arias placed his cup back on the bench from whence it came.

"Recognise these?" Arias asked as he ran his hand along the woven metal.

"Yes, Master," Kitara replied. "Relics from another time, from another life."

"And seeing them now, how do they make you feel?"

She shrugged in reply, "I feel nothing."

"Nothing?" Arias stroked his jaw. "Forgive me, but I do not believe that."

"Believe what you will," Kitara told him. "For as far back as I can remember I have been abandoned, beaten, or betrayed by everyone that I have ever known. I stole to survive. I killed to survive, yet had no more for it save the clothes on my back. At least here I have a roof over my head. I came from nothing, now I have something. Perhaps one day I shall have it all."

Arias gave her a curious look and stepped toward her. "One day? Why say one day when you have the means to have it all right now?"

"What means?" Kitara asked.

Kitara stiffened as the Aureian reached out with hungry hands. One went behind her head, the other to her lower back. She drank in his stench. She saw the look in his eye. Her heart pounded. Her veins ran cold.

Kitara remembered Barboza.

Her hand shot out and snatched Arias' knife from his belt.

The hilt connected heavily with the Aureian's jaw. Steel sliced through the air, and then the blade slid across Arias' cheek.

Blood flowed and the Aureian cried out. The guards seized her with rough hands. The knife rang as it hit the stone floor. Kitara felt horror claw at her as Arias touched his wound and stared at the red blood upon his fingers. Her heartbeat quickened. What had nearly happened. What *had* happened. Arias Nilor bared his teeth.

"Were you not fighting tomorrow I would have you whipped. When this is over, you will hear from me again. Take her away."

FORTY-EIGHT

City of Lumis, Isle of Vay'kis, The Valkir Isles

Erik Farrin marched into the great hall of Lumis with the crew of the Ravenheart at his back. Before him sat Arndyr Scaeva's throne, above which hung the griffin and dragon banners of Scaeva and the empire. Erik felt his blood boil as the rage clawed at him and fought to consume him. He resisted the urge to let it. He resisted the impulse to let his darkest dreams come to life.

The bloodsworn pulled his helmet from his head and cast it to the side, striding toward the throne. The crew said nothing as their leader walked by Scaeva's chair and made his way to the tapestries. The two monstrous sigils flew with bared teeth and wild eyes. The silver griffin, symbol of the greatest empire that the land had ever seen, was graceful and glorious.

The dragon of Vay'kis was a scaled beast, that all but belonged to Aureia and served the emperors as if an obedient pet. The bloodsworn's arm snaked out and in a single move he tore the banners down.

"Such a small thing, to have caused so much pain," Erik muttered as he ran his hands through the purple fabric of the Aureian flag. "These people have no honour."

"Aureia is a mighty empire, towering above all," Torben told him. "Yet so was Delios. In time all kingdoms crumble, all empires fall to ruin, yet the Valkir survive."

Erik walked into the centre of the hall with the twin flags

tightly in his grasp. He had not yet cleaned the blood from his armour, not yet removed the stench of battle. In this moment, he did not care. Erik reached the fire that burned brightly. The blaze had been lit to ward off the encroaching chill *before* the warriors of Agartha had landed.

"In time," Erik began, "the dust from our bones will be gone, and all memory of us with it, but before I die I will see the griffin *fall*."

He cast the banners into the flame.

The crew watched in silence as the fire consumed the cloth. The dragon burned first, and the griffin of Aureia shortly after. The doors of the hall flew open and Jarl Ulfric entered. The old captain nodded to Erik before he stepped aside and gestured to the prize held tightly by two of his warriors. A prize more valuable than all the gold and riches in Vay'kis.

"Jormund Scaeva," Ulfric said, as his warriors tossed the man to the ground.

Erik looked down at his foe. The brother of Earl Arndyr. The great warrior who had once been of the Arkin Garter, private guard to the emperor, now knelt before him.

"You stole my honour," Jormund growled as he stared up at his captor. "Stole my chance of death in battle."

"You talk about honour?" Erik hissed, shaking his head. "*You?*"

"Why did you spare me?"

"Because I want the truth," the bloodsworn strode toward him as he snarled. "What has been spoken of, Jormund? What has been agreed?"

"*Nothing* has been agreed," the prisoner shot back.

Erik stood before Jormund and bared his teeth. "Then tell me why my sister is dead."

"I don't know."

"You actually expect me to believe that?" the bloodsworn scoffed. "Your brother killed Astrid with his own hand. *Your* brother.

And now you tell me that what? He acted alone?"

Jormund was silent.

"Speak," Torben snarled.

"He will tell us what he knows," Nenrir said. "We can *make* him."

Erik crouched before Jormund. "I suggest that you speak," he said. "The people loved their Jarl. She was the best among us. A captain who would have led us to the edge of the world. Those who stand with me were her crew; her scâldir. Hold your tongue if you wish yet do not believe that there is one man or woman here who would not *gladly* tear it out."

Jormund did not look away from Erik, and he did not let his glare waver.

"If Arndyr planned to take her life then he did not inform me," Jormund said. "None of us here knew of his intent. When he left our shores, we did not expect him to return for many months. Right now, he should have been sailing south with Astrid."

Erik frowned. "Before he took his own life, Arndyr spoke of Aureia. *For the empire.* That is what he said. What meaning did he have?"

Jormund shook his head as he replied, "I do not know of what you speak, yet my brother's tongue has always been his own."

"Evidently it belongs to your empire," Laerke Redleaf spat.

"No," Jormund countered and turned his glare toward the man. "You're wrong."

Mayrun rolled her eyes and stepped before the prisoner. "Wrong about what exactly?" she said. "He spoke the words. We *all* heard them."

"I say we kill him," Fargrim said and spat at Jormund's feet. "Send this liar to join his traitor brother."

"I am no liar," the prisoner growled.

"Your brother murders one of the greatest captains that the Isles have ever known under the order of a crown that *you* once served, and yet you knew nothing?" Torben hissed.

Jormund lifted his eyes to the older warrior. "Yes," he said.

Erik snorted and turned from his kneeling enemy. "I do not believe you," he said.

Torben approached Jormund from behind and placed a hand upon the captive's shoulder.

He glanced at Erik. "Jarl?" Torben called.

Erik nodded.

Without a word, the old warrior slammed Jormund into the ground. There was a crack as the prisoner's nose shattered against the wooden floor. Blood splashed across the floor. Torben heaved him back to his knees.

"Tell me why my sister is dead," Erik's hands balled into fists.

Jormund bared his bloody teeth and glared back without reply.

"WHY!" Erik roared.

"I had nothing to do with her death!" Jormund shouted. "I only know that days before my brother set sail, he received a letter marked with the sun and moon. Arndyr burned it and did not tell me of its contents. He only said that things were about to change. I thought he meant the war and did not question him."

Erik crossed his powerful arms and met Torben's eye.

"The sun and moon? That can only mean one thing."

"A holy order," Torben nodded as he replied.

"So your peace-loving cardinal commanded her death," Erik hissed at Jormund. "What did he promise your family in return for sundering my own? What was the price? When our line is gone, you will add Agartha to your empire?"

"An empire that poisons all with lies and treachery," Mayrun said angrily. "Arndyr ate our food and drank our ale. He stood beside us. Stood beside Astrid. More than that even, and yet you say he killed her for empty words and the promise of land. Did he have no loyalty? Do you?"

"Do not act so mighty. Everybody has their price. Even you,"

Jormund told her. He gestured toward Erik, "Even him."

Erik stood over Jormund and took hold of the kneeling man's hair. He tipped his head back so that he could gaze into Jormund's eyes. "No. I would *never* betray by family, never betray my people," Erik growled. "Death before dishonour. That is my way. I reward loyalty with loyalty. I reward disloyalty with justice."

Erik released the man's hair and stepped away as he turned his back. He looked to the throne of Vay'kis.

"Justice?" Jormund spat to the side. "And what justice would that be?"

Erik's hand fell to his sword. "You have told us no lie, and for that I thank you. Yet what happened in Agartha cannot go unpunished, and with his own hand Arndyr stole our vengeance."

Erik drew his weapon. The light of the fire danced along the steel of the blade, kissed its surface, and brought it to life. Erik looked at the throne. It was no more than an ornate wooden chair. A symbol of power to some, yet not to him. Power was gained through the respect of those whom you lead. You were not born with it. He would rather stand beside his people in the shield wall, in an unwinnable battle, and fall, than sit idly by on a throne and live.

"If I am to die, give me a sword," Jormund Scaeva called to him. "I am Valkir. Do not deny me this, Erik. Do not deny me Ra'Haven."

"You were gone from your people for too long, Jormund," Erik told him darkly. "You have forgotten what it means to be Valkir, forgotten what it means to have honour. You are no more Valkir than the cardinal."

His grip tightened on the hilt of the sword. The wooden floor creaked under the weight of his boots as he walked toward Jormund. His people were silent, yet words were spoken in their eyes. Erik did not look away from Jormund. He did not tear his gaze from the empire's puppet. Once again, the Isles would be ruled by the Valkir. Not these pretenders.

He raised his sword.

Jormund looked up without fear. Erik felt the anger call to him. It was begging to be unleashed. He took a breath and then let it *flow*. Everything that he felt, everything that warred within the warrior, was let free. The pain of losing his sister. The last of his family. He would never again hear words from her lips, see the spark in her eyes, nor feel the warmth of her embrace. With the sorrow came pure rage. She had been slaughtered without cause, without reason. Erik brought the sword down and painted the floor with Jormund's blood.

Hours passed, yet Jormund Scaeva's words lived on in Erik's mind. He stared into the fire and watched as the flames flickered and danced. Erik had cleaned the blood from his face, his clothes, and weapons. He stood in the hall. What would Astrid do now? He had killed Scaeva and taken Vay'kis, yet in doing so Erik may have divided the Isles. He had been given a choice, and he had made it. Now he would live with it.

"Jarl Erik."

The bloodsworn tore his gaze from the fire as the voice broke his peace. He saw the grey-haired jarl approaching.

"Ulfric," Erik greeted him.

"It has been hours since we took this hall," the older man told him. "What comes next? What does your heart tell you?"

"What comes next?" Erik frowned. "That is not for me to decide."

Ulfric pursed his lips. "Is it not? The men... they look to you now."

"Ulfric, I am *no* earl or leader," Erik replied. "I am *bloodsworn*. Forbidden from carrying any such title."

"And yet it is you they have chosen," the man shrugged.

"I only ever wanted to avenge my sister," Erik told him. "I came here for justice, and yet I have only found more questions. I am a *warrior*, Ulfric, and yet you wish to place a crown upon my head. I do *not* want it."

"Your words are your own but mirror those spoken by your sister," Jarl Ulfric met his companion's eye as he spoke. "There was not a warrior who sailed with us who would not have followed her."

"I know," Erik said quietly.

"Nor anyone from home who would not have stood by her side."

"I know."

"The people chose Astrid as their leader. A woman who was both jarl and hero," Ulfric told him. "And yet it was not a famous captain that they followed to Vay'kis."

Erik's brow furrowed. "The people wanted justice," Erik said. "They came here to avenge their jarl."

"Any man could have led them here in their quest for vengeance," the jarl gestured toward the entrance of the hall. "Hundreds stand outside those very doors. It was *you* that they flocked to. *You* that they put their hopes into."

"I am no earl or great leader," Erik snapped back. "I am bloodsworn. I am a warrior. Ulfric, I am not *her*. I am not Astrid."

"No, you are not," Ulfric replied. "But perhaps that is what we need right now."

The bloodsworn's frown deepened. "You're speaking in riddles."

"In every man's life there comes a time when he must choose between who he is and who he wants to be. This choice is upon you now. Just as it once was for Astrid. You started this fire, Erik, and once started, whichever way it burns, be it good or bad, that is your doing."

Erik looked back to the fire. His hand rose in search of the raven head amulet at his throat. He ran his weathered fingers across the carved surface. For years it had been in his family. His mother had carved the raven and given it life. When she died it had passed to Lief and then in turn to Astrid. He could feel the strength of the Farrin clan within the wood. A strength that gave him hope.

"Your will, my strength," he whispered.

They were words that he had often shared with Astrid. Words that he would never again be able to say to her.

"What was that?" Ulfric asked.

"Remember why," Erik told him. "Those were Astrid's last words."

"What did she mean?"

"For a long time, I asked myself the very same question, yet now I think my heart has told me their truth," the bloodsworn said. "Ready the men. Ready ship and boat. There are messages to be sent, Ulfric."

Ulfric pursed his wizened lips, "Messages? To whom?"

"We must call *every* jarl and *every* earl. From Mikon to faraway Nesoi. They must all gather. Right here. Right in this city that we have taken."

"And what makes you believe that they will come? What words can you conjure to draw them from hearth and hall?"

Erik folded his arms and did not turn from the fire. "You ask me how to summon them here? You do it with the truth. Tell them that the greatest navigator in the history of our people is dead. Tell them that she was murdered. Tell them that I took Vay'kis in payment of this debt. But more importantly tell them that I have a grand tale to tell."

Erik watched from the cliff tops as ships and boats entered the Lupentine. Twenty-one vessels were launched. They were bound for each of the Valkir Isles. One by one they would gather, and then the jarls and earls of his people would hear his words. Erik could only pray that his tale, his song, would reach into the heart of every man and woman that came. He wished that he could still the rapid beating in his heart. He wished that he could calm himself and be nothing but composed, just as Astrid had always been.

"Erik?" a woman's voice called out.

The warrior glanced over his shoulder to see Mayrun walking

toward him. He gave her a short nod before he looked back toward the bay.

"The message has been sent," Erik said. "Who answers its call, who arrives upon these shores... I do not know."

"They will come," Mayrun told Erik, standing to his side. "All of them."

"We will see."

The woman turned to him, and her eyes softened. "How are you?"

Erik waved a hand absently. "I'm alright."

Mayrun reached out a hand and touch his arm gently. "Astrid is watching you, Erik. She will *always* be with you."

Erik brushed his fingers against the raven head amulet as he replied, "I know."

Mayrun turned her gaze toward the sea. "What you are feeling now, I understand it," Mayrun said. "All of the rage, all of the sorrow... nothing can compare. When Raol was killed, a part of myself died with him. In dark moments I wanted to die. Astrid gave me strength when I had none. She told me to embrace the present and live each day as it comes. That is something that she would want for you now. Astrid stood by me in my darkest days when the sun had set. Now I will stand by your side."

"Words of comfort," Erik told her sincerely. "Raol, Astrid, Hélla, my father, countless others. All were taken by the greed of others. An earl, a cardinal, an empire. Greed comes in many forms. We cannot change the past, cannot go back and save everyone that we have lost. But what we can do is make sure that no more of our people have to suffer the same fate."

"You speak of war, a war that I will gladly follow you into," Mayrun begun. "But with whom? The war with Magnus is over. The war with Scaeva is won."

"I do not think it was ever over," Erik replied. "If you cut the head off one tyrant, another grows in its place. Magnus weakened

Agartha and Arndyr sought to claim it. As foolish as it may seem, my heart tells me that both of them were connected. I do not know how, yet I feel it. This war has only just begun."

"And so now you wish to unite our people? Is that the purpose of summoning all our leaders?"

"Aye. Astrid was right," Erik told her. "There has been too much bloodshed of late. Our people fight among themselves and bicker. We murder and deceive each other. There is another way, another path. Astrid's eyes were open to it, Mayrun. The Valkir must build bridges if we are to survive. Yet for that I see only one course for our people to charter. A course that my sister would have *hated*. Yet not to pursue it, I believe, would be an insult to her memory."

"And this plan of yours, this road you wish to take has two paths," Mayrun murmured softly. "One would have led to no conflict yet would dishonour Astrid. The other quite the opposite. And this choice has torn you."

"A choice had to be made, and I have made it," Erik told her. "When I close my eyes, I see her ghost. When I open them, all I see is fire."

FORTY-NINE

City of Elara, the League of Trecento

Tariq led them across the bridge and back into the Pits. They found refuge in his home. Cleander had stayed behind to lead the soldiers that pursued them away. Without her aunt and uncle, without hope of bringing the magister to justice, Elise broke.

She left Tariq and Marshall alone in the house while she made her way into the alley behind it. Tears fell from her red rimmed eyes as she cast her cloak and mask aside. Two years ago she had been happy. She had barely been nineteen summers. Her fist smashed into the side of a clay walled building. The drive she had once felt had dissipated like smoke. It had been all that had kept her going, all that had kept her from falling into darkness. Her fist smashed into clay. It chipped and splintered and cut her hands. She could see her mother dying in that cold bed. She could see her father's mangled corpse in that mud filled alley.

She punched again and again as her tears fell. Elise could hear the whispers of disgust and contempt wash over her from those she had been sent to live among. She had been alone among enemies. The exhaustion of so many sleepless nights crashed down upon her. The pain of her wounds. Tears of blood fell from her fingers. Cirillo. Casimir Dusan. Her only allies had died because of her. Halina had died because of her. Her aunt and uncle had died because of her.

Elise screamed as she drove her fist into the wall. Her knuckles were coated in blood. She fell against the wall as what little remained of her heart shattered. Sobs shook her body as she cried. Her tormented scream echoed down the alley.

"Elise," Tariq called her name as he saw her.

Elise did not look toward him. She could barely see anything beyond the wall of tears. She was colder than she had ever been before. The world was darker than it had ever been before. Tariq reached her. He made to hug her, to pull her into his embrace. Elise shouted and shoved him away. She lashed out. Her bloodied fist caught his jaw. All she saw was black. She fell to her knees as her world fell apart around her. It took her a long time for her to realise that Tariq knelt before her. She'd hit him. She'd hit her friend.

"I'm sorry," Elise choked as she looked up at him. "I'm sorry."

"It's alright," he told her softly.

Elise shook. She glanced at the knuckles of her hands. Her skin was torn. Blood trailed down her fingers and dropped into the mud.

"My whole life, I grew up looking across the river believing that I was less than them," Elise managed. "Now I know that I am."

"That isn't true," Tariq told her.

"Isn't it?" Elise replied as a tear slid down her cheek. She watched it fall into the dirt. She trailed her fingers through the mud and scooped up a handful. "They killed my parents like they were *nothing*, because to them they *were* nothing," Elise said as she watched the mud drip from her hand. "Nothing but dirt. I was forced to live among them. I lived with my family, but I was alone. The others around me... even though we walked the same streets, ate the same food, and drank the same drink, I was never their equal. It was there. The look. I saw it in their faces every day. The disgust. Pit rat, mud dweller, dirt from across the river. They never hid the looks they gave me. They never hid the words that they spoke to my face. As much as it clawed at me. As much as it tore at me. I ignored it because I knew that one day I would bring those who murdered my parents to justice. That was how I survived. No matter the wounds I suffered. No matter the indignities. No matter the exhaustion."

The last of the mud slipped between her fingers. Her face ached from crying.

"After so long, I had almost given up hope right up until I met Cirillo Eris and uncovered the magister's plot. At last I had a name. Imrohir. I thought perhaps that I could make sense of it all, make sense of the world. That I could bring justice to the man who had taken my family from me. But that was a dream. A dream that Imrohir washed away like mud. Those who tried to help died because of me. Halina died because of me. My aunt and uncle… the *last* of my family died because of me. And now I know. The magister was right. The Riversiders were right."

Elise stared down into the dirt. Her hair had slipped from its braids and hung wild. Her will to fight was gone along with her heart. Nothing remained. She was empty.

"I am the dirt beneath their feet," she admitted quietly. "I am less than them."

"Don't you ever say that," Tariq told her fiercely. He extended a gentle hand and brushed a tear from her cheek. Elise felt nothing as Tariq wrapped his arms around her.

The day wore on and Elise sat in silence. She had barely uttered a word since returning to the Pits. Her hands had been washed and wrapped. Her kukri and knives lay on the table before her alongside her mask.

The room in Tariq's house was silent as the grave. No words were spoken between the three, for they all felt a deep grief at the loss of the Delfeyre family. Marshall, the captain and lone survivor of the house guard, ran a whetstone down the length of his already razor-edged sword. He had been with the family for over two decades, since before Elise had even been born, and he had failed them. Tariq watched the closed door with wary eyes.

He did not trust the gangs any more than he trusted the magister's soldiers. Elise was glad that her friend did not look to her. She would see only the pity in his eyes.

The door opened.

Tariq rose to his feet and his hands curled into powerful fists. Marshall flicked his gaze up toward the man who entered, and his grip tightened on the hilt of his blade.

It was Cleander.

Elise said nothing. He had saved her at the hanging and then again at her family's house, yet none of them trusted him. She did not even look up as he entered. The man glanced from Tariq, to Marshall, and then back to her.

"I led the soldiers away," Cleander told them before he crossed the room toward Elise.

He knelt on a single knee before her and tried to meet her eyes. "I am so sorry," Cleander murmured.

His words were sincere. Elise barely had the strength to look into his gaze. She felt numb, as if she was merely watching another act as Elise Delfeyre.

"What do you want, Cleander?" Marshall asked the man.

Cleander turned to reply.

"You're *sorry*?" Elise snarled, baring her teeth as rage consumed her. "My aunt and uncle are dead. They're dead! Their blood is on my hands and it will *never* wash off."

"No," Cleander told her. "You did not do this. It was Imrohir and his schemes."

Elise rose to her feet and turned away. Cleander made to move to Elise's side, to offer some form of comfort, but Tariq stepped between them. He gestured to Marshall who watched with wary eyes.

"The man asked you a question," Tariq said. "What is it that you seek here, for if it is pain… look around you."

"Straight to it then," Cleander said as he stared at the Berenithian.

"We plan to take this city from Imrohir."

"Madness," Marshall scoffed.

"No," the Annoran shook his head. "The whole city rises against Imrohir. It will be tonight that we cross the bridge. It will be tonight that every man and every woman this side of the river takes up arms, and they will not be alone. We have allies from the south who will gladly aid us in deposing the tyrant. We have the steel, and we have the warriors to wield it."

Elise barely heard Cleander's words. Her mind was filled with noise. It was so loud and its pitch so high that she could almost taste it.

"What we do not have is a way to prevent the alarm from being raised," Cleander finished.

"You speak of the belltower," Elise said as his final words broke through the noise. "What is that to us?"

Cleander looked to her as he replied, "We can get to the tower, yet we are without the means of disabling its song before it sounds. The soldiers who guard it are too strong and too many to be so easily overcome. We need someone who could slip in, disable the bell, and vanish into the night absent discovery. Only you can do this."

Elise stared at him. "Do you not understand? I have lost *everything*," her voice cracked. "I am not the person that you think that I am! The Nightingale was never real. It was a dream. I am done fighting. I am done."

"Imrohir took that choice from you long ago," Cleander countered. "Do not fool yourself into thinking that you can walk away now."

"She has lost *enough*," Tariq growled. "She has lost her entire family and now you want what? For her to give more when she has no more to give?"

Marshall adjusted his grip upon his sword. "The lady gave you answer," he told Cleander. "I suggest you leave."

"How many more must die for the city? How many must fall for the magister and his greed? In one move we could change all of that," Cleander said. "You may not be–"

"Do you know where the name 'Del' comes from?" Elise cut in darkly. "Do you know why my family is called Delfeyre? For that was not always our name. Once it was Dhara. My ancestors came from a small town in Aureia called Feyre. For generations we had a different name, a different home. When the Delions came and took our lands it was my ancestor who first rose against them. Bastian Dhara, Lord of Feyre, rose to meet the Delions. It was he who *killed* Alekos Gaedhela, eldest son of the great Nykalous, and liberated his people. In old Aureian the word 'del' means 'great one.' A title only given to those who have done a great deed. Once granted, the name of the town or city is taken along with it. The house of Dhara was no more. On that day, we became Delfeyre," Elise pulled a cloak around her shoulders and turned away from Cleander as she spoke. "My family have been liberators for hundreds of years. It is in my blood so do not tell me what will happen when I refuse you. I am *leaving*, Cleander. Never to return to this cursed city."

The Annoran nodded slowly and knew that he could not change her mind.

"Where will you go?" he asked.

"Where I belong."

They had been on the road for hours when they stopped for respite. They were not the only ones. A small caravan of two small carts and dozens of people dressed in rags had set up by the edge of the road. Men and women, children and old folk alike watched as the three newcomers dismounted opposite them. They came from the Pits and the other lower districts. Elise could see the fear in their eyes. The hunger.

"Who are these people?" Marshall asked.

"Refugees," Tariq replied sadly. "They will have been displaced by the war in Elara. More likely the magister's greed cost them their homes and livelihoods."

Elise could see the despair in their faces. One of the older men approached. His skin was lined and wrinkled while his hair was the colour of fresh snow. He reached out with his gnarled fingers toward Elise. He took hold of her cloak, as she took a startled step backward.

"Begging your pardon, lady–"

Steel rasped as Marshall half drew his sword.

"Easy there," the captain said.

"It's alright, Marshall," Elise replied and met the old man's tired gaze. "Can I help you?"

"Water," he murmured. "Could you spare a drop of water?"

She gave him her flask,

"Thank you," he told her and gave a weak smile before he took a long draught from the skin.

"What happened to you?" Elise asked.

The smile faded and suddenly the man's face was a mask of pain. "I had little enough before the magister seized all the houses by the river. Said I owed him taxes. I am a working man, always gave what was due but my house was mine. I earned it with blood, paid in full. He took everything that I had worked for, everything that I owned... and the magister," the man gestured to his travelling companions, "he took all they have too! We tried to stop him... but my son, he's dead. He's dead."

The old man dropped to his knees, as if he no longer had the strength to stand. Elise was not expecting the tears that poured from his eyes and rolled down his pale cheeks. She was not expecting to be holding a man old enough to be her grandfather.

"It's alright," Elise told him softly. "Everything is going to be alright."

Her eyes swept from the elder to the rest of the refugees. They were half starved, their eyes sunken and devoid of hope. They had no food, no coin, no home. They had nothing. She saw a girl, no more than sixteen or seventeen sitting against the wheel of a cart, her knees pull up to her chest as she wept. Perhaps she had lost a mother or father. Perhaps she was alone now. The girl met Elise's eyes. The memories came back.

When her parents had been killed, before Tariq had found her and brought her to Raphael's house, it had been her sitting on the steps to her family's house staring into the street hopelessly. None stopped to ask if she was alright. None had done *anything* until Tariq had appeared out of the darkness. Elise looked from the girl to Tariq and Marshall. The last friends that she had left. Together they had planned to ride to Tallis, and from there return to the empire. They had talked of travelling to Feyre and starting a new life there. In the wagon was a chest filled with gold and jewels. The sum of the Nightingale's work.

But what was the Nightingale? A thief who ran when it became too much? A thief who fought against the magister yet turned its back upon the people?

Elise turned back down the road, gazing to the south toward Elara. It was as if her body moved without command. She gathered up the reins of her horse before anyone had noticed and swung herself into her saddle. Tariq saw her first as she dug her heels in.

"ELISE!" he cried her name.

It was too late. She thundered back toward Elara.

The sun had started to slip beyond the horizon when they left the inn. They wore chainmail under their cloaks and kept their hands close to their swords. Crestless helms sat atop their heads, while shields were slung across their backs. Kyler and Alarik were ready to meet whatever awaited them. The Red Rose, that had been the name of the inn that

Mellisanthi had given them the name of the place wherein they would meet their foe. The knights wound their way through the streets, careful to keep to the shadows. They had enough to worry about without attracting the attention of city guards.

All too soon they made it to the inn. All too soon they were standing outside its large wooden door. Kyler shared a glance with Alarik. Here they were at the end of the line. What lay beyond the door, what face would greet them, they did not know. Would it be death that met them? The battlemaster pounded his fist upon the door. Kyler gripped the hilt of his sword tight.

The door opened.

The Medean made ready to fight. A man's face greeted then.

"Can I help you, sirs?"

Kyler let his hand relax.

"Apologies for the intrusion, my friend," Alarik said. "But we are to meet with Cleander in your establishment. The Lady Mellisanthi sent us."

"Ah yes, right you are, sir," he stepped back and gestured for them to enter. "Right this way."

They followed him into the empty inn, and then down into the basement. Kyler kept his head on a swivel, taking in everything. Every shadow could be hiding a knifeman. Every bench could conceal a killer lying in wait. The innkeeper led them to a tapestry that hung across a wall and pulled it back to reveal a locked door. He pulled the bolt and drew it open. A long, stone corridor stretched out before them.

"He awaits you down there," the innkeeper told them, pointing down into the dark.

Kyler wrinkled his nose as he caught a whiff of the stench that came from the tunnels. "You have led us to the sewers," he said.

"I did as I was asked," the man replied with a shrug.

"The tunnels provide a quick way to navigate the city," Alarik muttered. "Quite remarkable really."

The battlemaster took a torch from where it hung by the door and swiftly lit it with his flint stone. He handed the torch to Kyler, before using it to light a second one for himself. Alarik gave the innkeeper a nod before walking into the tunnel.

They had not made it ten paces before they heard the door shut behind them and the bolt driven home. Kyler looked back toward the inn and his skin crawled.

"We now have but one path," the battlemaster said. "We face whatever trap they have prepared for us."

"Words of comfort." Kyler rolled his eyes as he pushed passed his mentor and began to make his way deeper into the bowels of Elara. Without the sun or moon to guide them they lost track of time. They could have been walking the labyrinth of tunnels for moments or hours and would not know.

Was it midnight yet, or was it nearly dawn? Every sound that echoed through the stone maze, every splash and ripple that broke the still waters in the stream chilled Kyler to his core. He had known blood and battle, yet never anything like this. His eyes stayed alert, just as his hand stayed by his sword. They came to a large chamber where four tunnels met.

Kyker looked from left to right. "Now what?" he muttered.

Alarik ran his eyes across the ground as if looking for some kind of clue. "There has to be something."

"We did not come this far to be beaten by a maze," Kyler grimaced. He could see nothing. No clues or etchings upon the stone. No arrows directing them.

Footsteps.

Kyler spun around. The faint orange glow of a torch shone from the tunnel that they had come from. He half drew his blade. His eyes narrowed as the light came closer and closer. He made out the dark clothing and hood first. Alarik stood to his side, turned his sweeping gaze all around them, searching down the other dark paths. Nothing. The figure reached the entrance to the chamber.

Kyler felt his heart almost stop. His breath caught.

"Maija?" Alarik said as confusion distorted his voice.

"I was," the woman replied. She held her torch out with one hand and with the other pulled back her hood. It was Elena.

"*You!*" Alarik hissed. He took a furious step toward her, "I should have guessed you would be involved in this, demon."

"I *followed* you," Elena replied. She held her hands out to her sides, showing that she meant no harm, "No more than that."

"You lie!" Alarik snarled.

"No!" Kyler leapt between them. He stared at his mentor, "Alarik, she had *no* part in this."

The battlemaster released his sword and shoved Kyler hard. "You take her side. The side of a monster? Did you ever truly believe in the Order or were you a demon loving traitor the whole time?"

Still Kyler stayed between them. "You know that I would do anything for my faith, *you know it!* But I will not stand aside."

Alarik gave a mirthless chuckle. "So now we see the heart of it. It is not the Order for which you fight, it's for her."

"You know that is not true," Kyler countered and moved to counter Alarik as he tried to pass.

"I came here to help you," Elena cried. "You do not know what lies around the next corner. You know nothing of the gangs or their ways."

"And you do?" the battlemaster scoffed. Again, Alarik tried to shove passed Kyler, and again the Medean moved to intercept him.

Kyler squared his jaw as he saw fury contort his friend's face. "I try to do what is right," he said. "For my Order and for my gods."

"Then stand aside!"

"No."

"Stand aside!" Alarik spat. "We fight for the gods just as we are judged by the gods. You know what her people did, what they still do, and yet there you stand."

"Yet here I stand," Kyler growled. "Please, brother. Stop this.

Do not make me choose between you. Do not."

Alarik grabbed his pupil's shoulder.

"Kyler, I... Kyler!"

The Medean saw Alarik's eyes widen even as the battlemaster leapt backward. The Aureian stared over his shoulder, yet this time his hateful gaze was not directed at Elena. Kyler spun around. The light from burning torches lit the corridor behind. It lit *all* the tunnels. They were surrounded.

"We will deal with this later," Alarik growled as the soldier in him took over. "Now, as one."

The knights and the maija cast their torches down upon the floor of the chamber. Kyler followed his mentor's lead and strapped his shield to his arm and slid his sword free of its sheath. The running footfalls grew louder as the shadowy figures closed in.

Kyler pulled his knife free and handed it to Elena. He met her eyes and his gaze said it all. All that she needed to know, all that she already knew. The words went unspoken.

"Back to back," Alarik roared as he lowered into a fighting crouch.

Kyler followed his mentor's lead. He raised his shield and rested the blade of his sword atop its steel rim.

The gangmen swarmed into the chamber. Torches were tossed aside, while club, axe, spear, and sword were taken up. They stared at the knights with malicious intent. Kyler shifted his gaze from man to man. There would have been nearly twenty of them. The Medean sent a wordless prayer to the heavens. They had the armour and the training. Better yet, they had the gods on their side. Durandail and Azaria would see them free from this hole.

Or so he hoped.

A man armed with sword and shield pushed his way through the throng and stared at the three companions. He saw Kyler, and his lips curled upward. His *scarred* lip curled. It was the man from Odrysia. The man who had shot Hugh Karter. The man who had murdered his parents.

"I thought I smelt a baby knight," Scar Lip grinned savagely. "My prayers have been answered and now at last you stand before me."

It took all of Kyler's strength to not break ranks and charge the man who goaded him. All of his rage, all of his anger, it consumed him.

"You *killed* my family."

"And how they *screamed*," came the reply.

"Only a coward kills the innocent," the Medean snarled.

"Revenge is not cowardly," the man with the scarred lip said. "Do you deny killing my brother in Odrysia?"

Kyler adjusted his grip on his sword. "I killed only those who tried to kill me," he said. "Do not try to compare your deed to my own. Your brother was armed. My parents *innocent*."

"None of us are innocent, Kyler Landrey," the gang man muttered.

"You there," Alarik called out. "We have not properly been introduced."

Scar Lip glanced at the older knight as he replied, "My name is Olivera."

"Olivera," Kyler repeated, letting the name flow from his tongue. "You will die today."

"A touching thing to say with my sword at your throat," the man smirked back.

Kyler met his enemy's eye, "The wolf is born knowing that it is the predator, while the sheep knows that it is the prey. I know what I am, do you?"

"Such arrogance, boy," Olivera told him. "It will destroy you. Kill them."

FIFTY

City of Vesuva, Aureian Empire

Kitara stared through the steel bars of the tall gate and her gaze ran across the rough sands of the arena. She wore an embellished cuirass of gold over a gilded red, thigh-length tunic. A double layered battle kilt of leather hung from her hips, while bracers and greaves to match her cuirass were strapped to her arms and legs atop scarlet wraps. A thick ruby sash was wrapped around her waist with its end falling to her knee. A knife adorned the belt tightly bound over the sash, while her sword was held in her grasp.

To her side stood Yeomra, dressed to match in red and gold. A spear was held in his right hand, while a shield was buckled to his left. The colours that they wore united them in a single purpose; victory. Where before Kitara had fought alone on the sands, this time she stood shoulder to shoulder with an ally.

"I heard about what you did," Yeomra said without so much as looking at her.

"I am *not* a whore," Kitara replied with a growl.

"No, you are not," the champion told her. "Alessandra, despite your victories upon the sands, despite your glory and how they chant your name, you are a *slave*. The Nilor family are proud, and you made Arias bleed. He will not forget that. He will not forgive that."

In her heart she knew it to be true. What awaited her after the games, she dreaded to guess.

Lashings? Beatings? Worse? Only Arias Nilor knew.

Kitara smirked. "If I die today then it does not matter."

Yeomra turned on her. He pointed to the sands. "If you go out there seeking death then you will find it. If you become a hindrance to my victory and put my life in the balance, then I will kill you myself."

"Emotion without focus makes the eager man fall," Kitara told him as she echoed the words of her mentor Calvillo, as they had been spoken a decade before. "I am *not* going to die today. Look to yourself Yeomra."

"If we are to fight as one, then we must have a single purpose."

Kitara returned the glare that burned in Yemora's eyes. "My purpose is what it has always been," she said. "Victory will come with what I am about to do."

A great cheer came from the arena.

The steel doors groaned open.

Kitara's green eyes danced around the sands of the arena. Seven other pairs entered one by one, each dressed in a different colour yet each with the same goal. Victory. They were tall and strong, while their armour glistened under the sun. The steel of sword, axe, and spear shone as the light kissed it.

Yeomra raised his arms as the roar of the crowd rained down upon them. Kitara beat her sword on her chest and thrust it high. She took a breath and slowed her racing heart. Fire burned through her veins, yet all the emotion died within. It was a lesson that she had been taught long ago. When you fight with emotion you make mistakes. If you made a single mistake in battle, the cost would be high. Yeomra paced back and forth as his hand tightened upon the shaft of his spear. Kitara stood as still as stone. Watching. Waiting.

Her breathing was steady. Her muscles relaxed. The signal came with the blaring of a horn. It blasted from the stands down into the square arena. A great roar, screamed by hundreds, fell upon the fighters from above. Kitara barely heard the sound.

Her feet slid across the sand as the first pair moved to face them. Yeomra engaged the first With a war cry upon his lips as his spear darted forward. The swordsman came at Kitara, his two-handed blade ready to create a dance of death. Kitara was not there to dance. She was there to sing a song. She was there to sing the swordsong.

She sent her sword toward his eyes with a deadly lunge. The fighter parried as he skipped to the side, before he drove his weapon toward her. Steel kissed steel. Kitara slid to the left and cut off her opponent's movement. The fighter's sword created a deadly whirlwind as he attacked. Kitara blocked again and again as she gauged his speed. She deflected the third strike, feinted left, and then went right. He danced back, moved to block the blow that never came. Only his speed saved his life. Instead of ripping into his throat, Kitara's sword slid across the hard steel of his pauldron. She ducked his counter, came up inside his strength, and sliced her sword up the inside of his arm. Blood flowed from the wound as they fought.

Kitara's song grew louder.

She parried a blow and skipped to the right as their blades met. Instead of sliding away, she countered and sent a one-armed thrust over the top of her opponent's sword. Her steel bracer caught his blade, while her sword skewered his throat. He fell back as the wound opened. Kitara pushed his sword arm to the side as he froze before she flicked her blade up and sent a two-handed blow toward his neck. Blood-stained steel as the sword cut through his throat. He toppled over. His weapon fell from his nerveless fingers. Kitara held her poise as she turned. Her feet slid through the sand.

Her eyes darted toward Yeomra just in time to see the champion thrust his spear through the chest of his half-armoured opponent. It was a precise blow and the lance drove home into the man's heart. Yeomra kicked the man to the ground as he ripped his spear free. They had no time for celebration. No time for pause. Another pair came at them. Their eyes filled with dark intent. A fighter armed with a small shield and war hammer angled to face Kitara.

The hammer came toward her.

Kitara deflected the blow and countered, only to find his shield waiting. The hammer came back around. Its wicked spike drove toward her head. She ducked, slid forward, and lunged. Again, her attack found only the shield. They circled. Kitara kept her sword up and levelled. The other man whirled his hammer and then leapt toward her. His hammer came first. Kitara stepped back and narrowly avoided the blow. The man continued his assault. He lashed out with his shield. Kitara sent her sword over its rim, yet the man shifted his position and brought his shield up. It sent her blade skyward away from his face. They entered a dance of steel. Where a sword could slice flesh and leave nothing but a scar, a war hammer could easily break the bone beneath. They exchanged a deadly flurry as their feet constantly moved atop the sands. The hammer came around. Kitara stepped forward and brought her arm down. Her movement was precise.

The head of the hammer missed while her cuirass took the shaft. It hurt yet Kitara was true to her purpose. She wrapped her left arm around the weapon before her opponent could react and lashed out with a pommel strike. She spun as the blow connected with his helm, pirouetted, and tore the hammer from his grasp. It flew through the air and crashed down into the sand. Her sword sliced through the flesh of his eyebrow as he leapt backward. Blood erupted from the shallow wound. Kitara skipped to the side, as the man's companion drove his blade toward her. She blocked the blow, countered, and then the wounded man charged. He barrelled at her with a great roar. His arms wrapped around her waist as he stole her footing.

They hit the ground.

Pain lanced through Kitara's head. She grimaced and fought hard as her opponent forced his weight down upon her. His wound leaked down like a bloody waterfall. She could taste the crimson liquid as it splashed across her face. She could feel the warm stench of his breath upon her cheek. He raised his shield, and then brought it down hard. Kitara barely got her arms up in time to shop it shattering her face. Her forearms screamed despite the bracers. She grabbed the shield's rim and kept it tightly wedged to her chest. He stared down at her with hate-filled eyes, as his blood painted her armour and skin.

His blood was all she could feel, all she could smell, all she could taste. She reached out with her spare arm, as her fingers searched across the sands. He tore his shield free, gripped it with both hands and angled the sharp rim at her head. She raised an arm to shield her face. Her fingers found pommel and latched around it.

His body tensed as he made to bring it down. Kitara roared and brought her sword up. It sliced through the side of his neck. The man gurgled and the shield fell as he reached for his throat.

Kitara heaved and drove up with her hips as she pushed him to the side. Her sword came free. She rolled away, leapt to her feet, and brought her blade to bear.

He was already dead.

Kitara sucked in a lungful of air but all she tasted was blood. His blood. She wore it as a mask. Yeomra gave her a nod as they regrouped. One final pair remained. One final fight.

The crowed went into a frenzy. Their screams rolling down like a storm. Instead of sword, spear, or hammer, Kitara found herself standing opposite a man wielding a vicious two-handed axe.

She crossed the distance between them in half-a-dozen steps. The axe looped through the air. It cut through the wind and sliced toward her chest. Kitara danced to the side and countered but he was fast. Her sword met the shaft of his weapon. He did not pause and instead flicked his wrists to send the steel head of the axe toward her neck. Kitara leapt back, the blow missing by a hair's breadth. She circled him. Her eyes did not move away from his own. She tried to read them. He feinted. Kitara did not react.

Her breathing was steady. Her poise light.

He darted forward, and the axe came down. Kitara skipped to the side, but he followed as he changed his grip upon the shaft of the weapon. His right hand slid upward and gripped the axe behind the head, as he lashed out again and the weapon drove toward her side. Kitara's feet slid upon the sand as she brought her sword around. She grabbed the blade of her weapon with her left hand and caught his blow halfway down her sword. The weapons met. He was far stronger, yet her poise was *perfect*. The sword stopped the axe as her steel met with its shaft and kept it from carving into her ribs. Kitara heaved her arms to the side and then wrenched them up to free sword from axe. The tip of her sword flew up and slid along the side of the man's helmet.

The man fell back. Kitara skipped to the side as and his companion angled a sword toward her. She ducked beneath the blow as she deflected steel.

Yeomra leapt past her and engaged the axe wielding warrior. The swordsman lunged with his steel and barely missed as Kitara stepped back. He parried her lunge and replied in kind. She took her sword by the blade and blocked once, twice. Each time her arms rang ever more. Kitara leaned back as his blade shot up from close range. It flew before her eyes and then she was back in. Her halfsword strike sliced across his thigh. Blood flowed yet the fighter gave no more than a grunt. Instead, he barrelled forward before she could regain proper footing. She avoided his first attack, deflected the second, and blocked the third.

He pushed forward and locked their weapons together. Kitara snarled, and heaving as he forced their weapons up. She flicked her wrist, angled her body, and slid her weapon free. He was too fast. The crossguard of his axe cracked heavily into her head. The pommel followed as she made to retreat, smashing into her temple. The heavy blow widened her eyes and threatened to take her balance. Her helmet took the brunt of the force and kept her up.

He followed through, his sword hungry for blood. The first blow barely missed her chest, the second was closer still, and then her senses returned. Kitara deflected the third and thrust toward his face. He leapt back and brought his blade up. Kitara stepped in close, her second hand pulling forth her knife. The man brought his weapon around. Kitara raised her sword and dagger. She danced closer and caught the blade of the sword with both of her weapons. He was strong, but the muscles of leg, back, shoulder, and arm kept him at bay. Before he could react, before he could so much as think about stepping back, Kitara made her move. Her knife held the Blade up, while her sword came down.

Her arm drove forward and sent steel with it. The blade tore into the man's unarmoured chest. He leapt back and Kitara stepped with him. With her knife she knocked his sword to the side, while she brought her sword around and sliced it across his mid-section. He staggered backward. Kitara was relentless. She dropped her dagger and carved him from shoulder to hip, before she stepped in *close* and drove her sword through his body. The axe fell into the sand. The man's balance failed him. Kitara wrenched her sword free of his body's embrace. And then he was gone, toppling over into a lifeless heap.

She turned back to aid Yeomra, but it was over. His opponent was face down in the sand with Yeomra's spear embedded in his back.

Kitara nodded to her companion as blood dripped down from her face. He returned the bow, and then together their raised their crimson stained weapons. The people cheered.

The cheers had not yet faded when the victors were led from

the sands. Kitara plunged her head into a bowl of water before she scrubbed her skin free of blood with a rough cloth. Her face and cheek still ached from the blows she had taken, and bruising had begun to appear upon her skin. She took a long breath and leaned upon the table. Her armour had been cleaned, yet remained on her body. She had long since been deprived of her weapons.

"You have heart," Yeomra called from across the room, "and a talent for the sword."

She glanced over at the fighter.

"This is no talent," she replied. "I'm good because I work at it."

The champion did not rise from his seat, did not even turn to face her. Instead he stared at the wall opposite.

"You have the makings of a fine champion, Alessandra. In time perhaps you could become one of the best among us. Though something tells me that you take little joy in what you do."

Kitara sighed.

"It is sometimes hard to remember when I learned to fight yet in all the years that have followed one thing has remained true. I despise killing for sport. Now that I am forced upon a path where that is what I must do. I begin to feel its pull. It is a poison, Yeomra, a poison that is as intoxicating as it is deadly. With each victory it grows stronger."

"We walk a narrow road, Alessandra," he replied. "You are a survivor, like me. The will to live comes before all else. The poison that you speak of… there is no resisting its pull."

They shared a brief look. It had become hard in recent days to fight against the pull. Each day it grew harder. Yet she had to keep her mind on why she was truly fighting.

The doors opened and an Aureian soldier appeared.

"It is time," he said.

The ride back to the Nilor villa was long and silent. Only Kitara and Yeomra were in the covered wagon, yet no words were shared.

Kitara stared at her hands for her mind was taken.

Arias had only spared her from harm because she was fighting in the games, but now the games were *over*. What awaited her at the villa, she feared to guess. Men with clubs sent to give her a warning, chains, a whip? Whatever it was she would meet it head on as she always did.

The steel gates of the yard were thrown open and the wagon was led inside. The fighters gathered around as it came to a halt. The last rays of the dusk light spilled into the cart as the door was pulled back. Kitara glanced at Yeomra, and then the pair stepped out into the light. Clad in their brilliant armour, they appeared as gods of the arena.

The fighters of the Nilor house cheered as they emerged. Arms were clasped, and hands clapped upon backs. Kitara barely noticed Vidarr throwing an arm around her shoulders, barely heard his roaring laugh. She searched the crowd, looking for soldiers, looking for Arias Nilor. *Nothing*.

"Alessandra?"

Kitara shook her head and looked to Vidarr. "What?"

"You did not hear?" he chuckled. He shoved a full cup toward her. Kitara saw the movement and acted. Her hand shot forward and latched around his wrist. Her heart pounded, and then she realised what she had done. Vidarr stared at her for a moment. Kitara released her grip.

"Sorry," she told him. "My mind was elsewhere."

"Drink," he commanded. "You have won a great victory!"

She forced a laugh and took the cup. The warmth of the fighters slowly began to put her at ease. There were no soldiers. No blades waiting for her. No Arias Nilor seeking revenge. Perhaps her victory had earned her safety from the man. She could only pray.

The night wore on and the drink flowed. When at last the fighters began to drift off into slumber, Kitara bid Vidarr farewell and headed for her cell. Her head was still sore, partly from the arena, and partly from drink. The corridor was silent. Her eyes widened slightly.

The door to her room was open.

Kitara glanced all around yet saw nothing. Her pace quickened. Her hands balled into fists. She reached the cell, stepped inside, and then saw the blood. Kitara froze. Her heart stilled in her chest. A small body lay upon the stone floor. Her dress stained red from the knife wound in her belly.

"Sereia?" Kitara breathed and she rushed to the girl's side. "Sereia!"

She dropped to her knees beside the Káli girl. Sereia's eyes flickered open. She was alive but Kitara knew death was near. She would be gone within moments.

"Kitara?" Sereia murmured.

"Hush now," Kitara told her as she cradled the girl in her arms.

"They came from the blackness… the master's son and his men," she said softly as tears began to roll from her eyes. "Kitara… I'm scared."

"It's alright. Everything is going to be alright."

Kitara held the girl's hands and felt her lifeblood upon them. She met Sereia's gaze and would not look away. Kitara fought back the emotion that threatened. She stroked Sereia's wet cheek and gently ran her hands through her hair. Kitara held her close as she felt her heart break. She kissed the girl's brow… and then Sereia was gone. Kitara felt the first of her tears begin to spill.

"Rest easy now, Sereia. Drift deeper and deeper. The sirens are calling your name."

A sob wracked her body and then she began to weep. She had promised to free Sereia. Promised to get her home.

She was dead.

Kitara held the girl tightly in her arms as she cried. A glint of blue between Sereia's fingers caught her eye. She opened the girl's hand and there is at. A sapphire ring. Her mother's ring. This was

Arias Nilor's message. Kitara looked up toward the cell door as fury ignited in her eyes. All thoughts of escape were gone. All thoughts of glory were gone.

She filled her heart with hate.

FIFTY-ONE

"Tell them what you saw," Cailean commanded as he glanced at the Annorans that Bellec had sent.

"A great army," Layan told Lukas and his companions. "Thousands of men and horses. Medea is uniting."

One-Eye pursed his lips. "For the first time in a hundred years, the Houses have common cause," he said. "Aureia is on the march, Annora is on the march, and meanwhile the League has struck at the Belcar and Niavenn."

"The world rises against us," Cailean muttered. "We do not know how far away they are but if there is one thing that is certain, it is that they are coming."

Lukas stared into the flames of the fire and gently ran his fingers across his arm ring.

"We should not just sit here and wait for them," he said.

"What do you suggest?" the Aedei chief asked.

"There is still much that is unknown about your people, much that the west fears, and yet that fear is being shed with every step that they take toward us," Lukas looked from Maevin to Rodion, and then to Cailean as he spoke. "I suggest that we remind them what it means to be afraid. I suggest that we take Bandujar."

Eyes widened and jaws dropped.

"Bandujar is protected by hundreds of soldiers and thick walls," Rodion said.

"Yes, well, there is *always* a way in, Rodion," Lukas told him as a plan began to form.

"The city has always been a foothold in these lands for Aloys and his people. The land is fertile, and I can only imagine how much grain is stored behind Bandujar's walls."

"Armies cannot march on empty bellies," Maevin murmured. "If we get in and set the grain alight it would send a strong message to our enemy."

Cailean folded his arms and nodded thoughtfully.

"I will not risk my people in a fight that they cannot win," he said. "Do you have a plan?"

Lukas looked to the Annoran mercenaries as he spoke, "When Bellec sent you here did he give orders upon what to do once you arrived and delivered his message?"

"Told us to stay with the chief until he returned," Hadwin replied.

"And how does that make you feel?" Lukas asked. "Standing with Salvaar against your own people."

Bellec's men exchanged a look.

"Our people?" Layan replied with a shrug. "Our people are Jaimye and Galadayne, Bellec and Kompton. All of them. Brothers that we have ridden with for two long decades. They are our people. Not those who banished us for no cause or crime."

"Our ties to Annora were cut long ago," Hadwin added. "Now we are soldiers of fortune.

Offer us enough and we will fight Medea, Miera, Annora… it matters not."

"We are loyal to Bellec," Layan said. "It is obvious to me which side he will choose when he returns."

Lukas smiled. He understood them perfectly. "You are mercenaries," he said, "what if I was to pay for your services until your brothers arrive?"

"Then your enemies are *our* enemies," Layan said with a grin.

Lukas led his company of Káli southward to the road between Bandujar and Cacera. With less than a day between the Medean towns riders frequented the tracks. Scouts, soldiers, horses, and supply convoys. It did not take long for them to come across a place where the road cut down between a pair of ridges.

There they waited.

Lukas dropped from his saddle and made his way toward a great oak tree. From behind it he stared out across the land. His eye searched for movement. It came with a small glimmer of silver. The sun's light reflecting upon polished armour. The Káli fanned out, hidden by rock, bush, and the ridgeline. They dismounted and moved to the very top of the hills. They crouched behind the ridge or made shelter in the shadows of trees. The Salvaari horses were as silent and unmoving as their riders.

The first sounds of the Medean riders reached them. There were four men clad In chain armour and steel helmets. They held spears upon which banners flew. Banners marked with the colours of House Aloys. The white lion was their symbol, but they would have been foolish to believe themselves as anything more than mortal men. They rode between the ridges unaware of the danger that awaited them. Lukas watched them from his vantage point, his hand slowly rising. The Káli remained silent and unmoving, eyes fixed upon their leader.

One-Eye dropped his hand.

Bows sang.

A storm of arrows broke upon the Medeans. Man and horse screamed, yet there was no time to react. Within two heartbeats the Medeans lay still upon the hard earth.

Lukas rode down to the track and dismounted among the dead. He stared down at one of the dead men and stroked his bearded jaw. His plan had born fruit and now it was time to see it to its end.

"Strip their armour," he said, glancing at Layan and Hadwin.

"Remove all Aloys' markings. We do not ride to Bandujar as Salvaari or sellswords. We do so as Annoran scouts."

One-Eye cleaned himself of war paint before he donned his new set of armour. A hard mail shirt covered his torso, while bracers and greaves of steel protected arm and leg. He buckled a Medean sword to his waist and shoved his hammer through the belt.

"Here," Maevin held out a helmet.

Lukas pulled his coif up before he took the helm and placed it atop his head. He strapped it on. Though it had been months since he had worn a helmet it was a feeling most familiar.

One-Eye glanced down at his wrist and let his gaze wash across the silver arm ring. He took it from his wrist and extended it to Maevin.

"Look after it for me," he said.

Maevin took the ring and met his eye. "With or without this, the spirits ride with you," she said.

"They have not yet led me astray," Lukas replied. "I pray that they do not now."

The priestess placed the ring upon her arm and joined it with her own. "I will protect it with my life."

One-Eye nodded slowly and the words between them went unspoken. What he was about to do was reckless and foolish. An action that his father would have chastised him for. The Salvaari thought it brave. He would soon find out which it was. Lukas tore his gaze away from her as he pulled himself up into the saddle.

"We all know what happens next," he told his companions. "Rodion, take your people and meet with Cailean. We will take Bandujar and show the Medeans that they are right to fear us."

The party split. Rodion, Maevin, and the Káli rode east toward Cailean and his Aedei. Lukas, Hadwin, and Layan took the road north toward Bandujar.

Hadwin took the lead as the walls of Bandujar rose before them. The large gates were shut to the outside world. A barrier between the townspeople and any who would do them harm. Above the city flew the white lion banners, while upon the walls stood men of the city watch. They stared down at the three riders with wary eyes. Lukas took it all in and searched for any sign of weakness. If these people knew who he was, if they knew that he killed Emilian Aloys, his blood would be spilled in the street.

"Who goes there?" called out one of the soldiers.

"Hadwin Weles of Torosa," the Annoran replied. "And you, sir?"

"Javier Alvaro," the Medean told them. "What brings you this far north, Annoran?"

"King Dayne sent us as scouts," Hadwin said. He glanced at Layan, "We served King Dorian in the last war against the heathen. It is a bad omen to be caught beyond walls when the night comes, for when it comes the Salvaari come with it."

Javier nodded, as if satisfied. "You are welcome in Bandujar. Open the gates."

The three riders rode through the open threshold and into the city. The Medeans had welcomed them, yet still watched them suspiciously. They were at war, and the people of Bandujar lived close to the border. They did not trust outsiders, and that distrust had kept them alive.

"I am sorry to hear about your King's passing," Javier told them as he approached the horsemen. "He was a strong man, a godly man, and the Twins will watch over him in paradise."

"Thank you," Layan replied, "and our condolences to your Lord."

"Betrayal can only be betrayal when it comes from those closest to us," Javier said. "The Black Eagle shall pay for his treachery."

"The Black Eagle?" Lukas asked with a frown.

"That's what they're calling him now," the Medean spat. "Lukas Raynor, the banished prince. He is unfit to be called a son of Dorian."

One-Eye bit back a chuckle. So, he had been given a new name. Lukas Raynor, the Black Eagle, One-Eye, the Banished Prince… so many names, so many titles. He had begun to lose count.

"The traitor will get what he deserves, I am sure," Lukas replied. He froze as his eye locked with a new banner. This one did not bear the white lion over a golden field. This one was of midnight blue, emblazoned with a silver sun and moon. Then he saw the knights. There were six of them In deep conversation with the lord of Bandujar.

"Sir Draven Hanniel of the Order of Kil'kara," Javier explained. "The Warden, William Peyene, sent them to assist us in the war effort. Told us that your King had just left Kilgareth."

"Should be here in a matter of days," Layan said without missing a beat.

The Medean smiled. "And then we can finally be rid of those Salvaari devils," he said.

Lukas and his companions were given quarters in an inn near to the city entrance. Their horses were stabled and then they found their room.

"So the knights of Kil'kara have come," Lukas muttered.

The three companions sat awake as the moon rose.

"A wise man once told me that you should never provoke a knight of Kil'kara, and that you should never ever fight him," Hadwin replied.

"They are just men," Lukas said. "If you cut them, they will bleed."

"They are far from common men," Layan told him. "I've seen them fight before. The strongest iron is forged in the hottest flame, and that is how they are born. You take a man and mould him. Teach him the art of war. Make it all that he studies. You grant him faith greater than any other, a faith that welcomes those who die for it. Such a man will go into battle without fear for his own life. This faith grants him strength over vast armies."

Lukas gathered up his sword belt from the table that sat between them.

"If it is death at a knight's blade that you fear, you should have stayed in the forest," he said.

"I did not say that I feared them," Layan replied. "I only heed caution."

"The time for caution is over," One-Eye told him as he rose to his feet and strapped on his sword. "We are committed."

"Then tonight we meet our fate," Hadwin said.

The Annorans buckled on helmets and took up their weapons. Lukas took a breath and bit back a grimace as he picked up his crutch. He tightened his grip on the handle and forced the pain back. His knee would not fail him this night.

The armour and gambeson beneath kept the cool air at bay as the three made their way through the almost empty streets. Few men traversed the roads and those who did paid them no heed, for soldiers at night were commonplace in Bandujar. A pair of Medeans stood atop the gatehouse, while others were spread along the vast walls. All were watching the fields beyond the city. None were watching what was happening *within*. Only two other soldiers patrolled gate courtyard within the city walls. Without a word the three men separated. Lukas walked toward the gate while his companions vanished into side streets.

"Sleepless night?" Javier called as he spotted Lukas.

"One of many," One-Eye told him as he reached the Medeans.

"Your injuries?"

"The pain remains, yet I am at peace with what happened."

Javier glanced from the crutch to the bandage that covered his empty eye socket.

"How did you come to be so wounded?" he asked.

"A traitor's blade in Salvaar," Lukas replied.

"Forgive me, but you seem too young to have fought in the last war with the heathen," the Medean said with a frown.

"It is true that I was only a child then," he said. "These wounds are from a far more recent fight." Lukas slowly moved his hand behind his back. His fingers latched around the hilt of his dagger. He saw Layan emerge from the shadows behind the Medeans.

"Emilian Aloys," Lukas whispered.

His hand shot forward and drove the knife deep into Javier's throat. Before the second Medean could so much as scream Layan's fingers covered his mouth while a dagger was driven into the side of his neck. Lukas leapt forward, his second hand going to Javier's mouth, as he shoved him into the side of a building. Blood spurted from his gruesome wound and then the light left his eyes. Slowly, One-Eye lowered the lifeless body to the ground in the shadows of the building. Layan followed suit.

The pair exchanged a nod, and then the mercenary was gone. Lukas took up his crutch and watched from the darkness as his companions crept up the stairs and onto the wall. They were silent. They were precise. Within moments the men of the gatewatch were sent to the afterlife. Their lifeblood dripped onto the structure they had been sent to protect.

Lukas made his move, leaving the shadows and hobbling over to the gate as fast as his crutch would allow. They did not have long. If Rodion and his Káli were not in position, then they would all be undone.

Layan and Hadwin descended to the courtyard and moved over to the gate. Lukas gathered up a torch that hung from the gatehouse. He nodded to the mercenaries, who planted their shoulders against the locking bar and heaved. Teeth were made bare, and muscles were strained. The large wooden plank moved and was forced from its mooring. The mercenaries carried the bar away from the gate and placed it gently upon the ground. Lukas pushed the gate open just wide enough to slip through and left the city walls. He stood tight against the gate and then waved the torch from side to side. One-Eye waited a moment before handing the torch back to Layan.

He stared out across the fields, hoping, praying. The cry of a bird reached his ear, and then moments later a group of dark shapes appeared against the wall. *Rodion.*

The Káli said nothing as he approached, twenty other Salvaari in tow. He held a bow in his hand, while his face was a mask of black. One by one they slipped inside, opening the gates fully as they did so. Each moment that they were not discovered was a blessing.

The Káli held formation in front of the gatehouse, weapons held tightly in hand. Lukas drew his war hammer and moved to Maevin's side. A wicked spear was grasped in her hand, while her expression was even more vicious. Lukas cast his crutch to the side and tested his weight upon his injured leg. It held. Rodion handed One-Eye a shield.

A shadow flickered in the torchlight, and then soldiers appeared down the street. They froze as they saw the open gate and the dark clad Salvaari before it. Hands went to sword, spear, and shield.

"GATEHOUSE!" one of the Medeans screamed and he pulled his blade free.

"Make ready," Lukas adjusted his grip upon his hammer.

"Tanris, we come to you," Rodion growled.

More Medeans began to appear and then as one they charged. Rodion launched the first arrow, and then his people followed suit. Soldiers fell left and right as shafts found their targets. Layan and Hadwin led the Káli to meet their enemy. Hadwin deflected a spear with his shield, before he ripped his sword through his attacker's chest.

A Medean came at Lukas; he must have seen the bandage over his eye and suspected a weak foe. One-Eye caught his sword upon his shield. He grimaced as he slid his foot forward and blocked another blow as he did so. He brought his hammer around and smashed the steel head into his enemy's cheek. Bones splintered and blood erupted, before the man crashed to the ground screaming. Lukas brought his shield up just in time to stop the thrust of a spear. Before he could retaliate, Maevin replied with her own and buried it in the man's throat. One of the Káli fell to the blades of the enemy, and then another. Rodion put an arrow into a spearman before he pulled forth his axe.

A blue crest appeared through the chaos. The beat of hooves reached Lukas' ear. A knight of Kil'kara materialised and cut down a Káli with a single swing of his sword. The beat of hooves grew into a thunder. More knights appeared. Lukas looked over his shoulder and saw the riders.

"NOW!" he roared and leapt aside from the gate.

The Káli moved as one and cleared a path.

Cailean of the Aedei let loose a vicious war cry as he charged into the fray with over a hundred blue painted mounted Salvaari at his back. The fighting grew fierce.

"With me!" Lukas cried as he cut down a Medean. He reached the stairs to the wall with the surviving fifteen Káli in tow. They clambered up onto the stonework. Those without bows snatched them from racks along the walls. They turned to the battle. "Kill them all!" One-Eye commanded.

Bows sang and arrows rained down upon the defenders. They fell in droves. Those who raised their shields to stem the rain were killed by axe and spear, while those who didn't were taken by the deadly downpour. Pathways were opened in the thinning Medean defence, allowing the Aedei to gallop through and charge into the city.

Lukas turned his attention to the blue clad knights. Five remained. They stood back to back over a pile of corpses. Any who attacked them fell to sword and spear. None could stand against them and live. Two of the Aedei charged a single knight. He felled them both in as many moves, jammed his sword into the chest of a third, and then spun to a fourth. His armour took the weight of an axe. He fell to a knee as his chainmail tore.

With a ferocious scream the knight leapt to his feet and took the head of the man who had so wounded him. A spear was driven into his thigh, while a second glanced off his pauldron. Still he fought on. His companions charged at their mighty foe and carved a bloody path through the Aedei. They reached the walls, and then the gate. The last knight armed with a spear launched his weapon. His aim was true and an Aedei rider was cast from his saddle.

Lukas' eye widened as he realised what was happening.

The knight leapt up into the horse's saddle as his companions cleared his way. One of the knights slapped the horse's flank and then the rider thundered out. One-Eye gestured toward the rider as he fled.

"Take him!"

Arrows sped after the horseman. Two found their target. Both ripped into the man's shoulder. None felled him. Then he was gone.

The only defenders left within Bandujar were the knights of Kil'kara. One of the remaining holy warriors fell as a spear ripped through the back of his neck. Then there were three. They were battered and bleeding from a thousand wounds.

"Hold!" Lukas cried.

Aedei and Káli alike stepped back from their foe as One-Eye descended from the wall. He ran his gaze over the knights and came to a halt before them.

He gestured to the corpse of a Medean soldier. "These are not your people. Why do you choose to protect them, to stand with them even when you know that you cannot win?"

"I swore an oath of honour to my gods. We all did," an Aureian voice replied. "I am a knight of Kil'kara. Knights of Kil'kara do not retreat, nor surrender. We fight, no matter the odds."

"You would forsake your life for what?" Lukas frowned. "Your gods? Do they wish you to die?"

"I will gladly die for my gods, pagan," the knight replied. "I fight for a cause beyond your understanding."

"What is your name, knight?"

"Draven Hanniel," came the reply. "You are Annoran?"

"I was. I am Lukas, son of Dorian Raynor," Lukas told him as he squared his jaw. "You shall die for that cause, Sir Draven Hanniel, and you shall die today. But know that you have my respect." He said nothing else as he raised his arm. Bows came up.

"Areut talc cuun'etc!" roared Sir Draven.

"Areut talc cuun'etc!" the knights echoed.

They charged. The bows sang.

Lukas took a breath as he surveyed the battlefield. Corpses filled the streets from the gatehouse to the heart of the city. Yet the day was won. He approached Sir Draven's body and gathered up the knight's sword. The sun and moon marked its pommel, yet it was good steel. A sword such as this would serve him well. A warrior's sword. Maevin found him.

"The day is ours," she said simply. "The spirits are with you." She held out his arm ring. He took it.

"I begin to believe that you may be right," Lukas told her.

Maevin cupped his head and pressed her forehead to his own. They were both covered in the blood of their enemies, yet they did not care.

"Lukas," Cailean called as he approached the pair. "Because of you we have won a great victory and in so doing inflicted mighty blow to our enemy. But we cannot stay here. The rider who escaped will warn his people and more will come."

"Let him carry the tale, let it spread, and fear along with it," One-Eye replied. "Find the grain stores and burn them. Then we ride for Salvaar."

Myrdren of the Káli stared through the blackness, his silver eyes able to see all. "Steady girl," he murmured as he ran a hand down his steed's neck.

A great army sat encamped before him. An army thousands

strong. An army bearing the red eagle of Annora. King Dayne Raynor had come.

And his people were *alone*. The moonseer turned his horse and galloped back toward Vaylin and his kin.

FIFTY-TWO

"If I can get my men in, there is a chance that I would take down the bell," Cleander said.

"Getting in is the easy part," Bhaltair replied. "You can use the tunnels. But taking out the guard *before* they sound the alarm could be impossible.'"

"We need a way to draw the magister's attention away from us," Cleander told him.

The gang leader stroked his jaw. "What if I were to attack the arsenal? We have men enough to give them a fight at least for a time."

"Sting them from a dozen directions and keep their attention fixed upon us," Priamos Stentor added. "My men hunger for blood and battle."

"Many would fall," Cleander told him. "Yet they will fall regardless. Whether it is at the end of a rope or upon the walls of the arsenal. That is for every man to decide."

Bhaltair nodded. "Even if I get you in," he begun, "even if we draw the defenders to the walls, there is no guarantee that you will succeed."

Cleander leaned forward on the table and met his friend's eyes. "I know that it is almost hopeless. I know that. Give me this chance Bhaltair."

"And if you die?"

"Then I die." Cleander shrugged. "That is the fate of all men. I will go to my gods proudly. There may only be a small chance of success, yet even that chance is better than being condemned to a life in the shadows. I am ready to die for my beliefs. If I don't try, then what is the point? We will have been for nothing."

Bhaltair was quiet for a moment as he weighed the odds. By now Teague and his pirates would be on their way. The attack was coming and there was no stopping it. He did not turn away from his friend and instead nodded.

"Then let it be done," Bhaltair said.

Cleander held out a hand. "It has been an honour, my friend," he said.

Bhaltair took it.

"Godspeed, Cleander."

The Annoran left without looking back. The tunnels were filled with gang men and Stentor's soldiers. They were armed and ready for war. Their swords were sharp and their nerve sharper still. Cleander walked through their midst as he made his way toward his men. Only a small force could get inside the arsenal unnoticed, and so he had chosen the best. Without a way to disable the bell before they attacked the tower their cause was all but lost. Yet there was no choice. If he were to die, then at least he would go down fighting. Cleander would show the magister's soldiers why he was feared.

"Tonight," Cleander begun as he reached his men, "we have a task far greater than any before. If the belltower remains under the magister's control when Teague arrives then we are finished. So, it now falls to us to take it."

Eyes widened and breath fled lips.

"Even if we reach the tower, how do you propose we deal with the guard before they ring the bell?" one of the men asked.

"In truth, I do not know," Cleander admitted. Lies would do no good here. "Yet if we are to stand a chance this night then we have to. There is no other choice. I know that this will likely end with our deaths, so I will not ask you to come with me. If I am to stand alone before the tower, then I shall do so."

The man who had spoken rose to his feet and placed a fist over his heart. "You won't stand alone," he said. "Our swords are yours. Our lives are yours."

One by one, the other men rose and placed their fists on their chests as if it were a final salute.

"You will need me as well," a new voice called from behind Cleander.

The Annoran turned to see the Nightingale.

Elise's breathing was steady as they ran through the tight confines of the sewer network. There was no torch to light their way, no fire to give them away. They ran in silence with only the knowledge of Cleander to stop them from straying. They took a few turns through the never-ending maze of brick and mortar before the passage began to slant upward.

They slowed to a walk. Hands lowered to weapons as they approached the doors above. These were more than just simple gang men. Though they carried an array of swords, hammers, shields, and bows, it was in their eyes that she saw the danger lurking. Perhaps they had once been soldiers or mercenaries. Elise paid the notion little heed as they reached the tunnel entrance. The mask and scarf that covered her face hid the emotion that she felt stirring within. This was it. This was the endgame. What came tonight would be justice for her parents, for her aunt and uncle. Or it could be her death.

Cleander reached the barred door first. He held up a hand to stop the company from following him to the steel gateway. He peered through it, watching, waiting.

Shouts filled the air, followed by the blaring of a horn.

Soldiers stampeded down the streets and the sounds of battle began. Bhaltair had launched his attack. Cleander snatched out a pick and swiftly dealt with the door's lock. Elise took a breath as the Annoran pushed upon the gate, edging it open. He led them out into the street. The tunnel had directed them to a back alley, free from the sight of the magister's soldiers. The last man through shut the steel door, and then they began to make their way deeper into the arsenal. A second horn's sound echoed through the streets, swiftly followed by a third. The gangs were making their presence known. A storm of arrows filled the air between the walls and the buildings beyond. Screams and shouts arose in a deadly chorus.

Cleander led them true and with purpose. The soldiers that they passed paid them no mind, for many mercenaries worked under Imrohir's employ. One by one more horn blasts sounded in the night.

At last, the belltower rose before them. It stood at over a hundred feet of stone and wood, topped by an open lookout post. The great bell hung within. A wall surrounded the massive structure. A wall manned by bow wielding guards.

"You know what you must do," Cleander said to the Nightingale.

"Climb the tower and disable the bell," she replied.

"Signal us when you reach the peak and then we will come for you."

Without another word, Elise left them and vanished into the night.

Getting to the wall was easy, for she had buildings to conceal her. Once she crossed that last defence she would have to rely upon the darkness of night and her own skill. A great roar went up and then flames blazed to life upon the eastern wall of the arsenal. The tower guards turned as the orange glow lit the sky. Elise used the chaos to fly up the western wall. Her fingers latched onto one of the merlons and then she swept her gaze up and down the wall. None were looking toward her.

The Nightingale did not hesitate.

She heaved herself up onto the wall and then silently dropped beyond. She crossed the small yard in five strides and kept to the shadows. Elise glanced back. Her eyes darted along the line of soldiers. If they turned, she was dead. One false move and either they, or the men within the tower, would discover her and see the plan to ruin. The Nightingale ran her fingers across the stonework of the tower. Her fingers searched for holds. The stone was thick and its mortar strong yet holds were plentiful. Elise began to climb.

She moved as fast as she dared, barely breathing, and careful not to make a sound. She was ten feet above the ground and then twenty. The wind grew stronger, and her arms began to ache. Sixty feet. She could see the fights breaking out along the arsenal walls now. The gangs and Stentor's soldiers were using ladders to take the fight to the defenders. Thousands of those from across the river surged forward in their wake. Fire had begun to burn within the arsenal as the attackers sent flaming arrows toward vulnerable buildings. Eighty feet, one hundred. Her breathing became laboured. Despite years of training nothing could have prepared her for this. The Nightingale gritted her teeth and bit back the pain. She willed herself onward. Elise avoided the many windows and lookout points as she climbed. At times she took a longer route to avoid discovery.

After an eternity she reached the balcony that surrounded the great bell. She glanced through the small arches that ran along the balcony wall. A single guard stood within. She waited. She prayed that Cleander had been right, prayed that the changing of the guard would be upon them when the moon reached its peak. She dug her fingers in, dug her toes in, and waited.

The moon rose higher. The fighting grew fierce.

Only her willpower stopped the pain from sending her to her death. She held on and focussed on controlling her breath. The guard moved. Elise's eyes followed him. He made his way to the entrance to the balcony. A narrow doorway in the floor led to a staircase that ran down the inside of the tower. She waited until his head was beyond sight before she heaved herself up onto the balcony.

The Nightingale crept passed the bell. She was careful to avoid the gaping hole down which the massive ropes hung. She snatched at the wooden door. A shadow flickered below. The next guardsman was coming. Elise clenched her teeth and pulled with all her fading strength. The door lifted, and then with a push, Elise slammed it shut. Shouts came from below. There was a lock upon the door designed to protect whoever stood watch. A lock to which only the tower guards held a key. A lock which could only be unlocked from above. A bang came from below as a fist pounded into wood. Elise leapt atop the door as a soldier drove his weight into it. Her heart raced and her fingers searched. The door shuddered. The Nightingale shoved the bolt home.

Shouts grew louder from below. They were going to ring the bell.

Elise snatched out her kukri and raced toward the bell. She saw the men beneath as she reached the hole. Without a second thought for her own life, she snatched at the bell clapper. A spear darted though the hole. The Nightingale saw it coming and leapt across the gap. Steel grazed her leg.

She lashed out with her kukri and pulled the clapper tight. The curved knife bit into leather bell loop and severed the clapper from its mooring. The Nightingale jumped back from the gap and skipped aside from another spear. Elise cast the clapper down, swivelled around, and snatched a torch from its holder. She launched the brand over the edge of the balcony. It tumbled down end over end.

The attack began before the torch hit the ground. Tower guards were cast from the walls as arrows flew from the darkness. There was no alarm, and their cries went unanswered. The screams all but covered by the battle raging along the arsenal wall. Elise turned to the south as solders tried to force their way to the lookout to no avail. She saw a dark shape emerge from the blackness.

The first ship came into sight.

"Kill them," Olivera commanded.

Kyler swivelled his gaze from man to man and prepared for the charge. The gang men began to move. They were outnumbered, but not outmatched. Kyler was a knight, and if the gods willed it, he would *die* a knight.

"Wait!"

Elena pushed passed him.

"Elena, no!" Kyler hissed as she stepped out in front.

She held her hands out and let her dagger fall to the stones. Elena spread her arms as if to create a shield between the gang men and the knights. "Look at me," she called to Olivera. "Look into my eyes."

Unable to help himself, Olivera met her gaze. It burned red like fire. Elena's teeth sharpened into fangs and then there she stood. The power of the ruskalan ran through her veins. Kyler felt his blood chill as he saw Olivera stiffen.

"Are you looking?" Elena asked.

"Yes," the man replied, his voice as distant as his eyes now were.

"You will *not* harm us," she told him.

Olivera stared at her gaze fixated by the flames within. "I will not," he said.

Kyler looked left and right as the other gang men stared at their leader. They looked confused, as if not sure what to do. It was as if Olivera was captured by some kind of spell.

"What magic is this?" one of the men hissed.

Elena did not turn her gaze from Olivera and instead flicked a hand toward him.

"Ricard you will say nothing," Olivera commanded yet his eyes never wavered from those of the Medean woman.

"Lower your sword," Elena called to Olivera, her voice as powerful as the magic that flowed through her.

Without hesitation, Scar Lip tossed his blade to the ground.

"Boss?" questioned Ricard.

"Do it," came the reply.

"Olivera!"

"DO IT NOW!" Scar Lip snarled and still did not turn from Elena. The gang man froze. Kyler watched him closely and waited for Ricard to break ranks and attack. It did not come. With a grimace, Ricard cast his weapon aside. One by one the others followed suit. Kyler felt his heart race as he watched on. He glanced back at Alarik, and for the first time saw a flicker of doubt cross the veteran's face.

"Kyler, we have to go," Elena murmured without looking back. "We have to go now."

Slowly, the three began to back toward the path from which they had come.

"Olivera, they are getting away," Ricard spat.

"We hold," Scar Lip replied, still enthralled by Elena and those burning eyes.

"They are going to escape!"

Olivera said nothing.

"OLIVERA!"

The three reached the circle of gang men. Upon a gesture from Scar Lip his men began to move aside.

Thud.

Kyler stopped in his tracks. The sound echoed down from one of the tunnels. Footsteps.

They grew into a thunder as dozens of footfalls joined the first. They came from north and south, east and west.

Olivera's men turned as torches lit the passages. Kyler swept his gaze from tunnel to tunnel. They were trapped. He exchanged a glance with Alarik. Who was it? Olivera's men were not acting as if a friend was coming. They arrived in their dozens, clad in garments from rags to armour. Some carried swords, others axes. They wore dark expressions, as if they were men pushed to the edge, men who only thought about revenge. The only thing that united them were the bands of coloured cloth tied around their waists beneath their belts. They were savage men. They were dark men.

"Pirates," Alarik hissed.

Kyler's heart dropped. Somehow the Sacasian raiders had found a way into the north and had breached the city walls. They could only have come here with the aid of the gangs and that meant only one thing. Invasion.

"Are you the one they call Olivera?" a pirate stepped toward Scar Lip. "We were told to meet you."

Kyler readied his sword. There was only one choice now. They had to fight. Between the gangs and the pirates there could be no victory. Only death. But he would fight none the less.

"Are you Olivera?" the pirate repeated as he stepped closer to the man.

Elena flicked her wrist. It was a single, simple gesture.

Olivera spun toward the man and thrust a knife into his chest. The pirate roared in defiance. His hand reached for his sword. He was too late. Olivera's second blow opened his throat.

As the pirate fell to his knees, Scar Lip shook his head as if waking from a dream. His gaze was no longer locked with Elena's and once more he was free. He stared in horror from the blood covered knife to the dead pirate at his feet.

"You killed him!" another of the Sacasians bellowed. "Kill him! Kill them all!"

There was a pause, and then the pirates charged into the ranks of gang men. Kyler saw Olivera shout before gathering up his sword and turning to face the pirates.

"Kyler!" Alarik's cry brought the knight back to the present.

The Medean spun back as a Sacasian angled toward the knights. Alarik caught the man's blow upon his shield, while Kyler skewered him from the side. More pirates came.

Blood flowed as the knights fought side by side. Elena took up a fallen blade and joined them as the last of the crimson light faded from her eyes.

Through the chaos of battle, Olivera turned to the companions, his face now covered in a red mask. "Join us or we all die here!" he cried.

"Together then," Alarik growled.

Kyler bared his teeth as a war was fought inside him. He felt himself torn between two worlds. The man had murdered his parents, but his very survival called upon the knight to ally himself with their killer. Elena's survival depended on it.

"Kyler," Elena took hold of his arm. "Kyler, we have no choice." He saw the pain in her eyes, yet he knew that she was right.

"Together," Kyler hissed as he made his choice.

Kyler barrelled into the fray as more and more pirates began to descend upon them from the tunnels. He caught an axe upon his shield, before he countered and drove his sword through the man's heart. Kyler turned without pause, wrenching his sword free and sending the dying pirate crashing to the ground. His shield came up and deflected a sword aimed to skewer him. He felled the pirate in three moves. The first beating down his blade, the next carving him from hip to shoulder, while the third caught the man across the throat. Kyler blocked a blow aimed at Elena. Before he could move to finish the man, Elena cut him down. She was untrained and the kill wasn't clean, but the pirate fell all the same.

Another pirate rose to meet him. He battered at the knight's shield with his hammer. Kyler knocked the weapon aside, and then Olivera took him from behind and drove his sword through the man's body.

Olivera heaved the man aside. "If we stay here everybody dies!"

he roared. "Follow me!"

Kyler charged after Olivera as he led the gang from the chamber. Elena stayed tightly by his side. Pirates spilled from every direction. They emerged from every tunnel and passage. Sacasians and gang men fell in droves. Kyler cut a man down as he ran, skipped over the body, and thrust his weapon deep into the chest of another. He tore his sword free just as a blade slammed into his back. His armour held yet the blow drove him to one knee. Kyler turned and lunged upward. The knight caught his assailant in the neck with his sword before he hammered him from his feet with his shield. Blood cascaded over Kyler as he rose to his feet. There was no time to stop. No time for pause.

Kyler glanced over his shoulder and saw more pirates charging after them. He could no longer see Alarik. The battlemaster was gone.

"Run!" Kyler shouted as he engaged the pirates. "Run!"

Kyler felled one, two. A spear glanced off his helmet and the blade of an axe parted mail upon his sword arm. Still, he fought and killed both his assailants in as many moves. Gang men fell all around him, as the Sacasians came on without mercy. But Elena was with him. He would not, could not, stop fighting.

A pirate charged at Elena as Kyler killed another. The knight turned to see Elena barely get her blade up in time to stop the attack. Kyler roared and leapt at the man. The Sacasian blocked his blow, while a second latched his hands onto the knight's shield. Kyler heaved but could not tear his shield from the man's grip. More came. The knight released his grip on the shield and ripped his arm free of its embrace. He cut one down before they could act. A second followed him into the afterlife. The third jumped on Kyler and sent them both to the ground. A knife bit into Kyler's shoulder. The knight bellowed and brought the crossguard of his sword up. He slammed it into his attacker's head. The pirate rolled to the side with a scream.

Kyler leapt to his feet and carved his weapon across the man's body twice. Flesh parted and bone splintered. Something bit into Kyler's leg. He turned toward his new foe and killed him with a single swing of his sword. Pirates closed in around them. He heard Olivera's defiant roar as he fought against the ever-growing odds. Kyler pushed Elena further down the tunnel as the enemy grew. Weapons rained down. He blocked some with his sword while his armour turned away others. His body began to ache, and his blood began to flow from a dozen wounds. He saw Elena through the breaks in the fighting. She fought back, unwilling to yield.

"GO!" Kyler shouted as he backed down the tunnel and fought for every inch. "GO!"

Elena did not. She stayed by his side, stayed with what remained of the gang. Olivera led them into a round chamber with tunnels branching in every direction. Kyler's blade bit into a pirate's thigh, before it found a home between his ribs. He blocked a blow aimed at his head and heaved the blade up. A second man attacked and sliced his sword into Kyler's stomach.

The mail held but the knight fell back. He barely blocked a second blow before another connected heavily to his side. With a scream, Kyler launched himself forward at the pirates. He drove his sword through one, even as the second attacked. Kyler ducked the blow, ripped free a knife, and jammed it into the man's throat. The knight tore his sword from the falling pirate's body before it hit the ground.

More came.

More fell.

He stood between Elena and death. A bloody gash was opened on her arm before she replied and killed the man who had wounded her. Bodies filled the chamber. Blood covered the stonework. Kyler's own body was a canvas of red. His armour held. His faith held. A pirate armed with a war hammer angled toward Elena. Kyler threw a second Sacasian to the side as he charged toward the man. Elena's sword was knocked from her hands. The hammer came up. Kyler shoved her to the side as the blow came down. He leapt forward, and the hammer glanced upon his armour as he tackled the pirate down. Kyler fought for top position as he forced his sword up. Fear lit the man's eyes as Kyler overpowered him. The knight snatched at the weapon's blade and drove the edge down into the pirate's neck. Another pirate descended upon him, and then another. Kyler's sword was torn from his grasp. His back hit the stone floor. He blocked a knife with his bracers and caught a sword blow upon his pauldron. The knife was driven up. Kyler grabbed at the man's arms, but the blade drew closer. He saw the hatred in the man's face, tasted the stench of his breath. His weight was crushing.

The knife neared his throat, its tip digging into his coif.

Then the man was gone. Elena's blade was buried in his side. Kyler rolled to his feet as another pirate came at him. Kyler's empty hands balled into fists as he stepped to meet the man. The pirate's wicked axe rose. Too late. Olivera rushed past Kyler and thrust his sword home, killing the man before he had a chance to swing his axe. The knight barely acknowledged Scar Lip as he snatched up his fallen sword. His armour was stained red. All he could smell, all he could *taste,* was blood.

The remnants of the gang formed a circle as their foe came at them. Kyler pushed Elena behind him and used an arm to shield her. The pirates held for a moment as they eyed off their weakened foe. Kyler swept his gaze from man to man. He adjusted his grip and felt the weight of the sword. The pirates surged toward them.

Kyler roared. His cry was taken up by his allies.

They charged to meet their foe. The knight killed one, killed two. A knife was driven into his body, yet Kyler barely felt it. His armour turned aside a sword, while his own blade replied in kind. Kyler lashed out and felled the man. He tore the knife free and gave it a new home in another's neck. He turned left and right as they came on. Gang men fell all around him. Six pirates stood to his front. If they got past him Elena died. They both died. Kyler snarled and moved to meet them. He levelled his sword.

The first came at him.

Kyler stepped to the side and sliced him across the chest. He did not stop as he slid away from a second man, thrusting his sword into his attacker's heart. He blocked a third attack high. Kyler heaved the second mortally wounded man into the third, before he killed him with a sword strike. His blade sliced the stomach of a fourth as he ducked beneath a wild swing. The man did not fall, yet the knight kept moving. He blocked the next pirate's strike and then opened his throat. Kyler spun back to the wounded man and moved to finish him. The full force of a sword slammed into his back. Kyler fell to his knees with a scream. The mail and gambeson saved him. He spun upon the ground, barely able to get his blade up to block the blow that followed. He parried, countered, and savagely drove his sword up into the man's body. Heaving himself to his feet, he shoved the man to the ground. Only the wounded pirate remained. Kyler staggered toward him. He blocked once, twice. He switched his grip, took his sword by the blade and carved a bloody path across the man's torso. Flicking his sword up, he took the pirate's head.

A scream met his ears.

The knight turned toward it. He saw Elena, he saw the pirate. The *last* pirate.

He saw the sword embedded in Elena's body.

She staggered, struggling to keep her footing.

"ELENA!" Kyler roared as he felt his heart freeze.

Her weapon fell and rang as it hit the stone floor. Her jaw trembled. Kyler ran toward Elena, as the pirate pulled his bloody blade free. She stared at her wound, stared at the blood covering her hands. Then she began to fall.

Olivera reached them first. He barrelled into the Sacasian and drove him across the chamber. Kyler cast his sword to the side as he ran, all but ignoring the fight. He only had mind for the woman he loved. She fell but his arms were waiting. Her breathing was laboured and her eyes wide. Kyler gently lowered her down and held her tight. The blood was spreading across her robe.

The knight snatched at his helmet strap, pulled it loose and tossed it away. Kyler wrenched back his coif, and then slowly moved his hand to her cheek. Blood flowed, and her life flowed with it. Kyler ran his fingers through her hair and caressed her cheek.

"Kyler," Elena murmured as she reached up toward him.

He took her hand as she stroked his jaw. "I'm here," he told her. "I'm here."

"I'm sorry," Elena murmured as her voice began to fail.

"You have *nothing* to be sorry for," Kyler said, his voice as gentle as his caress.

"I am sorry that we did not have enough time. Not nearly enough time."

"But your blood–"

"It doesn't work like that, Kyler," Elena's voice was quiet. "Only on humans."

The knight squeezed her hand. "I don't want the sun to burn without you," he murmured as his voice broke.

Her lips managed to form a pained smile. "We will be together for eternity," Elena said. "In this life and the next."

Tears filled Kyler's eyes as he stared down at her. He was afraid to look away even for a single moment. Elena reached for her neck. Her fingers found the silver necklace that lay at her throat. A crystal as white as snow was cradled within a knotwork of silver. Kyler recognised it and its meaning. With a grimace Elena pulled it free. She pressed it into Kyler's hand and closed his fingers over the silver.

"Do you remember when you gave me this?" she managed.

Kyler nodded as he took the medallion. "In Adrestia. A lifetime ago."

"No… my life started when I met you."

"Whatever happens," he told her, fighting back the agony that tore at him from within, "you are half of my soul and all of my heart."

"Just as mine belongs to you," she whispered as she gripped his hand. "Always forward, my sweet Kyler. Always forward."

Kyler leaned down and placed his forehead upon Elena's. Her face was wet with tears, and her eyes revealed the pieces of her shattered heart. The sight tore the last strength from the knight.

"I love you, now and forever," Kyler murmured. "I love you. I love you…"

He kissed her, felt the warmth of her breath, the softness of her lips. Her hand slowly fell from his cheek.

"Elena," Kyler murmured, desperate to hear her voice. "Elena."

The light faded from her eyes. She was gone.

FIFTY-THREE

City of Lumis, Isle of Vay'kis, the Valkir Isles

It took many days for the messengers to return to Lumis yet when they did, they were not alone. A great fleet of ships followed in their wake. From Mikon and Kattir, Ramier and Nesoi, had they come. Dozens of ships and hundreds of warriors, while among them were every jarl and every earl of the Valkir.

"Bloodaxe is here," Torben called as he burst into the hall of Lumis.

Erik turned toward the entrance to see a great bear of a man enter. His hair was long and dark, while his beard was darker still. A thick woolly cloak was wrapped around the Jarl's large frame. He wore armour, while a deadly axe hung from his belt. The crew of the Ravenheart cheered as he entered the hall.

The Jarl greeted many of them by name, just as they too greeted him.

Erik's lips curled into a grin as he moved to greet the newcomer. "Jorun, my friend."

"Erik Farrin," the older jarl clasped Erik's arm and clapped a hand upon his shoulder. "It is good to see you."

Jorun Thorkel of Agartha was the last to arrive. Once Erik's shield brother upon the Wind Rider, the man now stood as a bloodsworn and jarl in his own right. The captain of the Harpy was the last to arrive for he had sailed from Nesoi to the east.

"Astrid was a great woman," Jorun told him. "I am sorry that I was not in Agartha, that I was not there for Magnus and all that followed."

"What's done is done. You had your own path to follow," Erik replied, before he turned to Torben. "Gather the earls, gather the jarls. It's time we talked."

Erik waited in the hall alone as his people gathered. He held the raven head amulet in his hand. He felt everything the medallion's previous bearers had known: the hope of his mother, the strength of his father, the wisdom of his sister. It was all there, in the carved wood. He would need it all now more than ever.

"Your mother's necklace," Jorun called as he approached and saw the amulet in is friend's hand.

"She carved it before I was born," Erik told him, not looking from the wooden surface. "She told me once that our family had the spirit of the raven, that their wisdom guided us. My family's strength is in this amulet, Jorun. I can feel it."

"They will always be with you, and when at last you ascend to Ra'haven, they will bask in your tales of glory," Bloodaxe said.

"The Sea-Father will welcome me," Erik replied before he let go of the amulet and turned to face his friend.

"They're ready, everyone is assembled," Jorun told him.

The Jarl of the Ravenheart squared his jaw and made for the entrance.

They met in the great stone courtyard of Lumis where there was plentiful room for both jarl and earl alike. The men and women that led the Valkir wore the powerful expressions and strong poise that could belong to only those who spent a lifetime at sea. Some were old, their hair and beards the colour of winter snow, while others stood young and proud.

"The whole world mourns the loss of Astrid," Earl Einri of Kattir said, stepping forward into the yard. His hair held more grey than black, and his weathered face was lined, yet the Earl gave no signs of age in his stature or voice. He gestured around at the gathered Valkir.

"We came here today to honour her memory, yet why did you call us Erik?"

"Your messenger spoke of murder," Earl Imelda added as she turned her blue eyes to Erik. "Is this true?"

"As true as the sea," Erik replied. He pointed up the hill toward the hall, "My sister was murdered by Earl Arndyr Scaeva. I came here to avenge her death, and to get answers for the most dangerous of questions. Some of you may know that Astrid shared a bond with Arndyr. That he aided us in defeating the tyrant Magnus. That Astrid's murder came at the hands of one so trusted was a blow felt by us all."

"Tell us what you know," Jorun spoke up.

Blaring came from the harbour. It echoed through the streets of Lumis.

"Horns!" Torben yelled as the song reached the company.

Someone approached Lumis. As one, the Valkir turned to the bay toward the sound of the horns. A single ship cut through the water. A ship with purple sails.

A ship bearing the silver griffin.

"Aureia," Einri spat.

"I have seen those ships before," Jorun said. "That is no trader or warship. That is an imperial delegation."

Erik looked to his crew and his eyes burned as a great rage stirred within. "Torben, Fargrim, go now and meet the Aureians. Tell them that I wish to speak."

There were five men in the company. Four wore the silver armour and violet cloaks of the Arkin Garter. They were Valkir, strong and broad yet without the olive skin of those native to the empire. Dark looks were exchanged between the Valkir who awaited them. To some of them those men who served the empire were seen as traitors.

The fifth man wore a shirt of mail beneath his embellished

plate armour. A purple half cloak hung from his pauldron, while a shortsword swung at his hip. His face was lined and hair was thin, yet he stood dignified and proud.

Erik stared at the Aureian and his eyes glowed with anger. The man returned the hard look. He knew that to turn away was a sign of weakness.

"Let me guess," the Aureian begun. "You would be Erik Farrin."

"I am," the bloodsworn replied.

"My name is Valan Azure Aldrich." The Aureian placed a fist over his chest and gave Erik a bow, "emissary to the silver court. I must admit, Jarl Erik, that I have heard your name before."

Erik fingered the hilt of his sword and did not return the gesture. "Unfortunately, *Valan Azure Aldrich*, I cannot say the same."

If Valan cared about the insult he did not show it.

"When I sailed into Lumis I had expected to see the dragon banner of Scaeva flying," he said calmly. "Not that of the raven."

"Why are you here, emissary?" Earl Einri asked.

"Unfortunately, the war," Valan clasped his hands.

"And what war might that be?" Jarl Ulfric of Agartha spoke up.

The Aureian glanced from man to man and nodded. "By now you will be aware of the fight against the eastern barbarians," Valan said. "Wars such as these open many doors, and it was one of these doors that I had intended to speak to Earl Arndyr about."

"Arndyr is dead," Erik growled. "His brother, Jormund, as well."

The bloodsworn looked to the four men of the Arkin Garter. None of them so much as flinched, yet he could see a flicker of anger emerge in their eyes. Arndyr and Jormund had been with the Garter for many years, and these men had obviously known them.

"That is most unfortunate," Valan continued. He gestured to Erik, "By your hand?"

"I killed Jormund," Erik replied. "But his brother, the traitor, took his own life."

"I see." The emissary pursed his lips. "And how did this tragedy come to pass?"

"You don't know?" the bloodsworn was incredulous.

"Of course, he knows," Torben spat. "Poison drips from his fangs just as it did from Arndyr's."

Valan spread his arms. "Forgive me but I do not know of what you speak."

"Arndyr killed Astrid," Erik glowered at the man. He pounded his fist to his chest, "My sister. He murdered her in cold blood atop a field of snow. Killed someone who trusted him above all else, before he in turn took his own life. That is why we came here, *Valan Azure Aldrich*, in pursuit of answers. That is why the Scaeva line is ended."

Valan turned to Erik and a flicker of sadness dancing through his eyes. "The death of family is a hard thing," he said. "I weep for you."

"Crocodile tears will not heal this wound," Erik told him.

"And who are you to say that they are crocodile tears?"

The bloodsworn took a step toward the emissary. The Aureian was shorter yet did not back down. "A letter commanded her death," Erik snarled down at him, "a letter bearing the sun and moon brand."

"The empire had nothing to do with her death," Valan countered. "If it did, I would know."

Jorun stepped to Erik's side. "The sun and moon is the mark of the cardinal is it not?" he said.

"His Holiness would not have–"

"Do you deny it?" Jorun Bloodaxe continued.

"If the cardinal–"

"Do you deny it?"

"No," Valan glared back at the man. "But why would Cardinal Aleksander wish for her death? From what I hear Astrid was no raider or pillager. She had no plans on bringing war to the empire.

Indeed, the last I heard was that she intended on sailing south and that is of no concern to the cardinal *or* the empire."

"Then why is she dead?" Erik roared.

Hands went to swords as the jarl's voice rose. The Arkin Garter stepped forward to stand between Erik and their master.

Valan held out a hand to stop his guard. "The jarl is grieving," he told them. "We need not resort to violence."

The Garter halted but did not remove their hands from their weapons.

"If your people did *not* command her death, then why was the letter marked with the cardinal's brand?" Earl Imelda asked.

"I could not say," Valan admitted. "All I know is that right now Cardinal Aleksander is in the north and will soon do battle with the heathen. He is *not* a murderer, Erik."

"I do not believe you," Erik told him.

"Then align yourself with me," the emissary pressed. "Join the empire in Arndyr's place and together we can win a great victory. In so doing perhaps we could even unshroud the mystery that led to Astrid's death."

"Align with you?" Ulfric snorted. "To what end?"

"Victory."

"To what end?" Ulfric said again.

Valan begun to pace around the courtyard. "All eyes are fixed upon Salvaar," he said. "Medea has pledged her troops, Annora has marshalled, and the Order of Kil'kara have left their fortresses. The time for action is now. Right in this moment, the League of Trecento have voted to rescind the accords struck with Miera. While the savage horsemen are watching the north, Tallis, Kiriador and Elara have prepared. Their armies gather, awaiting command. That command will come in the form of a great fleet that is assembling to the south. Soon that fleet will sail. Dozens of ships, thousands of soldiers. We will land in Miera, we will fight in Miera, and we will conquer Miera."

Erik frowned. For the empire to move against both Salvaar *and* Miera was bold. It was well known that fighting the horsemen on open ground could lead to only one path. Defeat. With the armies of both Aureia and the League it would be possible, yet if Annora and Medea decided to get involved then Miera would burn.

"And what is that to us?" Erik questioned.

"A path to glory," Valan told him, "a path to friendship between our two peoples."

"A path to friendship," Erik muttered.

He could see the wars being fought in the eyes of his people as they looked to him. Dozens of plays being acted in their minds. Yet it was in his own heart that Erik had found the answer.

"Remember why," Erik murmured.

"Pardon me?" Valan frowned.

"Those were her last words, Astrid's last words. Remember why," Erik told them all. "I did not understand them then, but now I see their truth. It was not herself that she wanted remembered, nor even her deeds. Astrid never wanted glory, never wanted fame, never even wanted a crown. All she ever wanted was to follow her heart, and it was a good heart, a peaceful heart. What she wanted remembered was why she had chosen to sail south. Astrid was not a fighter or warrior. She wanted peace. She wanted to escape the lies, the backstabbing, and the blood. She wanted to follow her heart. To follow a path away from fighting, away from war. She wanted peace. That is what she wanted us to remember. And you killed her for it."

Valan's face paled as he stared at the Jarl. Erik's words had shocked him to his core. "The empire did not–"

"It was all written neatly upon that letter," Erik snarled. "Holy orders condemning her to death. She was a woman of peace. She wanted peace! And you killed her. She was going to sail south to see what lay beyond. All she wanted was freedom. The freedom to sail. The freedom to choose her own destiny. The freedom to love.

That was her heart's desire. That was her song, and you killed her."

"You speak of war," Valan said, and his voice filled with the arrogance that belonged to a man of his station, a man who did business for the greatest empire to have ever been. "And swiftly do words of war become more than words."

"If you do not want war then bring your cardinal to me in *chains*," Erik told him.

"That will never happen."

The bloodsworn spat to the side before turning his furious gaze upon the Aureian." Then I say that the empire is as weak as it is cowardly," Erik snarled. "The dead will be avenged."

"The empire kneels to no man," Valan gloated with superiority. "If you want war then we will give you war. But make no mistake, if you choose this path then you are choosing death. Your warriors will be slain, your ships will burn, your women, your *children,* will be sold as slaves. Any mention of the Valkir will be erased from history. I *will* erase you."

The emissary began to stride around courtyard and looked to every one of the Valkir in turn. "Oh, you may sting us as you raid our shores, yet it is we who control the Lupentine, not *you*. Do you recall what happened when last you rose against us? The Isles burned for days, your people were carrion for wolves and crows. We outnumber you like you are nothing, for that is what you are. *Nothing.* An insignificant speck on the pages of history. Go down this path and we will wipe you out. All of you. What we do here will be spoken of for a thousand years, long after our bones have turned to dust. And yet you come to me and speak of war? Will you make that mistake? Will you be the one fool enough to destroy your own people? Or will you kneel and seek forgiveness for your insolence?"

The cool air ran through Erik's hair and caressed his cheek. He looked into the eyes of his people. He looked into their hearts. The jarls and earls had come when he had sent the call, and he could ask no more than that. In the eyes of his crew, he saw nothing but naked anger.

Ulfric had been right all along. What had happened here was his doing, and its consequences could only fall upon his shoulders. What happened next would only happen if he made it so. Could he set his people upon the path of his choosing? He saw Torben, his oldest friend. The closest people he had left to family. The old warrior nodded, and in that moment he knew. Erik's hand fell to his sword. He spun toward the Aureian as he drew his blade and placed it against the man's neck.

"We will have war!" His voice was as thunder. He saw fear in Valan's eyes as he gazed into them. The Garter drew their blades.

"Kill the traitors!" bellowed Torben as he leapt at the closest guardsman with his axe.

With a roar, the crew of the Ravenheart charged the four men. They had no time to react as they were swarmed. Within moments it was over. The blood of the Arkin Garter stained the frozen stone beneath.

Valan made to speak but Erik flicked his wrist. Steel cut into flesh and then the emissary was silenced forever. He crashed to the ground as blood poured from his ruined throat. Crimson spread across the courtyard, and then it was over.

"What have you done?" Earl Einri shouted. "You are no earl or king. You are bloodsworn. You swore an oath never to wear a crown!"

Erik tossed his sword to the ground and tore free his knife. In a single move he made bare his serpent tattoo and then sliced the blade through the markings. "Then I am bloodsworn no more," Erik cried as his wound bled. "I am not beholden to the laws and traditions of the serpent's creed. I am Jarl Erik Farrin, son of the slain Jarl Leif Farrin, brother of the slain Jarl Astrid Farrin, the greatest navigator of our time. And I will have my revenge whatever the cost."

Fires ignited in the eyes of the Valkir who watched. Fists began to beat upon chests.

"The empire has cast a shadow over these isles for too long. They have controlled us, murdered us, used us as soldiers in their wars. That ends now my brothers and sisters. That ends with our swords and our spears driven into the heart of the empire. This path was chosen by the empire, but by the Sea-Father it shall be us who decide our own destiny. I know that not all of you wished this, yet it is done. Friends… brothers, we have only one course now. We must unite in a way that our people have *never* done before. We must stand as one or fall as many. Astrid wanted a new future for us all, a future not darkened by the shadow of death. That future is within our grasp now. Fight with me and we shall claim it. What say you, Valkir? What say you? Don't fight for me. Don't fight for Astrid. Don't fight for crowns or gold because you won't get any. Fight for your homes. Fight for your sons. Fight for your daughters. Fight for your freedom. Fight for the Valkir!"

The warriors of the isles roared.

The crew of the Ravenheart roared.

FIFTY-FOUR

City of Vesuva, Aureian Empire

Kitara took a breath as she closed Sereia's unseeing eyes. The girl had been young. She'd still had so much to live for, yet she was gone. Kitara took the ring from Sereia's fingers and placed the cord that bound it around her neck. The sapphire ring hung at her throat once again. The ring of her mother. The ring of a Salvaari. Though Kitara knew that no one was coming to save her, she had a people, had a place. That place was not here, not in Aureia. It was in a distant land, so far away now that it may have been nothing but a whisper of her imagination. In Vesuva, Sereia had been all she had left.

Kitara rose to her feet and turned to the door as she heard footsteps fast approaching. Her breathing was steady. Her hands balled into fists. The first man appeared. His lips curled into a sneer. Kitara watched the soldier's eyes as he raised his wicked club. The blow was swift and thrown without mercy, but Kitara was ready. She leapt forward as she had once been taught. Her hands latched around his arm as she swivelled back. Kitara pulled hard and used the man's momentum against him. She threw him over her shoulder and slammed him hard into the ground. Kitara viciously tore the club from his hand and brought it up just in time to stop the second soldier's attack. A third club was driven hard into her stomach. Kitara doubled over as air fled her lungs. Soldiers poured into the room. They grabbed her arms and forced Kitara to her knees. She struggled and fought, clawed, and screamed.

A club smashed into the side of her head.

Kitara saw darkness.

As she came to, she heard footsteps upon stone. Kitara blinked as she awoke. Chains bound her hands, while her feet were dragged along the floor. Two men held her tight as they made their way through the villa. Kitara shook her head to clear the last of the darkness. She saw Arias Nilor talking to another man. His back was turned, yet she could see steel armour beneath his cloak.

"Senator Nilor," one of the soldiers called out, before the pair tossed Kitara before the Aureian lord. Her braids fell around her like a waterfall as she hit the ground. Her bound hands barely stopped her face from meeting stone.

Kitara stared up at Arias with bared teeth. "Why?" she growled. "Why?"

"She was good. She was kind. She was *innocent*, and you killed her," Kitara spat as she glared at the man with hate filled eyes.

"None of us are innocent, Alessandra," Arias replied. He placed a hand over the fresh scar upon his cheek, "You struck at me, so I struck back."

"A scar pales in comparison to a life that will no longer be lived," Kitara growled. "Sereia is dead. She is dead."

"You should have thought about that before you turned steel upon me," he countered, and met her hard stare with his own. "Sereia was a poor investment. She was a child who had no means of recovering the cost it took to purchase her. And do you know what else is a poor investment? A slave who does not know her place. A slave who injured relations between one house and another. You are a poor investment, Alessandra."

"That is *not* my name," Kitara snarled.

"It is now," Arias told her. "And it shall be the name you bear when you die."

"Then kill me. If I am such a poor investment, why am I not

dead?" Kitara snapped as she shrugged off the soldiers from her shoulder. "If I am to die today then I am ready."

The man in armour turned to face her. "No, you won't be dying today," a rough Medean voice said.

She recognised the voice as she recognised the face. "*You*," Kitara hissed as she saw Sir Rowan of Patchi. The very man who had condemned her and so many others to slavery and death. Morlag, Urlaigh, Sereia. The Medean mercenary knight nodded at her words.

"We meet again, Salvaari."

"Sir Rowan has graciously accepted an offer to work for me until such a time as he and his men wish to return home," Arias told her. "He shall be transporting you to your new owner come morning."

Kitara ground her teeth and barely kept her rage in check. Calvillo had once taught her to never fight with emotion, and never ever make decisions with it. At a gesture from Nilor, the two soldiers hoisted Kitara to her feet.

"I fought for you," she told Arias. "I killed for you."

"You killed for me?" the Aureian snorted contemptuously. "You're a slave! You do what you do, and you fight who you fight because you have to."

Kitara's hands curled around her restraints. "I am not your *slave*," she snarled. "I was *never* your slave. Oh, I played your games and I played them well, but do not ever think that I was serving you."

"That is of no consequence," Arias shrugged. "Tonight you will sleep in chains. Tomorrow I will sell you to Ceolsige Teora. By day you shall fight in his pits, by night you shall service whomever he chooses. You will never see the sun again. That is my promise."

"That is your promise?" Kitara hissed back. "Then allow me to make one. Before I die, I will look down upon you at my feet, as life flees your breath, and I will *smile*. That is my promise."

"Sir Rowan, escort the slave to her cell."

The Medeans led her down into the depths of the villa. Kitara had not seen nor heard of the tunnels in which they walked. A bad sign. A maze of corridors led to a jail cell. The door was made of steel bars, while the small chamber was cold stone. It was no more than a cage. Sir Rowan gathered up a large chain anchored to the far wall and began to attach it to Kitara's bindings. One of the Aureian soldiers drew his blade and held it to her throat as the mercenary worked. Kitara did not react as the steel touched her neck. She would show no weakness, least of all to her enemy. Sir Rowan turned his furious gaze toward the guard as he locked the bindings together.

"Lower your sword," he commanded. "Can't you see that she is in chains? Show her some respect."

The Aureian frowned before he did as he was bid and returned his weapon to its sheath.

Kitara glanced at the Medean. His words surprised her. The man who had condemned her to slavery and killed so many of her people was talking about *respect*.

"Respect?" Kitara muttered. "You know *nothing* of respect. You know nothing of compassion, and even for a knight you know little about honour."

"Honour doesn't feed a hungry family nor keep them warm in the coldest winter," Sir Rowan told her before he turned to his men. "Give us a moment."

Within moments they were alone.

"How can you serve him?" Kitara hissed and her hands balled into fists as she pulled the chains tight. "Arias Nilor is a monster."

"How can a mercenary serve one of the most influential families in the empire? Let me tell you something, *Kitara*. I was only ever taught two things," Rowan of Patchi said as he tapped the hilt of his longsword. "How to use a blade, and how to lead. With these skills I am a match for any man. That is not arrogance, that is the truth. Those skills set me upon the path that I now walk. They gained me reputation but understand this, reputation is no shield. I am a master of my craft and now I have obtained the patronage of the house of Nilor. This family plays host to one of the greatest magisters that the empire has ever seen. It has gained me both wealth and position. More than that even. It has made me a man of means. In a few years I will be able to lay down my sword."

"And what would a *mercenary* do without his sword?" Kitara scoffed.

"Watch his sons grow old without them ever knowing the weight of a spear, without ever knowing the chaos of battle, and without the chance of dying before their father," Rowan told her sincerely. "Yet you are right about Arias, you are right. You have my respect and for that reason I will tell you this. You cut him in front of his men. Arias will not forgive that. Tonight, he will come for you, he will stand before you and he will beat you."

Kitara sighed and gave him a slow nod. She had thought that to be true. "And you would tell me this out of respect?"

"We are not so different after all," Rowan replied.

Kitara rolled her eyes. She had heard those words countless times before and each time they had been proven to be false. "You know nothing about me," Kitara said.

The Medean pursed his lips. "I know that you are haunted by shadows of the past. I saw that on the ship. Though I do not know the names of your nightmares. I know that while you do not fear death, sometimes you wish for it."

She froze and for the first time was unable to speak. What he had said was true. The names of her demons had only ever been spoken to one person, and it had not been the knight who stood before her. They were names that terrified her. Names that had nearly broken her. Somehow, he knew about them, and it chilled her to the bone.

"You understand nothing," Kitara growled.

"I understand that you have will. That you have strength and that you conviction," Sir Rowan said as he closed the cell door. "If only you had been born Medean and stood by my side."

"It is a blessing then that I was born Salvaari," Kitara snarled.

"I am sorry that this is your fate," the knight told her sadly. "I should have killed you long ago."

The cell was cold and the chains that bound her were tight. They dug into her wrists, yet Kitara paid them no mind. A longer steel chain connected her bindings to an anchor upon the stone wall. Kitara sat against the wall staring toward the barred door of her cell. She did not know what time it was for there was no light in the bowels of the villa. She had not been able to sleep, nor turn her mind from what was about to come. Kitara had nothing, nowhere to run, and no friends to aid her.

Yet she would take whatever chance she had left at escape, and if in doing so she died then so be it. What she had told Arias Nilor had been the truth. If she were to die, then she was ready to meet her fate. She would not cry nor beg for more time. Kitara rested her arms upon her knees and waited. She closed her eyes. She still wore the armour from Vulir's games. She still felt its comforting weight. When the soldiers came to deprive her of it, perhaps she could act.

The cell door opened.

Kitara opened her eyes. Rowan had been right. It was Arias greeted who her. The nobleman turned to the soldier who guarded the cell and extended a hand. Without a word the guard handed Arias his wicked club. Kitara knew what was coming next. She rose to her feet in defiance.

"I have a question," Arias said.

"And what might that be?"

"From everything I have witnessed and from everything that I have been told by Sir Rowan, it seems clear to me that you fight without emotion and that you act without emotion," he begun. "Why then did you fight when your ring was first taken? Why then did you resist rather than submit?"

"I owe no man answers, least of all you."

"Even now you resist," Arias extended his club and placed it against her cheek. "Even when everyone that you have known or loved has abandoned you. Why?"

"I have been beaten, betrayed, and abandoned by them all since the day I was born. I have never had anyone to watch my back or stand by my side. Why do I resist? Because no one else will."

"You could have been so much more."

"Not if it meant serving you."

The club slammed into her side. Kitara grimaced, yet did not cry out. It cracked into her chest. She staggered yet did not scream. A third blow struck her shoulder. Kitara bared her teeth against the pain. The club met her stomach. She fell to a knee but did not shout. Her hands were balled so tight that her fingers grew white. Two times down, three times up. The words of her old mentor echoed through her mind and gave strength to her body. Another blow felled her. Kitara wheezed as she struggled for breath. She lay on her hands and knees, barely able to stay up. Only the armour was saving her. Arias Nilor turned. He thought her beaten when her body was merely bruised. He thought it over when life still roared in her veins.

Kitara heaved herself forward, pushed herself to her feet, and leapt at the Aureian's back. Her arms snaked out, bound by the chains. Kitara's bindings wrapped around his neck like a noose. They dug into his throat and strangled the breath from him. Arias reached for the chains, but Kitara had already pulled them tight. Her muscles strained hard. He reached for her yet a harsh tug from Kitara sent him to his knees. The guard bounded into the room as he heard his master's cries.

"Captain Nilor!" the soldier shouted as he ripped his sword free.

"Stand!" Kitara roared back. "Stand or your master dies!"

The guard made to move toward her. Kitara heaved on the chains, prompting a strangled cry from Nilor's lips. The soldier stopped in his tracks.

"Your sword," Kitara said and indicated the ground.

The guard complied and tossed steel onto stone.

Kitara nodded into the far corner of the cell. "Stand over there."

The guard grimaced but did as he was commanded. Kitara turned and took Nilor with her as the guard moved aside of the doorway. Her eyes went to the man's belt where they locked with a tiny piece of metal. "The key," she said as she opened her left hand.

She saw the war being fought in the man's heart and tightened the chains. With a curse the guard snatched up the key and tossed it into Kitara's awaiting hand. She reversed it in her grip, slid it into the lock that bound her chains to the wall. Kitara turned the key. The long chain fell away. Kitara had only moments. She could see Sereia in her mind. She could still hear the girl's voice. Kitara tensed and drove her full strength into the chain around Nilor's throat.

She gritted her teeth as she squeezed hard and gave a savage wrench.

Arias Nilor's neck snapped.

Kitara moved fast. She unwrapped her chains as the nobleman fell. The guard leapt for his blade with a shout, yet he was too slow. Kitara was closer to the fallen sword. It was in her hands in a heartbeat. Kitara's form was perfect and her movement fluid. Her sword sliced across the man's thigh as he tried to retreat. She saw the fear in his eyes. He had never faced anyone armed with the knowledge of tarkaras. It was over in moments. Her first strike took his balance, while her second took his head. Kitara flicked her sword and then turned back to Arias Nilor's body. His eyes were unseeing and his body limp; he was dead.

Kitara knelt beside the dead man and snatched up the key to free her hands of their bindings. The chains fell and rang as they hit the stone. She turned the body over and stared at the ornaments upon his wrist. Trophies taken from the dead. She ripped the collection of Salvaari arm rings from his forearm. Morlag's ring, Sereia's ring, her ring. They sat alongside others. Kitara took them all and in turn placed them along her own arm. She snatched up her sword before she moved to the cell's entrance.

Kitara stared down the long corridor and saw no one. No guards. No soldiers. Arias had been alone. Yet the passage was a maze. A maze which she had never seen before. She had no way of knowing which path was the right one or which passages held unseen enemies.

Then she remembered. It had been a long time since she had been awoken in the night. A long time since she had felt the gift.

Kitara closed her eyes. "Remember the sea… remember her voice," she murmured in Salvaari. Words that had once been spoken by Aeryn. Words that had calmed her. Words that tied her to the gift.

"Feel her anger as she rises around you, lashing as she reaches toward you, threatening a storm."

She felt it.

Kitara opened her eyes. Violet light ignited within them. She sensed everything around her. She could see it all. The passages, the soldiers, all of it. This time there was no pain. This time she could see clearly. Kitara knew where she had to go. She knew what path she had to take. She saw Rowan and his men. She saw them enter the corridor upon which her cell was joined. There was no time. Kitara blinked away the vision and walked out into the corridor.

Her hands tightly clasped her sword.

Sir Rowan saw her. A startled look crossed his face.

"She's escaping!" he bellowed.

One the Medeans charged. Kitara turned and ran in the opposite direction. Soldiers saw her from the far end of the corridor and angled to cut her off. Kitara felled one in two strikes, swivelled to the side, and then gutted the second. She hurried up the stairs and into the villa as the shouts were taken up. Torches lit the dark rooms. Servants watched in horror as Kitara ran through their midst. An Auriean charged from behind. Kitara blocked his blow, skipped to the side, and then opened his throat. She did not stop. She could not stop. Glancing over her shoulder Kitara saw Sir Rowan and his men appear.

They barrelled toward her. Kitara angled away, ducked into another room, and then charged up a set of stairs. She could hear their footsteps closing, hear their heavy breathing, and the shouts that echoed through the villa. Kitara barely avoided a spear as a soldier came at her from the side. She had no time to finish him and no time to engage. Kitara could only run. Her muscles ached from the beating, yet she would not let them slow her. She forced herself faster. Kitara glanced over her shoulder and saw yet more soldiers pursuing her. She sprinted into a wide corridor and ran for all she was worth. Her golden hair flew behind her like blonde fire.

A great window appeared at the corridor's end. She had no idea what lay beyond, no idea how far the drop would be. It was her only chance. Kitara charged at it. She leapt into the air and raised her left arm to shield her eyes. Kitara met the glass head on. It shattered. Shards bounced upon her armour and sliced through her skin. Then she was falling.

The drop was deep.

Her feet hit the ground and then she crashed into the mud. Breath fled her body and her ankle screamed. The darkness of night enveloped her in a blanket of shadows. Kitara groaned as pain rolled through her body. She barely noticed the rain that fell all around her. Blood wept from her arms and cheeks from the glass. A gash had opened in her thigh. Kitara heaved herself to her feet. She nearly fell as her ankle threatened to give way. Kitara took a breath, forced back the agony, and began to limp down the street.

The rain grew harder as she stumbled down the road. Kitara dragged her sprained ankle as fast as she could. She used the walls of buildings for support. Shouts had filled the streets of Vesuva and the blasting of horns swiftly followed. A pair of spear wielding city guards found her first. Kitara heaved herself from the wall of a house as the first lance darted her way. She knocked it aside with her arm and drove her sword through the man's neck. He fell with a cry, before his companion quickly followed him in death. Kitara snatched up one of the spears and, using it as a staff, began to hobble down the street once more. The rain chilled her skin and forced what little warmth she had from her bones. It hindered her vision and her hearing. Kitara grimaced as she used the spear to take her weight from her ankle.

The squelching of footsteps in mud came from behind. A shout came with them.

Dark shapes emerged from the shadows. The first to reach her was a steel-clad knight. One of the Medeans. A small shield covered his left arm, while he held a war hammer in his right hand. She jabbed the spear at his eyes, but the knight was fast. The shield came up and sent the lance skyward. Kitara barely slid aside from his counter. Her ankle cried out. She winced as she moved and was barely able to keep her footing. Kitara dropped her sword and took hold of the spear with both hands. She thrust once, twice. He blocked them both before he sent his hammer back toward her. Kitara raised her guard.

Steel splintered wood as the spear was snapped in half. The force of the blow took Kitara's balance, and her bad ankle gave way. She hit the ground and rolled to the side as the hammer bit into the ground next to her head. Kitara found the bladed end of the spear and rolled back on top of the war hammer to trap it beneath her body. She drove the broken spear up and thrust it into the knight's exposed neck. He screamed and crashed down upon her. His blood splashed upon her skin. Kitara heaved the dying Medean from her body. She pulled her spear free with her left hand and reached for her sword with her right. Kitara used the blade to push herself to her feet.

Aureians and Medeans alike came at her. She could not run and could not flee. She would not surrender. Kitara held her weapons high as she stood her ground. The sword of an Aureian descended. She caught it with her own blade before she thrust the spear up into his jaw. Kitara savagely wrenched the weapon free and sent the guard crashing into a lifeless pile of blood and bone. She tasted the rain, tasted the blood. Another knight came at her. She blocked with her spear and blocked with her sword. She could barely stand.

The spear found a home in the man's leg, before his shield sent her down into the mud. Her back hit the ground. Her head hit it hard. Her ears rung. Her body screamed. Kitara swivelled to her knees and lashed out with her spear. It kissed the knight's shield before it was ripped from her grasp. Her sword came around and slammed into his shin. The armour saved the man, but he fell. Kitara leapt on top of him. Her hands found his knife. She tore the blade from its sheath and plunged it down. The knight caught her arms with his hands. She heaved down and drove her full weight into the weapon.

Steel edged closer to his throat. A shield slammed into the side of her head. Kitara fell to the side as her vision flickered.

Two times down, three times up.

Her fingers found her spear. She sent it blindly toward her new foe. The shaft of a spear drove into her back and sent her face first into the mud. Earth and water filled her mouth and nose. She could barely see. She gasped for air.

Two times down, three times up.

She reached for her sword. The shaft cracked into her side and flipped Kitara onto her back. She felt blood roll from her nose and her split lip. She struggled to breathe, struggled to rise.

Two times down, three times up.

She would not give up. She would not give in. Kitara slowly rose to her knees and then her feet, as the Medeans circled like vultures. It was Rowan who held the spear. She met his eyes, saw the fury within them. Kitara had killed his benefactor. The spear came around. Its shaft connected heavily with her stomach. Kitara fell to her knees. She coughed as air fled her lungs. Mud ran through her fingers. Her own blood dripped down onto them. A shield slammed into her side and sent her to the ground.

Two times down, three times up.

Kitara heaved with her hands and pushed herself up. With her remaining strength, Kitara gathered up the fallen knight's dagger. She cried out as she drove it toward Rowan's thigh. He caught her wrist with his powerful grip and then battered the spear into the side of her head.

Two times down, three times up.

She tried to rise. The spear sent her down. The Medeans took her arms and lifted her to her knees. Rain mixed with the mud and blood upon her face and daubed her skin. It filled her senses. Her body ached from a thousand wounds. Her ankle was on fire. With a grimace she turned her head up toward the knight and gritted her teeth. Sir Rowan of Patchi cast his spear aside and pulled forth his longsword. Kitara met his eye as he raised the blade. So, it would be here in the streets of Vesuva that she met her fate. She felt the rain upon her skin, the cool northern breeze. A thin sliver of moonlight broke the dark clouds.

"Tanris, I come to you," she murmured.

Kitara did not close her eyes. She did not look away. There was a thud.

Sir Rowan staggered back. A broad bladed arrow fired from a Salvaari warbow embedded in his chest.

A second followed, and then a third. The knight toppled over. Death greeted Sir Rowan like a friend and welcomed him with gentle hands. More of the Medeans followed as arrows rained down. Kitara was released as her captors turned to face a line of charging horses. She fell into the mud. She heard the shouts and screams, the sounds of battle. Warriors fell all around her, Medean and Aureian alike. The blasting of horns filled the air. Boots splashed into the street beside Kitara.

"Kitara," a woman called her name. "Kitara!"

She looked toward the voice as she was pulled to her knees by her bow wielding saviour. Kitara saw the dark hair and the silver eyes.

"Aeryn?" she murmured, unsure if she was in a dream or a dream of a dream.

The moonseer pressed her forehead to Kitara's, before she snatched at her arm and heaved her to her feet. Bellec leapt down beside them and charged into the fray. He cut down Aureians left and right. Galadayne fought by his side.

"Kitara!" Bellec bellowed to his companion.

Without hesitation, Galadayne broke from the fight and ran to Kitara and Aeryn. "We have to go!" he shouted and took Kitara's other arm. Together they dragged her to a riderless horse and heaved her up into the saddle.

Aeryn heaved herself up behind Kitara, took the reins with her right hand, and used her bow to hold her companion tight. All of the mercenaries were fleeing and mounting their horses to make their escape. All but one. All but he. All but Bellec. A soldier came at the mercenary's back as he cut down another. The moonseer felled him with a single arrow. The wounded mercenary struggled to his feet as blood poured from his leg.

"Bellec!" Galadayne roared. "We have to go now!"

Aureians appeared from the street and surged toward them. Bellec roared. He cut down one, cut down two. Sakkar dropped another with his bow.

"BELLEC!" Galdayne shouted once more. "THERE ARE TOO MANY!"

Bellec barely heard. These people had enslaved his daughter. All he saw was death. He *became* death. Arrows and spears flew from the mercenaries' hands and bows as soldiers and knights charged at Bellec. His sword sang as it moved. Blood painted the street.

"BELLEC!" Aeryn cried as she killed another.

Galadayne kicked his heel in and charged back into the fray with Bellec's horse in tow. He took the wave of Aureians head on. His mount sent the first of the soldiers crashing to the ground while his sword took a second. The arrows of the mercenaries forced the Aureians back.

Galadayne lept from his horse and shoved his friend back toward the mercenaries.

"She's safe!" he shouted. "More come! We have to leave!" His words broke through the red mist.

Bellec snarled and then heaved himself up onto his horse. "Out now!" Bellec roared.

Aeryn kicked her heels in as the company fled back from whence they came. The Aureians screamed from behind but it there was nothing they could do. The mercenaries were gone.

FIFTY-FIVE

City of Elara, the League of Trecento

Kyler knelt amidst a field of corpses. Yet he did not care. His body was battered and bruised. His face and armour covered in blood. His blood and that of his enemies. Yet he did not care.

The woman that he loved was dead. Her life extinguished forever.

"Cuun'etca hĕy'læn," the knight murmured as he closed her unseeing eyes.

He did not know if she truly believed in the heavens, nor if she would be walking in the paradise of his gods. Elena was dead and the words of his faith were the only ones he knew. Tears streaked down from his eyes, and everything was cold. Kyler gently stroked her cheek. There was no light, not anymore. Elena was gone and his future gone with her. He had lost her once before, yet now it was forever. Like his parents, Kyler would never be able to hold her again. The pain began like a spear driven into his mind. The constant ache that had plagued him for days began to burn. Kyler winced and raised a hand to his pounding brow.

"Landrey," Olivera's voice broke the quiet.

The knight did not reply as he fought back the agony.

"Landrey!" the cutthroat repeated. "Your woman... what did she do?"

"She's dead," Kyler managed as his face contorted into a grimace and the pain worsened.

"She took my mind, seized my tongue and body. I could not fight her, could not resist. Yet it was as if I wanted to do what I did," Olivera growled. "What did she do? Answer me!"

"I don't know," the knight told him. He stared at Elena's body. He knew that she was not fully human, and that her existence was against the very nature of his order. He had seen the red eyes glowing like fire, and seen what she was capable of, yet he did not care.

"Tell me what happened," Olivera spat.

Kyler bared his teeth as his breathing began to grow ragged. His mind *burned*. He turned toward Scar Lip, and for the first time saw the other two surviving members of their company. Though they had fought side by side, the three gang men were no friends of Kyler. They were armed, and their faces awash with anger and fear.

"I don't know," Kyler said again.

Olivera spread his arms. "Was she a witch?"

"No," the knight could barely speak, and when he did it was pained. Everything burned.

"A monster then."

Kyler panted. The veins of his hands begin to blacken.

"Shut your mouth," the knight snarled. He slammed his fist into the ground. The agony grew into an inferno.

Olivera watched as Kyler stiffened. "Struck a nerve, did I?" the cutthroat chuckled.

The knight slowly turned to face the three men. Olivera's face paled and his skin crawled. Kyler's face was tired and worn. A web of dark veins ran across it. The knight's eyes burned brighter than the sun and were as crimson as fresh blood.

"Landrey?" Olivera called as he saw the bloodstained sword in Kyler's hand.

The knight said nothing as he moved toward them as if in a

trance. The three gang men exchanged glances. Olivera felt fear begin to gnaw at him. He raised his blade.

"Landrey!"

The sword came up.

Kyler came to as if he were awaking from a dream. He blinked and shook his head to fight off the last of the cloud that darkened his mind. It was only then that Kyler realised that he was standing, and only then that he felt the sword in his hand. He ran his gaze along the blade. Blood dripped from the steel and splashed upon the cold stone floor.

Then he saw the bodies.

Not the field of Sacasian pirates and gang men that surrounded him, but those of Olivera and his two companions. They weren't just dead. They were almost unrecognisable, torn apart by a sword. The last thing that he could remember was kneeling by Elena's side, yet in his heart Kyler knew what had happened. His hand went to his sun and moon amulet as fear took him.

"Dear gods… what have I done?" he murmured. Kyler stared at the bodies that surrounded him. He was frozen. His hand unconsciously tightened upon the hilt of his sword. His head still ached.

"Pisspot?"

The words woke him. He glanced toward their owner and saw Alarik standing across the chamber. The battlemaster's armour was as bloody as Kyler's, while a pair of arrows protruded from his shield. Three of Olivera's men stood with him.

"What happened here?" Alarik called as he approached.

Kyler met his mentor's eyes and saw the worry within them. "Elena is dead," he replied as he turned his gaze back to her body.

Alarik placed a comforting hand upon Kyler's shoulder. "I'm sorry."

Landrey said nothing as once more he knelt beside the woman he loved.

"The city has been overrun," Alarik told him.

"They were supposed to be our allies," one of the men murmured as he knelt beside a fallen comrade.

The battlemaster turned on him. "You let them in?" Alarik asked.

"While the Elaran fleet was chasing a single ship through the seas, dozens sailed from the south. Some we led through the tunnels, others will land in the bay," he replied. "By dawn Elara will belong to the people once again."

"Or your people will fall from the city walls," Alarik told him bitterly before glancing back at Kyler. "The gangs and pirates have flooded the streets. We need to leave this place."

Landrey could only nod.

"More will be coming," Alarik turned to the three men. "How do we get out?"

"Because of *you* our brothers lie dead," one of them growled.

The battlemaster gave them a venomous glare and placed a hand atop his sword. "I have no quarrel with you," Alarik said. "But if you stand in my way you will never see your families again."

The man grimaced before he gestured toward one of the tunnels. "That tunnel leads to the bazaar. Once you reach the crossroads, take the path on the right.

Alarik nodded his thanks and turned back to his companion. Pity filled his eyes. "We have to leave Elara before everything burns," he said. "Arntair will give us a way out."

"Why would the trader help us?" Kyler asked as he glanced up at his mentor.

"I was in Elara months before your arrival to the Order. He helped me in gathering supplies for the maija. We have to leave, Kyler," Alarik told him. "We have to leave *her*."

He was talking about Elena.

"No," Landrey replied.

"We have no choice," the battlemaster said. "More will be coming."

"Then her fate will be our fate," Kyler sheathed his sword and then gently gathered Elena's body in his arms and rose to his feet. "She deserves more than a tomb down here in the darkness."

Alarik stared at him, and his face showed the anger that burned within. "So be it," he muttered.

They walked for a while before the tunnel slowly began to lead upward. The higher they climbed the more screams they heard. People were fighting, *dying* in the streets above. Eventually they came to a barred door that led into the bazaar. Alarik drew his sword and in two strikes severed the chain that locked it. The two men shared a look before they walked out into the city.

Kyler could hear the shouts and the clashing of steel, as the battle raged through the city. The bazaar hadn't yet been breached. It was only a matter of time before the fighting spilled into the great market. The only life within the bazaar were the groups of Elaran soldiers rushing through. They did not stop to question the knights. They saw the armour, saw the blood, saw the body, yet did not call out.

"Arntair!" Alarik shouted as he pounded his fist upon the trader's door. "Arntair!"

The door was unbolted and then pulled open. The knights were greeted by the naked steel of a sword.

"You," Arntair muttered he saw the battlemaster.

"We need your help."

The trader looked to Kyler and saw the body that he carried. "What can I do?"

Arntair led Kyler through the market as the shouts and screams drew nearer. He took him beyond the walls and pavilion and to his warehouse. Within they found a cart and a horse to lead it. Kyler gently placed Elena's body in the back of the wagon. It took all of his strength to hold his emotion at bay. He turned to Arntair.

"Your cloak," Kyler said.

The trader must have seen the pain in his eyes, saw that there was no room for argument, and so passed the garment to the knight.

Kyler wrapped Elena in the fine blue silk and then looked at her face. It was as if she were only sleeping, yet her chest did not rise.

"What was her name?" Arntair asked.

"Her name is Elena," Kyler told him, unable to look away from her. His hand reached toward his throat, though instead of clasping the sun and moon, it turned to the silver necklace. The jewellery that he had once given to Elena. It had been on the day that she had left Adrestia. The day that had changed both of their lives. How he longed to return to that moment.

"She was dear to you?"

"She was my heart," Kyler told him quietly.

"Your friend will return with your horses soon," Arntair said after a moment. "You will soon be free of this city."

Kyler sighed and at last turned from Elena. He felt the weight begin to crush him. First his parents had been claimed by the pale horseman, and now in turn Elena had been taken from his arms. Always forward, that was what Elena had said. He would not give up. He would not let the loss destroy him.

"I wish that we had never come here," Kyler said as he held the necklace tight. "If I could turn back the sun I would."

"Your friend will be back soon."

"Thank you for helping us. Alarik told me that you had met before."

Arntair hesitated for a moment as he looked to Kyler. "Yes... he was in the city not so long ago to find recruits."

Kyler frowned. That was not what the battlemaster had told him.

Sir Alarik arrived shortly afterward. He rode his black steed with Asena's reins clasped in his left hand and a bloody sword in his right. He had been forced to fight to retrieve the horses, forced to kill to get back to the warehouse. The knight grimaced as Arntair closed the doors behind him.

"Pisspot, we need to leave *now*," Alarik shouted as he rode into the warehouse. "The pirates are being held by Elaran steel but will soon break through. This place will burn. Our only way out is the northern gate. Mount up."

"Yes, sir," Kyler replied on instinct as he hurried toward the front of the wagon.

Within moments he was seated atop the cart and had gathered up the reins.

"Arntair," Alarik called to the other man, "the doors."

The trader heaved the huge wooden doors of the warehouse open.

The battlemaster gave Arntair a nod. "Light of the gods be with you," Alarik said.

"And with you."

Kyler flicked his wrists, and the cart began to move. The knights rode out into the city.

Elise Delfeyre watched from the belltower as the streets were overrun. Fires began to burn and a great horde of pirates, gang men, and Stentor soldiers swarmed through Elara. From her vantage she could see it all and it chilled her to the bone.

The fighting within the tower had long since stopped, and now there was only the faint sound of battle coming from the city a hundred feet below.

She felt a great wave of sadness. The magister and many of the nobility deserved this fate, yet how many innocents would be caught up in the storm? Elise reached into her jacket and pulled out a single feather. The feather of a nightingale. She ran her fingers along its soft length.

A knock came from the trapdoor.

"Elise?"

It was Cleander's voice. The Nightingale made her way over to the door and heaved the lock open. The Annoran climbed up the last of the stairs and joined her in the tower. Together the pair gazed out from the railing and watched as their city burned.

"How did it come to this?" Elise murmured as she stroked the feather. "When I first wore my mask, it was to uncover answers yet now I find myself fighting in a war."

"Things rarely happen as they are intended," Cleander replied. "Weeks ago, you were only a thief. A thief who became a symbol that the people put all their hope and dreams into. Whether intentionally or not, this could not have happened without you."

"This is the Nightingale's shadow," Elise murmured and echoed the words of the poem.

"Everything is in the hands of the gods. I can only hope that they have some kind of purpose for all of this."

Elise glanced at him, more surprised than she would care to admit. "You have faith?" she asked.

"I was once a knight," he told her. "I served the Twins alongside the Order of Kil'kara... so much has changed since then."

"Some days I hardly recognise myself," Elise replied.

Cleander reached beneath his shirt and pulled out his sun and moon amulet. "There are days like that, aye," he said. "Let me tell you something. You and I are not the gentle people from stories. We are not the people who sleep in the streets below, who worry about no more than food and the roof over their heads. The people who call our city home. We are their voice. We fight because they cannot. Perhaps that was not always your calling, but now it is so. The only way to remain sane in this world is to find a purpose to live your life. I know who I am. I know what I am. I know what I believe, and only when we admit what we are can we truly do what needs to be done."

"And what are you, Cleander?"

The Annoran brushed his fingers along his amulet. "My name is Markus. Markus Harvarder."

The pair drifted into silence as they watched the fighting engulf the city.

Elise glanced down at the feather. She released it and let it glide from the tower and be swept up in the wind. She watched the nightingale feather fall until it vanished into the darkness.

The knights followed the road for miles as they travelled north. Refugees fled Elara in their hundreds as the hordes closed in. They did not know what their fate would be. They only knew that their city was on fire.

Kyler and Alarik ventured off the main road and made their way up into the hills. They were tall but were rarely travelled and the forests provided cover. Bushes and wildflowers lined the bottom of the woodland. The trees began to give way as they reached the ridge. It was there that Kyler brought the cart to a halt. He said not a word for none were needed. Alarik saw the wagon halt and paused.

Kyler dropped down to the ground and gazed around the small clearing. The stars shone and the only sounds were those of the nature.

"This is the place," Kyler said as he took it all in. "It's peaceful here. I did not know about her people or about her true beliefs. But from what I have heard, the stars are as important to them as they are to us. She can rest here beneath the stars. Here where she is free. Here she can be at peace," he looked to Alarik as he spoke. "I have to do this myself."

"Aye, lad," the battlemaster replied with a nod.

Kyler gathered his axe from Asena's saddlebags and made his way into the woods alone. He cut and broke branches from trees. He gathered bark and sticks from the forest floor. Kyler created a small pyre with the wood. The knight worked with purpose and a squared jaw. He focussed on his task and the purpose for which he worked. It gave his weary body strength, and his mind and shattered heart the will to go on. Next, he gathered wildflowers and placed them atop the pyre like a bed. They covered the branches with a magnificent riot of colour amidst a darkening world. The brown wood was hidden by a bed of green, red, yellow, white, and blue.

At last, Kyler put down his axe and used his water skin to clean his hands and face of earth, blood, and filth. He was tired, so tired.

Kyler returned to the cart and with hands as tender as a soft breeze, he took Elena in his arms once again. Each step toward the pyre was harder than the last. Each step meant that he was closer to a final goodbye. Kyler lightly placed her upon the bed of flowers and stared down at her pale face as the moonlight caressed her skin. He pushed a stray lock of hair aside before he placed a final kiss upon her brow. Kyler took a step back from the pyre as Alarik walked to his side.

The battlemaster held a burning torch in his hand.

Kyler did not take his eyes from Elena. He did not acknowledge his mentor's presence.

"I do not know if there are words or prayers that your people have for when you are gone too soon. Who knows what the gods have in store for us? Who can divine their will?" Kyler said softly as he held Elena's necklace tight. "If you have gone to your gods then I do not know if we will meet again. I can only pray that when my time comes, that my gods and yours will bring us together. We will meet again. In my dreams we are always together. I will never stop loving you. Not for a single moment, my Elena. My sweet Elena. I will live this life for you and, when my time comes then, we will be together again. No man or god will dare come between us. May you at last know peace, my Elena, my heart, my love. I will see you in heaven."

Kyler took the torch from Alarik who placed a comforting hand upon his shoulder. The young knight stepped toward the pyre and took a breath. It took all of his strength to join the flames with the wood and flowers. Kyler tossed the torch aside as he watched the pyre ignite. The flames burned bright. A sob shook his body, and then the tears came.

"You're not alone," Alarik said quietly as they stood together.

Kyler could not tear his gaze from the fire. "You hated everything she was, everything she stood for."

"You are my friend, my brother," Alarik told him sadly. "Be strong, be strong for her. When there is nothing else to hold on to, hold on to your faith."

They stood in silence as the flames sent Elena to the heavens.

Only when the fires had at last faded did they leave the clearing. Only then did they return to their horses. Kyler did not feel the earth underfoot or the wind against his cheek.

His body was numb. He could barely think. He barely had the power to do anything but walk.

"We have to get to the coast," Alarik said. "We have to get to Tallis." The battlemaster cut Arntair's horse from the cart and tied a lead from its reins to the saddle of his own steed.

"We have no time to linger and we cannot take the cart," Alarik continued as he mounted his horse. "Gods willing, I will live to repay my debt to Arntair."

Kyler froze as he heaved himself up into Asena's saddle. Alarik knew the trader and seemed to have known him well. Arntair was more than just a man whom he had retrieved information. They had been friends. The trader had told Kyler that he had procured poison for a soldier. A soldier of the empire. The same poison that had been used mere months ago within the walls of Kilgareth.

"In Elara you told me that you first met Arntair months ago while gathering supplies for the Order."

"I did," Alarik frowned.

"He told me that you met while searching for recruits," Kyler murmured as he pieced it all together. "He also told me that not so long ago an Aureian soldier came to him looking for poison."

Alarik stiffened yet said nothing.

Kyler turned to his mentor and the words left his mouth before he could stop them, "Alarik, you killed Amaris."

The battlemaster paused and met Kyler's stare.

"Aye."

FIFTY-SIX

Káli Lands, Forest of Salvaar

The tribes came one by one. Their faces masked in red, black, white, blue, and green. From the northern sea tribes to the highlanders and the deep forest clans, they had come. Ten tribes. *Thousands* of warriors. The morning was young, and a faint mist hung over the city of tents. Already the Salvaari were awake. Most had been before light had crept through the trees. Something was drawing near. They all felt it. The lifeblood of the forest, some had called it.

Here in Salvaar, they were all connected. Whatever affected one of them, affected them all.

Lukas grimaced as he limped from his tent. The pain in his knee was a constant reminder of the burden that he carried. He rubbed his wound as he stared out across the great war camp. Lukas had fought in many battles and skirmishes in his lifetime, yet never had he seen such numbers before. Never had he fought in such an army. The men and women of the forest sat around fires or walked in small groups. Most were readying weapons or fletching arrows. They told stories and sang songs. They were intriguing people, even so close to battle and death they acted as if today were like any other day.

"You would not have thought that they stood upon the edge of a knife," One-Eye said quietly as he heard Maevin emerge from the tent behind him.

"If you spent each day worrying about death, then that fear will kill you," Maevin replied with a shrug. "Each day could be their last and so they live it with a full heart."

Lukas could only nod as she passed him a cup of his medicine. He closed his eye as he drank the sweet tasting brew, feeling the ache vanish as if it had never been there.

"Morning, Lord," Hadwin called out as the Annoran mercenaries approached.

They were armoured in chainmail and plate, while weapons hung at their sides and shields were slung across their backs. They were ready for the battle that was looming.

"Myrdren rode into camp before dawn," Layan told them. "Think he may have seen something."

"Or someone," Lukas replied thoughtfully. "How are the men?"

"Prepared for whatever end," Hadwin said.

"Lukas," a strong voice called out. One-Eye glanced toward the man who called him name. It was Cailean, and the Aedei was not alone. A woman with fiery hair and a face striped in green paint walked toward the companions.

"Meet Etain of the Icari," Cailean said, gesturing to the woman.

Lukas clasped her proffered arm. So, this was his friend's betrothed. The great Chief of the Mountain Tribe. Her grip was as strong as her arm.

"Chief Etain, your reputation as a warrior proceeds you," One-Eye told her.

"As does your loyalty to your beliefs," Etain replied.

"What has happened?" Lukas asked. He saw a shadow pass through Cailean's eyes as he spoke.

"The Belcar and Niavenn are not yet here," Cailean said. "And word came in the night. You must come with us. The chiefs are waiting."

Lukas followed his friend through the maze of tents that filled the forest. The eight other chieftains of the Salvaari sat and stood in a small clearing. They argued beneath the trees. Henghis of the

Catuvantuli, the great chief who led this coalition, the man who all others had pledged their support, rose to greet them. Lukas bowed his head.

"King Henghis," he greeted the leader.

"Annora has come," the red painted Catuvantuli replied.

One-Eye's stomach turned. Of all the news he had been expecting, it was this that he had feared the most.

"What of Auriea, the Order, and the houses of Medea?"

"No word," Vaylin told him. "Annora stands alone."

"You know them better than any of us. You know your *brother* better than any of us," Cailean began. "We thought it best to hear your voice as we plan our attack."

Lukas placed his hands upon his crutch as he thought. "What path do they take?" he asked.

"North, they march north," Balor of the Sagailean spoke up. "When they sun reaches its peak, they shall be no more than a few miles west of here."

"I know the plains," Lukas nodded. He closed his eye as he searched for the right words. "My brother is nothing like my father. Nothing like any foe that you have ever fought before. He is clever. Everything that you are thinking, he has already thought. Every move that you plan he has already made. Even alone, even outnumbered, he will triumph just as he has countless times before. If we are to face him, as I believe we must, we have to do so with the greatest of caution."

"The time is right," Henghis nodded, "and the time is now. If we can defeat the army of Annora before it is reinforced, then we have a chance to win this war before it truly begins."

"They march from dawn until a few hours before dusk," Lukas explained. He used his crutch to draw a line in the earth. "They will set up camp," he said and prodded a hole into the ground and then drew a circle around it, "and then reinforce their position. Medea, the empire, they will not be far behind my brother and he will wait for them. What comes next... they will march into the forest and take the land inch by inch. They will build walled camps each night so that they cannot be ambushed. If they get into Salvaar it may already be too late."

"What if we were to attack before they could fortify their position?" Henghis said. "What if we struck them today, when they are tired from the march?"

"We would need to be swift. There would be no time to use our skirmishers against them," Cailean added. "I remember stories from the last war. The Annorans' love of the bow is a thing that will not soon be forgotten by our people. We will have to charge and cross the plains, before they have the chance to kill us in our hundreds with their arrows."

One-Eye nodded. "The archers will slip back through their own lines, and in that chaos perhaps we have been presented a chance."

Henghis turned to one of the other chieftains. "Daire, your people are renowned for their skill with the horse," he said. "If you take the fight to the Annoran cavalry, can you hold them?"

"Or die trying," the chief of the Coventina replied.

"Vaylin, Balor, prepare your own riders," Henghis commanded. "When the Coventina have engaged their enemy, your people will ride out from the trees and sow panic and confusion among the Annoran horse. Use poison. Whatever weapons you can muster. Then you *must* wrap around our enemy and drive into their archers from behind."

"Their gods will weep, and their blood will flow," Vaylin growled.

Her eyes darted up to the steel blade atop her spear. It seemed to glisten under the rays of sunlight. The steel was poisoned.

"We shall see it done."

"Annora is strong, disciplined," Lukas told them. "It may yet be difficult to achieve victory through strength of arms upon an open battlefield."

"We do not need to crush them today," Henghis replied as he walked into the centre of the group. He took Vaylin's spear, "We only need to hold them until night falls. The darkness is no place for men. The darkness is the place for wolves. The moonseer shall pierce the night with their arrows. Make no mistake, my brothers and sisters in blood, if the spirits are with us then we will have victory this day. I am not fighting as your King, nor even fighting as your Chief, but as a father, a son, a brother. I fight for all of you, for all of my people that call Salvaar home. I fight for your stolen lives, yours bruised bodies, and your lost freedom. Consider why you are fighting, and then together we shall win this battle or perish. Let every man and woman know that we stand in the face of a mighty foe and give our lives for freedom."

The commands were given, and the chiefs divided. Before long, the mood of the Salvaari changed. No longer did they laugh and joke, no longer did they sing and dance. Now they prepared for war. They moved quickly around the campsite to join with their tribes and kin. They gathered up weapons and horses, prayed to their spirits, and marked themselves with colour.

Maevin led Lukas into their tent and turned to face him. "And so the choice is at last upon you," she said.

"I had thought myself ready for this moment, thought myself ready to decide, yet now that I am here, I find myself torn," One-Eye replied. "Annora has come to burn all that I have come to love, and I wish to fight, to repel all outsiders. Yet the other part of me *is* the outsider."

Maevin took Lukas' hand and placed it over his chest. "You have a Salvaari heart. You are wild and reckless, untamed like the wind. That drew me to you. That is why men so willingly follow you. You are Salvaari to the spirits, to them," she nodded toward the tent flap as she spoke, "and to me. Have faith in us, have faith in the spirits, have faith in me."

Lukas looked down at her and into those enchanting emerald

eyes. "I do," he replied, truthfully. He believed her words. He believed in her. She kissed him. Deeply, hungrily. Maevin pulled him closer. Her scent filled his senses, alluring him, intoxicating him. Her lips brushed his neck, and her hair tickled his skin.

"Come," she murmured. "Salvaar will need children."

Their time together passed all to swiftly. Soon the horns were blowing. He tied on bracers and greaves of steel. Steel taken from the Medeans. A shirt of mail sat over a padded gambeson. A black sash was wrapped from his left shoulder to his right hip. It was held in place by a pin and his belt. He gathered up his war hammer and pushed it through his belt so that it hung freely at his side. Lukas' face was once more marked with black paint. One-Eye slung his dark shield over his shoulder before at last turning to Maevin. She held out his helmet without a word. One-Eye took the helm, seeing that like his face, the steel had been decorated with ebony.

He had chosen the Salvaari over his own family and now the fates would decide.

They had ridden through the night, and they had ridden hard. They did not know if Vesuva had sent forth a pursuit. They did not know if they were being hunted. The company had arrived at the coast as the first rays of the dawn sun had crept forward from the east. The mercenary band had halted by the northern cliffs that overlooked the Mithramir Sea for food, drink, and much needed respite.

Kitara had walked alone to the cliff tops. Her ankle still hurt, yet for the first time in months she was free. The warmth of the sun upon her skin, the caress of the gentle sea breeze, the *taste* of the ocean, all of it reminded her of what had been taken from her for many weeks. She had been a slave. No longer.

Kitara closed her eyes and sucked in a long draught of air. It tasted like freedom. She gazed down at her feet as they moved to the edge of the cliff. Waters churned nearly a hundred feet below and broke upon rock. The sea sang to her. It whispered her name. The abyss called, speaking of her demons, saying their names.

Rowan had been right. They still haunted her.

She thought of Calvillo and Luana Marquez. People who had called her family and then in turn betrayed her. She thought of Barboza. She thought of the slums in Annora and the dark streets of Miera. Treachery was all she had ever known. She thought of Sereia and Morlag, of Urlaigh and Vasquez who had died to save her. She had been enslaved and beaten again. Was that all she was?

The waters called.

Kitara felt a single tear fall from her cheek. She watched it drop. The tear vanished before it could meet the sea and for a moment Kitara thought about following it over the cliff.

Warm fingers entwined with her own. "I'm here," Aeryn told her.

"I was a slave," Kitara murmured. "I was sold like livestock. The others that were captured are all dead. They're dead. Some died because of me."

"No," Aeryn shook her head. "They died because of cruel men with an appetite for coin and the suffering of others. Do not ever say that their deaths were your fault."

"I spilled blood for the pleasure of the Aureians," she almost spat. "I killed for *sport*."

"You did what you had to do to survive."

Kitara squeezed her hand, yet was unable to face her companion. "Then why do I feel ashamed?"

"The demon's call is a powerful thing, Kitara," Aeryn replied. "You have spent so long in darkness, yet now you have begun to emerge into the light. The darkness does not want to let you go, and yet you will defeat it."

"You came for me," Kitara said quietly. "From the moment I was taken I thought myself alone, as I have always been. Yet you came for me."

"I will always come for you, Kitara, always. I know you. I know your heart and I know your worth. I will never abandon you, never leave your side."

"Kitara?" she whispered. "I had almost forgotten the sound of my own name. But who am I? I am not of Lamrei or Miera. I am no one of nowhere."

Aeryn pulled on her hand, turning Kitara to face her. In her other hand she held a sword of Tariki steel. Her sword. "You are Kitara of Salvaar," Aeryn told her. "It's time you learned that."

Kitara hesitantly felt the worn leather of the blade's handle. It fit her fingers perfectly, as if it were made for her. Kitara took the sword and felt its strength flow through her. The Tariki believed that the sword was their soul. A belief that had long since been instilled in her. She ran her eyes over the steel, from pommel to tip, as she raised it toward the sun. The light kissed the blade and swam down its naked edge.

Kitara sheathed the sword and looked to the moonseer. "Aeryn, I–"

Aeryn pulled her into a hug. She returned the embrace, feeling more than just the warmth that came with it. She felt the softness of Aeryn's cheek, and the light brush of her hair. The smell of wildflowers.

"Sometimes the face we show the world needs to be of strength, no matter the turmoil we harbour within," Aeryn whispered.

Kitara felt a warmth flow inside. Months ago, she had told Aeryn the names of her demons. She had given the Aedei her trust and it had not been in vain. For the first time perhaps, she had been right. Kitara pressed her forehead to Aeryn's. The moonseer met her eyes and then placed a tender kiss upon her lips.

The corridors of the citadel in Kilgareth were silent.

The knights had ridden to war and had taken many of the

maija with them. The arc'maija Lysandra had been chosen to remain behind and overlook the fortress home of the Order of Kil'kara. The cardinal and his guard remained as well, for this was the time for war. War was no place for old priests. Left to defend the castle were no more than two dozen maija and fewer than three hundred knights. They stayed to protect the families of their brothers along with the followers' camp that had travelled with the Annoran company.

The sound of a scream pulled Princess Kassandra Raynor from sleep. She gasped as the cry echoed in her mind. Her eyes flew open… all was silent. There was nothing save a pull that seemed to call her.

Kassie rolled from her bed, pulled on her shoes, and wrapped a thick cloak around her shoulders. Next came the deep hood. The *call* seemed to grow, and the princess felt herself almost being pulled toward the door of her chamber. She opened the door and peered down the corridor. Nothing. The blackness of night coated Kilgareth in a dark shroud. Kassandra began to walk down the hallways of stone, somehow knowing exactly where she had to go.

A feeling told her to be silent, and so she walked as silent as a shadow. Eventually she came to a magnificent midnight blue tapestry. Upon it the silver sun and moon burned brightly. Kassie reached out a hand and pushed the cloth back to reveal a wooden door. She pulled on the latch, and the door creaked open. Kassie looked left and right.

There was nothing save the empty voices of the wind. The pull grew with each step. The doorway led to a staircase that took her deep into the ground. It was dark and cold, yet somehow Kassandra knew the way. The stairs ended and led out into a new corridor. Light flickered at the end of the passage.

Curious.

She reached the corner and peered around. A pair of the white clad cardinal's guard stood before what seemed to be the steel barred door of a prison. Kassandra frowned. *What was Aleksander hiding so far beneath ground?*

The call drew her back to the stairs. Instead of going back up, the pull led her to the right. A small flight of steps led her into a second tunnel. She followed the passage around into a storage room. Weapons, armours, and other supplies were all neatly laid out. Kassandra peered around the room and noticed a grill at the very bottom of one of the walls. It could have been a drainage grill, or it could be a window into the cell that lay beyond. Kassandra made her way over to the steel bars and knelt upon the stone. The princess looked through the grill. The light of the guards' brazier beyond the far side of the cell lit the small room. There was only one inmate in the prison, only one who sat upon the cold floor. Long white hair fell from the woman's head, tumbling down her shoulders like a waterfall of snow. Slowly the woman turned toward Kassandra, as if somehow sensing the princess' presence.

Long, pointed ears cut through the snowy locks like daggers, yet it was the woman's gaze that captivated her. Ice cold eyes of frozen blue that burned brightly like an inferno of sapphire pierced deep into the princess' soul. White cracks in the blue burned dangerously.

The woman was an elf.

FIFTY-SEVEN

Fields of Bandujar, Duchy of Bailon, Medea

The sun had begun to lower when the army of Annora marched into the fields north of Bandujar. It marched under the eagle. It marched to meet its fate.

With the Aureian legions within their midst, they numbered nearly thirty thousand. Their number that would swell beyond measure when the armies of Medea and the Order joined them. King Dayne's orders had been simple. Begin to set up camp yet be prepared for the attack that was undoubtedly coming. Salvaari scouts had been spotted by his own outriders. It would not be long now.

The King waited in his tent. His eyes were drawn to a banner of the great red eagle that sat atop the table before him. Dayne ran his hand across the crimson silk and felt the might of the great bird of prey beneath his fingers. His father's symbol, his country's symbol, and now it was *his* symbol. He would not dishonour the eagle.

The tent flap opened unannounced.

Dayne turned to see Sir Garrik shove a cloaked person inside. Behind him came the general, Tristayn Martyn. He glanced at the cloaked figure. Their face was shrouded by a hood. Their hands were bound by chains. The king reached for a small wooden box as the master at arms shoved the prisoner into the ground. Dayne opened the wooden box and withdrew a thin strand of golden cloth.

"She who strives to topple a kingdom stumbles at a single thread," the king said as he looked to the prisoner now made hoodless by Sir Garrik. "Is that not right, Lady Eveline?"

The Medean noblewoman stared up at him defiantly, despite the chains that bound her and said nothing.

"Come now, my Lady, we both know that you killed my father," Dayne dropped the golden strand.

"My King, I did *not*."

The king clasped his hands and stared down at her without emotion. "You had grown close to King Dorian, had you not?" he said.

"The king trusted me and would often speak of his kingdom, his plans, and his *children*," Eveline replied.

"It is no secret to me that you shared his confidence just as you shared his bed."

"*What?*"

Dayne's eyes hardened like ice. "I will warn you once, so listen well. You do not play games with me," Dayne told her. "You were the only person outside his family that the king trusted so fully. You shared his bed, and he in turn shared his secrets, his fears, his truths. Oh, you wormed your way into my household, but I see everything. Only you could have been so close to him on the night of his murder. Only you could have convinced Dorian to send his guards away."

"My King I did not–"

Dayne spoke louder and cut off her plea. "Only you had the means and the opportunity to kill him. And then I found the golden thread, a thread which unless I am very much mistaken, came from your dress."

"I did not kill him... I couldn't," Eveline stammered.

King Dayne looked down. "There it is. I can see it in your eyes," he said. "Fear. I see through your lies, my Lady, and you *know* it. Strange isn't it, that my father would die so soon after his heir is about to provide him with a grandchild. A *new* claimant to the throne. A claimant of *Caspin* blood."

Eveline glared back at him. "And if I am the murderer that you claim, why is it that on the very same night that Dorian died, that Emperor Darius was killed?" she said. "I suppose that you believe that *I* had some hand in that as well."

"Actually, Lady Eveline, I do not," King Dayne told her. "I do not believe that the two were connected as much as they appear to be. Call it instinct if you will, but something tells me that there is another player in this game yet to reveal themself. Would you like to know why? Assassins of Kings have two purposes. To start wars, or to end them before they ever begin. If only Darius had been slain, then both ends would have been accomplished. The blame for the Emperor's death would have fallen solely on my people. Right now, Annora would be contending with the full might of Aureia and the war with Salvaar would have never begun. Yet with Dorian's passing that same anger cannot be directed at my people. While you slew my father, it was an ally of Salvaar who killed Dorian. And so now it falls to you and the death of my father to begin to unshroud this mystery."

Eveline said nothing.

"I don't want to hurt you," Dayne told the Medean woman.

"If you don't want to hurt me then you *won't* hurt me," she countered.

The king crouched before her and knelt upon one knee. "I will tell you something about myself, something that no one will have told you," Dayne said. "When the men follow me into battle it is not because they are commanded to do so. I tell them the truth. I tell them that they will have victory, no matter the odds. If another man said the same when faced with superior numbers, even the hardest of soldiers may feel the fear that seeks to control all men. Yet when they see me shed blood beside them, when they see me fight a master of the sword and risk my life to save thousands, when they see me lead the charge, when they look into my eyes, they know that there is no *lie* there. So, when I say that I do not wish to harm you, that is the truth. Yet do not believe that I will not."

Dayne reached out a hand and plucked the pin from Eveline's hair. He held it before her, revealing the sharpened steel blade. Eveline's eyes widened and her face paled.

"I have sent for my wife," Dayne said as he rose to his feet. "After the battle is won, I shall meet her at Kilgareth and then we will find answers. This plot is unravelling, my Lady, and I will follow it to the ends of the world if I must. Take her away."

"My King," Sir Garrik bowed before he pulled the prisoner to her feet and dragged her from the tent.

Dayne watched them go, before at last he reached for his stomach with a grimace. The ache had begun to grow before Eveline had been brought before him, yet he would not and did not show her weakness.

"So Caspin moves against us?" Tristayn murmured.

"It appears," Dayne replied, fighting back the pain.

"The alliance between our nations hangs by a thread and they seek to sever it," the general growled.

"I will not allow that to happen," the king told him.

The horns began to blow. They were long and loud. "Salvaar is here," Tristayn cried.

Dayne took a step toward the table that held his sword, and then he fell forward. The pain grew into an agony, seeking to tear him apart. His hands barely managed to take hold of the lip of the table and stop his fall. Everything tightened, everything sought to destroy him. He began to cough, to retch.

"King Dayne!" Tristayn turned to the tent flaps. "I will call the physician."

"NO!" shouted the king as he continued to cough. He raised a hand to his mouth and when he took it away, he saw the blood.

His fingers curled into fists as he struggled to stand straight.

"Give me my sword."

"My King, I cannot."

Dayne turned his murderous eyes to the general as he fought against the agony. "I will *not* allow this illness to make me doubt any longer," he growled. "I will *not* hide behind it any more than I will hide behind my people as they fight, and bleed, and die in my name. Now give me my sword." Dayne could see the pain in the general's eyes. He could see how torn he was.

"My King–"

"I gave you an order!" Dayne snarled as he squared his shoulders.

Tristayn hesitated, before handing over the eagle blade.

Henghis of the Catuvantuli, great Chief of all Salvaar led his people from the forest and out onto the plains. He could hear the sound of Annoran horns. He could see the might of its army marshalling opposite them in the field. He looked up and down the line with his burning eyes and beat his axe into his shield twice.

"Yorath, Warlord of the Plain, lift up your sword and stand beside these warriors of Salvaar who fight in your name," Henghis said before he beat his shield once more as his people roared. Fire filled his veins, "The spirits are with us!"

The chief began to march out into the plains of Bandujar. The horsemen who rode at the flanks of the great Salvaari army started to move.

Dayne watched from the right flank of his army as the Salvaari made the first move. Thousands of Annoran archers stood before the hidden Aureian legions. Their bows began to sing just as the pagans began to charge. They sought to close the distance quickly and save many lives, just as he had foreseen. Arrows rained down like a storm and Salvaari fell in droves. Shield and flesh alike were turned into pin cushions. Blood began to flow.

The Salvaari horseman began to accelerate and galloped across the plain. Around the king rode Sir Garrik and the rest of his guard. The Lords Balderik and Galan of Leaoflaed and Torosa were mounted with them.

King Dayne of Annora rose in his saddle and thrust his spear high toward the heavens. "FOR THE GODS, FOR ANNORA, AND FOR THE WEST!"

A great cry went up from the Annoran ranks as the king slammed his visor shut. Dayne kicked his heels in, and the heavy cavalry surged forward. The plains sped by under hoof as they charged. Each stride drove them forward faster. Dayne could hear the wild cries and screams of the Salvaari. He levelled his spear and adjusted his grip upon his shield. The king saw the whites of their eyes. The two sides crashed together. Earth sprayed all around them. Men and horses fell.

Dayne thrust his spear forward and drove steel deep into the chest of a Salvaari screamer. The man was thrown from his mount and his blood painted the air red.

Ilaros Arryn stood ready, his body angled, the grip upon his spear tight. He had seen the horseman come together. He had seen the collision between the eastern pagans and the men of the west. A horn blew, and then the Annoran archers began to run back through the ranks of Aureian soldiers.

"Make ready!" the general cried.

His soldiers remained silent, disciplined. The last of the Annorans fled and then, with an unspoken command, the Aureians closed ranks. The Salvaari closed in, barely thirty paces from their position.

"SHIELDS!"

A wall of steel and wood appeared as the legions linked their shields and raised their spears.

There was no time for the Salvaari to panic, no time for them to scream a warning, as an unbroken line of Aureian steel materialised before them. The Salvaari fell upon them like water on rock. They crashed and roiled, yet the steel of Aureia was strong. The steel of Aureia held.

Lukas watched from the trees as the Salvaari army surged into that of Annora. Hadwin, Layan, and Rodion rode by his side, while all around them were Lukas' black painted warband of Káli. The company were amidst the riders of Vaylin. Thousands of warriors and horse awaited her command. Further through the trees Balor and his own people would be waiting.

One-Eye looked down the line toward Vaylin and Eirian. The chief of the Káli silently levelled her spear. Without a word, the Káli began to walk their horses from the trees. The walk turned into a canter, which grew into a thunderous gallop. They would scream no war cries nor sound any horns, for they could not afford to give their charge away before it was too late. The Salvaari riders began to angle around the battlefield, aiming to strike the Annorans from the side. Arrows were nocked and readied, arrows *covered* in Káli poison.

They began to wrap around the churning mass of cavalry like a glove. The Káli riders unleashed a storm of arrows into the rear of the Annoran line. Men and horses screamed as the shafts found homes in flesh. Within moments the poison began to work its deadly magic. Knights clad in armour began to fall, for a wound no bigger than a scratch became mortal.

Eirian angled his mount and half of the Káli turned with him. They charged into the Annoran cavalry with savage screams. They had to hold the armoured horse.

Vaylin led the rest of the company west, around the cavalry and the flank of the infantry. Lukas looked to the battle. His eye squinted as he tried to make out who was gaining the advantage. The Annorans were holding. Then he saw them among the chaos. Aureian shields.

The soldiers of the silver army were pushing the Salvaari back as if they were nothing. Their spears and swords cutting through the tribes like a blade through water. They fell in droves to the imperial soldiers. If the men of the empire fought in the frontline, then where were the Annoran warriors?

Too late, Lukas realised.

The Káli crashed into what was thought to only be the archers and skirmishers of Annora. Instead, they were greeted by Annoran spearmen. The spearmen who were supposed to be fighting the Salvaari *in front* of the archers.

Annorans fell. Káli fell. Lukas took a spear upon his shield and replied in kind, skewering his attacker through the throat with his own lance. The Annoran crashed down.

"VAYLIN!" One-Eye cried as he fought through the battlefield. "VAYLIN!" Lukas' warband carved a bloody path toward the chief. One-Eye lost his spear in the chaos and tore free his hammer. He brought it down hard on the skull of an Annoran soldier.

"VAYLIN!"

The chieftain was surrounded. Her spear was like a viper's fang, fast and deadly. Her dark hair was like a whirlwind of black. Lukas charged her attackers without thought for his own life. He cut down one, two. Hadwin and Layan angled their horses as they felled spearman and archer alike to create a wall between the Annorans and the Káli leader. Rodion and the warband surged forward to aid them.

"Vaylin!" Lukas called as he reached her.

"What is it? What have you seen?"

"The Empire is here!"

Vaylin's eyes widened, "Impossible, they—"

"This is a trap," One-Eye told her.

Bavarian Delrovira stared ahead. He could hear the screams of men, the cries of horses and the song of steel coming from beyond the ridge. It was time.

The might of Rovira were mounted at his back. The might of Kilgareth stood with them. Corvo Alaine and William Peyene were mounted at his side. The grand master drove his lance into the earth and took a hold of his medallion.

Bavarian's eyes turned to the heavens. "Unto thee Durandail do I give my soul. Father of all Fathers, guide me in judgment and lead me in truth. Keep my soul and deliver me. Grant me strength. Grant me victory upon this day. Areut talc cuun'etc."

"Areut talc cuun'etc," the Knights of Kil'kara echoed.

The grand master tore his spear free and kicked his heels in, unleashing the Knights of Kil'kara. The ground sang beneath them as hooves churned the earth. They breached the ridgeline and for the first time saw the battle.

"KIL'KARA!" roared Bavarian.

"KIL'KARA!" the knights answered.

They crashed into the side of the Salvaari formation.

Dayne heard the cries of the knights of Kil'kara as they joined the battle. Within moments the song of Medean horns greeted his ears. He cut down a Sagailean rider and then through the battle, he caught a glimpse of the stag and bear banners, the viper and the lion. The tiger of Reyna. The full strength of Medea had come.

General Ilaros and his men were forcing the Salvaari back inch by inch. They were slaughtering them in their hundreds. Against the might of the silver army the heathens had no answer. The

Salvaari had tried to flank the Annoran position, but Dayne had foreseen it. He saw everything. His own infantry had met them and had all but crushed the opposing force.

With Kil'kara riding from the south, and Medea from the north, they began to encircle the Salvaari. It was far from over, yet the battle was won. Soon the Salvaari would run.

"Lord Galan," the King called to the great lord of Leaoflaed and gestured toward the Salvaari infantry. "Break from the pagan horse and flank their position."

"My King," the lord bowed before he thundered away.

Horns blew and the riders of Laeflaed broke from the Salvaari cavalry and charged deep into their lines of foot warriors.

"ANNORA!" King Dayne yelled as he charged back into the fray with his eagle sword held aloft.

Cailean heaved his way through the battlefield. The ground had become a slurry of earth and blood. He could feel it covering his body. He could taste it in the air.

"Henghis!" he cried as he reached the great Chief.

The pair fought side by side as their enemy closed in around them.

"They're all here!" Henghis shouted above the din and thrust his axe toward a fallen shield bearing the insignia of the griffin. "Annora did not march alone!"

"We have to fall back," Cailean told him, and the words broke his heart, "or we all die!"

Henghis froze and the Aedei could see the shattered soul in his leader's eyes. They had been so close to glory. So close to victory. With a snarl, Henghis shoved his way through his people.

"FALL BACK!" he bellowed. "FALL BACK!"

Lukas saw the Salvaari begin to stream away before he heard the shouts.

The retreat had been called. He spun on his saddle and cut down a Medean rider with his hammer.

"RUN!" he roared before kicking his heels in. "RUN!"

Man and horse began to flee. A great trail streaming back toward the forest. They left a field of death in their wake. Henghis felled an Aureian as a gap began to open between the lines.

"We need to get to the river!" Henghis shouted before he killed a second man. "FALL BACK! FALL BACK!"

Cailean watched as his people began to run. They reached the edge of the forest, yet there were still miles between them and the Arwan River. The enemy pursued. They would not make it to the river without losing thousands to the onslaught. The Aedei chief stopped in his tracks and snatched at the man who ran beside him.

"Bleddyn, we cannot run! Our people will die, all of them!"

The Aedei chief's guard met his eyes and gave a slow nod. He understood.

"AEDEI!" Cailean roared and his powerful voice carried in the wind. "AEDEI!"

Many stopped their retreat. Many turned to their chief.

"THIS IS WHERE WE HOLD THEM!" Cailean bellowed as he faced the oncoming enemy. He readied his sword and his shield. "Tanris, I come to you."

Lukas glanced over his shoulder as the Salvaari fled for all they were worth. The horsemen covered the flanks, yet the army of the west cut the people of the forest down in dozens as they ran. He had seen Cailean's sacrifice, and though the Aedei had held the west for a time it had been in vain. The trail of fleeing warriors had left a trail of bodies behind them. A feast for the crows.

Lukas angled his horse into an Annoran rider, even as he cut down a retreating Salvaari. The fallen man turned in the mud and reached for his axe as the rider raised his spear. Lukas' hammer caught him from behind and shattered armour and bone as if it were nothing. The man screamed as he fell. A second rider slammed into Lukas' horse.

One-Eye fell.

He hit the hard earth and rolled toward his hammer. His fingers found the hilt. Lukas rose to meet the rider, only to see the man be cut down from his saddle. A flame haired woman leapt atop the fallen man and finished him with her sword. It was Etain.

"With me!" the Icari Chief cried and reached out a hand.

One-Eye took it, and then Etain wrapped Lukas' arm around her shoulder. She took his weight from his aching knee.

Together they began to make for the river. Icari warriors formed up all around them and joined with Lukas' warband.

Annora began to close in.

Medea began to close in.

The Empire and the Order came with them.

Lukas could see the sun reflecting on water. The river was nearly upon them. Too late.

The cries of their enemy were drowned out by the thundering of their horses' hooves.

They turned to meet their fate.

It started with a whisper in the wind. It was so soft that it may have been a dream. Then came the ravens. The music of their flapping wings rose in chorus with their eerie song.

The air grew damp. A thin mist started to arise following in the wake of the ravens.

It began in the east and flowed like a surging river. A fog which flooded west even as it thickened. The Salvaari tribes stopped and stared. The western army came to a halt. Hands flew to holy amulets. The fog shrouded the river, shrouded the trees and earth, as the whispers grew. The forest seemed to come alive even as it was taken by the mist. The Salvaari began to vanish into the whiteness. The mist reached the enemy and began to weaken their sight.

Henghis stared across the river as the fog grew.

He saw the faint outline of a figure upon the other bank. The figure knelt at the water's edge. A staff was clasped in their hand.

It was a woman. A woman with flaming red hair and blazing eyes of violet fire. It was she who spoke. She who commanded the ravens and the ever-growing mist. He knew her name and her power.

The phantom reached down and placed her fingers into the river. She whispered words and the wind became her voice as it gusted through the forest. The water began to freeze at her touch.

"Sylvaine," Henghis murmured in awe.

The spirit mother had come to make safe her people. Ice spread across the river and froze it all. Ice conjured by the Great Queen.

Henghis stepped out onto the ice. He was unable to tear his gaze from Sylvaine. The spirit enthralled him with her purple eyes and her inaudible voice. The ice held. Sylvaine met his gaze. Her burning eyes stared deep into the chief's soul. Her stare chilled him, yet sent fire coursing through his veins. She did not tear her enthralling gaze from him. Her hand tightened upon her gnarled staff. Then she bowed to him.

Henghis shivered.

The ravens cried out. The mist took Sylvaine. The spirit vanished as swiftly as she had come, as if she had never been. Henghis stared at the riverbank. His eyes were fixed upon the spot that the Great Queen had knelt. A tremble ran through his body, and then he blinked as if awakening from a dream.

"Back," Henghis called as he made his retreat across the frozen river. The Salvaari began to fall back across ice at his command.

The Chief of the Catuvantuli made it to the far bank and turned back toward the enemy that had killed so many of his people. He could no longer see them, yet their cries echoed through the fog. Cries of confusion and cries of fear. He felt the rage burn within.

So many had been lost. So many of his people slain. The mist was thick. It consumed all, yet in the mist there be monsters. Monsters with silver eyes that would make the west bleed.

"Send in the moonseer."

King Dayne could only stare as the thick fog descended upon them.

He clenched his fists as the Salvaari were secreted away by the fog. His army had won the great battle upon the plains of Bandujar, yet the unnatural mist sought to claim the victory that was so rightfully his. Dayne heard the screams echoing through the mist. They came from north and south, east and west. Shouts and cries as men were slaughtered by an unseen foe. One by one the screams began to be silenced, and the King knew what it meant.

The stories his father had told him were *true*. He saw Alejandro Aloys through the whiteness. He saw the pale lion banner. A hornbearer rode with the duke.

"Call the men back," Dayne ordered as they reached him. He realised the horror that was about to become their reality if they did not retreat.

"They are defeated," Duke Alejandro cried and thrust his spear toward their hidden enemy. "We can crush them now!"

"I *said* call them back," King Dayne turned on him with furious eyes. "We will not follow them into their hell."

A small earthen mound sat within the dark clearing. Four standing stones encircled the hillock as they drove up toward the heavens like spears. They were ancient, covered in moss, and as old as the forest itself. A thin ray of light broke the thick canopy high above and illuminated the wisp of mist that arose from the forest floor.

She knelt between the stones and her hands encircled her gnarled staff. Her lips moved and her voice carried like a soft whisper through the mist. The Great Queen had long since crossed into the Plain and sent her mind forth. Something called to Sylvaine. Something had brought her back into the spirit world. Her brow furrowed. A wince contorted her face. A blazing inferno that burned sapphire flames sung her name. She felt a presence that she had not felt in a century. A familiar presence. That of her own blood. That of her own *tears*. Sylvaine's gaze snapped open.

Hundreds of miles away the she-elf's eyes opened. Blue eyes. Eyes like burning sapphires. Eyes covered in a web of white cracks. The First Woman's hands tightened upon her staff. Ravens cried around her. They beat their wings. Crows circled the standing stones. Then Sylvaine was gone.

She appeared in the deep forest to the song of ravens. There were six of them, men and women both, dark of clothes, sharp of ear, hair the colour of midnight, fangs like daggers, and eyes of ruby flame.

"First Woman," Harkan of the ruskalan bowed in reverence.

His people followed suit.

"Did you feel it?" Sylvaine asked. "Did you see it?"

"See what, Great Queen?"

"The she-elf Naidra has called to us," the spirit told him.

"Snowflame is close now," Harkan replied. "Just as was always intended."

"She is held captive in the mountain fortress beneath the cold iron earth. I made safe my people once in this war and it must be the last time. We spirits do not deal or meddle in the affairs of the mortal world, and my power wanes beyond the trees. Yet Naidra must be liberated. Balance must be restored."

The leader of the ruskalan did not look away from the First Woman. "Everything will soon be as it once was," he said. "My blood flows like a river reaching far beyond the edge of the forest. Through courts and palaces, even breaching the stone walls of the Citadel itself. Decades ago, when I first heard rumour of Snowflame's survival I prepared. She of my kin will find Naidra."

"Our enemy has chosen to reveal his hand at a most perilous time," Sylvaine's violet gaze shone as she spoke. "You know of what I speak. The eyes of Tanris have indeed opened."

"They were first felt by the Dark One over two decades ago, and we ruskalan were warned," Harkan said. "Moons ago the druids foretold that the eyes of Tanris would open and when they did, fire will follow. All of the death, all of the slaughter that followed, when the children of Salvaar spilled their own blood, when the west marshalled against them... that was the fire, and it has not yet finished burning. It has been over a year since Tanris came to me. He told me that the revenge that we seek will be ours on the day that the eyes of Tanris slay the cursed blood. What meaning this carries, what form it takes, I do not know. She of my kin walks among our foe. She pulls their strings, and in time will set them upon their fate."

"When I created the elves with my tears, they were born to be free," the First Woman told the ruskalan. "They are creatures of the heart. They are wild and passionate. They feel everything far more than any other. Love and loss, hate and rage. They feel everything. They are everything, and they were slaughtered for it. Your people, born of my son's blood, are of the mind. You think where the elves feel. You are patient where the elves were reckless. Two sides of mortal nature entangled in the dark. One cannot exist without the other. The world cannot be balanced without both peoples. You know this. You have seen it. The mortal world is *never* right unless there is balance. So now it falls to the ruskalan to make safe the *last* elf."

"For a century I have planned for this moment. For a century I have worked in the dark to grant us this chance," Harkan said. "One hundred years ago the humans believed that they had burned the last of my kind, yet here we stand. An echo of the ashes. We have hidden away and been forgotten by the world, yet we have not been silent. We waited. We prepared. This war is our doing and if it leads to my death, if it sets me upon my fate, then I will sing such a song as to be worthy of remembrance in the histories of even our greatest enemy. Everything is unfolding exactly as I have foreseen, exactly as the Dark One has foreseen. Everything happening now, in this moment, is my doing. I have killed their leaders and marshalled their armies. My people will free the she-elf, Naidra, and bring her back unharmed. You have my word, Great Queen. On the day of the summer solstice, she of my blood will divide our enemy and the Whisperer will draw their gaze. The night shall be pierced by silver. It is written."

"I stand with you in this revenge for it is mine as well, yet do not forget that the children of the forest are my people too," Sylvaine stepped closer to the ruskalan as she spoke, and a glare ignited her venomous eyes.

It was piercing and drove deep into Harkan's heart. For the first time Harkan felt fear. It shackled him and sought to destroy his soul.

The Great Queen bared her teeth as she spoke again, "You are the Firstborn, yet if your plan leads to the suffering and death of my people, if it leads them to their doom, I will kill you."

Ravens shrieked as they dove into the clearing, encircling the pair. The First Woman stepped forward. The ravens rained down, their screams and flapping wings beat Harkan's ears. She walked into Harkan as she vanished. Sylvaine was gone, taken by the darkness like smoke. She left nothing behind but the burning brand of fear.

Shawline Publishing Group Pty Ltd
www.shawlinepublishing.com.au

SHAWLINE
PUBLISHING
GROUP

Milton Keynes UK
Ingram Content Group UK Ltd.
UKHW020744231123
433129UK00017B/1225